The Year's Best Fantasy and Horror

THIRD ANNUAL COLLECTION

Edited by Ellen Datlow and Terri Windling

ST. MARTIN'S PRESS   NEW YORK

Design by Judy C. Dannecker

ISBN 0-312-04447-X (hbk)
ISBN 0-312-04450-X (pbk)

First Edition
10 9 8 7 6 5 4 3 2 1

A Bluejay Books Production

The Year's Best Fantasy and Horror

CONTENTS

Acknowledgments

I'd like to thank Merrilee Heifetz; Stuart Moore; Gordon Van Gelder; Robert Killheffer; the American and British contributors, editors, and publishers who provided material and background; and particularly I'd like to thank Jim Frenkel, who was invaluable.

Also, thanks to Charles N. Brown, whose magazine *Locus* (Locus Publications, Inc., P. O. Box 13305, Oakland, CA 94661; $40.00 for a one-year first-class subscription, 12 issues) was used as a reference source throughout the Summation and to Andrew Porter, whose magazine *Science Fiction Chronicle* (*S.F. Chronicle*, P. O. Box 2730, Brooklyn, NY 11202-0056; $33.00 for a one-year first-class subscription, 12 issues) was also used as a reference source throughout.

—Ellen Datlow

Many thanks to all the publishers, writers, artists, booksellers, librarians, and readers who sent me material, recommended favorite titles, and shared their thoughts on the year in fantasy publishing with me; and to *Locus, SF Chronicle, Library Journal, Horn Book*, and *Folk Roots* magazines, which are helpful sources for seeking out fantasy material. Special thanks go to Ellen Kushner, Sylvia Peretz, Elisabeth Roberts and Craig Gardner, Will Shetterly and Emma Bull, Valerie Smith, Jane Yolen; to Stuart Moore and Gordon Van Gelder of St. Martin's Press; to the helpful people at the Boston Public Library and Wordsworth Books; to Tappan King and Beth Meacham for providing a desert haven to finish the work on this year's volume (and to TK for looking over my introduction); and most of all to Thomas Canty, Ellen Datlow, and Jim Frenkel. Anyone wishing to recommend fantasy stories, novels, music, or art released in 1990 for next year's volume should do so c/o The Endicott Studio, 63 Endicott Street, Boston, MA 02113.

—Terri Windling

Summation 1989: Fantasy

The "Adult Fantasy" book genre, as we know it, barely existed at the beginning of the 1980s. As we enter the 1990s, it is interesting to take a look back over the last decade to see how the fantasy field has developed.

Fantasy stories, of course, have always been with us, an important part of every culture on this planet since the earliest myths, hero tales, and fairy tales, as well as a staple of English-language literature from Mallory to Shakespeare; from Yeats and Oscar Wilde to T. H. White and C. S. Lewis. It was a twentieth century, and particularly American, notion that fantasy was fit only for children—a notion dispelled in the latter half of this century by the popularity of British author J. R. R. Tolkien's books among readers of all ages, and by the acceptance by American literati of works of "magic realism" as popularized by Latin American writers such as Gabriel García Márquez, Miguel Asturias, and Jorge Luis Borges.

On the heels of the enormous popularity of Tolkien's *The Hobbit* and the *Lord of the Rings* trilogy came the first modern publishing venture expressly aimed at adult fantasy readers: the Sign of the Unicorn line, published by Ian and Betty Ballantine at Ballantine Books, edited by Lin Carter and beautifully illustrated by Gervasio Gallardo, in the early 1970s. Although this line failed to establish itself successfully in the commercial marketplace, editor Carter was able, for a short while, to bring classic literary fantasy works back into print, introducing such authors as George McDonald, William Morris, Lord Dunsany, E. R. Eddison, James Branch Cabell, and Mervyn Peake to readers hungry "for more stuff like Tolkien," thereby influencing what was to become the next generation of fantasy writers.

Judy-Lynn and Lester del Rey, founders of the Del Rey Fantasy imprint—under their Gryphon logo—at Ballantine, were more successful at providing readers with Tolkien-esque fantasy, particularly with *The Sword of Shannara* by Terry Brooks—which was accused of being too derivative of Tolkien, but which hit the best-seller lists and got the Del Rey Fantasy line off to a running start. Picking up selected titles and authors (such as Evangeline Walton, Poul Anderson, Peter Beagle, and Patricia A. McKillip) from the Lin Carter line, and introducing new authors (like Stephen R. Donaldson), Del Rey quickly had a thriving fantasy publishing program—and little competition.

As the 1980s began, Del Rey was the only American publisher with an adult fantasy imprint. Other houses published the occasional fantasy title under a science fiction label—a system that made some sense at the time because the little adult fantasy that was published then was largely of the Howardian "sword-and-sorcery" kind (as typified by the Conan stories of Robert E. Howard) which, like American science fiction, grew out of the pages of the old pulp magazines. The Del Rey line included both Howardian pulp fantasy and "high" fantasy a la Tolkien. Lester del Rey created strict guidelines, based on his own years as an SF/fantasy writer beginning in the 1940s, of what constituted a "Del Rey Fantasy," and what did not (such as magic realism and other less traditional forms.) The Del Rey line established the commercial viability of adult fantasy books and Judy-Lynn del Rey, a brilliant publisher, invented the current model for marketing fantasy best-sellers. Yet the boundary lines of the adult fantasy genre were at that time still quite narrowly drawn.

Ace Books, where I worked at the beginning of the decade, was the next publisher to create a separate adult fantasy imprint, and it was difficult to convince editorial boards and booksellers to commit advance monies and rack space to this upstart genre. Much of what was in print in those early days was pulp magazine-style stories aimed at a largely male readership, with covers sporting large-breasted women swooning at the feet of muscle-bound men. Little wonder then that the literary establishment dismissed the genre as a whole—an attitude that unfortunately lingers in some quarters today. High fantasy was in short supply at that time and reader demand for it was greater than the few contemporary fantasy writers could keep up with. It was a great time to be a young fantasy author seeking a first novel publication, and an exciting time to be a fantasy editor with a mandate to find and develop new talent. Thus a whole generation of writers who had whetted their teeth on Tolkien and on classic Sign of the Unicorn fantasies appeared on the American publishing scene.

Most major publishing houses now have adult fantasy imprints (run side-by-side with their science fiction lists, despite the fact that editing SF and fantasy are very different skills, which factor has had its effect on the genre). Annual combined sales of all fantasy titles currently exceed that of science fiction. The World Fantasy Award, originally established primarily as an award for horror fiction, now regularly honors high fantasy and magic realism as well; fantasy books are placing on the national best-seller lists; and a magic realist novel, *The Satanic Verses* by Salman Rushdie, has—in a most unfortunate manner—become the most notorious novel of the century.

In looking back over the last ten years, I see a field that has diversified and matured. Once the field, with a few laudable exceptions, could be boiled down to Howardian sagas with Frazetta-inspired covers and Celtic epics with Hildebrandt-inspired covers; early attempts to deviate from these areas, such as with the magic realism of Patricia McKillip's *Stepping from the Shadows* or Megan Lindholm's *The Wizard of the Pigeons*, did not have the reader and bookseller support such novels can expect today. Now the field encompasses works as diverse as Craig Shaw Gardner's light-hearted spoofs and Charles de Lint's urban faery stories, Lisa Goldstein's surrealistic explorations and Raymond Feist's dark epic sagas. Design-oriented book cover illustrations, owing more to Mucha and the Pre-Raphaelites than to Pyle or Frazetta, are now sharing the book stands with more standard works by Boris, Sweet, and the Hildebrandts; and the evolving technology of computer art promises to take cover designs in interesting new directions. Small presses are becoming more sophisticated in their marketing and distribution, and picking up—particularly in the short fiction market—where the large publishing houses leave off.

As we look into the 1990s, I think it is this diversity that will continue to make the fantasy field lively for both writers and readers. That new generation of fantasy writers is "growing up" and the field is growing up with them, resisting the trap of being genre-bound and cut off from the mainstream of American fiction. At the same time, writers from outside the genre are increasingly drawn to fantastic and magic realist themes, due to the influence of foreign writers and to the popularity of Joseph Campbell and his work in the area of myth and the function of the hero in our modern world. This cross-pollination between genre and mainstream writers holds promise of riches to come in both fields in the 1990s in the area of magic realism. It strikes me as the literary equivalent of Worldbeat music: a creative mixing of different styles and cultural rhythms to create a synthesis that is at once fresh and timeless.

More traditional fantasy fare is still a large staple of the genre, however, dominating the bestseller lists—and although I admit to groaning when yet another Young-Girl/Boy-with-Sword-in-Vaguely-Celtic-World manuscript finds its way to my desk, I don't think the continuing popularity of these books among the mass audience is hard to understand. Like fairy tales, these tend to be coming-of-age stories in the literal or psychological sense, speaking with age-old symbols (the magic sword, the poison apple, the hero who must count on wit or honor to survive) directly to the heart; and like fairy tales, their appeal is not in novelty or innovation, but in retelling a familiar tale so that it resonates anew. The best writers—Ursula K. Le Guin, Peter Beagle, Patricia A. McKillip, Robin McKinley and their ilk—write on two levels: on the surface is a colorful tale of a magical adventure, but beneath that a second tale is being told about deeper human issues such as good and evil, courage and despair, honor and betrayal, reflecting something of the author's own experience (just as Frodo Baggins's quest to save his beloved Middle Earth is given resonance by Tolkien's strong love of rural England and his experience of the horrors of World War II), and told with a clear lyricism of language that reflects the elegant simplicity of age-old, time-polished tales. To be sure, many of the high fantasies written and sold today are derivative tales that work only on the first level—but even these appeal to many readers by echoing the experience they had reading a master story-teller like Tolkien, tiding them over until the "real thing" comes along again.

While publisher expansion into the fantasy field in the last few years has glutted the market with more titles than the marketplace can sustain—making it harder for new writers to find an audience and for discriminating readers to tell the good from the bad—I don't think the 1990s will see the demand for high fantasy die out. And for those of us who have become wary of it due to all the second-rate books pushed onto the stands, I see a promising trend as talented authors with strong literary values—like Gwyneth Jones, C. J. Cherryh, and Ellen Kushner—turn to traditional stories, and as the line between high fantasy and dark fantasy/horror becomes thinner. Urban fantasy, of the kind pioneered by Charles de Lint, Michael de Larrabeiti, Emma Bull, Rick Bowes and others, continues to be a fascinating exploration of the interconnection of myth and folklore with modern society. Writers such as John Crowley, Orson Scott Card, Tom Dietz, Matt Ruff, Greg Bear, Elizabeth Ann Scarborough and Lisa Goldstein are developing a distinctly American brand of magic realist fantasy that seems particularly suited to the 1990s. We're seeing the American fantasy field come of age, and I find that exciting.

With this diversity of fantasy in mind, the following is a list of recommended fantasy in fiction and other arts which appeared in 1989. While I can't claim to have seen every fantastic or surrealistic work published here or abroad, I hope my readings and discussions with fantasy writers, artists, publishers, booksellers and readers across the U.S. and England will lead you to some works you might have overlooked, and some new authors who you might enjoy.

1989 was the year of the short story. So many excellent works of short fiction were published in magazines, anthologies, and single-author collections that they quite overshadowed novel-length works—but in fact it wasn't a bad year for novels either. If you can read only a few of the fantasy novels published in 1989, the following is a baker's dozen of works, by established and new authors, you shouldn't miss (in alphabetical order):

Prentice Alvin, Orson Scott Card (Tor). The latest volume in Card's excellent American historical fantasy epic, *The Tales of Alvin Maker*.

A Child Across the Sky, Jonathan Carroll (Legend, U.K.). Dark fantasy, loosely connected to Carroll's *Bones of the Moon* and *Sleeping in Flames*—he just keeps getting better and better.

Sunglasses After Dark, Nancy A. Collins (NAL). This wild, dark fantasy novel about inner-city vampires will appeal to non-horror readers as well.

The Whim of the Dragon, Pamela Dean (Ace). Traditional high fantasy with young protagonists, beautifully written by an author with a superior prose style; ends the Secret Country trilogy.

Geek Love, Katherine Dunn (Knopf). A strangely wonderful literary fantasy about an American family that breeds its own mutants.

Tourists, Lisa Goldstein (Simon & Schuster). American tourists in a surrealistic imaginary land, from one of the field's best young writers.

Gate of Darkness, Circle of Light, Tanya Huff (DAW). Urban fantasy set in contemporary Canada, well-crafted and enjoyable, from a promising new writer who is probably getting tired of being compared to Charles de Lint.

New Moon, Midori Snyder (Ace). Refreshingly original high fantasy set in a city wonderfully reminiscent of Dickensian London from another promising new writer.

The Stress of Her Regard, Tim Powers (Ace). Dark, dark fantasy about Byron and Shelley from one of the most twisted—I mean that as a compliment—and original minds in the fantasy field.

Kindergarten, Peter Rushford (David R. Godine). One of the very best novels of this or any other year, finally back in print—a contemporary reworking of the Hansel and Gretel tale, set in a small English town, expertly crafted.

The Coachman Rat, David Henry Wilson (Carroll & Graf). A good literary fantasy retelling of Cinderella from the coachman's point of view.

Soldier of Arete, Gene Wolfe (Tor). A masterful prose stylist continues the "diary" of a flawed hero begun in *Soldier in the Mist*.

White Jenna, Jane Yolen (Tor). Invented myth, history, folklore, and high fantasy adventure are beautifully woven together by one of the most respected authors in the children's and adult fantasy fields.

The Best Peculiar Book of the Year "award" goes to *The Cockroaches of Stay More*, a satiric fantasy by Donald Harrington (Harcourt Brace Jovanovich). Two excellent novels that straddle the line between SF and fantasy, Bruce McAllister's *Dream Baby* (Tor) and Pat Murphy's *The City, Not Long After* (Doubleday/Foundation), will also be of interest to fantasy readers and are among the very best books of the year. And I would, of course, heartily recommend the latest offering in my own Adult Fairy Tales series: *Snow White and Rose Red* by Patricia C. Wrede (Tor).

Other recommended titles of 1989:

From Ace Fantasy/The Berkley Publishing Group: *The Stone Giant*, James P. Blaylock (highly recommended sequel to *The Elfin Ship* and *The Disappearing Dwarves*, traditional fantasy infused with Blaylock madness); *Marianne, The Madame and the Momentary Gods* and *Marianne, the Matchbox and the Malachite Mouse*, Sheri S. Tepper (the surrealistic Marianne books are among her best works); *The Fortress of the Pearl*, Michael Moorcock (a fun new Elric novel, although I miss the striking Gould covers); *A Disagreement with Death*, Craig Shaw Gardner and *The Sword of Sagamore*, Kara Dalkey (both are humorous fantasy, a cut above most of the rest); *The Willow Garden*, Kathryn Grant (nicely written oriental fantasy); *The Tangled Lands*, Will Shetterly (terrific, strange SF novel with more than a touch of fantasy); and the following well-written adventure fantasy books: *Luck of the Wheels*, Megan Lindholm; *On the Seas of Destiny*, Ru Emerson; *The Schemes of Dragons*, David Smeds; and *Blood Storm*, Heather Gladney.

From Atheneum: *The Dogs of Paradise*, Abel Posse (the story of Columbus, aptly described by one reviewer as "history performed by the Monty Python troupe"; first English language publication by this Argentine author).

From The Atlantic Monthly Press: *Blue Fruit*, Adam Lively (literary time-travel novel).

From Avon Books: *The Gryphon King*, Tom Dietz (Dietz, a talented new writer, is at his best with contemporary fantasy like this one, set in Georgia—highly recommended); *Beauty and the Beast*, Barbara Hambly (don't be put off because this is based on a TV show—Hambly is, as always, superb).

From Baen/Sign of the Dragon: *Apocalypse*, Nancy Springer (Springer started out writing very traditional fantasy and keeps surprising me with books that are anything but; set in near-future Pennsylvania, this hard-hitting book is highly recommended); *The Complete Compleat Enchanter*, L. Sprague de Camp and Fletcher Pratt (note humorous fantasy fans—these guys practically invented it); and *Piper at the Gate*, Mary Stanton (a gentle fantasy novel that horse lovers will particularly enjoy).

From Bantam/Doubleday/Dell: *Sleeping in Flames*, Jonathan Carroll (first U.S. edition of a splendid novel by one of the best dark fantasy writers around); *The Coming of the King*, Nikolai Tolstoy (first U.S. edition of this British Arthurian saga); *A Wind in Cairo*, Judith Tarr (pleasant oriental fantasy); *Philip Jose Farmer's the Dungeon #3*, Charles de Lint (a cut above the rest of these packaged series books); the above-mentioned *The City, Not Long After*, Pat Murphy (a magical near-future tale set in San Francisco); and *Lord Byron's Doctor*, Paul West (the invented memoirs of Byron's companion, Polidori).

From Jonathan Cape, U.K.: *The Child of Good Fortune*, Tom de Haan (sequel to the quirky *A Mirror for Princes*, highly recommended).

From Crossing Press: *The Fablesinger*, Judith Woolcock Colombo (flawed but intriguing Caribbean fantasy).

From Crossway: *Arthur*, Stephen Lawhead (nice Arthurian retelling).

From DAW: *Magic's Pawn*, Mercedes Lackey (Lackey has come into her own with this latest novel); *The Heroine of the World*, Tanith Lee (one of fantasy's masters—she's in good form with this one); and the above-mentioned *Gate of Darkness, Circle of Light* by Tanya Huff.

From Del Rey: *Rusalka*, C. J. Cherryh (traditional fantasy from a respected SF writer, set in mythical Russia, highly recommended); *Sorcess of Darshiva*, David Eddings (traditional fantasy, well crafted); *The Curse of Slagfid*, Elizabeth R. Boyer (traditional fantasy with a nice Scandinavian touch); and *The Harrowing of Gwynedd*, Katherine Kurtz (the latest entry in Kurtz's long-running Deryni series).

From GW Books: *Drachenfels*, Jack Yeovil (written for Warhammer fantasy gaming enthusiasts, it's surprisingly good).

From Harcourt Brace Jovanovich: *Foucault's Pendulum*, Umberto Eco (occult conspiracy novel by the author of *The Name of the Rose*).

From Hunter House: *On the Road to Baghdad*, Guneli Gun (flawed but interesting Arabian feminist fantasy).

From Knopf: *The Golden Ball*, Hanne Marie Svendsen: (a lovely, dreamlike magic realist fantasy translated from the Danish); *The History of the World in 10½ Chapters*, Julian Barnes (mad literary fantasy by the author of *Flaubert's Parrot*); *Changing the Past*, Thomas Berger (one of America's preeminent magic realists and satirists with a story about a man who changes his past with disastrous results); *The History of Luminous Motion* by Scott Bradfield (all right, it's really stretching things to list this as a fantasy—but it's by a writer well-known for his fantasy short stories and it's one of the best books of the year, about a young boy's journey across the U.S.); and the above-mentioned *Geek Love*, Katherine Dunn.

From William Morrow: *Lavondyss*, Robert Holdstock (first U.S. edition of this wonderful dark mythological fantasy, highly recommended); *Red Branch*, Morgan Llyewelyn (fantasy based on Irish history and mythology from an author who handles this material better than most); *Knight of Shadows*, Roger Zelazny (the ninth book in his Amber series).

From NAL: *Mort*, Terry Pratchett, and *Sphynxes*, Esther M. Friesner (both for fans of humorous fantasy); *The Dark Tower II: The Drawing of the Three*, Stephen King (surrealistic "gunslinger" fantasy from King with interesting experimental illustrations by Phil Hale); and, the above-mentioned *Sunglasses After Dark*, Nancy A. Collins.

From Peter Owen/Dufour Editions: *Parsival*, Peter Vansittart (interesting, somewhat obscure retelling of the Parsival legend).

From Poseidon Press: *Tours of the Black Clock*, Steve Erickson (literary alternate history novel, recommended).

From Random House: *Dollarville*, Peter Davies (peculiar magic realist novel); *Cannibal Kiss*, Daniel Odier (literary fantasy translated from the French about an author's character who comes to life).

From Tor: *Nemesis* and *Inferno*, Louise Cooper (fans of Moorcock's Elric series will likely enjoy Cooper's work, too); *The Woman Who Loved Reindeer*, Meredith Ann Pierce (lyrically written high fantasy tale, originally published in hardcover as a young adult book); and, the previously mentioned titles: *Prentice Alvin*, Orson Scott Card; *White Jenna*, Jane Yolen; *Soldier of Arete*, Gene Wolfe; and *Snow White and Rose Red*, Patricia C. Wrede.

From Underwood-Miller: *Madouc*, Jack Vance (sequel to *Lyonesse*, beautifully illustrated by James Christiansen), and a cloth edition of Nancy Springer's *Apocalypse*.

From Viking/Penguin: *Mascara*, Ariel Dorfman (first novel in English by this Chilean author, this magic realism story is about a man so nondescript no one can remember him); and, *There's Something in the Back Yard*, Richard Snodgrass (a magic realist novel about a university professor who gets tangled up with a Hopi kachina spirit).

From Walker: *Hong on the Range*, William F. Wu (American Chinese fantasy, illustrated by Darrel Andersen and Phil Hale).

From Warner/Questar: *The Fool on the Hill*, Matt Ruff (paperback reprint of a first novel from The Atlantic Monthly Press, delightful magic realism, highly recommended); *Queen's Gambit Declined*, Melinda Snodgrass (historical fantasy set in the seventeeth century).

The best first novel of the year: the above-mentioned *Sunglasses After Dark* by Nancy A. Collins (NAL). Runner up: Randall Kenan's *A Visitation of Spirits*, a magic realism novel about black family and community life in North Carolina (Grove Press.) Other interesting debuts: Teresa Edgerton's nicely written Celtic-style fantasies: *Child of Saturn* and *The Moon in Hiding* (Ace); Alidia van Gores's sea lore fantasy *Mermaid's Song* (NAL); and Jeanne Larsen's *Silk Road*, an oriental fantasy (Henry Holt).

1989 produced a bumper crop of short story collections, despite the fact that readers don't buy them with the same frequency that they purchase novels, leading some publishers to avoid them altogether. Happily, small presses are becoming more skilled in picking up the slack.

The best collections of 1989 were:

Novelty, John Crowley: four novellas—magic realism and a lovely original fairy tale (Doubleday/Foundation); *Hot Jazz Trio*, William Kotzwinkle: three wonderful, wild magic realist novellas, illustrated by Joe Servello (Houghton Mifflin); *Casting Fortune*, John M. Ford: a tour-de-force original Liavekan novella and two reprint stories (Tor); *Provençal Tales*, Michael de Larrabeiti: beautifully crafted adult fantasy tales based on French folklore (St. Martin's Press); *Forests of the Night*, Tanith Lee: a collection of superb original and reprint stories with an overall dark fantasy tone (Unwin Hyman, U.K.); *Escape from Kathmandu*, Kim Stanley Robinson: humorous fantasy adventure stories—hard to describe, wonderful to read (Tor); *Author's Choice Monthly, Issue Three*,

Lisa Goldstein: a monthly small press "magazine" series published in hardcover book format, *Issue Three* contains Goldstein's excellent work—both fantasy and SF, all reprint (Pulphouse Publishing); *Antique Dust*, Robert Westall: a dark fantasy collection, the first for adults from a master of children's fantasy (Viking); *The Faery Flag*, Jane Yolen: thirteen faery and supernatural stories and poems in an illustrated book for children (Orchard); and *A Romance of the Equator*, Brian Aldiss: twenty-six of his best fantasy stories (Gollancz, U.K.)

Other recommended collections that contain at least some fantasy stories: *Women as Demons*, Tanith Lee (The Women's Press, U.K.); *Patterns*, Pat Cadigan (Ursus); *Endangered Species*, Gene Wolfe (Tor); *Frost and Fire*, Roger Zelazny (William Morrow); *Children of the Wind*, Kate Wilhelm (St. Martin's Press); *The Yellow Wallpaper*, Charlotte Perkins Gilman—contains selections from her feminist utopian fantasy *Herland* as well as short fiction and nonfiction (Bantam); *Nantucket Slayrides*, Lucius Shepard and Robert Frazier (Mark V. Ziesing); *The Heliotrope Wall and Other Stories*, Ana Maria Matute (Columbia University Press); *Man Without Memory*, Richard Burgin (University of Illinois Press); *Red Moon, Red Lake*, Archer/Straus (McPherson & Co.); *The Magic Deer*, by Conger Beasley, Jr. (Wordcraft Press); *The Boy Who Set Fire*, tales translated from the Moroccan Moghrebi by Paul Bowles; *Crackling Mountain and Other Stories*, Osamu Dazai, translated from the Japanese by James O'Brien; and *The Book of Frog*, Jeff Vandermeer, amphibian fantasy stories, a collection notable for its peculiarity (The Ministry of Whimsy Press).

Five excellent fantasy novellas published as small press chapbooks: Lucius Shepard's *Father of Stones*, sequel to last year's "The Scalehunter's Beautiful Daughter," and Howard Waldrop's *A Dozen Tough Jobs*, the Labours of Hercules set in the rural South (both from Mark V. Ziesing); Charles de Lint's urban Canadian fantasy *Westlin Wind* (Axolotl Press) and Borderland story *Berlin* (Fourth Avenue Press); and, Greg Bear's urban fairy tale *Sleepside Story* (Cheap Street.)

Notable anthologies published in 1989: *Masterpieces of Fantasy and Wonder*, edited by David G. Hartwell (Literary Guild), useful reprint anthology; *Full Spectrum II*, edited by Aronica, LoBrutto, McCarthy and Stout (Bantam), original SF anthology that contains some nice fantasy pieces too, as well as a truly lovely Kim Stanley Robinson story that isn't really either one; *Pulphouse Spring Fantasy Issue*, edited by Kristine Kathryn Rusch (Pulphouse), not as strong as their horror issues, but still worth picking up; *Don't Bet on the Prince*, edited by Jack Zipes (Routledge), excellent collection of feminist/humanist fairy tale-inspired fiction by authors such as Angela Carter, Anne Sexton, Tanith Lee, Jane Yolen, reprint; *Razored Saddles*, edited by Joe R. Lansdale and Pat LoBrutto (Dark Harvest), good collection of seventeen western horror and fantasy stories; *What Might Have Been*, Vols. I and II, edited by Gregory Benford and Martin H. Greenberg (Bantam), for alternate history fans; *The Best from Fantasy and Science Fiction: A 40th Anniversary Anthology*, edited by Edward L. Ferman (St. Martin's), stories reprinted from the venerable SF and fantasy digest; *Thieves' World #12: Stealer's Sky*, Robert Asprin and Lynn Abbey (Ace), notable as the final volume of the series that pioneered the "shared world anthology" concept; *Dark Fantasies*, edited by Chris Morgan (Legend, U.K.), original horror and dark fantasy; *Zenith*, edited by David Garnett (Sphere, U.K.), SF anthology with some fantasy, notably good stories by Robert Holdstock and Colin Greenland; *Other Edens III*, edited by Christopher Evans and Robert Holdstock (Unwin Hyman, U.K.), contains both SF and fantasy; not as strong in fantasy as in past volumes but still better than most; *Hidden Turnings*, edited by Diana Wynne Jones (Methuen), highly recommended original young adult collection containing several good fantasy stories and a terrific mainstream story by Robert Westall; *Things That Go Bump in the Night*, edited by Jane Yolen and Martin H. Greenberg (Harper & Row), highly recommended original children's fantasy collection; *The Green Ghost and Other Stories*, edited by Mary Danby (Armada, U.K.), forty-two reprint children's fantasy stories; *Sweeping Beauties*, (Attic Press, U.K.), original feminist fairy tales; *Talk That Talk*, edited by Linda Gross and Marian E. Barnes (Simon and Schuster), anthology of African-American storytelling; *The Best Japanese Science Fiction Stories*, edited by John L. Apostolou and Martin H. Greenberg (Dembner Publishing), contains both SF and fantasy stories; and, *Korean Classical Literature*, edited and translated by Chung Chong-wa, (Paul Kegan International), contains a section devoted to folk and fairy tale-based literature.

Good short fantasy fiction was also to be found in magazines both large and small in 1989. The most reliable sources remain: *Omni, The Magazine of Fantasy and Science Fiction*; the British *Interzone*; and *Isaac Asimov's Science Fiction Magazine* (despite its name)—particularly now that *Twilight Zone*, which published some excellent dark fantasy under editor Tappan King, sadly has disappeared. A number of innovative small press magazines specializing in fantasy and speculative fiction have popped up alongside more traditional efforts like *Dragon* and *Weird Tales*. The best of these is *Pulphouse*, published in an interesting hardback book format out of Oregon; the same folks are responsible for the nice new series *Author's Choice Monthly*. *Ice River*, a good little magazine of speculative writing, new music, and fantastic art also comes out of Oregon.

New Pathways into SF & Fantasy is a fun and always interesting cutting edge magazine published in Texas; and, *Strange Plasma*, published in Massachusetts, debuted this year with a promising first issue containing work by Gene Wolfe and R. A. Lafferty. There's also some interesting work to be found in the *Jabberwocky* (premier issue), *EUTO, Pandora, The Magazine of Speculative Poetry* (from the Midwest), and in *POLY*, a beautifully produced speculative poetry edition from Ocean View Press. University press magazines (such as the *Iowa Review* and the *Antioch Review*) are a good place to watch for magic realist stories and surrealist poetry by mainstream writers, as well as the international quarterlies and journals sponsored by large publishing houses (like *Granta* and *The Quarterly*). This year, unfortunately, marked the last edition of *Pulpsmith*, a literary magazine that grew out of *The Smith*, published in New York.

The best children's fantasy I read this year was *Baylet* by Patricia Wrightson, based on Australian aboriginal legend (Macmillan/Colliers). *The King's Fountain* by children's fantasy master Lloyd Alexander is also particularly noteworthy. Other recommended children's fantasy titles that adult readers may enjoy include: *The Golden Thread* by Suzy McKee Charnas (Bantam); *The Trolley to Yesterday* and *The Chessmen of Doom* by John Bellairs (Dial); *An Acceptable Time*, the latest sequel to *A Wrinkle in Time* by Madeleine L'Engle (Farrar, Straus & Giroux); *Seal Child* by Sylvia Peck (Morrow); *The Rainbow People* by Lawrence Yep (Harper & Row), *The Hidden Ones* by Gwyneth Jones (The Women's Press, U.K.), and, *The Daymaker* by Jones writing as Ann Halam (Puffin, U.K.); *High Wizardry* by Diane Duane (Delacorte); *Son of Two Worlds*, a "Pyrderi" retelling by Haydn Middleton (Ballantine/Available Press); *Melusine* by Lynn Reid Banks (Harper & Row); *A Night of Birds* by Katherine Scholes (Doubleday); *Catwings Returns*, an illustrated story for younger children by Ursula K. Le Guin (Orchard Books); and, reissues of classic fantasy tales by Edward Eager: *Half Magic, Magic by the Lake* and *Magic or Not*, with the original N. M. Bodecker illustrations (Harcourt Brace Jovanovich).

There were a number of good fairy tale and folk tale books published in the last year—particularly stories from the French, highlighting that country's rich fantasy tradition. Besides the above-mentioned *Provençal Tales* by Michael de Larrabeiti (St. Martin's Press), there were four titles I'd recommend, the first book, in particular: *Beauties,*

Beasts and Enchantments: Classic French Fairy Tales, edited and translated by Jack Zipes; *French Folktales* (Pantheon), a selection of over one hundred tales from Henri Pourrat's "Les trésor des contes," tales from Auvergne, selected by C. G. Bjurström (Pantheon has an excellent Fairy Tale and Folk Tale Library series); *Proud Knight, Fair Lady: The Twelve Lais of Marie de France*, a contemporary prose translation by Naomi Lewis of a twelfth century fairy tale collection (Viking/Kestral); and, *Cinderella and Other Tales from Perrault*, a picture book selection of Charles Perrault's tales, illustrated by Michael Hague (Henry Holt & Co). A related title is Betsy Hearne's interesting and beautifully packaged *Beauty and the Beast*, which is a nonfiction work tracing the folkloric roots, literary variations, and illustrative interpretations of the fairy tale best known in its classic French version by Madame Leprince de Beaumont (Random House).

Other recommended titles: *Little Red Riding Hood; A Casebook*, twelve essays by fairy tale scholars, edited by Alan Dundes (University of Wisconsin Press); *The Brothers Grimm and Folktale*, a collection of essays edited by James M. McGlathery (University of Illinois Press); *Russian Folk Beliefs*, by Linda J. Ivanits (M. E. Sharpe, Publisher); *The Japanese Psyche: Motifs in the Fairy Tales of Japan*, by Hayao Kawai (Spring Publications); *Italian Folktales in America: The Verbal Art of Immigrant Women*, by Elizabeth Mathias and Richard Raspa (Wayne State University Press); *Under the Starfruit Tree*, folktales from Vietnam told by Alice M. Terada (University of Hawaii Press); *The Shining Princess and Other Japanese Legends*, retold by Eric Quayle and illustrated by Michael Foreman (Little, Brown); *The Irish Folk and Fairy Tale Omnibus*, edited by Michael Scott (Penguin); *Gypsy Folk Tales*, retold by Diane Tong (Harcourt Brace Jovanovich); *Folktales and Legends from the South*, edited by John H. Burrison and illustrated with lovely photographs (University of Georgia Press); and, three nicely produced Green Tiger Press books of classic fairy tale illustrations compiled by Cooper Edens: *Beauty and the Beast*, *Goldilocks*, and *Cinderella*.

There were a number of lovely fantasy picture books published for children in 1989. Two books that may appeal more to adult readers: *Ophelia's Shadow Theater* by Michael Ende (author of *The Never-Ending Story*), illustrated by Friedrich Hechelman and translated from German by Anthea Bell (The Overlook Press); and, *The Voice of the Wind* by Claude Clément, illustrated by Frédéric Clément and translated from the French by Lenny Hort (Dial). They are both surrealistic and gorgeous, and I strongly urge you to seek them out.

I also highly recommend *Dove Isabeau*, an English folk ballad-inspired story by Jane Yolen, beautifully illustrated by Dennis Nolan, from an author and an artist also active in the adult fantasy field (Harcourt Brace Jovanovich); and, *The Sand Horse*, by Ann Turnbull with lovely illustrations by British artist Michael Foreman (Atheneum).

There were some terrific illustrators working in the children's picture book field this year. In addition to the above-mentioned titles, one of America's preeminent illustrators and small press bookmakers, Barry Moser of Pennyroyal Press, has illustrated *The Adventures of Brer Rabbit and His Family*, by Joel Harris (Harcourt Brace Jovanovich); award-winning Viennese illustrator Lizbeth Zwerger's picture book *Hansel and Gretel* has been brought out in an American edition (Picture Book Studio); Peter Weevers has illustrated a new edition of *Alice in Wonderland* (Philomel); David Wiesner has illustrated Marianne Mayer's retelling of *The Sorcerer's Apprentice* (Bantam/Skylark); Jan Brett illustrated a Walter Crane-inspired version of *Beauty and the Beast* (Clarion Books) and Mordicai Gerstein's *Beauty and the Beast* (Dutton) has been made into an animated video (Stories to Remember, available on VHS); P. J. Lynch has illustrated E. Nesbit's

Melisandre (Harcourt Brace Jovanovich); Maria Danley has written and illustrated *Lullabye River*, released with a cassette of lullabies by herself and her sister, Linda Danly (Knopf); and, Alix Berenzy has written and illustrated a delightful variation of *The Frog Prince* (Henry Holt & Co).

The most talked-about children's fantasy book of the year was *Swan Lake* by Mark Helprin (author of the magic realist novel, *A Winter's Tale*) and World Fantasy Award-winning illustrator Chris van Allsburg. *Swan Lake* found its way to bestseller lists after having already made publishing news with the extremely sizable advance Houghton Mifflin paid Ariel Books, a book packager, to acquire it.

In addition to children's picture books, there were four art books of particular interest to lovers of fantasy art and illustration: *Rossetti*, a new collection of the works of the English romantic Dante Gabriel Rossetti, notable for including reproductions of his pencil and watercolor work which is in many cases finer than his better-known oil paintings (Abbeville Press); *Shaman*, the beautiful, mystical paintings of southwest American artist Susan Seddon Boulet (Pomegranate Press Art Books); *Hiten*, the art of Yoshitaka Amano, who was feted as the Artist Guest of Honor at the 1989 World Fantasy Convention (Asahi Sonorama); and *The Art of Stephen Hickman*, illustrations by the popular book cover artist (Donning/Starblaze).

There is little new, innovative work being done in adult fantasy book cover illustration right now—however, it should be noted that these illustrators are working under the direction of art directors and editors who are in turn responding to what bookstore managers, buyers, and book distributors consider to be acceptable "looks" for genre covers. Thus, it is not a reflection on the talent of the genre artists that our field lags behind some others (mysteries, for example) in creating interesting new contemporary work. Some notable exceptions to this that stand out from the look-alike books on the racks deserve commendation:

Yvonne Gilbert's Bilibin-like illustration for *Heroine of the World*/Tanith Lee (DAW); Jody Lee's graceful design-oriented work on the Lackey books for DAW; Kinuko Craft's Persian miniature painting for *The Shining Fountain*/Josepha Sherman (Avon); Robert Gould's Burne-Jones influenced painting for *Queens Gambit Declined*/Melinda Snodgrass (Questar) and *Mirage*/Louise Cooper (Tor); Thomas Canty's Mucha-like romantic design work on the Patricia A. Kennealy books for NAL and the Fairy Tale series for Tor, as well as his strikingly different ultra-modern computer style for *Scare Care*/edited by Graham Masterton and *Dream Baby*/Bruce McAllister (both Tor); Bob Hicksons's contemporary treatment of *Deserted Cities of the Heart*/Lewis Shiner (Bantam/Spectra); Arnie Fenner's splashy work for Mark V. Ziesing; Michael Whelan's moody, memorable covers for *The Changeling Sea*/Patricia A. McKillip (Del Rey) and *The Snow Queen*/Joan D. Vinge (Questar, reissue); Jim Burns's surrealistic painting for *Other Edens III*/Chris Evans and Robert Holdstock (Unwin Hyman); Alan Lee's lovely mythic forest watercolor for *Lavondyss*/Robert Holdstock (Morrow); and, Brian Froud's signature twilight faery land for *The Irish Folk and Fairy Tale Omnibus*/Michael Scott (Penguin).

Graphic novels and adult-oriented comics are becoming in the U.S. (as they have been in Europe for years) an area where fantasy artists can be more innovative. Some of the best combine fine art values with commercial illustrative technique. For instance, Jon J. Muth's gorgeous, painterly work in his graphic novel *Dracula: A Symphony in Moonlight and Nightmares* is reminiscent, in more than the title, of Whistler, and of the romantic work of Jeffrey Jones, to whom it is dedicated (Marvel Comics). Muth is also in good form, along with artists Kent Williams, George Pratt, Sherri Van Valkenburgh, and Glenn Pepple, in *The Moonshadow*, graphic novel by J. M. DeMatteis (Epic).

The Town That Didn't Exist, written by Pierre Christin and translated by Tom Leighton, is a French graphic novel charmingly illustrated by Enki Bilal, in its first U.S. publication (Catalan Communications).

Fantasy readers might also take a look at some of the interesting adult comics being put out by DC these days, in particular *The Sandman* series, illustrated by a number of talented artists and excellently written by Neil Gaiman, a writer to watch. And, DC's Piranha Press line of whimsically nasty books like *Gregory* (about a little boy in an insane asylum, including "The Incredibly Odd and Mystifying Spectacle of Herman Vermin," which I thank Craig Shaw Gardner for pointing out to me) and *Beautiful Stories for Ugly Children*. Eclipse Comics published several high fantasy titles this year, including *The Hobbit*, adapted from Tolkien's novel by Charles Dixon and illustrated by David Wenzel, and *Ariane and Bluebeard*, the latest of Craig Russell's graphic adaptations of operas (he's previously adapted *Pelleas and Melisande*, *Salome*, and *Parsifal*). You might also take a look at: Roy Thomas's adaptation of *The Ring of the Nibelung* (DC); the work of Hayao Miyazaki in the Japanese comic *Nausicaa in the Valley of the Wind* (English language edition published by Viz Select Comics); and *The Bank Street Book of Fantasy*, a graphic work for children developed by Byron Preiss Visual Publications.

The Delaware Art Museum, known for their collection of Howard Pyle and Brandywine School illustration, held an extensive exhibition of fantasy and science fiction art in 1989; artists Janny Wurts and Don Maitz were among the people who put this exhibit together, and most of the major illustrators in the field were represented.

Traditional folk music is of special interest to many fantasy readers because the old ballads, particularly in the English, Irish, and Scots folk traditions, are often based on the same folk and fairy tale roots as fantasy fiction. And the current generation of folk musicians, like contemporary fantasy writers, are taking traditional material and adapting it to a modern age. New listeners might try *Flight of the Green Linnet: Celtic Music—The Next Generation* as an introduction to the music; it features a number of the best new Celtic bands such as Silly Wizard, Capercaillie, and Patrick Street. Silly Wizard has just released a concert video, "Live Wizardry," from Green Linnet on VHS. Phil Cunningham, of Silly Wizard, has released a solo album, *The Palomino Waltzes*, reflecting his musical evolution journeying across Ireland, the U.S. and his own native Scotland; he also produced *Horse with a Heart* for the Irish band Altan, featuring the voice and fiddling of Mairead Ni Mhaonaigh. The other Cunningham brother, Johnny, has produced *Playing with Fire: The Celtic Fiddle Collection*, a compilation album featuring some of the best fiddlers in Ireland, Scotland and Brittany, and *The Best of the Tannahill Weavers 1979–1989*, ten years of music from one of Scotland's premier folk bands.

From the Ladle to the Grave is the new and best album from Boiled in Lead, a Minneapolis "Celtodelic and Worldbeat rock-and-reel" band, highly recommended (particularly in the CD version, which contains the extra track "My Son John," an evocatively performed old anti-war ballad). The same description can also be used for the Massachusetts band The Horseflies, with their latest album *Human Fly*. And for the music of Canada's Rare Air, with their wonderful new instrumental album *Primeval*; Rare Air's compositions are original, but their traditional roots run deep. *Ad Vielle Que Pourra* is the debut of an instrumental band from France with an album of new folk music—traditional Breton music mixed with jazz and cajun rhythms. Singer June Tabor has released a new album of traditional English and Scottish songs, *Aqaba*. Tabor gave the best U.S. concert tour of the year with her powerful performance of the darker Celtic ballads; you have to hear her in concert to appreciate her range. And Capercaillie—a band that sounds like Silly Wizard crossed with early pre-pop Clannad—has released *Sidewaulk*, possibly the best album of the year.

The 1989 International Conference on the Fantastic in the Arts was held in March in Ft. Lauderdale, Florida, with Doris Lessing as the Guest of Honor and C. N. Manlove from the University of Edinburgh as the Guest Scholar. The conference awarded Michaela Roessner, author of *Walkabout Woman*, the William Crawford Award for best new writer in the fantasy field.

The 1989 Fourth Street Fantasy Convention was held in June in Minneapolis, Minnesota; writer Guest of Honor was Tim Powers, and editor Guest of Honor was Beth Meacham of Tor Books.

The 1989 World Fantasy Convention and Awards Ceremony was held in October in Seattle, Washington. The writer Guest of Honor was Avram Davidson and the artist Guest of Honor was Yoshitaka Amano. Winners of the World Fantasy Award (for work in 1988) were: Best Novel: *Koko* (horror) by Peter Straub; Best Novella: *The Skin Trade* (horror) by George R. R. Martin; Best Short Fiction: "Winter Solstice, Camelot Station" (poem) by John M. Ford; Best Short Story Collection (tie): *Storeys from the Old Hotel* by Gene Wolfe and *Angry Candy* by Harlan Ellison; Best Anthology: *The Year's Best Fantasy, First Annual Collection*, edited by Ellen Datlow and Terri Windling; Special Award/Professional (tie): Terri Windling (editor, Tor Books/Endicott Studio) and Robert Weinberg (author of *The Biographical Dictionary of SF and Fantasy Artists*); Special Award/Nonprofessional: Kristine Kathryn Rusch and Dean Wesley Smith (editor and publisher of Pulphouse small press); Best Artist: Edward Gorey; Life Achievement Award: writer Evangeline Walton. Judges for the awards were: Susan Allison, Edward Bryant, Lisa Goldstein, Peter D. Pautz, and Jon White. Next year's World Fantasy Convention will be held in Chicago.

The British Fantasy Awards were announced at Fantasycon 14 in Birmingham, England, in October. They were as follows: Best Novel, *The Influence* (horror) by Ramsey Campbell; Best Short Story, "Fruiting Bodies" (horror) by Brian Lumley; Best Artist, Dave Carson; Best Small Press, *Dagon* edited by Carl T. Ford; Best Newcomer, John Gilbert, editor of *Fear*; Special Award, R. Chetwynd-Hayes.

The Mythopoeic Society Annual Convention gave the Mythopoeic Award for Best Fantasy Novel of 1988 to *Unicorn Mountain* by Michael Bishop.

Ian and Betty Ballantine, whose contribution to American fantasy publishing is immeasurable, celebrated their fifty year anniversary in publishing at the 1989 World SF Convention in Boston, Massachusetts.

James P. Blaylock had his story "Unidentified Objects" (included in this volume, originally published by *Omni*) chosen by the Society of Arts and Sciences for inclusion in *Prize Stories 1990: The O. Henry Awards*. Jane Yolen, author and editor-in-chief of the new Jane Yolen Books, a children's SF/fantasy imprint of Harcourt Brace Jovanovich, won the National Jewish Book Award for her 1988 children's time-travel novel, *The Devil's Arithmetic*, which also won the Sydney J. Taylor Award from the Association of Jewish Libraries, the Judy Lopez Honor Book Award, and it was a nominee for the World Fantasy Award.

Atheneum announced a new children's fantasy line, Dragonflight Books, packaged by Byron Preiss with art direction by Robert Gould. The first two titles are by Robert Silverberg (illustrated by Gould) and Charles de Lint (illustrated by Brian Froud).

Recommended nonfiction about the fantasy field published in 1989: *Dancing at the Edge of the World*, essays by Ursula K. Le Guin (Grove Press); *G.K. Chesterton and C. S. Lewis: The Riddle of Joy*, edited by Michael H. Macdonald and Andrew H. Tadie

(Eerdmans); *Lewis Carroll: Interviews and Recollections*, edited by Morton H. Cohen (University of Iowa Press); *Pathways to Elfland: The Writings of Lord Dunsany*, Darrell Schweitzer (Owlswick Press); *Welsh Myth in Modern Fantasy*, C. W. Sullivan (Greenwood Press); and a reissue of Jonathan Cott's excellent look at Victorian fantasy, *Beyond the Looking Glass* (Viking/Overlook Press.)

The fiction and poetry in this volume comes from a broad range of American and foreign sources including genre anthologies, out-of-genre collections, children's books, magazines, large and small presses. The superabundance of fantasy short fiction published in 1989 made selecting stories both delightful and difficult; there were too many good stories—particularly longer works—that could not be included in this volume because of space limitations. These stories deserve special mention because they are among the very best of the year, and I wish we had the space to reprint them here:

"The Father of Stones" by Lucius Shepard (Ziesing chapbook); "A Dozen Tough Jobs" by Howard Waldrop (Ziesing chapbook); "The Nightingale Sings at Night" by John Crowley (*Novelty*); "Sedalia" by David Schow (*Razored Saddles*); "Juniper, Gentian and Rosemary" by Pamela Dean (*Things That Go Bump in the Night*); "Django Reinhardt Played the Blues" by William Kotzwinkle (*Hot Jazz Trio*) and "The Happy Turnip" by Thomas M. Disch (*The Magazine of F and SF*).

I hope you will seek these stories out. And I hope you will be entertained and enchanted by the stories in the following pages, as I was. Enjoy.

—Terri Windling

Summation 1989: Horror

For fantasy/horror writers and the publishing industry, the most significant event of the year was the furor over Salman Rushdie's novel *The Satanic Verses*. To summarize: The novel contains dream sequences of a fraudulent prophet Mahound, who fundamentalist Muslims assert is a thinly disguised Mohammed. For radical Moslems, it is considered blasphemy to depict the prophet in word or portrait. The novel, first published in Great Britain and winner of the Whitbread Prize, has provoked protest rallies in England, book banning in Islamic countries around the world, violent demonstrations in Pakistan, and, most disturbing—the setting of a price on Rushdie's head by clerics in the Ayatollah Khomeini's Iran.

Many publishers and booksellers courageously supported Viking/Penguin's American publication and continued distribution of the book. Waldenbooks and B. Dalton bookstores temporarily ordered it removed from their shelves to protect employees from potential terrorist acts. In October, *Publishers Weekly* ran an editorial suggesting that the novel not be published in paperback to avoid further offense to Moslem moderates. The editorial was fiercely criticized, but as this volume goes to press, Rushdie remains in hiding. By the end of January 1990 it was unclear when or if Viking/Penguin would issue a paperback edition. The hardcover edition was a phenomenal bestseller and is still available in most bookshops.

Other events in book publishing that directly or indirectly affected the horror field include: Viking/Penguin's announcement in October that it would no longer operate the adult division of E. P. Dutton, the 137-year-old publishing house that it acquired four years previously, as a separate unit. The entire editorial department and support staff (about 20 people) was let go. Ironically, Robert G. Diforio, the chief executive of Dutton and NAL who notified the employees, was himself ousted three days later. Viking has been beset by distribution problems both before and since it moved its warehouses last summer from New Jersey to Tennessee. At the same time, the company had to tighten security as a result of *The Satanic Verses* controversy.

Several companies went under. Pageant Books, foundering in 1988, officially closed down operations in 1989 (although as of January 1990 no decision had been made as to inventory disposition). Critic's Choice Paperbacks ceased publication after four years. Consulting editor Martin H. Greenberg's SF reprint line for Bart Books has been suspended. The purchase of Paperjacks by Zebra has been put on hold. Tudor Books, an occasional publisher of horror founded in 1987, closed its New York editorial office and moved in with Leisure Books; Tudor's three member staff, including editorial director Kate Duffy, left at the end of July. The trade division of The Donning Company/Publishers has been sold to Schiffer Publishing Ltd. of West Chester, PA and will no longer publish fiction. (Donning published the hardcover of S. P. Somtow's novel *Vampire Junction*). Less than two weeks before its 150th birthday, Dodd, Mead & Company, one of the oldest privately owned publishers in the country, went out of business. According to industry sources, poor business decisions ran Dodd, Mead into the ground. Dodd, Mead had published such distinguished titles as *The Island of Dr. Moreau* by H. G. Wells, *The Dodd, Mead Gallery of Horror* edited by Charles L. Grant, and several books by Edward Gorey.

On the positive side, Dell will be launching a new horror imprint called Abyss in February 1991 leading off with Kathe Koja's first novel, *The Funhole*. Daniel Levy was named editor of Citadel Press, a fifty-year old imprint acquired in January 1989 by the Carol Publishing Group: they launched the Citadel Twilight series which publishes "fiction of the imagination." The first titles, released this spring, were the first five volumes of *The Collected Stories of Philip K. Dick* and the first three volumes of *The Selected Stories of Robert Bloch*. Elsewhere, the Book-of-the-Month Club is creating a twenty-title Stephen King Library, which will be offered to members singly or collectively, beginning in 1990.

In Great Britain: William Kimber, Ltd. long known in the field as a publisher of collections and anthologies (mostly library sales), was bought by Thorsons. William Collins turned around and bought Thorsons and dumped Kimber and Equation (the Thorson horror line). And so it goes. Victor Gollancz Ltd., one of Britain's last major privately owned publishing houses, was bought by Houghton Mifflin. Not long before the announcement, SF publishing director Malcolm Edwards left Gollancz to take on the same post at Grafton Books. He, Nick Austin, and John Boothe are developing a new imprint for all Grafton fantasy and SF in hardcover, trade and mass market.

Mandarin, a newly created mass-market paperback imprint from the Octopus Group, was launched in 1989. The editorial director is Max Eilenberg, formerly of Secker & Warburg. Science fiction, fantasy and horror will be an important part of the program, and Jo Fletcher is their genre consultant.

Pan Books is expanding its presence in horror. There will be a complete relaunch of the thirty-year-old Pan Book of Horror series with number thirty-one appearing in 1990. Herbert van Thal edited the series for twenty years. The first volume used all reprints and its success surprised the publisher; from number five on, the series contained all original stories. The earlier volumes had a great impact on both British and American horror writers, including Charles L. Grant, F. Paul Wilson, Clive Barker, Shaun Hutson,

Ramsey Campbell and Dennis Etchison. When van Thal died, Clarence Paget, the former editorial director of Pan, took over as editor. To celebrate the revival of the series, Pan is releasing *Dark Voices: The Best from the Pan Book of Horror Stories*, edited by Stephen Jones and David Sutton, who will also co-edit the overhauled series. Pan has also recently bought horror novels by K. W. Jeter, and Thomas Sullivan, *Faces of Fear* edited by Douglas E. Winter, and a couple of non-fiction Stephen King books.

Futura is also actively buying horror, adding Jonathan Carroll and Ramsey Campbell to their list. Robinson Publishing, which publishes *Fantasy Tales* and the British edition of Gardner Dozois's *Best SF*, is planning to publish a companion volume to the latter. The new annual will contain selections from a variety of horror writers—more a sampling of the horror available than a "best of" according to co-editor Stephen Jones, who will be sharing duties with Ramsey Campbell. The volume will include an overview of the field and obituaries. It will debut in October 1990 to tie in with the British Fantasy Convention. Robinson is also publishing Thomas Ligotti with a paperback version of his collection, *Songs of a Dead Dreamer*.

In general, although horror continues to maintain a hold on the market, book publishers across the board—not just in horror—are cutting back. Editors feel that there's a glut of horror novels and that too many generic covers are being produced—confusing and frustrating readers. The cover problem is worsened by pressure from sales to use more and more special effects to ace out the competition. This gets expensive and defeats the original purpose of trying to make a line's covers stand out from the pack. In another trend, some psychological horror fiction is being packaged as general fiction or like mainstream bestsellers; there's more mixing of the genres of SF and horror, spurred on by recent novels from Dean R. Koontz and Stephen King. Bantam continues to publish about six horror titles a year and starting in 1990 plans a new look for their covers; Tor has cut back to two horror paperbacks (instead of four) a month but is still publishing four to eight hardcovers a season. While Warner Books has no established monthly horror program, they've bought paperback rights to World Fantasy Award winner Dan Simmons's opus *Carrion Comfort*, previously published in a sold-out, limited hardcover edition by Dark Harvest. The book will be released in October 1990, and the company has high hopes for it and for Simmons. Warner has also bought rights to Garfield Reeves-Stevens's first three novels, previously published only in Canada. Onyx, NAL's horror line, continues to publish one paperback a month. As of August, 1990, Ace/Charter will become Charter/Diamond and eventually just Diamond. This line will be generating two original horror titles a month (which won't preclude Jove or Berkley from doing their own horror material).

What follows is an admittedly biased novel reading list—as often as not these novels were not published as genre but I feel they could be of interest to horror readers:

Midnight by Dean R. Koontz (Putnam) is a Dr. Moreau techno-horror thriller with the typical "family" grouping of Koontz characters. Effective and fast-paced.

Dead Lines by John Skipp and Craig Spector (Bantam) is about a suicide victim whose horror stories are found in the loft where he died by the next tenant. The "discovered" stories are interspersed throughout the book. They show the wide range and control Skipp and Spector *can* wield in their work.

In Darkness Waiting by John Shirley (Onyx, 1988) is ambitious, powerful, and scary, if a bit overlong. It's about a pop psychologist playing around with the mind and releasing violent impulses better left alone in his patients (not unlike David Cronenberg's *The Brood*). Psychological and supernatural. A good read.

Antibodies by David J. Skal (Congdon & Weed/Worldwide Library). To escape their bodies and all the attendant needs of the flesh, the adherents of a weird sect embrace the idea that only by becoming one with machines can they reach a higher spiritual plane. Well-written, terrifying SF/horror. One of the best 1989 paperbacks.

In the Land of the Dead by K. W. Jeter (Onyx) is completely unpredictable, wonderfully portentous, and very, very dark. There are some supernatural elements in the character of Fay, a witchy woman who may or may not be able to talk to, listen to, and reanimate the dead. Disturbing, depressing and bleak but awfully good. Highly recommended.

The Hunting Season by John Coyne (Macmillan, 1987) is a disturbing novel about an anthropologist who moves to the Catskills for the summer to research inbreeding in isolated communites. Fascinating, though it has annoying loose ends.

Body Mortgage by Richard Engling (Onyx) is about a Chicago detective and his very bright side-kick facing the millennium. There are some unresolved plot threads but basically it's a good, tightly-paced suspense novel with very likable protagonists. Excellent SF/horror.

Geek Love by Katherine Dunn (Knopf). If you can buy the premise—that a carny couple decide to breed their own freak show by taking thalidomide and other awful drugs to birth their own monster children—the rest of the novel's a breeze. Shocking, perhaps, and a bit overlong, but it's a rich and colorful work.

Ash Wednesday by Chet Williamson (Tor, 1989) is about the dead coming back to life in a small Pennsylvania town, forcing the townspeople to come to terms with various forms of guilt. The most chilling thing about the existence of the ghosts, at least for the townspeople, is that they seem to want nothing. They do nothing. They just *are*. And no one can explain them. Not all that frightening, but beautifully written and haunting.

Cold Eye by Giles Blunt (Arbor House) is a terrifying first novel which snuck up on me despite my resistance to the protagonist, a rather unlikable, ambitious, and temper-amental artist. He meets an ugly dwarf who promises to make him a success with no strings attached (sure). The dwarf is precognitive and knows when violent acts will be committed, and has the artist meet him to "witness" and later paint the events. Nick, the artist, is so arrogant from the get-go that you want to smack him—so the loss of his "soul" doesn't seem very meaningful. Some flat characterizations mar the work, but it's still more interesting and more ambitious than most of the genre horror being published today.

Sunglasses After Dark by Nancy Collins (Onyx) is an excellent first novel about a vampire. Much better than most of the stuff being published today. Well-written for the most part, it's violent and sexy without being misogynistic. Some loose ends but it's really hot, and highly recommended.

Carrion Comfort by Dan Simmons (Dark Harvest) is an intricate interwoven story of mind vampires, and the victims-turned-hunters in pursuit of the amoral creatures. The story also pits the older "vampires" against new ones who have their own special games and agenda. Long, ambitious novel about violence in the twentieth century and those who feed off it. By the author of the World Fantasy Award-winning first novel *Song of Kali*.

Nightshade by Jack Butler (Atlantic Monthly Press) is by the author of *Jujitsu for Christ*. This is an odd SF novel about a vampire on twenty-first century Mars. Readable, energetic but somewhat pretentious; Butler claims to have written the "first full-boogie *literary* science fiction novel." If he'd paid more attention to why his protagonist is a vampire from the nineteenth century who lives in the twenty-first century, and less with the so-called literary aspects, he'd have written a better novel. As it is, Butler uses a lot of slang that needs a glossary and then spends the last chapter trying to tie up all his many loose ends. Ambitious failure.

The Coachman Rat by David Henry Wilson (Carroll & Graf) is Cinderella from the point of view of the rat that was changed into a coachman for a night. In it, Cinderella and the prince do not live happily ever after. It's a charming fable about power and man's inhumanity to man. Fantasy/horror. Lovely, powerful, sad.

Those Who Hunt the Night by Barbara Hambly (Del Rey, 1988) is one of the best vampire novels I've ever read. It opens with a mystery: Some time in the early 1900s, Oxford don James Asher is hired by a vampire to find a vampire murderer in London. Hambly's writing and characterizations bring new energy and life to the vampire novel. Why this didn't win the horror/fantasy awards in 1988 (it wasn't even nominated) is a mystery to me.

The Grotesque by Patrick McGrath (Poseidon) is a brilliant first novel, essentially a murder mystery told by a paralyzed mute in a wheelchair who is, as the reader discovers, a very unreliable narrator. Unlike McGrath's short stories, this novel is under control; it's beautifully wrought with an ambiguous denouement.

Reaper by C. Terry Cline (Donald I. Fine) is a psychological suspense novel about a serial killer who hates old women, cats, and astrology, and the disgraced detective who hunts him down. Interesting plot, good characterizations, suspenseful—what more could you ask for? I'm impressed. It's the first Cline novel I've read.

The Wolf's Hour by Robert R. McCammon (Pocket Books) is an entertaining thriller about a British spy during World War II who happens to be a werewolf. His travails in occupied France and Germany while on a secret mission are interwoven with his past—how he became a werewolf and his life up until he leaves his native Russia for England.

A *Child Across the Sky* by Jonathan Carroll (Legend, U.K.) is slightly connected to *Bones of the Moon* and *Sleeping in Flame*, his last two novels. The book opens with the suicide of Philip Strayhorn, maker of slasher films. His friend Weber Gregston tries to discover why Strayhorn killed himself. The novel is about art and the creative process and artistic responsibility. Brilliant and intense although I'm not entirely convinced it hangs together. Still, highly recommended.

My Pretty Pony by Stephen King and designed by Barbara Kruger (Knopf/Whitney Museum) is about the nature of time and our perception of it during different periods of our lives. This coffee table book is a slight story and more a collectible for King fans than anything else.

Dreamthorp by Chet Williamson (Avon) combines psycho-horror with the supernatural and makes it work. Excellent characterizations and writing. It's an example of what horror writing should and can be. One of the year's best.

The Perfect Place by Sheila Kohler (Knopf) is a first novel that the publisher accurately depects as a "psychosexual striptease." Kohler's control over the material and structure dazzles as the reader realizes what the author is trying for and ultimately accomplishes. This short, subtle mystery won't be for everyone but I think it's quite brilliant.

Ancient Images by Ramsey Campbell (Scribner's) is an excellent melding of contemporary concerns with the occult past. Like Carroll's A *Child Across the Sky*, this novel's centerpiece is a horror film that may or may not be evil. The two books also share excellent characterizations and an ability to scare the reader.

John Dollar by Marianne Wiggins (Harper & Row) has echoes of Golding's *Lord of the Flies* but manifests its own originality. Eight young girls, their schoolteacher, and their teacher's lover (a sailor) are washed up onto the shore of an island off their home of Burma and try to survive. Beautifully written with a wonderful depiction of the British colonial mentality.

* * *

Horror or borderline horror novels published in 1989 include: *Webs* by Scott Baker (Tor); *The Axman Cometh* by John Farris (Tor); *The Influence* by Ramsey Campbell (Tor); *Haunted* by James Herbert (Putnam); *Mindbender* by James Cohen and Peter Rubie (Lynx); *Vampyr* by Brian Lumley (Tor); *Resurrection Dreams* by Richard Laymon (Onyx); *The Black School* by J. N. Williamson (Dell); *The Dream of a Beast* by Neil Jordan (Random House); *A Candle for D'Artagnan* by Chelsea Quinn Yarbro (Tor); *Night Things* by Michael Talbot (Avon); *Walkers* by Graham Masterton (Tor); *Playing for Keeps* by Jack Kendall (Avon); *The Spirit Stalker* by Nina Romberg (Pinnacle); *Monocolo* by Theodore Taylor (Donald I. Fine); *Black Horizon* by Robert Masello (Jove); *Thunder Rise* by G. Wayne Miller (Arbor House/Morrow); *Fury* by John Coyne (Warner); *The House of Stairs* by Ruth Rendell writing as Barbara Vine (Harmony); *Oktober* by Stephen Gallagher (Tor); *Christopher Unborn* by Carlos Fuentes (Farrar, Straus & Giroux); *Shattered Glass* by Elizabeth Bergstrom (Jove); *The Bridesmaid* by Ruth Rendell (Mysterious Press); *In a Dark Dream* by Charles L. Grant (Tor); *Eva* by Peter Dickinson (Delacorte); *Full Moon* by Mick Winters (Berkley); *Resurrection, Inc.* by Kevin J. Anderson (Signet); *Night Angel* by Kate Green (Delacorte); *Charades* by Janette Turner Hospital (Bantam); *Grace* by Michael Stewart (Atheneum); *Blackground* by Joan Aiken (Doubleday); *Nighteyes* by Garfield Reeves-Stevens (Doubleday); *The Mummy: or Ramses the Damned* by Anne Rice (Ballantine); *While My Pretty One Sleeps* by Mary Higgins Clark (Simon & Schuster); *Deliver Us from Evil* by Stephen Smoke (Berkley); *She Wakes* by Jack Ketchum (Berkley); *The Place* by T. M. Wright (Tor); *The Great and Secret Show* by Clive Barker (Harper & Row); *Julian's House* by Judith Hawkes (Ticknor & Fields), *The Dark Half* by Stephen King (Viking), *Mystery* by Peter Straub (Dutton); *Pulse* by William R. Dantz (Avon); *The Encyclopedia of the Dead* by Danilo Kiš (Farrar, Straus); *Dreamspy* by Jacqueline Lichtenberg (St. Martin's); *The Bad Place* by Dean R. Koontz (Putnam); *Dream Baby* by Bruce McAllister (Tor), *The Paradise Motel* by Eric McCormack (Viking); *Beneath Still Waters* by Matthew J. Costello (Berkley); *The History of Luminous Motion* by Scott Bradfield (Knopf); *The Woodwitch, A Tale of Horror* by Stephen Gregory (St. Martin's); *Next, After Lucifer* by Daniel Rhodes (St. Martin's/Tor); *The Ridge* by Lisa Cantrell (Tor); *Night of the Moonbow* by Thomas Tryon (Knopf); *The Drive-in* 2 by Joe Lansdale (Bantam); *Creature* by John Saul (Bantam); *The Dwelling* by Tom Elliott (St. Martin's); and, *The Story-Teller* by Mario Vargas Llosa (Farrar, Straus).

1989 was an excellent year for short horror fiction despite the demise of some major magazine markets. First, the bad news. *Twilight Zone* put out its last few issues and David Silva's *The Horror Show* announced there would be one last special double issue in the spring of 1990. *The Horror Show* had been improving steadily over the years, and while still not officially a pro market because of low payment rates, it certainly published professional-quality fiction. Still unconfirmed rumor has it that *Amazing Stories* (which published the occasional horror story or poem) has suspended publication. Editor Patrick Price quit TSR last year and has been editing the magazine on a freelance basis. Publisher Mike Cook left late in 1989. All new material sent to the magazine has been returned without comment via *Dragon* magazine's fiction editor (another TSR publication). *Slaughterhouse Magazine* died after its fifth issue. Apparently, the sixth issue was ready for the printer when the publisher pulled the plug. Among reasons cited were problems with the distributor.

This leaves even fewer prozines regularly running horror fiction. Nevertheless, the short fiction field seems quite healthy, as will be seen by the amount of stories that made my recommended list at the back of this book. Right now, though, this is a result of the unusually large number of original anthologies published in 1989—from both specialty presses and larger publishers, in paperback and hardcover.

But first the magazines:

Several horror and horror-related magazines published good fiction in 1989. *Midnight Graffiti*, edited by Jessica Horsting and James Van Hise is by far the best-looking horror magazine around, although it hasn't yet gotten onto a regular schedule—only two issues came out in 1989. The art is wonderful (but not always credited) and the magazine is attractively designed. There's good news coverage of the field, but not enough fiction, and what is run should have more of an edge to it.

Fear, edited by John Gilbert, is the only slick horror magazine published in Great Britain. *Fear* provides thorough coverage of filmed horror and slightly less adequate coverage of print. It also runs interesting profiles and occasionally, thoughtful essays. The amount of fiction published has increased but remains inconsistent in quality. There were good stories by Jonathan Carroll, Steve Rasnic Tem, Nicholas Royle, Ian Watson, Tony Reed, Simon D. Ings, and Rod Pike. I think the grisly, over-the-top covers probably turn off readers who would otherwise be interested in the magazine. *Fear* is now monthly and recently achieved professional status, with a paid circulation of 19,000.

Weird Tales, edited by Darrell Schweitzer, John Betancourt, and George H. Scithers, accomplishes what it set out to do—it is a premier purveyor of dark fantasy. But the emphasis is on "fantasy" rather than "dark," or in any case, usually not dark enough for my taste. The fall 1989 issue is, overall, the best one since the magazine's most recent resurrection: there's very good fiction by Nina Kiriki Hoffman, Jonathan Carroll, and Brian Lumley, a powerful cover, interiors, and portfolio by J. K. Potter; plus an interview to go with a rare new novelette by Karl Edward Wagner. The winter 1989 issue allowed SF artist Vincent Di Fate to stretch and featured good stories by Brian Lumley, Anne Goring and Larry Walker.

The Twilight Zone, edited by Tappan King, published its last three issues. One of the magazine's best stories, by Reginald Bretnor, appeared in February.

Pulphouse, edited by Kristine Kathryn Rusch, officially put out one horror issue in 1989, but in fact its "genres" overlapped quite a bit. There was good horror fiction in the fantasy issue by William F. Wu, Ken Wisman, David B. Silva and Charles de Lint. There was also notable fiction in the science fiction issue by Rick Lawler and in the horror issue by Elizabeth Hand, Francis Matozzo, John Maclay, Darrell Schweitzer, Esther M. Friesner, J. N. Williamson and Adam-Troy Castro.

The Magazine of Fantasy & Science Fiction, edited by Edward L. Ferman, published excellent horror by Lucius Shepard, Nancy Etchemendy, Garry Kilworth, Gene Wolfe, Orson Scott Card, Patricia Anthony, Marc Laidlaw, Brian Aldiss, and Esther M. Friesner.

Isaac Asimov's Science Fiction Magazine, edited by Gardner Dozois, published fine horror by Charles Sheffield, Steven Utley, Gregory Benford, Richard Kadrey, Rory Harper, Kathe Koja, Suzy McKee Charnas, and Lucius Shepard.

Omni, (edited by myself) published horror by Gahan Wilson, Joyce Carol Oates, and Jonathan Carroll, Richard Christian Matheson, and Michaelene Pendleton.

Amazing Stories, edited by Patrick Price, published good horror by Kristine Kathryn Rusch, E. W. Smith, and an excellent poem by Amy Schaefer.

Ellery Queen's Mystery Magazine, edited by Eleanor Sullivan, published borderline horror by Andrew Vachss, Takashi Atoda, Reginald Hill, and Antonia Fraser.

Alfred Hitchcock's Mystery Magazine, edited by Cathleen Jordan, published borderline horror by Nancy Simpson Hoke and Gregory Robinson.

Interzone, edited by David Pringle, is primarily a science fiction magazine but has been publishing more and more excellent material that could be considered horror or fantasy. Among the best in 1989 were pieces by Karen Joy Fowler, Ramsey Campbell, Kim Newman, Nicholas Royle, J. G. Ballard, and Ian R. MacLeod.

Weirdbook 23/24, published by Paul Ganley, was the twentieth anniversary issue (pub date was late 1988 but copies arrived in early 1989). The magazine hadn't been out for a long time before that, however, this venerable magazine carries a good variety of a certain kind of dark fantasy—perhaps more mannered than I like. There were good stories by Brian Lumley, Joseph Payne Brennan, Al Sarrantonio, Gerald Page, and Delia Sherman.

Nocturne is a new magazine edited and published by Michael J. Lotus and Vincent L. Michael. In late 1988 and 1989 there were two issues. At $7.00 a pop it's expensive, but *Nocturne* looks good, and features interesting art by contemporary artists (Harry O. Morris, Leilah Wendell, H. E. Fassl, Thomas Willoch, T. M. Caldwell and Rick Lieder), plus old woodcuts and photographs. Also published are excerpts from the critical writing on the supernatural by writers such as Baudelaire. The magazine features better than average poetry and good fiction by Bruce Boston, Patricia Russo, and Mark Rainey.

The Scream Factory, edited by Clifford V. Brooks, Peter Enfantino and Joe Lopez, had a thoughtful, critical essay on "The Chronicles Of Anne Rice," book and film reviews, and some interviews. There was also impressive fiction by A. R. Morlan in issue two.

Deathrealm, edited by Mark Rainey, is definitely on the upswing. Issue eight was an excellent one, with terrific stories by Thomas Ligotti, Jeffrey Osier, and Ken Wisman. The cover by Alan Rainey was nicely atmospheric. Also included was a strange interview with Ligotti, who, judging from the tone of his responses in this interview, would seem to wish to remain as mysterious as possible. There was more Lovecraftian horror than I would have liked in issue nine but the quality was very good. The best illustrations were by Timothy Standish, Rodger Gerberding, and Robert Troy Jamison; there was good fiction and poetry by John Maclay, Fred Chappell, and Shawn Ramsey. In issue ten I was impressed by the art of Osier, Gerberding, Harry Fassl, and Cathy Buburuz and the stories by Yvonne Navarro and Jeffrey Goddin.

New Pathways, edited by Michael G. Adkisson, generally has good interior art and covers. Horror fiction is not regularly published, but issue fourteen, the third anniversary issue, featured a quiet little chiller by Steve Rasnic Tem, along with some horror reviews by Misha and an excellent cover by Mark Bilokur. Issue fifteen had good horror by George W. Smyth, a great cover by Brad Foster and good interiors by Richard Schindler. Some horror reviews.

Skeleton Crew, #V, edited by Dave Hughes, contained some good articles and art, but not enough fiction. The effective cover was by Martin McKenna. There were so many typos in the Lumley story that it was distracting. Issue #VI, which I haven't seen, was supposed to be their first full-color issue.

Back Brain Recluse, edited by Chris Reed, is a combination of horror, fantasy and SF with tiny but readable type and a nice design. There was a good story by Steve Sneyd in issue twelve.

Dagon, edited by Carl T. Ford, is excellent for what it does, which is to specialize in the Cthulhu mythos. Issue 22/23 includes some excellent essays on horror and there are fine stories by Thomas Ligotti and Mark Morrison.

Eldritch Tales, edited by Crispin Burnham, continues to publish some excellent stories. Those I was most impressed with were by A. R. Morlan, Bentley Little, Don Webb, and Christina Kiplinger. Good art by Ron Leming, Harry O. Morris, Rodger Gerberding, Charles Dougherty, and Augie Weidemann. I received the last 1989 issue too late to review this year.

Grue, edited by Peggy Nadramia, has improved more in general quality than any other small press magazine this year. Issue ten presents very good fiction by Randolph Cirilo, Thomas Ligotti, Eugene Marten, Gery Whetter, Wayne Allen Sallee, George W. Smyth, and an excellent poem by Bruce Boston.

The Horror Show, edited by David B. Silva, put out two issues in 1989, both with creepily effective Harry O. Morris covers. This magazine featured consistently good fiction; I especially liked stories by Darrell Schweitzer, Susan M. Watkins, G. L. Raisor and Brian Hodge.

2 A.M. edited by Gretta M. Anderson put out four issues in 1989 and published noteworthy fiction by Keven J. Anderson, Jeffrey Osier, C. S. Fuqua, Donald R. Burleson.

Carnage Hall, edited by David Griffin, made its debut at the Horror Writers of America meeting last summer. It's the best new small press horror magazine I've seen in some time. Griffin starts with an editorial criticizing the critics of SF/horror/fantasy. The magazine features excellent illustrations throughout by Grandville, Edmund V. Gillion Jr. and Davli Poli; a good (although not particularly horrific) story by Kim Sterling; an interesting interview with Peggy Nadramia; and a painfully honest and perceptive commentary by Melli Morrison on small press publications. A high quality, thoughtful magazine, willing to offend. I just wish there were more fiction pieces and that the typeface was slightly larger. I look forward to the second issue.

A bunch of weird magazines from Cryptic Publications, published and/or edited by Robert M. Price, ranged from the regular *Crypt of Cthulhu* and *Tales of Lovecraftian Horror*, and *Revelations from Yuggoth* to the new *Tales of the Episopals* and various Lin Carter material. Most of it is exactly what the titles say.

Not One of Us #5, edited by John Benson, is difficult to read (because of the reproduction) but nonetheless contained one of the best stories of the year, by Gary A. Braunbeck.

Finally, we'll see if the newest kid on the block, *Iniquities* ("The Magazine of Great Wickedness and Wonder"), can live up to its great advance p.r., when and if it appears sometime in 1990.

In addition, there was fine horror or borderline horror in *The New Yorker* (poem), *The Nation* (poem), *Another Dimension* (Special Report), *Witness Magazine*, *Argonaut*, *Gorezone*, *Thin Ice*, *Cemetery Dance*, *Granta 28*, *Esquire*, and *Playboy*, by, respectively, Dana Gioia, Michael Ryan, Dorothy Cannell, Misha, Charles R. Saunders, Albert J. Manachino, Dale Hammell, J. R. Ericson, Timothy M. Swain, Lucy Taylor, William Relling, Jr., Jeannette Winterson, Mario Vargas Llosa, Steven Millhauser, and T. Coraghessan Boyle.

Many of the small press magazines come out irregularly and are only available through subscription. Here are some addresses and prices. Only U.S. subscription prices are listed. For overseas information, query the publication. I've included pro or semi-pro magazines unavailable on newsstands. *Fear*, P. O. Box 20, Ludlow, Shropshire SY8 1DB, England, thirty-six pounds sterling outside Europe (airmail) for twelve issues. *Midnight Graffiti*, 13101 Sudan Road, Poway, CA 92064, $24.00 for a first-class, one-year subscription. *Weird Tales*, P. O. Box 13418, Philadelphia, PA 19101, $18.00 for six quarterly issues, $34.00 for twelve quarterly issues. *Grue* Magazine, Hell's Kitchen Productions, P. O. Box 370, Times Square Station, New York, NY 10108, $11.00 for a three-issue subscription (one year). *Deathrealm*, 3223-F Regents Park, Greensboro, NC 27405, $13.00 for four issues (one year). *2 A.M.*, P. O. Box 6754, Rockford, IL 61125-1754, $19.00 for four issues. *Weirdbook*, P. O. Box 149, Buffalo, NY 14226-0149, $25.00 for seven issues. *Nocturne*, P. O. Box 1715, Chicago, IL 60690, $6.00 plus $1.50 postage for the second issue. *Back Brain Recluse*, 16 Somersall Lane, Chesterfield, Derbyshire S40 3LA, England, $14.00 (cash only, no coins) for a four-issue subscription. *Carnage Hall*, P. O. Box 7, Esopus, NY 12429, $3.00 for the second issue. *Dagon*, 11 Warwick Road, Twickenham, Middlesex TW2 6SW, England, $20.00 surface mail or $30.00 airmail (cash only) for a six-issue subscription. *Not One of Us*, 44 Shady Lane, Storrs, CT 06268, $10.50 for a three-issue subscription. *Crypt of Cthulhu, Tales of Lovecraftian Horror*, and other related magazines, Cryptic Publications, 107 East James Street, Mount Olive, NC 28365, various prices, please write for subscription information. *Thin Ice*, Kathleen Jurgens, 379 Lincoln Avenue, Council Bluffs, IA 51503, $4.50 per issue. *Eldritch Tales*, Crispin Burnham, 1051 Wellington Road, Lawrence, KS 66049, $24.00 for four issues. *The Scream Factory*, 145 Tully Road, San Jose, CA 95111, $17.00 for four issues. For more information on small press magazines get *The Scavenger's Newsletter*, 519 Ellinwood, Osage City, KS 66523-1329, $12.50 for a first class one-year subscription (twelve issues), payable to Janet Fox.

Even with small press magazines booming, the best place to find consistently good short horror fiction is in original anthologies. The general feeling among publishers is that theme anthologies work better than single author collections—except for those by bestselling authors—probably because theme anthologies are easier to package. Original anthologies are more in demand right now than reprint ones, with follow-up editions promised for *Hot Blood, Book of the Dead, Blood Is Not Enough, Architecture of Fear* and *Stalkers*. Also, several new original anthologies are in the works for 1990 and 1991.

The *Shadows* anthology series has been discontinued by Charles L. Grant. Grant says he's tired of editing them and wants to concentrate more on his writing. He also contends that the quality of writing has dropped drastically in the last five years, making it hard to find publishable material. There will be a major volume (200,000 words) of *Final Shadows* published by Bantam in the fall of 1991. Grant is not giving up editing, however. He plans to publish a biannual professional horror magazine to be called *Shadows* beginning in the summer of 1993. It will be digest size, contain only fiction, and have no illustrations.

Post Mortem, edited by David B. Silva and Paul F. Olson (St. Martin's), is a consistently entertaining anthology of ghost stories. My only criticism is that an amateurish introduction belies the excellence of its contents. The editors pretend the book is a "phantom" like the *Necronomicon*. Yet another attempt at cuteness makes the contributor's page all but useless (match the authors to their past works). Good fiction by Kathryn Ptacek, Charles de Lint, Steve Rasnic Tem and Melanie Tem, Thomas Tessier, Charles L. Grant, P. W. Sinclair, and David B. Silva.

Phantoms, edited by Martin H. Greenberg and Rosalind M. Greenberg (DAW), capitalizes on the popularity of the musical *Phantom of the Opera*, but doesn't contain enough stories that *run* with the theme. Most stay close to the background of the opera house, which is too limiting. The best stories are those which only peripherally refer to the phantom, like those by Daniel Ransom, Karen Haber, and, particularly, Steve Rasnic Tem's "The Unmasking." (A word about Tem—he has produced a number of outstanding short stories in 1989 including: "Merry-Go-Round," in *New Pathways*; "Hooks," in *Fear*; "Resettling," with Melanie Tem in *Post Mortem*; "Nocturne," (poem) in *Blood is Not Enough*; and, "The Strangers," in *Scare Care*. Isn't it time for a collection?)

Book of the Dead, edited by John Skipp and Craig Spector (Bantam)—I'm not sure what to make of this original anthology set in George Romero's cannibal zombie universe. There's a sameness of tone to most of the stories and even the best—by Edward Bryant, Joe R. Lansdale, Chan McConnell, Ramsey Campbell, Steven R. Boyett, Robert R. McCammon and Brian Hodge—suffer because of the company they keep. There are four (count 'em, four) stories featuring castration, and too many with gory murder and mayhem as their climaxes. Basically, my feeling is that zombies are rather boring as characters unless you give them some humanity, but once you do they're no longer zombies—a bit of a problem.

Hot Blood, edited by Jeff Gelb and Lonn Friend (Pocket): This anthology of erotic horror boasts some excellent reprints, but the originals are fairly mediocre—with a few exceptions, specifically Ray Garton's "Punishments."

Blue World, by Robert R. McCammon (Grafton, U.K.), is an excellent collection of McCammon's shorter work including the novella "Blue World" (which if it hasn't been optioned yet for a movie it should be any second). It's a thriller about a priest tempted by a porn star, who in turn is being stalked by a serial killer. Most of the stories are a combination of horror, SF and the unclassifiable. McCammon, who began his writing career as a novelist, has developed into an exceptional short story writer.

The New Frontier, edited by Joe R. Lansdale (Doubleday), while definitely a western anthology, also contains some excellent fantasy and a bit of very good horror as well. Surprisingly varied in tone and theme. Good stuff, particularly the stories by Leif Enger, Loren D. Estleman, Scott Cupp, and Gary L. Raisor.

Heatseeker, by John Shirley (Scream/Press), is a collection with mostly reprints and three excellent originals. A combination of SF, horror, and fantasy.

Scare Care, edited by Graham Masterton (Tor): The introduction claims, "with few exceptions, the stories in *Scare Care* are brand new, written specifically for this volume"; in fact, at least thirteen of the thirty-eight stories are reprints, most uncredited to their original source of publication. Regardless of the origins of stories, this volume is published to benefit a worthy cause: The earnings go to aid abused children. There are good originals by Felice Picano, J. N. Williamson, John Maclay, William Relling, Jr., Steve Rasnic Tem, Gary A. Braunbeck, and Chris Lacher.

Blood Is Not Enough, edited by Ellen Datlow (William Morrow). Stories and poems concentrating on vampirism rather than the vampire, with original material by Scott Baker, Chet Williamson, Susan Casper, Tanith Lee, Steve Rasnic Tem, Harvey Jacobs, Edward Bryant, Joe Haldeman, Garry Kilworth, and Pat Cadigan.

Masques III, edited by J. N. Williamson (St. Martin's), is a really good looking anthology. The cover (using a Hieronymus Bosch painting) and typeface are quite elegant. Credit for the jacket design should go to Raquel Jaramillo. Even though there are excellent stories by Dan Simmons, Joseph A. Citro, Wayne Allen Sallee, Bill Ryan, Diane Taylor, William F. Nolan, Melissa Mia Hall and Doug Winter, and Jeannette M. Hopper, as well as an excellent poem by Bruce Boston and Robert Frazier, unfortunately the overall impression is mediocrity. I suspect the anthology's unevenness is related to the large number of stories and poems (33); too many of them are short toss-offs. Still, recommended.

Dark Fantasies, edited by Chris Morgan (Legend, U.K.), is disappointing on the whole, despite good work by R. M. Lamming, Stephen Gallagher, Christopher Evans, Nicholas Royle, and Chris Morgan. Not enough edge to the collection.

The 30th Pan Book of Horror Stories, selected by Clarence Paget (Pan, U.K.), was also fairly unimaginative. Good stories by Christopher Fowler and Jack Wainer.

Razored Saddles, edited by Joe R. Lansdale and Pat LoBrutto (Dark Harvest), is a collection of the weirdest western fiction you'll ever read, ranging from transvestites at the Alamo to a nasty nasty about a romance novelist who goes west to fulfill his lifelong dream (reprinted in this volume). Good horror and dark fantasy by David J. Schow, Chet Williamson, F. Paul Wilson, Robert R. McCammon and Ardath Mayhar. A terrifically creepy dust jacket by Rick Araluce.

Patterns, by Pat Cadigan (Ursus Press), is a collection of some of her horror, fantasy and SF stories with one terrific original (included here). Excellent.

Night Visions VII edited by Stanley Wiater (Dark Harvest) is disappointing: the Gary Brandner novella, while not all that original, is entertaining; Chet Williamson's novella is excellent, his short stories good (but not among his best); Richard Laymon's story "Wishbone" isn't bad. But no real standouts.

The Bureau of Lost Souls, by Christopher Fowler (Century Hutchinson, U.K.), reprints seven stories from his two *City Jitters* collections last year. The five new stories are much better.

Christmas Ghosts, edited by Kathryn Cramer and David G. Hartwell (Wynwood), is a good collection of ghost stories including originals by Gene Wolfe, Chet Williamson and a knockout by Martha Soukup. Not all that horrific but definitely for anyone interested in fantasy and dark fantasy.

Forests of the Night, by Tanith Lee (Unwin Hyman, U.K.), is a combination of horror, SF, and fantasy, including her World Fantasy Award-winning story "The Gorgon" and eight originals.

Antique Dust, by Robert Westall (Viking), is his first adult collection of short stories. He's better known in England than in the U.S. Even if the stories aren't always original in plot, the writing freshens them; all are about an antique dealer named Geoff Ashdon, his friends, family and acquaintances in England—and the ghostly doings around them. It's an excellent collection.

Arrows of Eros, edited by Alex Stewart (NEL, U.K.), has a terrible cover and a gimmicky title, but there's some decent fiction. It's a combination of SF and horror, and better than it looks.

In the Hollow of the Deep-Sea Wave, by Garry Kilworth (The Bodley Head, U.K.), contains a novella and several stories (including fantasy and SF published in *Omni* and *Asimov's*) and one marvelous mainstream story ("The Blood Orange") which was short-listed for a British award and chosen by Ruth Rendell for a British mainstream *Best of Year* collection. Excellent work by the author of *The Songbirds of Pain*.

Things That Go Bump in the Night, edited by Jane Yolen and Martin H. Greenberg (Harper & Row), is a young adult collection of dark fantasy and a wee bit of horror. That wee bit includes stories by William Sleator and Mary K. Whittington.

Stalkers, edited by Ed Gorman and Martin H. Greenberg (Dark Harvest), has some excellent stories of "terror and suspense" by James Kisner, F. Paul Wilson, Robert R. McCammon, Ed Gorman, Al Sarrantonio, and Charles de Lint.

Zenith, edited by David S. Garnett (Sphere, U.K.), is an original anthology of science fiction, some with horrific overtones. There were excellent SF/horror stories by Garry Kilworth and Andrew Stephenson (both included here).

Other anthologies and collections with some good original horror fiction were: *Warhammer: Ignorant Armies*, edited by David Pringle (GK Books, U.K.); *Full Spectrum II* edited by Lou Aronica, Shawna McCarthy, Amy Stout, and Pat LoBrutto (Bantam); *Memories and Visions; Women's Fantasy and Science Fiction*, edited by Susanna Sturgis (Cross Press), *The Further Adventures of Batman* edited by Martin H. Greenberg (Bantam); *Fear and Trembling* by Robert Bloch (Tor); *The End of Tragedy* by Rachel Ingalls (Simon & Schuster); *Somewhere in the Night*, edited by Jeffrey N. McMahan (Alyson Publications) supernatural stories featuring gay men; *Sisters in Crime* edited by Marilyn Wallace (Berkley); *Wild Cards V: Down and Dirty*, edited by George R. R. Martin (Bantam); *Three Dreams and a Nightmare, and Other Tales of the Dark*, by Judith Gorog (Philomel); *Other Edens III* edited by Christopher Evans and Robert Holdstock (Unwin, U.K.); *October Dreams* (Kubicek & Associates); *Winter's Tales*,

New Series Five, edited by Robin Baird-Smith (St. Martin's); *The Omni Book of SF #6,* edited by Ellen Datlow (Zebra); *Soft and Other Stories* by F. Paul Wilson (Tor); *Blackbeard's Cup: And Other Stories of the Outer Banks* by Charles Harry Whedbee (John F. Blair).

The following reprint anthologies were published in 1989: *The Year's Best Horror,* edited by Karl Edward Wagner (DAW); *Tales of the Occult,* edited by Isaac Asimov, Martin H. Greenberg, and Charles G. Waugh (Prometheus); *The Compleat Werewolf* by Anthony Boucher (Carroll & Graf), *East Coast Ghosts* edited by Charles G. Waugh and Martin H. Greenberg (Middle Atlantic Press); *The Amber Gods and Other Stories* by Harriet Prescott Spofford, edited by Alfred Bendixen (Rutgers University Press); *The Best Horror Stories of Arthur Conan Doyle* (Academy Chicago Publishers) *The Dark Side: Tales of Terror and the Supernatural* by Guy de Maupassant (Carroll & Graf); *If The River Was Whiskey* by T. Coraghessan Boyle (Viking); *Triumph of the Night: Tales of Terror and the Supernatural* edited by Robert Phillips (Carroll & Graf); *What Did Miss Darrington See? An Anthology of Feminist Supernatural Fiction* edited by Jessica Amanda Salmonson (The Feminist Press); *Pack of Cards* by Penelope Lively (Grove Press); *Salvage Rights* by Ian Watson (Gollancz, U.K.); *Tales by Moonlight II* edited by Jessica Amanda Salmonson (Tor); *The Best from Fantasy & Science Fiction: A 40th Anniversary Anthology* edited by Edward L. Ferman (St. Martin's); *Victorian Ghost Stories by Eminent Women Writers* edited by Richard Dalby (Carroll & Graf); *The Anastasia Syndrome and Other Stories* by Mary Higgins Clark (Simon & Schuster); *Nectar at Noon* by Sheila Cudahy (Harcourt, Brace); *Intensive Scare* edited by Karl Edward Wagner (DAW); *Beauties, Beasts, and Enchantment: Classic French Fairy Tales* edited by Jack Zipes (NAL); *Lighthouse Horrors* edited by Charles G. Waugh and Martin H. Greenberg (Middle Atlantic Press); *Tales of Natural and Unnatural Catastrophies* by Patricia Highsmith (Atlantic Monthly Press); *The Horror Hall of Fame* edited by Robert Silverberg and Martin H. Greenberg (Lynx); *Isaac Asimov's Magical Worlds of Fantasy #11: Curse* edited by Isaac Asimov, Martin H. Greenberg and Charles G. Waugh (NAL/Signet); *Dialing the Wind* by Charles L. Grant (Tor); *Endangered Species* by Gene Wolfe (Tor); *Ghosts for Christmas* edited by Richard Dalby (Carroll & Graf); *The Weird Gathering and Other Tales from the Enchanted World of Dark Legends* edited by Ronald Curren (Fawcett Crest).

There are a number of magazines covering events and/or reviews in the horror field, including *Fear, Gorezone, Locus, Science Fiction Chronicle, SF Eye, New Pathways, The New York Review of Science Fiction,* the Horror Writers of America newsletter and *The Scavenger's Newsletter.* In addition, *Mystery Scene* magazine, published by Ed Gorman and Bob Randisi, now covers horror and science fiction as well as the mystery and crime genres. It's valuable for its reviews, market reports and essays. *The Blood Review: The Journal of Horror Criticism,* published by Ruben Sosa Villegas, is a new literary quarterly journal specializing in the horror genre and featuring reviews, interviews and essays. Its first issue looked promising. According to the HWA newsletter, the journal is looking for fiction to run in its Halloween 1990 issue.

Science Fiction Eye, P. O. Box 43244, Washington, DC 20010-9244, $10.00 for three issues (one year); *New Pathways,* MGA Services, P. O. Box 863994, Plano, TX 75086-3994, write for new rates; *The New York Review of Science Fiction,* P. O. Box 78, Pleasantville, NY 10570, $32.00 payable to Dragon Press for a one-year first class subscription (twelve issues), $24.00 for a second-class subscription; *The Blood Review,* P. O. Box 4394, Denver, CO 80204-9998, $35.00 for a one-year subscription; *Mystery Scene,* 3840 Clark Road S.E., Cedar Rapids, IA 52403, $35.00 for seven issues).

* * *

The small specialty presses remained active in 1989. Arkham House published *The Horror in the Museum and Other Revisions* by H. P. Lovecraft, with texts edited by S. T. Joshi. Included is an introduction by August Derleth. Dust jacket is by Raymond Bayless. Mark V. Ziesing published *The Anubis Gates* by Tim Powers, with dust jacket by J. K. Potter and interiors by Mark Bilokur; *By Bizarre Hands*, a collection by Joe R. Lansdale (two originals) with dust jacket by J. K. Potter and interior illustrations by Mark Nelson; and *Book of the Dead* edited by John Skipp and Craig Spector, with dust jacket and interior illustrations by J. K. Potter. All of Ziesing's books were designed by Arnie Fenner and most are available in both signed limited editions or less expensive trade editions. Scream/Press published *Heatseeker*, John Shirley's collection (three originals), with dust jacket and interior illustrations by Harry O. Morris, introduction by William Gibson, and foreword by Stephen P. Brown. The Dream/Press imprint published *Collected Stories* by Richard Matheson, clothbound, no dust jacket. Most Scream/Press titles are published in either signed limited volumes or less expensive trade editions.

Underwood-Miller published *Screams: Three Novels of Terror* by Robert Bloch (first hardcover publication of three tales of psychological suspense) with dust jacket by Ned Dameron, and *Horrorstory: The Collectors Edition, Volume Five*, edited by Karl Edward Wagner, the first of five hardcover volumes collecting Wagner's *Year's Best Horror Stories* (DAW)—three of the original annuals per volume. Volume Four has just been published—they're working backwards—and all volumes will have dust jackets by Michael Whelan. Other Underwood-Miller books published in 1989 were: *Apocalypse*, by Nancy Springer, in a trade edition with dust jacket by Ned Dameron; *Harlan Ellison's Watching*, a collection of Ellison's commentary on film and modern culture, with dust jacket by Ilene Meyer; and *Feast of Fear: Conversations with Stephen King*, with a dust jacket by Clark Ashton Smith. Most Underwood-Miller books are available in signed limited and trade editions. Eel Grass Press (through Mark V. Ziesing) published *Nantucket Slayrides*, which contains three short novels—two reprints by Lucius Shepard and one original by Robert Frazier, in a signed limited and trade edition, with dust jacket by J. K. Potter. Charnel House published *The Stress of Her Regard*, a new novel by Tim Powers, illustrated by the author with an introduction by Dean R. Koontz and an afterword by James P. Blaylock. There are two signed limited editions.

Dark Harvest published *Carrion Comfort* by Dan Simmons, illustrated by Simmons and Kathleen McNeil Sherman with dust jacket by Dan Simmons. Other Dark Harvest books were *Swan Song*, by Robert R. McCammon, in its first hardcover edition; *The Eyes of Darkness* and *The Key to Midnight*, both by Dean R. Koontz (originally released under the Leigh Nichols pseudonym), with illustrations by Phil Parks; *Night Visions VII*, edited by Stanley Wiater, featuring short fiction by Richard Laymon, Chet Williamson and Gary Brandner, illustrated by Charles Lang; the above-mentioned *Razored Saddles*, illustrated by Rick Araluce, and *Stalkers*, with dust jacket and interior art by Paul Sonju. Most of Dark Harvest's publications come in signed limited and trade editions. Morrigan Publications (U.K.) published *Winterwood and Other Hauntings* by Keith Roberts, a compilation of previously uncollected stories and one original with artwork by Roberts, and an introduction by Robert Holdstock, available in a signed limited and trade edition; *In the Land of the Dead* by K. W. Jeter, with dust jacket by Ferret, in a signed limited and trade edition; and *Alligator Alley* by Mink Mole and Dr. Adder, with a dust jacket by Ferret, in a signed limited (with cassette and T-shirt) and trade editions.

Donald M. Grant published *Adventures of Lucius Leffing*, a new collection by Joseph Payne Brennan, illustrated by Luis Ferreira, in a signed limited edition. The Whitney Museum of American Art published Stephen King's story "My Pretty Pony" with photographic art and design by Barbara Krueger in a signed limited edition. Kerosina Publications published Gene Wolfe's collection *Storeys from the Old Hotel* with a dust jacket by Pete Lion in a signed limited as well as unsigned limited edition. Nantier Beall Minoustchine (NBM) published a graphic novel version of *Vic and Blood*, art by Richard Corben, text by Harlan Ellison, in a signed limited and trade edition.

Several small presses published chapbooks in 1989, including: Axolotl's (recently taken over by Pulphouse Press) *Westlin Wind* by Charles de Lint, cover by Donna Gordon and introduction by Emma Bull, in a signed limited and trade edition; and its *Axolotl Special* edited by John Pelan, with stories by Lucius Shepard, Michael Shea and Jessica Amanda Salmonson, also in a signed limited and trade edition. Cheap Street published John Sladek's original short story, "Blood and Gingerbread," illustrated by Judy King-Rienerts (available only by subscription). Footsteps Press published Chet Williamson's original story "House of Fear" in a signed limited edition with illustrations by Douglas Klauba, and "Hurry Monster," by Graham Masterton with illustrations by Ken Snyder in a signed limited edition. Hell's Kitchen Productions published *Narcopolis*, an original anthology of dark fantasy poetry, edited by Peggy Nadramia with cover artwork by Harry O. Morris. Available in a trade edition. Dagon Press published *Haunters of the Dark*, an art portfolio by Dave Carson, consisting of six black and white plates depicting works by Lovecraft, Derleth, Campbell, Bloch and Lumley. Introduction by Ramsey Campbell, afterword by Carl T. Ford. Signed limited edition. Gryphon Publications published *Doctor Departures and Others*, a collection of stories by Alan Nelson from *Weird Tales* and *F&SF* in a limited edition. Lord John Press published Stephen King's novella "Dolan's Cadillac" in two signed limited editions; 2 A.M. Publications put out 'Wishes and Fears," a novelette by David Starkey with cover and interior art by Douglas C. Klauba. Ministry of Whimsy Press published *The Book of Frog* by Jeff Vandermeer, illustrated by Penelope Miller. Triskell Press published "The Stone Drum," by Charles de Lint, illustrated by Donna Gordon with an introduction by James P. Blaylock in a signed limited edition.

The production of graphic novels for adults has increased, with news of more to come. Some of the more interesting ones:

Blood by J. M. DeMatteis and Kent Williams (Epic), great artwork, imaginative plot (except for taking the easy way out with a cyclical ending). Lovely impressionistic artwork. Vampires, mutants and mystics. One reservation: the two main characters are both nude most of the time so why is there full frontal female nudity and not male full frontal?

The Tell-Tale Heart and Other Stories by Edgar Allan Poe (Fantagraphics), illustrated by Daryl and Josef Hutchinson. Nice production.

Pigeons from Hell by Robert E. Howard (Eclipse), introduction by Ramsey Campbell, adapted by Scott Hampton. Beautifully rendered adaptation of Howard's horror story (although I haven't read the original, I gather the racial overtones have been removed) but the story as told in this version has very little depth.

The Magician's Wife by Jerome Charyn and François Bouq (Catalan 1987), won a French award for best comic book. Mysterious, sensuous, lovely, and depressing. Most definitely worth a look. *Pioneers of the Human Adventure* by Francois Bouq (Catalan), is a group of eleven absurdist vignettes, most of them strange and wonderful.

Taboo 2, edited by Stephen Bissette (Spiderbaby Graphics), excellent cover art by John Totleben, some good pieces by Eddie Campbell, and a collaboration by Tim Lucas and Simonida Perica; fourth called "Sweet Nothings," which is a lovely surreal piece. While the rampant sexism in "Wet" and the heavy duty misogyny of S. Clay Wilson's pieces are offensive, there isn't much that is actually taboo except for pieces by Rick Grimes and Tom Marnick. There are some other good chillers by Stephen Bissette, Mark Askwith and Rick Taylor, Michael Zulli, Richard Sala, and Cara Sherman-Tereno, who has produced one of the best AIDS/vampire stories I've seen.

Horror: The Illustrated Book of Fears, edited by Mort Castle (Northstar Publishing) is kind of a combo graphic novel/magazine. This premiere issue has a good cover by Mark Bernal—a strangled Raggedy Ann doll—and some good illustrated stories by Richard Christian Matheson (illustrated by Bernal) and Mort Castle (illustrated by Gary McClusky). Also, what I take to be an original short story by J. N. Williamson along with an interview with him. A promising debut, but the material is inconsistent in quality.

Tapping the Vein Book I by Clive Barker (Eclipse), features stories from the *Books of Blood*. The first, "Human Remains," adapted and illustrated by P. Craig Russell—disappointingly vague and not scary enough. "Pig Blood Blues," adapted by Chuck Wagner illustrated by Scott Hampton is much more amorphous and evocative. *Tapping the Vein Book II*, "Skins of Our Fathers," illustrated by Klaus Janson is, to me, too unsophisticated for the subject matter. John Bolton's "In the Hills, In the Cities," in contrast, is terrific. Powerful, realistic illustrations with a dark brooding feel.

Clive Barker's *Hellraiser* (Epic) is a new series of original stories by various writers and artists that take place in the Hellraiser universe. Barker was the consultant on the "bible" for the project but doesn't seem to be involved otherwise. This first issue features several original stories, most of them being variations on some poor jerk opening one of the Lament Configurations (puzzle boxes), summoning up a cenobite and paying the grisly price. Despite the cover blurb, they're not as horrifying as the films. Some of the art is good, though, specifically that of Kent Williams, Mark Chiarello and Ted McKeever (who also provides the most original story). Upcoming issues will have stories and art by Phil Nutman, Neal Gaiman, Dave McKean, and Bill Sienkiewicz. Their abilities could make a big difference to the product.

RAW Volume 2, Number 1 Open Wounds from the Cutting Edge of Comix: Great graphics, incomprehensible texts. The best are "Paul," by Pascal Doury, "Bulemic," by Villard and Jacques Loustal, the new installment of *Maus* by Art Spiegelman, and "Here," by Richard McGuire.

Beautiful Stories for Ugly Children, (Piranha Press), a series of fractured fairy tales for adults with macabre humor. All written and illustrated by Dave Louapre and Dan Sweetman. The series includes: *Volume 1*, "A Cotton Candy Autopsy," unhappy clowns go on a brutal trip; *Volume 2*, "The Deadjohnsons' Big Incredible Day," regular middle class couple and their dog go out for an adventure—only they're dead (this doesn't seem to bother them and no one else seems to notice); *Volume 3*, "Diary of a Depressed Tap Dancer," "Olga Schump was a tap dancer, and not happy about it in the least . . . the depression born of tap dancing clung to her back like some insane organ grinder's monkey"; *Volume 4*, "The Black Balloon (A Happy Story),"—Happy if, like the protagonist, you don't mind being born and living your life strapped to an electric chair; *Volume 5*, "The Crypt of the Magi," a horror parody of O. Henry's classic "The Gift of the Magi," it's silly but strangely effective, although the characters are much too old for the plot—weakest of the lot but still not bad; *Volume 6*, "Happy Birthday to Hell," Wally (aka Satan) tells his side—funny and weird. The entire series is highly recommended. I can't wait for the next installments.

Stray Toasters by Bill Sienkiewicz (Epic). The first three volumes of the series came out in 1988, the fourth in 1989. A gorgeous, eerie, frightening, and ultimately incomprehensible story about child abuse. It's also beautiful to look at, fascinating, and worthwhile.

Lea: The Confessions of Julius Antoine by Serge LeTendre and Christian Rossi (Fantagraphics). An odd, morally shaky story about a man on the edge whose obsession with young girls destroys his life (kind of like Lolita, which it's compared to in the blurbs). The blurbs seem to imply that he is an innocent persecuted for his fantasies and that the book "exposes the hypocrisy that surrounds sexual crime." Frankly, I'm not sure what they're referring to. It's quite clear that Julius is no innocent.

Fires by Mattotti (Catalan, 1988) is brilliant. Beautiful and mysterious, it's about a magical island, its inhabitants, and their encounter with a battleship and its crew.

Bell's Theorem by Schultheiss (Catalan) is a three volume SF/adventure series about a convict offered freedom if he takes part in some medical experiments. He proceeds to search for his identity while being hunted by unknown parties. Visually evocative and sensual as well as frightening and nightmarish.

Last year the hottest new item on the scene was graphic novels. They're still proliferating like mad, but this year trading cards are making their mark. A sampling:

Jonestown Massacre Memorial Cards edited by Dennis Worden and Wayne Honath (Carnage Press, Box 301, West Somerville, MA 02144). Black and white cards illustrated by KAZ, Charles Burns and other artists. Some amazing art for collectors. Basically, a history of the cult. Really bizarre.

Freakards with art by Drew Friedman, "cool cards for collectors" (Shel-Tone Publications, Larry Shell, P. O. Box 45, Irvington, NJ 07111). Fascinating trading cards with capsule descriptions (no writers' credit) of a wide variety of genetic freaks, mostly members of circus sideshows—midgets, dog-faced boys, Siamese twins, etc. The subtitle is "portraits of peculiar people."

Iran-Contra Scandal Trading Cards by Paul Brancato and Salim Yaqub (Eclipse Enterprises, P. O. Box 1099, Forestville, CA 95436) are thirty-six cards delineating who was who and the intertwining connections in the biggest federal scandal since Watergate. The information was compiled by the Christic Institute, a non-profit public interest law firm that has filed suit against key figures involved in the scandal. Covers everyone's involvement from Ollie North to Joseph Coors through John Hull and the Medellín cocaine cartel up to Ronald Reagan. Brilliant job. Order before the CIA confiscates them.

Friendly Dictator Trading Cards: Featuring Thirty-six of America's Most Embarrassing Allies, written by Dennis Bernstein and Laura Sydell, illustrated by Bill Sienkiewicz in his best expressionistic style (Eclipse). A disturbing and depressing overview of American involvement in other countries' affairs (primarily Central and Latin America with a bit of Africa and the Mid- and Far East thrown in). These are the leaders our self-righteous government has propped up for economic/political reasons without regard to rampant human rights abuses. Terrifying, even taking into account the political bias. A must buy for learning your government's miserable history since World War II.

The Bush League trading cards written by Paul Brancato and illustrated by Salim Yaqub (Eclipse). This batch, done up as baseball cards, is a fascinating and appalling history of our current president, following his career as an oilman circumventing Mexican law (a practice that made him a millionaire), through his rumored long-term affair with his personal appointments secretary, to what would happen if Quayle took over. It implies that the current and Reagan administrations made dirty deals with foreign nations and leaders in order to make political capital. Most of the information has been published in various sources, but this series sets it all down starkly and puts it into perspective.

Rotten to the Core Trading Cards: The Best and Worst of New York City's Politics written by Peggy Gordon and Dean Mullaney, illustrated by Rick Bryant and George Kochell (Eclipse), should be mandatory for all public schools. A civics lesson on how a big city works—and doesn't work—and how corruption can become endemic.

* * *

As usual, here are some odds and ends I've come across in the past year that may be of interest:

Nightsounds–Horror Stories on Tape (Embassy Cassette) is a good idea with lousy material for those who are completely unfamiliar with horror. Good special effects and production.

Horror House, produced by Berl Boykin, is another "audio series of the macabre." I haven't heard these so I don't know about the production qualities, but the material is good—adaptations include "The Dunwich Horror" and "Pickman's Model."

Tales from the Crypt, a series of six half-hour excursions into the bizarre, was presented on Home Box Office during the summer of 1989. The directors included Walter Hill (*Streets of Fire*), Richard Donner (*Superman*) and Robert Zemeckis (*Who Framed Roger Rabbit*).

You Never Believe Me by Davis Grubb (St. Martin's). Grubb is best known for his novel *The Night of the Hunter*, which was made into a powerful movie by Charles Laughton (his only chance as a director because the film flopped) with a crazed Robert Mitchum, Shelley Winters, and Lillian Gish. There's some horror in this collection of short stories, and the best is the title story, which became an Alfred Hitchcock episode under the title, "Where the Woodbine Twineth." Mostly associational; the mainstream material is uneven and none of it lives up to *The Night of the Hunter*.

About the Body, by Christopher Burns (Secker & Warburg). Some of the stories have been published in *Interzone*, the British science fiction and fantasy magazine, but many are mainstream. They are for the most part intelligent, mysterious, and haunting, and some definitely have horrific undertones. "Fogged Plates," "Among the Wounded," and "Embracing the Slaughterer" are the best. Some originals are also included. Highly recommended for a mindstretch.

Blind Side by William Bayer (Villard) is a compelling psychological thriller with film noir undertones. A blocked photographer falls in love with a beautiful, mysterious woman he photographs, and they become embroiled in a web of sexual perversion, blackmail and betrayal. A good read.

Bone by George C. Chesbro (Mysterious Press) is another entertaining thriller/psychological horror novel from the creator of the dwarf/circus performer/professor/detective Mongo and the clairvoyant Veil (although this one isn't in either series). In *Second Horseman Out of Eden*, also Chesbro (Atheneum), Mongo and his brother Garth are again teamed up. Mongo has quit his academic post and, with Garth, who's no longer a cop, has set up a detective agency. In volunteering to answer Christmas mail, they find a letter from a little girl who says she's abused. Their search leads them to a reclusive billionaire and a dangerous cult that plans for the end of the world. Though some of the series is supernatural, this one isn't, but it's an engrossing thriller.

The Fall of the House of Usher, by Philip Glass and Richard Foreman, was performed as an opera in New York to mixed reviews. Odd, expressionistic sets and acting reminiscent of the film, *The Cabinet of Dr. Caligari*.

Send Bygraves, by Martha Grimes, illustrated by Devis Grebu (Putnam), is a bizarre mystery poem by the well-known American mystery writer. Beautifully illustrated line drawings. Almost Goreyesque, but not quite as nasty. Dark, strange, provocative. The most mysterious figure in the book is the Scotland Yard detective Bygraves, whom no one ever sees.

Macho Sluts, by Pat Califia (Alyson Publications, 1988), is a profoundly disturbing collection of erotic stories about sadomasochism, mostly lesbian. In the introduction, the author tells how she had to take out any portrayals of "unsafe" sex, for the publisher, which is promoting safe sex.

Visions of Poe: A Selection of Edgar Allan Poe's Stories and Poems, with photographs and an introduction by Simon Marsden (Knopf, 1988) is exactly what the title says, with effective, haunting, surreal photographs. A lovely coffee table book.

Dreams and Nightmares: The Fantastic Visions of Winsor McCay, edited by Richard Marshall with an introduction by Gary Groth (Fantagraphics, 1988), is a collection—gathered for the first time—of fantasies, allegories and political cartoons by the creator of Little Nemo.

News of the Weird: Over 500 Bizarre But True Stories That Reveal Weirdness, Weirdness Everywhere, by Chuck Shepherd, John J. Kohut, and Roland Sweet, illustrated by Drew Friedman (Plume). Funny compendium of incompetent bank robbers, weird pieces of legislation, peculiarly motivated homicides and more.

In the Forbidden Zone, by Michael Lesy (Anchor), the author of *Wisconsin Death Trip* interviews people whose professions force them to deal with death on a daily basis —undertakers, detectives, slaughterhouse workers, the officials in charge of death row, people who work with AIDS patients, a professional soldier, etc. Although it takes a few chapters to figure out where he's going and if it's worth it, stick with him: the cumulative effect is quite fascinating and powerful. Highly recommended.

The Grand Guignol; Theatre of Fear and Terror, by Mel Gordon (Amok, 1988), is a history of the theatre of Grand Guignol, which began in turn-of-the-century Paris and lasted more than sixty years. The theatre, celebrating horror, fear, sex, and violence, was a progenitor of the splatter film. The text includes a history of the theatre, one hundred plots of the Grand Guignol, photo-documentation of three plays, and the scripts of two full plays. A must read for anyone interested in influences on the horror field.

Rants and Incendiary Tracts, Voices of Desperate Illumination 1558-Present, edited by Bob Black and Adam Parfrey (Amok Press and Loompanics Unlimited), is great stuff from the people who brought you *Apocalypse Culture*. From Marat to Ayatollah Ruhollah Khomeini to Valerie Solanas (the woman who tried to assassinate Andy Warhol in the late sixties) to Kathy Acker.

Modern Primitives (Re/Search) is the newest of this publisher's volumes on the avant-garde. The growing revival of tattooing, piercing, and scarification is examined in text and photos. Practitioners are interviewed in depth. Some of the photos are pretty rough, but this is fascinating and highly recommended.

The Torture Garden by Octave Mirbeau (Re/Search) is a beautiful new reprint of an 1899 classic calleed "the most sickening work of art of the nineteenth century." The book follows a dissolute Frenchman to a garden in China where torture is practiced as an art form.

Giger's Alien (Morpheus International) is a hardcover with wraparound dust jacket, over 150 detailed color reproductions, design sketches, paintings, scenes from the movie, and on the set photos. With an introduction by Timothy Leary.

Notable nonfiction books of interest to the horror reader:
Dracula: Prince of Many Faces by Radu R. Florescu and Raymond T. McNally (Little, Brown); *Modern Fantasy: The Hundred Best Novels* by David Pringle (Peter Bedrick Books); *Harlan Ellison's Watching* (Underwood-Miller Books); *Mary Shelley* by Muriel Spark, a trade paperback edition of the Bram Stoker Award-winner (Meridian); *Mary Shelley: Romance and Reality* by Emily W. Sunstein (Little, Brown); *American Vampires: Fans, Victims, Practioners* by Norine Dresser (Norton); *Stigmata* by Ian Wilson (Harper & Row); *Horror: A Connoisseur's Guide to Literature and Film* by Leonard Wolf (Facts

on File); *Vampires, Burial, and Death: Folklore and Reality* by Paul Barber (Yale University Press); *Horrors!* by Drake Douglas (The Overlook Press); *Permanent Californians: An Illustrated Guide to the Cemeteries of California*, by Judi Culbertson and Tom Randall (Chelsea Green); *The Encyclopedia of Monsters* by Jeff Rovin (Facts on File); *The Stephen King Companion* by George Beahm (Andrews & McMeel); *The Highest Altar: The Story of Human Sacrifice* by Patrick Tierney (Viking); *Strange Shadows: The Uncollected Fiction and Essays of Clark Ashton Smith*, edited by Steve Behrends (Greenwood); *From Satire to Subversion: The Fantasies of James Branch Cabell* by James D. Riemer (Greenwood); *H. P. Lovecraft* by Peter Cannon (G. K. Hall/Twayne); *Stephen King: The First Decade, Carrie to Pet Sematary* by Joseph Reino (G. K. Hall/Twayne); *Science Fiction, Fantasy and Horror: 1984* by Charles L. Brown and William G. Contento (Locus Press); *Science Fiction, Fantasy and Horror: 1988* by Charles L. Brown and William G. Contento (Locus Press); *H. P. Lovecraft and the Cthulhu Mythos* by Robert M. Price (Starmont); *Discovering Classic Horror Fiction I* edited by Darrell Schweitzer (Starmont); *The Vampire: In Legend and Fact* by Basil Copper (Lyle Stuart); *Redefining the American Gothic: From Wieland to Day of the Dead* by Louis S. Gross (UMI); *Vampirism in Literature: An Annotated Bibliography* edited by Margaret L. Carter (UMI); *Dr. Jekyll and Mr. Hyde After One Hundred Years* edited by William Veeder and Gordon Hirsch (University of Chicago Press); *Contemporary Science Fiction, Fantasy, and Horror Poetry: A Resource Guide and Biographical Dictionary* by Scott E. Green (Greenwood Press).

The Horror Writers of America held a banquet and other events the weekend of June 16–18 at the Warwick Hotel in New York City. Ace Books sponsored a party Friday evening and Saturday morning there was an HWA business meeting and several panel discussions. The Bram Stoker Awards for outstanding achievement in horror literature were presented at a banquet on Saturday, June 17. Laurence Kirshbaum, president of Warner Books, was the keynote speaker. The recipients of the awards were: Life Achievement: Ray Bradbury and R. Chetwynd-Hayes; Best Novel: *The Silence of the Lambs* by Thomas Harris (St. Martin's); First Novel: *The Suiting* by Kelly Wilde (Tor); Novella: "Orange Is for Anguish, Blue for Insanity" by David Morrell, published in the anthology *Prime Evil* (NAL); Short story: "Night They Missed the Horror Show" by Joe R. Lansdale, published in the anthology *Silver Scream* (Dark Harvest/Tor); Collection: *Selected Stories of Charles Beaumont* (Dark Harvest). Following the banquet, another party was hosted by HWA and Tor Books. For information on the Horror Writers of America, contact HWA c/o Lisa Cantrell, P. O. Box 655, Madison, NC 27025.

Flyers have been sent out announcing the first World Horror Convention to be held in Nashville, Tennessee, February 28–March 31, 1991. It will be organized by the same staff who ran the 1987 World Fantasy Convention in Nashville, and it will concentrate on all forms of the genre, including fiction, art and movies. Writer Guest of Honor will be Clive Barker, with Jill Bauman as artist Guest of Honor and David J. Schow, Craig Spector, and John Skipp as masters of ceremonies. For the first two years the convention will remain in Nashville. Membership is limited to one thousand.

The winners of the 1988 Rhysling Awards sponsored by the SF Poetry Association were: Long Poem: "White Trains," by Lucius Shepard (*Night Cry*); Short Poem (a tie): "Rocky Road to Hoe," by Suzette Haden Elgin (*Star * Line*) and "The Nightmare Collector" by Bruce Boston (*Night Cry*).

Because of limited space in this volume, I was unable to publish some excellent novellas that I would have otherwise included. I'd like to strongly recommend the following: *I, Said the Fly* by Michael Shea, *Children of the Wind* by Kate Wilhelm, *The Ends of the Earth* by Lucius Shepard, *Dirty Work* by Pat Cadigan, *The Place Where all*

Things Go to Die by Susan M. Watkins, *The Boy in the Tree* by Elizabeth Hand, *On the Far Side of the Cadillac Desert with Dead Folks*, by Joe R. Lansdale, *At First Just Ghostly* by Karl Edward Wagner, *The Devil and Clocky Watson* by Robert Westall, and, *Confessions of St. James* by Chet Williamson.

Also, because there were so many strong stories to choose from this year, it was very difficult to make some final decisions. I'd like to cite a few fine stories that I just couldn't fit: "Stalker" by Ed Gorman, "Models" by John Maclay, "Each Night, Each Year" by Kathryn Ptacek, "The Sculptor's Hand" by Nicholas Royle, "Third Rail" by Wayne Allen Sallee, "Children of Cain" by Al Sarrantonio, "I Live in Elizabeth" by John Shirley, "Brothers" by David B. Silva, "The Unmasking" and "Hooks" by Steve Rasnic Tem, "The Last Day of Miss Dorinda Molyneaux" by Robert Westall, "Leavings" by Gahan Wilson, and "In the Heart of the Blue Caboose" by Ken Wisman.

—Ellen Datlow

Horror and Fantasy on the Screen: 1989

Let me quote from Gustav Hasford's *The Phantom Blooper*, the exemplary and fabulous sequel (in both the strict and figurative sense) to *The Short-Timers*, his Vietnam novel that was the basis for *Full Metal Jacket*: "Americans are prisoners of their own mythology, having watched too many of their own movies. If they ever want to send Americans to the gas chambers, they won't tell us we're going to take showers, they'll herd us into cinder-block movie houses." That was true during the Vietnam era, the novel's setting. These days, the author would probably substitute "video stores" for movie houses, alas.

Film is still big, big business, but the scene is changing. For half a century, our society let movie palaces be the community center for the happy ritual of shared tribal excitement. But now ticket prices are going up and the palaces are coming down. Such innovative enterprises as Super Saver Cinemas ("$1 any movie anytime—see our "Star Wars" tunnel and magic light show—digital sound") valiantly attempted to head off the stampede of couch potatoes renting stacks of video cassettes, but it's a tough, and perhaps quixotic, battle. More and more films, aimed originally at theatrical release, are being consigned directly to video, particularly films of the fantastic. Note such 1989 non-theatrical features as *Moon Trap* and *Slipstream*. The word is out: horror, fantasy, and science fiction don't sell at the theaters.

They don't? Part of the problem is definition. Stuff in our little genre doesn't seem to work when it's labeled as such. But when it's released as a general film, well. . . . In the twenty-five top grossing films of 1989, six out of the top ten were SF or fantasy. Ditto twelve out of the top twenty-five. I didn't bother stoking up the calculator to add the year's proceeds for all the dozen films in question. I could add the top two in my head.

Batman and *Indiana Jones and the Last Crusade* made, between them, nearly half a *billion* dollars. That's a figure even the Pentagon might notice. So here's a quick once-over of what made the money.

Batman ($251.2 million) was in first place, of course—not just as a film, but as a marketing phenomenon. Director Tim Burton (*Beetlejuice*) ensured his continued career. But money isn't everything. So many viewers, after reveling in Jack Nicholson's sublimely scenery-chewing performance as the villainous Joker, and the *Blade Runneresque*, parallel-world Gotham City sets, didn't have a lot more to compliment. Michael Keaton was okay as the Caped Crusader. Kim Basinger was okay as Vicky Vale. Lots of things were just . . . okay.

Indiana Jones and the Last Crusade ($196.2 million) was another okay film—but again, like *Batman*, still a reasonable and diverting way to kill a summer night. Sean Connery did quite a fine job playing Harrison Ford's dad. Every once in a while, the script was able to capitalize on that. Unfortunately, the intrinsic mythology (the quest for the Holy Grail), powerful stuff, was pretty much frittered away. So much for learning lessons at the knee of Joseph Campbell.

Down in fifth place, *Honey, I Shrunk the Kids* ($130.2 million, Disney). Microscopic kids lost in the backyard. This film utilized some good special effects, but the sheer excitement and wonder of exploring the world of smallness was much more effectively captured by *The Incredible Shrinking Man* way back in 1957.

At number six, *Look Who's Talking* ($114.4 million) was Tri-Star's indifferent comedy. Director Amy Heckerling used the voice of Bruce Willis to personalize a baby's sensibility. Interestingly, she also inadvertently managed to turn the otherwise innocuous entertainment into a de facto anti-abortion screed with an initial stretch of animation shouting out the assertion that human sentience begins at the very moment of conception. Unintentionally effective propaganda, but Woody Allen it wasn't.

Ghostbusters II ($112.5 million) rose to number seven, but didn't come close to the ticket sales for its predecessor. Most of the old cast was back, but there wasn't anything fresh in the script. It was retread city. Ditto *Back to the Future Part II* ($95.2 million) at number nine. Although Michael J. Fox became a good-looking teenage girl in one scene, and the script did a more than fair job of trying to introduce the general movie audience to the wild, wacky, wonderful sci-fi world of time-travel paradoxes, this was not even so much of a sequel as it was a two-hour trailer for *Back to the Future Part III*. Cleverness was overwhelmed by what appeared to be crass cynicism.

National Lampoon's Christmas Vacation ($60.5 million) made it to number fourteen by brightening the holidays with a predictably twisted portrayal of our most productive shopping season. It contained some fine scenes, such as Chevy Chase finally turning on the Christmas lights suffocating his gaily decorated house—as the entire city dims and blacks out in the background—and a cautionary sequence in which a heedless kitty learns it shouldn't gnaw on wires leading to Christmas trees. This was hardly *The Ruling Class*, but then it was intended for the whole family.

Finally, at number fifteen, there was a fantasy I could recommend wholeheartedly. It's *Field of Dreams* ($63.3 million), Phil Robinson's version of the W. P. Kinsella novel, *Shoeless Joe*. Kevin Costner did fine as the decent guy building a baseball field in the middle of an Iowa cornfield on faith—and waiting for the ghosts of the Black Sox to show up to play. Amy Madigan played his wife, and James Earl Jones was fabulous as a reclusive writer and former radical. Strong men wept during this sentimental comedy-drama. There were those who accused *Field of Dreams* of being crassly manipulative. I'd agree, but strike the "crassly." The nicest aspect of this film is that it treats its fantastic element the way the Latin American fantasists do—or just as *The Milagro Beanfield War* did a year or two ago. Nobody in the movie feels constrained to offer long rationalizations about why something weird is happening. It simply appears as a given and the characters adapt. Magic is validated as a natural—and reasonable—part of life.

Pet Sematary ($57.5 million), at number sixteen, was the top-grossing out-and-out horror movie for the year. A product of the independent Laurel team, the script was from Stephen King, adapting his own novel. Unfortunately, it duplicated the critical flaw of the book. Director Mary Lambert, fresh from her *homage* (unconscious, I think) to *Carnival of Souls*, *Siesta*, did well with location filming in Maine. This dark and brooding story of a genuinely frightening issue—parents' fears for the safety of their children— did fine until the melodramatic ending. But at least it tried, and it did so very well.

The most lucrative science fiction film came in at number twenty. This was *The Abyss* ($54.8 million), James Cameron's thriller about undersea drillers having a first contact with aquatic aliens. The production was marvelous—everyone's favorite claustrophobic fantasies about drowning were exploited to great effect. While Ed Harris did fine as the prickly hero, Cameron wasn't able to get his ensemble cast of grunt-level blue-collar workers to jell as effectively as they did in *Aliens*. Everything from special effects to sheer suspense went gangbusters until the aliens finally appeared on-screen. Those big-eyed E. T. swimmers were enough to make all viewers require insulin shots. The word is that Fox made the director cut a hefty chunk out of the final print that will be restored in the video release. Since the picture's excessive cost to make was close to what it grossed, *The Abyss* wasn't considered a success by the studio.

Star Trek V: *The Final Frontier* made it to number twenty-two ($52.2 million), a lot by my standards, but not too impressive compared to the balance sheets for previous *Star*

Trek pictures. Directed by William Shatner, this episode was neither terribly amusing nor especially exciting. It was somewhere below okay. Examining futuristic metaphysics didn't save it. The philosophic content slogged. This could be the end of the orbit for the old *Enterprise*.

Disney's *The Little Mermaid* rounded out the top twenty-five ($49.4 million). This new animated feature brightened up the Christmas season, though it played a bit fast and loose with Hans Christian Andersen's tale. The holidays were also brightened by Don Bluth's animated *All Dogs Go To Heaven*, another charmer, though probably not one for the ages.

The most interesting mainstream animated pieces in theaters were *Tummy Trouble*, (a *Roger Rabbit* short that played before screenings of *Honey, I Shrunk the Kids*), and *The Brave Little Toaster*, based on Thomas M. Disch's novel. *Tummy Trouble* successfully harkened back to everybody's favorite violent cartoons of the 1940s. *The Brave Little Toaster* used fairly limited animation (done in Asia), but still did a good job of suggesting a nostalgic 1940's style. This $2.3 million dollar feature follows a band of plucky household appliances as they attempt to rejoin the human boy they think has abandoned them. It's funny, smart, and engaging. It's also, as a friend astutely pointed out, politically unsound. The film works fine so long as you can avoid drawing slave/master parallels to humans. It's a tricky little devil.

Here's a scattershot look at some of the other films of 1989 that didn't make it into the financial stratosphere. Among them are both the best and the worst of the year. There were more horror sequels, of course. *Friday the 13th: Part VIII: Jason takes Manhattan* had a terrific trailer. Disappointingly, most of the slashing took place aboard a cruise ship rather than in Central Park—a true bait-and-switch. *Nightmare on Elm Street* V drew, to some degree, on the talents of John Skipp and Craig Spector, as well as David J. Schow, but that couldn't save it. You could see the touches of innovation and literacy. Only the touches, alas. And as with *Nightmare, Halloween* V made one wish for the fresh, scary, creative horror of the original version. Michael Myers and his knife returned to his hometown in this one, marking the (presumably) final appearance of Donald Pleasance as the increasingly battered shrink charged with Mikey's therapeutic doom. *The Fly II* was the teen version of its predecessor. It had lots of ick and yuck, but, unfortunately, no David Cronenberg or Jeff Goldblum. *Fright Night II* had all the original good guys, save the prize, Evil Ed. Unfortunately it did not have the original charm and wit either. The sister of the original deceased vampire returns for revenge. At a loss for originality, the sequel borrows its best offbeat horrific qualities from *Near Dark*.

The Abyss wasn't the only subsurface thriller of the year. *Deep Star Six* was cheap and cheesy, posing the intellectual puzzle of how a large and nasty crustacean could get through the airlock into an undersea habitat. It was the basic problem of how a starving camper might open a can of Spam without any directions. . . . The viewer did, however, have the opportunity to see Miguel Ferrer explode in retribution for clumsily causing *two* nuclear accidents in one day. *Leviathan* solved the puzzle by having the deadly menace portable enough to be brought inside by the human characters. That didn't make the movie successful, but at least the viewer didn't guffaw quite so loud.

In terms of deliberate comedy, there were those who decried the time-travel spoof, *Bill and Ted's Excellent Adventure* as a *"Time Bandits* for morons." I wasn't among those nay-sayers. Admittedly skeptical at first, I came out of the theater charmed by the film. Silly, yes; stupid, no. *Earth Girls Are Easy* was another one with a bit of charm, though more slapstick than wit. While Jeff Goldblum and Geena Davis headlined the cast, Julie "The Prom Queen Has a Gun" Brown stole the show as bewildered aliens explored suburbia.

For a peculiar low-budget first-contact picture, there was *Communion*. Based on Whitley Strieber's asserted nonfiction account of alien abduction, this was intended as an earnest biography of a writer and his family being contacted by extraterrestrials. Christopher Walken did a wonderful job as Whitley—I know *I'd* be flattered to have an actor like that playing me. Unfortunately the film was neither convincing as a fact-based piece, nor engaging as science fiction. Perhaps if the aliens had played themselves, rather than relying upon substandard special effects.

Probably the most disappointing science fiction movie of the year was the long-awaited *Millennium*, scripted by John Varley and based on his short story, "Air Raid." One got the feeling that all the writer's intentions were not reflected in the final product. This melodrama of time travelers kidnapping present-day air crash victims to repopulate a nearly destroyed future was doomed by everything from a hashed-up plot to maladroit casting (Kris Kristofferson, Cheryl Ladd, and Daniel J. Travanti). Much like an elephant trapped in warm tar, it kept trumpeting and attempting to climb out; finally it just gave up and sank.

Stephen Spielberg made a sentimental film with *Always*, a romantic ghost story and updated remake of *A Guy Named Joe*. Good cast (John Goodman, Richard Dreyfuss, Holly Hunter), but soggy melodrama. Spielberg changed the original's wartime pilots to contemporary slurry-bomber jocks. Finally, he got to use all that models-and-miniatures technology developed for *1941*.

For a much more effective tearjerker (in the sense that you felt less guilt groping for the Kleenexes), you should have seen the Christmas release, *Prancer*. This movie portrayed a little girl with a gruff father and a dead mother, terrified that her home is about to be split even further. Then she finds a wounded reindeer in the woods and comes to believe it's one of Santa's own. Sam Eliot is, as always, great as the father.

Timothy Dalton was again a sex symbol as James Bond in *Licence to Kill*. Though the studio kept the British spelling of "licence," they did change the title from *Licence Revoked* because—it's alleged—marketing people said American audiences didn't understand the word "revoked." As usual, with Hollywood, the story's probably true.

More disappointments. The *Monty Python*'s Terry Jones made *Erik the Viking*. Such potential. It seemed to be trying desperately to come off as either exciting or funny, and succeeded at neither. Wes Craven's *Shocker* was a deliberate and defensible attempt to recreate the director/writer's success with the original *Nightmare on Elm Street*. Alas, there seemed to be too much calculation about this electrocuted killer returned to life in the electrical grid, and not enough of Craven's patented to-hell-with-the-consequences-let's-pull-out-the-stops attitude.

Robert Englund got to ditch the Freddy makeup and play the Phantom in Dwight Little's remake of *Phantom of the Opera*. The new makeup was great, the story had a chance of involving the viewer for the first half—and then everything fell apart. Lon Chaney, Jr. is still unthreatened. Anthony Perkins presumably spent a brief European vacation playing Dr. Jekyll and Mr. Hyde in *The Edge of Sanity*. While a period piece, there were some intriguingly peculiar scenes of MTV-inspired back alleys infested with hookers in minidresses and contemporary makeup. We also got to see Dr. J., with the help of a lab monkey, invent freebasing. Just say no, thank you.

If you miss the Disney nature epics of the 1950s—mixed with a lot of high-tech special effects work—there was Jean-Jacques Annaud's *The Bear*. The only thing missing from this beast epic of an orphaned grizzly cub's search for a new parent after its mother is killed in a rockslide, is narration by Winston Hibler. This is a prime opportunity to see a bear cub having animated hallucinogenic mushroom fantasies, as well as contemplating Jim Henson's animatronic bears.

On a less impressive level than performing bears, one could catch Jean-Claude Van Damme in *Cyborg*, a futuristic action-adventure vehicle in which a cyborg, with Van Damme's help, has to get the serum to Nome, er, to Atlanta. Lots of survivalist fun here in a plague-devastated North America. You get to wince while Van Damme eludes crucifixion through brute strength. You get to wonder about characters who absolutely cannot figure out the shortest distance between two points when it comes to East Coast American geography. Director Albert Pyun gives the picture some touches of style, but the movie as a whole illustrates exactly why Cannon Pictures went down the tubes.

Here are some movies that, with varying degrees of success, were intended to be funny. *UHF* and *Young Einstein* are opposing sides of the same comedic coin. Each is essentially a one-man vehicle. In *UHF*, Weird Al Yankovic—he of such musical parodies as "Yoda" and "Eat It"—just didn't come across as weird enough as a young man taking over a down-at-the-rheostats TV station. There were moments, but no consistent humor. *Young Einstein* was wrapped around Yahoo Serious, a young Australian comedy star. I thought the movie—and Yahoo—worked surprisingly well. This is effectively a parallel-universe bio-pic of the twentieth century's great genius, mixing real-life events with outrageously cobbled-up fabrication. Everything from the Tasmanian devil to the kitchen sink is in here. One of its tangential charms is the use of honest-to-god scientific terminology and concepts as part of the dialogue. Neat.

Actor Bob Balaban made his directing debut with *Parents*, a black comedy. "Now there's a new name for terror . . ." said the publicity sheet. It all looks good in theory. Set in the sterile, modernist 1950s, the film revolves around a young boy's paranoid fear that his parents, Randy Quaid and Mary Beth Hurt, are complete psychopaths behind their smug exteriors. This idea worked better in the original *Invaders From Mars*. Here it comes across as merely a one-trick pony.

For genuine—and genuinely uncomfortable—laughter mixed with wit and panache, try *Heathers*. Not to everyone's taste, this movie follows Winona Ryder becoming involved with a psychopathic killer, Christian Slater, in a nastily berserk comedy about contemporary high school life. The laughs are genuine and frequent, but dark verging on the ultra-violet. Murder has rarely been so amusing.

Another first-rate and darkly hued comedy is *Vampire's Kiss*. Directed by Robert Bierman from a script by Joseph Minion, this Hemdale release features Nicholas Cage as a literary agent (appropriately enough) who fears and hopes he is becoming a Manhattan vampire. Cage pushes his role about as far as he can without actually reaching out of the screen and devouring your popcorn. Maria Conchita Alonso is terrific as the meek secretary who becomes the object of Cage's increasingly vampiric tendencies. It's a wonderful film that strikes to the heart of how deeply—and how weirdly—humans will search to find love.

In the mood for unashamed violence—but with humor? Martin Donovan's *Apartment Zero* is an over-the-top Hitchcockian thriller filmed in Buenos Aires. Colin Firth plays a repressed young movie theater owner and Hart Bochner surprises the audience as an American mercenary and sociopathic killer. When the laughs come, they are surprising for their very nature. Rather more sober, but just as claustrophobically suspenseful, Australian director Phillip Noyce's *Dead Calm* is a minimalist off-beat thriller. It's about an Aussie couple on a healing voyage aboard their boat after their child is killed in an accident. They encounter a derelict vessel inhabited by one survivor—an American psycho. The film has a particularly nice little scene involving both drowning and large, marine cockroaches. . . . Eric Red, veteran writer of both *The Hitcher* and *Near Dark*, wrote and directed *Cohen and Tate*. The titular bad guys, played by Roy Scheider and Adam Baldwin, have kidnapped a young boy who their hoodlum bosses want to question and then kill. The kid has to be transported from Oklahoma to Houston. The plot flow isn't nearly as seamless as it should be, but the film is full of wonderful images and memorable moments. And then for psychological violence rapidly escalating to physical mayhem, there's Danny DeVito's *War of the Roses*. Depicting a yuppy couple's (Michael Douglas and Kathleen Turner) complete and grotesque dissolution as husband and wife, this bitterly funny film culminates in a disturbingly over-the-top image not usually allowable in a major studio production.

The most interesting failures in the films of the fantastic this past year were probably *The Navigator* and *Girl in a Swing*. The first was a fascinating time-travel fantasy in which fourteenth century Cumbrian miners, beset by the Black Plague, heed the vision of a young boy and start digging a tunnel through the earth. Sure enough, they come out in twentieth century Auckland. This is a movie much more in love with terrific images than common sense. There should have been room for both. *Girl in a Swing*, based on the Richard Adams novel, stars Meg Tilly as a mysterious young woman who completely overturns the staid existence of a British antiques dealer, Rupert Frazer. The viewer can figure out that this is about supernatural vengeance, but the script (as filmed) seems to be missing a fair amount of connective tissue. Still, the movie gets points both for its intermittent creepiness and Tilly's erotic and enigmatic portrayal.

Here are a couple of wonderfully weird ones. The French *La Lectrice* is of that rarest breed—a warm, surreal, pro-literacy sex comedy. The plot's about a woman who hires out as a reader to others. There are stories within stories here, and the characters in one story frequently affect the characters in others. I think Italo Calvino would have approved. This is a splendid explanation and defense of an individual's interior life, a portrait in which the imagination is a predominating feature—and virtue. But for complete strangeness, try the Canadian *Tales from the Gimli Hospital*. On the surface, this looks like the grainy black-and-white print of an ancient silent movie—until then you realize it's about such things as plague and necrophilia, and it's very funny indeed. Set in a backwoods Canadian plague hospital at the turn-of-the-century, it depicts the convoluted and bizarre relationship of two Icelandic fishermen who discover that they both loved the same woman, but on different sides of her demise. Made on weekends over a ten-month period, for a budget of $16,000, writer/director Guy Maddin has created a masterpiece of midnight screenings.

I'll wrap up the feature section of this eye-strain marathon with modest suggestions for several "best" categories.

The best horror film of the year? I think my favorite was the British *Paperhouse* directed by Bernard Rose, a veteran of music videos. In this film of interior dreams, a young girl (Charlotte Burke) confronts very real childhood terrors of threat and abandonment. The movie has some terrifying moments, but relies on suspense, timing, and editing for its shocks, rather than on graphic violence. This is a movie about kids for adults, recapturing the true horror and triumph of childhood. Part of its ambition and attraction is its ambiguous nature: is *Paperhouse* the depiction of a girl's fever-dream hallucinations, or is it a literal exploration of someone's uncharted dreamscape?

Best science fiction film of the year? I've become very fond of *Miracle Mile*, Steve De Jarnatt's black comic melodrama about the last night of Los Angeles before the nuclear firestorm. Months after seeing this small movie about the countdown to Armageddon, I find myself still recalling a hell of a lot of splendid moments, such as the immaculately groomed Denise Crosby, dressed in powder blue yuppie garb, sitting at a nighttime diner counter with her attaché case full of computerware and cellular phones, drinking coffee and speed-reading the Cliff's Notes version of *Gravity's Rainbow*. And I probably shall never forget the year's most nightmarish happy ending, in the movie's final moments in the La Brea tarpits.

The best fantasy film? There can be no other choice than Terry Gilliam's magnificent *The Adventures of Baron Munchausen*. It's too soon to tell, but I suspect this will become a classic, though whether minor or major it's hard to say. This is a fantastical comic epic suitable for both children and adults. As ever with Gilliam's movies, the background is full of busy, fascinating things, and violence is accepted as a normal part of life. Magic is real here, and reality is relative. *Baron Munchausen* was not an instant financial hit. I think that will come gradually, over the years, as new and appreciative audiences discover this marvel and enjoy it.

What about the small screen—television? There were (pixel) spots both memorable and forgettable. On NBC, *ALF* continued for those who like cutesy aliens. ABC's *Quantum Leap* allowed Scott Bakula as time-traveler Sam Beckett to continue literally jumping into other people's lives. It's admittedly a gimmick, but *Quantum Leap* allows a low-key SF series to tell human stories and make some social commentary. CBS cancelled *Beauty and the Beast* after trying to revamp the romantic series into less of a fairy tale and more of a tough, mean-streets adventure.

On cable, HBO's *Tales from the Crypt* did well in creating a continuing anthology series with scripts directed by such notables as Walter Hill and Robert Zemeckis. Syndication saw a nice selection of low-budget SF and horror series. *Freddy's Nightmares* is continuing, despite its frequently incoherent nature. Paramount has cancelled *Friday the 13th*, now that three seasons have provided enough episodes for packaged syndication. It also canned *War of the Worlds*; despite good ratings, they weren't good enough to justify the show's high budget.

Perhaps the greatest success story in syndicated SF is Fox's *Alien Nation*, the weekly alien/human buddy-cop series based on Rockne O'Bannon's 1988 theatrical feature. The gimmick works better as a TV series than as a movie. The characters are sympathetic and involving, and the scripts have been fairly well-written. In time-honored tradition, the show frequently uses the distance of science fiction as a means of presenting fairly sharp-edged social commentary. Since the basic plot device is the resettling of a quarter million stranded alien "boat people" in Los Angeles, there is a splendid opportunity to examine everything from racism to sexism. The writers have done well at this. And the frequent humor often works. All in all, this is a credible and creditable job.

Now let's not discount live theater. Forget the endless Broadway and touring shows of *Phantom of the Opera*—here's a grass roots effort from middle America that amazes, astonishes, and delights. Yes, *live, on stage*, direct from Kansas City, it's *Plan 9 from Outer Space—The Musical!* I'm not kidding. David G. Smith, Mark Knowles, and David Brisco Luby have created an adaptation of Edward D. Wood, Jr.'s immortal screenplay. With music and lyrics by Smith, and directed by Rick Cowan, this amazingly brash production is getting ready to hit the road on a national tour. Watch for it in your town. I saw it in Kansas City last Halloween and was properly amazed, not to mention amused. How can a company, you may ask yourself, do justice to a musical comedy adaptation of a camp film that already serves as its own best parody? I don't know either. But it does.

Finally, a few words about yet another medium—music. I won't attempt to cover all the tunes that included references to dark fantasy—talk to Tipper Gore about *those*. But here are several noteworthy examples of the fantastic as translated to listenable, danceable music.

You can't really call Tom Petty's *Full Moon Fever* (MCA) an album about fantasy.

But he's a good example of a performer who can load the lyrics with fantastical resonances. Take "Free Fallin'," an uptempo ballad about Los Angeles. Watch the MTV video. Whether you want to be figurative or literal, this is a tune about vampires. For those readers who have consumed Douglas Winter's "Less Than Zombie" in *Book of the Dead* (Bantam), Petty's "Zombie Zoo" makes perfect musical accompaniment.

White Zombie's *Make Them Die Slowly* (Caroline), titled after the Italian cannibalism horror flick, is its own horror show of downbeat songs such as "Demonspeed," "Acid Flesh," "Murder World," and "Godslayer." Needless to say, these are not gentle love ballads.

Ace song writer/performer Warren Zevon's *Transverse City* (Virgin) is his self-acknowledged cyberpunk album. This is not a direct translation of William Gibson at all. Rather, it's a talented artist's listening to what Gibson's been saying, reflecting for a time, and then letting some of the feeling and vocabulary osmose through into the music. It's a fine album and a flattering cross-pollination between popular science fiction and pop music.

Check your vinyl, tape, and CD collections. There's more interchange going on in the vocabulary of SF, fantasy, and horror with popular music than you might have consciously thought. The process shows no signs of slacking off.

Finally, back to movies for just a second. Whether films are on the large or small screen, they're still a primary reflection, trigger, and reinforcer of our cultural myths. But did any of 1989's films of the fantastic come close to the deliberate provocation, unflinching candor, and scathing insight of, say, Spike Lee's *Do the Right Thing*? Too damn few.

Maybe next year.

—Edward Bryant

Obituaries

Among those who died in 1989 were a number of people who made profound contributions to the shaping of fantasy and horror over many years. Perhaps the loss that stands out as the most significant is that of **Samuel Beckett**, 87, whose *Waiting for Godot* was a landmark in existential literature. Born in Ireland but living abroad for many years, Beckett gave unique and original voice to *Godot* and works like *Endgame* and *Krapp's Last Tape*. His works bridged many cultures in posing fundamental questions about the nature of reality and existence.

Daphne du Maurier, 81, is best known for her seminal novel of gothic horror, *Rebecca* (1938), which became the model for hundreds of imitations. Her short story, "The Birds," was filmed by Alfred Hitchcock. Du Maurier was for decades an exceedingly popular writer whose work transcended the genre in which she worked, touching the lives of millions with portraits of the evil that lives in seemingly ordinary people.

Donald Barthelme, 58, was an important literary fantasist whose work was often blackly humorous, surreal, and almost always sardonic. He used myth, fable, and other fantasy forms in his short stories, and in the early novel, *Snow White* (1967), a satire of the fairy tale.

Mel Blanc, 81, was known as "the man of a thousand voices." He was the voice of the great Warner Bros. cartoon characters, including Bugs Bunny, Porky Pig, Daffy Duck, Yosemite Sam, Tweety, Sylvester, Foghorn Leghorn, and many others. He was also the voice of *The Flintstones*' Barney Rubble, and of Woody Woodpecker. In addition to his animated work, he had a long career in radio and television, notably with the Jack Benny Show in both mediums. Blanc was one of the great original voice men, starting in the late 1930s with Warner, almost singlehandedly creating the famous Warner Bros. "sound," which remains popular on TV fifty years later. **Dik Browne**, 71, created and produced the comic strip *Hägar the Horrible*, and collaborated with Mort Walker on *Hi and Lois*. Hägar, now continued by his sons, is enormously popular, appearing in over 1,800 newspapers. Early in his career he was an advertising artist, creating, among other images, Chiquita Banana. **Jay Ward**, 68, was the co-creator and moving force behind the *Rocky and Bullwinkle* show that stood out as the most original and creative animated TV series in the 1960s. The show featured such delightful lunacies as "Fractured Fairy Tales," "Professor Peabody's Improbable History," and the characters Boris and Natasha, soon to star in a major motion picture. Ward also created an earlier series of note, *Crusader Rabbit*.

Sir Lawrence Olivier, 82, the acclaimed Shakespearean actor and star of stage and many films, was possessed of tremendous intensity and great range. His fantasy roles included turns as Professor Moriarty in *The Seven Percent Solution* and as Professor Von Helsing in the 1979 production of *Dracula*. **Bette Davis**, 81, was a Hollywood legend, a great actress and star whose career spanned six decades. From early roles as ingenues and then romantic leads, she endured as her looks faded by successfully taking on such parts as one of the crazy sisters in *What Ever Happened to Baby Jane*, and a chilling role in *Hush, Hush, Sweet Charlotte*. She won the Academy Award for her role in *All About Eve*. **Graham Chapman**, 48, was a member of the troupe and creative team of *Monty Python's Flying Circus*, a British television series that shocked and delighted audiences in the 60s and 70s on both sides of the Atlantic. He also wrote the screenplays for and starred in *Monty Python and the Holy Grail* and *The Life of Brian*. **Jim Backus**,

76, was a character actor in films and on television, who left his most lasting impression as the voice of the lovable curmudgeon Mr. Magoo, in a series of animated cartoons. **Maurice Evans**, 87, a renowned Shakespearean actor, played major roles in several fantasy films, most notably *Rosemary's Baby*. **John Cassavetes**, 59, an actor who gained fame for his role starring in that film, was also known for his own films, mostly low-budget, which he wrote and directed and which often starred his wife, Gena Rowlands, and sometimes his colleague Peter Falk.

Walter Farley, 74, was famous for *The Black Stallion*, one of some twenty novels for children he wrote. Geoffrey Household, 87, was a British author of many popular thrillers, and of *The Sending* (1980) a novel of black magic. **Aeron Clement**, 52, was the author of *The Cold Moons*, a bestselling British fantasy novel about badgers that was published first as a small-press hardcover and then was bought for paperback, film, and U.S. publication this year. **Sammy Fain**, 87, was a well-known songwriter whose hits included "Love Is a Many-Splendored Thing." He wrote the songs for Disney's *Alice in Wonderland* and, with Sammy Cahn, "Peter Pan." **C.C. Beck**, 79, co-created the comic book hero *Captain Marvel*. **Jean Paiva**, 45, was the author of *The Lilith Factor* which, as we went to press, was a strong contender for the Bram Stoker Award for best horror novel of 1989. **John Payne**, 77, acted in over fifty films. He's best known as the lawyer who defended Santa Claus in the 1947 classic, *Miracle on Thirty-fourth Street*. **Cornel Wilde**, 74, best known for his Oscar-nominated role in *A Song to Remember*, appeared in many films and television productions, including *A Thousand and One Nights* (1945) in which he played Aladdin. **Richard Quine**, 68, was an actor/director known for some fine films in the 1950s and 1960s, including *Bell, Book and Candle* (1959). **John W. Wall**, 78, wrote fantasies under the name "Sarban." His works included *The Sound of His Horn* (1952), an alternate world novel in which Germany won World War II, and *Ringstones and Other Curious Tales* (1951), a collection of dark fantasies, some quite original. **Guy Williams**, 65, gained fame as Zorro in the Disney television series. **Frank S. Pepper**, 78, was a British comic strip writer who wrote, in the comic *Lion* the superhero Captain Condor and later the "spellbinder" series. **Norman Saunders**, 82, was a prolific pulp magazine and paperback cover illustrator whose career spanned decades. **Lionel Newman**, 73, was an Oscar-winning composer of music for more than 250 films, including some fantasy classics. **Osamu Tezuka**, 62, was a Japanese cartoonist whose work included *Jungle Emperor* and *Ambassador Atom*, the latter of which became the animated TV series, *Astroboy*. **Sylvia Cassedy**, 59, wrote young adult fiction and poetry, including *Behind the Attic Wall* (1983). **Frank O'Rourke**, 72, was a prolific and talented author of westerns, mysteries, and sports novels. His novel, *A Mule for the Marquesa*, was filmed as *The Professionals*. His 1957 novella, *The Man Who Found His Way*, was about witchcraft in the Southwest U.S. **Maurice Seiderman**, 82, was a makeup artist on many fantasy films in the 1940s. **Robert J. Wilke**, 77, was a character actor who appeared in many films and television shows from the 1940s to the 1970s, including *The Wild, Wild West*. **Ben Wright**, 74, was a British character actor who appeared in numerous theatrical and television productions, including *The Pharaoh's Curse* (1957). **J. Allen Highfill**, 42, was a costume designer whose credits include Shelley Duvall's *Faerie Tale Theatre*. **Nat Levine**, 89, was a partner in Republic Pictures, which produced many film serial fantasies. **Anton Diffring**, 72, was a German actor featured in Francois Truffaut's production of *Fahrenheit 451* and many other film and television features. **Karel Zeman**, 78, was a leading Czech filmmaker known for his fantasies that combined animation and live action. **David Buck**, 53, was a British actor featured in many British television productions. He was the voice of Gimli in the 1978 animated *Lord of the Rings*. **Harry Andrews**, 77, was a veteran British actor featured in many films, including *The Ruling Class*. George

Coulouris, 79, was a character actor who appeared in numerous film and television productions, including a number of fantasy and horror films. **Clyde Geronimi**, 87, was an Oscar-winning animator for Disney. He directed Disney's *Peter Pan*, *Cinderella*, and *Sleeping Beauty*, among others. **Charles Lampkin**, 76, veteran character actor, had supporting roles in many films, including *Cocoon*.

—James Frenkel

The Year's Best Fantasy and Horror

MICHAEL SWANWICK

The Edge of the World

Michael Swanwick is a writer who has received considerable acclaim since the publication of his first novel, *In the Drift*, as part of Terry Carr's exceptional Ace Science Fiction Specials series. His first two published stories were Nebula Award finalists, as were four subsequent stories; he has also had short fiction nominated for the Hugo Award and the World Fantasy Award. His second novel is *Vacuum Flowers*, and a third is forthcoming.

"The Edge of the World" is a beautifully told story of magic realism, deftly working fantasy elements into a contemporary, real world setting. Swanwick is an author we've come to expect a lot of, and he doesn't let us down.

Swanwick makes his home in Philadelphia, Pennsylvania. His story comes from the pages of the Bantam anthology *Full Spectrum II*.

—T.W.

The Edge of the World

MICHAEL SWANWICK

The day that Donna and Piggy and Russ went to see the Edge of the World was a hot one. They were sitting on the curb by the gas station that noontime, sharing a Coke and watching the big Starlifters lumber up into the air, one by one, out of Toldenarba AFB. The sky rumbled with their passing. There'd been an incident in the Persian Gulf, and half the American forces in the Twilight Emirates were on alert.

"My old man says when the Big One goes up, the base will be the first to go," Piggy said speculatively. "Treaties won't allow us to defend it. One bomber comes in high and *whaboom*"—he made soft nuclear explosion noises—"It's all gone." He was wearing camouflage pants and a khaki T-shirt with an iron-on reading: KILL 'EM ALL AND LET GOD SORT 'EM OUT. Donna watched as he took off his glasses to polish them on his shirt. His face went slack and vacant, then livened as he put them back on again, as if he were playing with a mask.

"You should be so lucky," Donna said. "Mrs. Khashoggi is still going to want that paper done on Monday morning, Armageddon or not."

"Yeah, can you believe her?" Piggy said. "That weird accent! And all that memorization! Cut me some slack. I mean, who cares whether Ackronnion was part of the Mezentian Dynasty?"

"You ought to care, dipshit," Russ said. "Local history's the only decent class the school's got." Russ was the smartest boy Donna had ever met, never mind the fact that he was flunking out. He had soulful eyes and a radical haircut, short on the sides with a dyed-blond punklock down the back of his neck. "Man, I opened the *Excerpts from Epics* text that first night, thinking it was going to be the same old bullshit, and I stayed up 'til dawn. Got to school without a wink of sleep, but I'd managed to read every last word. This is one weird part of the world; its history is full of dragons and magic and all kinds of weird monsters. Do you realize that in the eighteenth century three members of the British legation were eaten by demons? That's in the historical record!"

Russ was an enigma to Donna. The first time they'd met, hanging with the misfits at an American School dance, he'd tried to put a hand down her pants, and she'd slugged him good, almost breaking his nose. She could still hear his surprised laughter as blood ran down his chin. They'd been friends ever since. Only there were limits to friendship, and now she was waiting for him to make his move and hoping he'd get down to it before her father was rotated out.

In Japan she'd known a girl who had taken a razor blade and carved her boyfriend's name in the palm of her hand. How could she do that, Donna had wanted to know? Her friend had shrugged, said, "As long as it gets me noticed." It wasn't until Russ that Donna understood.

"Strange country," Russ said dreamily. "The sky beyond the Edge is supposed to be full of demons and serpents and shit. They say that if you stare into it long enough, you'll go mad."

They all three looked at one another.

"Well, hell," Piggy said. "What are we waiting for?"

The Edge of the World lay beyond the railroad tracks. They bicycled through the American enclave into the old native quarter. The streets were narrow here, the sideyards crammed with broken trucks, rusted-out buses, even yachts up in cradles with staved-in sides. Garage doors were black mouths hissing and spitting welding sparks, throbbing to the hammered sound of worked metal. They hid their bikes in a patch of scrub apricot trees where the railroad crossed the industrial canal and hiked across.

Time had altered the character of the city where it bordered the Edge. Gone were the archers in their towers, vigilant against a threat that never came. Gone were the rose quartz palaces with their thousand windows, not a one of which overlooked the Edge. The battlements where blind musicians once piped up the dawn now survived only in Mrs. Khashoggi's texts. Where they had been was now a drear line of weary factory buildings, their lower windows cinderblocked or bricked up and those beyond reach of vandals' stones painted over in patchwork squares of gray and faded blue.

A steam whistle sounded and lines of factory workers shambled back inside, brown men in chinos and white shirts, Syrian and Lebanese laborers imported to do work no native Toldenarban would touch. A shredded net waved forlornly from a basketball hoop set up by the loading dock.

There was a section of hurricane fence down. They scrambled through.

As they cut across the grounds, a loud whine arose from within the factory building. Down the way another plant lifted its voice in a solid wham-wham-wham as rhythmic and unrelenting as a headache. One by one the factories shook themselves from their midday drowse and went back to work. "Why do they locate these things along the Edge?" Donna asked.

"It's so they can dump their chemical waste over the Edge," Russ explained. "These were all erected before the Emir nationalized the culverts that the Russian Protectorate built."

Behind the factory was a chest-high concrete wall, rough-edged and pebbly with the slow erosion of cement. Weeds grew in clumps at its foot. Beyond was nothing but sky.

Piggy ran ahead and spat over the Edge. "Hey, remember what Nixon said when he came here? *It is indeed a long way down*. What a guy!"

Donna leaned against the wall. A film of haze tinted the sky gray, intensifying at the focal point to dirty brown, as if a dead spot were burned into the center of her vision. When she looked down, her eyes kept grabbing for ground and finding more sky. There were a few wispy clouds in the distance and nothing more. No serpents coiled in the air. She should have felt disappointed but, really, she hadn't expected better. This was of a piece with all the natural wonders she had ever seen, the waterfalls, geysers and scenic vistas that inevitably included power lines, railings and parking lots absent from the postcards. Russ was staring intently ahead, hawklike, frowning. His jaw worked slightly, and she wondered what he saw.

"Hey, look what I found!" Piggy whooped. "It's a stairway!"

They joined him at the top of an institutional-looking concrete and iron stairway. It zigzagged down the cliff toward an infinitely distant and nonexistent Below, dwindling into hazy blue. Quietly, as if he'd impressed himself, Piggy said, "What do you suppose is down there?"

"Only one way to find out, isn't there?" Russ said.

Russ went first, then Piggy, then Donna, the steps ringing dully under their feet. Graffiti covered the rocks, worn spraypaint letters in yellow and black and red scrawled one over the other and faded by time and weather into mutual unreadability, and on the iron railings, words and arrows and triangles had been markered onto or dug into the paint with knife or nail: JURGEN BIN SHEISSKOPF. MOTLEY CRUE. DEATH TO SATAN AMERICA IMPERIALIST. Seventeen steps down, the first landing was filthy with broken brown glass, bits of crumbled concrete, cigarette butts, soggy, half-melted cardboard. The stairway folded back on itself and they followed it down.

"You ever had *fugu*?" Piggy asked. Without waiting for an answer, he said, "It's Japanese poisonous blowfish. It has to be prepared very carefully—they license the chefs—and even so, several people die every year. It's considered a great delicacy."

"Nothing tastes that good," Russ said.

"It's not the flavor," Piggy said enthusiastically. "It's the poison. Properly prepared, see, there's a very small amount left in the sashimi and you get a threshold dose. Your lips and the tips of your fingers turn cold. Numb. That's how you know you're having the real thing. That's how you know you're living right on the edge."

"I'm already living on the edge," Russ said. He looked startled when Piggy laughed.

A fat moon floated in the sky, pale as a disk of ice melting in blue water. It bounced after them as they descended, kicking aside loose soda bottles in styrofoam sleeves, crushed Marlboro boxes, a scattering of carbonized spark plugs.

On one landing they found a crumpled shopping cart, and Piggy had to muscle it over the railing and watch it fall. "Sure is a lot of crap here," he observed. The landing smelled faintly of urine.

"It'll get better farther down," Russ said. "We're still near the top, where people can come to get drunk after work." He pushed on down. Far to one side they could see the brown flow from the industrial canal where it spilled into space, widening and then slowly dispersing into rainbowed mist, distance glamoring its beauty.

"How far are we planning to go?" Donna asked apprehensively.

"Don't be a weak sister," Piggy sneered. Russ said nothing.

The deeper they went, the shabbier the stairway grew, and the spottier its maintenance. Pipes were missing from the railing. Where patches of paint had fallen away the bolts anchoring the stair to the rock were walnut-sized lumps of rust.

Needle-clawed marsupials chittered warningly from niches in the rock as they passed. Tufts of grass and moth-white gentians grew in the loess-filled cracks.

Hours passed. Donna's feet and calves and the small of her back grew increasingly sore, but she refused to be the one to complain. By degrees she stopped looking over the side and out into the sky, and stared instead at her feet flashing in and out of sight while one hand went slap-grab-tug on the rail. She felt sweaty and miserable.

Back home she had a half-finished paper on the Three Days Incident of March, 1810, when the French Occupation, by order of Napoleon himself, had fired cannonade after cannonade over the Edge into nothingness. They had hoped to make rainstorms of devastating force that would lash and destroy their enemies, and created instead only a gunpowder haze, history's first great failure in weather control. This descent was equally futile, Donna thought, an endless and wearying exercise in nothing. Just the same as the rest of her life. Every time her father was reposted, she had resolved to change, to be somebody different this time around, whatever the price, even if—no, especially if—it meant playacting something she was not. Last year in Germany when she'd gone out with that local boy with the Alfa Romeo and instead of jerking him off had used her mouth, she had thought: Everything's going to be different now. But no.

Nothing ever changed.

"Heads up!" Russ said. "There's some steps missing here!" He leaped, and the landing gonged hollowly under his sneakers. Then again as Piggy jumped after.

Donna hesitated. There were five steps gone and a drop of twenty feet before the stairway cut back beneath itself. The cliff bulged outward here, and if she slipped she'd probably miss the stairs altogether.

She felt the rock draw away from her to either side, and was suddenly aware that she was connected to the world by the merest speck of matter, barely enough to anchor her feet. The sky wrapped itself about her, extending to infinity, depthless and absolute. She could extend her arms and fall into it forever. What would happen to her then, she wondered. Would she die of thirst and starvation, or would the speed of her fall grow so great that the oxygen would be sucked from her lungs, leaving her to strangle in a sea of air? "Come on Donna!" Piggy shouted up at her. "Don't be a pussy!"

"Russ—" she said quaveringly.

But Russ wasn't looking her way. He was frowning downward, anxious to be going. "Don't push the lady," he said. "We can go on by ourselves."

Donna choked with anger and hurt and desperation all at once. She took a deep breath and, heart scudding, leaped. Sky and rock wheeled over her head. For an instant she was floating, falling totally lost and filled with a panicky awareness that she was about to die. Then she crashed onto the landing. It hurt like hell, and at first she feared she'd pulled an ankle. Piggy grabbed her shoulders and rubbed the side of her head with his knuckles. "I knew you could do it, you wimp."

Donna knocked away his arm. "Okay, wise-ass. How are you expecting to get us back up?"

The smile disappeared from Piggy's face. His mouth opened, closed. His head jerked fearfully upward. An acrobat could leap across, grab the step and flip up without any trouble at all. "I—I mean, I—"

"Don't worry about it," Russ said impatiently. "We'll think of something." He started down again.

It wasn't natural, Donna realized, his attitude. There was something obsessive about his desire to descend the stairway. It was like the time he'd brought his father's revolver to school along with a story about playing Russian roulette that morning before breakfast. "Three times!" he'd said proudly.

He'd had that same crazy look on him, and she hadn't the slightest notion then or now how she could help him.

Russ walked like an automaton, wordlessly, tirelessly, never hurrying up or slowing down. Donna followed in concerned silence, while Piggy scurried between them, chattering like somebody's pet Pekingese. This struck Donna as so apt as to be almost allegorical: the two of them together yet alone, the distance between filled with noise. She thought of this distance, this silence, as the sun passed behind the cliff and the afternoon heat lost its edge.

The stairs changed to cement-jacketed brick with small buttresses cut into the rock. There was a pile of stems and cherry pits on one landing, and the railing above them was white with bird droppings. Piggy leaned over the rail and said, "Hey, I can see seagulls down there. Flying around."

"Where?" Russ leaned over the railing, then said scornfully, "Those are pigeons. The Ghazoddis used to release them for rifle practice."

As Piggy turned to follow Russ down again, Donna caught a glimpse into his eyes, liquid and trembling with helplessness and despair. She'd seen that fear in him only once before, months ago when she'd stopped by his house on the way to school, just after the Emir's assassination.

The living room windows were draped and the room seemed unnaturally gloomy after being out in the morning sun. Blue television light flickered over shelves of shadowy ceramic figurines: Dresden milkmaids, Chantilly Chinamen,

Meissen pug-dogs connected by a gold chain held in their champed jaws, naked Delft nymphs dancing.

Piggy's mother sat in a limp dressing gown, hair unbrushed, watching the funeral. She held a cup of oily-looking coffee in one hand. Donna was surprised to see her up so early. Everyone said that she had a bad problem with alcohol, that even by service wife standards she was out of control.

"Look at them," Piggy's mother said. On the screen were solemn processions of camels and Cadillacs, sheikhs in jellaba, keffigeh and mirrorshades, European dignitaries with wives in tasteful gray Parisian fashions. "They've got their nerve."

"Where did you put my lunch?" Piggy said loudly from the kitchen.

"Making fun of the Kennedys like that!" The Emir's youngest son, no more than four years old, salaamed his father's casket as it passed before him. "That kid's bad enough, but you should see the mother, crying as if her heart were broken. It's enough to turn your stomach. If I were Jackie, I'd—"

Donna and Piggy and Russ had gone bowling the night the Emir was shot. This was out in the ruck of cheap joints that surrounded the base, catering almost exclusively to servicemen. When the Muzak piped through overhead speakers was interrupted for the news bulletin, everyone had stood up and cheered. *Up we go*, someone had begun singing, and the rest had joined in, *into the wild blue yonder. . . .* Donna had felt so sick with fear and disgust she had thrown up in the parking lot. "I don't think they're making fun of anyone," Donna said. "They're just—"

"Don't talk to her!" The refrigerator door slammed shut. A cupboard door slammed open.

Piggy's mother smiled bitterly. "This is exactly what you'd expect from these ragheads. Pretending they're white people, deliberately mocking their betters. Filthy brown animals."

"*Mother!* Where is my fucking lunch?"

She looked at him then, jaw tightening. "Don't you use that kind of language on me, young man."

"All right!" Piggy shouted. "All right, I'm going to school without lunch! Shows how much you care!"

He turned to Donna and in the instant before he grabbed her wrist and dragged her out of the house, Donna could no longer hear the words, could only see that universe of baffled futility haunting Piggy's eyes. That same look she glimpsed today.

The railings were wooden now, half the posts rotting at their bases, with an occasional plank missing, wrenched off and thrown over the side by previous visitors. Donna's knees buckled and she stumbled, almost lurching into the rock. "I have to stop," she said, hating herself for it. "I cannot go one more step."

Piggy immediately collapsed on the landing. Russ hesitated, then climbed up to join them. They three sat staring out into nothing, legs over the Edge, arms clutching the rail.

Piggy found a Pepsi can, logo in flowing Arabic, among the rubble. He held it in his left hand and began sticking holes in it with his butterfly knife, again and again, cackling like a demented sex criminal. "Exterminate the brutes!" he said happily. Then, with absolutely no transition he asked, "How are we ever going to get back up?" so dolorously Donna had to bite back her laughter.

"Look, I just want to go on down a little bit more," Russ said.

"Why?" Piggy sounded petulant.

"So I can get down enough to get away from this garbage." He gestured at the cigarette butts, the broken brown glass, sparser than above but still there. "Just a little further, okay guys?" There was an edge to his voice, and under that the faintest hint of a plea. Donna felt helpless before those eyes. She wished they were alone, so she could ask him what was wrong.

Donna doubted that Russ himself knew what he expected to find down below. Did he think that if he went down far enough, he'd never have to climb back? She remembered the time in Mr. Herriman's algebra class when a sudden tension in the air had made her glance across the room at Russ, and he was, with great concentration, tearing the pages out of his math text and dropping them one by one on the floor. He'd taken a five-day suspension for that, and Donna had never found out what it was all about. But there was a kind of glorious arrogance to the act; Russ had been born out of time. He really should have been a medieval prince, a Medici or one of the Sabakan pretenders.

"Okay," Donna said, and Piggy of course had to go along.

Seven flights farther down the modern stairs came to an end. The wooden railing of the last short, septambic flight had been torn off entire, and laid across the steps. They had to step carefully between the uprights and the rails. But when they stood at the absolute bottom, they saw that there were stairs beyond the final landing, steps that had been cut into the stone itself. They were curving swaybacked things that millennia of rain and foot traffic had worn so uneven they were almost unpassable.

Piggy groaned. "Man, you *can't* expect us to go down that thing."

"Nobody's asking you," Russ said.

They descended the old stairway backwards and on all fours. The wind breezed up, hitting them with the force of an expected shove first to one side and then the other. There were times when Donna was so frightened she thought she was going to freeze up and never move again. But at last the stone broadened and became a wide, even ledge, with caves leading back into the rock.

The cliff face here was green-white with lichen, and had in ancient times been laboriously smoothed and carved. Between each cave (their mouths alone left in a natural state, unaltered) were heavy-thighed women—goddesses, perhaps, or demons or sacred dancers—their breasts and faces chipped away by the image-hating followers of the Prophet at a time when Mohammed yet lived. Their hands held loops of vines in which were entangled moons, cycling from new through waxing quarter and gibbous to full and then back through gibbous and waning quarter to dark. Piggy was gasping, his face bright with sweat, but he kept up his blustery front. "What the fuck is all this shit, man?"

"It was a monastery," Russ said. He walked along the ledge dazedly, a wondering half smile on his lips. "I read about this." He stopped at a turquoise automobile door someone had flung over the Edge to be caught and tossed by fluke winds, the only piece of trash that had made it down this far. "Give me a hand."

He and Piggy lifted the door, swung it back and forth three times to build up momentum, then lofted it over the lip of the rock. They all three lay down on their stomachs to watch it fall away, turning end over end and seeming finally to flicker as it dwindled smaller and smaller, still falling. At last it shrank below the threshold of visibility and became one of a number of shifting motes in the downbelow, part of the slow, mazy movement of dead blood cells in the eyes' vitreous humors. Donna turned over on her back, drew her head back from the rim, stared upward. The cliff seemed to be slowly tumbling forward, all the world inexorably, dizzyingly leaning down to crush her.

"Let's go explore the caves," Piggy suggested.

They were empty. The interiors of the caves extended no more than thirty feet into the rock, but they had all been elaborately worked, arched ceiling carved with thousands of *faux tesserae*, walls adorned with bas-relief pillars. Between the pillars the walls were taken up with long shelves carved into the stone. No artifacts remained, not so much as a potsherd or a splinter of bone. Piggy shone his pocket flash into every shadowy niche. "Somebody's been here before us and taken everything." he said.

"The Historic Registry people, probably." Russ ran a hand over one shelf. It was the perfect depth and height for a line of three-pound coffee cans. "This is where they stowed the skulls. When a monk grew so spiritually developed he no longer needed the crutch of physical existence, his fellows would render the flesh from his bones and enshrine his skull. They poured wax in the sockets, then pushed in opals while it was still warm. They slept beneath the faintly gleaming eyes of their superiors."

When they emerged it was twilight, the first stars appearing from behind a sky fading from blue to purple. Donna looked down on the moon. It was as big as a plate, full and bright. The rilles, dry seas and mountain chains were preternaturally distinct. Somewhere in the middle was Tranquility Base, where Neil Armstrong had planted the American flag.

"Jeez, it's late," Donna said. "If we don't start home soon, my mom is going to have a cow."

"We still haven't figured a way to get back up," Piggy reminded her. Then, "We'll probably have to stay here. Learn to eat owls and grow crops sideways on the cliff face. Start our own civilization. Our only serious problem is the imbalance of sexes, but even that's not insurmountable." He put an arm around Donna's shoulders, grabbed at her breast. "You'd pull the train for us, wouldn't you, Donna?"

Angrily she pushed him away and said, "You keep a clean mouth! I'm so tired of your juvenile talk and behavior."

"Hey, calm down, it's cool." That panicky look was back in his eyes, the forced knowledge that he was not in control, could never be in control, that there was no such thing as control. He smiled weakly, placatingly.

"No, it is not. It is most emphatically not 'cool.' " Suddenly she was white and shaking with fury. Piggy was a spoiler. His simple presence ruined any chance she might have had to talk with Russ, find out just what was bugging him, get him to finally, really notice her. "I am sick of having to deal with your immaturity, your filthy language and your crude behavior."

Piggy turned pink and began stuttering.

Russ reached a hand into his pocket, pulled out a chunk of foil-wrapped hash, and a native tin pipe with a carved coral bowl. The kind of thing the local beggar kids sold for twenty-nine cents. "Anybody want to get stoned?" he asked suavely.

"You bastard!" Piggy laughed. "You told me you were out!"

Russ shrugged. "I lied." He lit the pipe carefully, drew in, passed it to Donna. She took it from his fingers, felt how cold they were to her touch, looked up over the pipe and saw his face, thin and ascetic, eyelids closed, pale and Christlike through the blue smoke. She loved him intensely in that instant and wished she could sacrifice herself for his happiness. The pipe's stem was overwarm, almost hot, between her lips. She drew in deep.

The smoke was raspy in her throat, then tight and swirling in her lungs. It shot up into her head, filled it with buzzing harmonics: the air, the sky, the rock behind her back all buzzing, ballooning her skull outward in a visionary rush that forced wide-open first her eyes and then her mouth. She choked and spasmodically coughed. More smoke than she could imagine possibly holding in her lungs gushed out into the universe.

"Hey, watch that pipe!" Piggy snatched it from her distant fingers. They tingled with pinpricks of pain like tiny stars in the darkness of her flesh. "You were spilling the hash!" The evening light was abuzz with energy, the sky swarming up into her eyes. Staring out into the darkening air, the moon rising below her and the stars as close and friendly as those in a children's book illustration, she felt at peace, detached from worldly cares. "Tell us about the monastery, Russ," she said, in the same voice she might have used a decade before to ask her father for a story.

"Yeah, tell us about the monastery, Unca Russ," Piggy said, but with jeering undertones. Piggy was always sucking up to Russ, but there was tension there too, and his sarcastic little challenges were far from rare. It was classic beta male jealousy, straight out of Primate Psychology 101.

"It's very old," Russ said. "Before the Sufis, before Mohammed, even before the Zoroastrians crossed the gulf, the native mystics would renounce the world and go to live in cliffs on the Edge of the World. They cut the steps down, and once down, they never went back up again."

"How did they eat then?" Piggy asked skeptically.

"They wished their food into existence. No, really! It was all in their creation myth: In the beginning all was Chaos and Desire. The world was brought out of Chaos—by which they meant unformed matter—by Desire, or Will. It gets a little inconsistent after that, because it wasn't really a religion, but more like a system of magic. They believed that the world wasn't complete yet, that for some complicated reason it could never be complete. So there's still traces of the old Chaos lingering just beyond the Edge, and it can be tapped by those who desire it strongly enough, if they have distanced themselves from the things of the world. These mystics used to come down here to meditate against the moon and work miracles.

"This wasn't sophisticated stuff like the Tantric monks in Tibet or anything, remember. It was like a primitive form of animism, a way to force the universe to give you what you wanted. So the holy men would come down here and they'd wish for . . . like riches, you know? Filigreed silver goblets with rubies, mounds of moonstones, elfinbone daggers sharper than Damascene steel. Only once they got them they weren't supposed to want them. They'd just throw them over the Edge. There were these monasteries all along the cliffs. The farther from the world they were, the more spiritually advanced."

"So what happened to the monks?"

"There was a king—Althazar? I forget his name. He was this real greedhead, started sending his tax collectors down to gather up everything the monks brought into existence. Must've figured, hey, the monks weren't using them. Which as it turned out was like a real major blasphemy, and the monks got pissed. The boss mystics, all the real spiritual heavies, got together for this big confab. Nobody knows how. There's one of the classics claims they could run sideways on the cliff just like it was the ground, but I don't know. Doesn't matter. So one night they all of them, every monk in the world, meditated at the same time. They chanted together, saying, It is not enough that Althazar should die, for he has blasphemed. He must suffer a doom such as has been visited on no man before. He must be unmade, uncreated, reduced to less than has ever been. And they prayed that there be no such king as Althazar, that his life and history be unmade, so that there never had been such king as Althazar.

"And he was no more.

"But so great was their yearning for oblivion that when Althazar ceased to be, his history and family as well, they were left feeling embittered and did not know why. And not knowing why, their hatred turned upon themselves, and their wish for destruction, and they too all of a single night, ceased to be." He fell silent.

At last Piggy said, "You believe that crap?" Then, when there was no answer, "It's none of it true, man! Got that? There's no magic, and there never was." Donna could see that he was really angry, threatened on some primal level by the possibility that someone he respected could even begin to believe in magic. His face got pink, the way it always did when he lost control.

"No, it's all bullshit," Russ said bitterly. "Like everything else."

They passed the pipe around again. Then Donna leaned back, stared straight out, and said, "If I could wish for anything, you know what I'd wish for?"

"Bigger tits?"

She was so weary now, so pleasantly washed out, that it was easy to ignore Piggy. "I'd wish I knew what the situation was."

"What situation?" Piggy asked. Donna was feeling langorous, not at all eager to explain herself, and she waved away the question. But he persisted. "What situation?"

"Any situation. I mean, all the time, I find myself talking with people and I don't know what's really going on. What games they're playing. Why they're acting the way they are. I wish I knew what the situation was."

The moon floated before her, big and fat and round as a griffin's egg, shining with power. She could feel that power washing through her, the background radiation of decayed chaos spread across the sky at a uniform three degrees Kelvin. Even now, spent and respent, a coin fingered and thinned to the worn edge of nonexistence, there was power out there, enough to flatten planets.

Staring out at that great fat boojum snark of a moon, she felt the flow of potential worlds, and within the cold silver disk of that jester's skull, rank with magic, sensed the invisible presence of Russ's primitive monks, men whose minds were nowhere near comprehensible to her, yet vibrated with power, existing as matrices of patterned stress, no more actual than Donald Duck, but no less powerful either. She was caught in a waking fantasy, in which the sky was full of power and all of it accessible to her. Monks sat empty-handed over their wishing bowls, separated from her by the least fictions of time and reality. For an eternal instant all possibilities fanned out to either side, equally valid, no one more real than any other. Then the world turned under her, and her brain shifted back to realtime.

"Me," Piggy said, "I just wish I knew how to get back up the stairs."

They were silent for a moment. Then it occurred to Donna that here was the perfect opportunity to find out what was bugging Russ. If she asked cautiously enough, if the question hit him just right, if she were just plain lucky, he might tell her everything. She cleared her throat. "Russ? What do you wish?"

In the bleakest voice imaginable, Russ said, "I wish I'd never been born."

She turned to ask him why, and he wasn't there.

"Hey," Donna said. "Where'd Russ go?"

Piggy looked at her oddly. "Who's Russ?"

It was a long trip back up. They carried the length of wooden railing between them, and every now and then Piggy said, "Hey, wasn't this a great idea of mine? This'll make a swell ladder."

"Yeah, great," Donna would say, because he got mad when she didn't respond. He got mad, too, whenever she started to cry, but there wasn't anything she could do about that. She couldn't even explain why she was crying, because in all the world—of all his friends, acquaintances, teachers, even his parents—she was the only one who remembered that Russ had ever existed.

The horrible thing was that she had no specific memories of him, only a vague feeling of what his presence had been like, and a lingering sense of longing and frustration.

She no longer even remembered his face.

"Do you want to go first or last?" Piggy had asked her.

When she'd replied, "Last. If I go first, you'll stare at my ass all the way up," he'd actually blushed. Without Russ to show off in front of, Piggy was a completely different person, quiet and not at all abusive. He even kept his language clean. But that didn't help, for just being in his presence was enough to force understanding on her: that his bravado was fueled by his insecurities and aspirations, that he masturbated nightly and with self-loathing, that he despised his parents and longed in vain for the least sign of love from them. That the way he treated her was the sum and total of all of this and more.

She knew exactly what the situation was.

Dear God, she prayed, let it be that I won't have this kind of understanding when I reach the top. Or else make it so that situations won't be so painful up there, that knowledge won't hurt like this, that horrible secrets won't lie under the most innocent word.

They carried their wooden burden upward, back toward the world.

FRED CHAPPELL
The Adder

Fred Chappell teaches at the University of North Carolina, Greensboro. His new novel is *Brighten the Corner Where You Are* (St. Martin's Press) and his latest collection of poetry is *First and Last Words* (Louisiana State University Press).

Just when I think there couldn't possibly be another interesting Cthulhu Mythos story, one appears in print that seems fresh and clever, and maybe even frightening. "The Adder" is all that, with a touch of humor. And it's that rarest of tales—one that contains an element of bibliophilic horror. Mr. Chappell, known for his fine, literate stories of the contemporary South, has deftly created a gem.

—E.D.

The Adder

FRED CHAPPELL

My Uncle Alvin reminds the startled stranger of a large happy bunny. He is pleasantly rotund, and with silver blond hair that makes him look a full decade younger than his sixty years. His skin has a scrubbed pink shine that the pale complexions of English curates sometimes acquire, and he has a way of wrinkling his nose that one irresistibly associates with—well, I've already named rabbits. He is a kindly, humorous, and often mildly mischievous fellow.

My admiration of Uncle Alvin has had a large measure of influence upon my life. His easygoing manner has seemed to me a sensible way to get along in the world. And his occupation is interesting and leisurely, though it's unlikely he'll ever gain great wealth by it. I can support this latter supposition by my own experience; I followed my uncle into the antiquarian book trade and I am not—please let me assure you—a rich man.

We don't compete with one another, however. Uncle Alvin lives in Columbia, South Carolina, and runs his mail order business from his home. The bulk of my trade is also mail order, but I run it from a shopfront in Durham, North Carolina. My shop sells used paperbacks, mostly to Duke University students; in the back I package and mail out rare and curious books of history, the occult, and fantasy, along with some occasional odd science fiction. Uncle Alvin specializes in Civil War history, which in South Carolina almost guarantees a living income, however modest.

But anyone in the trade is likely to happen upon any sort of book, whether it belongs to his specialty or not. When Uncle Alvin called one Saturday morning to say that he had come into possession of a volume that he wanted me to see, I surmised that it was more in my line than his, and that he thought I might be interested in making a purchase.

"What sort of book is it?" I asked.

"Very rare indeed—if it's genuine. And still rather valuable if it's only a forgery."

"What's the title?"

"Oh, I can't tell you that on the telephone," he said.

"You can't tell me the title? It must be something extraordinary."

"Caution never hurts. Anyway, you can see it for yourself. I'll be by your place with it on Monday morning. If that's all right with you."

"Say, that's grand," I said. "You'll stay overnight, of course. Helen will be thrilled to see you."

"No," he said. "I'm driving through to Washington. I'll stop off on the way. Because I don't want to keep this book in the car any longer than I have to."

"We'll have lunch, at least," I said. "Do you still crave lasagne?"

"Day and night," he replied.

"Then it's settled," I said and we chatted a little longer before ringing off.

Monday morning he entered my shop—called Alternate Histories—carrying a battered metal cashbox and I knew the book was inside it. We sounded the usual pleasantries that friendly kinfolk make with one another, though ours may have been more genuinely felt than many. But he was anxious to get to the business he had in mind. He set the cashbox on top of a stack of used magazines on the counter and said, "Well, this is it."

"All right," I said, "I'm ready. Open her up."

"First, let me tell you a little bit about what I think we have here," he said. "Because when you see it you're going to be disappointed. Its appearance is not prepossessing."

"All right."

"In the first place, it's in Arabic. It's handwritten in a little diary in ordinary badly faded ink and it's incomplete. Since I don't read Arabic, I don't know what's missing. I only know that it's too short to be the full version. This copy came to me from the widow of a classics professor at the University of South Carolina, an Egyptologist who disappeared on a field excursion some thirty years ago. His wife kept his library all this time, hoping for his return. Then, last year, she offered up the whole lot. That's how I happen to be in possession of this copy of *Al Azif*."

"I never heard of it," I said, trying not to show the minor disappointment I felt.

"It's the work of a medieval poet thought to have been insane," Uncle Alvin said, "but there is debate as to how crazy he actually was. His name was Abdul Alhazred and he lived in Yemen. Shortly after composing *Al Azif* he met a violent and grisly death—which is all we know about it because even the eye-witnesses dispute the manner of his dying."

"Abdul Alhazred. Isn't that—?"

"Yes indeed," he said. "The work is more recognizable under the title of its Greek translation. *The Necronomicon*. And the most widely known text—if any of them can really be said to be widely known—is the thirteenth century Latin translation of Olaus Wormius. It has always been surmised that the original

Arabic text perished long ago, since every powerful government and respected religious organization has tried to destroy the work in all its forms. And they have largely succeeded in doing so."

"But how do you know what it is, if you don't read Arabic?"

"I have a friend," he said proudly. "Dr. Abu-Saba. I asked him to look at it and to give me a general idea of the contents. When I handed it to him and he translated the title, I stopped him short. Better not to go on with *that*. You know the reputation of *The Necronomicon*."

"I do indeed," I said, "and I don't care to know what's in it in any detail. In fact, I'm not really overjoyed at finding myself in such close company."

"Oh, we should be safe enough. As long as we keep our mouths closed so that certain unsavory groups of cultists don't hear that we've got it."

"If you're offering it to me for sale—" I began.

"No, no," he said hastily. "I'm trying to arrange to deposit it in the Library of Congress. That's why I'm going to Washington. I wouldn't put my favorite nephew in jeopardy—or not for long, anyway. All I would like is for you to keep it for a week while I'm negotiating. I'm asking as a personal favor."

I considered. "I'll be happy to keep it for you," I said. "To tell the truth, I'm more concerned about the security of the book than about my own safety. I can take care of myself. But the book is a dangerous article, and an extremely valuable one."

"Like an atomic weapon," Uncle Alvin said. "Too dangerous to keep and too dangerous to dispose of. But the Library of Congress will know what to do. This can't be the first time they've encountered this problem."

"You think they already have a *Necronomicon*?"

"I'd bet money," he said cheerfully, "except that I wouldn't know how to collect. You don't expect them to list it in the catalogue, do you?"

"They'd deny possession, of course."

"But there's a good chance they won't have an Arabic version. Only one is known to have reached America and it was thought to have been destroyed in San Francisco around the turn of the century. This volume is probably a copy of that version."

"So what do I do with it?" I asked.

"Put it in a safe place. In your lockbox at the bank."

"I don't have one of those," I said. "I have a little old dinky safe in my office in back, but if anyone came to find it, that's the first place they'd look."

"Do you have a cellar in this shop?"

"Not that I'd trust the book to. Why don't we take a hint from Edgar Allan Poe?"

He frowned a moment, then brightened. "A purloined letter, you mean?"

"Sure. I've got all sorts of books scattered about in cardboard boxes. I haven't sorted them yet to shelve. It would take weeks for someone to hunt it out even if he knew it was here."

"It might work," Uncle Alvin said, wrinkling his nose and rubbing his pink ear with a brisk forefinger. "But there's a problem."

"What's that?"

"You may wish to disregard it because of its legendary nature. I wouldn't. In the case of *Al Azif*, it's best to take every precaution."

"All right," I said. "What's the legend?"

"Among certain bookmen, *The Necronomicon* is sometimes known as *The Adder*. Because first it poisons, then it devours."

I gave him a look that I intended to mean: not another one of your little jokes, Uncle Alvin. "You don't really expect me to believe that we've got a book here that eats people."

"Oh no." He shook his head. "It only eats its own kind."

"I don't understand."

"Just make sure," he said, "that when you place it in a box with other books, none of them is important."

"I get it," I said. "Damaged cheap editions. To draw attention away from its true value."

He gave me a long mild stare, then nodded placidly. "Something like that," he replied at last.

"Okay," I agreed, "I'll do exactly that. Now let's have a look at this ominous rarity. I've heard about *The Necronomicon* ever since I became interested in books. I'm all a-flutter."

"I'm afraid you're going to be disappointed," Uncle Alvin said. "Some copies of this forbidden text are quite remarkable, but this one—" He twitched his nose again and rubbed it with the palm of his hand.

"Now don't be a naughty tease, Uncle Alvin," I said.

He unlocked the metal box and took out a small parcel wrapped in brown paper. He peeled away the paper to reveal a rather thin octavo diary with a worn morocco cover that had faded from what would have been a striking red to a pale brick color, almost pinkish. Noticing the expression on my face, he said, "See? I told you it would be a disappointment."

"No, not at all," I said, but my tone was so obviously subdued that he handed it to me to examine without my asking.

There was little to see. The pinkish worn binding felt smooth. The spine was hubbed and stamped *Diary* in gold, but the gold too had almost worn away. I opened it at random and looked at incomprehensible Arabic script so badly faded that it was impossible to say what color the ink had been. Black or purple or maybe even dark green—but now all the colors had become a pale uniform grey. I leafed through almost to the end but found nothing in the least remarkable.

"Well, I do hope this is the genuine article," I said. "Are you sure your friend, Dr. Hoodoo—"

"Abu-Saba," said Uncle Alvin primly. "Dr. Fuad Abu-Saba. His knowledge of his native tongue is impeccable, his integrity unassailable."

"Okay, if you say so," I said. "But what we have here doesn't look like much."

"I'm not trying to sell it. Its nondescript appearance is in our favor. The more undistinguished it looks, the safer we are."

"That makes sense," I admitted, handing it back to him.

He glanced at me shrewdly as he returned it to the cashbox, obviously thinking that I was merely humoring him—as to a certain extent I was. "Robert," he said sternly, "you're my favorite nephew, one of my most favorite persons. I want you to follow my instructions seriously. I want you to take the strongest precautions and keep on your guard. This is a dangerous passage for both of us."

I sobered. "All right, Uncle Alvin. You know best."

He wrapped the volume in the brown paper and restored it to the scarred box and carried it with him as we repaired to Tony's Ristorante Venezia to indulge copiously in lasagne and a full-bodied Chianti. After lunch he dropped me back at Alternate Histories and, taking *Al Azif* out of the metal box, gave it over to my safekeeping with a single word of admonition. "Remember," he said.

"Don't worry," I said. "I remember."

In the shop I examined the book in a more leisurely and comprehensive fashion. But it hadn't changed; it was only one more dusty faded stained diary like thousands of others and its sole distinction to the unlearned eye was that it was in handwritten Arabic script. A mysterious gang of sinister thieves would have to know a great deal about it merely in order to know what to search for.

I decided not to trust it to a jumble of books in a maze of cardboard boxes. I took it into my little backroom office, shoved some valueless books out of the way, and laid it flat on a lower shelf of a ramshackle bookcase there that was cluttered with every sort of pamphlet, odd periodical, and assorted volume from broken sets of Maupassant, Balzac, and William McFee. I turned it so that the gilt edge faced outward and the word "Diary" was hidden. Then I deliberated for a minute or two about what to stack on top of it.

I thought of Uncle Alvin's warning that no important books were to be placed with *Al Azif* and I determined to heed it. What's the point in having a favorite uncle, wise and experienced in his trade, if you don't listen to him? And besides that, the dark reputation of the book was an urgent warning in itself.

I picked up an ordinary and utterly undistinguished copy of Milton's poems. Herndon House, New York, 1924. No introduction and a few sketchy notes by an anonymous editor, notes no doubt reduced from a solid scholarly edition. It was a warped copy and showed significant water damage. I opened to the beginning of *Paradise Lost* and read the first twenty-six lines, then searched to find my favorite Miltonic sonnet, number XIX, *On His Blindness*.

> *When I consider how my light is spent*
> *Ere half my days, in this dark world and wide,*
> *And that one Talent which is death to hide,*
> *Lodg'd with me useless, though my Soul more bent*
> *To serve therewith my Maker, and present*
> *My true account, lest he returning chide . . .*

Well, you know how it goes.

It's a poem of which I never tire, one of those poems which has faithfully befriended me in periods happy and unhappy since the years of my majority. Milton's customary stately music is there, and a heartfelt personal outcry not often to be found in his work. Then there comes the sternly contented resolution of the final lines. Milton requires, of course, no recommendation from me, and his sonnet no encomium. I only desire to make it clear that this poet is important to me and the sonnet on his blindness particularly dear.

But not every copy, or every edition, of Milton is important. I have personal copies of fully annotated and beautifully illustrated editions. The one I held in my hand was only a cheap mass edition, designed in all probability to be sold at railway bookstalls. I placed it on top of the Arabic treasure and then piled over both books a stack of papers from my desk which is always overflowing with such papers: catalogues, booklists, sale announcements, and invoices. Of this latter item especially there is an eternal surplus.

Then I forgot about it.

No, I didn't.

I didn't in the least forget that I almost certainly had in my possession *Al Azif*, one of the rarest documents in bibliographic annals, one of the enduring titles of history and legend. And one of the deadliest. We don't need to rehearse the discomfiting and unsanitary demises alleged of so many former owners of the book. They all came to bad ends, and messy ones. Uncle Alvin had the right idea, getting the volume into the hands of those prepared to care for it. My mission was merely a holding action—to keep it safe for a week. That being so, I resolved not to go near it, not even to look at it until my uncle returned the following Saturday.

And I was able to keep to my resolution until Tuesday, the day after I'd made it.

The manuscript in its diary format had changed when I looked. I noticed right away that the morocco covers had lost their pinkish cast and taken on a bright red. The stamped word *Diary* shone more brightly too and when I opened the volume and leafed through it, I saw that the pages had whitened, losing most of the signs of age, and that the inked script stood forth more boldly. It was now possible to discern, in fact, that the writing actually was clothed in different colors of ink: black, emerald green, royal purple, Persian rose.

The Necronomicon, in whatever version, is a remarkable book. All the world knows something of its reputation, and I might have been more surprised if my encounter with it had been uneventful than if something unusual transpired. Its history is too long, and a knowledgeable scholar does not respond to mysterious happenings in the presence of the book by smiting his breast and exclaiming, "Can such things be?"

But a change in the physical makeup of the book itself was something I had not expected and could not account for. Not knowing yet what to think, I replaced it just as it had been, beneath the random papers and the copy of Milton, and went on with my ordinary tasks.

There was, however, no denying the fact of the changes. My senses did not belie me. Each time I examined it on Tuesday and Wednesday—I must have picked it up a dozen times all told—our *Al Azif* had grown stronger.

Stronger. As silly as that word seems in this context, it is still accurate. The script was becoming more vivid, the pages gleamed like fresh snowbanks, the staunch morocco covers glowed blood-red.

It took me too long to understand that this manuscript had found something to feed upon. It had discovered a form of nourishment which caused it to thrive and grow stout. And I am embarrassed to admit that more hours elapsed before I guessed the source of the volume's food—which had to be the copy of Milton's poems I had placed on top of it.

Quickly then I snatched up the Milton and began to examine it for changes. At first I could discover no anomalies. The print seemed perhaps a little greyer, but it had already been rather faded. Perhaps too the pages were more brittle and musty than I'd thought—but, after all, it was a cheap book some sixty-odd years old. When I turned to the opening of *Paradise Lost*, all seemed well enough; the great organ tones were as resonant as ever:

> *Of Man's First Disobedience, and the Fruit*
> *Of that Forbidden Tree, whose mortal taste*
> *Brought Death into the World, and all our woe . . .*

And I thought, Well, I needn't have worried. This poetry is immune to the ravages of time and of all circumstance.

So it was in anticipation of a fleeting pleasure that I turned idly to glance at sonnet XIX:

> *When I consider how my loot is spent*
> *On Happy Daze, a fifth of darling wine . . .*

But the familiar opening of the sonnet had lost much of its savor; I was missing something of that intimate stateliness I was accustomed to. I set down my pallid reaction to tiredness and excited nerves. Anxiety about Uncle Alvin's treasure was beginning to tell on me, I thought.

I shook my head as if to clear it, closed my eyes and rubbed them with both hands, then looked once more into the volume of Milton open on the counter, sonnet XIX:

> *When I consider how my lute is bent*
> *On harpy fates in this dork woolly-wold,*
> *And that dung-yellow witches' breath doth glide,*
> *Lobster and toothless . . .*

No use. I was too confused to make sense of the lines at all. It's only nerves, I thought again, and thought too how glad I would be for my uncle's return on Sunday.

I laid the copy of *Al Azif* and determined to put the puzzle out of my mind.

I couldn't do that, of course. The idea had occurred that our particular copy of Abdul Alhazred's forbidden work was changing the nature of Milton's lines. What was it Uncle Alvin had compared it to? An adder, was it? First it poisons, he'd said, then it devours. Was it indeed poisoning the lines of the great seventeenth century poet? I took up the Milton again and opened to the beginning of his immortal religious epic:

> *Of a Man's First Dish of Beetles, and the Fat*
> *Of that Forboding Fay, whom Myrtle Trent*
> *Brought fresh into the World, and Hollywood . . .*

The words made no sense to me, none at all—but I couldn't remember them any differently than how they appeared on the page. I couldn't tell whether the fault lay in the book or in myself.

A sudden thought inspired me to go to my poetry shelves and find another edition of Milton's poems so that I could cross-check the strange-seeming verses. If *Al Azif* truly was changing the words in the other, then a book untouched by the diary would render up only the purest Milton. I went round to the front and took down three copies of Milton's poems in different editions and used my favorite sonnet as touchstone. The first one I examined was Sir Hubert Portingale's Oxbridge edition of 1957. It gave me these lines:

> *When I consider to whome my Spode is lent,*
> *Ear-halves and jays on this dank girlie slide . . .*

It seemed incorrect somehow. I looked at the poem in Professor Y. Y. Miranda's Big Apple State University Press volume of 1974:

Winnie's Corn Cider, how my lust is burnt!

That line was wrong, I felt it in my bones. I turned to the more informal edition edited by the contemporary poet Richmond Burford:

> *When I consider how a lighter splint*
> *Veered off my dice in this dour curled end-word*
> *And that wan Talent . . .*

I shook my head. Was that correct? Was it anywhere near correct?

The trouble was that I couldn't remember how the lines were supposed to read. I had the vague feeling that none of these versions was the right one. Obviously, they couldn't all be right. But why couldn't I remember my favorite poem, more familiar to me than my Social Security number?

Uncle Alvin's warning had been: "First it poisons, then it devours."

Now I began to interpret his words in a different way. Perhaps *The Necronomicon* didn't poison only the book it was in physical contact with, perhaps it poisoned the actual content of the work itself, so that in whatever edition it appeared, in whatever book, magazine, published lecture, scholarly essay, commonplace book, personal diary—in whatever written form—a polluted text showed up.

It was an altogether terrifying thought. Uncle Alvin had not warned against placing it with an important *edition*; his warning concerned an important *book*. I had placed it with Milton and had infected the great poems wherever they might now appear.

Could that be right? It seemed a little farfetched. Well no, it seemed as silly as picturing Milton, the poet himself, in a Shriner's hat. It seemed just dog-dumb.

But I determined to test my wild hypothesis, nevertheless. I got to the telephone and called my old friend and faithful customer in Knoxville, Tennessee, the poet Ned Clark. When he said Hello, I was almost rude: "Please don't ask me a lot of questions, Ned. This is urgent. Do you have a copy of Milton's poems handy?"

He paused. Then: "Robert, is that you?"

"Yes it is. But I'm in an awful hurry. Do you have the poems?"

"In my study."

"Can you get the book, please?"

"Hold on," he said. "I have an extension. I'll pick up in there." I waited as patiently as I was able until he said, "Here we are. What's the big deal?"

"Sonnet XIX," I said. "Would you please read it to me?"

"Right now? Over the phone?"

"Yes. Unless you can shout very loud."

"Hey, man," he said. "Chill out, why don't you?"

"I'm sorry, Ned," I said, "but I think I may have made a big mistake. I mean, a heavy *bad* mistake, old son. So I'm trying to check up on something. Could you read the poems to me?"

"Sure, that's cool," he replied, and I heard him leafing through his book. "Okay, Robert. Are you ready? Here goes: 'When icons in a house mild lights suspend, Or half my ties in this stark world have died . . .'"

I interrupted. "Okay, Ned. Thanks. That's all I need to hear right now."

"That's all? You called long distance to hear me say two lines of your favorite poem?"

"Yes I did. How did they sound to you?"

"As good as Milton gets."

"Did they sound correct? Are those the words as you've known them all your life?"

"I haven't known them all my life," he said. "You're the wild-haired Milton fan. He's too monumental for my taste, you know? I mean, massive."

"Okay, but you've read the poem, at least."

"Yes, indeed. It's a big-time famous poem. I read all those babies, you know that."

"And these lines are the ones you've always known?"

Another pause. "Well, maybe not exactly," he admitted. "I think the punctuation might be a little different in this book from what I'm used to. But it mainly sounds right. Do you want publication information?"

"Not now," I said, "but I may call back later for it." I thanked my friend and hung up.

It seemed that my surmise was correct. All the texts were now envenomed.

But I wanted to make certain of the fact and spent the next four hours telephoning friends and acquaintances scattered throughout America, comparing the lines. Not every one answered, of course, and some of my friends in the western states were groggy with sleep, but I got a large enough sample of first lines to satisfy me.

Walt Pavlich in California: *One-Eye can so draw my late sow's pen* . . .

Paul Ruffin in Texas: *Wind I consider now my life has bent* . . .

Robert Shapard in Hawaii: *Wound a clean liver and the lights go out* . . .

Vanessa Haley in Virginia: *Wind a gone slider and collide a bunt* . . .

Barbara Smith in West Virginia: *Watch a corned beef sandwich bow and bend* . . .

These were enough and more for me to understand the enormity of my mistake. All the texts of Milton that existed were now disfigured beyond recognition. And I had noted a further consequence of my error. Even the texts as they resided in memory were changed; not one of my friends could remember how the lines of sonnet XIX were *supposed* to read. Nor could I, and I must have been for a decade and a half one of the more constant companions of the poem.

The copy of *Al Azif* was flourishing. I didn't need even to pick it up to see that. The gilt edge shone like a gold bar fresh from Fort Knox and the morocco binding had turned ruby red and pulsed with light like a live coal. I was curious how the inks would glitter, so now I did pick up the volume—which seemed as alive in my hands as a small animal—and opened it at random.

I was right. The different colors of the inks were as vivid and muscular as kudzu and looked as if they were bitten into the thick creamy pages like etching. However disquieting these changes, they had resulted in a truly beautiful manuscript, a masterpiece of its kind. And though I knew it to be a modern handwritten copy, it also seemed to be regaining some of its medieval characteristics. Most of the pages were no longer totally in Arabic; they had become macaronic. Toward the end pages a few English words were sprinkled into the eastern script.

Oh, no.

As long as *Al Azif* was in Arabic it was relatively harmless. Most people would be unable to read the spells and incantations and the knowledge to be found there that is—well, the traditional epithet is "unspeakable," and it is accurately descriptive. I certainly would not speak of the contents, even if I were able to read them.

I flipped to the front. The first lines I found in the first page were these:

> *Wisely did Ibn Mushacab say, that happy is the tomb where no wizard hath lain, and happy the town at night whose wizards are all ashes. For the spirit of the devil-indentured hastes not from his charnel clay, but feeds and instructs the very worm that gnaws. Then an awful life from corruption springs and feeds again the appointed scavengers upon the earth. Great holes are dug hidden where are the open pores of the earth, and things have learned to walk that ought to crawl.*

I snapped the cover shut. Those phrases had the true stink of *The Necron-omicon*. You don't have to be an expert upon the verses of Alhazred to recognize his style and subject matter.

I had read all of these pages that I ever wanted to read, but even so I opened the volume again, to the middle, to confirm my hypothesis. I was right: *Al Azif* was translating itself into English, little by little. There was only a sprinkling of English in the latter pages; the early pages were English from head to foot; the middle pages half Arabic, half English. I could read phrases and sentences, but not whole passages. I could make out clearly, "they dwell in the inmost adyta;" then would follow lovely Arabic calligraphy. Some of the passages I compre-hended were these:

> *Yog-Sothoth knows the gate; in the Gulf the worlds themselves are made of sounds; the dim horrors of Earth; Iä ïa ïa, Shub-Niggurath!*

Nothing surprising, and nothing I wanted to deal with.

But I did understand what had happened. When I had so carelessly allowed this copy of *Al Azif* to batten upon Milton's poetry, it took the opportunity to employ Milton's language in the task of translating itself. With a single thought-less act, I had given *The Necronomicon*—call it accursed or unspeakable or maddening, call it whatever minatory adjective you choose—both life and speech and I saw the potential for harm that I had set in place.

I flung the volume into my flimsy little safe, clanged shut the door, and spun the dial. I put up the CLOSED sign on my shop door, called my wife Helen to tell her I wouldn't be home, and stood guard like a military sentinel. I would not leave my post, I decided, until Uncle Alvin returned to rescue me and all the rest of the world from a slender little book written centuries ago by a poet who ought to have known better.

Nor did my determination falter.

As soon as Uncle Alvin laid eyes on me Sunday morning, he knew what had gone wrong. "It has escaped, hasn't it?" he said, looking into my face. "*Al Azif* has learned English."

"Come in," I said. When he entered I glanced up and down the empty street, then shut the door firmly, and guided my uncle by his arm into my office.

He looked at the desk, at the crumpled brown paper bags that held my meals and at the dozens of empty styrofoam cups. He nodded. "You set up a watch post. That's a good idea. Where is the volume now?"

"In the safe," I said.

"What's in there with it?"

"Nothing. I took everything out."

"There's no cash in the safe?"

"Only that book you brought upon me."

"That's good," he said. "Do you know what would happen if this copy were brought into contact with cash money?"

"It would probably poison the whole economy of the nation," I said.

"That's right. All U.S. currency everywhere would turn counterfeit."

"I thought of that," I said. "You have to give me some credit. In fact, this never would have happened if you had given me a clearer warning."

"You're right, Robert, I'm sure. But I feared you'd think I was only pulling your leg. And then I thought maybe you'd experiment with it just to see what would happen."

"Not me," I said. "I'm a responsible citizen. *The Necronomicon* is too powerful to joke around with."

"Let's have a look," he said.

I opened the safe and took the volume out. Its outward appearance was unchanged, so far as I could tell. The ruby morocco was rich as a leopard pelt and the gilt edge and gold stamping gleamed like fairy tale treasure.

When I handed it to Uncle Alvin he didn't bother to glance at the exterior of the book, but turned immediately to the latter pages. He raised his eyebrows in surprise, then began reading aloud: "The affair that shambleth about in the night, the evil that defieth the Elder Sign, the Herd that stand watch at the secret portal each tomb is known to have and that thrive on that which groweth out of the tenants thereof: All these Blacknesses are lesser than He Who guardeth the Gateway—"

"Stop, Uncle Alvin," I cried. "You know better than to read that stuff aloud." It seemed to me that it had grown darker in my little office and that a certain chill had come into the room.

He closed the book and looked at it with a puzzled expression. "My word," he said, "that is an exotic and obsolescent diction. What has *Al Azif* been feeding on?"

"Milton," I answered.

"Ah, Milton," he said and nodded again. "I should have recognized that vocabulary."

"It has poisoned all of Milton's works," I said.

"Indeed? Let's see."

I picked up one of the copies on the desk and handed it to him.

He opened it and, without showing any expression, asked, "How do you know this book is Milton?"

"I brought all my copies in here and stacked them on the desk. I've been afraid to look at them for two days, but I know that you're holding a fairly expensive edition of John Milton's poetic works."

He turned the open book toward me. The pages were blank. "Too late."

"It's eaten all the words," I said. My heart sank. I tried to remember a line of Milton, even a phrase or a characteristic word. Nothing came to mind.

"Well, maybe not *eaten*," Uncle Alvin said. "Used up, let's say. *Absorbed* might be an accurate term."

"No more Milton in the world . . . How am I going to live my life, knowing I'm responsible for the disappearance of Milton's works?"

"Maybe you won't have to," he replied. "Not if we get busy and bring them back."

"How can we do that? *Al Azif* has—swallowed them," I said.

"So we must get the accursed thing to restore the poems, to spit them up for us, the way the whale spat Jonah whole and sound."

"I don't understand."

"We must cause this manuscript to retract its powers," he said. "If we can reduce it to its former state of weakness, the way it was when I first met it in Columbia, the works of John Milton will reappear on the pages—and in the minds of men."

"How do you know?"

"You don't think this is happening for the first time, do you? It has been such a recurring event that restoration procedures have been designed and are followed in a traditional—almost ritualistic—manner."

"You mean other authors have been lost to it and then recovered?"

"Certainly."

"Who?"

"Well, for instance, the works of all the Cthulhu Mythos writers have been lost to the powers of the evil gods that they describe. Stories and poems and novels by Derleth, Long, Price and Smith have all had to be recovered. The works of Lovecraft have been taken into the domain of *Al Azif* at least a dozen times. That's why his work is so powerfully pervaded by that eldritch and sinister atmosphere. It has taken on some of the shadow of its subject."

"I never thought of that, but it makes sense. So what are the restoration procedures?"

"They're simple enough," he said. "You keep watch here while I go to my car."

He gave me the book and I set it on the edge of the desk, well away from any other written matter. I couldn't help thinking that if Uncle Alvin succeeded in defeating the powers of *Al Azif* and rescuing the hostage works of Milton, these moments represented my last opportunity to read in the great bibliographic rarity. And simply as a physical object it was inviting: the lush red glow of the binding offered a tactile pleasure almost like a woman's skin and I knew already how the inks shone on the white velvety pages. *The Necronomicon* seemed to breathe a small breath where it lay on the desk, as if it were peacefully dozing like a cat.

I couldn't resist. I picked it up and opened it to a middle page. The seductive Persian rose ink seemed to wreathe a perfume around the couplet that began the fragment of text: *That which is not dead can eternal lie, And with strange aeons even death may die.* A large green fly had settled on the bright initial that stood at the beginning of the next sentence, rubbing its legs together and feasting on the ink that shone as fresh and bright as dripping blood. I brushed at it absent-mindedly and it circled lazily toward the ceiling.

That which is not dead . . .

The lines sang hypnotically in my ear, in my head, and I began to think how I secretly longed to possess this volume for myself, how indeed I had burned to possess it for a long time, and how my ridiculous rabbit-faced Uncle Alvin was the only obstacle in my way to—

"No, no, Robert," Uncle Alvin said from the doorway. "Close the book and put it down. We're here to break the power of the book, not to give in to its spells."

I snapped it shut in a flash and flung it onto the desk. "Wow," I said. "Wow."

"It's an infernal piece of work, isn't it?" he said complacently. "But we'll have a hammerlock on it shortly."

He set down the metal cashbox he had formerly carried the book in and opened it up. He then laid *The Necronomicon* inside and produced from a brown paper bag under his arm a small book bound in black cloth and placed this second book on top of the other and closed the metal box and locked it with a key on his key ring. I noticed that the black book sported no title on cover or spine.

"What are we doing now?" I asked.

"The inescapable nature of this book is to cannibalize other writings," he said. "To feed upon them in order to sustain its ghoulish purposes. If it is in contact with another work, then it *must* try to feed, it cannot stop itself. The method of defeating it is to place it with a book so adamantine in nature, so resistant to evil change, to the inimical powers of darkness, that *The Necronomicon* wastes all its forces upon this object and in exhausting itself renders up again those works it had earlier consumed. It simply wears itself out and that which formerly had disappeared now reappears."

"Are you certain?" I asked. "That seems a little too simple."

"It is not simple at all," he said. "But it is effective. If you'll open up one of your copies of Milton there, we ought to be able to watch the printed words return to the pages."

"All right," I said and opened one of the blank-paged books to a place toward the front.

"The process is utterly silent," he said, "but that is deceptive. Inside this box, a terrific struggle is taking place."

"What is the unconquerable book that you put in with it?"

"I have never read it," he said, "because I am not worthy. Not yet. It is a great holy book written by a saint. Yet the man who wrote it did not know he was a saint and did not think of himself as writing a book. It is filled with celestial wisdom and supernal light, but to read it requires many years of spiritual discipline and ritual cleansing. To read such a holy book one must first become holy himself."

"What is the title?"

"Someday soon, when I have accomplished more of the necessary stages of discipline, I will be allowed to say the title aloud," he told me. "Till then I must not."

"I am glad to know there is such a book in the world," I said.

"Yes," he said. "And you should look now to see if Milton is being restored to us."

"Yes he is," I said happily. "Words are beginning to reappear. Wait a second while I find our control poem." I leafed through rapidly to find sonnet XIX and read aloud:

> *"When I consider how my light is spent*
> *Ere half my days—"*

"Why are you stopping?" he asked.

"It's that damned pesky green fly again." I brushed at the page. "Shoo!" I said.

The fly shooed, lifting from the book in a languorous circle, buzzing around the office for a moment, and then departing the premises through the open window there beside a broken bookshelf.

"You need to put in a screen," Uncle Alvin said. He wrinkled his nose, pawed at his ear.

"I need to do a lot of things to this old shop," I replied. "Let's see now, where were we?" I found my place on the page and began again:

> *"When I consider how my light is spent*
> *Ere half my days, in this dark world and weird—"*

"Wait a minute," my uncle said. "What was that last word?"

I looked. "Weird," I said.

He shook his head. "That's not right."

"No, it's not," I said. "At first I didn't see it was wrong because the fly covered it, the same old fly that was gobbling up the ink in *The Necronomicon*."

"A carrier," he said slowly. "It's carrying the poison that it contracted from the ink."

We looked at each other and, as the knowledge came clear to me, I cried out: *"The fly!"* Then, just as if we had rehearsed to perform the single action together, we rushed to the window.

But out there in the sleepy southern Sunday morning would be countless indistinguishable green flies, feeding, excreting, and mating.

NANCY ETCHEMENDY

Cat in Glass

Nancy Etchemendy lives in Menlo Park, California. She is the author of three young adult novels with a fourth on the way, and has sold stories to various magazines.

In the chilling "Cat in Glass," a priceless sculpture is imbued with its creator's soul, bringing horror into the lives of its owners. When boiled down to its essential elements, this story is about the persistence of utter evil, and the impossibility of avoiding to deal with those effects. While not the most gruesome of tales, "Cat in Glass," originally published in *The Magazine of Fantasy and Science Fiction*, is one of the most disturbing of the year.

—E.D.

Cat in Glass

NANCY ETCHEMENDY

I was once a respectable woman. Oh yes, I know that's what they all say when they've reached a pass like mine: I was well educated, well traveled, had lovely children and a nice husband with a good financial mind. How can anyone have fallen so far, except one who deserved to anyway? I've had time aplenty to consider the matter, lying here eyeless in this fine hospital bed while the stench of my wounds increases. The matrons who guard my room are tight-lipped. But I heard one of them whisper yesterday, when she thought I was asleep, "Jesus, how could anyone do such a thing?" The answer to all these questions is the same. I have fallen so far, and I have done what I have done, to save us each and every one from the *Cat in Glass*.

My entanglement with the cat began fifty-two years ago, when my sister, Delia, was attacked by an animal. It happened on an otherwise ordinary spring afternoon. There were no witnesses. My father was still in his office at the college, and I was dawdling along on my way home from first grade at Chesly Girls' Day School, counting cracks in the sidewalk. Delia, younger than I by three years, was alone with Fiona, the Irish woman who kept house for us. Fiona had just gone outside for a moment to hang laundry. She came in to check on Delia, and discovered a scene of almost unbelievable carnage. Oddly, she had heard no screams.

As I ran up the steps and opened our door, I heard screams indeed. Not Delia's—for Delia had nothing left to scream with—but Fiona's, as she stood in the front room with her hands over her eyes. She couldn't bear the sight. Unfortunately, six-year-olds have no such compunction. I stared long and hard, sick and trembling, yet entranced.

From the shoulders up, Delia was no longer recognizable as a human being. Her throat had been shredded and her jaw ripped away. Most of her hair and scalp were gone. There were long, bloody furrows in the creamy skin of her arms and legs. The organdy pinafore in which Fiona had dressed her that morning was clotted with blood, and the blood was still coming. Some of the walls were even spattered with it where the animal, whatever it was, had worried her in its frenzy. Her fists and heels banged jerkily against the floor. Our pet dog, Freddy, lay beside her, also bloody, but quite limp. Freddy's neck was broken.

I remember slowly raising my head—I must have been in shock by then—and meeting the bottomless gaze of the glass cat that sat on the hearth. Our father, a professor of art history, was very proud of this sculpture, for reasons I did not understand until many years later. I only knew that it was valuable and we were not allowed to touch it. A chaotic feline travesty, it was not the sort of thing you would want to touch anyway. Though basically catlike in shape, it bristled with transparent threads and shards. There was something at once wild and vaguely human about its face. I had never liked it much, and Delia had always been downright frightened of it. On this day, as I looked up from my little sister's ruins, the cat seemed to glare at me with bright, terrifying satisfaction.

I had experienced, a year before, the thing every child fears most: the death of my mother. It had given me a kind of desperate strength, for I thought, at the tender age of six, that I had survived the worst life had to offer. Now, as I returned the mad stare of the glass cat, it came to me that I was wrong. The world was a much more evil place than I had ever imagined, and nothing would ever be the same again.

Delia died officially in the hospital a short time later. After a cursory investigation, the police laid the blame on Freddy. I still have the newspaper clipping, yellow now, and held together with even yellower cellophane tape. "The family dog lay dead near the victim, blood smearing its muzzle and forepaws. Sergeant Morton theorizes that the dog, a pit bull terrier and member of a breed specifically developed for vicious fighting, turned killer and attacked its tragic young owner. He also suggests that the child, during the death struggle, flung the murderous beast away with enough strength to break its neck."

Even I, a little girl, knew that this "theory" was lame; the neck of a pit bull is an almost impossible thing to break, even by a large, determined man. And Freddy, in spite of his breeding, had always been gentle, even protective, with us. Simply stated, the police were mystified, and this was the closest thing to a rational explanation they could produce. As far as they were concerned, that was the end of the matter. In fact, it had only just begun.

I was shipped off to my Aunt Josie's house for several months. What Father did during this time, I never knew, though I now suspect he spent those months in a sanatorium. In the course of a year, he had lost first his wife and then his daughter. Delia's death alone was the kind of outrage that might permanently have unhinged a lesser man. But a child has no way of knowing such things. I was bitterly angry at him for going away. Aunt Josie, though kind and good-hearted, was a virtual stranger to me, and I felt deserted. I had nightmares in which the glass cat slunk out of its place by the hearth and prowled across the countryside. I would hear its hard claws ticking along the floor outside the room where I slept. At those times, half-awake and screaming in the dark, no one could have comforted me except Father.

When he did return, the strain of his suffering showed. His face was thin and weary, and his hair dusted with new gray, as if he had stood outside too long on a frosty night. On the afternoon of his arrival, he sat with me on Aunt Josie's sofa, stroking my cheek while I cuddled gladly, my anger at least temporarily forgotten in the joy of having him back.

His voice, when he spoke, was as tired as his face. "Well, my darling Amy, what do you suppose we should do now?"

"I don't know," I said. I assumed that, as always in the past, he had something entertaining in mind—that he would suggest it, and then we would do it.

He sighed. "Shall we go home?"

I went practically rigid with fear. "Is the cat still there?"

Father looked at me, frowning slightly. "Do we have a cat?"

I nodded. "The big glass one."

He blinked, then made the connection. "Oh, the Chelichev, you mean? Well . . . I suppose it's still there. I hope so, in fact."

I clung to him, scrambling halfway up his shoulders in my panic. I could not manage to speak. All that came out of my mouth was an erratic series of whimpers.

"Shhhh, shhhh," said Father. I hid my face in the starched white cloth of his shirt, and heard him whisper, as if to himself, "How can a glass cat frighten a child who's seen the things you've seen?"

"I hate him! He's glad Delia died. And now he wants to get *me*."

Father hugged me fiercely. "You'll never see him again. I promise you," he said. And it was true, at least as long as he lived.

So the Chelichev *Cat in Glass* was packed away in a box and put into storage with the rest of our furnishings. Father sold the house, and we traveled for two years. When the horror had faded sufficiently, we returned home to begin a new life. Father went back to his professorship, and I to my studies at Chesly Girls' Day School. He bought a new house. The glass cat was not among the items he had sent up from storage. I did not ask him why. I was just as happy to forget about it, and forget it I did.

I neither saw the glass cat nor heard of it again until many years later. I was a grown woman by then, a schoolteacher in a town far from the one in which I'd spent my childhood. I was married to a banker, and had two lovely daughters and even a cat, which I finally permitted in spite of my abhorrence for them, because the girls begged so hard for one. I thought my life was settled, that it would progress smoothly toward a peaceful old age. But this was not to be. The glass cat had other plans.

The chain of events began with Father's death. It happened suddenly, on a snowy afternoon, as he graded papers in the tiny, snug office he had always had on campus. A heart attack, they said. He was found seated at his desk, Erik Satie's Dadaist composition "La Belle Excentrique" still spinning on the turntable of his record player.

I was not at all surprised to discover that he had left his affairs in some disarray. It's not that he had debts or was a gambler. Nothing so serious. It's just that order was slightly contrary to his nature. I remember once, as a very young woman, chiding him for the modest level of chaos he preferred in his life. "Really, Father," I said. "Can't you admire Dadaism without living it?" He laughed and admitted that he didn't seem able to.

As Father's only living relative, I inherited his house and other property, including his personal possessions. There were deeds to be transferred, insurance reports to be filed, bills and loans to be paid. He did have an attorney, an old school friend of his who helped a great deal in organizing the storm of paperwork from a distance. The attorney also arranged for the sale of the house and hired someone to clean it out and ship the contents to us. In the course of the winter, a steady stream of cartons containing everything from scrapbooks to Chinese miniatures arrived at our doorstep. So I thought nothing of it when a large box labeled "fragile" was delivered one day by registered courier. There was a note from the attorney attached, explaining that he had just discovered it in a storage warehouse under Father's name, and had had them ship it to me unopened.

It was a dismal February afternoon, a Friday. I had just come home from teaching. My husband, Stephen, had taken the girls to the mountains for a weekend of skiing, a sport I disliked. I had stayed behind and was looking forward to a couple of days of quiet solitude. The wind drove spittles of rain at the windows as I knelt on the floor of the front room and opened the box. I can't explain to you quite what I felt when I pulled away the packing paper and found myself face-to-face with the glass cat. Something akin to uncovering a nest of cockroaches in a drawer of sachet, I suppose. And that was swiftly followed by a horrid and minutely detailed mental re-creation of Delia's death.

I swallowed my screams, struggling to replace them with something rational. "It's merely a glorified piece of glass." My voice bounced off the walls in the lonely house, hardly comforting.

I had an overpowering image of something inside me, something dark and featureless except for wide white eyes and scrabbling claws. *Get us out of here!* it cried, and I obliged, seizing my coat from the closet hook and stumbling out into the wind.

I ran in the direction of town, slowing only when one of my shoes fell off and I realized how I must look. Soon I found myself seated at a table in a diner, warming my hands in the steam from a cup of coffee, trying to convince myself that I was just being silly. I nursed the coffee as long as I could. It was dusk by the time I felt able to return home. There I found the glass cat, still waiting for me.

I turned on the radio for company and made a fire in the fireplace. Then I sat down before the box and finished unpacking it. The sculpture was as horrible as I remembered, truly ugly and disquieting. I might never have understood why Father kept it if he had not enclosed this letter of explanation, neatly handwritten on his college stationery:

To whom it may concern:

This box contains a sculpture, *Cat in Glass*, designed and executed by the late Alexander Chelichev. Because of Chelichev's standing as a noted forerunner of Dadaism, a historical account of *Cat*'s genesis may be of interest to scholars.

I purchased *Cat* from the artist himself at his Zurich loft in December 1915, two months before the violent rampage that resulted in his confinement in a hospital for the criminally insane, and well before his artistic importance was widely recognized. (For the record, the asking price was forty-eight Swiss francs, plus a good meal with wine.) It is known that Chelichev had a wife and two children elsewhere in the city at that time, though he lived with them only sporadically. The following is the artist's statement about *Cat in Glass*, transcribed as accurately as possible from a conversation we held during dinner.

"I have struggled with the Devil all my life. He wants no rules. No order. His presence is everywhere in my work. I was beaten as a child, and when I became strong enough, I killed my father for it. I see you are skeptical, but it is true. Now I am a grown man, and I find my father in myself. I have a wife and children, but I spend little time with them because I fear the father-devil in me. I do not beat my children. Instead, I make this cat. Into the glass I have poured this madness of mine. Better there than in the eyes of my daughters."

It is my belief that *Cat in Glass* was Chelichev's last finished creation.

> Sincerely,
> Lawrence Waters
> Professor of Art History

I closed the box, sealed it with the note inside, and spent the next two nights in a hotel, pacing the floor, sleeping little. The following Monday, Stephen took the cat to an art dealer for appraisal. He came home late that afternoon excited and full of news about the great Alexander Chelichev.

He made himself a gin and tonic as he expounded. "That glass cat is priceless, Amy. Did you realize? If your father had sold it, he'd have been independently wealthy. He never let on."

I was putting dinner on the table. The weekend had been a terrible strain. This had been a difficult day on top of it—snowy, and the children in my school class were wild with pent-up energy. So were our daughters, Eleanor and Rose, aged seven and four, respectively. I could hear them quarreling in the playroom down the hall.

"Well, I'm glad to hear the horrid thing is worth something," I said. "Why don't we sell it and hire a maid?"

Stephen laughed as if I'd made an incredibly good joke. "A maid? You could hire a thousand maids for what that cat would bring at auction. It's a fascinating piece with an extraordinary history. You know, the value of something like this will increase with time. I think we'll do well to keep it awhile."

My fingers grew suddenly icy on the hot rim of the potato bowl. "I wasn't trying to be funny, Stephen. It's ugly and disgusting. If I could, I would make it disappear from the face of the earth."

He raised his eyebrows. "What's this? Rebellion? Look, if you really want a maid, I'll get you one."

"That's not the point. I won't have the damned thing in my house."

"I'd rather you didn't swear, Amelia. The children might hear."

"I don't care if they do."

The whole thing degenerated from there. I tried to explain the cat's connection with Delia's death. But Stephen had stopped listening by then. He sulked through dinner. Eleanor and Rose argued over who got which spoonful of peas. And I struggled with a steadily growing sense of dread that seemed much too large for the facts of the matter.

When dinner was over, Stephen announced with exaggerated brightness, "Girls. We'd like your help in deciding an important question."

"Oh goody," said Rose.

"What is it?" said Eleanor.

"Please don't," I said. It was all I could do to keep from shouting.

Stephen flashed me the boyish grin with which he had originally won my heart. "Oh, come on. Try to look at it objectively. You're just sensitive about this because of an irrational notion from your childhood. Let the girls be the judge. If they like it, why not keep it?"

I should have ended it there. I should have insisted. Hindsight is always perfect, as they say. But inside me a little seed of doubt had sprouted. Stephen was always so logical and so right, especially about financial matters. Maybe he was right about this, too.

He had brought the thing home from the appraiser without telling me. He was never above a little subterfuge if it got him his own way. Now he carried the carton in from the garage and unwrapped it in the middle of our warm hardwood floor with all the lights blazing. Nothing had changed. I found it as frightening as ever. I could feel cold sweat collecting on my forehead as I stared at it, all aglitter in a rainbow of refracted lamplight.

Eleanor was enthralled with it. She caught our real cat, a calico named Jelly, and held it up to the sculpture. "See, Jelly? You've got a handsome partner now." But Jelly twisted and hissed in Eleanor's arms until she let her go. Eleanor laughed and said Jelly was jealous.

Rose was almost as uncooperative as Jelly. She shrank away from the glass cat, peeking at it from between her father's knees. But Stephen would have none of that.

"Go on, Rose," he said. "It's just a kitty made of glass. Touch it and see." And he took her by the shoulders and pushed her gently toward it. She put out one hand, hesitantly, as she would have with a live cat who did not know her. I saw her finger touch a nodule of glass shards that might have been its nose. She drew back with a little yelp of pain. And that's how it began. So innocently.

"He bit me!" she cried.

"What happened?" said Stephen. "Did you break it?" He ran to the sculpture first, the brute, to make sure she hadn't damaged it.

She held her finger out to me. There was a tiny cut with a single drop of bright red blood oozing from it. "Mommy, it burns, it burns." She was no longer just crying. She was screaming.

We took her into the bathroom. Stephen held her while I washed the cut and pressed a cold cloth to it. The bleeding stopped in a moment, but still she screamed. Stephen grew angry. "What's this nonsense? It's a scratch. Just a scratch."

Rose jerked and kicked and bellowed. In Stephen's defense, I tell you now it was a terrifying sight, and he was never able to deal well with real fear, especially in himself. He always tried to mask it with anger. We had a neighbor who was a physician. "If you don't stop it, Rose, I'll call Dr. Pepperman. Is that what you want?" he said, as if Dr. Pepperman, a jolly septuagenarian, were anything but charming and gentle, as if threats were anything but asinine at such a time.

"For God's sake, get Pepperman! Can't you see something's terribly wrong?" I said.

And for once he listened to me. He grabbed Eleanor by the arm. "Come with me," he said, and stomped across the yard through the snow without so much as a coat. I believe he took Eleanor, also without a coat, only because he was so unnerved that he didn't want to face the darkness alone.

Rose was still screaming when Dr. Pepperman arrived fresh from his dinner, specks of gravy clinging to his mustache. He examined Rose's finger, and looked mildly puzzled when he had finished. "Can't see much wrong here. I'd say it's mostly a case of hysteria." He took a vial and a syringe from his small brown case and gave Rose an injection, ". . . to help settle her down," he said. It seemed to work. In a few minutes, Rose's screams had diminished to whimpers. Pepperman swabbed her finger with disinfectant and wrapped it loosely in gauze. "There, Rosie. Nothing like a bandage to make it feel better." He winked at us. "She should be fine in the morning. Take the gauze off as soon as she'll let you."

We put Rose to bed and sat with her till she fell asleep. Stephen unwrapped the gauze from her finger so the healing air could get to it. The cut was a bit red, but looked all right. Then we retired as well, reassured by the doctor, still mystified at Rose's reaction.

I awakened sometime after midnight. The house was muffled in the kind of silence brought by steady, soft snowfall. I thought I had heard a sound. Something odd. A scream? A groan? A snarl? Stephen still slept on the verge of a snore; whatever it was, it hadn't been loud enough to disturb him.

I crept out of bed and fumbled with my robe. There was a short flight of stairs between our room and the rooms where Rose and Eleanor slept. Eleanor, like her father, often snored at night, and I could hear her from the hallway now, probably deep in dreams. Rose's room was silent.

I went in and switched on the night-light. The bulb was very low wattage. I thought at first that the shadows were playing tricks on me. Rose's hand and arm looked black as a bruised banana. There was a peculiar odor in the air, like the smell of a butcher shop on a summer day. Heart galloping, I turned on the overhead light. Poor Rosie. She was so very still and clammy. And her arm was so very rotten.

They said Rose died from blood poisoning—a rare type most often associated with animal bites. I told them over and over again that it fit, that our child had indeed been bitten, by a cat, a most evil glass cat. Stephen was embarrassed. His own theory was that, far from blaming an apparently inanimate object, we ought to be suing Pepperman for malpractice. The doctors patted me sympathetically at first. Delusions brought on by grief, they said. It would pass. I would heal in time.

I made Stephen take the cat away. He said he would sell it, though in fact he lied to me. And we buried Rose. But I could not sleep. I paced the house each night, afraid to close my eyes because the cat was always there, glaring his satisfied glare, and waiting for new meat. And in the daytime, everything reminded me of Rosie. Fingerprints on the woodwork, the contents of the kitchen drawers, her favorite foods on the shelves of grocery stores. I could not teach. Every child had Rosie's face and Rosie's voice. Stephen and Eleanor were first kind, then gruff, then angry.

One morning I could find no reason to get dressed or to move from my place on the sofa. Stephen shouted at me, told me I was ridiculous, asked me if I had forgotten that I still had a daughter left who needed me. But, you see, I no longer believed that I or anyone else could make any difference in the world. Stephen and Eleanor would get along with or without me. I didn't matter. There was no God of order and cause. Only chaos, cruelty, and whim.

When it was clear to Stephen that his dear wife Amy had turned from an asset into a liability, he sent me to an institution, far away from everyone, where I could safely be forgotten. In time, I grew to like it there. I had no responsibilities at all. And if there was foulness and bedlam, it was no worse than the outside world.

There came a day, however, when they dressed me in a suit of new clothes and stood me outside the big glass and metal doors to wait; they didn't say for what. The air smelled good. It was springtime, and there were dandelions sprinkled like drops of fresh yellow paint across the lawn.

A car drove up, and a pretty young woman got out and took me by the arm.

"Hello, Mother," she said as we drove off down the road.

It was Eleanor, all grown up. For the first time since Rosie died, I wondered how long I had been away, and knew it must have been a very long while.

We drove a considerable distance, to a large suburban house, white, with a sprawling yard and a garage big enough for two cars. It was a mansion compared to the house in which Stephen and I had raised her. By way of making polite small talk, I asked if she were married, whether she had children. She climbed out of the car looking irritated. "Of course I'm married," she said. "You've met Jason. And you've seen pictures of Sarah and Elizabeth often enough." Of this I had no recollection.

She opened the gate in the picket fence, and we started up the neat stone walkway. The front door opened a few inches and small faces peered out. The door opened wider and two little girls ran onto the porch.

"Hello," I said. "And who are you?"

The older one, giggling behind her hand, said, "Don't you know, Grandma? I'm Sarah."

The younger girl stayed silent, staring at me with frank curiosity.

"That's Elizabeth. She's afraid of you," said Sarah.

I bent and looked into Elizabeth's eyes. They were brown and her hair was shining blonde, like Rosie's. "No need to be afraid of me, my dear. I'm just a harmless old woman."

Elizabeth frowned. "Are you crazy?" she asked.

Sarah giggled behind her hand again, and Eleanor breathed loudly through her nose as if this impertinence were simply overwhelming.

I smiled. I liked Elizabeth. Liked her very much. "They say I am," I said, "and it may very well be true."

A tiny smile crossed her face. She stretched on her tiptoes and kissed my cheek, hardly more than the touch of a warm breeze, then turned and ran away. Sarah followed her, and I watched them go, my heart dancing and shivering. I had loved no one in a very long time. I missed it, but dreaded it, too. For I had loved Delia and Rosie, and they were both dead.

The first thing I saw when I entered the house was Chelichev's *Cat in Glass*, glaring evilly from a place of obvious honor on a low pedestal near the sofa. My stomach felt suddenly shrunken.

"Where did you get that?" I said.

Eleanor looked irritated again. "From Daddy, of course."

"Stephen promised me he would sell it!"

"Well, I guess he didn't, did he?"

Anger heightened my pulse. "Where is he? I want to speak to him immediately."

"Mother, don't be absurd. He's been dead for ten years."

I lowered myself into a chair. I was shaking by then, and I fancied I saw a half-smile on the glass cat's cold jowls.

"Get me out of here," I said. A great weight crushed my lungs. I could barely breathe.

With a look, I must say, of genuine worry, Eleanor escorted me onto the porch and brought me a tumbler of ice water.

"Better?" she asked.

I breathed deeply. "A little. Eleanor, don't you realize that monstrosity killed your sister, and mine as well?"

"That simply isn't true."

"But it is, it is! I'm telling you now, get rid of it if you care for the lives of your children."

Eleanor went pale, whether from rage or fear I could not tell. "It isn't yours. You're legally incompetent, and I'll thank you to stay out of my affairs as much as possible till you have a place of your own. I'll move you to an apartment as soon as I can find one."

"An apartment? But I can't. . . ."

"Yes, you can. You're as well as you're ever going to be, Mother. You liked that hospital only because it was easy. Well, it costs a lot of money to keep you there, and we can't afford it anymore. You're just going to have to straighten up and start behaving like a human being again."

By then I was very close to tears, and very confused as well. Only one thing was clear to me, and that was the true nature of the glass cat. I said, in as steady a voice as I could muster, "Listen to me. That cat was made out of madness. It's evil. If you have a single ounce of brains, you'll put it up for auction this very afternoon."

"So I can get enough money to send you back to the hospital, I suppose? Well, I won't do it. That sculpture is priceless. The longer we keep it, the more it's worth."

She had Stephen's financial mind. I would never sway her, and I knew it. I wept in despair, hiding my face in my hands. I was thinking of Elizabeth. The sweet, soft skin of her little arms, the flame in her cheeks, the power of that small kiss. Human beings are such frail works of art, their lives so precarious, and here I was again, my wayward heart gone out to one of them. But the road back to the safety of isolation lay in ruins. The only way out was through.

Jason came home at dinnertime, and we ate a nice meal, seated around the sleek rosewood table in the dining room. He was kind, actually far kinder than Eleanor. He asked the children about their day and listened carefully while they replied. As did I, enraptured by their pink perfection, distraught at the memory of how imperfect a child's flesh can become. He did not interrupt. He did not demand. When Eleanor refused to give me coffee—she said she was afraid it would get me "hyped up"—he admonished her and poured me a cup himself. We talked about my father, whom he knew by reputation, and about art and the cities of Europe. All the while I felt in my bones the baleful gaze of the *Cat in Glass*, burning like the coldest ice through walls and furniture as if they did not exist.

Eleanor made up a cot for me in the guest room. She didn't want me to sleep in the bed, and she wouldn't tell me why. But I overheard Jason arguing with her about it. "What's wrong with the bed?" he said.

"She's mentally ill," said Eleanor. She was whispering, but loudly. "Heaven only knows what filthy habits she's picked up. I won't risk her soiling a perfectly good mattress. If she does well on the cot for a few nights, then we can consider moving her to the bed."

They thought I was in the bathroom, performing whatever unspeakable acts it is that mentally ill people perform in places like that, I suppose. But they were wrong. I was sneaking past their door, on my way to the garage. Jason must have been quite a handyman in his spare time. I found a large selection of hammers on the wall, including an excellent short-handled sledge. I hid it under my bedding. They never even noticed.

The children came in and kissed me good night in a surreal reversal of roles. I lay in the dark on my cot for a long time, thinking of them, especially Elizabeth, the youngest and weakest, who would naturally be the most likely target of an animal's attack. I dozed, dreaming sometimes of a smiling Elizabeth-Rose-Delia, sifting snow, wading through drifts; sometimes of the glass cat, its fierce eyes smoldering, crystalline tongue brushing crystalline jaws. The night was well along when the dreams crashed down like broken mirrors into silence.

The house was quiet except for those ticks and thumps all houses make as they cool in the darkness. I got up and slid the hammer out from under the bedding, not even sure what I was going to do with it, knowing only that the time had come to act.

I crept out to the front room, where the cat sat waiting, as I knew it must. Moonlight gleamed in the chaos of its glass fur. I could feel its power, almost *see* it, a shimmering red aura the length of its malformed spine. The thing was moving, slowly, slowly, smiling now, oh yes, a real smile. I could smell its rotten breath.

For an instant I was frozen. Then I remembered the hammer, Jason's lovely short-handled sledge. And I raised it over my head, and brought it down in the first crashing blow.

The sound was wonderful. Better than cymbals, better even than holy trumpets. I was trembling all over, but I went on and on in an agony of satisfaction while glass fell like moonlit rain. There were screams. "Grandma, stop! Stop!" I swung the hammer back in the first part of another arc, heard something like the thunk of a fallen ripe melon, swung it down on the cat again. I couldn't see anymore. It came to me that there was glass in my eyes and blood in my mouth. But none of that mattered, a small price to pay for the long-overdue demise of Chelichev's *Cat in Glass*.

So you see how I have come to this, not without many sacrifices along the way. And now the last of all: the sockets where my eyes used to be are infected. They stink. Blood poisoning, I'm sure.

I wouldn't expect Eleanor to forgive me for ruining her prime investment. But I hoped Jason might bring the children a time or two anyway. No word except for the delivery of a single rose yesterday. The matron said it was white, and held it up for me to sniff, and she read me the card that came with it.

"Elizabeth was a great one for forgiving. She would have wanted you to have this. Sleep well, Jason."

Which puzzled me.

"You don't even know what you've done, do you?" said the matron.

"I destroyed a valuable work of art," said I.

But she made no reply.

RORY HARPER

Monsters, Tearing Off My Face

Rory Harper lives in Texas. His first novel, *Petrogypsies* (Baen) was published last fall.

"Monsters, Tearing Off My Face," originally published in *Isaac Asimov's Science Fiction Magazine,* packs a powerful punch for such a short tale. It was written after Harper learned that his wife was pregnant.

—E.D.

Monsters Tearing Off My Face

RORY HARPER

I was drawing a true picture.

Miss Kendall asked me. "What is that picture, Eileen?"

I told her. "Mommy and Daddy and me."

She made a noise. "Oh, no, sweetheart, those are monsters. That can't be your mommy and daddy."

"Yes. Mommy and Daddy."

"But they're blue and they have long claws and teeth. That's what monsters have, not mommies and daddies."

"Yes." I don't argue. "Monsters. Mommy and Daddy."

"What are they doing?"

I looked at the picture. It isn't finished. "They are tearing off my face. So I won't be a little girl any more."

Miss Kendall looked sad.

I told her. "I don't mind when they do it. They love me."

After nap time, Miss Kendall taked me to the office. A nice lady was there. She sitted in a chair beside me. "Hello, Eileen. I'm Patricia Adler."

"Hello, Miss Adler."

"I'm with the Children's Protective Service. Do you know what that is?"

I shaked my head from side to side like a little girl. "No."

"How old are you, dear?"

I showed her my fingers. "One-two-three-four."

"Well, Eileen, we try to help children who may be having problems. With their Mommy or Daddy."

"Oh. Okay."

She taked the picture I made. It is finished now. "You told Miss Kendall that these blue monsters are your Mommy and Daddy. Is that right?"

I shaked my head up and down like a little girl. "Yes."

"What are they doing?"

I told her. "Tearing off my face. So I won't be a little girl any more."

"Does it hurt when they do that?"

"Yes. I am crying. But I don't mind. They love me."

"Is this something you saw on television, dear?"

I shaked my head. "No. It is a true picture."

"It happened to you?"

"Yes."

"Did it happen more than once?"

"Yes."

"Did you bleed, like in the picture?"

"Yes. And then they teared off the rest of my body and I am not a little girl any more."

Miss Adler looked sad.

Miss Adler taked me to the place where I stayed now. She bringed the picture, too.

Mommy taked me to my room. I sitted on the stairway and listened.

Daddy telled Miss Adler. "She was about two years old. A security guard found her on the roof of a downtown building. If you'd check with your agency, there should be a file."

Miss Adler asked. "You didn't go through Child Welfare for the adoption?"

Mommy telled Miss Adler. "No. When her parents couldn't be located, she was placed into a foster home with a private agency. The Christian Child Aid Society. We adopted her through them."

"Was there any evidence of physical abuse when they found her?"

"Not by the time we got her. But there may be something in your files that we haven't seen. She cried a lot for the first six months we had her, but that's gone completely away. She has nightmares occasionally, wakes up screaming in the middle of the night, but she claims not to remember what she was dreaming about."

"She hasn't been a difficult child?"

Daddy telled Miss Adler. "Oh, no. She's a delightful, wonderful little girl. We love her very much. I can't even imagine why anyone would have abandoned her."

Mommy telled Miss Adler. "It gives me the shudders to think this picture is how she remembers her real parents. What kind of monsters could they have been? Would you like some more coffee?"

It was dark. I looked out the window, into the dark. They would come from the dark for me.

Under my bed was dark. I looked under my bed, too.

Then it was bed time. I looked in the dark closet and then I climbed in the bed.

I woked up when Mommy and Daddy opened the door. Their face was dark in the dark room. Daddy turned on the light. He looked mad. Mommy looked mad, too.

He picked me up in the air and shaked my little girl body. "Eileen, you have been a very bad little girl."

I did not cry. I telled him. "I am sorry, Daddy."

"Don't you ever, ever draw pictures like that again." He shaked me more. "Don't tell lies about Mommy and Daddy like that."

I don't argue. "I am sorry, Daddy."

"You've been very bad and I'm going to have to punish you." He throwed me on the bed.

He taked off my nightie again. Mommy watched.

I started to cry.

Then the window breaked from the outside and the dark came in.

I looked. On the window sitted my real Mommy and Daddy. I runned to my real Mommy.

My real Daddy teared off the face of my other Daddy and Mommy with his claws. Underneath was a red and white face. My other Mommy and Daddy cried and cried. Then my real Daddy teared off the body of my other Mommy and Daddy. Underneath was a red and white body.

Then my real Mommy teared off my face with her claws. I could not see my new face. Then she teared off my body so I wouldn't be a little girl any more. Underneath was a pretty blue body. It hurt. I cried and she holded me.

Then my real Daddy picked up my new body and taked me to the window.

Then we went away into the dark, where the monsters stay.

JOYCE CAROL OATES
Family

Joyce Carol Oates, when inspired, is immediate in her response to requests for stories. I commissioned a short-short from her for *Omni* and a couple of weeks later I received it, as well as "Family," which is certainly science fiction, definitely horrific, and has all the earmarks of an Oates gem. The basic plot is simple: An isolated family adapts to changing times. It's only when one considers the nature of the changing outside world, and the bizarre nature of the family's adaptations, that "Family" achieves its full effect.

—E.D.

Family

JOYCE CAROL OATES

The days were brief and attenuated and the season appeared to be fixed—neither summer nor winter, spring nor fall. A thermal haze of inexpressible sweetness (though bearing tiny bits of grit or mica) had eased into the valley from the industrial regions to the north and there were nights when the sun set slowly at the western horizon as if sinking through a porous red mass, and there were days when a hard-glaring moon, like bone, remained fixed in a single position, prominent in the sky. Above the patchwork of excavated land bordering our property—*all* of which had formerly been our property, in Grandfather's time: thousands of acres of fertile soil and open grazing land—a curious fibrillating rainbow sometimes appeared, its colors shifting even as you stared, shades of blue, turquoise, iridescent green, russet red, a lovely translucent gold that dissolved to moisture as the thermal breeze stirred, warm and stale as an exhaled breath. And if I'd run excited to tell others of the rainbow, it was likely to have vanished when they came.

"Liar!" my older brothers and sisters said, "—don't promise rainbows when there aren't any!"

Father laid his hand on my head, saying, with a smiling frown, "Don't speak of anything if you aren't certain it will be true for others, not simply for yourself. Do you understand?"

"Yes, Father," I said quietly. Though I did not understand.

This story begins in the time of family celebration—after Father made a great profit selling all but fifteen acres of his inheritance from Grandfather; and he and Mother were like a honeymoon couple, giddy with relief at having escaped the fate of most of our neighbors in the Valley, rancher-rivals of Grandfather's, and their descendants, who had sold off their property before the market began to realize its full potential. ("Full potential" was a term Father often uttered, as if its taste pleased him.) Now these old rivals were without land, and their investments yielded low returns; they'd gone away to live in cities of ever-increasing disorder, where no country people, especially once-aristocratic country people, could endure to live for long. They'd virtually prostituted themselves, Father said—"And for so little!"

It was a proverb of Grandfather's time that a curse would befall anyone in the Valley who gloated over a neighbor's misfortune but, as Father observed, "It's damned difficult *not* to feel superior, sometimes." And Mother said, kissing him, "Darling—you're absolutely right!"

Our house was made of granite, limestone, and beautiful red-orange brick; the new wing, designed by a famous Japanese architect, was mainly tinted glass, overlooking the Valley where on good days we could see for many miles and on humid-hazy days we could barely see beyond the fence at the edge of our property. Father, however, preferred the roof of the house: in his white suit (linen in warm weather, light wool in cold), cream-colored fedora cocked back on his head, high-heeled leather-tooled boots, he spent most of his waking hours on the highest peak of the highest roof, observing through high-powered binoculars the astonishing progress of construction in the Valley—for overnight, it seemed, there had appeared roads, expressways, sewers, drainage pipes, "planned communities" with such melodic names as Whispering Glades, Murmuring Oaks, Pheasant Run, Deer Willow, all of them walled to keep out trespassers, and, even more astonishing, immense towers of buildings made of aluminum, and steel, and glass, and bronze, buildings whose magnificent windows winked and glimmered like mirrors, splendid in sunshine like pillars of flame . . . such beauty, where once there'd been mere earth and sky, it caught at your throat like a great bird's talons. "The ways of beauty are as a honeycomb," Father told us mysteriously.

So hypnotized was Father by the transformation of the Valley, he often forgot where he was; failed to come downstairs for meals, or for bed; if Mother, meaning to indulge him, or hurt by his growing indifference to her, did not send a servant to summon him, he was likely to spend an entire night on the roof. . . . In the morning, smiling sheepishly, he would explain that he'd fallen asleep; or, conversely, he'd been troubled by having seen things for which he could not account—shadows the size of longhorns moving ceaselessly beyond our twelve-foot-high barbed-wire fence, and inexplicable winking red lights fifty miles away in the foothills. "Optical illusions!" Mother said, "—or the ghosts of old slaughtered livestock, or airplanes. Have you forgotten, darling, you sold thirty acres of land, for an airport at Furnace Creek?" "These lights more resemble fires," Father said stubbornly. "And they're in the foothills, not in the plain."

There came then times of power blackouts, and financial losses, and Father was forced to surrender all but two or three of the servants, but he maintained his rooftop vigil, white-clad, a noble ghostly figure holding binoculars to his eyes, for he perceived himself as a *witness*; and believed, if he lived to a ripe old age like Grandfather (who was in his hundredth year when at last he died

—of a riding accident), he would be a chronicler of these troubled times, like Thucydides. For, as Father said, "Is there a new world struggling to be born— or only struggle?"

Around this time—because of numerous dislocations in the Valley: the abrupt abandoning of homes, for instance—it happened that packs of dogs began to roam about looking for food, particularly by night, poor starving creatures that became a nuisance and should be, as authorities urged, shot down on sight— these dogs being not feral by birth but former household pets, highly bred beagles, setters, cocker spaniels, terriers, even the larger and coarser type of poodle— and it was the cause of some friction between Mother and Father that, despite his rooftop presence by day and by night, Father nonetheless failed to spy a pack of these dogs dig beneath our fence and make their way to the dairy barn where they tore out the throats—surely this could not have been in silence!—of our remaining six Holsteins, and our last two she-goats, before devouring the poor creatures; nor did Father notice anything unusual the night two homeless der- elicts, formerly farmhands of ours, impaled themselves on the electric fence and died agonizing deaths, their bodies found in the morning by Kit, our sixteen- year-old.

Kit, who'd liked the men, said, "—I hope I never see anything like that again in my life!"

It's true that our fence was charged with a powerful electric current—but in full compliance with County Farm and Home Bureau regulations.

Following this, Father journeyed to the state capital with the intention of taking out a sizable loan, and re-establishing, as he called it, old ties with his political friends, or with their younger colleagues; and Mother joined him a few days later for a greatly needed change of scene—"Not that I don't love you all, and the farm, but I need to see other sights for a while!—and I need to be *seen*." Leaving us when they did, under the care of Mrs. Hoyt (our housekeeper) and Cory (our eldest sister), was possibly not a good idea: Mrs. Hoyt was aging rapidly, and Cory, for all the innocence of her marigold eyes and melodic voice, was desperately in love with one of the National Guardsmen who patrolled the Valley in a jeep, authorized to shoot wild dogs, and, when necessary, vandals, arsonists, and squatters who were considered a menace to the public health and well-being. And when Mother returned from the capital, unaccompanied by Father, after what seemed to the family a long absence (two weeks? two months?), it was with shocking news: she and Father were going to separate.

Mother said, "Children, your father and I have decided, after much soul- searching deliberation, that we must dissolve our wedding bond of nearly twenty years." As she spoke Mother's voice wavered like a girl's but fierce little points of light shone in her eyes.

We children were so taken by surprise we could not speak, at first.

Separate! Dissolve! We stood staring and mute; not even Cory, Kit, and Dale—not even Lona who was the most impulsive of us—could find words with which to protest; the younger children began whimpering helplessly, soon joined by the rest. Mother clutched at her hair, saying, "Oh please don't! I can hardly bear the pain as it is!" With some ceremony she then played for us a video of Father's farewell to the family, which drew fresh tears . . . for there, framed astonishingly on our one-hundred-inch home theater screen, where we'd never seen his image before, was Father, dressed not in white but in somber colors, his hair in steely bands combed wetly across the dome of his skull, and his eyes puffy, an unnatural sheen to his face as if it had been scoured, hard. He was sitting stiffly erect; his fingers gripped the arms of his chair so tightly the blood had drained from his knuckles; his words came slow, halting, and faint, like the faltering progress of a gut-shot deer across a field. *Dear children, your mother and I . . . after years of marriage . . . of very happy marriage . . . have decided to . . . have decided . . .* One of the vexatious low-flying helicopters belonging to the National Guard soared passed our house, making the screen shudder, but the sound was garbled in any case, as if the tape had been clumsily cut and spliced; Father's beloved face turned liquid and his eyes began to melt vertically, like oily tears; his mouth was distended like a drowning man's. As the tape ended we could discern only sounds, not words, resembling *Help me* or *I am innocent* or *Do not forget me beloved children I AM YOUR FATHER* —and then the screen went dead.

That afternoon Mother introduced us to the man who was to be Father's successor in the household!—and to his three children, who were to be our new brothers and sister, and we shook hands shyly, in a state of mutual shock, and regarded one another with wide staring wary eyes. Our new father! Our new brothers and sister! So suddenly, and with no warning! Mother explained patiently, yet forcibly, her new husband was no mere *step*father but a true *father*; which meant that we were to address him as "Father" at all times, with respect, and even in our most private innermost thoughts we were to think of him as "Father": for otherwise he would be hurt, and displeased. And moved to discipline us.

So too with Einar and Erastus, our new *brothers* (not *step*brothers), and Fifi, our new *sister* (not *step*sister).

New Father stood before us smiling happily, a man of our old Father's age but heavier and far more robust than that Father, with an unusually large head, the cranium particularly developed, and small shrewd quick-darting eyes beneath brows of bone. He wore a tailored suit with wide shoulders that exaggerated his bulk, and sported a red carnation in his lapel; his black shoes, a city man's shoes, shone splendidly, as if phosphorescent. "Hello Father," we murmured shyly, hardly daring to raise our eyes to his, "—Hello Father." The man's jaws were strangely elongated, the lower jaw at least an inch longer than the upper, so that a wet malevolent ridge of teeth was revealed; as so often happened in those days, a single thought passed like lightning among us children, from one to the other to the other, each of us smiling guiltily as it struck us: *Crocodile! Why, here's Crocodile!* Only little Jori burst into frightened tears and New Father surprised us all by stooping to pick her up gently in his arms and comfort her . . . "Hush, hush little girl! Nobody's going to hurt *you*!" and we others could see how the memory of our beloved former Father began to pass from her, like dissolving smoke. Jori was three years old at this time, too young to be held accountable.

New Father's children were tall, big-boned, and solemn, with a faint greenish-peevish cast to their skin, like many city children; the boys had inherited their father's large head and protruding jaw but the girl, Fifi, seventeen years old, was striking in her beauty, with pale blond fluffy hair as lovely as Cory's, and thickly lashed honey-brown eyes in which something mutinous glimmered. That evening certain of the boys—Dale, Kit, and Hewett—gathered around Fifi to tell her wild tales of the Valley, how we all had to protect ourselves with Winchester rifles and shotguns, from trespassers, and how there was a mysterious resurgence of rats on the farm, as a consequence of excavation in the countryside, and these tales, just a little exaggerated, made the girl shudder and shiver and giggle, leaning toward the boys as if to invite their protection. Ah, Fifi was so pretty! But when Dale hurried off to fetch her a goblet of ice water at her request she took the goblet from him, lifted it prissily to the light to examine its contents, and asked rudely, "Is this water *pure*? Is it safe to *drink*?" It was true, our well water had become strangely effervescent, and tasted of rust; after a heavy rainfall there were likely to be tiny red-wriggly things in it, like animated tails; so we had learned not to examine it too closely, just to drink it, and as our attacks of nausea, diarrhea, dizziness, and amnesia were only sporadic, we rarely worried but tried instead to be grateful, as Mrs. Hoyt used to urge us, that unlike many of our neighbors we had any drinking water at all. So it was offensive to us to see our new sister Fifi making such a face, handing the goblet back to Dale, and asking haughtily how anyone in his right mind could drink such—*spilth*. Dale said, red-faced, "*How*? This is *how*!" and drank the entire glass in a single thirsty gulp. And he and Fifi stood staring at each other, trembling with passion.

As Cory observed afterward, smiling, yet with a trace of envy or resentment, "It looks as if 'New Sister' has made a conquest!"

"But what will she do," I couldn't help asking, "—if she can't drink our water?"

"She'll drink it," Cory said, with a grim little laugh. "And she'll find it delicious, just like the rest of us."

Which turned out, fairly quickly, to be so.

Poor Cory! Her confinement came at a time of ever-increasing confusion . . . prolonged power failures, a scarcity of all food except canned foods, a scarcity too of ammunition so that the price of shotgun shells doubled, and quadrupled; and the massive sky by both day and night was criss-crossed by the contrails of unmarked jet planes (Army or Air Force bombers?) in designs both troubling and beautiful, like the web of a gigantic spider. By this time construction in most parts of the Valley, once so energetic, had been halted; part-completed high-rise buildings punctuated the landscape; some were no more than concrete foundations upon which iron girders had been erected, like exposed bone. How we children loved to explore! The "Mirror Tower" (as we called it: once, it must have had a real, adult name) was a three-hundred-story patchwork of interlocking slots of reflecting glass with a subtle turquoise tint, and where its elegant surface had once mirrored scenes of sparkling natural beauty there was now a drab scene, or succession of scenes, as on a video screen no one was watching: clouds like soiled cotton batting, smoldering slag heaps, decomposing garbage, predatory thistles and burdocks grown to the height of trees. Traffic, once so congested on the expressways, had dwindled to four or five diesel trucks per day hauling their heavy cargo (rumored to be diseased livestock bound for northern slaughterhouses) and virtually no passenger cars; sometimes, unmarked but official-looking vehicles, like jeeps, but much larger than jeeps, passed in lengthy convoys, bound for no one knew where. There were strips of pavement, cloverleafs, that coiled endlessly upon themselves, beginning to be cracked and overgrown by weeds, and elevated highways that broke off abruptly in midair, thus as state authorities warned travelers they were in grave danger, venturing into the countryside, of being attacked by roaming gangs—but the rumor was, as Father insisted, the most dangerous gangs were rogue Guardsmen who wore their uniforms inside-out and gas masks strapped over their faces, preying upon the very citizens they were sworn to protect! None of the adults left our family compound without being armed and of course we younger children were forbidden to leave at all—when we did, it was by stealth.

All schools, private and public, had been shut down indefinitely.

"One long holiday!" as Hewett said.

The most beautiful and luxurious of the model communities, which we called "The Wheel" (its original name was Paradise Hollow), had suffered some kind of financial collapse, so that its well-to-do tenants were forced to emigrate back to the cities from which they'd emigrated to the Valley only about eighteen months before. (We called the complex "The Wheel" because its condominiums, office buildings, shops, schools, hospitals, and crematoria were arranged in spokes radiating outward from a single axis; and were ingeniously protected at their twenty-mile circumference not by a visible wall, which the Japanese architect who'd designed it had declared a vulgar and outmoded concept, but by a force-field of electricity of lethal voltage.) Though the airport at Furnace Creek was officially closed we sometimes saw, late at night, small aircraft including helicopters taking off and landing there; were wakened by the insectlike whining of their engines, and their winking red lights; and one night when the sun remained motionless at the horizon for several hours and visibility was poor, as if we were in a dust storm, yet a dust storm without wind, a ten-seater airplane crashed in a slag heap that had once been a grazing pasture for our cows, and some of the older boys went by stealth to investigate . . . returning with sober, stricken faces, refusing to tell us, their sisters, what they had seen except to say, "Never mind! Don't ask!" Fifteen miles away in the western foothills were mysterious encampments, said to be unauthorized settlements of city dwellers who had fled their cities at the time of the "urban collapse" (as it was called), as well as former ranch families, and various wanderers and evicted persons, criminals, the mentally ill, and victims and suspected carriers of contagious diseases . . . all of these considered "outlaw parties" subject to severe treatment by the National Guardsmen, for the region was now under martial law, and only within family compounds maintained by state-registered property owners and heads of families were civil rights, to a degree, still operative. Eagerly, we scanned the Valley for signs of life, passing among us a pair of heavy binoculars, unknown to Father and Mother—like forbidden treasure these binoculars were, though their original owner was forgotten. (Cory believed that this person, a man, had lived with us before Father's time, and had been good to us, and kind. But no one, not even Cory, could remember his name, nor even what he'd looked like.)

Cory's baby was born the very week of the funerals of two of the younger children, who had died, poor things, of a violent dysentery, and of Uncle Darrah, who'd died of shotgun wounds while driving his pickup truck along a familiar road in the Valley; but this coincidence, Mother and Father assured us, was only that—a coincidence, and not an omen. Mother led us one by one into the drafty attic room set aside for Cory and her baby and we stared in amazement at the puppy-sized, florid-faced, screaming, yet so wonderfully alive creature . . . with its large soft-looking head, its wizened angry features, its smooth, poreless skin. How had Cory, one of us, accomplished *this*! Sisters and brothers alike, we were in awe of her, and a little fearful.

Mother's reaction was most surprising. She seemed furious with Cory, saying that the attic room was good enough for Cory's "outlaw child," sometimes she spoke of Cory's "bastard child"—though quick to acknowledge, in all fairness, the poor infant's parentage was no fault of its own. But it was "fit punishment," Mother said, that Cory's breasts ached when she nursed her baby, and that her milk was threaded with pus and blood . . . "fit punishment for shameful sluttish behavior." Yet, the family's luck held, for only two days after the birth Kit and Erastus came back from a nocturnal hunting expedition with a dairy cow: a healthy, fat-bellied, placid creature with black-and-white-marbled markings similar to those of our favorite cow, who had died long ago. This sweet-natured cow, named Daisy, provided the family with fresh, delicious, seemingly pure milk, thus saving Cory's bastard-infant's life, as Mother said spitefully, "Well, the way of Providence *is* a honeycomb!"

Those weeks, Mother was obsessed with learning the identity of Cory's baby's father; Cory's "secret lover," as Mother referred to him. Cory, of course, refused to say—even to her sisters. She may have been wounded that the baby's father had failed to come forward to claim his child, or her; poor Cory, once the prettiest of the girls, now disfigured with skin rashes like fish scales over most of her body, and a puffy, bloated appearance, and eyes red from perpetual weeping. Mother herself was frequently ill with a similar flaming rash, a protracted respiratory infection, intestinal upsets, bone aches, and amnesia; like everyone in the family except, oddly, Father, she was plagued with ticks—the smallest species of deer tick that could burrow secretly into the skin, releasing an analgesiac spittle to numb the skin, thus able to do its damage, sucking blood contentedly for weeks until, after weeks, it might drop off with a *ping*! to the floor, black, shiny, now the size of a watermelon seed, swollen with blood. What loathsome things! Mother developed a true horror of them, for they seemed drawn to her, especially to her white, wild-matted hair.

By imperceptible degrees Mother had shrunk to a height of less than five feet, very unlike the statuesque beauty of old photographs; with that head of white hair, and pebble-colored eyes as keen and suspicious as ever, and a voice so brassy and penetrating it had the power to paralyze any of us where we stood . . . even the eldest of her sons, Kit, Hewett, Dale, tall bearded men who carried firearms even inside the compound, were intimidated by Mother, and, like Cory, were inclined to submit to her authority. When Mother interrogated Cory, "*Who* is your lover? Why are you so ashamed of him? Did you find him in the drainage pipe, or in the slag heap?—in the compost?" Cory bit her lip, and said quietly, "Even if I see his face sometimes, Mother, in my sleep, I can't recall his name. Or who he was, or is. Or claimed to be."

Yet Mother continued, risking Father's displeasure—for she began to question *all males* with whom she came into contact, not excluding Cory's own blood relations—cousins, uncles, even brothers!—even those ravaged men and boys who made their homes, so to speak, beyond the compound, as she'd said jeeringly, in the drainage pipe, in the slag heap, in the compost. (These men and boys were not official residents on our property but were enlisted by the family in times of crisis and emergency.) But no one confessed—no one acknowledged Cory's baby as his. And one day when Cory lay upstairs in the attic with a fever and I was caring for the baby, excitedly feeding it from a bottle, in the kitchen, Mother entered with a look of such determination I felt a sudden fear for the baby, hugging it to my chest, and Mother said, "Give me the bastard, girl," and I said weakly, "No Mother, don't make me," and Mother said, "Are you disobeying me, girl? *Give me the bastard*," and I said, backing away, daringly, yet determined too, "No Mother, Cory's baby belongs to Cory, and to all of us, and it isn't a bastard." Mother advanced upon me, furious; her pebble-colored eyes now rimmed with white; her fingers—what talons they'd become, long, skinny, clawed!—outstretched. Yet I saw that in the very midst of her passion she was forgetting what she intended to do, and that this might save Cory's baby from harm.

(For often in those days when the family had little to eat except worm-riddled apples from the old orchard, and stunted blackened potatoes, and such game, or wildlife, that the men and boys could shoot, and such canned goods as they could acquire, we often, all of us, young as well as old, forgot what we were doing in the very act of doing it; plucking bloody feathers from a quail, for instance, and stopping vague and dreamy wondering what on earth am I doing? here? at the sink? *is* this a sink? what is this limp little body? this instrument— a knife?—in my hands? and naturally in the midst of speaking we might forget the words we meant to speak, for instance *water, rainbow, grief, love, filth, Father, deer tick, God, milk, sky* . . . and Father, who'd become brooding with the onset of age, worried constantly that we, his family, might one day soon lose all sense of ourselves as a family should we forget, in the same instant, all of us together, the sacred word *family*.)

And indeed, there in the kitchen, reaching for Cory's baby with her talonlike fingers, Mother was forgetting. And indeed within the space of a half-minute she had forgotten. Staring at the defenseless living thing, the quivering, still-hungry creature in my arms, with its soft flat shallow face of utter innocence, its tiny recessed eyes, its mere holes for nostrils, its small pursed mouth set like a manta ray's in its shallow face, Mother could not, simply could not, summon back the word *baby*, or *infant*, nor even the cruel *Cory's bastard*, always on her lips. And at that moment there was a commotion outside by the compound gate, an outburst of gunfire, familiar enough yet always jarring when unexpected, and Mother hurried out to investigate. And Cory's baby returned to sucking hungrily and contentedly at the bottle's frayed rubber nipple, and all was safe for now.

But Cory, my dear sister, died a few days later.

Lona discovered her in her place of exile in the attic, in her bed, eyes opened wide and pale mouth contorted, the bedclothes soaked in blood . . . and when in horror Lona drew the sheet away she saw that Cory's breasts had been partly hacked away, or maybe devoured?—and her chest cavity exposed; she must have been attacked in the night by rats, and was too weak or too terrified to scream for help. Yet her baby was sleeping placidly in its crib beside the bed, miraculously untouched . . . sunk in its characteristic sleep to that profound level at which organic matter seems about to revert to the inorganic, to perfect peace. For some reason the household rats with their glittering amaranthine eyes and stiff hairless tails and unpredictable appetites had spared it!—or had missed it altogether!

Lona snatched the baby up out of its crib and ran downstairs screaming for help; and so fierce was she in possession she would not give up the baby to anyone, saying, dazed, sobbing, yet in a way gloating, "This is my baby. This is Lona's baby now." Until Father, with his penchant for logic, rebuked her: "Girl, it is the family's baby now."

And Fifi too had a baby; beautiful blond Fifi; or, rather, the poor girl writhed and screamed in agony for a day and a night, before giving birth to a perfectly formed but tiny baby weighing only two pounds, that lived only a half hour. How we wept, how we pitied our sister!—in the weeks that followed nothing would give her solace, even the smallest measure of solace, except our musical evenings, at which she excelled. For if Dale tried to touch her, to comfort her, she shrank from him in repugnance; nor would she allow Father, or any male, to come near. One night she crawled into my bed and hugged me in her icy bone-thin arms. "What I love best," she whispered, "—is the black waves that splash over us, endlessly, at night—do you know those waves, sister? and do you love them as I do?" And my heart was so swollen with feeling I could not reply, as I wished to, "Oh *yes*."

Indeed, suddenly the family had taken up music. In the evenings by kerosene lamp. In the pre-dawn hours, roused from our beds by aircraft overhead, or the barking of wild dogs, or the thermal winds. We played such musical instruments as fell into our hands discovered here and there in the house, or by way of strangers at our gate eager to barter anything they owned for food. Kit took up the violin shyly at first and then with growing confidence and joy for, it seemed, he had musical talent—practicing for hours on the beautiful though scarified antique violin that had once belonged to Grandfather, or Great-grandfather (so we surmised: an old portrait depicted a child of about ten posed with the identical violin tucked under his chin); Jori and Vega took up the piccolo, which they shared; Hewett the drums, Dale the cymbals, Einar the oboe, Fifi the piano . . . and the rest of us sang, sang our hearts out.

We sang after Mother's funeral and we sang that week a hot feculent wind blew across the Valley bearing the odor of decomposing flesh and we sang (though often coughing and choking, from the smoke) when fires raged out of control in the dry woodland areas to the east, an insidious wind then too blowing upon our barricaded compound and handsome house atop a high hill, a wind intent upon seeking us out, it seemed, carrying sparks to our sanctuary, our place of privilege, destroying us in fire as others both human and beast were being destroyed . . . and how else for us to endure such odors, such sights, such sounds, than to take up our instruments and play them as loudly as possible, and sing as loudly as possible, and sing and sing and sing until our throats were raw, how else.

Yet, the following week became a time of joy and feasting, since Daisy the cow was dying in any case and might as well be quickly slaughtered, when Father, surprising us all, brought his new wife home to meet us: New Mother we called her, or Young Mother, or Pretty Mother, and Old Mother that fierce stooped wild-eyed old woman was soon forgotten, even the mystery of her death soon forgotten (for had she like Cory died of household rats? or had she, like poor Erastus, died of a burst appendix? had she drowned somehow in the cistern, had she died of thirst and malnutrition locked away in the attic, had she died of a respiratory infection, of toothache, of heartbreak, of her own rage, or of age, or of Father's strong fingers closing around her neck . . . or had she not "died" at all but passed quietly into oblivion, as the black waves splashed over her, and Young Mother stepped forward smiling happily to take her place).

Young Mother was so pretty!—plump, and round-faced, her complexion rich and ruddy, her breasts like large balloons filled to bursting with warm liquid, and she gave off a hot intoxicating smell of nutmeg, and tiny flames leapt from her when in a luxury of sighing, yawning, and stretching, she lifted the heavy mass of red-russet hair that hung between her shoulder blades, and fixed upon us her smiling-dark gaze. "Mother!" we cried, even the eldest of us, "—oh Mother!" hoping would she hug us, would she kiss and hug us, fold us in those plump strong arms, cuddle our faces against those breasts, each of us, all of us, weeping, in her arms, those arms, oh Mother, *there*.

Lona's baby was not maturing as it was believed babies should normally mature, nor had it been named since we could not determine whether it was male or female, or somehow both, or neither; and this household problem Young Mother addressed herself to at once. No matter Lona's desperate love of the baby, Young Mother was "practical minded" as she said: for why else had Father brought her to this family but to take charge, to reform it, to give *hope*? She could not comprehend, she said, laughing incredulously, how and why an extra mouth, a useless mouth, perhaps even a dangerous mouth, could be tolerated at such a time of near famine, in violation of certain government edicts as she understood them. "Drastic remedies in drastic times," Young Mother was fond of saying. Lona said, pleading, "I'll give it my food, Mother—I'll protect it with my life!" And Young Mother simply repeated, smiling, so broadly her eyes were narrowed almost to slits, "Drastic remedies in drastic times!"

There were those of us who loved Lona's baby, for it *was* flesh of our flesh, it *was* part of our family; yet there were others, mainly the men and boys, who seemed nervous in its presence, keeping a wary distance when it crawled into a room to nudge its large bald head or pursed mouth against a foot, an ankle, a leg. Though it had not matured in the normal fashion Lona's baby weighed now about thirty pounds; but it was soft as a slug is soft, or an oyster; with an oyster's general shape; apparently boneless; the hue of unbaked bread dough, and hairless. As its small eyes lacked an iris, being entirely white, it must have been blind; its nose was but a rudimentary pair of nostrils, holes in the center of its face; its fishlike mouth was deceptive in that it seemed to possess its own intelligence, being ideally formed, not for human speech, but for seizing, sucking, and chewing. Though it had at best only a cartilaginous skeleton it did boast two fully formed rows of tiny needle-sharp teeth, which it was not shy of using, particularly when ravenous for food; and it was often ravenous. At such times it groped its way around the house, silent, by instinct, sniffing and quivering, and if by chance it was drawn by the heat of your blood to your bed it would burrow beneath the covers, and nudge, and nuzzle, and begin like a nursing infant to suck virtually any part of the body, though preferring of course a female's breasts . . . and if not stopped in time it would start to bite, chew, *eat* . . . in all the brute innocence of appetite. So some of us surmised, though Lona angrily denied it, that the baby's first mother (a sister of ours whose name we had forgotten) had not died of rat bites after all but of having been attacked in the night and partly devoured by her own baby.

(In this, Lona was duplicitous. She took care never to undress in Mother's presence for fear Mother's sharp eye would discover the numerous wounds on her breasts, belly, and thighs.)

As the family had a time-honored custom of debating issues, in a democratic manner, for instance should we pay the exorbitant price a cow or a she-goat now commanded on the open market, or should the boys be given permission to acquire one of these beasts however they could, for instance should we try to feed the starving men, women, and children who gathered outside our fence, even if it was food too contaminated for the family's consumption—so naturally the issue of Lona's baby was taken up too, and soon threatened to split the family into two warring sides. Mother argued persuasively, almost tearfully, that the baby was "worthless, repulsive, and might one day be dangerous,"—not guessing that it had already proved dangerous; and Lona argued persuasively, and tearfully, that "Lona's baby," as she called it, was a living human being, a member of the family, one of us. Mother said hotly, "It is not one of *us*, girl, if by *us* you mean a family that includes *me*," and Lona said, daringly, "It is one of *us* because it predates any family that includes *you*—'Mother.' "

So they argued; and others joined in; and emotions ran high. It was strange how some of us changed our minds several times, now swayed by Mother's reasoning, and now by Lona's; now by Father who spoke on behalf of Mother, or by Hewett who spoke on behalf of Lona. Was it weeks, or was it months, that the debate raged?—and subsided, and raged again?—and Mother dared not put her power to the vote for fear that Lona's brothers and sisters would side with Lona out of loyalty if not love for the baby. And Father acknowledged reluctantly that however any of use felt about the baby it *was* our flesh and blood, and embodied the Mystery of Life: ". . . Its soul bounded by its skull and its destiny no more problematic than the sinewy tubes that connect its mouth and its anus. Who are we to judge!"

Yet Mother had her way, as slyboots Mother was always to have her way . . . one March morning, soliciting the help of several of us, who were sworn to secrecy and delighted to be her handmaidens, in a simple scheme: Lona being asleep in the attic, Mother led the baby out of the house by holding a piece of bread soaked in chicken blood in front of its nostrils, led it crawling across the hard-packed wintry earth, to the old hay barn, and, inside, led it to a dark corner where we helped her lift it and lower it carefully into an aged rain barrel empty except for a wriggling mass of half-grown rats, that squealed in great excitement at being disturbed, and at the smell of the blood-soaked bread which Mother dropped with the baby. We then nailed a cover in place; and, as Mother said, her skin warmly flushed and her breath coming fast, "There, girls—it is entirely out of our hands."

And then one day it was spring. And Kit, grinning, led a she-goat proudly into the kitchen, her bags primed with milk, swollen pink dugs leaking milk! How grateful we all were, those of us who were with child especially, after the privations of so long a winter, or winters, during which time certain words have all but faded from our memories, for instance *she-goat*, and *milk*, and as we realized *rainbow*, for the rainbow too reappeared, one morning, shimmering and translucent across the Valley, a phenomenon as of the quivering of millions of butterflies' iridescent wings. In the fire-scorched plain there grew a virtual sea of fresh green shoots and in the sky enormous dimpled clouds and that night we gathered around Fifi at the piano to play our instruments and to sing. Father had passed away but Mother had remarried: a husky bronze-skinned horseman whose white teeth flashed in his beard, and whose rowdy pinches meant love and good cheer, not meanness. We were so happy we debated turning the calendar ahead to the New Year. We were so happy we debated abolishing the calendar entirely and declaring this the First Day of Year One, and beginning Time anew.

JAMES POWELL

A Dirge for Clowntown

James Powell is known as a writer of mystery fiction, and the following story comes from the pages of *Ellery Queen's Mystery Magazine*.

"A Dirge for Clowntown" is a police procedural tale, a satiric fantasy, a circus story, and half-a-dozen other things rolled into one, by a writer tap-dancing on the genre boundary lines. This story won the *EQMM* readers' poll as best short story of the year.

—T.W.

A Dirge for Clowntown

JAMES POWELL

"Ringling-ringling!" shouted the bedside telephone. When he fumbled the receiver out of its cradle, a familiar voice at the other end of the line said, "We've got a live one, Inspector. Three seventy-one Pagliacci Terrace, Apartment 2C."

Forcing a grunt as close to "I'm on my way" as he could muster, the man in the bed got his feet on the floor and staggered toward the bathroom, hitting a chair and the doorjamb on the way. Grabbing two tight fistfuls of sink porcelain, he stared down at the drain for a long moment. Then he raised his head and saw himself in the mirror. By Jumbo, he looked as bad as he felt! The dead-white skin, the great bloody slash of smile, the huge round maraschino nose, the perfect black triangles of his eyebrows, the dead white skullcap with the two side-tufts of bright-orange hair. There he was, Clowntown's finest, Inspector Bozo of the Homicide Squad. Talk about a three-ring hangover! Bozo ran the tips of his trembling fingers across his cheek. A trip to Makeup was long overdue. Well, it would have to wait. When Homicide said they had a live one, they meant they had a dead one.

Splashing water on his face, Bozo hurried back to the bedroom. The clock-radio on the bedside table said 11:15 in the morning. Shaking his head at himself, he got into his baggy pants, pulled the suspenders up over his shoulders, and sat down on the edge of the bed to put on his long yellow shoes. (Shoe length indicated rank on the Clowntown force. When two deputy chiefs met toe to toe, they had to raise their voices to communicate.)

Next came the high celluloid collar with the big bow tie of fluorescent orange and purple lightning bolts. Then he slipped into the paddy-green-plaid trenchcoat with all the belts and flaps, tabs and buttons, and the three-pound brass police badge pinned to a lapel. Slapping the pockets to make sure he had his revolver and his bicycle horn, he headed for the front door. He took the expensive pearl-grey fedora from the hatrack, set it carefully and properly on his head, and stepped out into the hall. Years ago, when he'd designed his outfit, he could have chosen one of those little umbrellas with the water spout in the ferrule or a squirting flower as the finishing touch. Instead he'd picked this perfect hat, feeling it set off the rest of his exaggerated costume. Yes, all in all he'd put together a damn good act. Why was it starting to fall apart?

As he passed through the lobby, Bozo exchanged horn-honk greetings with the building superintendent. Outside, a crew of Sanitation Department clowns armed with pushbrooms were sweeping spotlights out of the gutters. The Saturday-morning street was cold and blustery beneath an elephant-grey sky. Clowntown's wind was legendary, with newspapers scuttling around every corner and flags snapping like tent canvas overhead. The rawness came with early December.

Bozo decided to walk. Pagliacci Terrace wasn't that far and he needed to clear his head. He stumbled going up a curb and felt his nose budge. Damn, not that again. Almost twenty years on the force and the best nose he could afford was a wobbly mail-order number from Mr. Snoot. Last month, coming down the crowded City Hall steps with some buddies from Vice, the thing had dropped right off and gone bouncing high, wide, and handsome down the steps with Bozo cursing and chasing after it.

Oh, no one laughed. His embarrassed friends pretended not to notice. His Honor and the police chief and the rest of the brass looked the other way. They were all great admirers of his father, Big Bozo, who'd made the family name synonymous with clown. But Bozo knew they'd soon be clucking among themselves about how Big Bozo's boy was hitting the bottle, how he was going to seed, how he'd been in a tailspin since his divorce.

No, Bozo couldn't let that happen again. He made a mental note to have the nose looked after at the next sporting-goods store. The same people who custom-drilled the holes in bowling balls did nose refitting. And they always tried to sell him one of those flashy new Japanese noses all the trendy young clowns were wearing. But ever since the india-rubber-cartel people got their act together, the price of noses had gone through the roof.

Bozo reached the Pagliacci Terrace address and took the steps two at a time. The uniformed clown policeman guarding the apartment door saluted, using the hand holding his nightstick, rapping himself on the head and knocking his tall blue helmet askew. It was a stunt he did well and Bozo could see he was proud of it.

The dead clown lay on his back on the floor, toes pointed at the ceiling, the wreckage of a whole custard pie on his face. He was dressed in a convict's uniform of broad black and white horizontal stripes and brimless cap and had a black-plastic ball-and-chain shackled to one leg. Retrieving the victim's wallet, Bozo found the man's union card. He recognized the ferret face staring out at him from the photograph. Yes, he knew Clown Bunco very well. Like a few other clowns on the shady side of the law, Bunco, a small-time confidence man and hustler, had taken to wearing a convict outfit as if to openly challenge society and its values. Bozo glanced at the card again. Today was Bunco's birthday.

Sending a friend a custard pie in the face on his birthday was an old Clowntown custom.

Over in the corner, the police medical examiner was cramming an immense cleaver, a butcher knife as big as a scimitar, and a vast hypodermic needle back into his black bag. "Well, Doctor?" asked Bozo coldly as he knelt down to clear away some of the custard and make sure it really was Bunco under the mess. He'd never cared for the medical examiner. The man had fled Clowntown soon after graduating from the Emmett Kelly School of Medicine to take a fling at burlesque, slouching across the stage and leering at females in low comic routines. When burlesque died, he'd crept back, happy to eke out a living as a police medical examiner. His lewd eyebrows, glasses, red nose, and moustache looked made from one piece and he walked like his tie was caught in the zipper of his fly. For Bozo the man would always have the smell of the rim-shot about him.

"Strychnine," said the doctor. "A massive dose in the birthday boy's custard pie." Reading Bozo's look of disbelief, he gave a take-it-or-leave-it shrug and loped for the door, adding over his shoulder, "The delivery man's waiting for you in there."

Bozo followed the direction of the medical examiner's cocked thumb into the bedroom, where a clown wearing a bright-yellow bellboy's uniform sat waiting with a very depressed look. His chest was decorated with large brass buttons and the words MIDWAY BAKING COMPANY were printed in chartreuse on his pillbox hat. "What the hell happened?" demanded Bozo.

"Search me," said the delivery man in a reedy, nervous voice. "This was almost my last stop of the day. I parked my van on the street. Up I came and honked at his keyhole. When he opened the door, I was standing there holding the pie behind my back. 'Clown Bunco?' I asked. 'Yeah, so what?' sez he. 'So Happy Birthday,' sez I and I let him have it right in the kisser. You know, the secret of my marksmanship is never taking my eyes off the target.

"But it's funny the reaction you get in that split second while the pie's in the air. Clown A's pleasantly surprised. Clown B's smug—he's already had so many pies in the face he hasn't gotten the custard out of his ears from the last one and I know there are three more pie-delivery men stacked up out on the staircase. But Bunco there gave me the kind of look you don't see very often, a kind of tearing up in the eyes like he was remembering how long a time it had been since anybody'd remembered his birthday. Then the pie hit." The delivery man looked at Bozo helplessly. "Then he fell over dead."

"The doctor says the pie was poisoned," said Bozo. "Which would mean he got custard in his mouth or up his nose. Well, I can't buy that." One of the first things a clown learned was the right way to take a custard pie in the face. Just before impact you closed your mouth tightly and breathed out through your nose.

"Believe me, it was the finger schtick that did him in," insisted the delivery man.

The great clown, Josef Schtick, the originator of many little routines clowns still use, came up with the business in question as a follow-up to being hit with a custard pie. He would stand there, a forlorn laughingstock, with the mess sliding down his face. Then he would take a scoop of the custard on his forefinger, look at it curiously, taste it, smile, smack his lips, and start eating. Bozo cursed his own obtuseness. The finger schtick. Of course.

Bozo sent the delivery man home, confident he couldn't have known the pie was poisoned. Clowns were totally incapable of causing direct physical harm to another person. That didn't mean a clown couldn't commit murder, only that he couldn't do it directly.

Bozo spent a good hour searching the apartment for something that might give him a clue to the murderer's identity. He found nothing until almost the last place he looked. In an envelope taped to the underside of the drawer in the telephone table, he discovered a manila envelope. Inside were a sheaf of sales receipts for furniture and other household furnishings made out to Bunco. He skimmed through them quickly. It was all expensive stuff and it wasn't anything here in the apartment. Strange.

But stranger still, why would a man hide sales receipts? Bozo made the envelope into a tube and stuffed it into his pocket. He left the apartment not sure what his next move should be. But back out on the sidewalk, he saw a Dinero's hamburger place across the street. All he'd found in Bunco's refrigerator was a wizened lemon and a moldy quart of buttermilk. Well, the guy had to eat somewhere. And that reminded Bozo he could use a shot of the feedbag himself.

The girl behind the lunch counter wore a blonde fright wig, a fashionable nose, an immense greasepaint smile, and, under her uniform, a big set of inflatable breasts. The portside one seemed to have a slow leak. When Bozo came in, she put down her copy of *Big Top Tid Bits* and ducked behind the coffee urn. He was sure he heard several strokes of a tire pump before she reappeared in full repair. "What'll it be?" she asked.

Bozo ordered his burger and sat watching the waitress prepare it. He knew her type well. The young girl fresh from Pratt Falls comes to Clowntown with stars in her eyes, so sure she'll land a job with the circus she can already smell the cotton candy. It ached to think about it. It made him remember his ex-wife, Calliope. She'd been new in town, too, the first time he met her, and hell-bent to make her name in the circus. What a knockout she'd been, with her carrot-red hair done up in braids and her great big freckles and the tasteful way she'd only blacked out a single tooth.

Those first years of their marriage had been times of big change for Clowntown. Until then, the city'd been a solidly blue-collar community. A lot of clowns worked for Ringmeister, the center-city brewery, or in the textile mills of Clown-town Tinsel and Spangle. But one of the biggies bought out Ringmeister and closed it down and the Japanese computerized the hell out of the spangle industry. Center city declined and the clowns began their flight out to the suburbs, to Carneyville and Highwire.

Bozo and Calliope hadn't made the move. He was glad they hadn't. He had watched the suburban clowns trade in their floppy shoes for expensive sneakers and their baggy pants for designer jeans. And he saw their red-nosed faces at the commuter-train windows on the elevated tracks, looking sad—not clown sad, but stark, lonely, three-piece-suit sad. And he knew how their stories would end. Each year they'd buy a smaller-size nose until they got down to one no bigger than an angry boil. One morning they'd arrive at work with a Band-Aid on their nose and tell their secretary they'd had the boil lanced. When the band-aid came off, it would be goodbye, Clowntown.

But looking back on it, Bozo knew that he and his wife should have started a family. They put it off too long. Then all of a sudden Calliope wanted her own career. Bozo had argued strongly against it, but Calliope stood firm. "I can hear my slapstick clock ticking," she insisted. "It's now or never."

"Then it's never!" Bozo had shouted.

After the divorce, Calliope went to circus winter quarters in Florida. Bozo missed her. He tried not to think of her down there, just one more big red smile among a thousand big red smiles waiting for the big break. He got a card from her now and then. Sometimes he sent her money. But he knew he'd never see her again.

Bozo's food arrived. He ate it warily, unsure of his stomach, and set about organizing his thoughts on the case. So what did he have? The business of breathing out through the nose when you take a custard pie in the face was a clown trade-secret. So the murderer had to be a clown, a clown who knew Bunco well enough to know he still did the finger schtick.

And what about the hidden envelope? Bozo pulled it out and examined the contents again. A receipt from Crystal Palace Furniture for a bedroom and a living-room set. Another from S-T Molding and Shelving for a fireplace mantel. A third from a company called PlexiGrandi for a piano. All were marked with the special instruction that the customer would pick them up at the warehouse. Why was stuff like this important enough for Bunco to hide? And was it connected with his murder?

Bozo pondered for a moment and then called the waitress over and showed her Bunco's union card. "Ever see this guy in here?"

She looked at the picture. "Him and his ball and chain? Sure—he was a regular," she said. "My first day here he gave me the honk and said if I played my cards right he'd introduce me to his bigwig pals in the circus. What a laugh. I sure told him where to get off."

"Somebody just told him where to get off permanently," said Bozo. "Bunco's been murdered." He waited for that to register before asking her, "Did he ever come in with anybody else?"

She snapped her gum thoughtfully before answering. "There was Waco. He was a rodeo clown—purple suspenders, hairy chaps, red-flannel long johns, a cowboy hat with the brim turned up in front—the whole ten yards. Distracting Brahman bulls from thrown riders was his life until rodeos went the way of the buffalo. He was a nice guy, Waco. Too nice to have anything to do with Bunco, I always thought. They used to sit over in that corner booth and talk. I haven't seen Waco for—how long's it been? Two months? Six weeks?"

She thought for a minute. "I let him take me out once. Oh, it was no big deal. He'd just come into some money and wanted to celebrate. He took me to one of those new wine bars where the mimes go. How harmless can it get, right, standing around for an hour or so pretending to drink?"

Bozo wasn't sure. In a recent try at cutting down on his own intake, he'd visited a wine bar some mimes had opened where Trapezio's, the great old Italian clown restaurant, used to be. It'd been a pleasant evening. A couple of those mime women would've been real knockouts if only they'd had big red noses. And the drinks had gone down smooth. But there'd been nothing pretend about the hangover he woke up with next day.

Over the past few years, mimes had started moving into center city Clowntown, renting apartments, restoring brownstones. Now they were a familiar sight every weekday morning, going off to their jobs wearing the tight jumpsuits of their class, striped jerseys, a white oval on the front of their faces, their hats decorated with a flower or a butterfly on a wire. And all of them, all, relentlessly walking against some wind that only they could feel. A lot of clowns resented the mimes, claiming they were standoffish and wouldn't give you the time of day. Bozo knew that wasn't true. Mimes were kind, gentle folk, quick, at the slightest encouragement, with the big smile and the gift of an imaginary flower.

"Boy, Waco really got a charge out of watching those mimes go through their paces—like sitting on bar stools that weren't there or leaning on empty air like it was the most natural thing in the world," said the waitress. " 'I've seen the future and it works,' he said as we walked out the door. Afterward we went around the corner to his place. He didn't try anything funny. We just had coffee and he showed me pictures of his kids."

"Where was this?" demanded Bozo.

"Corner of Pantaloon and Rigoletto," she said. "But don't waste your time. That was a couple of months ago. He said he was moving. He said the owner of his apartment building wanted to renovate and rent the place out for big bucks to the mimes. Hey, maybe he left his landlord a forwarding address."

She thought for a moment and said, "The only other guy I ever saw with Bunco was this big-jawed, big-chested clown in a red bowler and a tight orange suit."

Bozo drummed four fingers against his white cheek. "A tough-looking customer with a skull-and-crossbones on his left hand?" he asked. When she nodded, he had his clown. The only trouble was Mugo had been in jail for the last ten days on the charge of mime-bashing. But he had friends. Mugo could have arranged to have Bunco killed from there.

Mime-bashing was the crime of the moment among trendy clown criminals, a shameful business made all the more so by the victims' peaceful natures. Where clowns were incapable of harming another directly, mimes couldn't knowingly do harm to anyone, period. Except, of course, to themselves.

Unfortunately, a bad clown element had gotten wise to this. They would prowl the streets at night with their noses in their pockets so they couldn't later be identified in a police lineup. If they ran across a mime, they'd take a swing at him, being careful to miss by a good six inches. But mimes being what they were, they had to snap their heads around as though struck or hurl themselves backward into the nearest wall or down a flight of steps. Last month Mugo and a bunch of his friends had set upon four mimes, throwing punches at them until the mimes knocked themselves unconscious. Then the clowns had stripped them and left them naked and bloody in the street. Fortunately, two of the victims had been able to identify Mugo by his tattoo. Could Mugo be the murderer? Why would he want to kill Bunco?

"Hey," said the waitress, looking down at Bozo's empty plate. "It's fresh—how about a slice of custard pie?"

Bozo headed off for Pantaloon and Rigoletto. But in the next block he saw a sporting-goods store and decided to get his nose tended to.

The dark, old-fashioned shop smelled of leather and the rosin bag. Bozo's honk was answered by one from the back room and a moment later a dusty old clown with a burly grey moustache appeared, cleaning his wire-framed glasses on his striped apron. He spotted Bozo's problem at once and without a word ushered the Inspector into a small curtained alcove.

There Bozo handed over the nose and sat with a hand modestly covering his naked undernose. The old man put a jeweler's loupe in his eye and examined the inside of the rubber nose. He sighed and was about to start his sales pitch when he saw Bozo's name inscribed on the rim of the hole. "Inspector," he asked in a voice filled with awe, "was your father by any chance Big Bozo?"

Bozo nodded. His father had been a three-star general in the Clown Marines. Strutting out there at the head of his crack clown drill-team in his uniform of electric-blue with all the gold frogging and gold stripes on the sleeve and his shako with its immense pompom, he'd been the hit of every parade. The drill-team's trips and stumbles were all coordinated to perfection. When one marching clown slipped on a banana peel, a hundred did.

"Let me shake your hand," said the little old clown, doing just that. "The way I see it, Big Bozo and his drill-team set war back a hundred years. And isn't that what the military's supposed to be all about?" Then he returned to the matter at hand. "Inspector, this nose of yours has gone to the well once too often. I can fix it for now, but what you really need—"

"Is a new nose? Forget it," said Bozo. "Not on a police inspector's salary."

"I was thinking of maybe something nice in the second-hand line," said the nose-auger man.

Bozo frowned. Since the india-rubber cartel, there'd been a sharp rise in the theft of noses for resale. There were even stories of ghoulish clowns haunting midnight cemeteries to desecrate the graves of the recent dead.

The old man had produced a small box lined with white velvet. Inside was a smart red nose. "This has you written all over it," he said. "A match made in heaven. That undernose of yours is a real honker. This little honey belonged to one of your small-nosed rodeo clowns. It'll auger out real nice."

Bozo blinked and snatched the nose. The name *Waco* was inscribed around the rim. "How'd you come by this?"

"Last week this rodeo clown in chaps and cowboy hat walked in off the street," explained the old man. "He said he had this spare that was just collecting dust. He said he could use the cash. So we struck a deal. Trust me. Like I said, it'll auger out real nice."

The old man was clearly disappointed when Bozo told him he'd have to get back to him on that. He shrugged and set about repairing the old nose as best he could.

Bozo sat there patiently, considering this new development. Here was this rodeo clown, a friend of Bunco's who comes into some money and then drops out of sight. A couple of months later, Waco pops up again out of nowhere to sell a spare nose. A week later more or less and Bunco gets killed. What the hell did it all mean? Bozo didn't know. But as he paid for the repair job, he decided to flash Bunco's picture. "Seen this guy around?"

The old man looked at him like he was joking. "The outfit's all wrong, of course," he said, "but I swear that there's the Waco character I was just telling you about."

Bozo strode down the street puzzling out this new development. Then he heard an approaching siren and stopped to watch as a Clowntown Fire Department ladder truck, a caricature of a vehicle, rushed down the street with clown firefighters falling off and chasing after it on all sides. Bozo smiled, knowing the bumble and ineptitude was part of the clown's art. That ladder truck would arrive at the fire as quickly if not quicker than any non-clown ladder truck. And, yes, the buckets of confetti they threw on the fire would extinguish it as effectively as any modern chemical mix. Clowns were proud of that.

As he resumed his walk, Bozo mused on why some clowns hated the mimes so much. He thought he knew the answer. It'd come to him a while back when he'd been eating his lunch on a park bench. Along came this mime, walking against the wind, and sat down across the path from him as though there was a bench there, which there wasn't. From an imaginary brown bag, he drew this imaginary napkin and tucked it under his chin. Next came an imaginary sandwich, which he unwrapped and smiled down at before eating with visible relish, scattering the crumbs for the real pigeons.

Then he peeled and ate an invisible banana while he watched the birds crowd around his feet. When he was through, he put the sandwich wrapper and banana peel into the paper bag, which he crushed into an imaginary ball and tossed at a wire trash-container twenty feet away. The mime's anxious face told Bozo about the flight of the ball. He knew it rimmed the target once, twice, three times before body English knocked it into the container. Delighted, the mime got up and strode happily back in the direction he'd come, still walking against the wind.

Sitting chewing on his baloney sandwich, which now tasted like ashes, Bozo decided clowns resented mimes not because the pigeons preferred their imaginary bread crumbs to a clown's substantial ones or because a mime's invisible tears seemed larger, his silent laughter louder than clown sorrow or joy. No, in the end he decided that the mimes made the clowns feel clumsy, coarse, material, and utterly earthbound.

Not that that justified mime-bashing.

* * *

The brick facade of Waco's old apartment building had been sandblasted. A spanking new canopy flapped over the front door with *Pierrot Plaza* written across it in cursive script. While Bozo stood there at the curb, a mime couple arrived, pushing their child in an imaginary stroller. As more mimes entered and left the building, Bozo noticed the fat clown in top hat, cutaway, and baggy striped trousers standing nearby watching the come and go with a big red smile and rubbing his gloved hands together vigorously. The man was the epitome of the old plutocrat clown so popular in the Twenties and Thirties. Here was clown avarice—greed carried to the point of laughter. Here was the Pierrot Plaza's landlord.

Honking his horn and wagging his badge with a thumb behind his lapel, Bozo stepped forward. "Bozo's the name, Homicide's the game," he said. "I'm trying to track down an old tenant of yours, a rodeo clown called Waco."

The landlord clown turned pale. Glancing quickly left and right, he led Bozo by the elbow down the sidewalk to the next apartment building. "If we're going to talk murder," he murmured, "let's do it here in front of my competitor's building. Violence makes mimes very nervous. But Waco didn't leave any forwarding address, if that's what you're after. I guess he's living somewhere in the high-rent district. Did you know he hit it big with the ponies a couple of months ago? He bet his bankroll. 'Play Animal Act in the fifth,' he told me. I wish I had. It paid a bundle."

Bozo frowned. Without a forwarding address, where did he go from here? "I don't suppose you caught the name of the people who moved his furniture?" he asked.

"That junk?" said the landlord. "He gave it all to the Poor Souls Rescue Mission. They fix up stuff like that for resale and use the money to help tramp and hobo clowns." He shook his head. "Boy, what a bunch of dodos they sent round to pick it up! Those clowns broke half the stuff on the way down, not counting what they did to the paint on the stairwell."

The landlord winced at the memory. Then he chuckled. "You want to hear something real funny? A month later when I'd fixed the place up for my new tenants, I was down in the lobby when this mime Pip, who I rented Waco's old apartment to, drives up in a truck with four mime buddies and they go through the rigmarole of unloading invisible furniture and carrying it up the stairs. Laugh, I thought I'd die. But here's what really got to me. Those mimes were a hell of a lot more careful moving furniture that only existed in their heads than those rescue-mission clowns were with the real McCoy.

"No, sir, I've got no complaints with the mimes," he continued, counting the reasons on his gloved fingers. "They're polite as hell. They're neat as pins. Maybe they're a bit emotional, but they don't talk your arm off. They don't trash the building. They pay their rent on time."

Warming to his subject, he added, "Look, I'm as big a clown booster as the next guy. But the circus doesn't stop here any more. We've got to move with the times. Sure, Waco was a nice guy and he got lucky—good for him. But he never did a lick of work, nothing but mope around in his apartment all day or hang out at the track. Now take the mimes. Five mornings a week there they go, all heading for the financial district, all walking against the wind. And after work, here they all come back, still walking against the wind."

Bozo knew the mimes were highly favored by the financial community. The banks and brokerage houses liked them because of their honesty. As the saying goes, there are no pockets in mime jumpsuits.

The landlord barked a short laugh. "No, what I just said isn't quite right, come to think of it. They go and come back together, all except this Pip I was telling you about. He works down in the financial district like the rest of them, but with him you never know what way he's going to go when he leaves for work or which way he'll come back. Strange, right?"

"Well, maybe not," said Bozo thoughtfully. "Wasn't it the great clown philosopher Plato who said that the only thing you could say for sure about the wind was that it didn't always blow from the same direction?"

He left the puzzled landlord scratching his head, went into the apartment building, and took the elevator to the fifth floor where the directory said this Pip character lived. Suppose the guy wasn't a mime? Suppose he couldn't fake the walking-against-the-wind bit? Suppose he actually had to be walking against the wind? That would mean sometimes he'd have to head off in a different direction from the others. But if the guy wasn't a mime, who was he? Bozo thought he knew.

The door to Pip's apartment was wide open. The place was quite empty of furniture. A pug-nosed man in the usual mime getup sat in midair in the middle of the room, seemingly engrossed in the play of his wrists and fingers along the keys of a baby grand that wasn't there. Bozo's polite horn-honk made the mime jump and look up quizzically.

"I'm Inspector Bozo of the Clowntown Police, Mr. Pip," said Bozo. "I'm selling tickets for our annual Policeman's Ball."

Pip smiled broadly and nodded his head. Crossing the room, he seemed to sit down at an imaginary desk, pull out an imaginary drawer, take out an imaginary checkbook, and with a visible flourish, make out an invisible check, which he handed over.

"You're very generous, Mr. Pip," said the police inspector. When the mime cocked his head modestly, Bozo continued, "You'll get your tickets in the mail, sir." Politeness made him add, "It's a nice place you've got here."

The mime beamed and, getting up, reached out his elbow and leaned with perfect ease on the precarious perch of a mantel Bozo could not see.

Back in the elevator, Bozo had to admit that Pip was one of the best mimes he'd ever seen. Boy, that mantel routine, that was really some—Bozo frowned and tugged thoughtfully at the ends of his bright bow tie. Reaching in his pocket, he pulled out the manila envelope of sales receipts and went through them until he came to the word he was looking for. When the elevator doors opened, he crossed to the lobby phonebooth and skimmed through the classified ads, stopping to read in several places. Then he phoned for a police backup.

Rejoining the landlord out on the street, Bozo asked, "Did one of the mimes who helped Pip move in have a skull-and-crossbones tattoo on his hand?"

"Now that you mention it, one did. Strange. Mimes aren't much for tattoos. What's going on?"

"That's easy," said Bozo. "Those weren't mimes moving mock furniture. They were clowns in stolen mime outfits lugging real furniture up the stairs."

The landlord looked bewildered.

"Okay," said Bozo. "Do you know what the S-T in S-T Furniture Company stands for? See-Through, that's what. They make transparent home furnishings like fireplaces and mantels. And Crystal Palace Furniture only deals in glass tables and chairs and things like that. And surprise, surprise, PlexiGrandi Company makes Plexiglas pianos."

"So what're you telling me?"

"That your old tenant, Waco the clown, moved right back in again as Pip the mime. For him, clowning was a dead-end street. He dreamed of sending his kids to mime school to learn the basics—the tough stuff, like sitting on chairs and leaning on mantels that aren't really there. That meant passing himself off as a mime. Transparent furniture seemed the easiest way."

"So he wants his kids to have a better future than he did," said the landlord. "Since when was that a crime? Just between us, and in case you hadn't noticed, being a clown isn't what it used to be. So big deal. Listen, you don't tell anybody about Waco, I won't either."

"I wish it was that simple," said Bozo. "You see, Waco paid a shady clown named Bunco to set up his operation, like getting the fake mime union card, the furnishings, and the bogus mime movers. It looks like Waco gave this Bunco his clown nose as payment for all his help. And his costume, too. After all, he wasn't going to need the stuff any more. But Bunco had a little shakedown in mind. He calculated that Waco would end up in some mime job with a lot of money or insider-information lying around. Well, he was right. Where he made his mistake was thinking Waco would sit still for a lifetime of being blackmailed. Waco decided to have him killed with a custard pie."

As he spoke, a little fluorescent-yellow car with a big star on the door pulled up to the curb. Bozo's police backup had arrived. Fourteen uniformed officers got out and lined up in order of height, from a seven-foot beanpole to a dwarf no more than three feet tall. Back in the days before the cuts in the police budget, they could have gotten nineteen men out of the same car.

They were a smart-looking bunch of clowns, full of ginger and bicycle horns, eager to get the job done. Bozo divided them into two groups, one to take the stairs and his own assault group that would go up by elevator. At Bozo's signal, the policemen started tripping over themselves, bumping into each other, and trying to get through the apartment-building doorway at the same time. They were a crack unit. Even with a good dose of gaston-and-alphonsing on top of the obligatory clowning around, they were in position in record time.

The door to the false mime's apartment was closed. Signaling his men to keep clear, Bozo honked his bicycle horn at the keyhole and shouted, "Open up, Waco, it's the police! We're onto your game!"

From inside, a voice shouted, "There's nobody here named Waco! I'm Pip!

I'm a—" Then, realizing he'd given himself away, Waco snarled a defiant, "Come and get me, coppers!"

Bozo heard the sound of a window opening. He signaled his men to break down the door, and followed in after them. Later he would remember the sorry dash of the Clowntown Police across a room filled with transparent furniture with a smile, but at the time the sight filled him with dismay. His men looked like a charge of stumblebums, barking their shins on the crystal coffee table and crashing into the Plexiglas piano and falling over the sofa and chairs.

Bozo rallied his men and, hot on Waco's trail, he led them out the window and up onto the roof. They got there just in time to see the fugitive clown cross over to the neighboring roof on a narrow plank. Sprinting as fast as his big shoes would allow, Bozo reached the edge just as Waco toppled the plank down between the two buildings. Bozo knew there'd be no catching him now.

Waco knew it, too. He lingered for a moment as Bozo's men came running up. "Doing things on too big a scale was my only mistake!" he called. "Next time I'll make do with a glass cardtable and folding chair, max! I'll sleep on the floor! I'll send the kids to mime boarding school! I won't tell them the truth about their daddy until they're old enough to understand! Then it'll be our little secret!"

"You'll never pull it off!" shouted Bozo earnestly. "Every time you sat down, it'd be a lie! And what kind of life would it be for your kids, always afraid to invite their friends home, always having to hide the dark secret that their dad was a clown?"

"I'm not a clown! I never was a clown! I'm a mime!" Waco cried in a fury. Then, as if he realized his anger belied his words, he forced himself to be calm. "All my life I've felt like an outsider," he said. "I told myself it was because I was a rodeo clown in a world where the rodeos are few and far between. But deep down in my bones, I always knew I was a mime. I think maybe the Gypsies stole me from a mime cradle and sold me to a nice childless couple of rodeo clowns. Okay, I can't recapture my mime heritage for myself, but I can damn well do it for my kids."

"You lost any chance of that when you killed Bunco," said Bozo.

"Bunco deserved what he got!" shouted Waco, turning away from the edge of the roof and starting toward the top of the metal ladder that would take him down to a fire escape and safety. "He would have sucked me dry! Then he'd have started on my kids! I don't regret what I did!"

It was cold on the roof. The sun poked through the dull winter sky like a nose of brass. A mere summer ago the same sun had set, a perfect fit, soft, warm, and red, down the slot of any Clowntown street. Bozo sighed to himself. He knew what he had to do. "I've got to take you in, Waco!" he called.

The murderer continued walking toward the ladder.

Bozo's men were lined up along the edge of the roof. They turned to him for instructions, honking their horns nervously. Bozo had hoped it wouldn't come to this, but police regulations were clear—he knew what he had to do. He drew his weapon. "Stop or I'll shoot, Waco!" he ordered.

The fugitive clown had reached the roof parapet now, his hands on the metal uprights of the ladder. He gave Bozo and the other policemen standing with their drawn weapons a pitying look and shook his head.

Bozo had no other choice. As humiliating as it would be, he pulled the trigger and the flag popped out of the end of the barrel. BANG! said the flag. In the next moment, all the clown policemen fired and all the flags at the ends of their pistol barrels said BANG! One policeman had a submachine gun. Its longer flag read RATATAT! What other kinds of weapons would be issued to clowns who by nature were unable to hurt anyone directly?

Waco knew that and he should have made his escape, but when the barrel flags appeared his body gave a sudden jump and spun as though hit with a fusillade of bullets. The horrified clowns watched Waco's grip on the ladder give way finger by finger until he fell back into that long emptiness that led to the street below.

Bozo watched in sad amazement. Could Waco's parents really have been mimes? Or was his desire to be a mime so strong that when the flag fire came he'd done what any real mime would have done even if it cost him his life?

Bozo sat on the edge of his unmade bed massaging his big bare left foot, which rested on his knobby right knee. He'd been thinking about the day's events. But now he turned his thoughts to Calliope hanging around circus winter quarters with clown stars in her eyes. It seemed to him that she'd been right to go and try. And he'd been right to stay, to see in his own small way that clowns got a fair shake and gave a fair shake. After all, wasn't justice as rare as stardom?

And when push came to shove, the mimes were right, too. They'd pared things down to the essentials—a jumpsuit, a hat, imaginary flowers and butterflies. It looked like the kind of act the world needed now. Maybe the doomsayers were right. Maybe the clown days *were* numbered. Maybe they'd played the game with too heavy a hand.

Well, what the hell, clown or mime, hadn't they all sprung from the same crazy pair of ancestors, sitting arm in arm, fishing for the moon in a bucket?

Bozo reached for the bottle of Old Roustabout on the bedside table, drew out the stopper with his teeth, and looked around for his well thumbprinted glass from the night before. When he couldn't find it, he grunted and spat out the stopper. Then he turned out the light, rolled over in bed, and fell quickly into clown slumber.

DELIA SHERMAN

Miss Carstairs and the Merman

Delia Sherman is a gifted new writer in the fantasy field. In 1989 she was a Campbell Award nominee on the basis of her first novel, *Through a Brazen Mirror*, and stories such as "The Maid on the Shore" (reprinted in *The Year's Best Fantasy, First Annual Collection*), which were based on traditional British folk ballads. She is currently at work on a second novel, an historical fantasy set in France.

The following story is set, like so much of Sherman's short fiction, on the edge of the sea—not some misty fairyland shore, but the hard rocky coast of New England. It is a wistful story of a Massachusetts bluestocking who finds magic . . . and cannot let it go.

Sherman lives in Boston, Massachusetts. Her story is reprinted from *The Magazine of Fantasy and Science Fiction*.

—T.W.

Miss Carstairs and the Merman

DELIA SHERMAN

The night Miss Carstairs first saw the merman, there was a great storm along the Massachusetts coast. Down in the harbor town, old men sat in the taverns drinking hot rum and cocking a knowledgeable ear at the wind whining and whistling in the chimneys. A proper nor'easter, they said, a real widow-maker, and they huddled closer to the acrid fires while the storm gnawed at the town. It ripped shingles from roofs; it tore small boats from their moorings and flung them against the long piers. Strong gusts leaped across the dunes and set Miss Carstairs's tall white house surging and creaking like a great ship.

High on the bluffs above the town, Miss Carstairs was sitting by the uncurtained window of her study, watching the lightning dazzle on the water, and peering, from time to time, through a long telescope. With her square hands steady upon the telescope's barrel, she watched the windblown sand and rain scour her garden and pit the glass of her window. In kinetoscopic bursts, she saw a capsized dinghy scud past her beach and a gull beaten across the dunes; and at about midnight, she saw a long, dark, seal-sleek shape cast up on the rocky beach, flounder for a moment in the retreating surf, and then lie still.

Miss Carstairs calculated that the shape lay not two hundred yards from her aerie in a shallow tidal pool, which was, for the moment, holding it safe. She put aside the telescope and hesitated for a moment with her hand upon the bellpull. It was a filthy night. Yet, if it really was a seal washed into that tidal pool, she wanted to secure it before it washed out again.

The peculiarities of ocean storms and seals had been familiar to Miss Carstairs since earliest childhood. Whenever she could slip away from her nurse, she would explore the beach or the salt marshes behind her father's house, returning from these expeditions disheveled: her pinafore pockets stuffed with shells, her stockings torn and sodden, her whole small person reeking, her mother used to say, like the flats at low tide. On these occasions, Mrs. Carstairs would scold her daughter and send her supperless to bed. But her father usually contrived to slip into her room, bearing a bit of cranberry bread, perhaps, and would read to her from Linnaeus or Hans Andersen's fairy tales or Lyell's *Natural History*.

Mr. Carstairs, himself an amateur ichthyologist, delighted in his daughter's intelligence. He kept her crabs and mussels in the stone pond he had built in the conservatory for his exotic oriental fish. When Charles Darwin's *The Origin of Species* was published, he presented her with a copy for her fifteenth birthday. He would not hear of her attending the village school with the children of the local fishermen, but taught her mathematics and Latin and logic himself, telling her mother that he would have no prissy governess stuffing the head of his little scientist with a load of womanish nonsense.

By the time Mr. Carstairs died, his daughter had turned up her hair and let down her skirts; but she still loved to tramp all day along the beaches. Her mother lectured her daily on the joys of the married state and drained the pond in the conservatory. Miss Carstairs was sorry about the pond, but she knew she had only to endure and she would eventually have the means to please herself. So endure she did for five years, saying, "Yes, Mama," and "No, Mama," until the day when Mrs. Carstairs followed her husband to the grave, a disappointed woman.

As soon as her mother died, Miss Carstairs ordered a proper collecting case and a set of scalpels and an anatomy text from Codman and Shurtleff in Boston. She lived very much alone, despising the merchants' and fish-brokers' wives who formed the society of the town. They, in turn, despised her. Wealth, they whispered over cups of Indian tea, was utterly wasted on a woman who would all too obviously never marry, being not only homely as a haddock, but a bluestocking as well.

A bluestocking Miss Carstairs may have been, but she looked nothing like a fish. She had a broad, low brow; a long jaw; and her Scottish father's high, flat cheekbones. Wind and cold had creased her skin and made it brown as a fisherman's, and her thin hair was silver-gray like the weathered shingles on the buildings along the wharf. She was tall and sturdy and fit as a man from long tramps on the marshes. She was patient, as a scientist must be, and over the years had taught herself classification and embryology and enough about conventional scientific practices to write articles acceptable to *The American Naturalist* and the Boston Society of Natural History. By the time she was forty-nine, "E. Monroe Carstairs" had earned the reputation of being very sound on the *mollusca* of the New England coast.

In the course of preparing these articles, Miss Carstairs had collected hundreds of specimens, and little jars containing pickled *Cephalopoda* and *Gastropoda* lined her study shelves in grim profusion. But she had living barnacles and sea slugs as well, housed in the pool in the conservatory, where they kept company with lobsters and crabs and feathery sea worms in a kind of miniature ocean. When she had her father's goldfish pond repaired, Miss Carstairs had fitted it out with a series of pumps and filters to bring seawater up from the bay and keep it clean and fresh. In shape the pond was a wide oval, built up at the sides with a mortared stone coping, and it nestled in an Eden of Boston ferns and sweet-smelling mint geraniums. Miss Carstairs was very proud of it, and proud of the collection of marine life it housed. Stocking it with healthy specimens of rare fauna was the chief pleasure of her life, and summer and winter she spent much of her time out stalking the tidal flats after a neap tide or exploring the small brackish pools of the salt marshes. But nothing was as productive of unusual specimens as a roaring gale, which, in beating the ocean to a froth, swept up shells and crabs from its very floor.

As Miss Carstairs stood now with her hand upon the bellpull, her wide experience of such storms told her that she must either bring in the seal immediately, or watch it wash away with the tide. She pulled sharply on the bell, and when the maid Sarah sleepily answered it, ordered her to rouse Stephen and John without delay and have them meet her in the kitchen passage. "Tell them to bring the lantern, and the stretcher we used for the shark last spring," she said. "And bring me my sou'wester and my boots."

Soon the two oilclothed men, yawning behind their hands, awaited Miss Carstairs in the dark kitchen. Although they had been rousted out of their beds in the middle of the night and knew they were in for a wet and dangerous scramble over slippery ground, the men were unresentful. Truth to tell, they were secretly proud of the forthright eccentricity of their mistress, who kept lobsters in a fancy pool instead of eating them, and traipsed manfully over the marshes and mud flats in all weather. If Miss Carstairs wanted to go out into the worst nor'easter in ten years to collect some rare grampus or other, then the least they could do was to go along and help her.

Miss Carstairs led the way with the lantern, and the little company groped its way down the slippery wooden stairs to the beach. The thunder had rolled away, taking with it the confusing spurts of lightning. The lantern illuminated glimpses of scattered flotsam: gouts of seaweed and beached fish, broken seagulls and strange shells. Miss Carstairs, untempted, ran straight before the wind toward the rocks at the lip of the bay and the tidal pool imprisoning her quarry.

Whatever the creature was, it was not a seal. The dim yellow lantern gave only the most imperfect outline of its shape, but Miss Carstairs could see that it was more slender than a seal, and lacked a pelt. Its front flippers looked peculiarly long and flexible, and it seemed to have a crest of bony spines down its back. Something was familiar about its shape, about the configuration of its upper body and head.

Miss Carstairs was just bending to take a closer look, when Stephen's "Well, Miss?" drew her guiltily upright. The wind was picking up; it was more than time to be getting back to the house. She stood out of the way while the men unfolded a bundle of canvas and sticks into a wide stretcher like a sailor's hammock suspended between two long poles. Into this contrivance they bundled their find and, in case it might still be alive, covered it with a blanket soaked in seawater. Clumsily, because of the wind and the swaying weight of their burden, the men crossed the beach and labored up the wooden stairs, wound through the garden and up two shallow stone steps to the large glass conservatory built daringly onto the sea side of the house.

When Miss Carstairs opened the conservatory door, the wind extinguished most of the gaslights Sarah had thoughtfully lit there. So it was in a poor half-light that the men hoisted their burden to the edge of the pool and tipped the creature out onto the long boulder that had once served as a sunning place for Mr. Carstairs's terrapins. The lax body rolled heavily onto the rock; Miss Carstairs eyed it doubtfully while the men panted and wiped at their streaming faces.

"I don't think you should submerge it entirely," she said finally. "If it's still alive, being out of the water a little longer shouldn't hurt it, and if it is not, I don't want the lobsters getting it before I do." The men positioned the creature, then shut off the gas cocks and squished off to their beds.

For a few minutes, Miss Carstairs stood biting thoughtfully at her forefinger and looking down at her new specimen. Spiky and naked, it did not look like anything she had ever seen or read about in Allen, Grey, or von Haast. But many common objects look strange in the dark, and calling Sarah back to relight the gas hardly seemed worthwhile. She might as well go to bed and study her find by the light of day. But when she ascended the stairs, her footsteps led her not to her bedroom but to her study, where she spent the rest of the night in restless perusal of True's *Catalog of Aquatic Mammals*.

At six o'clock, Miss Carstairs rang for Sarah to bring her rolls and coffee. By 6:30 she had eaten, bathed and dressed herself, and was on her way to the conservatory. Her find lay as she had left it, half in and half out of the water. Growing from its muscular tail was a powerful torso, scaleless and furless and furnished with what looked like arms, jointed like a human's and roped with long, smooth muscles under a protective layer of fat. Its head was round and flanked by a pair of ears shaped and webbed like fins.

At first, Miss Carstairs refused to believe the evidence of her eyes. Perhaps, she thought, she was overtired from reading all night. The creature, whatever it was, would soon yield its secrets to her scalpel and prove to be nothing more wonderful than a deformed porpoise or a freak manatee.

She took its head in her hands. Its skin was cool and pliant and slimy: very unpleasant to touch, as though a fish had sloughed its scales but not its protective mucus. She lifted its thick, lashless lids to reveal pearly eyes, rolled upward. She had never touched nor seen the like. A new species, perhaps? A new genus?

With a rising excitement, Miss Carstairs palpated its skull, which was hairless and smooth except for the spiny ridge bisecting it, and fingered the slight pro-trusion between its eyes and lipless mouth. The protrusion was both fleshy and cartilaginous, like a human nose, and as Miss Carstairs acknowledged the sim-ilarity, the specimen's features resolved into an unmistakably anthropoid ar-rangement of eyes, nose, mouth, and chin. The creature was, in fact, neither deformed nor freakish, but in its own way as harmoniously formed and perfectly adapted to its environment as an elephant or a chimpanzee. A certain engraving in a long-forgotten book of fairy tales came to her mind, of a wistful child with a human body and a fish's tail.

Miss Carstairs plumped heavily into her wicker chair. Here, lying on a rock in her father's goldfish pond, was a species never examined by Mr. Darwin or classified by Linnaeus. Here was a biological anomaly, a scientific impossibility. Here, in short, was a mermaid, and she, Edith Carstairs, had collected it.

Shyly, almost reverently, Miss Carstairs approached the creature anew. She turned the lax head toward her, then prodded at its wide, lipless mouth to get a look at its teeth. A faint, cool air fanned her fingers, and she snatched them back as though the creature had bitten her. Could it be alive? Miss Carstairs laid her hand flat against its chest and felt nothing; hesitated, laid her ear where her hand had been, and heard a faint thumping, slower than a human heartbeat.

In a terror lest it awake before she could examine it properly, Miss Carstairs snatched up her calipers and her sketchbook and began to make detailed notes of its anatomy. She measured its cranium, which she found to be as commodious as most men's, and traced its webbed, four-fingered hands. She sketched it full-length from all angles, then made piecemeal studies of its head and finny ears, its curiously muscled torso and its horny claws. From the absence of external genitalia and the sleek roundness of its limbs and body, she thought her specimen to be female even though it lacked the melon breasts and streaming golden hair of legend. But breasts and streaming hair would drag terribly, Miss Carstairs thought: a real mermaid would be better off without them. By the same token, a real merman would be better off without the drag of external genitals. On the question of its sex, Miss Carstairs decided to reserve judgment.

Promptly at one o'clock, Sarah brought her luncheon—a cutlet and a glass of barley water—and still the creature lay unconscious. Miss Carstairs swallowed the cutlet hastily between taking wax impressions of the creature's claws and scraping slime from its skin to examine under her microscope. She drew a small measure of its thin scarlet blood, and poked curiously at the complexity of tissue fringing the apparent opening of its ears, which had no parallel in any lunged aquatic animal. It might, she thought, be gills.

By seven o'clock, Miss Carstairs had abandoned hope. She leaned over her mermaid, pinched the verdigris forearm between her nails, and looked closely at the face for some sign of pain. The wide mouth remained slack; the webbed ears lay flat and unmoving against the skull. It must be dead after all. It seemed that she would have to content herself with dissecting the creature's cadaver, and now was not too early to begin. So she laid out her scalpels and her bone saw, and rang for the men to hoist the specimen out of the pool and onto the potting table.

"Carefully, carefully, now." Miss Carstairs hovered anxiously as Stephen and John struggled with the slippery bulk, and sighed as they dropped it belly-down over the stone coping. Suddenly the creature gave a great huff of air and twitched as though it had been electrified. Then it flopped backward, twisted eel-quick under the water, and peered up at Miss Carstairs from the bottom of the pool, fanning its webbed ears and gaping. Stumbling and slipping in their haste, the men fled.

Fairly trembling with excitement, Miss Carstairs leaned over the water and stared at her acquisition. The mer-creature, mouthing the water, stared back. The tissue in front of its ears fluttered rhythmically, and Miss Carstairs knew a moment of pure scientific gratification. Her hypothesis was proved correct; it did indeed have gills as well as lungs.

The mer undulated gently from crest to tail-tip, then darted from one extremity of the pool to the other, sending water slopping into Miss Carstairs's lap. She recoiled, shook out her skirts, and looked up to see the mer peering over the coping, its eyes deep-set, milk-blue, and as intelligently mournful as a whipped dog's.

Involuntarily, Miss Carstairs smiled, then frowned again hastily. Had not Mr. Darwin suggested that to most lower animals, a smile is a simple baring of the teeth, a sign of dominance and not of friendship? If the creature was the anthropomorph it appeared to be, a kind of oceanic ape, then might it not, as apes do, find her well-meant smile as sinister and challenging as a shark's grinning maw? Was a mer a mammal, or was it a fish, an amphibian, even a reptile? Did it properly belong to a genus at all, or was it, like the platypus, sui generis? She must reread Mr. Gunther's *The Study of Fishes* and J. E. Grey on seals.

While Miss Carstairs was pondering its origins, the mer seemed to be pondering Miss Carstairs. It held her eyes steadily with its pearly gaze, and Miss Carstairs began to fancy that she heard—no, it was rather that she sensed—a reverberant, rhythmic hushing like a swift tide withdrawing over the sand of a sea cave.

The light shimmered before her eyes, and she shook her head and recalled that she had not eaten since lunch. A glance at the watch pinned to her breast told her that it was now past nine o'clock. Little wonder she was giddy, what with having had no sleep the night before and working over the mer-creature all day. Her eyes turned again to her specimen. She had intended ringing for fish and feeding it from her own hand, but now thought she would retire to her own belated supper and leave its feeding to the servants.

The next morning, much refreshed by her slumbers, Miss Carstairs returned to the conservatory armored with a bibbed denim apron and rubber boots. The mer was sitting perched on the highest point of the rock with its long fish's tail curled around it, looking out over the rose beds to the sea.

It never moved when Miss Carstairs entered the conservatory, but gazed steadily out at the bright vista of water and rocky beach. It sat extremely upright, as if disdaining the unaccustomed weight of gravity on its spine, and its spiky crest was fully erect. One clawed hand maintained its balance on the rock; the other was poised on what Miss Carstairs was obliged to call its thigh. The wide flukes of its yellow-bronze tail draped behind and around it like a train and trailed on one side down to the water. This attitude was to become exceedingly familiar to Miss Carstairs in the weeks and months that followed; but on this first morning, it struck her as being at once human and alien, pathetic and comic, like a trousered chimpanzee riding a bicycle in a circus.

Having already sketched it from all angles, what Miss Carstairs chiefly wanted now was for the mer to do something. Now that it was awake, she was hesitant to touch it, for its naked skin and high forehead made it look oddly human, and its attitude forbade familiarity. Would it hear her, she wondered, if she called it? Or were those earlike fans merely appendages to its gills?

Standing near the edge of the pool, Miss Carstairs clapped her hands sharply. One fluke stirred in the water, but that might have been coincidence. She cleared her throat. Nothing. She climbed upon a low stool, stood squarely in the creature's field of vision, and said quite firmly, "How d'ye do?" Again, nothing, if she excepted an infinitesimal shivering of its skin that she might have imagined. "Boo!" cried Miss Carstairs then, waving her arms in the air and feeling more than a little foolish. "Boo! Boo!"

Without haste, the mer brought its eyes to her face and seemed to study her with a grave, incurious attention. Miss Carstairs climbed down and clasped her hands behind her back. Now that she had its attention, what would she do with it?

Conquering a most unscientific shrinking, Miss Carstairs unclasped her hands and reached one of them out to it, palm upward, as if it had been a strange dog. The mer immediately dropped from its upright seat to a sprawling crouch, and to Miss Carstair's horrified fascination, the movement released from a pouch beneath its belly a boneless, fleshy ocher member that could only be its— unmistakably male—genitalia.

Feeling a most uncomfortable heat in her cheeks, Miss Carstairs hid her confusion in a Boston fern, praying that the merman would withdraw his nakedness, or at least hide it in the water. But when she turned back, he was still stretched at full length along the stone, his outsized privates boldly—Miss Carstairs could only think defiantly—displayed. He was smiling.

There was nothing pleasant, welcoming, friendly, or even tangentially human about the merman's smile. His mouth gaped and was full of needle teeth. The palate was deeply ridged, the gorge pale rose and palpitating. He had no tongue.

Although she might be fifty years old and a virgin, Miss Carstairs was no delicate maiden lady. Before she was a spinster or even a woman, she was a naturalist, and she immediately forgot the merman's formidable sexual display in wonder at his formidable dentition. Orally, at least, the merman was all fish. His gaping grin displayed to advantage the tooth plate lining his lower jaw, the respiratory lamellae flanking his pharynx, the inner gill septa. Miss Carstairs seized her notebook, licked the point of her pencil, and began to sketch diligently. Once she glanced up to verify the double row of teeth in the lower jaw. The merman was still grinning at her. A moment later she looked again; he had disappeared. Hurriedly, Miss Carstairs laid aside her book and searched the pool. Yes, there he was at the deep end, belly-down against the pebbled bottom.

Miss Carstairs seated herself upon the coping to think. If the merman had noted her shock at the sight of his genitals, then his flourishing them might be interpreted as a deliberate attempt to discomfit his captor. On the other hand, the entire display could have been a simple example of instinctive aggression, like a male mandrill presenting his crimson posterior to an intruder. Had the merman acted from instinct or intelligence?

A light touch on her hand roused Miss Carstairs from her meditations. Considerably startled, she nonetheless refrained from snatching her hand away, instead slowly moving her head until she could see into the pool. The merman floated just below her, his hand alone breaking the surface of the water, and Miss Carstairs found herself staring full into his iridescent eyes. She heard—or thought she heard—a noise of water rushing over sand; saw—or thought she saw—a glimmer as of sun filtered through clear water. Then the merman somersaulted neatly and dove into a hollow under the rock.

Miss Carstairs mounted to her study and picked up her pen to record her observations. As she inscribed the incident, she became increasingly convinced that the merman's action must be the result of deliberate intention. No predator—and the merman's teeth left no doubt that he was a predator—would instinctively bare rather than protect the most vulnerable portion of his anatomy. He must, therefore, have exposed himself in a gesture of defiance and contempt. But such a line of reasoning, however theoretically sound, did not go far in proving that her merman was capable of reasoned behavior. She must find a way to test his intelligence empirically.

Lifting her eyes from her notebook, Miss Carstairs looked blindly out over the autumn-bright ocean glittering below her. The duke of Argyll had written that Man was unique among animals in being a tool-user. On the other hand, Mr. Darwin had argued persuasively that chimpanzees and orangutans commonly use sticks and stones to open hard nuts or knock down fruit. But surely no animal lower than an ape would think to procure his food using anything beyond his own well-adapted natural equipment?

Since he was immured in a kind of free-swimming larder, Miss Carstairs could not count upon the merman's being hungry enough to spring her trap for the bait alone, so the test must engage his curiosity. Trap: now there was an idea. What if she were to use one of the patent wire rattraps stacked in the garden shed? She could put a fish in a rattrap—a live fish, she thought, would prove more attractive than a dressed one—and offer the merman an array of tools with which to open it—a crowbar, perhaps a pair of wire snips. Yes, thought Miss Carstairs, she would put the fish in a rattrap and throw it in the pool to see what the merman would make of it.

Next morning the merman had resumed his station on the rock looking, if anything, more woebegone than he had the day before. Somewhat nervously, Miss Carstairs entered the conservatory carrying a bucket of water with a live mackerel in it. She was followed by Stephen, who was laden with the rattrap, a crowbar, a pair of wire snips, and a small hacksaw. With his help, Miss Carstairs introduced the mackerel into the trap and lowered it into the deep end of the pool. Then she dismissed Stephen, positioned herself in the wicker chair, pulled *Descent of Man* from her pocket, and pretended to read.

For a quarter of an hour or so, the tableau held. Miss Carstairs sat, the merman sat, the rattrap with its mackerel rested on the sandy bottom of the pool, and the tools lay on the coping as on a workbench, with the handles neatly turned toward their projected user. Finally, Miss Carstairs slapped over the page and humphed disgustedly; the merman slithered off the rock into the pool.

A great rolling and slopping of briny water ensued. When the tumult ceased, the merman's head popped up, grinning ferociously. He was clearly incensed, and although his attitude was comic, Miss Carstairs was not tempted to laugh.

With an audible snap, the merman shut his gaping mouth, lifted the rattrap onto the rock, hauled himself up beside it, and carefully examined the tools set out before him. The wire snips he passed over without hesitation. The hacksaw he felt with one finger, which he hastily withdrew when he caught it upon the ragged teeth; Miss Carstairs was interested to see that he carried the injured member to his mouth to suck just as a man or a monkey would. Then he grasped the crowbar and brought it whistling down upon the trap, distorting it enough for him to see that one end was not made all of a piece with the rest. He steadied the trap with one hand and, thrusting the crowbar through the flap, pried it free with a single mighty heave. Swiftly, he reached inside and grabbed the wildly flapping mackerel.

For a time the merman held the fish before him as if debating what to do with it. He looked from the fish to Miss Carstairs and from Miss Carstairs to the fish, and she heard a sound like a sigh, accompanied by a slight fluttering of his gill flaps. This sigh, combined with his habitual expression of settled melancholy, made his attitude so like that of an elderly gentleman confronted with unfamiliar provender that Miss Carstairs smiled a little in spite of herself. The merman stiffened and gazed at her intently. A long moment passed, and Miss Carstairs heard once more a low susurration, saw once more a silver-blue glittering.

Now, Miss Carstairs was not a woman given either to the vapors or to lurid imaginings. Thunderstorms that set more delicate nerves quivering merely stimulated her; bones and entrails left her unmoved. Furthermore, she was never ill and had never been subject to sick headaches. So, when her head began to throb and her eyes to dazzle with sourceless pinwheels of light, Miss Carstairs simply closed her eyes to discover whether the effect would disappear. The sound of rushing waters receded; the throb subsided to a dull ache. She opened her eyes to the merman's pearly stare, and sound and pain and glitter returned.

At this point she thought it would be only sensible to avert her eyes. But being sensible would not teach her why the merman sought to mesmerize her or why his stare caused her head to ache so. Briefly, she wondered whether he intended to crawl from his rock and tear out her throat with his needle teeth when she was sufficiently stupified. She dismissed the thought half conceived and abandoned herself to his gaze.

All at once, Miss Carstairs found herself at sea. Chilly green-gray depths extended above and below her; fishy shadows darted past the edges of her vision. She was swimming in a strong and unfamiliar current. The ocean around her tasted of storm and rocks and fear. She knew beyond doubt that she was being swept ever closer to a strange shore, and although she was strong, she was afraid. Her tail scraped sand; the current crossed with windblown waves and conspired to toss her ashore. Bruised, torn, gasping for breath in the thin air, Miss Carstairs fainted.

She came to herself some little time later, her eyes throbbing viciously and her ears ringing. The merman was nowhere to be seen. Slowly, Miss Carstairs dragged herself to her chair and rang for Sarah. She would need tea, perhaps even a small brandy, before she could think of mounting the stairs. She felt slightly seasick.

When Sarah came into the conservatory, she exclaimed in shock at her mistress's appearance. "I've had a bit of a turn," said Miss Carstairs shortly. "No doubt I stayed up too late last night reading. If you would bring me some brandy and turn down my bed, I think I should like to lie down. No,"—in answer to Sarah's inquiring look—"you must not call Dr. Bland. I have a slight headache; that is all."

Some little time later, Miss Carstairs lay in her darkened bedroom with a handkerchief soaked in eau de cologne pressed to her aching forehead. She did not know whether to exult or to despair. If her recent vision had been caused by the feverish overexcitement of an unbridled imagination, she feared that excessive study, coupled with spinsterhood, had finally driven her mad as her mother had always warned her it would.

But if the vision had been caused by the merman's deliberate attempt to "speak" to her, she had made a discovery of considerable scientific importance.

Miss Carstairs stirred impatiently against her pillows. Suppose, for the sake of argument, that the experience was genuine. That would suggest that some-where in the unexplored deeps of the ocean was a race of mermen who could cast images, emotion, even sounds, from mind to mind. Fantastic as the thing sounded, it could be so. In the first edition of the *Origin*, Mr. Darwin had said that over the ages a bear might develop baleen and flippers, evolving finally into a kind of furry whale, if living upon plankton had become necessary to the species' survival. Why should not some ambitious prehistoric fish develop arms and a large, complex, brain, or some island-dwelling ape take to the sea and evolve gills and a tail?

The general mechanism of evolution might, given the right circumstances, produce anthropoid creatures adapted for life in the sea. And evolution could also account for a telepathic method of communication, just as it accounted for a verbal one. To Miss Carstairs's mind, the greater mystery was how she could have received and understood a psychic message. Presumably, some highly evolved organ or cerebral fold peculiar to mermen transmitted their thoughts; how could she, poor clawless, gill-less, forked creature that she was, share such an organ?

A particularly stabbing pain caused Miss Carstairs to clutch the handkerchief to her brow. She must rest, she thought. So she measured herself a small dose of laudanum, swallowed it, and slept.

Next morning, armed with smelling salts and a pair of smoked glasses that had belonged to her mother, Miss Carstairs approached the conservatory in no very confident mood. Her brain felt sore and bruised, almost stiff, like a long-immobilized limb that had been suddenly and violently exercised. Hesitantly, she peered through the french doors; the merman was back on his rock, staring out to sea. Determined that she would not allow him to overcome her with his visions, she averted her gaze, then marched across the conservatory, seated herself firmly in her chair, and perched the smoked glasses on her nose before daring to look up.

Whether it was the smoked glasses or Miss Carstairs's inward shrinking that weakened the effect of the merman's stare, this second communion was less intimate than the first. As if they were images painted on thin silk, Miss Carstairs saw a coral reef and jewellike fish darting and hovering over the seafloor. This picture was accompanied by a distant chorus of squeaks, whistles, and random grunts, but she did not feel the press of the ocean upon her or any emotion other than her own curiosity and wonder.

"Is that your home?" she asked absurdly, and the images stopped. The merman's face did not, apparently could not, change its expression, but he advanced his sloping chin and fluttered his webbed fingers helplessly in front of his chest. "You're puzzled," said Miss Carstairs softly. "I don't wonder. But if you're as intelligent as I hope, you will deduce that I am trying to speak to you in my way as you are trying to speak to me in yours."

This speech was answered by a pause, then a strong burst of images: a long-faced grouper goggling through huge, smoky eyes; a merman neatly skewered on a harpoon; clouds of dark blood drifting down a swift current. Gasping in pain, Miss Carstairs reeled as she sat and, knocking off the useless smoked spectacles, pressed her hands to her eyes. The pain subsided to a dull ache.

"I see that I shall have to find a way of talking to you," she said aloud. Fluttering claws signed the merman's incomprehension. "When you shout at me, it is painful." Her eye caught the hacksaw still lying by the pool. She bent, retrieved it, offered it to the merman blade-first. He recoiled and sucked his finger reminiscently. Miss Carstairs touched her own finger to the blade, tore the skin, then gasped as she had when he had "shouted" at her and, clutching her bleeding finger dramatically, closed her eyes and lolled back in her chair.

A moment passed. Miss Carstairs sat slowly upright as a sign that the performance was over. The merman covered his face with his fingers, webs spread wide to veil his eyes.

It was clearly a gesture of submission and apology, and Miss Carstairs was oddly moved by it. Cautiously, she stood, leaned over the coping, and grasped him lightly on one wrist. He stiffened, but did not pull away. "I accept your apology, merman," she said, keeping her face as impassive as his. "I think we've had enough for one day. Tomorrow we'll talk again."

Over the course of the next few weeks, Miss Carstairs learned to communicate with her merman by working out a series of dumb shows signifying various simple commands: "Too loud!" and "Yes" and "No." For more complex communications, she spoke to him as he spoke to her: by means of images.

The first day, she showed him an engraving of the Sirens that she had found in an illustrated edition of *The Odyssey*. It showed three fishtailed women, rather heavy about the breasts and belly, disposed gracefully on a rocky outcropping, combing their long falls of hair. The merman studied this engraving attentively. Then he fluttered his claws and sighed.

"I don't blame you," said Miss Carstairs. "They look hardly able to sit on the rocks and sing at the same time, much less swim." She laid aside *The Odyssey* and took up a tinted engraving of a parrot fish. The merman advanced his head and sniffed, then snatched the sheet from Miss Carstairs's fingers and turned it this way and that. Catching her eyes, he sent her a vision of that same fish, shining vermilion and electric blue through clear tropical waters, its hard beak patiently scraping polyps out of coral dotted with the waving fronds of sea worms. Suddenly one of the coral's thornier parasites revealed itself as a merman's hand by grabbing the parrot fish and sweeping it into the predator's jaw. "Oh," said Miss Carstairs involuntarily as she became aware of an exciting, coppery smell and an altogether unfamiliar taste in her mouth. "Oh my."

She closed her eyes, and the vision dispersed. Her mouth watering slightly and her hands trembling, she picked up her pen to describe the experience. Something of her confusion must have communicated itself to the merman, for when she next sought his eyes, he gave her a gossamer vision of a school of tiny fish flashing brilliant fins. Over time, she came to recognize that this image served him for a smile, and that other seemingly random pictures signified other common expressions: sunlight through clear water was laughter; a moray eel, heavy, hideous, and sharply toothed, was weeping.

Autumn wore on to winter, and Miss Carstairs became increasingly adept at eliciting and reading the merman's images. Every morning she would go to the conservatory bearing engravings or sepia photographs and, with their help, wrestle some part of the merman's knowledge from him. Every afternoon, weather permitting, she would pace the marshes or the beach, sorting and digesting. Then, after an early dinner, she would settle herself at her desk and work on "A Preliminary Study of the Species *Homo Oceanus Telepathicans*, With Some Observations on His Society."

This document, which she was confident would assure E. Monroe Carstairs a chapter of his own in the annals of marine biology, began with a detailed description of the merman and the little she had been able to learn about his anatomy. The next section dealt with his psychic abilities; the next was headed "Communication and Society":

> As we have seen (Miss Carstairs wrote), quite a sophisticated level of communication can be achieved by an intelligent merman. Concrete as they necessarily are, his visions can, when properly read and interpreted, convey abstract ideas of some subtlety. But they can convey them only to one other mer. Chemical exudations (*vide supra*) signal only the simplest mer emotions: distress, lust, fear, anger, avoidance; booms and whistles attract a companion's attention or guide cooperative hunting maneuvers. All fine shades of meaning, all philosophy, all poetry, can pass from one mer to another only by direct and lengthy mutual gazing.
>
> This fact, coupled with an instinctive preference for solitude similar to that of the harlequin bass (*S. tigrinus*) and the reef shark (*C. melanopterus*), has prevented *H. oceanus* from evolving anything that *H. sapiens* would recognize as a civilized society. From the time they can safely fend for themselves at about the age of six, mer-children desert their parents to swim and hunt alone, often faring from one ocean to another in their wanderings. When one of these mer-children meets with another of approximately its own age, it will generally pair with

that mer-child, whether it be of the same or of the opposite sex. Such a pairing, which seems to be instinctive, is the merman's only means of social intercourse. It may last from a season or two to several years, but a couple with an infant commonly stay together until the child is ready to swim free. Legends exist of couples who swam faithfully together for decades, but as a rule, the enforced and extreme intimacy of telepathic communication comes to wear more and more heavily on one or both members of a pair until they are forced to part. Each mer then swims alone for whatever period of time fate and preference may dictate, until he meets with another receptive mer, when the cycle begins again.

Because of this peculiar behavioral pattern, the mer-folk can have no government, no religion, no community; in short, no possibility of developing a civilization even as primitive as that of a tribe of savages. Some legends they do have (*vide* Appendix A), some image-poems of transcendent beauty remembered and transmitted from pair to pair over the ages. But any new discovery made by a merman or merwoman swimming alone may all too easily die with its maker or become garbled in transmission between pair and pair. For, except within the pair-bond, the mer's instinct for cooperation is not strong.

The more she learned about the customs of the mer-folk, the more conscious Miss Carstairs became of how fortunate she was that the merman had consented to speak to her at all. Mermen swimming solitary were a cantankerous lot, as likely to attack a chance-met pair or single mer as to flee it.

So Miss Carstairs realized that the merman must look upon her as his companion for the duration of his cycle of sociability, but she did not understand the implications such a companionship had for him. When she thought of his feelings at all, she imagined that he viewed her with the same benevolent curiosity with which she viewed him, never considering that benevolent curiosity is a peculiarly human trait.

The crisis came in early December, when Miss Carstairs determined that it was time to tackle the subject of mer reproductive biology. She knew that an examination of the rituals of courtship and mating was central to the study of any new species, and no scientist, however embarrassing he might find the subject, was justified in shirking it. So Miss Carstairs gathered together her family album and a porcelain baby doll exhumed from a trunk of old toys in the attic, and used them, along with an old anatomy text, to give the merman a basic lesson in human reproduction.

At first, it seemed to Miss Carstairs that the merman was being particularly inattentive. But close observation having taught her to recognize his moods, she realized at length that his tapping fingers, gently twitching crest, and reluctance to meet her eyes, all signaled acute embarrassment.

This, Miss Carstairs found most interesting. She tapped on his wrist to get his attention, then shook her head and briefly covered her eyes. "I'm sorry," she told him, then held out a sepia photograph of herself as a stout and solemn infant propped between her frowning parents on a horsehair sofa. "But you must tell me what I want to know."

In response, the merman erected his crest, gaped fiercely, then dove into the deepest cranny of the pool, where he wantonly dismembered Miss Carstairs's largest lobster. In disgust, she threw the baby doll into the pool after him and stalked from the room. She was furious. Without this section, her article must remain unfinished, and she was anxious to send it off. After having exposed himself on the occasion of their first meeting, after having allowed her to rummage almost at will through his memories and his mind, why would he so suddenly turn coy?

All that afternoon, Miss Carstairs pondered the merman's reaction to her question, and by evening had concluded that the mer had some incomprehensible taboo concerning the facts of reproduction. Perhaps reflection would show him that there was no shame in revealing them to her, who could have only an objective and scientific interest in them. It never occurred to her that it might bewilder or upset the merman to speak of mating to a female to whom he was bonded, but with whom he could never mate.

The next morning, Miss Carstairs entered the conservatory to see the merman sitting on his rock, his face turned sternly from the ocean and toward the door. Clearly, he was waiting for her, and when she took her seat and lifted her eyes to his, she felt absurdly like a girl caught out in some childish peccadillo and called into her mother's sitting room to be chastised.

Without preamble, the merman sent a series of images breaking over her. Two mer—one male, one female—swam together, hunted, coupled. Soon they parted, one to the warm coral reefs, the other to arctic seas. The merwoman swam, hunted, explored. A time passed: not long, although she could not have told how she knew. The merwoman met a merwoman, drove her away, met a merman, flung herself upon him amorously. This exchange was more complex than the earlier couplings; the merman resisted and fled when it was accomplished.

The merman began to eat prodigiously. He sought a companion and came upon a merman, with whom he mated, and who hunted for him when he could no longer easily hunt for himself. As the merman became heavier, he seemed to become greedier, stuffing his pouch with slivers of fish as if to hoard them. How ridiculous, thought Miss Carstairs. Then, all at once, a tiny crested head popped up from the merman's pouch, and the scales covering it gave a writhing heave. Tiny gills fluttered; tiny arms worked their way out of the pouch. Claiming its wandering gaze with iridescent eyes, the merman's companion coaxed the infant from its living cradle and took it tenderly into his arms.

Three days later, Miss Carstairs sent John to the village to mail the completed manuscript of her article, and then she put it out of her mind as firmly as she could. Brooding, she told herself, would not speed it any faster to the editor's desk or influence him to look more kindly upon it once it got there. In the meanwhile, she must not waste time. There was much more the merman could tell her, much more for her to learn. Her stacks of notes and manuscripts grew.

In late January, "Preliminary Study of the Species *Homo Oceanus Telepathicans*" was returned with a polite letter of thanks. As always, the editor of *The American Naturalist* admired Mr. Carstairs's graceful prose style and clear exposition, but feared that this particular essay was more a work of imagination than of scientific observation. Perhaps it could find a more appropriate place in a literary journal.

Miss Carstairs tore the note into small pieces. Then she went down to the conservatory. The merman met her eyes when she entered, recoiled, and grinned angrily at her; Miss Carstairs grinned angrily back. Obscurely, she felt that her humiliation was his fault, that he had misled or lied to her. She wanted to dissect his brain and send it pickled to the editor of *The American Naturalist*; she wanted him to know exactly what had happened and how he had been the cause of it all. But since she had no words to tell him this, Miss Carstairs fled the house for the windy marshes, where she squelched through the matted beach grass until she was exhausted. Humanity had always bored her, she thought, and now scholarship had betrayed her. She had nothing else.

Standing ankle-deep in a brackish pool, Miss Carstairs looked back across the marshes to her house. The sun rode low in a mackerel sky; its light danced on the calm water around her and glanced off the conservatory's glazing. The merman would be sitting on his rock like the Little Mermaid in the tale her father had read her, gazing out over the ocean he could not reach. She had a sudden vision of a group of learned men standing around the pond, shaking their heads as they stroked their whiskers and debated whether or not this so-called merman had an immortal soul. Perhaps it was just as well the editor of *The American Naturalist* had rejected the article. Miss Carstairs could imagine sharing her knowledge of the merman with the world, but not sharing the merman himself. He had become necessary to her, she realized, her one comfort and her sole companion.

Next morning she was back in the conservatory, and on each morning succeeding that. Day after day she gazed through the merman's eyes as if he were a living bathysphere, watching damselfish and barracuda stitch silver through the greenish antlers of elkhorn coral, observing the languorous unfurling of the manta ray's wings and the pale groping fingers of hungry anemones. As she opened herself to the merman's visions, Miss Carstairs began not only to see and hear, but also to feel, to smell, even to taste, the merman's homesick memories. She became familiar with the complex symphony of the ocean, the screeching scrape of the parrot fish teeth over coral, the tiny, amatory grunts of frillfins. In the shape of palpable odors present everywhere in the water she learned the distinct tastes of fear, of love, of blood, of anger. Sometimes, after a day of vicarious exploration, she would lie in her bed at night and weep for the thinness of the air around her, the silent flatness of terrestrial night.

The snow fell without Miss Carstairs's noticing it, and melted and turned to rain, which froze again, then warmed and gentled toward spring. In her abandoned study, the ink dried in the well, and the books and papers lay strewn around the desk like old wrecks. Swimming with the merman in the open sea, Miss Carstairs despised the land. When she walked abroad, she avoided marshes and clambered instead out over the weed-slick rocks to the end of the spit, where she would stand shivering in the wind and spray, staring into the waves breaking at her feet. Most days, however, she spent in the conservatory, gazing hungrily into the merman's pearly eyes.

The merman's visions were becoming delirious with the need for freedom as, in his own way, he pleaded with Miss Carstairs to release him. He showed her mermen caught in fishermen's nets, torn beyond recognition by their struggles to escape the ropes. He showed her companions turning on each other, mate devouring mate when the cycle of one had outlasted the cycle of the other. But Miss Carstairs viewed these horrific images simply as dramatic incidents in his submarine narrative, like sharks feeding, or grouper nibbling at the eyes of drowned sailors.

When at last the merman took to sulking under the rock, Miss Carstairs sat in her wicker chair, like a squid lurking among the coral, and waited patiently for him to emerge. She knew the pond was small; she sensed that the ocean's limitless freedom was more real to him when he shared his memories of it. She reasoned that no matter how distasteful the process had become, he must eventually rise and feed her the visions she craved. If, from time to time, she imagined that he might end her tyranny by tearing out her throat, she dismissed the fear. Was he not wholly in her power? When she knew the ocean as well as he, when she could name each fish with its own song, then she might let him swim free.

Early one morning the merman woke and slithered over the rim of his gray stone prison. Seal-like, he humped himself toward the door, pulled himself up the doorframe, pressed the handle, and fumbled open the door. He crawled down the two wide steps to the garden and across the path toward the beach stair. His scales scraped off onto the sharp pebbles; his skin dulled and puckered as its protective mucus dried in the sun. When he reached the sundial in the center of the garden, he heaved himself up on his tail and sought the sea. Then he collapsed.

Some little time later, Miss Carstairs came down to find the rock empty. At first she thought the merman was hiding; only when she moved toward the pool did she notice that the floor of the conservatory was awash with water and that the door was ajar. Against all odds, her merman had deserted her.

Miss Carstairs groped for her wicker chair and sat, bereaved and betrayed as she had not been since her father's death. Her eye fell on the open door; she saw the blood and water smeared over the steps. Rising hurriedly, she followed the trail through the garden to where the merman lay sprawled across the gravel. With anxious, delicate fingers, she caressed his mouth and chest to feel the thin breath coming from his lips and the faint rhythmic beat under his ribs. His tail was scored and tattered where the scales had been torn from it.

Somewhere in her soul, Miss Carstairs was conscious of dismay and tenderness and horror. But in the forefront of her brain, she was conscious only of anger.

She had fed him, she thought; she had befriended him; she had opened her mind to his visions. How dare he abandon her? Grasping him by the shoulders, she shook him violently. "Wake up and look at me!" she shouted.

Obediently, the merman opened his opalescent eyes and conjured a vision: the face of a middle-aged human woman. It was a simian face, slope-jawed and snub-nosed, wrinkled and brown.

The ape-woman opened her mouth and spoke, showing large, flat teeth. Harsh noises scraped over Miss Carstairs's ears, bearing with them the taint of hunger and need and envy as sweat bears the scent of fear. Grimacing fearfully, the ape-woman stooped toward Miss Carstairs and seized her shoulders with long fingers that burned and stung her like anemones. Miss Carstairs tore herself from the ape-woman's poisonous grasp and covered her face with her hands.

A rough claw gripped her wrist, shook it to get her attention. Reluctantly, Miss Carstairs removed her hands and saw the merman, immovably melancholy, peering up at her. How could he bear to look at her? she wondered miserably. He shook his head, a gesture he had learned from her, and answered her with a kind of child's sketch: an angular impression of a woman's face, inhumanly beautiful in its severity. Expressions of curiosity, wonder, joy, discovery darted across the woman's features like a swarm of minnows, and she tasted as strongly of solitude as a free-swimming mer.

Through her grief and remorse, Miss Carstairs recognized the justice of each of these portraits. "Beast and angel," she murmured, remembering old lessons, and again the merman nodded. "No, I'm not a mer, am I, however much I have longed for the sea. And it isn't you I want, but what you know, what you have seen."

The merman showed her a coral reef, bright and various, which seemed to grow as she watched, becoming more complex, more brilliant with each addition; then an image of herself standing knee-deep in the sea, watching the merman swim away from her. She smelled of acceptance, resignation, inwardness—the taste of a mer parting from a loved companion.

Wearily, Miss Carstairs rubbed her forehead, which throbbed and swelled with multiplying thoughts. Her notebooks, her scholarship, her long-neglected study, all called to her through the merman's vision. At the same time, she noted that he was responding directly to her. Had she suddenly learned to speak visions? Had he learned to see words? Beyond these thoughts, Miss Carstairs was conscious of the fierce warmth of the spring sun, the rich smell of the damp soil, and the faint green rustle of growing leaves. She didn't know if they were the merman's perceptions or her own.

Miss Carstairs pulled herself heavily to her feet and brushed down her skirts with a shaking hand. "It's high time for you to be off," she said. "I'll just ring for Stephen and John to fetch the sling." Unconsciously, she sought the savor of disapproval and rum that was John's signal odor; it was several hours stale. At the same time, she had a clear vision of Stephen, wrapped in a disreputable jacket, plodding with bucket and fishing pole across the garden to the seawall. She saw him from above, as she had seen him from her bedroom window early that morning. So it was her vision, not the merman's. The scientist in her noted that fact, and also that the throbbing in her head had settled down to a gentle pulse, discernible, like the beating of her heart, only if she concentrated on it.

A laughing school of fish flashed through the ordered currents of her thoughts, and Miss Carstairs understood that the merman found her new consciousness amusing. Then a searing sense of heat and a tight, itching pain under her skin sent her running into the house shouting for John. He appeared from the kitchen. "Get a bucket and a blanket and wet down the merman," said Miss Carstairs. "You'll find him in the garden, near the sundial. Then bring the stretcher." He gaped at her uncomprehendingly. "Hurry!" she snapped, and strode off toward the seawall in search of Stephen.

Following his odor, she soon found him sitting hunched over his fishing pole and his pipe. He tasted of wet wool, tobacco, and solitude. "Stephen," she began. "I have learned everything from the merman that he is able to tell me."

Stephen turned, looked up inquiringly, and lowered his pipe.

"I have decided to release him."

"Yes, Miss," he said.

The tide was going out, and the men had to carry their burden far past the spit and the tidal pool where the merman had first washed ashore. It was heavy going, for the wet sand was soft and the merman was heavy. When they came at last to the water, Miss Carstairs stood by as they released the merman into the shallows, then waded out up to her knees to stand beside him. The sun splintered the water into blinding prisms; she turned her eyes inshore, away from the glare. Behind her, Stephen and John were trudging back toward the beach, and above them the conservatory glittered like a crystal jewel box. Sharp tastes of old seaweed and salt-crusted rocks stung her nose. Squinting down, Miss Carstairs saw the merman floating quietly against the pull of the sea, one webbed hand grasping the sodden fabric of her skirt. His crest was erect, his mouth a little open. When he turned his pearly eyes to her, Miss Carstairs read joy in them, and something like regret.

"I shall not forget what you have shown me," said Miss Carstairs, although she knew the words to be superfluous. Mentally, she called up the ape-woman and the scientist, and fused them into a composite portrait of a human woman, beast and angel, heart and mind, need and reason; and she offered that portrait to the merman as a gift, an explanation, a farewell. Then he was gone, and Miss Carstairs began to wade back to shore.

REGINALD BRETNOR

Unknown Things

"Unknown Things" has absolutely nothing supernatural in it and there is no onstage violence. That doesn't stop it from being one of the most disturbing pieces in this book. Nor did it keep it from being published in the final issue of *Twilight Zone* magazine.

The author of this piece, Reginald Bretnor, has been a prolific writer of short fiction for many years. He is known particularly for his humorous work, especially the long-running "Adventures of Ferdinand Feghoot Through Time and Space," which has brightened the pages of *The Magazine of Fantasy and Science Fiction* for decades. His novel, *Schimmelhorn's Gold* was published in 1988.

—E.D.

Unknown Things

REGINALD BRETNOR

I have met any number of collectors during my thirty years in the antique trade, greedy ones (though of course they're all greedy one way or another,) and some with superb taste and a deep understanding of their fields, some with book knowledge and no taste at all, others who collect status symbols or security blankets, rare people with whom it is a joy to converse and many more utter bores, and others still so unbelievably eccentric that they defy classification. But Andreas Hoogstraten was strangest of them all. Always polite, almost always smiling, he still seemed to carry with him that eerie coldness you find in haunted houses. Neither his obvious wealth nor his perfect tailoring, neither his patrician nose, sleek blond hair, and thick, impossibly yellow eyebrows, nor a voice as soft and gentle as a wooing dove's could conceal it, at least from me.

I met him first in a Glastonbury pub. Every year, I'd go to England, buy an ancient van, and spend two months at least driving around and about, through Scotland and back down to Wales and Cornwall, buying big antiques and filling them with little antiques, then for the last third of my time crossing over to the continent and doing the same thing in France and the Low Countries. When the van was full, I'd ship it back as deckload on a freighter—this was in the days when you could do that—and drive it home to Saybrook from wherever it landed. It was a lot of fun, and I enjoyed every bit of it.

The Glastonbury pub was called the Weeping Nun—after some local ghost story—with an eighteenth-century sign that showed its dismal subject against a background of ancient tombstones and a silver moon—but inside it was the essence of English country hospitality, with all the dark wood and pewter and hunting prints you might expect, a great fireplace fit for roasting haunches of beef but cold now in the summertime, and neither a jukebox nor a telly to ruin the atmosphere. I went there with a local dealer, Tod Bardsley, with whom I had done business for several years, and we were just about to have lunch when Hoogstraten came in. He waved. He strode over to our table, carrying his cold aura with him.

"Mr. Bardsley, they said you'd be here, but I see you're with a friend?"

Bardsley nudged my foot under the table. He moved over. "Ah, do sit down, Mr. Hoogstraten," he invited. "Charles here won't mind. He's a fellow dealer—" he chuckled, "—always happy to meet another customer, like all of us."

We were introduced. I shook Hoogstraten's tense, cold hand. I was, I said, pleased to meet him. I was indeed a dealer, but I was a long way from home.

Briefly, Bardsley told him about my yearly trips, while the girl brought us two half-and-halfs and took his order for a whiskey and soda.

"You really must get around," he commented, looking at me intently. "I imagine you see a far greater variety of things than the average dealer, don't you?"

"Rather!" laughed Bardsley. "There's not a shop from Land's End to John o' Groat's Charlie's not been in, to say nothing of across Channel. I daresay he's probably seen a thing or two that'd strike your fancy."

"What do you collect?" I asked.

He turned his head, and I found myself looking directly into his lashless eyes. They were almost a matte blue, reminding me of Wedgwood Parian ware, and they looked dry, as though they'd never known tears. "What do I collect?" he said, "As our friend here will tell you, I buy anything I do not understand. I do not mean the expert's understanding of antiques and works of art. If I do not know what a thing is, if I cannot imagine what it was made for, it intrigues me, and if it's for sale I buy it. You see, if I do not know, and if nobody can tell me, it makes me determined to find out, to solve the problem. Where is your shop?"

"In Saybrook, in Connecticut."

"Well, that's certainly near enough to me. My apartment's in New York."

We exchanged cards, and he said he'd take a run up one of these days and have a look around and made me promise to keep my eyes peeled for any of his mysterious objects. He was, he told me, on his way to Istanbul and the Near East generally, and perhaps to Nepal and, now that the Chinese were letting down the barriers, to Tibet.

Shortly after our lunch arrived, he rose to go, saying he'd see Bardsley later at the shop, and once more he made me promise to look out for him.

He left, and I asked Tod about him.

"He's a rum one, Charlie. Buys anything if you can't tell him what it is, and pays well too. Last time in my place, he saw a weird cast-iron tool with a lot of cogs and a twisty handle that somehow didn't seem to connect with anything. He peered at it and peered at it, and finally took it with him looking like the cat fresh from the cream jug. A year or so back, too, I found him a painting— a dark thing like something seventeenth-century Dutch—but not like any you ever saw. The more you tried to make out what the subject was, the odder it looked. But it was done by a real artist, you could tell that. He paid me seven hundred without a quiver. And the real beauty of it is, he buys things that otherwise you'd have on hand forever—so what if he is strange looking, with those crazy eyebrows and blue-blue eyes?"

I told him then about the coldness, but he said the man had never affected him that way, so I put the thought aside as a quirk of my own.

Now I know that it was not.

Actually, Hoogstraten never did take the trouble to come up to Saybrook and visit my shop, and for three or four months I almost forgot about him. Then, at a flea market, I found a gadget I couldn't make head or tail of—one which ordinarily I'd have passed by without a second look. It was beautifully made of brass and polished steel, and its fitted mahogany box clearly went back to the last decade of the nineteenth century. Cased with it were eight or ten brass wheels, the rim of each serrated with geometrical neatness and with its individual pattern. It had a central axis to which these might have been affixed, a plunger like a date-stamp's, a spirit level, and two calibrated dials the purpose of which I couldn't even guess at. The man who had it thought it might have been a check-writing device, but he couldn't tell me how it possibly could have worked.

I bought the thing for less than twenty dollars, and that night I phoned Hoogstraten and was pleased to find him back from his journeyings. I described it to him, and instantly his voice came alive with interest. No, he couldn't possibly come up to Saybrook, not then, but would I bring it to New York?

I hesitated, for it seemed like quite an expedition for what I assumed would be a pretty petty deal, and at once he answered my unspoken question. "You needn't worry about the money part, Mr. Dennison—it is Dennison, isn't it? I am accustomed to paying well for anything that meets my criteria—at least in three figures—unless, of course, the seller has already set a lower price. In this case, even if I do not buy it, I'll make the trip worth your while."

So I agreed to bring it to him on the Sunday, and he gave me an address near Sutton Place—his card had carried only his phone number. The cab dropped me off at two in the afternoon in front of a several-story, obviously very expensively converted brownstone, with a martial doorman mounting guard at the entrance. I waited humbly while he made his phone call, and saw that there was only a single flat on each floor.

"Mr. Hoogstraten is waiting for you," he told me finally, giving my shoes and sports coat a supercilious farewell appraisal. "Take the elevator to the third floor."

The elevator was smooth and swift and new, and I was whisked to my destination in an instant. There a man-servant was waiting for me—I won't say a butler. He was short and muscular and massive, with a pale square face and huge hands. I judged him to be some sort of general factotum—chauffeur perhaps? Guard? He looked more like a hit-man. But he was polite enough, bowing me through the hall and opening the door for me.

I don't know exactly what I had expected, but it was not the Museum of Modern Art decor that greeted me, spare and stark and rectilinear, self-consciously manipulating mass and light and shadow in grays and blacks, startling whites, intrusive yellows, solid reds, some of the furniture echoing it, some tortured, twisted, with a thin scattering of anomalous ornaments. Of the objects he collected, there was no sign.

My face, I know, must have mirrored my astonishment, but he did not notice. He had eyes only for the package I was carrying, and I saw how hard his small black pupils were in their Wedgwood settings. He did not ask me to sit down. Dressed like something from a *Vanity Fair* men's fashions ad, he seized it without a word, opened it. His lips now drawn back from his almost too even teeth, he plucked the gadget from its box, hastily put the box down on a table, seated himself. For several minutes, he examined it, testing this, trying that, while I stood there uncomfortably.

Finally, "What do you suppose it is?" he said.

"I haven't the foggiest," I answered. "The man I bought it from thought it might have been intended as some sort of check protector."

He said that this was nonsense, and went back to his examination for several more long, silent minutes.

Then he looked up at me. He smiled, and again I felt wrapped in coldness. "It is satisfactory," he told me. "Yes, it is completely satisfactory. I shall derive pleasure from it." He nodded. "Indeed yes. Will five hundred be adequate?"

"You are very generous," I said, accepting the five hundred-dollar bills.

And at that point, a door opened and a woman entered. The effect was unbelievable. She paused, regarding us—and suddenly, as far as I was concerned, no one else was in the room. Her presence dominated it. She was tall, her hair coal black, as were her eyes. Her cheekbones were high. But the physical details were nothing compared with the totality. Suddenly I knew why men had imagined goddesses, and sacrificed to them, why there had been tilting in the lists and knightly quests, why late Victorian artists like Burne-Jones had so idealized the beauty of womankind. And simultaneously there was another surge, one I still feel when I remember her, that very natural one that sets your loins afire.

She turned toward us, and against all reason I was quite sure that she did not walk, but flowed, floated. Nor was she gowned for any such effect. She was dressed simply, in a tailored suit with white lace at the throat, and almost no jewelry; a brooch, a wedding ring.

Hoogstraten looked up, frowning slightly. "You're going out?" he asked.

"Yes, dear," she answered—and at the word irrational jealousy flamed in me. "Only for a—how do you say it?—for an hour or two perhaps? You do not need me here?"

She had the strangest accent I've ever heard, one I was quite unable to identify. All I can say is that somehow, to my ear, it sounded archaic.

He didn't even answer, his attention once more on the thing I'd sold him.

"Goodbye," she said, smiled very slightly at me, and left.

I had to interrupt him. "Mrs. Hoogstraten?" I asked.

"Yes, yes," he replied, a hint of irritation in his voice. "Pretty, isn't she?"

She's magnificent! I thought. But I had sense enough not to say it. It took him a moment more to remember I was there, but with a sigh he put the object down again. "Thank you, Dennison," he said. "You will call me if you find anything else, won't you? Yes, yes. Now Varig will show you out."

He must have pressed a button, because immediately the servant was at the door. Hoogstraten did not say goodbye.

That night I dreamed of her, a dream which Tennyson might have written for me, or one of the Cavalier poets, and I had a hard time explaining my abstraction to the sweet girl I was going with. *She* was in my mind, and would not leave, and I began to hope I'd never find another object for her husband, no matter how profitable the find might be.

As it turned out, during the next several months I found three things that seemed to have been made especially for him, and on each occasion he demanded that I bring them to him in New York. I justified it by telling myself that, after all, I was a dealer and could not forego such easy money, but I know now that it was far more the hope of seeing her even for a moment, of hearing her speak a few casual words. I dreamed of her time and again, and tormented myself with the thought of her embraced in her husband's coldness.

My second visit went much like the first, except that she was in the room when I arrived, again attired very simply in—but what she wore is of no moment. She stood up when I walked into her presence, and though again Hoogstraten did not introduce us, she thanked me for the machine—was it not a machine?—I had sold Andreas, which had pleased him. He was a genius. His mind, it demanded problems. . . . It was very nice of. . . .

I stood there tongue-tied, trapped by the magic radiating from her. Hoogstraten was already opening what I had brought him—a clock but not a clock. A thing with complicated clockwork in a case which could have been made by some exotic Fabergé, which told something, but not time—at least not any time that might make sense to us. After a moment, his voice still soft, he told her to leave the room, and without demur, as I stood there grinning at her foolishly, she left. For that I hated him, and almost for spite I asked him seven thousand for the thing. He paid me seventy-five hundred, again in cash, and sent me on my way.

Two months passed before I went again, two months during which I still dreamed of her, still thought of her, wondered at whatever power she had over me, at what her life might have been before she married Hoogstraten and, indeed, why she had married him.

This time, again, she was in the room when I arrived, and again she spoke to me, nothing memorable, comments about the season possibly, or how very good I was to find another treasure for Andreas. Then, once more, he sent her out; and the performance was repeated. He first became wholly absorbed in what I'd brought—what was it? Half book, half Byzantine icon?—but written in a script completely alien to me, resembling none I'd seen before, which seemed to change as its pages turned, momentarily revealing illustrations that vanished almost instantly. He was delighted with it, and paid me far more than I would have dared to ask. Then, for the first time, he became almost friendly.

"Dennison," he said, "where do these come from? Why were they made? Was it simply as a challenge to me, to my intellect? I have no doubt that some of them came from hidden cultures, arts not permitted to the masses, lost civilizations, perhaps even other worlds! But *why*? Again, I ask you, is it delib- erate? A continuing contest? To see if I, Andreas Hoogstraten, have a breaking point?" He stood. From a skeletal cabinet as convoluted as the last agony of an El Greco saint, he lifted a vessel, which I had seen before, but which I had taken simply for some far-out potter's drug-dream. He handed it to me. Perhaps a foot high, almost opaque, it was enormously heavy.

"Look at it, Dennison," he said. "Do you know what it is?"

Up close, it looked like grayish glass, but with a higher lustre, and it was much, much heavier. Like any vase, it tapered to a neck, but there the resem- blance ceased, for the neck doubled back on itself to penetrate the body halfway down and emerge again in a mouth melding with the other side.

"It is a Klein bottle, Dennison. Are you familiar with the Moebius Strip?"

"You mean a strip of paper you give a sort of twist to and then join its ends so that in effect it has one side only?"

"Exactly. Well, a Klein bottle is like that, only in three dimensions. Its inside is its outside and vice versa. Do you understand?"

I said I understood.

He took it from me, looked at it with an expression of mixed pride and anger. "I have drilled into it, Dennison. I have used a little instrument with which surgeons look into our bodies' inmost secrets. Inside it is a complex of beautifully ground crystals, and what seem to be controls and things I cannot put a name to. So far, it is the only unknown thing that has defeated me. I have had it several years, and I know no more about it than when it came to me, but my getting it could not have been an accident. It was part of the test, the challenge."

Shocked at his megalomania, I fumbled for something innocuous to say. "I —I suppose you have a pretty large collection by this time, Mr. Hoogstraten?"

He replaced the Klein bottle in the cabinet. "A large collection?" He said it with a sneer. "Dennison, I have always two or perhaps three. They do not defeat me for very long. Indeed, this is the only one I have had to keep for several years."

"But what do you do with them?" I asked. "Do you give them away or sell them?"

"Certainly not. When I have solved them, when they have served their pur- pose, I destroy them. That is the only way for me perhaps to get revenge, you understand?"

Frankly, I was horrified. I started to protest that some of them were treasures, that they exhibited superb craftsmanship, that surely scientists would be interested in them.

He cut me off before I had three words out. "Never!" he cried. "When I have solved them, they are nothing! *Nothing!* They no longer have a soul!"

He paid me even more than he had previously, and exacted a promise that I'd keep hunting for him; and I left telling myself that no matter what I found, I'd never go back again.

It was five months before I did, just after I returned from my annual trip to England, and then it was because I knew I had to see her one more time. In a sense, she had never left me. I would wake at night from my Pre-Raphaelite dreams of her, despairing, wondering how ever she could have married him— not for his money, certainly. But why, why, *why?*

So I went back. The thing I'd found was simple—a crude tool, mysterious only in the fact that it had no discernible function. This time, when the man-servant admitted me, I saw that she wasn't in the room, and all the while Hoogstraten examined what I'd brought him, I kept looking at the door through which she had come and gone, wishing, hoping.

Finally he rose. "I will take the tool," he told me, "even though it is not of so high a quality. I shall pay four hundred only."

I could control myself no longer. "I haven't seen Mrs. Hoogstraten," I said, I hoped casually.

He stopped counting money. For moments, those cold, glistening pupils stared at me. Then, "No," he said, ever so gently. "You see—" he smiled, "—I found out what she was."

BRUCE BOSTON and ROBERT FRAZIER

Return to the Mutant Rain Forest

Bruce Boston has won the Rhysling Award for poetry and the 1976 Pushcart Prize for fiction. He's the author of six collections of fiction and poetry, including *The Nightmare Collector* and *Skin Trades*. His poem, "In the Darkened Hours," was chosen for *The Year's Best Fantasy: Second Annual Collection*.

Robert Frazier has sold poetry to *Night Cry*, *F&SF*, *Asimov's*, *Weird Tales* and *Omni*. His novella, *Summer People*, recently appeared in the collection *Nantucket Slayrides*.

"Return to the Mutant Rain Forest" first appeared in *Masques III*, and will also be in the Boston/Frazier collaborative collection *Chronicles of the Mutant Rain Forest*, forthcoming from Mark Ziesing. Part of the profits will be used to aid efforts to save the rain forest.

In this poem, luscious hallucinatory imagery combines with technologically created horrors to tell a powerful story in graceful poetic form.

—E.D.

Return to the Mutant Rain Forest

BRUCE BOSTON and ROBERT FRAZIER

*Years later we come back to find the fauna and flora
more alien than ever, the landscape unrecognizable,
the course of rivers altered, small opalescent lakes
springing up where before there was only underbrush,
as if the land itself has somehow changed to keep pace
with the metaprotean life forms which now inhabit it.*

*Here magnetism proves as variable as other phenomena.
Our compass needle shifts constantly and at random,
and we must fix direction by the stars and sun alone.
Above our heads the canopy writhes in undiscovered life:
tiny albino lemurs flit silently from branch to branch,
tenuous as arboreal ghosts in the leaf purple shadow.*

*Here time seems as meaningless as our abstracted data.
The days stretch before us in soft bands of verdigris,
in hours marked by slanting white shafts of illumination.
At our feet we watch warily for the tripvines of arrowroot,
while beetles and multipedes of every possible perversion
boil about us, reclaiming their dead with voracious zeal.*

*By the light of irradiated biota the night proliferates:
a roving carpet of scavenger fungi seeks out each kill
to drape and consume the carcass in an iridescent shroud.
A carnivorous mushroom spore roots on my exposed forearm
and Tomaz must dig deeply beneath the flesh to excise
the wrinkled neon growth which has sprouted in minutes.*

We have returned to the mutant rain forest to trace
rumors spread by the natives who fish the white water,
to embark on a reconnaissance into adaptation and myth.
Where are the toucans, Genna wonders, once we explain
the cries which fill the darkness as those of panthers,
mating in heat, nearly articulate in their complexity.

Tomaz chews stale tortillas, pounds roots for breakfast,
and relates a tale of the Parakana who ruled this land.
One morning the Chief's wife, aglow, bronzed and naked
in the eddies of a rocky pool, succumbed to an attack
both brutal and sublime, which left her body inscribed
with scars confirming the bestial origins of her lover.

At term, the massive woman was said to have borne a child
covered with the finest gossamer caul of ebon-blue hair.
The fiery vertical slits of its eyes enraged the Chief.
After he murdered the boy, a great cat screamed for weeks
and stalked about their tribal home, driving them north.
His story over, Tomaz leads our way into the damp jungle.

From base camp south we hack one trail after another
until we encounter impenetrable walls of a sinewy fiber,
lianas as thick and indestructible as titanium cables,
twining back on themselves in a solid Gordian sheath,
feeding on their own past growth; while farther south,
slender silver trees rise like pylons into the clouds.

From our campo each day we hack useless trail after trail,
until we come upon the pathways that others have forged
and maintained, sinuous and waist-high, winding inward
to still farther corrupt recesses of genetic abandon:
here we discover a transfigured ceiba, its rugged bark
incised with the fresh runes of a primitive ideography.

Genna calls a halt in our passage to load her Minicam.
She circles about the tree, shrugging off our protests.
As we feared, her careless movement triggers a tripvine,
but instead of a hail of deadly spines we are bombarded
by balled leaves exploding into dust—marking us with
luminous ejecta and a third eye on Genna's forehead.

Souza dies that night, limbs locked in rigid fibrogenesis.
A panther cries; Tomaz wants us to regroup at our campo.
Genna decides she has been chosen, sacrificed for passage.
She notches her own trail to some paradise born of dream

hallucination, but stumbles back, wounded and half-mad,
the Minicam lost, a cassette gripped in whitened knuckles.

From base camp north we flail at the miraculous regrowth
which walls off our retreat to the airstrip by the river.
The ghost lemurs now spin about our heads, they mock us
with a chorus as feverish and compulsive as our thoughts.
We move relentlessly forward, as one, the final scenes
of Genna's tape flickering over and over in our brains.

In the depths of the mutant rain forest where the water
falls each afternoon in a light filtered to vermilion,
a feline stone idol stands against the opaque foliage.
On the screen of the monitor it rises up from nowhere,
upon its hind legs, both taller and thicker than a man.
See how the cellular accretion has distended its skull,
how the naturally sleek architecture of the countenance
has evolved into a distorted and angular grotesquerie,
how the taloned forepaws now possess opposable digits.
In the humid caves and tunnels carved from living vines,
where leprous anacondas coil, a virulent faith calls us.
A sudden species fashions godhood in its own apotheosis.

TATYANA TOLSTAYA

Date with a Bird

Tatyana Vladimirovna Tolstaya was born in Leningrad in 1951, attended Leningrad University, and currently lives in Moscow. Her stories appear frequently in Soviet literary journals, including *Neva*, *Novy Mir*, and *Oktyabr*, she is one of the most widely admired young writers in the Soviet Union. *On the Golden Porch*, a collection of her short fiction published by Knopf in 1989, is her first American publication. It is a volume of stories about modern Soviet life, beautifully told by an author who is the great-niece of Leo Tolstoy and the granddaughter of Alexei Tolstoy.

"Date with a Bird" is a rare flight into the realm of fantasy. Tolstaya portrays the world through the eyes of a young boy for whom the world is built of magic—a magic as fragile and fleeting as a dream. It is translated from the Russian by Antonina W. Bouis.

—T.W.

Date with a Bird

TATYANA TOLSTAYA

"Boys! Dinner time!"

The boys, up to their elbows in sand, looked up and came back to the real world: their mother was on the wooden porch, waving; this way, come on, come on! From the door came the smells of warmth, light, an evening at home.

Really, it was already dark. The damp sand was cold on their knees. Sand castles, ditches, tunnels—everything had blurred into impenetrability, indistinguishability, formlessness. You couldn't tell where the path was, where the damp growths of nettles were, where the rain barrel was . . . But in the west, there was still dim light. And low over the garden, rustling the crowns of the dark wooded hills, rushed a convulsive, sorrowful sigh: that was the day, dying.

Petya quickly felt around for the heavy metal cars—cranes, trucks; Mother was tapping her foot impatiently, holding the doorknob, and little Lenechka had already made a scene, but they swooped him up, dragged him in, washed him, and wiped his struggling face with a sturdy terry towel.

Peace and quiet in the circle of light on the white tablecloth. On saucers, fans of cheese, of sausage, wheels of lemon as if a small yellow bicycle had been broken; ruby lights twinkled in the jam.

Petya was given a large bowl of rice porridge; a melting island of butter floated in the sticky Sargasso Sea. Go under, buttery Atlantis. No one is saved. White palaces with emerald scaly roofs, stepped temples with tall doorways covered with streaming curtains of peacock feathers, enormous golden statues, marble staircases going deep into the sea, sharp silver obelisks with inscriptions in an unknown tongue—everything, everything vanished under water. The transparent green ocean waves were licking the projections of the temples; tanned, crazed people scurried to and fro, children wept. . . . Looters hauled precious trunks made of aromatic wood and dropped them; a whirlwind of flying clothing spread. . . . Nothing will be of use, nothing will help, no one will be saved,

everything will slip, list, into the warm, transparent waves. . . . The gold eight-
story statue of the main god, with a third eye in his forehead, sways, and looks
sadly to the east. . . .

"Stop playing with your food!"

Petya shuddered and stirred in the butter. Uncle Borya, Mother's brother—
we don't like him—looks unhappy; he has a black beard and a cigarette in his
white teeth; he smokes, having moved his chair closer to the door, open a crack
into the corridor. He keeps bugging, nagging, mocking—what does he want?

"Hurry up kids, straight to bed. Leonid is falling asleep."

And really, Lenechka's nose is in his porridge, and he's dragging his spoon
slowly through the viscous mush. But Petya has no intention of going to bed.
If Uncle Borya wants to smoke freely, let him go outside. And stop interrogating
him.

Petya ate doomed Atlantis and scraped the ocean clean with his spoon, and
then stuck his lips into his cup of tea—buttery slicks floated on the surface.
Mother took away sleeping Lenechka, Uncle Borya got more comfortable and
smoked openly. The smoke from him was disgusting, heavy. Tamila always
smoked something aromatic. Uncle Borya read Petya's thoughts and started
probing.

"You've been visiting your dubious friend again?"

Yes, again. Tamila wasn't dubious, she was an enchanted beauty with a
magical name, she lived on a light blue glass mountain with impenetrable walls,
so high up you could see the whole world, as far as the four posts with the signs:
South, East, North, West. But she was stolen by a red dragon who flew all over
the world with her and brought her here, to this colony of summer dachas. And
now she lived in the farthest house, in an enormous room with a veranda filled
with tubs of climbing Chinese roses and piled with old books, boxes, chests,
and candlesticks; smoked thin cigarettes in a long cigarette holder with jangling
copper rings, drank something from small shot glasses, rocked in her chair, and
laughed as if she were crying. And in memory of the dragon, Tamila wore a
black shiny robe with wide sleeves and a mean red dragon on the back. And
her long tangled hair reached down to the armrests of the chair. When Petya
grew up he would marry Tamila and lock Uncle Borya in a high tower. But
later—maybe—he would have mercy, and let him out.

Uncle Borya read Petya's mind again, laughed, and sang—for no one in
particular, but insulting anyway.

> A-*a-ana was a seamstress,*
> *And she did embroidery.*
> *Then she went on sta-age*
> *And became an actress!*
> *Tarum-pam-pam!*
> *Tarum-pam-pam!*

No, he wouldn't let him out of the tower.

Mother came back to the table.

"Were you feeding Grandfather?" Uncle Borya sucked his tooth as if nothing were wrong.

Petya's grandfather was sick in bed in the back room, breathing hard, looking out the low window, depressed.

"He's not hungry," Mother said.

"He's not long for this world," Uncle Borya said, and sucked his tooth. And then he whistled that sleazy tune again: *tarum-pam-pam!*

Petya said thank you, made sure the matchbox with his treasure was still in his pocket, and went to bed—to feel sorry for his grandfather and to think about his life. No one was allowed to speak badly of Tamila. No one understood anything.

. . . Petya was playing ball at the far dacha, which went down to the lake. Jasmine and lilacs had grown so luxuriantly that you couldn't find the gate. The ball flew over the bushes and disappeared in the garden. Petya climbed over the fence and through the bushes—and found a flower garden with a sundial in the center, a spacious veranda, and on it, Tamila. She was rocking in a black rocker, in the bright-black robe, legs crossed, pouring herself a drink from a black bottle; her eyelids were black and heavy and her mouth was red.

"Hi!" Tamila shouted and laughed as if she were crying. "I was waiting for you."

The ball lay at her feet, next to her flower-embroidered slippers. She was rocking back and forth, back and forth, and blue smoke rose from her jangling cigarette holder, and there was ash on her robe.

"I was waiting for you," Tamila repeated. "Can you break the spell on me? No? Oh dear . . . I thought . . . Well, come get your ball."

Petya wanted to stand there and look at her and hear what she would say next.

"What are you drinking?" he asked.

"*Panacea*," Tamila said, and drank some more. "Medicine for all evil and suffering, earthly and heavenly, for evening doubts, for nocturnal enemies. Do you like lemons?"

Petya thought and said: I do.

"Well, when you eat lemons, save the pits for me, all right? If you collect one hundred thousand pits and make them into a necklace, you can fly even higher than the trees, did you know that? If you want, we can fly together, I'll show you a place where there's buried treasure—but I forgot the word to open it up. Maybe we'll think of it together."

Petya didn't know whether to believe her or not, but he wanted to keep looking at her, to watch her speak, watch her rock in that crazy chair, watch the copper rings jangle. She wasn't teasing him, slyly watching his eyes to check: Well? This is interesting, isn't it? Do you like it? She simply rocked and jangled, black and long, and consulted with Petya, and he understood: she would be his friend ages unto ages.

He came closer to look at the amazing rings shining on her hand. A snake with a blue eye circled her finger three times; next to it squatted a squashed silver toad. Tamila took off the snake and let him look at it, but she wouldn't let him see the toad.

"Oh no, oh no; if you take that off, it's the end of me. I'll turn into black dust and the wind will scatter me. It protects me. I'm seven thousand years old, didn't you know?"

It's true, she's seven thousand years old, but she should go on living, she shouldn't take off the ring. She's seen so much. She saw Atlantis perish—as she flew over the doomed world wearing her lemon-pit necklace. They had wanted to burn her at the stake for witchcraft, they were dragging her when she struggled free and soared up to the clouds: why else have the necklace? But then a dragon kidnapped her, carried her away from her glass mountain, from the glass palace, and the necklace was still there, hanging from her mirror.

"Do you want to marry me?"

Petya blushed and replied: I do.

"That's settled. Just don't let me down! We'll ratify our union with a word of honor and some chocolates."

And she handed him a whole dish of candies. That's all she ate. And drank from that black bottle.

"Want to look at the books? They're piled over there."

Petya went over to the dusty mound and opened a book at random. It was a color picture: like a page from a book, but he couldn't read the letters, and on top in the corner there was a big colored letter, all entwined with flat ribbon, grasses, and bells, and above that a creature, half-bird, half-woman.

"What's that?" Petya asked.

"Who knows. They're not mine," Tamila said, rocking, jangling, and exhaling.

"Why is the bird like that?"

"Let me see. Ah, that bird. That's the Sirin, the bird of death. Watch out for it: it will choke you. Have you heard somebody wailing, cuckooing in the woods at night? That's this bird. It's a night bird. There's also the Finist. It used to fly to me often, but then we had a fight. And there's another bird, the Alkonost. It gets up in the morning at dawn, all pink and transparent, you can see through it, and it sparkles. It makes its nest in water lilies. It lays one egg, very rare. Do you know why people pick lilies? They're looking for the egg. Whoever finds it will feel a sense of longing all their life. But they still look for it, they still want it. Why, I have it. Would you like it?"

Tamila rocked once on the black bentwood rocker and went into the house. A beaded cushion fell from the seat. Petya touched it; it was cool. Tamila came back, and in her hand, jingling against the inside of her rings, was the magical egg, pink glass, tightly stuffed with golden sparkles.

"You're not afraid? Hold it! Well, come visit me." She laughed and fell into the rocker, moving the sweet, aromatic air.

Petya didn't know what it was to be depressed for life, and took the egg.

Definitely, he would marry her. He had planned to marry his mother, but now that he had promised Tamila . . . He would definitely take his mother with him, too; and if it came to that, he could take Lenechka, as well . . . but Uncle Borya—no way. He loved his mother very, very much, but you'd never hear such strange and marvelous stories as Tamila's from her. Eat and wash up—

that was her whole conversation. And what they bought; onions or fish or something.

And she'd never even heard of the Alkonost bird. Better not tell her. And he'd put the egg in a matchbox and not show it to anybody.

Petya lay in bed and thought about how he would live with Tamila in the big room with the Chinese roses. He would sit on the veranda steps and whittle sticks for a sailboat he'd call *The Flying Dutchman*. Tamila would rock in her chair, drink the panacea, and talk. Then they would board *The Flying Dutchman*, the dragon flag on the mast, Tamila in her black robe on the deck, sunshine and salt spray, and they would set sail in search of Atlantis, lost in the shimmering briny deep.

He used to live a simple life: whittling, digging in the sand, reading adventure books; lying in bed, he would listen to the night trees anxiously moving outside his window, and think that miracles happened on distant islands, in parrot-filled jungles, or in tiny South America, narrowing downward, with its plastic Indians and rubber crocodiles. But the world, it turned out, was imbued with mystery, sadness, and magic, rustling in the branches, swaying in the dark waters. In the evenings, he and his mother walked along the lake: the sun set in the crenellated forest, the air smelled of blueberries and pine resin, and high above the ground red fir cones glimmered gold. The water in the lake looks cold, but when you put your hand in, it's even hot. A large gray lady in a cream dress walks along the high shore: she walks slowly, using a stick, smiles gently, but her eyes are dark and her gaze empty. Many years ago her little daughter drowned in the lake, and she is waiting for her to come home: it's bedtime, but the daughter still hasn't come. The gray lady stops and asks, "What time is it?" When she hears the reply, she shakes her head. "Just think." And when you come back, she'll stop and ask again, "What time is it?"

Petya has felt sorry for the lady ever since he learned her secret. But Tamila says little girls don't drown, they simply *cannot* drown. Children have gills: when they get underwater they turn into fish, though not right away. The girl is swimming around, a silver fish, and she pokes her head out, wanting to call to her mother. But she has no voice . . .

And here, not far away, is a boarded-up dacha. No one comes to live there, the porch is rotted through, the shutters nailed, the paths overgrown. Evil had been done in that dacha, and now no one can live there. The owners tried to get tenants, even offered them money to live there; but no, no one will. Some people tried, but they didn't last three days: the lights went out by themselves, the water wouldn't come to a boil in the kettle, wet laundry wouldn't dry, knives dulled on their own, and the children couldn't shut their eyes at night, sitting up like white columns in their beds.

And on that side—see? You can't go there, it's a dark fir forest; twilight, smoothly swept paths, white fields with intoxicating flowers. And that's where the bird Sirin lives, amid the branches, the bird of death, as big as a wood grouse. Petya's grandfather is afraid of the bird Sirin, it might sit on his chest and suffocate him. It has six toes on each foot, leathery, cold, and muscular, and a face like a sleeping girl's. *Cu-goo! Cu-goo!* the Sirin bird cries in the evenings, fluttering in its fir grove. Don't let it near Grandfather, shut the windows and doors, light the lamp, let's read out loud. But Grandfather is afraid, he watches the window anxiously, breathes heavily, plucks at his blanket. *Cu-goo! Cu-goo!* What do you want from us, bird? Leave Grandfather alone! Grandfather, don't look at the window like that, what do you see there? Those are just fir branches waving in the dark, it's just the wind acting up, unable to fall asleep. Grandfather, we're all here. The lamp is on and the tablecloth is white and I've cut out a boat, and Lenechka has drawn a rooster. Grandfather?

"Go on, go on, children." Mother shoos them from Grandfather's room, frowning, with tears in her eyes. Black oxygen pillows lie on a chair in the corner—to chase away the Sirin bird. All night it flies over the house, scratching at windows; and toward morning it finds a crack, climbs up, heavy, on the windowsill, on the bed, walks on the blanket, looking for Grandfather. Mother grabs a scary black pillow, shouts, waves it about, chases the Sirin bird . . . gets rid of it.

Petya tells Tamila about the bird: maybe she knows a spell, a word to ward off the Sirin bird? But Tamila shakes her head sadly: no; she used to, but it's back on the glass mountain. She would give Grandfather her protective toad ring—but then she'd turn into black powder herself. . . . And she drinks from her black bottle.

She's so strange! He wanted to think about her, about what she said, to listen to her dreams; he wanted to sit on her veranda steps, steps of the house where everything was allowed: eat bread and jam with unwashed hands, slouch, bite your nails, walk with your shoes on—if you felt like it—right in the flowerbeds; and no one shouted, lectured, called for order, cleanliness, and common sense. You could take a pair of scissors and cut out a picture you liked from any book—Tamila didn't care, she was capable of tearing out a picture and cutting it herself, except she always did it crooked. You could say whatever came into your head without fear of being laughed at: Tamila shook her head sadly, understanding; and if she did laugh, it was as if she were crying. If you ask, she'll play cards: Go Fish, anything; but she played badly, mixing up cards and losing.

Everything rational, boring, customary; all that remained on the other side of the fence overgrown with flowering bushes.

Ah, he didn't want to leave! At home he had to be quiet about Tamila (when I grow up and marry her, *then* you'll find out); and about the Sirin; and about the sparkling egg of the Alkonost bird, whose owner will be depressed for life. . . .

Petya remembered the egg, got it out of the matchbox, stuck it under his pillow, and sailed off on *The Flying Dutchman* over the black nocturnal seas.

In the morning Uncle Borya, with a puffy face, was smoking before breakfast on the porch. His black beard stuck out challengingly and his eyes were narrowed in disdain. Seeing his nephew, he began whistling yesterday's disgusting tune . . . and laughed. His teeth—rarely visible because of the beard—were like a wolf's. His black eyebrows crawled upward.

"Greetings to the young romantic." He nodded briskly. "Come on, Peter, saddle up your bike and go to the store. Your mother needs bread, and you can get me two packs of Kazbeks. They'll sell it to you, they will. I know Nina in the store, she'll give kids under sixteen anything at all."

Uncle Borya opened his mouth and laughed. Petya took the ruble and walked his sweaty bike out of the shed. On the ruble, written in tiny letters, were incomprehensible words, left over from Atlantis: *Bir sum. Bir som. Bir manat.* And beneath that, a warning: "Forging state treasury bills is punishable by law." Boring, adult words. The sober morning had swept away the magical evening birds, the girl-fish had gone down to the bottom of the lake, and the golden three-eyed statues of Atlantis slept under a layer of yellow sand. Uncle Borya had dissipated the fragile secrets with his loud, offensive laughter, had thrown out the fairy-tale rubbish—but not forever, Uncle Borya, just for a while. The sun would start leaning toward the west, the air would turn yellow, the oblique rays would spread, and the mysterious world would awaken, start moving, the mute silvery drowned girl would splash her tail, and the heavy, gray Sirin bird would bustle in the fir forest, and in some unpopulated spot, the morning bird Alkonost perhaps already would have hidden its fiery pink egg in a water lily, so that someone could long for things that did not come to pass. . . . *Bir sum, bir som, bir manat.*

Fat-nosed Nina gave him the cigarettes without a word, and asked him to say hello to Uncle Borya—a disgusting hello for a disgusting person—and Petya rode back, ringing his bell, bouncing on the knotty roots that resembled Grandfather's enormous hands. He carefully rode around a dead crow—a wheel had run over the bird, its eye was covered with a white film, the black dragged wings were covered with ashes, and the beak was frozen in a bitter avian smile.

At breakfast Mother looked concerned—Grandfather wouldn't eat again. Uncle Borya whistled, breaking the shell of his egg with a spoon, and watching the boys—looking for something to pick on. Lenechka spilled the milk and Uncle Borya was glad—an excuse to nag. But Lenechka was totally indifferent to his uncle's lectures: he was still little and his soul was sealed like a chicken egg; everything just rolled off. If, God forbid, he fell into the water, he wouldn't drown—he'd turn into a fish, a big-browed striped perch. Lenechka finished his milk and, without listening to the end of the lecture, ran out to the sand box: the sand had dried in the morning sun and his towers must have fallen apart. Petya remembered.

"Mama, did that girl drown a long time ago?"

"What girl?" his mother asked with a start.

"You know. The daughter of that old lady who always asks what time it is?"

"She never had any daughter. What nonsense. She has two grown sons. Who told you that?"

Petya said nothing. Mother looked at Uncle Borya, who laughed with glee.

"Drunken delirium of our shaggy friend! Eh? A girl, eh?"

"What friend?"

"Oh, nothing . . . Neither fish nor fowl."

Petya went out on the porch. Uncle Borya wanted to dirty everything. He wanted to grill the silver girl-fish and crunch her up with his wolf teeth. It won't work, Uncle Borya. The egg of the transparent morning bird Alkonost is glowing under my pillow.

Uncle Borya flung open the window and shouted into the dewy garden: "You should drink less!"

Petya stood by the gate and dug his nail into the ancient gray wood. The day was just beginning.

Grandfather wouldn't eat in the evening, either. Petya sat on the edge of the crumpled bed and patted his grandfather's wrinkled hand. His grandfather was looking out the window, his head turned. The wind had risen, the treetops were swaying, and Mama took down the laundry—it was flapping like *The Flying Dutchman*'s white sails. Glass jangled. The dark garden rose and fell like the ocean. The wind chased the Sirin bird from the branches; flapping its mildewed wings, it flew to the house and sniffed around, moving its triangular face with shut eyes: is there a crack? Mama sent Petya away and made her bed in Grandfather's room.

There was a storm that night. The trees rioted. Lenechka woke up and cried. Morning was gray, sorrowful, windy. The rain knocked Sirin to the ground, and Grandfather sat up in bed and was fed broth. Petya hovered in the doorway, glad to see his grandfather, and looked out the window—the flowers drooped under the rain, and it smelled of autumn. They lit the stove; wearing hooded jackets, they carried wood from the shed. There was nothing to do outside. Lenechka sat down to draw, Uncle Borya paced, hands behind his back, and whistled.

The day was boring: they waited for lunch and then waited for dinner. Grandfather ate a hard-boiled egg. It rained again at night.

That night Petya wandered around underground passages, staircases, in subway tunnels; he couldn't find the exit, kept changing trains: the trains traveled on ladders with the doors wide open and they passed through strange rooms filled with furniture; Petya had to get out, get outside, get up to where Lenechka and Grandfather were in danger: they forgot to shut the door, it was wide open, and the Sirin bird was walking up the creaking steps, its eyes shut; Petya's schoolbag was in the way, but he needed it. How to get out? Where was the exit? How do I get upstairs? "You need a bill." Of course, a bill to get out. There was the booth. Give me a bill. A treasury bill? Yes, yes, please! "Forging state treasury bills is punishable by law." There they were, the bills: long, black sheets of paper. Wait, they have holes in them. That's punishable by law. Give me some more. I don't want to! The schoolbag opens, and long black bills, holes all over, fall out. Hurry, pick them up, quick, I'm being persecuted, they'll catch me. They scatter all over the floor, Petya picks them up, stuffing them in any which way; the crowd separates, someone is being led through. . . . He can't get out of the way, so many bills, oh there it is, the horrible thing: they're leading it by the arms, huge, howling like a siren, its purple gaping face upraised; it's neither-fish-nor-fowl, it's the end!

Petya jumped up with a pounding heart; it wasn't light yet. Lenechka slept peacefully. He crept barefoot to Grandfather's room, pushed the door—silence.

The night light was on. The black oxygen pillows were in the corner. Grandfather lay with open eyes, hands clutching the blanket. He went over, feeling cold; guessing, he touched Grandfather's hand and recoiled. Mama!

No, Mama will scream and be scared. Maybe it can still be fixed. Maybe Tamila can help?

Petya rushed to the exit—the door was wide open. He stuck his bare feet into rubber boots, put a hood over his head, and rattled down the steps. The rain had ended, but it still dripped from the trees. The sky was turning gray. He ran on legs that buckled and slipped in the mud. He pushed the veranda door. There was a strong waft of cold, stale smoke. Petya bumped into a small table: a jangle and rolling sound. He bent down, felt around, and froze: the ring with the toad, Tamila's protection, was on the floor. There was noise in the bedroom. Petya flung open the door. There were two silhouettes in the dim light in the bed: Tamila's tangled black hair on the pillow, her black robe on the chair; she turned and moaned. Uncle Borya sat up in bed, his beard up, his hair disheveled. Tossing the blanket over Tamila's leg and covering his own legs, he blustered and shouted, peering into the dark: "Eh? Who is it? What is it? Eh!"

Petya started crying and shouted, trembling in horrible understanding, "Grandfather's dead! Grandfather's dead! Grandfather's dead!"

Uncle Borya threw back the blanket and spat out horrible, snaking, inhuman words; Petya shuddered in sobs, and ran out blindly: boots in the flowerbeds; his soul was boiled like egg white hanging in clumps on the trees rushing toward him; sour sorrow filled his mouth and he reached the lake and fell down under the wet tree oozing rain; screeching, kicking his feet, he chased Uncle Borya's horrible words, Uncle Borya's horrible legs, from his mind.

He got used to it, quieted down, lay there. Drops fell on him from above. The dead lake, the dead forest: birds fell from the trees and lay feet up; the dead empty world was filled with gray thick oozing depression. Everything was a lie.

He felt something hard in his hand and unclenched his fist. The squashed silver guard toad popped its eyes at him.

The match box, radiating eternal longing, lay in his pocket.

The Sirin bird had suffocated Grandfather.

No one can escape his fate. It's all true, child. That's how it is.

He lay there a bit longer, wiped his face, and headed for the house.

JOSEPH A. CITRO

Them Bald-headed Snays

Joseph A. Citro is a native Vermonter. He's published two novels, *Shadow Child* and *Guardian Angel*, and has sold two more.

"Them Bald-headed Snays" is his first published short story. It uses his home territory to excellent advantage, creating an odd family that could almost exist in the backwoods of Vermont. And it also puts a chilling twist on the classical concept of the sin-eater. It first appeared in *Masques III*.

—E.D.

Them Bald-headed Snays

JOSEPH A. CITRO

After the cancer got Mom, Dad took me way out in the Vermont countryside to live with my grandparents.

"I'll come back for you, Daren," he said. His eyes looked all glassy and sad. I bit my top and bottom lips together so I wouldn't cry when he started home without me. Sure, he'd come back, but he didn't say when.

Before that day I'd never seen too much of my grandparents. They'd come to visit us in Providence once, right after Mom got sick. But that was years ago, when I was just a kid. I remember how Dad and Grampa would have long, quiet talks that ended suddenly if Mom or me came into the room.

After that they never came to visit again. I don't think Mom liked them, though she never said why. "Their ways are different from ours," that's all she'd say.

And they sure weren't the way I remembered them! Grampa turned out to be sort of strange and a little scary. He was given to long, silent stretches in his creaky rocking chair. He'd stare out the window for hours, or read from big, dark-covered books. Sometimes he'd look through the collection of catalogs that seemed to arrive with every mail delivery. My job was to run to the bottom of the hill and pick up the mail from the mailbox. There were always the catalogs, and big brown envelopes with odd designs on them. There were bills, too, and Grampa's once-a-week newspaper. But there was never a letter from Dad.

"Can we call Dad?" I asked. Grampa just snorted as if to say, *You know we ain't got a phone.* Then he turned away and went back to his reading. Sometimes he'd stand, take a deep breath, and stretch, reaching way up toward the ceiling. Then he'd walk—maybe to the kitchen—bent over a little, rubbing the lower part of his back.

Grampa didn't talk to me much, but Gram was the quiet one. She'd move from room to room like a draft. Sometimes I'd think I was all alone, then I'd look over my shoulder and Gram was sitting there, watching me. At first I'd smile at her, but soon I stopped; I'd learned not to expect a smile in return, only a look of concern.

Sometimes she'd bring me a big glass of greenish-brown tea that tasted of honey and smelled like medicine.

"How you feeling today, Daren?" she'd ask.

"Good," I'd say.

"You drink up, now." She'd nod, pushing the glass toward me. "You'll feel even better."

When I'd take the glass away from my mouth she'd be gone.

Every other Friday, Grampa went into town to get groceries. After I'd been there about a month, he took me along with him. And that was another odd thing about him: he had a horse and buggy when everybody else had cars. I felt embarrassed riding through the downtown traffic beside an old man in a horse-drawn wagon.

Grampa said his back was acting up real bad, so he made me carry all the bags to the wagon. Then he told me to stay put while he made a second stop at the liquor store.

I didn't, though. I took a dime from my pocket and tried to make a collect call to my father. The operator said our number was no longer in service.

Grampa came back with his bottle before I'd made it back to the wagon. He yelled at me, told me he'd tan me brown if I ever disobeyed him again.

I'd lived in Stockton, Vermont, about two months before I saw Bobby Snay.

I was playing in the barn, upstairs in the hayloft, looking out the loading door toward the woods. I saw him come out from among the trees. He swayed when he walked, moving with difficulty, as if a heavy wind were trying to batter him back to where he'd come from.

He continued across the meadow, weaving through the tall grass and wild-flowers until he came to the road that ends in Grampa's dooryard. When he got closer I saw how funny he looked. His skin was the color of marshmallows, his eyes so pale it was impossible to say if they were blue or brown.

And it looked like his hair was falling out. Maybe it wasn't really, but it wasn't very plentiful. It looked limp and sparse and stuck out here and there in little patches, making his head look like it was covered with hairy bugs.

Back home he would have been the type of nerdy kid we'd pick on in school. But here, well, he was the only other kid I'd seen for a long time.

"Hey!" I called, "hey! Wait up!"

I dodged back into the barn and jumped down into the pile of hay below. I sneezed once, then made for the door, ran after him. But I didn't need to; he was in the barn waiting for me.

All of a sudden I wasn't so eager to say hi. In fact, I was kind of scared of him. He was taller than I, but he was spindly, weak-looking. I wasn't afraid he was going to beat me up or anything. It was something else. Maybe it was the way he had crossed the dooryard and entered the barn in less time than it took me to jump out of the loft. Maybe it was the way he stared at me as if there was no brain behind his washed-out eyes.

Or maybe it was the smell.

I didn't realize it at the time, but now I think that strange odor was coming from him.

It was like the odor of earth, the strange scent of things that were once alive—like rotting squirrels and leaves mixed with the smell of things that would never live. Like water and stones.

"I . . . I'm Daren Oakly."

"Bobby," he said. "Bobby Snay." His voice was windy-sounding, like air through a straw.

"Where you going?" I couldn't think of anything else to say.

"Walkin', jes' walkin'. Wanna come?"

"Ah . . . No. Grampa says I gotta stay here."

"You don't gotta. Nobody gotta. Nobody stays here."

It was warm in the barn. The smell seemed to get stronger.

"Where d'ya live?"

He pointed with his thumb, toward the woods.

"You *live* in *the woods*?"

"Yup. Sometimes."

"How old are you?"

He blinked. I hadn't noticed till then, but it was the first time he'd blinked since we stood face to face.

"I gotta go now," he said. "But I'll come again. I always come 'round when ya need me."

I watched him walk away, lurching, leaning, zigzagging through the field. He had no more than stepped back into the woods when I heard Grampa's wagon coming up the hill.

"You ain't to do it again!" Grampa raged. "I won't have it. I won't have you keepin' time with them bald-headed Snays! Not now, not till I tell ya. You don't know nothin' about 'em, so you stay clear of 'em, hear me?"

"But—"

"You see them around here again, you run an' tell me. That's the long an' short of it."

"But Grampa—!"

It was the fastest I'd ever seen him move. His hand went up like a hammer and came down like a lightning bolt, striking my cheek.

"An' that's so you don't *forget*."

Anger flared in me; adrenaline surged, uselessly. Then fear settled over everything. I couldn't look at Grampa. My nose felt warm. Red drops splatted on the wooden floor like wax from a candle. I bit my lips and fought away the tears.

Later, I heard him telling Gram, "They're back. The boy seen one of 'em just today." Grampa sounded excited—almost happy.

*   *   *

I woke up to the sound of shouting. Outside my bedroom window, near the corner of the barn, two persons were fighting. One of them, the one doing the hollering, was Grampa.

"I don't care *who* you come for, I'm the one's got you now!"

Grampa pushed the other away, butted him with his shoulder against the open barn door. The door flapped back, struck the side of the building like a thunderclap.

I could see the other person now. It was Bobby Snay.

Grampa hit him in the stomach. Bobby doubled up. Puke shot out of his nose and mouth.

Grampa lifted a boot and Bobby's head jerked back so hard I thought his neck would snap. He tumbled sideways, slid down the barn door and curled up on the ground.

Grampa stomped hard on his head, once, twice. Every time his boot came down he'd yell, "YEH!"

There was a big rock near the barn. Grampa kept it there to hold the door open. It was about the size of a basketball, yet Grampa picked it up like it were weightless.

I was surprised how easily Grampa lifted that rock all the way to his shoulders. Then he did something crazy: he let it drop. Bobby lay still after it had smashed against his head.

Grampa turned and walked toward the house. He was smiling.

All the rest of the day I tried to pretend I hadn't seen anything. I knew I couldn't tell Gramma, so I actually tried to forget how weird Grampa was acting. But I couldn't forget; I was too scared of him.

It was then I decided that staying clear of him wouldn't be enough. I'd have to sneak off, run away. Then I'd find my father and things would be pretty much the way they used to be.

Gramma watched me force down a bowl of pea soup at the silent dinner table. Then I got up and started toward the back door. My plan was to run through the woods to the main road, then hitch a ride.

When I opened the door, Grampa was in the yard. He stood tall and straight, hands on hips. That arthritic droop to his shoulders was gone now. His face, though wrinkled as ever, seemed to glow with fresh, pulsing blood. He was still smiling.

I knew he could tell by the terror on my face that I'd seen everything. "Get dressed," he said, "you got some work to do."

I thought he was going to make me bury Bobby Snay's body. Instead, he made me go down to the cellar to stack firewood he handed to me through a window. We did that all afternoon. After about an hour my back was hurting something awful, but Grampa never slowed up. Now and then he'd stand straight and stretch his arms wide. He'd smile; sometimes he'd laugh.

I didn't dare say anything to him.

I could hardly eat supper. I was tired and achy and I wanted to take a nap. Grampa wasn't tired at all. He ate lots of beans and biscuits, even carried on a conversation with Gramma. "I feel ten years younger," he said.

The next day Grampa went into town again. I asked him if I could go too. I wanted to get at least that far in the wagon, then . . . well, I wasn't sure. I'd go to the police, or run away, or something.

He said, "No. I'm goin' alone. I want you *here*."

I was sitting on the fence by the side of the barn, trying to decide what to do, when Bobby Snay stepped out of the woods.

I couldn't *believe* it.

As he got closer, I saw what was really strange: he wasn't bruised or cut or anything. I mean, I was sure Grampa had killed him, but here he was, without any trace of that awful beating.

He walked closer, weaving this way and that, as if one of his legs was shorter than the other. When he was near enough to hear me, I forced myself to ask, "Are you okay?"

He stopped walking. His eyes were pointed in my direction but I didn't feel that he saw me. "Yeah," he said, "yeah, sure, 'course I am."

Then he lurched to the right as if someone had shoved him, and he continued on his way.

I watched him go, not believing, not knowing.

Should I tell Grampa Bobby was okay? Should I talk to the law? Keep quiet? Or what? I had to decide; I had to do something.

Friday at supper Gramma had a heart attack.

She was spooning stew onto Grampa's plate when she dropped the pot. Grampa's hand went up like he was going to smack her. Then he saw what was happening.

She put both her hands on the tabletop, trying to steady herself. Her knuckles were white. Sweat popped out all over her face. "I . . . I . . . I . . . ," she said, as if her tongue was stuck on that one word.

Then her knees folded and she dropped to the floor.

Grampa said, "Jesus, oh Jesus . . . oh *God*."

But instead of bending over and helping Gramma, he did something awfully weird: he grabbed his shotgun and ran out the door.

Left alone with Gramma, I didn't know what to do. I knelt over her and tried to ask how I could help. I was crying so hard I was afraid she couldn't understand what I was saying.

Now her skin turned completely white; her lips looked blue. Her whole face was shiny with sweat. She whispered something: "Go get me a *Snay*, boy. Go quick."

I didn't argue. I ran toward the door.

Maybe Mr. Snay was a doctor, a preacher, or something, I didn't know. Whatever he was, Gramma seemed to need him. Somehow, I guessed, he'd be able to help her.

Quickly finding the path Bobby Snay had taken earlier, I entered the woods. Almost at once I heard noises. Grunting sounds. Soft *thupps*. Cracks and groans.

It was Grampa and one of the Snays—*not* Bobby this time, but surely one of his relatives. It was a girl. She had the same tall, frail body, the same mushroom-white complexion, the same patchy growths of hair.

Grampa was smashing her with a piece of pipe that looked like a tire iron. The Snay didn't fight back, didn't scream, she just stood there taking the blows. I saw Grampa jab at her with the flattened end of the metal rod. It went right through her eye, sinking halfway into her skull. She fell backwards, sat on the ground. Grampa jerked the rod up and down just like he was pumping the blood that spurted from her eye socket.

I couldn't look and I couldn't run away. "Grampa," I shouted, "stop it! You gotta *help Gramma!*"

Grampa finished what he was doing and looked up. His eyes were bright, fiery-looking. Then he took a step toward me, squeezing the bloody pipe in his slimy red hand.

He looked wild.

I backed away from him, thinking, He's going to brain me with that thing.

Then my heel hit something.

The shotgun!

I picked it up from where Grampa must have dropped it. I guessed he wanted to do his job by hand. I guessed he enjoyed it.

I pointed the gun at him.

"Put that down, boy!" His voice was as gruff as I'd ever heard it. When he stepped toward me I stepped backward, almost stumbled. I had the gun but that didn't keep me from being afraid.

"Put it *down*." He waved the tire iron, gesturing for me to drop the shotgun. Tears blurred my vision; the gun shook in my hands.

"Listen to me, boy . . ." His hand was reaching out.

I looked around. The Snay wasn't moving. There was no one to help me.

Grampa took another step.

"I'm *tellin*' you, boy—"

Closer.

I cried out and pulled the trigger.

If I hadn't been shaking so much, I might have killed him straight off. As it was, his shirt tore away and red, slimy skin exploded from his left side.

We both fell at the same time, me from the recoil, Grampa from the shot.

I stared at him. A white, red-glazed hipbone showed through his mangled trousers. Broken ribs bit through the shredded flesh.

"Daren," he said. This time his voice was weak.

I couldn't move. I couldn't go to him. I couldn't run away.

"Daren, you don't understand nothin'."

I could barely hear him. "The Snays," he said, "you gotta give 'em your pain. You gotta give 'em your troubles. You *can't* hurt 'em. You can't *kill* 'em. They jest keep comin' back . . ."

I found myself on my feet again, moving closer to Grampa dragging the shotgun by the barrel.

Suddenly, I was standing above him.

"You shot me, boy—but you can make it right. You gotta *do* one of 'em. You gotta do jes' like you're killin' one of 'em. Then I'll be all right. You gotta kill one of 'em, for me."

"But what about Gramma?"

"Please, boy . . ." His voice was weak. I could barely hear him. He lifted his finger toward the Snay with the ruined eye. "See that? I got to her in time. Your gramma's all right."

I needed proof, wanted to run back to the house to see for myself, but there was no time. And Grampa was dying.

The mangled Snay was moving now. She was using the tree trunk to work her way back up to her feet.

"See there, boy," Grampa wheezed. "*Get* her, boy, shoot her. Hit her with the gun!"

I lifted the shotgun, braced my shoulder for another recoil.

"Hurry, Daren, 'fore she gets away."

My finger touched the trigger. I was shaking so much the metal seemed to vibrate against my fingertip.

"*Please*, boy . . ." Grampa was propped up on his elbow. He watched the Snay lurch, stumble toward the shadowy trees—

"Now, boy, NOW!"

—and disappear.

Grampa collapsed on the ground. He was flat on his back, head resting on an exposed root. Now his eyes were all cloudy-looking. They rolled around in different directions.

I was still posed with the gun against my shoulder. When he tried to speak again, I just let it fall.

I had to kneel down, put my ear right up next to his mouth, to hear what the old man was saying.

"You shoulda *shot*, Daren . . ."

"I couldn't, Grampa." I was blubbering. "I can't shoot nobody . . ." My tears fell, splattered on his face.

"You *gotta*, son. Your daddy, he never had no stomach for it neither. Couldn't even do it to save your mama. That's why he brung you here. He knew old Gramp would know what to do. That cancer that got your mama, boy—that cancer that killed her? Well, Daren . . . you got it, too."

His words stopped in a gag, his eyes froze solid, and he was dead.

I looked up. Looked around. The Snay was gone. The birds were quiet. I was alone in the woods.

EDWARD BRYANT

A Sad Last Love at the Diner of the Damned

"A Sad Last Love at the Diner of the Damned" is a love story. It's one of the most romantic stories from *Book of the Dead*, the shared-world anthology based on George Romero's zombie-cannibal universe. If you think the living inhabitants of this story are bad, wait till you meet the dead ones. A warning: It's vicious and has graphic gore.

Edward Bryant, besides writing about film for this annual volume, is the author of many stories of science fiction, fantasy, and horror. He's won Hugo and Nebula awards for his trouble, and a reputation as one of the finest short fiction craftsmen in the field. Many of his pieces are hard to categorize. But not the tale that follows.

—E.D.

A Sad Last Love at the Diner of the Damned

EDWARD BRYANT

There once was a beautiful young woman with long hair the russet gold of ripe wheat. Her name was Martha Malinowski and her family had lived in Fort Durham for three generations. Martha was nineteen and had spent her entire life in the border area where southern Colorado shades subtly from browns and tans to the dark green mountains of northern New Mexico.

Martha's eyes were a startling blue that deepened or paled according to the season and her mood. Her temperament had begun to darken with the onset of early winter snows, and so her eyes began to reflect that. Now they appeared the color of the road ice that formed on the headlights and steel bumpers of the pickups lining the parking strip beside the Diner.

She waited on tables for one, sometimes two long shifts each day at the Cuchara Diner. Occasional tourists speculated aloud that the Diner was more properly called the Cucaracha. Henry Roybal, the owner, would gesture at the neon tablespoon suspended in the front window. That made little difference to the tourists who rarely understood Spanish. The locals around Fort Durham simply referred to the place as the Diner. The Diner itself was a sprawling stucco assemblage that had been added to many times over the decades. Its most notable feature was Henry Roybal's pride and joy, an eight-foot-high neon EAT that flashed from red to green and back again while a blue arrow pointed down at the Diner's front door.

Martha Malinowski's fair features haunted the illicit dreams of many in the community. She was largely oblivious to this and to the dreamers themselves. She ignored the ones she did notice. Her cap was set for Bobby Mack Quintana, the deputy sheriff. Bobby Mack was always cordial toward her, but that seemed to be about it. Martha wondered if he was just too shy to express his feelings.

Then there was Bertie Hernandez who openly lusted after Martha. Crude, rude, and vital, his buddies and he were among Henry's best customers. Martha was never glad to see them coming into the Diner. But a job was a job, and business was business in this world of sage, scrub grass, endless horizons, and Highway 159. Someday Martha would have saved enough cash to leave this place. Or if Bobby Mack wanted her, then perhaps she would stay. She was practical about romance, yet still maintained her dreams.

The men watched the little old ladies tap and scratch ineffectually against the Diner's thick plate-glass front window, their clawed fingers fluttering like the wings of injured birds.

"Don't look too mean to me," said Billy Gaspar, a strapping young man in a red plaid lumberjack shirt.

"You don't know squat about zombies," said Shine Willis, who was a few years Billy's senior and half a head taller. "I was up to the Springs last week when a bunch of 'em came boilin' out of a Greyhound bus downtown. They're faster than they look, and stronger too. Especially if they been eatin' good." He chuckled.

Billy looked a bit livid. "People."

"Yeah," said Shine. "People."

Bertie Hernandez glanced up from his breakfast plate. "Gimme another side of bacon, Martha," he said. "Have Henry make it good and chewy." The radio above the cash register was blaring out the Beat Farmers' cover of "Sweet Jane." "An' turn off that shit. I want to hear something good."

"Like what?" someone said from down the formica counter.

"Conway Twitty," said Bertie. "Good shit."

The radio stayed where it was set. The Beat Farmers' record segued into Joe Ely's "Crazy Lemon."

"Better," Bertie said.

"What we gonna do about the old ladies?" said Shine.

"Where'd they come from?" Billy Gaspar said. His fingers twitched around the handle of an untouched mug of cooling coffee.

"Eventide Manor, most like. The nursing home." Shine grinned mirthlessly. "Musta found a zombie in the woodpile sometime in the night, I'd judge."

"We gotta kill 'em?" said Billy.

"Too old to fuck," said Shine. "Too tough to eat."

Billy's complexion seemed to slide from white to greenish.

Somebody closer to the window said, "See the second from the left? That's ol' Mrs. Davenport, Kevin's grandma."

"The one in the center," said Bertie Hernandez, "is my mother. Fuck her. Let's do it." He swung around on the counter seat and stood in one fluid motion. He slid the big .357 magnum out of its holster and checked the cylinder.

"Nice piece," said Miguel Espinosa.

"Six old ladies," said Bertie. "I figure I can handle them."

"You want some help?"

Bertie shook his head. "Not unless they take a chunk out of me. Then shoot me quick." It all sounded matter-of-fact.

"Why don't all of you wait for Bobby Mack?" said Martha.

"Bobbee May-ack," Bertie mimicked her. "Your fag cop heartthrob? Fuck him. Let him find his own zombies to blow him."

Nose level with Bertie's Adam's apple, Martha looked up at him. "Don't say things like that. Not ever."

Bertie looked at her steadily for a moment. "Just watch what I do to the deadheads, darlin'. If it makes you wet enough, maybe I'll take you over to Walsenburg tonight for a movie show and then the Motel Six."

"Bertie," said Henry Roybal. "There's no call for talk like that." The Diner's owner had stuck his head out of the kitchen. "And don't get any mess on the window. I washed it just yesterday."

"They're smearin' the glass, right enough," said Shine. "Pus, blood, all sorts of shit."

"Okay," said Bertie, looking away from Martha toward the old ladies beyond the window.

Martha stood rigid. Then she turned toward Henry, whose corpulent body was still wedged in the kitchen doorway. "Can you get hold of Bobby Mack?"

Henry shook his head. "Tried. Can't raise nothing on the base station or the phone. Sheriff's number is busy. I figure everybody's calling to report a zombie or two. Sorry, *muchacha*."

"Back me up," Bertie said to Shine. "Just in case." The other man nodded and hefted his Remington pump. Bertie smiled at Martha. "Kiss for good luck? No?" He shrugged and called to the men lined along the counter, "Somebody decoy the fuckers long enough for me to clear the door."

At the end of the counter, a weathered cowboy in boot-cut jeans and a pearl-snap shirt strolled over to the front window. He stared into the faces of the zombie women for a moment, then he turned, skinned down his pants and mooned them. The zombies crowded toward the pressed ham.

"Gross," said Martha.

Bertie flipped the latch on the front door and crunched out onto the gravel. Shine relocked the door. "Don't nobody get in my way if he needs help."

"It's all yours, buddy," said Miguel Espinosa. "I don't want none of those ladies."

The zombies had evidently figured out that fresher meat was now outside and within chewing distance. Still, it took all six a few moments to lurch around vaguely and fix on Bertie Hernandez. Bertie held the magnum in the proper two-handed position and sighted down the barrel.

"Bertieee—" The squeal of expelled breath was loud enough even to hear inside the Diner. Bertie's mother lunged at her son. The muzzle of the .357 belched flame and the back of Mrs. Hernandez's skull exploded outward, the spray of blood and tissue coating the face of the zombie close behind her.

Inside the Diner, Billy said, "I didn't think they were supposed to remember anything human."

Miguel shrugged. "Reflexes, I'll bet. You know, like chickens when you pull off their heads."

Billy looked dubious.

Bertie blew away the faces of the next two zombies; ducked a fourth that had the smarts to flank him; then practically stuck the muzzle in the mouth of a fifth creature. The exiting slug nicked one front corner of the Diner's roof.

"*Dios!*" yelled Henry. "Be careful!"

Bertie had taken his eyes off the craftiest of the zombies. While he was watching the sixth go for him, the other survivor got in close enough to grab his gun hand. Then the last zombie wrapped her spindly arms around his lower leg and began to gnaw one Fry elephant-hide boot.

"Shit!" said Shine Willis, flicking the latch and pumping in a round as he slammed open the door. He had a clear shot at the zombie Bertie was fighting off with both hands. The old woman's head simply disintegrated and the body flopped backward, twitching as it hit the graveled parking apron.

"Jesus," Bertie cried. "I'm fuckin' deaf!"

Shine reversed the pump and swung the stock into the skull of the remaining zombie chewing on Bertie's boot. It took three blows before the creature's jaws stopped champing.

"Christ," said Shine, panting. "She's worse'n a Gila monster."

Bertie kicked free of the zombie's doubly dead body. "Shit, man, I had her —I had 'em both."

"Yeah, sure." Shine wiped the bloody stock of the pump on an old lady's flowered dress. "If I was a second longer, you'd be zombie jerky and I'd be obliged to blow your fuckin' head into the Arkansas."

Bertie said nothing; just thumbed some shells out of his right front pocket and began reloading the magnum. When he was done, he said, "Okay, bud, you got one on me. Let's go back in and I'll buy you a coffee."

"I need somethin' stronger than that," Shine said.

They both froze a moment when they heard the siren.

The county car slewed off the blacktop and into the gravel. Both Bertie and Shine jumped to avoid the spray of rocks. Bobby Mack Quintana got out of the car with his service revolver drawn. "What's going on here?"

"Fuck you," Bertie said. "Henry'll fill you in." He turned and walked back into the Diner, Shine following with the barrel of the Remington propped against one shoulder.

Bobby Mack stared after them. "Zombies?" he called.

"No shit, Sherlock."

The deputy took out a notebook and a ballpoint. He gingerly flipped over a body with his booted toe. He recognized the piece of face that remained.

Martha watched from inside. The body Bobby Mack was identifying was old Mrs. Hernandez. Martha had known her since she was a little girl. Mrs. Hernandez had read to her from the collection of P. G. Wodehouse books that had furnished Bertie's name.

Martha felt a sudden lurch in her belly. She barely made it to the ladies' room. As she hunched over the stool and heaved up her breakfast, she heard Bertie Hernandez complaining at the counter.

"Hey, Henry, get your buns out here. This bacon's *way* too done!"

*   *   *

"Bobby Mack, I want to talk to you," said Martha. Bertie and his friends were out back of the Diner in an open field, piling up the bodies of the six zombie ladies, dousing them with unleaded, and then holding out chilled masculine palms, calluses to the heat.

The deputy had reminded them about the recent state law. " 'You kill 'em, you burn 'em,' " Bertie had repeated somewhat derisively. "Sure enough, Deputy Dawg, we're good citizens. We'll have a little zombie roast . . . work up a healthy appetite for lunch."

"I can't wait around for this," whined Miguel Espinosa. "I gotta go to work down to the Quik-Lube."

"Just shut the fuck up," said Bertie. "We'll do it," he said to Bobby Mack. The deputy watched for a few minutes, then went back into the Diner.

When Martha asked to speak with him, he hesitated. "Official business?" he said.

Martha sighed. "You've got to be kidding. I just want to take a minute."

Bobby Mack looked doubting, then shrugged. "Okay, I can talk."

"Not here." She called to Henry in the kitchen, "Hey, boss, I'm taking my break." Without waiting for an answer, she led Bobby Mack out the door.

A cold autumn wind followed them a hundred yards across the highway and up a forested rise. The greasy black smoke curled over their heads. Martha wrinkled her nose. Bobby Mack Quintana looked fine in his tan uniform and Stetson. The black leather at his trimly belted waist didn't hurt.

"Just wanted to talk," she said, turning to face him. She had to tilt her face up to meet his dark eyes.

"Figured," Bobby Mack said. He smiled.

Shyly, she thought. Martha took a deep breath. "Would it be too bold," she said, "to ask why you don't like me?"

Bobby Mack looked stunned. "Don't like you? I *do* like you, Martha. Truly I do."

"You don't ever show it." She had amazed herself with her boldness. She knew she should be tongue-tied, but the words tumbled out anyway. "I want you to feel kindly toward me, Bobby Mack."

The deputy started to say something, but stuttered the words. He took a breath and started over. "I don't want to overstep what's right. I figured you and Carl Crump—"

"Carl Crump?" she said incredulously. Just what did Bobby Mack think was going on between her and the high school principal's son? "He's just a—just a horny jerk, just like—" His father, she started to say, but clipped off the words in time. No use aggravating things. She knew the Crumps square-danced with Bobby Mack's folks on Friday nights. "*Carl*?" she said again. "Why do you think he and I—?"

Bobby Mack seemed to be blushing. "Well, he was saying . . ."

"Who—Carl Crump?" The deputy nodded. "No way," said Martha. "I may not make much money at the Diner, but I've got some standards."

"And pride," Bobby Mack almost whispered.

"That too." Martha reached out and lightly grasped his hands. Their fingers touched warmly. "Any other gossip you want to ask me about?"

Bobby Mack met her eye. "No," he said.

She could have called him a liar, but didn't want to. She didn't want to think about it, but knew there were men in the town who talked about her, speculated, perhaps even claimed to have touched her in the dark, in the backseats of their cars, in the balcony of the movie theater in Walsenburg, on the grass along the bank of— "Okay," she said. It had never happened. But God knows, she had turned them down. They had said all the things that seemed harmless on the surface, but she knew meant something else if examined closely enough.

"Nice day," he said, as the shifting wind whipped corpse-smoke through the trees and into their faces.

Martha started to laugh and cough at the same time. When she could speak, she said, "No, it isn't."

Bobby Mack laughed too. "No, you're right. It's a bad day, a rotten day, except for this." His fingers tightened on hers.

She screwed up her courage. "Bobby Mack, do you think you might like to go out tonight and do something?" Smoke from the pyre curled over their heads and up into the pine branches. His fingers tightened so fiercely, she feared he'd bruise her. Yet she didn't mind.

"Yes," said Bobby Mack. "I get off patrol at six. Yes," he said again.

After a long moment they both smiled and began to walk back toward the Diner. The day was sufficiently overcast, Henry had turned on the neon sign. EAT, it flashed. EAT, EAT, EAT.

Bobby Mack checked in the county Ford by six and picked up Martha at the Diner in his Suzuki Samurai.

"How about the Lanes?" he said, glancing at her and then back at the road.

"Sure. That's fine."

"We can't bowl tonight," he said.

"I heard on the radio. The meeting's at seven."

"We should have time to eat."

"You want to stay for the meeting?" she said.

"I've got to. Sheriff's orders."

"Oh," she said.

"*Shit!*" Thump-*thump*. The Samurai bounced over something lying humped on the road. "Sorry about my language, Martha."

She ignored that. "What was it?"

"Looked like a dog." With a hunk taken out of its head. That's what he didn't say. "It was already dead."

"Poor thing." She stared out the side window. "It was all curled up the way Mrs. Hernandez was this morning."

Bobby Mack didn't say anything.

"This morning," Martha said, "is that how it's going to have to be from here on out?"

"I wish I knew." Bobby Mack's words were clipped. "The word from the legislature is that Bertie can do that sort of thing. Anyone can. They're looking at what happened back East. You don't argue with zombies. You just shoot them in the head."

"They can't all be bad," said Martha. "There have to be some that remember being alive."

"Maybe they do," answered Bobby Mack. "Maybe that's why they're so pi— irritated."

Martha was clearly not satisfied. "I don't think I could kill one if it was somebody I'd loved."

"Hard to say." Bobby Mack swung the Samurai off the blacktop. "I reckon we'd do most anything if we were pushed." The parking lot of the Chama Lake Lanes wasn't crowded. He parked by the row of elms bordering the near side of the lot.

"Not if I loved him," Martha muttered.

"Huh?" said Bobby Mack. "Sorry, I wasn't listening."

"Nothing. Let's go eat."

The cheeseburgers and fries were what she could have eaten anytime at the Diner, but these were prepared by a different cook. They tasted terrific. A Coke apiece. Hot fudge sundaes for dessert.

By seven o'clock the bowling alley had started to fill with the citizens of Fort Durham and the surrounding countryside. It was clear there would not be enough chairs in the area on the riser behind the alleys, so old MacFarland, the owner, handed out pairs of bowling shoes to the later arrivals. They had to seat themselves on the polished hardwood of the lanes.

"Looks like most everybody's here," said Bobby Mack. "Sheriff's over there, so's the mayor, most of the county commissioners."

Martha had noted all those, but also Carl Crump, both junior and senior, not to mention Father Sierra and Pastor Beecham, the latter accompanied by his wife. Both the pastor and the priest had come onto her—at least that was what she'd suspected. She was unsure how else to interpret their words and actions on separate occasions. It seemed tragic to her, sadder, somehow more shocking than something like the propositions of Principal Crump or his son. But the weirdest thing—She hardly wanted to think about that at all. The true strangeness was the overture she had received from Mrs. Beecham, the pastor's wife.

For an entire semester after that, the final term of her senior year, she had attempted to dress even more conventionally than she had before. It didn't seem to work. She could still interpret the smirks and smiles.

Mayor Hardesty levered his plump self upright behind the lectern. "Let's get this called to order, folks. Sooner we get started, the sooner we can get home and do whatever we need to do." The room quieted. "I figure you all pretty much know what's going on from listening to the TV and radio, and after hearing the Health Department lady at the meeting last week."

"Nobody believed her," said Bobby Mack in a low voice.

Martha knew that was true. At the time, the zombie stories on the hourly

KNBS news had been just that—stories. It was like a war in Central America or a volcano blowing up in Asia. You just couldn't believe in some things unless you actually saw them. Otherwise they weren't real.

The zombies were real enough now. The morning had proved that. Mayor Hardesty mentioned the massacre at Eventide Manor and briefly outlined Bertie's morning exploits at the Diner. "We all have to be heroes like that," said the mayor. "We've got to watch out for each other and do more than just our share."

"And arm civilians with automatic weapons," Bobby Mack said sarcastically into Martha's ear.

The mayor went on. It was an attempt at being inspirational. Then the time for questions came. Someone spoke up from the rear of the snack area.

"How long's this zombie thing gonna last, anyway?"

"Probably about as long," said the mayor, "as it takes for the army to get mobilized, come on in, and kick some butt."

"After what happened out at the old folks' home, what about maybe putting up some roadblocks? You know, like a quarantine."

The mayor smiled politically. "You folks probably saw the news shows tonight. Both Denver and Albuquerque are in pretty bad shape. But fortunately for people out in the sticks like us, the zombies don't drive much."

"*Somebody* got here and wiped out Eventide Manor."

The mayor looked as if he were strenuously attempting to think on his feet. "Maybe it was a virus or something." He shrugged. "Something in the air or the food we been getting—"

"Not a good move," said Bobby Mack, voice low. "He's just blowing smoke. Zombies can't infect you by sneezing or letting you use their towels. They've got to bite you."

Martha shivered and laid her hand across his.

The room started to dissolve into chaos. People shouted questions and opinions, paying no attention to the mayor's gavel. "Let's get out of here," said Bobby Mack. He kept hold of her hand and led her toward the door.

Martha saw stares following them, appraising expressions. Neither of the Crump men was smiling. Nor was the priest or the pastor and his wife. They hate me, she thought, somewhat startled by the epiphany. They want me, but they hate me too.

Outside, the chill night air took away the sweat and the stale cigar smoke. There was no need out here for them to hold hands, but they did it anyway. About halfway across the parking area, Bobby Mack let loose of her fingers and trotted on ahead.

"Hey! What the hell are you guys doing?"

When Martha caught up to him, she realized that Bertie Hernandez and his cronies were having some fun.

"We're havin' a tailgate party," said Bertie. "What's it look like? That we're stringin' us up a zombie?"

That was, indeed, what it looked like. Billy, Miguel, Shine, and the rest were gathered around Bertie's jacked-up old red Chevy pickup. The truck was parked under the elms. The tailgate was down, and on it stood a thoroughly bound man Martha didn't recognize. But then he would have been hard to identify in any case. One ear dangled freely, barely attached to a tattered strip of gray skin. Dark liquid hissed and frothed from ragged lips. Several twists of shiny barbed wire, wound around his head the long way, from crown to jaw, kept the man's mouth shut.

Bertie saw them both looking at the wire. "Gotta keep him from biting. This here's a zombie, *comprende?*"

"You're going to lynch him?" said Bobby Mack. "That's murder."

"Gotta be alive to be a murder," said Shine Willis, grinning.

"Mutilating a corpse, then," said the deputy.

"Come on, Bobby Mack, get off it," said Bertie. "You know as well as me that there ain't no laws at all protecting these things. It isn't like they're endangered species or whatever. They just gotta die, that's all."

"Who—who is he?" said Martha.

"The guy who got to the old folks' home," said Bertie. "I guess he was the one who was supposed to deliver the butt paper and towels. From the Springs, probably. Me and the boys went up to the home to check it out after lunch. We found this guy down in the basement munching down the last of Doctor Jellico's feet. There were pieces of some of the other people in the home too."

"He was a fag," said Shine.

Martha and Bobby Mack stared at Shine.

He shrugged. "Dunno really. But all the bodies he'd been chewin' on were men. Let the ladies go after he killed 'em. That's why they were all down to the Diner."

"Enough of this shit," said Bertie. "Bobby Mack, you gonna interfere, or can we get on with it?"

"I guess the governor says you can kill him if you burn him. But hanging's not going to do any good, is it?"

"It is," said Bertie, "when you use piano wire for the noose." He banged on the Chevy's fender. The driver gunned the engine, then popped the clutch. The truck lurched forward, leaving the zombie kicking.

With the creature's weight, it didn't take but for a few seconds before the wire loop twanged into a knot and the zombie's head and body took separate falls. The head bounced a few feet away, the eyes blinking. Miguel Espinosa gave it a hard rap with an irrigation shovel.

"Hey, Martha," said Bertie. "You still want to go on over to Walsenburg with me tonight?"

"I never said I wanted to go."

Bertie walked over to stand in front of them. "You gonna go out for a ride in the deputy's rice-burner?"

"I'm going to give her a ride home," said Bobby Mack.

"See that's the only ride you give her."

"Bertie—" Martha started to say.

"I mean it." Bertie showed a toothy smile. "It's the best for you or nothing, you know?"

"Go burn your corpse," said Bobby Mack. The two men stared at each other. Bertie lowered his eyes first.

Over beneath the tree, the men were playing kickball with the head.

Bobby Mack took Martha home the long way. "Probably shouldn't use the gas," he said. "Don't know when the tankers'll stop coming here. But I don't want to call it a night yet."

"Me neither," said Martha. The Samurai had bucket seats, but she did her best to lean into his shoulder.

They drove south, almost to the New Mexico line, stopping short and turning around when they saw the police flashers and the leaping flames from something burning on the road.

"It's either their state patrol or ours," said Bobby Mack. "I'm off duty. I figure they've got it under control, whatever it is. Those boys have firepower."

He drove north again, taking the county road south of Fort Durham that wound into the hills to the west of town. Headlights, one out of adjustment and too bright, paced them. Bobby Mack squinted at the glare, then pulled off on a hilltop turnout to let the other vehicle by. A black Ford quarter-ton roared past. "Looks like Billy Gaspar," Bobby Mack said. "Wonder what the heck he's doing up here?" The sound of the truck diminished.

They stayed in the Samurai and looked down at Fort Durham's scattered lights.

"It always looks bigger at night," Martha said.

"Lot of things do. I guess that's why most folks think the dark's scary. When I was a kid, I used to wake up in the summer around three, four in the morning. I'd set a mental alarm. Then I'd sneak out of the house and just explore around the ranch. The greatest thing was the milk cows. They'd be just standing there in the moonlight, big and quiet and warm."

Martha looked sidelong at him. "There weren't any zombies then."

"Not here, at least. I expect there were the first zombies, back down in Jamaica or wherever they come from."

"Radio says these aren't the same thing. I was listening to NPR—"

"You listen to public radio?" He sounded surprised, yet pleased. "Me too."

"I'm not stupid, Bobby Mack. Yes, I was listening to NPR. They had a voodoo priest on who was really mad about his people being blamed for the zombies."

"Can't say as I'd blame him."

She hugged herself. "I don't want to talk about zombies."

"It's pretty much all anybody's gonna want to discuss for a while. Biggest thing to happen in this town since I don't know when."

A long minute went by.

"Bobby Mack, do you ever think about getting out of here? Going somewhere else?"

"I did that," he said. "I went away to college."

She laughed, but gently. "A couple hundred miles to Fort Lewis College in Durango isn't a long way."

"You didn't say *long* way."

"You know what I meant."

After a while, he said, "I don't know if I'd like it anywhere else."

"I know what you mean." Martha unhugged herself. "But sometimes I wonder what it would be like to find out."

"To go to California or something," he said, "it'd get lonely if you were by yourself."

"Yes," she said quietly. "I get lonely right here."

He sounded surprised. "You were always the prettiest girl around. Lonesome?"

"You don't know much about me, do you?"

"Reckon I was scared to find out," he said.

"No reason for that." Martha gently touched the side of his face. "No reason at all."

He shrugged slightly. "Like I told you, I heard things."

"They were wrong."

He touched her hair, her face, her lips. "I need to think about this."

"Do you?" she said, looking at him steadily in the glow from the dash lights.

"Yes, I do."

She touched his cheek with her lips. "There may not be much time."

"What's that mean?"

"I don't know," she said. "Just a feeling."

"One way or another," he said, "there'll be time." He leaned forward and flicked on the headlights. "I'd better get you home. I don't want your folks to raise Cain."

"Bobby Mack," she said, amazed again at her boldness. "Just one hug? One kiss?"

He nodded, and then held her and kissed her. And drove her home.

"That's funny," said Martha as they drove into the Malinowski yard four miles north of town.

"What?" Bobby Mack coasted the Samurai up near the house and turned off the lights.

"Yard light's off. Dad just replaced the bulb last week."

"Maybe he turned it off."

"Never does that when he figures I'm going to be late." She shrugged. "Maybe he expected I'd come home right after the meeting."

"Don't get jumpy," said Bobby Mack, grinning. "You're with the deputy sheriff, remember?"

"I remember." Martha got out of the Samurai. Bobby Mack started around the front of the vehicle to meet her. The night was only a day removed from the new moon, and the darkness was deep.

"Give me your hand," said the deputy. "I don't want to break a leg. I figure you know the terrain."

At the front step, Martha fumbled in her handbag for a key. "What with the zombies, Dad said he was going to start locking up at night." Once she had key in hand, Martha leaned up toward him. "Good night, Bobby Mack."

Whatever he was going to say was lost as they both heard the sound of something heavy, lurching and crunching in the gravel behind them. An indistinct shape loomed out of the darkness.

"GRRROARRRR!"

Clawed hands reached for him.

"Sweet Jesus!" said Bobby Mack, trying to get in front of Martha and reaching at the same time for his holstered pistol. Arms grabbed him from both sides and he was held immobile in the night. The creature in front of him staggered close and Bobby Mack smelled alcohol.

"Evenin', Deputy Dawg." It was Bertie Hernandez.

"Hey, man! It's okay, it's okay." Billy Gaspar's voice in Bobby Mack's ear. "We just didn't want you shootin' no one." He let loose of Bobby Mack's right arm. Someone else set free the left.

"You bastards!" said Martha. "What are you doing?"

"Just checkin'," said Bertie. "We're the PDA monitors, just like in high school. Wanta make sure the neckin' don't go too far, unnerstand?"

Bobby Mack said angrily, "I ought to—"

"Oughtta what, college boy? Just a little joke." Bertie turned heavily away. "Just a little joke. Okay, guys, let's go."

Bobby Mack started for him, but Martha grabbed his arm. "No, Bobby Mack. This isn't the time."

Bertie and the others were laughing uproariously by the time they piled into Billy Gaspar's black Ford. It had been parked around the angle of the house. Billy floored the pedal and the truck whined away toward the blacktop. The night swallowed the laughter.

Bobby Mack and Martha stared after them. The deputy realized his fingers were still clamped to the flap of his holster. He took his hand away.

The yard light went on, bathing the whole area in mercury vapor glare. Mr. Malinowski stood framed in the doorway, yawning and rubbing sleep from his eyes.

"Hey, you kids! What the hell's going on out there? Some of us are tryin' to sleep."

Martha and Bobby Mack exchanged looks. She reached up and touched his lips. "I'll see you at the Diner."

Talk at the Diner in the morning centered around two things, football and zombies. The preseason game between Denver and the Seattle Seahawks had been canceled just before kickoff. The rumors mentioned locker-room atrocities and half-devoured tailbacks.

"Musta been Seattle zombies," said Shine Willis grimly. "'Bout the only way they could beat the Broncos." No one contradicted him.

"Okay, ace," said Bertie. "Listen up. I got a little question for you."

Everyone listened up, especially Shine.

"So can animals bite you and turn you zombie?"

"You mean like dogs?" said Shine. "Get bit by Cujo? Beats the shit out of me."

No one knew, but everyone had an opinion.

"I was wonderin'," said Bertie, "'cause when I come out of the trailer this morning, the Jergensons' mutt came for me and I had to put him down. He looked like he'd already been dead a couple days."

Billy Gaspar looked glum. "Cripes, all we need is for every critter to be set against us."

"I wouldn't worry," said Shine. "The Jergensons' dog always looks like twenty pounds of shit. Probably just didn't like your looks. You shower this morning?"

The men along the counter laughed. A bit nervously, Martha thought. She dispatched the plates of hotcakes, eggs, potatoes, bacon, toast. Poured the coffee. The real stuff. No one here drank decaf.

A rough hand gripped her wrist. The coffee pot sloshed. "No more for me," said Bertie. "I'm tryin' to cut down."

"Let go," she said.

He sat there; she stood waiting. A silent tableau. The men stared, then went back to talking. But glances kept flickering toward Martha and Bertie.

"Tipped a few with Carl Crump real late last night," said Bertie casually. "He talks real interesting."

"I doubt that," said Martha. "Now let me go."

"No." The thick fingers did not relax. "He says you got a little mark under your left titty. Looks like a bird. That true?"

"No." Martha switched the steaming coffeepot to her right hand. "Let me go right now or you're going to get this all down your front."

In the sudden silence, the radio playing John Hiatt's "I Don't Even Try" seemed to blare out. The men at the counter no longer pretended to look away.

"If you'll go down for Bobby Mack," said Bertie, "then how come you won't do nothing for me?"

"Carl's a liar," said Martha evenly.

Bertie looked into her eyes intently. "Sure," he said, and let her wrist go. "Maybe tonight we can go to Walsenburg?"

She didn't know why she said it. "I'd sooner fuck a zombie." She said it so low, no one heard but Bertie. He stared at her.

Martha turned away and walked back to the kitchen, trying to move straight and true, and not bolt. Once out of sight of the dining room, she rubbed at the quick tears. She felt a raw pain. Her wrist. She turned it over and saw the angry-looking black-and-blue marks. They looked like the wings of a bird.

Bobby Mack didn't come into the Diner for his mid-morning coffee stop. About eleven Martha called to Henry Roybal, "Hey, anything on the scanner? What's going on out there? Anybody hear tell of Bobby Mack?"

"Nary a word about your young man, Martha. Lots of other stuff, though."

She balanced a tray of dirty dishes and flatware into the kitchen. Jose, the dishwasher, took it away from her, grunting as the load clattered and splashed into a steel sink full of soapy water.

"What do you mean, other stuff?"

"Don't know, really. Lots of code things, like when they know people are listening and the sheriff don't want anything to hit the grapevine right away."

As if on cue, the police scanner crackled and hissed around a call: "Sheriff central, this is patrol three."

"Patrol three, come in."

"Hey, affirmative. Kenny and me, we got a confirmed patch of veggies just off country one-fiver at the Centennial Ditch. Must have been holed up in the First Baptist. We're gonna take actions as ordered."

"Veggies?" said Martha.

Henry Roybal nodded. "All mornin'."

The scanner crackled. "Patrol three, don't do nothing stupid."

"Central, can you send us backup?"

"That's a negatory, patrol three. Things are jumpin' all over the county."

"We copy, central. Do what we can. Got my old AK47 in the trunk. Worked on Charlie. Figure it'll harvest a whole row or two of veggies."

"My God," said Martha.

"Repeat, patrol three. Stay cool. We already lost a coupla harvesters this morning."

There was a silence on the scanner. Then the voice of patrol three said, "We know that, central. This one's gonna be for Dale and J.B."

Henry Roybal expelled a long breath. Martha looked at him. They both knew exactly whom the voice was talking about. Town cops. They hadn't come in for coffee either. Bobby Mack, she thought, staring intently at the scanner. Say something. Report in. Please.

"Hey, central, we got civilians back of us. It's Reverend Beecham and some others." There was a pause, and then the voice got fainter as though the speaker were sticking his head out the car window. "Hey, Pastor! You need some help? The cavalry's here—"

A strangled scream filtered through the scanner.

A second voice shouted, "Central, they're veggies too—" A crackle of shots. Another scream. Indistinguishable noises. Scratching. A sound like something chewing on the microphone. Silence.

"Patrol three, what's goin' down? Report, patrol three—"

Martha rushed from the kitchen, trying to blank the sounds from the speaker. Bobby Mack. At least he wasn't patrol three.

The radio on the shelf was playing Nick Cave's cover of "Long Black Veil."

"Why don't you give us some news!" Martha cried at it.

"Mayor Hardesty don't want none of us to panic," said Bertie Hernandez. His pals and he had evidently entered the Cuchara Diner in the last minute or so. They'd tracked in some of the thin skiff of snow that covered the Diner's parking lot. Brown water pooled on the tile floor.

"I think maybe *I'm* about ready to panic," said Martha candidly. "I want to know what's going on."

"Don't worry, darlin'," said Bertie. "We'll take good care of you, somethin' happens."

"You didn't see Bobby Mack out there this morning, did you?"

Bertie and Shine Willis exchanged glances. "Not lately," said Bertie. "He's a smart boy. I 'spect he's okay, but probably real busy. You won't see him before tonight."

"Just what's going on out there?" said Martha. "For God's sake, tell me!"

"It's the zombies," said Billy Gaspar.

"They're spreadin' faster'n AIDS," said Shine.

"Yeah," said Bertie. "Looks like maybe all they got to do is bite you, not even kill you. The bastards are all over town, lotta people you and me both know."

"We killed a bunch of them," said Billy Gaspar. "But there's so many—"

"Now," said Bertie, "we got to hole up and rest. Diner's as good a place as any. Anyhow, I figure we got to have lunch. What's the special?"

"Meat loaf," said Martha.

Billy Gaspar groaned. "I don't think my belly can take that."

"Eat or be eaten," said Bertie with a grin.

"This is KHIP," said the radio, "the kay-hip country voice of the southern Colorado empire. Pueblo to Durango, we bring you the absolutely latest news. . . ."

"Shut up," said Martha tightly. "Just tell me what's going on."

The recorded opening trailed off, and there was a moment of dead air. The announcer, when he came on, sounded dead tired and scared shitless. "This is Boots Bell at the kay-hip studios north of Fort Durham. I've got a whole raft of announcements and they're most all life and death, so listen up."

"We're listening, goddamn it," said Bertie Hernandez, sounding as tightly wound as Martha. "Get to it." The boys hadn't gone out much during the afternoon. They'd stayed close to the Diner, bringing in weapons from their trucks and drinking a lot of beer. A few of the other regulars had drifted in. There was very little traffic on 159.

Boots Bell riffled some papers over the radio. Then he said, "The main thing is, stay indoors. Lock your houses. Anybody comes to your door, check 'em out good. All of a sudden, there's dead folks walking everywhere. This is no joke, no test of the emergency broadcast system, nothing like that. It's the real thing."

"Damn straight," said Shine Willis.

"If you've got weapons," said Bell, "keep them loaded and handy. Shoot for the head. That's about the only way to kill a zombie."

"Hey, what about fire?" said Shine.

"—or burn 'em," Bell continued. "Remember they're quicker than they look, and real strong. They generally run in packs. If you see one, there's probably another ten sneaking up behind you."

Jose dropped a pan in the kitchen and half the guys at the counter twitched.

Bell said, "Here at the station, we've received word that the National Guard'll be moving in as soon as they finish mopping-up operations in Walsenburg." He hesitated. "Reckon that'll come after they clean up the Springs. And in Denver—well, we don't have much word at all." Papers rattled for a few moments. "We're keeping a map at the station of all sightings, so if you spot a zombie, give us a jingle and we'll pass the news along." There was a second voice, indistinguishable. Then Bell said, "We've already got so many reports of zombies, we can tell you it isn't safe to be anywhere outdoors in Fort Durham. Period. Sheriff and police officers are doing what they can, along with community volunteers. But if you don't have to be out, then don't go out. Not for any reason." Bell's voice cracked slightly. "The station manager just told me something, and I agree with it. If we stick together, we'll come out of this okay. Remember that."

In the Diner, the men with guns held them tight and exchanged looks.

"More news when it comes in," said Bell. "Now let's listen to some music." The speaker began to twang the opening chords of Tammy Wynette's "Stand by Your Man."

"At least," said Billy Gaspar, "they're not playing the Grateful fucking Dead." He tried to grin, but the effect was ghastly.

Martha set her tray down on the counter and went to the phone behind the cash register. She dialed her parents' number, knowing *of course they're all right*, but just wanting the reassurance. All she got in the earpiece was the soft buzz of a dead line.

By three o'clock, the first zombie appeared in the Diner's parking lot. It was Mrs. Dorothy Miller, who had been the head cashier at the Stockman's Bank.

"For Chrissake, kill her," said Bertie, waving Shine and Billy toward the door. "They're probably like ants, sending out scouts. We don't want the rest to know there's all sorts of food here."

The men nodded and went outside, Shine first. Billy put the butt of the 30.06 deer rifle against his shoulder and slowly squeezed off a round. The bullet went squarely through Mrs. Miller's left eye. The zombie flung out its arms and spun around. Shine raised his Remington pump at close range and blew Mrs. Miller's head completely off.

Shine and Billy dragged the body around the corner of the Diner and out of sight; then they came back in and shared a pull off Miguel Espinosa's flask of home brew.

Martha hardly noticed. She kept listening to the radio and badgering Henry Roybal to keep close track of both the CB base station and the police scanner. "Anything?" she'd say on her trips into the kitchen.

"Nothing," Henry would answer. "Listen, Bobby Mack's probably way too busy to use his radio. Try not to worry."

In the dining room, KHIP was playing Gordon Lightfoot's "Wreck of the Edmund Fitzgerald."

"Christ," said Shine, "who picks the music? I wish to hell Henry had a jukebox."

"But he don't," said Bertie. "We're just gonna have to make our own entertainment." He caressed the rifle lying across his lap. Then he looked up toward Martha and held out his cup.

Martha stared at him and started to turn away.

"Please?"

She thought about it a moment and then brought the pot over.

His expression was earnest. "Listen, Martha, if we all get out of this, think maybe we can start over?"

"No." She resisted the impulse to start laughing hysterically. "We can't start over what we never began in the first place."

Something seemed to smolder in Bertie's eyes. "I'm really on my best behavior now."

"I know that," she said quietly. "But I'm being honest with you."

"Me too," he said. "I really want you to be my girl."

She shook her head.

"Final word?" he said.

—*dangerously*, Martha thought. *He sounds like he'll do anything.* She nodded. Yes.

"Well, shoot," said Bertie. "I guess the only thing left is to fuck you till you can't see straight. Or walk straight, neither."

"Try it," said Martha, "and I'll kill you."

"And I'll come back," said Bertie. "And keep fucking you. Bet it doesn't do no good to kick a zombie in the nuts. What do you think?"

"I think you're disgusting." Martha held the handle of the coffeepot tightly. The temptation to blister his face so that it looked like a basic zombie visage of torn and rotting flesh was nearly irresistible. She turned away.

"I'll wait," said Bertie toward her back. "After you're done waitin' for Bobby Mack, I'll still be good and hard."

Without turning, she said, "I can wait too."

"Not long enough for the Deputy Dawg."

She whirled. "What do you *know*?"

Bertie ostentatiously licked his lips.

By six o'clock it was getting dark. Henry Roybal came out of the kitchen and switched on the EAT sign.

"Think that's a real good idea?" said Shine.

"You think zombies can read?"

"They could when they were alive," said Billy.

"They're animals," said Henry flatly. "Beasts. Probably color-blind too."

Nobody pushed the issue. The neon on the roof fizzed and crackled. The glow on the snow outside the window cycled from red to green.

"Maybe we should make a break for it," said Miguel Espinosa. "Head for New Mexico."

"Doubt there's anything different there," said Bertie. "May as well stay where there's lots of food and booze." He winked at Martha. "And a pretty lady."

"I got a full tank of gas," said Billy to Miguel.

"How come *you* don't leave?" Bertie said to Henry.

The owner of the Diner answered without hesitation. "My daddy stopped here in Fort Durham while he was on his way to California during the Dust Bowl. He loved this place." He shrugged. "I like it too. I been here for floods and droughts, blizzards and tornadoes. I'm not going to be driven off by a passel of flesh-eating sons of bitches."

The radio intermittently delivered repeats of the afternoon messages. There seemed to be few developments. The warnings continued. Stay indoors. Lock the doors. Load the weapons. Aim for the head. Boots Bell finally added a new one. Save a round for yourself.

The men in the Diner talked and drank. Bertie Hernandez mainly drank. By eight o'clock he was chasing shots of tequila with mescal rather than beers. Shine Willis wasn't far behind him.

At nine-oh-seven by the Hamm's clock beside the radio, Bertie hurled his glass against the far wall. It shattered below the mounted head of a twelve-point buck Henry's father had shot sometime around Pearl Harbor.

"I think," said Bertie, grinning horribly at Martha, "it's time for some real entertainment."

Miguel and Shine had moved into position to either side of her. Martha glanced at them, then back at Bertie. He stood up and played for a moment with his Peterbilt belt buckle.

"What I propose," said Bertie, "is to screw this little girl until my pecker comes out her asshole. Is there anybody here with an objection?"

"I don't think I can let you do that, Bertie," said Henry Roybal.

"Didn't think so. You're a good man, Henry." Bertie drew the .357 magnum from its holster and shot Henry Roybal through the heart. The impact threw the old man back against the kitchen doors. They flopped open as the body fell backward. The doors swung shut again, but now dappled with butterfly wings of blood.

"Anyone else?" said Bertie, surveying the silent men.

No one said anything. Not everyone looked wholly enthusiastic, but there were no objections voiced.

"Okay, then." Bertie set the pistol down on the table, then bent and grunted as he tugged his boots loose. His belt buckle followed.

Martha bolted. She was not quick enough to elude Shine's grasp. She struggled, trying to knee him, bite him, crush his instep—Miguel slugged her across the back of the neck and she sagged toward the floor.

She heard Bertie say, "Let's see some pussy."

She felt hands ripping her brown waitress dress down its buttoned front. Rough fingers hooked her pantyhose and rolled them down off her hips, along her legs, clear to her feet.

Martha opened her eyes and glared at Bertie. He had taken off his pants and briefs and stood there in his long-tailed blue work shirt and socks. She suddenly noticed that his socks were slightly mismatched—black and dark blue. "Bertie—" she said. "Don't do it."

He smiled almost cheerfully as he loomed over her, fingering his balls. His penis jutted out and up like a construction crane. Apparently all the alcohol he'd drunk hadn't done a thing to his erection.

"Martha," he said, sounding almost gentle. "I've *got* to." He spat into his hand and slicked up the head of his penis. "You know what's going on out there. This may be our only chance."

She didn't know how to answer him in a way that would mean anything.

Bertie smiled. "Oh," he said, "don't worry about a last-minute rescue by good ol' Bobby Mack Quintana."

She finally confronted what she suspected. What she didn't even want to *think*. As calmly as she could, she said, "What did you do to him?"

"It's not what *I* did to him," Bertie said, walking forward to stand between her spread legs. "It's what the Jergensons' Dobie did to him. I just put him out of his misery. It was a favor." Bertie laughed in a way that was almost a giggle. "Woulda done the same for a dog."

Martha felt the tears, willed them back. No time. Suddenly the radio came through, as though the sound were piped directly to her ears. KHIP was playing "Poor Poor Pitiful Me."

Bullshit! She arched her back, suddenly whipping her right leg up into Bertie's crotch.

Bertie twisted surprisingly fast, turning the blow on his thigh. He put one socked foot on her left ankle. Shine took her right.

Miguel snickered from up beside her head. "Make a wish."

"No gratitude in this pussy," said Bertie conversationally. "I expect there will be." He started to kneel down between her legs.

—as Bobby Mack Quintana came through the front door.

He didn't open it. He just came through it in a crash and chaos of shattered glass and yells from the men along the counter.

"What the fuck?" said Bertie, springing to his feet and lunging for the magnum on the table.

Men cursed and someone screamed, and everyone scattered to get out of Bobby Mack's path. He stood there for a moment and Martha could see he was not alive. He wore his uniform, but no hat. His khaki shirt was soaked with crusted blood that had obviously cascaded down much earlier from the shredded ruin where his throat had been. There were three black holes across his chest where large-caliber bullets had punched in. A fourth bullet had creased his face, laying open one cheek and setting his nose askew. Corruption had already set in. The flesh around his mouth seemed to be rotting. Fluids oozing from tatters in his face gleamed in the glow of the fluorescents.

"Christ, Bobby Mack," said Bertie, holding his pistol out in two shaking hands. "How many times I got to kill you?" The fire and noise reached out, slamming Bobby Mack backward, staggering his body but not felling him.

The zombie turned slightly to look at Martha still on the floor. Its mouth opened, and somehow sounds gurgled up through the torn throat. "Mar-thhha . . ."

Bobby Mack turned back toward Bertie, striding forward before the man could pull the trigger. The dead deputy reached down and grasped Bertie's penis, fingers wrapping around the thick base and the scrotum. With one powerful yank, he pulled back and up, the flesh giving way, tearing like rotten fabric.

The zombie's arm came up and Bertie's abdomen and stomach opened like someone had jerked the seam on a full Ziploc bag of lasagna. Viscera spewed across the dining room. If Bertie screamed, it was drowned out by the sounds of all the other men either frantically grabbing for their weapons or diving for a door.

Bertie's arms windmilled, spasming. Blood sprayed across the overheads and the light suddenly filtered red.

No one was holding onto Martha now, and she tried to scramble to her feet. Bobby Mack had turned to Shine and Miguel, digging fingers into the former's face and shoving the latter back into the glass shards protruding from the door frame. The zombie tossed Shine's face away as though it were a discarded Halloween mask and lurched toward Billy Gaspar.

"I didn't do it!" Billy screamed. "It was them. It was *them*—" Bobby Mack pulled off Billy's left arm and then pulped his head with the hard-muscled limb.

It suddenly seemed very quiet in the Diner. It was inhabited only by the dead and the dying. And Martha. She crouched back by the counter as Bobby Mack turned and came to her. They confronted each other and she stared sickly at his mutilated face.

He reached out jerkily, but his fingers were gentle as they touched her hair. He tried to say something, but the destroyed throat wouldn't let him.

"You too," Martha said, tears finally coming now. "I love you too."

Then she heard the screaming from outside.

Men were dying in the parking lot. In the glow from EAT —EAT—EAT, Martha could see the survivors of the Diner being torn apart by shadowy knots of zombies.

She turned toward Bobby Mack and took his hand. The skin felt as loose as an oversized cotton work glove. "We've got to get out of here," she said. "Come on."

He didn't move. Bobby Mack stared behind her. Slowly, unwillingly, she looked too.

Martha recognized most of the faces.

Some had recently fed—strings of meat hung slack and bloody from the corners of pursed-lip mouths. They were all there. Her nightmares: Carl Crump, Sr., dead eyes alight behind the smashed lenses of a pair of precariously balanced tortoise-shell glasses. Pastor Beecham, his clerical collar and black jacket streaked with gore that looked just as black, except that it glistened wetly in the light. Mrs. Beecham's red bouffant was in disarray, sodden ringlets hanging around her ears. Her gray A-line dress hung in tatters off one shoulder. Father Sierra's head was turned askew on the stalk of his neck by about forty-five degrees. He looked like an owl staring at its prey.

Carl Crump, Jr., reached out toward Martha, and Bobby Mack batted the blood-clotted nails away from her. The younger Crump wore a Maui shirt and ridiculous tropical flower-print jams.

He must be freezing, thought Martha irrelevantly. She realized she couldn't count all the zombies that were crowding into the Diner. Teachers, the night clerk from the 7-Eleven, some of the volunteer firefighters, the county librarian, her doctor. It looked like half the population of Fort Durham.

Carl Crump, Jr., groaned out something Martha couldn't understand. His father stirred beside him. Both zombies put their hands to their crotches like an obscene joke version of the see-no-evil, hear-no-evil monkeys.

She realized they both had enormous erections.

"No!" she said, huddling close to Bobby Mack. The dead deputy gurgled something and put one arm around her.

And then the zombies went for them.

There simply wasn't much maneuvering room, and so the mob surge did little good until the tidal force of corpses swung toward the Diner's front window and the glass exploded outward into the parking area.

Martha found herself on her back, both hands around Mrs. Beecham's neck, attempting to keep the snapping, pit-bull teeth from her own throat. Then a kick from Bobby Mack's boot caught Mrs. Beecham under the collarbone and the zombie twisted away.

Carl Crump, Sr.'s, fist slammed into Bobby Mack's mouth, crumbling teeth and disappearing up to the wrist.

"Bobby—!" Martha screamed.

The elder Crump's hand reappeared, the fingers dripping with blood, nails squeezing cartilage and gray matter. Bobby Mack's body began to spasm, arms jerking away at bizarre angles. Crump licked his own nails.

The crush of dead, writhing bodies bore Martha down into the freezing gravel. A clawing hand snatched away her bra and part of her right breast. At first she felt no pain—just the cold air on her nipples.

She saw the wild tangle of henna-red hair descend toward her crotch, felt the cold lips and icy tongue violate her vagina, tried to draw back against the unforgiving gravel as rotting teeth ground into her flesh. Mrs. Beecham's face, slick with Martha's blood, lunged against her repeatedly, until her husband shoved his wife aside.

Pastor Beecham mounted her as Martha raked at the vacant eyes. Other arms grabbed at her and she felt her left shoulder twist and separate. Her right arm flailed, fingers searching for any purchase at all among her attackers.

The clergyman's penis slid deep into her like a rod of absolute-zero ice. Then Carl Crump, Jr., was at her, rolling her on her side and shoving his erection up into her anus. Martha felt the tissues tear. This time there was no merciful shock. This *hurt* and she screamed.

As Carl, Jr., pushed at her from behind, the movement seemed to excite Reverend Beecham. He shoved back, bubbles of saliva and stale air grunting from his blue lips. Martha could see Carl's father and the others waiting like patient customers in a post office queue.

The pain was a grinding, broken-glass agony that drew out the cells of her brain, sucking them into infinity. "Damn you!" Martha cried. "Damn you *all*!"

The intrusions of the others within her inexorably pounded toward some sort of vanishing dead climax. At first Martha watched, increasingly distant. A frozen calm began to narcotize her. Then she realized how close Bobby Mack's mercifully inert body lay, twisted into the complex lovers' knot her body composed with the thrashing ministrations of Beecham and Carl Crump, Jr.

She could reach his holster flap with her right hand. Her fingertips touched the cold, still-bright leather. Surely one live round must remain in the cylinder of his .38 Police Positive. *Please.*

Carl Crump, Sr., squatted down above her face, runneled fingers moving back and forth along the purpling length of his erection.

Martha's numbed fingers twitched at the holster flap, tugged, pushed at the snap. The catch clicked free. She could feel the knurled walnut butt of the pistol. *Thank you, Bobby Mack.*

The zombies inside her grunted and heaved. Martha sensed others, many more, crowding around her. Dead eyes looked at her, but none of them *saw.* They never had. Her vision grayed.

The zombies kept coming—

—and coming—

Just one bullet, Martha thought.

There was.

MICHAEL MOORCOCK

Hanging the Fool

A British writer, editor, musician, and world traveler, Michael Moorcock is one of the most renowned authors in the fantasy field. He is best known among fantasy readers for his "Elric" series and his splendid fantasy romance *Gloriana*. Among literary mainstream readers he's best known for brilliant novels such as *Byzantium Endures*, *The Laughter of Carthage*, and last year's excellent *Mother London*. Other works include the "Count Brass" series, the "Jerry Cornelius" quartet, "The Dancers at the End of Time" series, *Behold the Man*, and *Wizardry and Wild Romance: A Study of Epic Fantasy* (highly recommended).

The following story was written for Rachel Pollack and Caitlin Matthews' anthology, *Tarot Tales* (Legend, U.K.), a collection of stories based on the imagery to be found in a deck of Tarot cards. Moorcock's contribution is a dark fantasy story of the decadent rich in pre-World War II Europe, and the Wheel of Fortune symbolizing fortune's rise and fall.

Moorcock—winner of The World Fantasy Award, the British Fantasy Award, the Nebula Award, the Guardian Fiction Prize and other honors—lives with his wife, Linda Steele, dividing his time between London, the British countryside, and North Africa.

—T.W.

Hanging the Fool

MICHAEL MOORCOCK

1 THE HERMIT

His wife, he said, had negro blood. "It makes her volatile, like Pushkin."

Watching him later, as he played the table, I saw him show panic twice. He recovered himself rapidly on both occasions. He would tap his wedding ring sharply with his right index finger. His hands were long, not particularly thin, and as tawny as the rest of him—a lion, lazy and cruel, quick as a dagger. "Lord, lord," he would say as his wife made her appearance every evening just before dinner, "she is magnificent!" And he would dart towards her, eager to show her off. Her name was Marianne Max and she loved him in her careless way, thought I thought it more a mother's affection, for she was at least ten years his senior.

He would escort her into the dining room and afterwards would never gamble. Together they would stroll for a while along the promenade. Frequently I saw them silhouetted with the palms and cedars, talking and sometimes embracing before returning to the hotel and the suite permanently booked to them. The Hotel Cumberland was older than most and cared more for pleasing its regular customers than attracting the new money which had come to St. Crim; it was a little run down but maintained its elegance, its superiority over more modern buildings, especially those revivalist deco monstrosities which had risen across the bay on the French side, upon the remains of the old Ashkanasdi mansion, where the so-called Orient Express brought rich Americans in large numbers.

I had been spending the summer with my ex-wife, who had a villa just above the town, in the pine woods. Every evening I would go down to dine at the hotel and perhaps indulge in a little baccarat.

De Passoni was the chief reason for the regularity of my visits. The man was so supremely unselfconscious, so unguarded, few would have believed him a

convicted murderer, escaped from the notorious Chatuz Fortress outside Buenos
Aires some years earlier. There was no sign that he feared recognition or recapture. He appeared to live entirely for the day. And there was, of course, no
deportation treaty between Argentina and St. Crim.

I had not by the middle of the season found any means of approaching him,
however. Every time I tried I had been rebuffed. His wife was equally impossible
to engage in anything but light conversation.

She was the Countess Max, one of the oldest titles in Wäldenstein. Her first
husband, Freddie Max, had been killed during the Siege, leading a cavalry
charge against the Prussians across the ruins of the St. Maria and St. Maria
Cathedral. She had remarried after a year, regaining her estates by her alliance
with Prince Osbert, the new prime minister. He had died of influenza in 1912,
whereupon she had appeared openly with de Passoni, who was already her lover,
until the scandal had forced them to St. Crim where they now lived in unofficial
exile.

De Passoni had his own money, from his father's locomotive works, and it
was this he gambled. He took nothing from her. Neither did she expect him to
take anything. Residents of the Hotel Cumberland said they were a bloodless
pair. I thought otherwise.

2 THE NINE OF PENTACLES

When I came home from North Africa, the following spring, my ex-wife told
me that the couple had disappeared from the Hotel Cumberland, although their
suite was still booked and paid for. There was a rumour that they were in the
hills outside Florence and that the Italian police were resisting an attempt to
extradite him. His father had investments in Milan and considerable influence
with the authorities. My ex-wife became vague when I asked her for more details,
a sure sign that she possessed a secret which she hoped would add to her power.

While she was in her private sitting room taking a telephone call my ex-wife's
companion approached me that evening. The woman, Pia, knew through a
friend of hers that Countess Max had been seen in Florence and then in Genoa.
There was talk of her having brought and equipped a steam yacht. De Passoni
had not been with her.

I asked Pia, who disliked me, why they should have left St. Crim. She did
not know. She shrugged. "Perhaps they were bored."

Returning, my ex-wife had laughed at this and then grown mysterious; my
sign for leaving them.

I borrowed her horse and rode down to the cliffs above Daker's Cove. The
Englishman's great Gothic house was a shell now, washed by the sea he had
attempted to divert. Its granite walls were almost entirely intact and the towers
showed well above the water line even at high tide, when waves washed foam
in and out of the tall windows, but the great weather vane in the shape of a
praying mantis had broken off at last and lay half-buried in the sand of the cove.
Daker himself had returned to England and built himself a castle somewhere

in the Yorkshire Dales. He lived there the year round, I heard, a disappointed recluse. The remains of his great garden were as beautiful as ever. I rode the chestnut down overgrown paths. Rhododendrons, peonies, lilac and great fox-gloves filled the beds, and the whole of the ground was pale blue with masses of forget-me-nots, the remaining memories of England.

What had he learned, I wondered, from all his experience? Perhaps nothing. This was often the fate of those who attempted to impose their own reality upon a resisting and even antagonistic world. It was both a failure of imagination and of spirit. One died frustrated. I had known so many politicians who had ended their days in bitterness. The interpreter, the analyst, the celebrant, however, rarely knew the same pain, especially in old age. Neither, I thought, was that the destiny of those whose politics sought to adjust genuine social ills, who responded to the realities of others' suffering.

The paths joined at an abandoned fountain, a copy of the Kassophasos Aphrodite. Even though she was half-obscured by a wild clematis which clambered over her torso and shoulders like a cloak, she retained her air of serene wisdom. I reined in my horse and dismounted.

Struck by her similarity to the Countess Max, I wondered if I, in my turn, were not imposing my own fancy on the reality.

3 THE ACE OF WANDS

I had returned to Paris for a few days. My investments there were under attack from some manipulations on the Bourse which it soon emerged were fraudulent. By careful covering I was able not only to counter the threat and recover my capital, but make a handsome and honest profit from those whose actions might well have caused me considerable financial embarrassment.

Hearing I was at my house my friend Frere came to see me. He had a message from my father to say that he had been taken ill and was in Lucerne to recover. My own business was over. I went immediately to Switzerland to find my father in reasonable health and breathing almost normally. He was working on his book again, a catalogue of the important buildings destroyed in France and Belgium during the Great War. It was to be his acknowledgement, he said, to an irrecoverable moment in our history, when peace had seemed a natural condition of civilized mankind.

My father asked me to visit my brother at our estates. I had not been to Bek since the last family gathering immediately following the Armistice. Uncle Ricky was long since gone to Italy, obsessed as usual, with a woman, but my brother Ulrich, whom we called Billy, was running the place very well. He was most like my father, more prepared than I to accept such rural responsibilities.

When I left Lucerne the summer had come. Mountains were brilliant with wild flowers and the lake shone with the tranquillity of steel. The train wound down to the French border first and then travelled across to Germany. I changed in Nuremberg, which always reminded me of a gigantic toy, like the one made by the Elastolin firm, with its red castle and walls, its neat cobbles and markets, the epitome of a Bavarian's dream of his perfect past. I had a light lunch at the excellent station restaurant and was disturbed only once, by a gang of men, evidently ex-soldiers, who marched in military style through the lanes shouting of revenge against the French. I found this singularly disturbing and was glad to get on the train which took me to Bek's timeless woods and towers, her deep, lush fields, so like the countryside of Oxfordshire which I had explored while at Balliol before the War.

Billy met me himself, in a dogcart, having received my telegram that morning. "You've been in Africa, I gather?" He looked me over. "You'll be black as an Abyssinian, at this rate!" He was curious about my mining interests in Morocco and Algeria, my relations with the French.

Since I had taken French citizenship, I explained, I had had no trouble. But I was disturbed by the Rif and Bedouin rebels who seemed to me to be growing in strength and numbers. I suspected German interests of supplying them with weapons. Billy said he knew little of international politics. All he hoped was that the Russians would continue fighting amongst themselves until Bolsheviks, Whites, Anarchists, Greens, and whoever else there were, had all wiped one another out.

I had less unsophisticated views, I said. But I laughed. Ivy-covered Bek came in sight at last. I sighed.

"Are you ever homesick?" Billy asked as he guided the dogcart up the drive.

"For which home?" I was amused.

4 THE HIGH PRIESTESS

From Marseilles I took the train down the coast. The sun had turned the olive trees and vines to an astonishing sharpness and the white limestone glared so fiercely that it became for a while unbearable. The sea lacked the Atlantic's profundity but was a flat, uncompromising blue, merging with a sky growing hotter and deeper in colour with every passing hour until by three o'clock I drew the blinds and sat back in my compartment to read.

I determined not to go to Cassis where Lorna Maddox, the American, had told me she would wait until she returned to Boston in September.

I had met her at dinner when I visited Lord St. Odhran at the opening of the grouse season, the previous summer. She had told an extraordinary story about her own sister receiving in the post a piece of human skin, about the size of a sheet of quarto writing paper, on which had been tattooed an elaborate and, she said, quite beautiful picture. "It was the Wheel of Fortune, including all the various fabulous beasts. In brilliant colours. Do you know the Tarot?"

I did not, but afterwards, in London, I purchased a pack from a shop near the British Museum. I was curious.

Lorna's sister had no idea of the sender, nor of the significance of such a grotesque gift.

I discovered that the card indicated Luck and Success.

For at least a week, whenever I had time on my hands, I would lay out sets of cards according to the instructions in the book I had bought at the same time. I attempted to tell my own fortune and that of my family. I recall that even my Uncle Ricky had "Safety" as his final card. But I made no notes of my readings and forgot them, though I still kept the pack in my luggage when I travelled.

"She was told by the police that the tattoo was quite recent," Lorna had said. "And that if the owner were still alive she would have a trace of the design still, on her flesh. The ink, apparently, goes down to the bone. The theory was that she had regretted having the thing made and had it removed by surgery only a month or so after it had been done."

"You're sure it was a woman's skin?" I had been surprised.

"The police were pretty certain."

"What did your sister do with the thing?" St. Odhran had asked.

"The police held it for a while. Then they returned it to her. There was no evidence of foul play, you see. My brother wanted it. It fascinated him. I believe she gave it to him."

I knew her brother. His name was Jack Hoffner and he often visited St. Crim. I had no great liking for him. He was a bad loser at the tables and was reputed to be a cruel womanizer. Possibly the piece of skin had belonged to some deserted paramour. Had she sent it to Hoffner's sister as an act of revenge?

5 THE NINE OF WANDS

It was raining by the time I reached St. Crim. Huge drops of water fell from the oaks and beeches on to tall irises and there was a sound like the clicking of mandibles. Mist gathered on the warm grass as my car drove from the station up the winding road to the white house with its gleaming red roof and English chimneys. The scent of gardenias in the rain was almost overwhelming. I found that I was suddenly depressed and looking back through the rain saw the sea bright with sunlight, for the cloud was already passing.

Pia waited for me on the steps, her hair caught in some multi-coloured gypsy scarf. "She's not here. But she'll be back." Pia signed for a servant to take my bags from the car. "She told me you were coming."

"She said nothing of leaving."

"It happened suddenly. A relative, I gather."

"Her aunt?"

"Possibly." Pia's tone had become almost savage and it was clear she had no intention of telling me anything else.

It had always been my habit not to enquire into my ex-wife's life but I guessed she had gone somewhere with a lover and that this was disturbing Pia unduly. As a rule she kept better control of herself.

My room was ready for me. As soon as I had bathed and dressed I took the car back to the Cumberland. Almost the first person I saw as I stepped through the revolving door into the foyer was the Countess Max who acknowledged my greeting with a warmer than usual smile. Her husband came hurrying from the elevator and shook hands with me. His palm was moist and cool. He seemed frightened, though he quickly masked his expression and his face grew relaxed as he asked after mutual friends.

"I heard you had gone to Genoa to buy a boat!" I said.

"Oh, these rumours!" Countess Max began to move away on de Passoni's arm. And she laughed. It was a wonderful sound.

I followed them into the dining room. They sat together near the open French doors, looking out to the harbour where a slender steam yacht was moored, together with several other large vessels chiefly the property of visitors. I was on the far side of the room and a party of Italians came in, obscuring my view, but it seemed to me that the couple talked anxiously while preserving a good appearance. They left early, after a main course they had scarcely started. About half-an-hour later, as I stood smoking on the balcony, I saw a motor launch leaving a trail of white on the glassy water of the harbour. It had begun to rain again.

6 THE LOVERS

By the following Sunday I suspected some radical alteration in the familiar routine of life at St. Crim. My ex-wife had not yet returned and it was impossible for me to ignore the gossip that she had gone to Tangier with Jack Hoffner. Further rumours, of them disappearing into the interior wearing Arab dress, I discounted. If every European said to be disguised as a Tuareg was actually in the Maghreb then I doubted if there were a single tribe not wholly Caucasian and at least ninety per cent female!

However, I began to feel some concern when, after a month, nothing had been heard from them while the *Shaharazaad*, the steam yacht owned by Countess Max, was reported to have docked in El Jadida, a small, predominantly Jewish port south of Casablanca. They had radio equipment aboard.

I took to laying out my Tarot pack with the Hermit as Significator. I constantly drew the Ten of Swords, the Ace of Wands and Justice, always for the future but the order frequently changed so that although sadness, pain and affliction lay forever in my future they were not always the finale to my life. The other card drawn regularly for the future was the Lovers.

We turn to such methods when the world becomes overly mysterious to us and our normal methods of interpretation fail.

I told myself that my obsession with the Tarot was wholesome enough. At least it lacked the spurious authenticity of psychoanalysis. That particular modern fad seemed no more than a pseudo-scientific form of Theosophy, itself pseudo-religious: an answer to the impact of the twentieth century which enabled us to maintain the attitudes and convictions of nineteenth-century Vienna. Every one I knew was presently playing at it. I refused to join in. Certain insights had been made by the psychoanalystic fraternity, but these had been elevated to the level of divine revelation and an entire mystical literature derived from them. I was as astonished by society's acceptance of these soothsayers as I was by the Dark

Age rituals in St. Crim's rather martial sub-Byzantine cathedral. At least these had the excuse of habit. Doctor Freud was a habit I did not wish to acquire.

I remained at St. Crim until early September when I received a letter from my ex-wife. She was recovering from typhus in a hospital run by the White Sisters in Tangier. She was alone and had no friends there. She asked me to cable funds to the British Embassy or have my agent help her. There was no mention of Jack Hoffner or de Passoni and the Countess Max.

I chose one card at random from my pack. It was the Wheel of Fortune. I went down to the hotel and telephoned my friend Vronsky. That afternoon his Van Berkel seaplane landed in the harbour and after a light supper we took off for North Africa, via Valencia and Gibraltar.

The machine was a monoplane of the latest type and was built to race. There was barely room for a small valise and myself. Vronsky's slightly bloated, boyish face grinned at me from the rear cockpit, his goggles giving him the appearance of a depraved marmoset. Since the Bolshevik counterrevolution Vronsky had determined to live life to the absolute, convinced that he had little time before someone assassinated him. He was a distant cousin of the Tsar.

The plane banked once over St. Crim, her wooded hills and pale villas, the delicate stone and iron of her harbour and promenade, the mock-Baroque of her hotels. It would only be a matter of seven years before, fearing the political situation in Italy, she gave up her independence to France.

The plane's motion, though fluid, filled me with a slight feeling of nausea, but this was quickly forgotten as my attention was drawn to the beauty of the landscape below. I longed to own a machine again. It had been three years since I had crashed and been captured by the Hungarians, happily only a matter of weeks before the end of the War. My wife, a German national, had been able to divorce me on the grounds that I was a traitor, though I had possessed French citizenship since 1910.

Gradually the familiar euphoria returned and I determined, next time I was in the Hague, to order a new machine.

After refuelling stops we were in sight of Tangier within a few hours. As always, the shores of Africa filled me with excitement. I knew how difficult, once one set foot on that continent, it was to leave.

7 THE PAGE OF WANDS

The Convent of the White Sisters was close to the British Consulate, across from the main gate to the Grand Socco, an unremarkable piece of architecture by Arab standards, though I was told the mosque on the far side was impressive. Apart from the usual mixture of mules and donkeys, bicycles, rickshaws, the occasional motor car and members of almost every Berber and Arab tribe, there was an unusually large presence of soldiers, chiefly of the Spanish Foreign Legion. Vronsky spoke to a tall man he recognized from before the War. The exchange was in Russian, which I understood badly. There had been some sort of uprising in a village on the outskirts of the city, to do with a group of Rif who had come in to trade. The uprising was not, as it had first seemed, political.

"A blood feud," Vronsky informed me as we crossed the square from the shade of the great palms, "but they're not complaining. It brought them in from the desert and now they have a day's unexpected leave. They are going in there"—he pointed through the gate—"for the Ouled Näil. For the women." And he shuddered.

We knocked on a rather nondescript iron door and were greeted by a small black nun who addressed me in trilling, birdlike French which I found attractive. Since they did not accept divorce, I simply told her I was visiting my wife and she became excited.

"You got the letter? How did you arrive so soon?"

"Our aeroplane is in the harbour." I lifted my flying helmet.

She made some reference to the miraculous and clapped her little hands. She asked us to wait but Vronsky said he had some business in the new town and arranged to meet me at the Café Stern in three hours. If I was delayed I would send a message.

The little negress returned with a tall olive-skinned old woman who introduced herself as the Mother Superior. I asked after my wife.

"She is well. Physically, she's almost fully recovered. You are Monsieur von Bek? She described you to me. You'll forgive me. She was anxious that it should only be you."

The nun led me down whitewashed corridors smelling of vinegar and disinfectant until we entered a sunny courtyard which contained a blue mosaic fountain, two Arab workmen repairing one of the columns and, in a deck chair reading a book, my ex-wife. She wore a plain lawn dress and a simple straw cloche. She was terribly pale and her eyes still seemed to contain traces of fever.

"Bertie." She put down her book, her expression one of enormous relief. "I hadn't expected you to come. At least, I'd hoped—" She shrugged, and bending I kissed her cheek.

"Vronsky brought me in his plane. I got your letter this morning. You should have cabled."

Her look of gratitude was almost embarrassing.

"What happened to Hoffner?" I asked. I sat on the parapet of the fountain.

"Jack's . . ." She paused. "Jack left me in Foum al-Hassan, when I became ill. He took the map and went on."

"Map?" She assumed I knew more than I did.

"It was supposed to lead to a Roman treasure—or rather a Carthaginian treasure captured by the Romans. Everything seemed to be going well after we picked up the trail in Volubilis. Then Michael de Passoni and Countess Max came on the scene. God knows how they found us. The whole business went sour."

"Where did Hoffner come by a map?"

"His sister gave it to him. That awful tattoo."

"A treasure map? The Wheel of Fortune?"

"Apparently." The memory appeared to have exhausted her. She stretched out her arms. "I'm so glad you're here. I prayed for you to come. I've been an absolute ass, darling."

"You were always romantic. Have you ever thought of writing novels? You'd make a fortune."

On impulse I moved into her embrace.

8 THE QUEEN OF PENTACLES

I remained at St. Crim for several months while my wife grew stronger, though her mental condition fluctuated considerably. Her nightmares were terrifying even to me and she refused to tell me what they involved.

We were both curious for news of Jack Hoffner and when his sister arrived at the Cumberland for a few days I went down to see her. My visits to the town had been rare. In the evenings my wife and I played cards. Sometimes we read each other's Tarot. We became quite expert.

Lorna Maddox believed that her brother was dead. "He hadn't the courage for any prolonged adventure—and North Africa sounds dangerous. I've never been there. Someone killed him, probably, for that map. Do you really think it was sent by a deserted mistress?"

"Perhaps by the one who actually inscribed the tattoo."

"Or the person who commissioned it? I mean, other than the recipient, as it were?"

"Do you know more about this now?" I asked. We sat indoors looking through closed windows at the balcony and the bay beyond.

"I'm not sure," she said. "I think Michael de Passoni had it done."

"To his victim?"

"Yes. To a victim."

"He's murdered more than once?"

"I would guess so. I heard all this from Margery Graeme who had quite a long affair with him. She's terrified of him. He threatened to kill her."

"Why would he have told her such secrets?" A waiter came to take our orders and there was a long pause before she could speak again.

She had magnificent blue eyes in a large, gentle face. She wore her hair down in a girlish, rather old-fashioned style identified with pre-War Bohemia. When she bent towards me I could feel her warmth and remembered how attractive I had found her when we had met in Scotland.

"Margery discovered some papers. Some designs. And a set of Tarot cards with the Wheel of Fortune removed. The addresses of several tattooists in Marseilles were there. And the piece of skin, you know, came from there. At least the postmark on the envelope was Cassis."

"Everyone goes to Cassis." I was aware of the inanity of my remark which had to do, I was sure, with my wish to reject her information, not because it seemed untrue but because it seemed likely. I was beginning to fear a moral dilemma where previously I had known only curiosity.

9 THE WHEEL OF FORTUNE

Business at last forced me to return to Paris. Dining at Lipp's in St. Germain on the first evening of my arrival I was disturbed to see the Countess Max. De Passoni was not with her. Instead she was in the company of a dark man who was either Levantine or Maghrebi. He was strikingly handsome and wore his evening clothes with the easy familiarity which identified him, as we used to say, as some sort of gentleman.

Countess Max recognized me at once and could do nothing but acknowledge me. When I crossed to greet her she reluctantly introduced me to her companion. "Do you know Moulay Abul Hammoud?"

"Enchanted, monsieur," he said in the soft, vibrant voice I associated always with the desert. "We have already met briefly, I believe."

Now that we stood face to face I remembered him from a Legation reception in Algiers before the War. He had been educated at Eton but was the religious leader of the majority of clans in the Southern and pre-Sahara. Without his control the clans would have been disunited and warring not only amongst themselves but making desultory raids on the authorities. Moulay Abul Hammoud not only kept order in large parts of the Maghreb but also maintained enormous political power, for upon his orders the desert Berbers as well as large numbers of urban Arabs, could forget all differences and unite to attack the French or Spanish.

It was commonly agreed that Moulay Abul was only awaiting the appropriate moment, while the benefits of colonial occupation outweighed the ills, before declaring the renewed independence of the Saharan kingdoms. His influence was also recognized by the British who acknowledged his growing power in North India and also in their own Middle Eastern interests.

"I'm honoured to meet you again, sir." I was impressed by him and shared a respect many had expressed before me. "Are you in Paris officially?"

"Oh, merely a vacation." He smiled at the Countess Max. She looked darker, even more exotic than when I had last seen her.

"Moulay Abul was of great service to me," she murmured, "in Morocco."

"My wife has only recently returned. I believe you met her there. With Jack Hoffner?"

The countess resumed her familiar detached mask, but in spite of seeming ill-mannered I continued. "Have you heard anything of Hoffner? He was meant to have disappeared in Morocco or Algeria."

Moulay Abul interrupted quickly and with considerable grace. "Mr. Hoffner was unfortunately captured by hostile Tuaregs in Mauretania. He was eventually killed. Also captured, I believe, was the poor countess's husband. The authorities know, but it has not been thought wise to inform the Press until we have satisfactory identification."

"You have some?"

"Very little. A certain map that we know was in Hoffner's possession."

It seemed to me that the Countess Max tried to warn him to silence. Unconsciously the Moulay had told me more than he realized. I bowed and returned to my table.

It seemed clear that Hoffner and de Passoni had failed in their adventure and had died in pursuit of the treasure. Possibly Moulay Abul and Countess Max had betrayed them and the treasure was in their hands. More likely the answer was subtler and less melodramatic.

I was certain, however, that Moulay Abul and the Countess Max were lovers.

10 THE TEN OF SWORDS

The tragedy eventually reached the Press. By coincidence I was in Casablanca when the news appeared and while the local journals, subject to a certain discretion, not to say censorship, were rather matter-of-fact in their reporting, the French and English papers were delighted with the story and made everything they could of it, especially since de Passoni was already a convicted murderer and Hoffner had a warrant for fraud against him issued in Berlin at the time of his disappearance.

The Countess Max emerged more or less with her honour intact. The Press preferred to characterize her as an innocent heroine, while my wife was not mentioned at all. Moulay Abul remained a shadowy but more or less benign figure, for the story had been given a Kipling touch by the time the writers had licked it into a shape acceptable to a wide public.

The opinion was that de Passoni and Hoffner had duped the Countess Max, getting her to buy the steam yacht they needed to transport the treasure back to Europe as soon as it was in their possession. The map, drawn on the skin of a long-dead Roman legionary, had become the conventional object of boys' adventure fiction and we learned how the two adventurers had dressed as Bedouin and ridden into the Sahara in search of a lost city built by Carthaginians who had fled conquering Rome. More in fact was made of the mythical city than the map, which suited Hoffner's family, who had feared the sensational use journalists would have made of the bizarre actuality.

I was invited to dinner by General Fromental and his wife and should have refused had not I heard that Moulay Abul was also going to be present.

By chance it was a relatively intimate affair at one of those pompous provincial mansions the French like to build for themselves in imitation of an aristocracy already considered impossibly vulgar by the rest of Europe. My fellow guests were largely of advanced years and interested neither in myself nor the Moulay, who seemed glad of my company, perhaps because we shared secrets in common.

When we stood together smoking on the terrace, looking out at palms and poplars, still a dark green against the deep blue of the sky, and listening to the night birds calling, to the insects and the occasional barking of a wild dog, I asked after the Countess Max.

"I gather she's in excellent health," he said. He smiled at me, as if permitting me a glimpse of his inner thoughts. "We were not lovers, you know. I am unable to contemplate adultery."

The significance of his remark completely escaped me. "I have always been fascinated by her," I told him. "We were frequently in St. Crim at the same time. She and de Passoni lived there for a while."

"So I understand. The yacht is moored there now, is it not?"

"I hadn't heard."

"Yes. Recently. She had expressed some notion of returning to Wäldenstein but the situation there is not happy. And she is a cold-natured woman needing the sun. You've a relative there, I believe."

"An ex-wife. You know her?"

"Oh, yes. Slightly. My other great vice is that I have difficulty in lying." He laughed and I was disarmed. "I make up for this disability by the possession of a subtle mind which appreciates all the degrees and shades of truth. Hoffner deserted her in Foum al-Hassan. I was lucky enough to play some small part in getting her back to Tangier. One should not involve women in these affairs, don't you think?"

"I rather understood they involved themselves."

"Indeed. A passion for excitement has overwhelmed Western females since the dying down of war. It seems to have infected them more than the men."

"Oh, our women have always had more courage, by and large. And more imagination. Indeed, one scarcely exists without the other."

"They do define each other, I'd agree."

He seemed to like me as much as I liked him. Our companionship was comfortable as we stood together in the warm air of the garden.

"I'm afraid my wife mentioned nothing of your help," I told him.

"She knew nothing of it. That man Hoffner? What do you think of him?"

"A blackguard."

"Yes." He was relieved and spoke almost as if to someone else. "A coward. A jackal. He had a family."

"Two sisters living. I know one of them slightly."

"Ah, then you've heard of the map?"

"The one you mentioned in Paris? Yes, I know of it. I don't think his sister recognized it for a map."

"Metaphysically, perhaps, only?" His humour had taken a different colour. "Oh, yes, there is a map involved in many versions of that design. I thought that was common knowledge."

"You're familiar with the Tarot?"

"With arcana in general." He shrugged almost in apology. "I suppose it's in the nature of my calling to be interested in such things. Hoffner's death was no more unpleasant than any he would have visited on—on me, for instance." He turned away to look up at the moon. "I believe they flayed him."

"So he's definitely dead. You saw the corpse?"

"Not the corpse exactly." Moulay Abul blew smoke out at the sky. It moved like an escaped ifrit in the air and fled into invisible realms. "Just the pelt."

11 JUSTICE

My return to St. Crim was in the saddest possible circumstances, in response to a telegram telling me that my wife was dead. When I arrived at the house Pia handed me a sealed envelope addressed to me in my wife's writing.

"You know she killed herself?" The voice was neutral, the eyes desolate.

I had feared this but had not dared to consider it. "Do you know why?"

"It was to do with Hoffner. Something that happened to her in Africa. You know how she was."

We went down to the kitchens where Pia made coffee. The servants were all gone, apart from the cook, who was visiting her sister in Monaco. The woman and her husband who had kept the house for her had found her body.

"She cut her wrists in the swimming pool. She used Hoffner's razor."

"You don't know why? I mean—there wasn't anything she discovered? About Hoffner, for instance?"

"No. Why, did you hear something?"

I shook my head but she had guessed I was lying. Handing me the coffee cup she said slowly: "Do you think she knew what was going on? With Hoffner and de Passoni?"

"She told you?"

"The Countess Max stayed with us for several days. She went down to the hotel. She plans to remain there until the funeral. Hoffner's sister is there, too. A bit of a reunion."

"You think my wife was guilty? That she had a hand in whatever happened in Morocco?"

"She knew Hoffner was involved in every sort of beastly crime and that half the Berlin underworld was after him—not to mention the New York police and the French Secret Service. He betrayed men as well as women. She told me he was threatening her but I think she loved him. Some bad chemistry, perhaps. He excited her, at least. The Countess Max, on the other hand, was thoroughly terrified of him. He had a hold over her husband, you know."

"So he forced them into his adventure?"

"Apparently. They needed a boat."

I found that I could not bear to open the envelope my wife had left for me and walked instead down to the Hotel Cumberland where I found Lorna Maddox and Countess Max taking tea together in the cool of the salon. They both wore half-mourning in honour of my wife and greeted me with sincerity when I presented myself, asking me to join them.

"It must have been frightful for you," said Lorna Maddox, "the news. We were appalled."

"Her nerves were terribly bad." The Countess Max remained distant, though less evasive, less cool. "I thought she was brave. To go inland with the men like that. I refused, you know."

"But you believed the map?"

"I had no reason to doubt. Jack was completely convinced. The woman— the woman on whom it had been inscribed was—well, you know, of very good family over there. She was no more than a girl. The secret was passed from mother to daughter, apparently. God knows where Jack heard the story originally, but he made it his business to find her."

"And seduce her," said Lorna in a small, chilling voice.

"He was proud of that. I gather it was something of a challenge." The Countess Max raised china to her lips.

"Surely he didn't—he couldn't . . . ?" I was glad to accept the chair Lorna Maddox offered me.

"Take the skin?" she said. "Oh, no. That was sent to my sister by the girl's uncle, I gather. There was for a while some suspicion of a blood feud between her family and mine."

"Moulay Abul put a stop to that." The Countess was approving. "Without his interference things might have become considerably worse." She frowned. "Though poor Michael's not entirely convinced of that."

I was shocked. "Your husband's still alive? I understood that he had died in North Africa."

"Moulay Abul saved him also. Through his influence he was given up to the French police and is now at sea, escorted back to Buenos Aires by two Sûreté sergeants. He was relieved at first. . . ."

"He'd heard what happened to Hoffner?"

She stared directly back into my eyes. "He saw it."

Although it was not yet five I ordered a cognac from their waiter. I marvelled at the self-control of such women. It was still impossible to guess their real feelings—one towards her brother, the other towards her husband.

There was little more to say.

"The matter's been resolved in the best possible way." Lorna Maddox sighed and picked up a delicate cup. She glanced at me almost in amusement. "You are very upset. I'm sorry. We were fond of your wife. But she would encourage men to such extremes, don't you think?"

I returned to the house and opened the packet, expecting some explanation of my wife's part in the affair. But she had written nothing.

The envelope contained a folded section of almost transparent skin on which had been tattooed a Wheel of Fortune. It had been wrapped around the Tarot card representing Justice. There was also a visiting card bearing the printed name of Moulay Abul Hammoud and on the reverse, in clear script, a few words— "With my compliments. I believe this is morally, madame, your property."

The note was, of course, unsigned.

LEIF ENGER

Hansel's Finger

"Hansel's Finger" is a beautifully crafted story that defies definition. It was published in *New Frontiers*, an anthology of new western stories edited by Joe R. Lansdale—although Lansdale admits that it's not really a western. His reason for including it in the anthology? It was too good to pass up.

It is easier to make a case for classifying the story as fantasy, for the events are certainly fantastical, if not impossible; it is set in Disney World, a place that is a monument to one man's fantasy; and the title refers to a well-known fairy tale. But when it comes right down to it, my reason for publishing it is the same as Lansdale's: it's just too good to pass up.

"Hansel's Finger" is Leif Enger's first published short work. He and his brother, Lin, wrote a mystery novel together, *Comeback*, published by Pocket Books.

—T.W.

The finger referred to in the story's title is a grotesque object that not only impinges on an ordinary day in the life of an ordinary guy at Disney World, but also abruptly and profoundly shatters that ordinariness. While the tone of the piece is rather cool, the disturbing nature of the disruption of life makes for a neatly horrific, effective tale.

—E.D.

Hansel's Finger

LEIF ENGER

In a painted plastic boat, the silver safety rail snug against your lap, you begin the little voyage: a cave is where it all starts, cement stalactites fingering the artificial river, which still manages to trick you with its salamander smell. Outside it is midafternoon, hot as bird screams, and heavy with the cumulative breath of exhausted tourists; here in the cave, bumping through the water, it is ten at night and twelve is just visible if you lean forward. There's a small skidding sound now as your shell accelerates. You scrape the bottom once more, tilt several degrees to the right and *floom*, into the dark and down a drop that makes your arms float up in front of you. Celia wouldn't have liked this, but you've left her back in Paradise Valley to eat onion rings until your return, which is tomorrow. Actually you could have gone back yesterday; the conference ended early when two vice presidents forsook their places at the table for a day of charter deep-sea fishing. But your reservations were already made, and here you are, waiting to be amazed in a cave, and the first of the celebrated pirates is now ahead, on your left.

It's a skeleton pirate, actually, the fake remains upright, pinned contrapposto by a cutlass. Disney *invented* pirates, Celia would have said; in your mind she walks the plank, leaving you alone, in danger, happy. The skeleton turns its head to watch as you scoot slowly past, and now you enter larger waters. The sea, apparently. It's nighttime on the coast of some homely Caribbean point of land, and offshore a ragged galleon is pouring a hell of ball and grapeshot into the streets of an honest village. This is long-distance battle; some of the cannon just don't have the range, and shipside ammo keeps pounding the water near your fragile craft. You're on the pirates' side, of course. If the villagers had wanted to avoid fire and pillage and all the rest of it, why didn't they set up shop further inland? But there they are, under siege, and evidently indignant about it. Landlubbers. They shout angrily, waving brooms.

You regret having to leave the invasion before it's finished—one of the fist-raising village viragoes, certain to get hers eventually, looks a little like Celia—but your boat's leaving now, and you have to go with it. Under a bridge, two loutish mannequins (my word, they even have hair on their *legs*) grin at you as you pass, offering the brown bottle. It's nearly done, so short a ride—and now, as the tunnel narrows down again and that midday heat shines from a hole in the distance, a final attraction. You cruise past so slowly, so close, you could reach out and brush a finger against his cheek. He is a strong, old pirate. He is the veteran of a million days on the water, a thousand years of breathing salt and gold. In the crow's-feet of his eyes are the weight of doubloons, the kisses of stolen women, the corpses of his mates. There are pistols braced in his belt, a huge throw of ale in one fist, and a cutlass in the other, which he pounds, in slow motion, upon a stump. The stump, you notice as you slip away, is the pirate's table: it holds a lump of cheese, black bread, and a bottle. The cutlass jerks firmly up and down, a robotic exercise, missing the cheese by an inch.

And after that it's over. You're in the last run now, surfacing, coming awake. The subterranean humidity begins baking away with the first breath of afternoon that reaches you, and you twist in your seat, checking the wallet, the keys. As you do so the butt of someone's old cigar rolls away from you and bumps into the corner of the car. Disgusting. You pick it up to toss it away, now while you're still in the water, and it surprises you and makes you stare. It isn't a cigar. It's someone's finger.

On September 24th, 1984, at approximately 2:30 in the afternoon, within the steaming confines of Disney World, Florida, Howard Arvis became the only person he knew ever to find a finger outside its normal scope of human involvement. Although his first impulse was to throw it away, he was unable to do it. He held it out in front of him, both of his hands gripping part of someone else's, the finger as black and vertical as an exclamation mark: *Look at me!* Howard Arvis looked, reaffirmed the rare digit for what it was, and remembered to close a fist around it before the ride dry-docked and was boarded by a bright new crew.

"When you're trapped with a finger in a crowded amusement park," Howard Arvis would later write to his brother in Iowa, "there are no conventional escapes." This was a truth he discovered as he was looking for a fitting dismissal of his new secret; when he tried dumping the finger into one of Disney's frequent trash bins, a corner of his conscience wouldn't let him. This wasn't a corn dog he was tossing away unfinished, or a chocolate-covered banana; this was someone's trusted finger, a once versatile index which had point at sunsets and rubbed the chins of chuckling babies. "With five fingers and a thumb in your right-hand pocket, there's very little else you can keep your mind on," Howard wrote.

He also found he couldn't leave the park. He hadn't intended to stay all day, under pre-trip admonitions from Celia that more than six hours of that bloated Florida sun was bad for one's body thermostat, but when he neared the outgate, still one finger richer than natural man, the thought of leaving and riding for an hour and then arriving back in his clean, white hotel room with that blackened holy object still on his person was too much for his honest mind. He'd parked the rented Skylark in the Goofy lane, row thirty-eight, at 9:05 that morning. Twenty minutes later, goosed into the park by shuttle and monorail, he had breakfasted on Mickey ice cream, vanilla-faced with two chocolate ears. Then he did all the rides he could find, sweating out the ice cream under the sun and a sport coat, ignoring his hollow stomach as the day got hotter and hotter because *Boy* there's so much to see here, and then he'd found that famous pirate ride. It was the one he'd seen film of on a Sunday-night TV show years before, when the Disney thing was just beginning. And the cave sure looked cool, and *was* cool, and he had gone into it thinking of Celia and come out with a sorry old finger which demanded proper disposal. He stepped out of the sidewalk crush and into a vast rest room, where he was able to examine the finger in the private blue light of a stall. Taking it from his pocket (it was rubbing against a load of change, he realized with disgust—he remembered putting pennies in his mouth as a child, and understood his mother's consternation to a degree *she* never had) he held it at eye level. It quelled his whining stomach. The finger had apparently been owned by a Caucasian male of medium size, and the amputation hadn't been clean. Howard closed his eyes. The finger, clasped between his own index and thumb, felt very dry and wrinkled and slightly rubbery, like a carrot forgotten over the summer in the refrigerator. Howard dropped it into a jacket pocket— no change there—and aimed his mind at a juniper bush he'd planted with Celia last spring. So wonderfully fragrant. So green and romantic and promising. Howard Arvis stepped from the stall with the dead stem in his pocket. He knew he would never eat again.

Howard had been just nine years old when his neighbor Hans Harrickson had dismembered a hand with a lawn mower. Hans' father owned a tired Minneapolis Moline tractor under which was wired a wide-swath grass-cutter, an arrangement which predated the Cub Cadet by decades. The Moline was fired up a couple of times a month to return a sense of domicile to the sage-grown Harrickson yard; one Saturday, only hours after Mr. Harrickson had sharpened the scary blades and lubed the rotor, Hans got off the tractor to snag a wayward garter snake, and as he fumbled in the grass a blade spun free and flicked off the leading edge of his right hand. It was pretty weird, he'd told Howard two days later while showing off the bandages. The ring finger and pinky, took right off. *Zippo,* he said, just like that. The snake got away. And long after the scar tissue had set and turned the color of regular skin and Hans had become used to giving less than he got in a handshake, the wound remained a sort of barometer. It predicted autumn, Hans said, a good six weeks before the last mowing of every summer. "Got to keep it in my pocket," he told Howard. "Or my armpit. Always July in there." No one had ever found Hans's fingers. "Didn't think to look," Hans said.

"When you find a finger in Disney World," Howard wrote to his brother in Iowa, "you quickly realize there's no Lost and Found." Actually Howard had walked right past the Lost and Found, but was preoccupied enough to miss it; if he had seen it, he probably would have passed it anyway, not wanting to approach the clear-faced girl behind the counter: "Here, found this on one of the rides. Has anyone been looking for it?" Howard Arvis was not a seeker of that sort of attention. Instead, he found he was gazing at the hands of men he passed on the walk—full, four-finger-and-a-thumb men without exception, the hands swinging at their sides mostly, though some were tucked into pockets. These he viewed with more care, looking at their faces, seeking concealed agony. He saw many smiles, many empty expressions, many squints from tired parents. It was too late anyway; the finger was beyond resuscitation, and its former owner was probably home from the hospital already, whiskeying down in preparation for the novocaine's fade-out. Howard thought, *Probably a college student, who was well watered when it happened and is going to be awfully surprised when he wakes up.* Howard imagined a new freshman on his first weekend home: "How was Hell Week?" his parents would ask. "Did you make the fraternity?" "Sure did," the kid would say. "Shake."

By dinnertime Howard Arvis had covered most of the Disney park on foot and needed to sit down. He headed on instinct for a neat quick-seafood shop with blue colonial siding and white Shaker chairs, but got a peek of someone's shrimp before he reached the counter and recommitted himself to starvation. The shrimp were curled, pinkylike, their still-attached tails spatulate, like fingertips slammed in a car door. Howard turned on his groaning soles and aimed for the closest ride.

It turned out to be the Snow White adventure, in which the main character was not Snow White or the Seven Dwarfs but a wart-ridden witch that darted out and offered him poisoned apples every time he turned a corner. Howard was grateful for the rest, but annoyed by the ride; there were too many witches here, and too few dwarfs. He had never seen Snow White on TV or read the story in a book, but it was his understanding there was only one witch in it. Maybe he'd been wrong. Howard's car bumped forward through a dark cardboard tunnel and, *bam*, another witch slid out, leering: *Have an apple, sonny.* He wanted to slap the witch, but instead closed his eyes and leaned back in his seat. Why didn't they build a story-ride you could understand? Something straightforward like Hansel and Gretel: it had a witch, just one, and there was even something about a finger in it. Yes. The blind old witch was fattening Hansel for a stew and was feeling his finger every day to check his rate of weight gain. Only he was tricking her, poking a bone through the bars: *Sorry, lady, fast metabolism.* It was pretty clever of Hansel, really, staving her off like that day after day, staying out of the pot by displaying a surrogate. Probably his real fingers were like link sausage. It worked though, and in the end he and Gretel had followed a trail of bread crumbs back to their quaint little woodcutter's hut in the forest. Helped by a substitute finger, they had turned the corner from the witch's nasty shop to the ultimate place of warmth and safety: an oven that presumably baked bread instead of children, and a father within yelling distance, whose job it was to carry an ax. Howard wondered if Hansel had then carried around his lucky finger bone, which had, after all, served him better than a plump rabbit's foot would have, or if he'd given it a decent burial. Probably neither, Howard decided; probably he just threw it at a tree stump or a sparrow on his walk home through the woods with Gretel. Just, *zing*, threw it away.

It would never work that way in Disney World.

After Snow White, Howard went on the Peter Pan ride, in which his car took off and flew, like Peter, only in slower motion, over the rooftops of a tiny London. He was not fooled, as he had tried to be among the Caribbean pirates, especially when he caught his first look at the Peter Pan pirate, Captain Hook. Even with a detached finger getting old in his pocket, it didn't bother Howard that the Captain was an amputee; the cartoonity of this particular ride was tiring to his mind and suggestive to his stomach. As a boy he had practiced a rigorous exercise of eating during cartoons, especially on Saturday mornings. One favorite show concerned the adventures of a boy, probably a cousin of the Pan family, who could fly, and young Howie Arvis had watched him do it week after week while eating yellow bowls of Cheetos. The taste, which had been hidden in his mouth just where the tongue joins the back of the jaw, came out now and began to tease the salivary glands. *I'm going to eat*, Howard thought. *Something huge and fried and salty*, he thought. *Finger or not.*

He did not eat something huge and fried, though his intention was firm. It was past nine o'clock when he got done with the Pan flight (it had ended with Captain Hook about to be reunited with his lost hand, in the belly of a crocodile which had swallowed it years before), and all visible venders were closing up. Not a taco, not a burger, not a godforsaken foot-long wiener was available, and to head for a sit-down place at this hour was to be a nuisance to the cooks and janitorial staff. Howard had, in the end, to settle for a watery malted which was like vanilla with a misplaced spurt of chocolate. A glass of melted Mickey Bars. *As I began*, Howard thought, *so shall I end. Hungry, and with only my fingers to count on.*

In his freshman year of college Howard Arvis had been taken with a girl, a woman, not Celia, and he had carried her lipstick in the glovebox of his Ford for six years. It was the only item he'd ever owned for which he felt the same solemnity and responsibility as the stale joint in his polyester pocket. Sheila. The "she" at the beginning of her name was perfect, a fitting prefix for a woman so inveterate at squeezing the nectar out of whatever crowd she happened to be with. Sheila wore whipstitched work shirts, a wild white grin, and peg-leg Levis that dove into sharkskin boots. The boots were Sheila: tall-heeled, narrow-toed, and white as the Western sun. Her smile made her invisible to the night guards at the all-male dorm. By herself she could create a mob, then pick out one soul from the condemned and gallop away like a high wind, leaving the rest grabbing at their hats. Howard had been the survivor one night, plucked from a pearl-snap bar and pulled along by Sheila's soft hands, blinking in surprise.

"Where should we go?" Howard had said, love-uncertain, struck by luck.

"To the country," said Sheila, and Howard was amazed at how faint and true her voice was away from people. Warm as new skin.

He angled the Fairlane off the highway and into a piñon stand, black in the high Nevada night. Just before they turned it off, the radio told them forty-nine degrees.

"Would you take off your shirt for me?" said Sheila.

Howard would have taken it off and then eaten it. When his torso was bare and chill as a brick, Sheila touched him with her fingers, then asked him to turn around and face out the window. He did, and heard her hands searching her purse. It clinked softly with combs, compacts, feminine things. She said, "Hold still." He held and in an instant arched high with the waxy tickle of her lipstick running patterns on his back. It dipped and dodged, and he laughed in fear and disbelief, squirming.

"Hold still," she said. "I'm drawing." She said it so quietly he gripped the door handle in one hand and the wheel in the other and let her draw. It was an abstract design, she told him, a series of up-and-down lines raked over by some side-to-side lines, not a real picture of anything at all.

"Like a fishnet?" said Howard, who couldn't see it.

"I suppose, if you've got to put a name on it," Sheila said.

He kept her lipstick after that, sliding the tube into the pocket of his on-again flannel shirt and later placing it gently into the corner of the Fairlane's glovebox. The fishnet attracted the envy of his roommate and came off during his next three showers. Sheila saved another soul the next week, and then another, leaving Howard as dry as a slow south breeze.

"To depart from a finger one is just beginning to know," Howard wrote to his brother in Iowa, torturing his brain to form the thought, "might be similar to divorce. There must be a good deal of grace present, and when it's over you just stand there by yourself."

With the light gone and the temperature down to sixty degrees in the Magic Kingdom, Howard cupped the finger in his pocket and made a glazed walk toward the exit gates. The alien felt cool as Sheila's lipstick in his palm and ticklish to his skin. It also felt bigger, heavier, important, a growing child to be responsible for. He did not want it, could not leave the park with it. He leaned forward against its tug.

In the flannel glow of blue-white Disney light, the cobblestones lead you over a bridge. The exit is ahead, an impossibility for you: your little passenger won't have it. The bridge arches more dramatically than it needs to, and at its peak you look down and see the swan. It's a Disney swan, but living; it shakes droplets from its beak like mercury and splays its feathers. The swan sways its neck and looks at you the way Sheila did. It is a good sign. The last of the tourists are at the exit now, boarding trams. The swan is waiting. With the mind of Hansel and the grip of a Barbary corsair, you pull the finger free and hold it high. You stretch back, whip forward, and release. The throw is better than you ever thought you could be, high and spinning, better than all the cucumbers you tossed growing up. The twig comes down, deflated now, black against the water. The swan lunges, its neck wand-white, and you look back toward the exit. Your plane leaves tomorrow, for Celia.

GARRY KILWORTH

Dogfaerie

British author Garry Kilworth is best known for adult fantasy and horror tales, but he also publishes work for children, such as the following gem from the children's anthology *Hidden Turnings*, edited by Diana Wynne Jones and published in the U.K.

"Dogfaerie" makes deft use of British folklore, reminding us that the wonders of the land of faery are surpassed only by its dangers . . . at least for the unwary. Like all the best works of "children's fantasy," this sparkling tale is ageless.

—T.W.

Dogfaerie

GARRY KILWORTH

There is some folk what say there bant no such creatures as faeries, but I knows different, see. Them folk is cockle-headed, as any totter, diddycoy, pikey and tinker would tell. Here's a tale as is proof of such.

More'n a hundred years since, a travelling man took himself from a life on the seaways to settle in the county of Rutland, far north of here. This man built himself a big house on a hill, making use of the woodland trees what covered his estate. While the house were being built, the seed of a dogfaerie blowed in from the woods and growed down below the floorboards. Soon after, afore this wildrose faerie were able to let go its roots, the forest had been cut back to a spinney, situated too far from the dwelling for the dogfaerie to reach. There were no escape for the little creature and it were trapped, tight and hard. Leastways, there were *one* way it could get out, but that were a drastic method, which the dogfaerie were not up to using at that time.

In the beginning, it were happy, see. The master married and filled the house with children, fizzy as lemonade, and the dogfaerie's eating habits were such it gobbled their feelings, the way we would a hunk o' cheese and bread. Them were days when the house smelled of fresh-cut timber and the oak and elm were still in it. The dogfaerie were much like a shrunk child itself, with gold tracers in its eyes, a-flashin' like polished brass on a harness.

Come winter the dogfaerie would curl up in the fire ashes, after all had gone to bed, to keep out the cold. Summertime, though, would find it crawling a-tween the kindling sticks, which was not likely to be touched at that point in the seasons. Fireplaces, with their stacked logs and smell of the forest, is true heart-o'-home for dogfaeries, and where they spend much of their forevers.

O' course, when folk was about the house, it spent much of its forever in hiding. It had the magic of shapechangers, so long as there were a copying image in sight, near human form. Like a statue or painting and such. It would stand close to, its eyes burning like candle-flames in a draught, and make itself into a copy of that painting afore burying itself deep in the brushstrokes. From that hidey-hole it would set to studying the folk coming and going, as snug and safe as woodworms in a beam. Folks would look on the eyes of such pictures and shiver a while from their toes without knowing the wherefores.

On such close-to lookings from human folks, the dogfaerie took to having feelings what bant known to you or me. It were both caught and thrown by such close proximities, since it liked the nearness of human folk but hated the stink of a real living soul. One Edward Ruttersdown, owner of this house at the century's change, would lean with his back up at the fireplace, warming his trouser-seat, never knowing what gases wafted from his soul and all but choked the poor dogfaerie's delicate senses.

Later on, of course, the house were full of photos, pictures of the family, old folks and babes, and the dogfaerie would flit from one to other, changing places as quick as a weasel swapping holes.

Listen in, though. There were one image what frit that dogfaerie more than Oberon himself: its very own likeness. When it stood to, afore a mirror and looking on its own form, it knew it were standing on the cliff edge of nowheres—of nowheres in nothingworld. A dogfaerie is eternal, never dying, but take away itself and there is nothing to hold it inside. If the dogfaerie went into its own image, inside the mirror, it would vanish away, for a looking-glass picture is only as lasting as the folk what stands afore it, be they human or faerie.

One night in May-time, when the cherry blossom were covering the windowpanes with pollen dust in the darkness, Edward Ruttersdown spoke a few words to his good wife. "Darlin'," he says, soft as you like, "the two of we must go from this here house and find another home. Business in London calls us to it, and we must move to the big city."

"Oh," she says in a voice what is tight with feeling, "and why might that be?"

"The business," he tells her, "has got to have me near it, now it's growed so big. There is a grand lady by the name of Wuthers, wishing to buy this old house with good cash. I will buy you a fine home in the town. I know you will like it as well as this one."

"Well," she says, looking around wistful like, "I don't know as I'll like no place as well as this, but if it's got to be I won't cause no argument. But let me tell you this, Teddy Ruttersdown, I shall miss our home, despite its funny ways."

The dogfaerie were naturally very saddened to hear these words from the human folk of the household. It wanted to make them stay but such power were not in its tiny hands. It could do many things, play many tricks with light and shadow, and send whispering voices from the woodwork of empty rooms. It could drive out spiders, silver the flies and gild the cockroaches. It could copy the bats and birds in the attic, their sounds, and leave peculiar scents in the corners of the hall. But it could not make the humans stay and be happy with their lot.

"And another thing," says Alice Ruttersdown, as she looks up from her embroidering to the photo of her mother above the fireplace, "have you told this

Wuthers lady that the house is haunted with a ghost? No, I can see it in your face you haven't."

"Well," says her Teddy, shifting his bottom as the hot coals send up steam from his shiny pants, "it would only give her the frits, and she's an old lady. The ghost won't harm her none and she's a very short-sighted woman, deaf as a post with it."

"Come away from that fire before it scorches," says Alice. And Teddy does as he's told in such small matters as this, knowing he has got the big one under his wing.

So the house fell into the wrinkled hands of its last mistress. Widow Wuthers were an ancient piece of flesh, dry as a husk of corn let lie in the sun. Her body had not the spark of the child still residing: all her feelings was stale and untasty, leaving a bitter flavour on the dogfaerie's tongue. The dogfaerie came to loathe her bad, since she would chase off young people what come to the garden. Once it even showed itself, but she spit at it and raised up her stout hickory-stick as if to strike. She were concerned by nothing in this life, for death were waiting not far off, crouched and ready to jump on her shoulders, and this squatter in her home worried her no more than ghosts or faeries.

The Wuthers woman did nothing to make repairs on the house and slowly the place fell into ruins from where it would not rise again. When the unwelcome squatter finally leapt and bore her creaky frame to the floor under its weight, the garden had growed tall with weeds what choked the air and fluffed-up the drainpipes with white seedballs, the window-sills of the house had rotted and new tenants moved into the cupboards on insecty legs. Widow Wuthers were taken away to her last narrow home, but no new folk came to fill the old place and stock its larder with tears or laughter.

Silence unpacked its bag and settled in.

The dogfaerie had a melancholy hunger. It missed, most of all, the scampering feet and voices of the children. Now it had only the wind in the chimney. Mice scuttled to and fro behind wainscots and nameless birds stamped across the roof, hollering at their own kind. On occasion, slates did death slides down the roof, to crash on the paths underneath. Moss crept in through chinks in the brickwork and toadstools growed on the inside ledges.

In the shafts of light what sparkled with dust, the dogfaerie sat and moped, its spirit growing lean. All around, the house shed its finery and the damp of the cellars moved up to the bedrooms.

The dogfaerie hated it. And it were not too long afore this hatred sizzled and spat like it were frying in grease, and this meal of emotions it were cooking were intended to be served to human folk, once they came into reach again. Humans had built the house, had trapped the faerie inside one of their dwellings, and lastly, had left it there to pine and starve. On days when Jack Frost twinkled in the grasses outside the windows, and copied the patterns of ferns on the panes themselves, the dogfaerie would go to the great oval mirror standing proud in the hall and think about what shouldn't be thought. It would take to staring at itself, its shape, born of dogrose and bryony during a stalking moon, and try to summon up its strength to enter nothingness, never getting there.

One day in spring it sat licking the cobwebs clean of housefly terror, when it seen two figures come into the garden. One were a tall man with black hair and a face bearing the marks of eighty winters. The other were a small boy with seven summers in his eyes. This pair had come in the grounds through a gap in the old red brick wall where ivy had tore out the mortar. They had fishing rods in their hands and they talked in high voices of finding the large pool half-hidden by thistles.

"This is a good place," says the boy. "An't nobody been here for years, have they, Grandpa? You can see that from the thistles. Nobody likes thistles in their garden, do they, Grandpa, eh?" And he laughs.

Fifty years since, the dogfaerie would have loved to hear that laugh, but now it rose fury in it. There were happiness outside, in the wilds of outdoors. It wanted to get to the little boy and poke his eyes out with a twig.

"Can't argue that, little man," says the child's companion. "Shouldn't think nobody's been here since the old woman died, when I were a boy. Long climb up that hill. And not much when you get here, except a few old crab apples. Place is filled with wilderness."

"But it's got this here pond," says the boy.

"Yep, the pond looks good. Shouldn't wonder there's a fish or two, 'neath that scumweed. Get a line out, boy—let's see what's what."

So the pair settled in to fish and chatter the sunshine away, while the dogfaerie fumed in the dust and damp of the house.

Later that night, when a rash of stars lighted up the garden, the dogfaerie set to scheming. There were one way it could leave the house, but it meant giving up its faerie form forever. It could, should it wish, take over and possess a child. In the same way it entered images, it could change its form to resemble the little boy and then take over his body. But to do this terrible thing, it had to get the child inside the house.

It gathered from all the nooks and crannies of the house the cast-off feathers of birds. It took some moss from one of the sills in the larder, and some clay what had seeped through cracks in the cellar walls. With these it wove a strange bird, which were sure to catch the eye of the little boy. The tail feathers was all of different lengths and the wings like the flaps of a child's kite. The beak were the tip of a dead rat's tail and the eyes come from two black beetles. Dried spiders made up the claws and its breast were fashioned of dandelion down, blown in fresh from the garden.

The dogfaerie put this decoy just inside the doorway of the house, where the great door hanged loose on its hinges, and waited for the return of the small boy.

The couple did not come for many days and though dogfaeries is eternal, time passes by as slowly for them as any human folk when nothing but expectancies float in the still air around their heads. Its tiny heart were pattering fast as it doodled with a splinter in the dust, waiting, waiting.

Just when hope were all but dry mould in its breast, it heard the sound of voices on the breeze. Into the sunlighted garden come the boy and his grandfather. They stared at the house for a handful of moments and then the boy tugged at the man's sleeve and pointed at the pond.

They sat down by the water, amid cow-parsley, and began to fish. Once or twice the child looked towards the house, but he showed no desire to wander near. The afternoon drifted away and the dogfaerie took to agitation. All it knowed of children told it that the boy would come, that boys like this was curious creatures by nature, following in the footsteps of cats.

Then comes that magical time, just near to sunset, when windows catch such violence as twilights want to offer, showing red and fierce reflections in their panes. The human folks showed no signs of leaving. Indeed, the man were intent on his line, fixing the fish with his determined stare.

The young boy, however, were watching the clouds of midges coming in, and the low-flying martins dipping in to meet them.

"Hey," cries the boy, jumping up on his feet. "Look, Grandpa, the house is on fire!"

The man looks up, briefly, but says no, it's only the sunset snared by the window-glass.

"I'm going to look," cries the child, and begins running to meet the house, while the man shouts to be careful, not to go inside as the boards is all rotten.

The dogfaerie's heart, small as that of a shrew, twitters inside it. The boy were coming. He were running to the house.

The boy stands at the bottom of the wooden porch steps, which lay at all angles and even have weeds poking sly heads through steps and rise.

Up! Climb up!

One foot on the bottom step, testing for strength.

Yes! Yes! Come. See the pretty bird.

Small light feet, finding their way to the top, to stand on the porch.

A hand on the crumbling doorjamb, skin as soft, pink and delicate as the vanes of a mushroom.

See. See. Look at the pretty bird.

The child's eyes open wide and blue as autumn skies.

"Hey! There's somethin' here. There's a funny bird . . ."

"Be careful," calls the man.

"It bant moving. Just sittin' still."

"Mind the boards," says the man.

One foot—

two feet—

inside.

The dogfaerie flashed bright as new gold, inside, quick as quick. Inside, deep inside the boy. The boy were caught, the boy were . . . something were wrong. The dogfaerie felt the boy's feelings, thought the boy's thoughts, and knowed that there had been no surprise. The child were in a thrall of triumphant feeling, knowing what he already knowed would happen.

"GOT YOU!" yells this boy, dashing from the house and down the wooden steps towards the man what stands, broad in his smile, by the pond.

"Grandpa, Grandpa, I got him."

There is slaps of delight.

"I just knowed you would. From the first day we see the house, I said there were one inside, didn't I, boy? It looked so right. No ghost, said I—that's one of *them* in there."

The boy looks up into the man's face.

"Will I live forever too, Grandpa? Now I've got him? Like you, Grandpa?"

The black-haired man with the gold-flecked eyes ruffles the boy's hair.

"Sure you will, son. And anybody says to you they don't believe in faeries, why you can tell 'em different, see. You can tell 'em the truthfulness of the thing."

And that's what I done, here in this book.

EMMA BULL

A Bird That Whistles

Emma Bull took the fantasy field by storm with her first novel, *War for the Oaks*, an urban fantasy pitting rock musicians against the faery folk on the streets of modern day Minneapolis. She then took on the science fiction field with her second novel, *Falcon*. In between these novels, Bull co-edited the five *Liavek* anthologies, wrote stories for both *Liavek* and the urban fantasy series *Borderland*, and composed songs for the Minneapolis band Cats Laughing, of which she is the lead singer. She is also a founding member of the Minneapolis Fantasy Writers Group, and publisher—with her husband, novelist Will Shetterly—of Steeldragon Press, producing limited edition fiction and comics.

"A Bird That Whistles" was written for Diana Wynne Jones's *Hidden Turnings*, a collection of stories for young adults published in the U.K. It features fiddle-player Willy Silver from *War for the Oaks*, but takes place some years before the events of that novel.

—T.W.

A Bird That Whistles

EMMA BULL

The dulcimer player sat on the back steps of Orpheus Coffeehouse, lit from behind by the bulb over the door. His head hung forward, and his silhouette was sharp against the diffused glow from State Street. The dulcimer was propped against his shoulder as if it were a child he was comforting. I'd always thought you balanced a dulcimer across your knees. But it worked; this sounded like the classical guitar of dulcimer playing. Then his chin lifted a little.

> 'Twas on one bright March morning, I bid New Orleans adieu,
> And I took the road to Jackson town, my fortunes to renew.
> I cursed all foreign money, no credit could I gain,
> Which filled my heart with longing for the lakes of Pontchartrain.

He got to the second verse before he stopped and looked up. Light fell on the side of his face.

"I like the bit about the alligators best," I said stupidly.

"So do I." I could hear his grin.

" 'If it weren't for the alligators, I'd sleep out in the woods.' Sort of sums up life." He sounded so cheerful, it was hard to believe he'd sung those mournful words.

"You here for the open stage?" I asked. Then I remembered *I* was, and my terror came pounding back.

He lifted the shoulder that supported the dulcimer. "Maybe." He stood smoothly. I staggered up the steps with my banjo case, and he held the door for me.

In the full light of the back room his looks startled me as much as his music had. He was tall, slender and pale. His black hair was thick and long, pulled into a careless tail at the back, except for some around his face that was too short and fell forward into his eyes. Those were the ordinary things.

His clothes were odd. This was 1970 and we all dressed the way we thought Woody Guthrie used to: blue denim and workshirts. This guy wore a white T-shirt, black corduroys, and a black leather motorcycle jacket that looked old enough to be his father's. (I would have said he was about eighteen.) The white streak in his hair was odd. His face was odd; with its high cheekbones and pointed chin, it was somewhere out beyond handsome.

But his eyes—they were like green glass, or a green pool in the shadow of trees, or a green gemstone with something moving behind it, dimly visible. Looking at them made me uncomfortable; but when he turned away, I felt the loss, as if something I wanted but couldn't name had been taken from me.

Steve O'Connell, the manager, came out of the kitchen, and the green-eyed man handed him the dulcimer. "It's good," he said. "I'd like to meet whoever made it."

Steve's harried face lit up. "My brother. I'll tell him you said so."

Steve disappeared down the hall to the front room, and the green eyes came back to my face. "I haven't forgotten your name, have I?"

"No." I put my hand out, and he shook it. "John Deacon."

"Banjo player," he added. "I'm Willy Silver. Guitar and fiddle."

"Not dulcimer?"

"Not usually. But I dabble in strings."

That's when Lisa came out of the kitchen.

Lisa waited tables at Orpheus. She looked like a dancer, all slender and small and long-boned. Her hair was a cirrus cloud of red-gold curls; her eyes were big, cat-tilted, and grey; and her skin was so fair you should have been able to see through it. I'd seen Waterhouse's painting *The Lady of Shalott* somewhere (though I didn't remember the name of the painter or the painting then; be kind, I was barely seventeen), and every time I saw Lisa I thought of it. She greeted me by name whenever I came to Orpheus, and smiled, and teased me. Once, when I came in with the tail-end of the flu, she fussed over me so much I wondered if it was possible to get a chronic illness on purpose.

Lisa came out of the kitchen, my heart gave a great loud thump, she looked up with those big, inquiring eyes, and she saw Willy Silver. I recognised the disease that struck her down. Hadn't she already given it to me?

Willy Silver saw her, too. "Hullo," he said, and looked as if he was prepared to admire any response she gave.

"Hi." The word was a little breathless gulp. "Oh, hi, John. Are you a friend of John's?" she asked Willy.

"I just met him," I told her. "Willy Silver, Lisa Amundsen. Willy's here for open stage."

He gave me a long look, but said, "If you say so."

I must have been feeling masochistic. Lisa always gets crushes on good musicians, and I already knew Willy was one. Maybe I ought to forget the music and just commit seppuku on stage.

But you can't forget the music. Once you get the itch, it won't go away, no matter how much stage fright you have. And by the time my turn came—after a handful of guys-on-stools-with-guitars, two women who sang *a capella* for too long, a woman who did Leonard Cohen songs on the not-quite-tuned piano, and the Orpheus Tin-and-Wood Toejam Jug Band—I had plenty of stage fright.

Then Willy Silver leaned over from the chair next to me and whispered, "Take your time. Play the chord progression a couple of times for an intro—it'll settle you down."

I looked up, startled. The white streak in his hair caught the light, and his eyes gleamed green. He was smiling.

"And the worst that can happen isn't very bad."

I could embarrass myself in front of Lisa . . . and everyone else, and be ashamed to ever show my face in Orpheus again. But Willy didn't look like someone who'd understand that.

My hands shook as if they had engine knock. I wanted to go to the bathroom. Steve clumped up on stage, read my name from the slip of paper in his hand and peered out into the dark room for me. I hung the banjo over my shoulder and went up there to die for my art.

I scrapped the short opening I'd practised and played the whole chord progression instead. The first couple measures were shaky. But banjos give out a lively noise that makes you *want* to have a good time, and I could feel mine sending those messages. By the time I got around to the words, I could remember them, and sing them in almost my usual voice.

> *I got a bird that whistles, honey, got a bird,*
> *Baby, got a bird that will sing.*
> *Honey, got a bird, baby, got a bird that will sing.*
> *But if I ain't got Corinna, it just don't mean,*
> *It don't mean a natural thing.*

At the back of the room, I could just see the halo of Lisa's hair. I couldn't see her face but at least she'd stopped to listen. And down front, Willy Silver sat, looking pleased.

I did "Lady Isabel and the Elf Knight" and "Newry Highwayman." I blew some chords and forgot some words, but I lived through it. And people applauded. I grinned and thanked them and stumbled off the stage.

"Do they clap because they like what you did," I asked Willy, "or because you stopped doing what they didn't?"

Willy made a muffled noise into his coffee cup.

"Pretty darn good," said Lisa, at my elbow. I felt immortal. Then I realised that she was stealing glances at Willy. "Want to order something, now that you're not too nervous to eat it?"

I blushed, but in the dark, who could tell? "PB and J," I told her.

"PB and J?" Willy repeated.

We both stared at him, but it was Lisa who said, "Peanut butter and jelly sandwich. Don't you call them that?"

The pause was so short I'm not sure I really heard it. Then he said, "I don't think I've ever been in a coffeehouse where you could order a peanut butter and jelly sandwich."

"This is it," Lisa told him. "Crunchy or smooth, whole wheat or white, grape jelly or peach preserves."

"Good grief. Crunchy, whole wheat, and peach."

"Non-conformist," she said admiringly.

He turned to me when she went towards the kitchen. "You *were* pretty good," he said. "I like the way you sing. For that last one, though, you might try mountain minor."

"What?"

He got an eager look on his face. "Come on," he said, sprang out of his chair, and led the way towards the back.

We sat on the back steps until the open stage was over, and he taught me about mountain minor tuning. His guitar was a deep-voiced old Gibson with the varnish worn off the strategic spots, and he flat-picked along with me, filling in the places that needed it. Eventually we went back inside, and he taught me about pull-offs. As Steve stacked chairs, we played "Newry Highwayman" as a duet. Then he taught me "Shady Grove," because it was mountain minor, too.

I'd worked hard at the banjo, and I enjoyed playing it. But I don't think I'd ever been aware of making something beautiful with it. That's what those two songs were. Beautiful.

And Lisa moved through the room as we played, clearing tables, watching us. Watching him. Every time I looked up, her eyes were following his face, or his long fingers on the guitar neck.

I got home at two in the morning. My parents almost grounded me; I convinced them I hadn't spent the night raising hell by showing them my new banjo tricks. Or maybe it was the urgency with which I explained what I'd learned and how, and that I had to have more.

When I came back to Orpheus two nights later, Willy was there. And Lisa, fair and graceful, was often near him, often smiled at him, that night and all the nights after it. Sometimes he'd smile back. But sometimes his face would be full of an intensity that couldn't be contained in a smile. Whenever Lisa saw that, her eyes would widen, her lips would part, and she'd look frightened and fascinated all at once. Which made me feel worse than if he'd smiled at her.

And sometimes he would ignore her completely, as if she were a cup of coffee he hadn't ordered. Then her face would close up tight with puzzlement and hurt, and I'd want to break something.

I could have hated him, but it was just as well I didn't. I wanted to learn music from Willy and to be near Lisa. Lisa wanted to be near Willy. The perfect arrangement. Hah.

And who could know what Willy wanted?

Fourth of July, Independence Day 1970, promised to be the emotional climax of the summer. Someone had organised a day of Vietnam War protests, starting with a rally in Riverside Park and ending with a torchlight march down State Street. Posters about it were everywhere—tacked to phone poles, stuck on walls, and all over the tables at Orpheus. The picture on the posters was the photo taken that spring, when the Ohio National Guard shot four students on the Kent State campus during another protest: a dark-haired woman kneeling over a dead student's body, her head lifted, her mouth open with weeping, or screaming. You'd think a photo like that would warn you away from protesting. But it gives you the feeling that someone has to do some-thing. It gets you out on the street.

Steve was having a special marathon concert at the coffeehouse: Sherman and Henley, the Rose Hip String Band, Betsy Kaske, and—surprise—Willy Silver and John Deacon. True, we were scheduled to go on at seven, when the audience would be smallest, but I didn't care. I had been hired to play. For money.

The only cloud on my horizon was that Willy was again treating Lisa as one of life's non-essentials. As we set up for the show, I could almost see a dotted line trailing behind Willy that was her gaze, fixed on him.

Evening light was slanting through the door when we hit the stage, which made me feel funny. Orpheus was a place for after dark, when its shabby, struggling nature was cloaked with night-and-music magic. But Willy set his fiddle under his chin, leaned into the microphone, and drew out with his bow one sweet, sad, sustained note. All the awareness in the room—his, mine, and our dozen or so of audience's—hurtled to the sharp point of that one note and balanced there. I began to pick the banjo softly and his note changed, multiplied, until we were playing instrumental harmony. I sang, and if my voice broke a little, it was just what the song required:

> The sun rises bright in France, and fair sets he,
> Ah, but he has lost the look he had in my ain country.

We made enough magic to cloak *three* shabby coffeehouses with glamour. When I got up the nerve to look beyond the edge of the stage, sometime in our fourth song, we had another dozen listeners. They'd come to line State Street for the march and our music had called them in.

Lisa sat on the shag rug in front of the stage. Her eyes were bright, and for once, her attention didn't seem to be all for Willy.

Traditional music mostly tells stories. We told a lot of them that night. I felt them all as if they'd happened to friends of mine. Willy seemed more consumed by the music than the words, and songs he sang were sometimes almost too beautiful. But his strong voice never quavered or cracked like mine did. His guitar and fiddle were gorgeous, always, perfect and precise.

We finished at eight-thirty with a loose and lively rendition of "Blues in the Bottle," and the room was close to full. The march was due to pass by in half an hour.

We bounded off stage and into the back room. "Yo," said Willy, and stuck out his right hand. I shook it. He was touched with craziness, a little drunk with the music. He looked . . . not quite domesticated. Light seemed to catch more than usual in his green eyes. He radiated a contained energy that could have raised the roof.

"Let's go look at the street," I said.

We went out the back door and up the short flight of outside stairs to State Street. Or where State Street had been. The march, contrary to the laws of physics governing crowds, had arrived early.

Every leftist in Illinois might have been there. The pavement was gone beneath a winding, chanting snake of marchers blocks and blocks and *blocks* long. Several hundred people singing, "All we are saying/Is give peace a chance," makes your hair stand on end. Willy nudged me, beaming, and pointed to a banner that read, "Draft Beer, Not Boys." There really were torches, though the harsh yellow-tinted lights of State Street faded them. Some people on the edge of the crowd had lit sparklers; as the line of march passed over the bridge, first one, then dozens of sparklers, like shooting stars, arced over the railings and into the river, with one last bright burst of white reflection on the water before they hit.

I wanted to follow the march, but my banjo was in the coffeehouse, waiting for me to look after it. "I'm going to see what's up inside," I shouted at Willy. He nodded. Sparklers, fizzing, reflected in his eyes.

The crowd packed the sidewalk between me and Orpheus's front door, so I retraced our steps, down the stairs and along the river. I came into the parking lot, blind from the lights I'd just left, and heard behind me, "Hey, hippie."

There were two of them, about my age. They were probably both on their school's football and swimming teams; their hair was short, they weren't wearing blue jeans, they smelled of Southern Comfort, and they'd called me "hippie." A terrible combination. I started to walk away, across the parking lot, but the blond one stepped forward and grabbed my arm.

"Hey! I'm talking to you."

There's nothing helpful you can say at times like this, and if there had been, I was too scared to think of it. The other guy, brown-haired and shorter, came up and jabbed me in the stomach with two fingers. "You a draft dodger?" he said. "Scared to fight for your country?"

"Hippies make me puke," the blond one said thoughtfully.

They were drunk, for God's sake, and out on the town, and as excited in their way by the mass of people on the street above as I was. Which didn't make me feel any better when the brown-haired one punched me in the face.

I was lying on my back clutching my nose and waiting for the next bad thing to happen to me when I heard Willy say, "Don't do it." I'd heard him use his voice in more ways than I could count, but never before like that, never a ringing command that could turn you to stone.

I opened my eyes and found my two tormenters bracketing me, the blond one's foot still raised to kick me in the stomach. He lost his balance as I watched and got the foot on the ground just in time to keep from falling over. They were both looking toward the river railing, so I did, too.

The parking lot didn't have any lights to reflect in his eyes. The green sparks there came from inside him. Nor was there any wind to lift and stir his hair like that. He stood very straight and tall, six metres from us, his hands held a little out from his sides like a gunfighter in a cowboy movie. Around his right hand, like a living glove, was a churning outline of golden fire. Bits of it dripped away like liquid from the ends of his fingers, evaporating before they hit the gravel. Like sparks from a sparkler.

I'm sure that's what my two friends told each other the next day—that he'd had a sparkler in his hand, and the liquor had made them see something more. That they'd been stupid to run away. But it wasn't a sparkler. And they weren't stupid. I heard them running across the parking lot; I watched Willy clench the fingers of his right hand and close his eyes tight, and saw the fire dim slowly and disappear. And I wished like hell that I could run away, too.

He crouched down beside me and pulled me up to sitting. "Your nose is bleeding."

"What are you?" I croaked.

The fire was still there, in his eyes. "None of your business," he said. He put his arm around me and hauled me to my feet. I'm not very heavy, but it still should have been hard work, because I didn't help. He was too slender to be so strong.

"What do you mean, none of my business? Jesus!"

He yanked me around to face him. When I looked at him, I saw wildness and temper and a fragile control over both. "I'm one of the Daoine Sidhe, Johnny-lad," he said, and his voice was harsh and coloured by traces of some accent. "Does that help?"

"No," I said, but faintly. Because whatever that phrase meant, he was admitting that he was not what I was. That what I had seen had really been there.

"Try asking Steve. Or look it up, I don't care."

I shook my head. I'd forgotten my nose; a few drops of blood spattered from it and marked the front of his white shirt. I stood frozen with terror, waiting for his reaction.

It was laughter. "Earth and Air," he said when he caught his breath, "are we doing melodrama or farce out here? Come on, let's go lay you down and pack your face in ice."

There was considerable commotion when we came in the back door. Lisa got the ice and hovered over me while I told Steve about the two guys. I said Willy had chased them off; I didn't say how. Steve was outraged, and Lisa was solicitous, and it was all wasted on me. I lay on the floor with a cold nose and a brain full of rug fuzz, and let all of them do or say whatever they felt like.

Eventually I was alone in the back room, with the blank ceiling tiles to look at. Betsy Kaske was singing "Wild Women Don't Get the Blues." I roused from my self-indulgent stupor only once, when Steve passed on his way to the kitchen.

"Steve, what's a—" and I pronounced Daoine Sidhe, as best I could.

He repeated it, and it sounded more like what Willy had said. "Elves," he added.

"What?"

"Yeah. It's an Irish name for the elves."

"Oh, Christ," I said. When I didn't add to that, he went on into the kitchen.

I don't know what I believed. But after a while I realised that I hadn't seen Lisa go by in a long time. And she didn't know what I knew, or almost knew. So I crawled up off the floor and went looking for her.

Not in the front room, not in the kitchen, and if she was in the milling people who were still hanging out on State Street, I'd never find her anyway. I went out to the back steps, to see if she was in the parking lot.

Yes, sort of. They stood in the deep shadow where Orpheus's back wall joined the jutting flank of the next building. Her red-gold hair was a dim cascade of lighter colour in the dark. The white streak in his was like a white bird, flying nowhere. And the pale skin of her face and arms, his pale face and white shirt, sorted out the rest of it for me. Lisa was so small and light-boned, he'd lifted her off her feet entirely. No work at all for him. Her arms were around his neck. One of his hands was closed over her shoulder—I could see his long fingers against her dark blouse—and the gesture was so intense, so hungry, that it seemed as if that one hand alone could consume her. I turned and went back into Orpheus, cold, frightened, and helpless.

Lisa didn't come back until a little before closing, several hours later. I know; I was keeping watch. She darted in the back door and snatched her shoulder bag from the kitchen. Her eyes were the only colour in her face: grey, rimmed with red. "Lisa!" I called.

She stopped with her back to me. "What?"

I didn't know how to start. Or finish. "It's about Willy."

"Then I don't want to hear it."

"But—"

"John, it's none of your business. And it doesn't matter now, anyway."

She shot me one miserable, intolerable look before she darted out the back door and was gone. She could look like that and tell me it was none of my business?

I'd helped Steve clean up and lock up, and pretended that I was going home. But at three in the morning I was sitting on the back steps, watching a newborn breeze ruffle a little heap of debris caught against the doorsill: a crushed paper cup, a bit of old newspaper, and one of the flyers for the march. When I looked up from it Willy was standing at the bottom of the steps.

"I thought you'd be back tonight," I said.

"Maybe that's why I came back. Because you thought it so hard." He didn't smile, but he was relaxed and cheerful. After making music with him almost every day for a month, I could tell. He dropped loose-limbed on to the bottom step and stretched his legs out in front of him.

"So. Have you told her? What you are?"

He looked over his shoulder at me with a sort of stunned disbelief. "Do you mean Lisa? Of course not."

"Why not?" All my words sounded to me like little lead fishing weights hitting the water: plunk, plunk.

"Why should I? Either she'd believe me or she wouldn't. Either one is about equally tedious."

"Tedious."

He smiled, that wicked, charming, conspiratorial smile. "John, you can't think I care if Lisa believes in fairies."

"What *do* you care about?"

"John . . ." he began, wary and a little irritable.

"Do you care about her?"

And for the second time, I saw it: his temper on a leash. "What the hell does it matter to you?" He leaned back on his elbows and exhaled loudly. "Oh, right. You want her for yourself. But you're too scared to do anything about it."

That hurt. I said, a little too quickly, "It matters to me that she's happy. I just want to know if she's going to be happy with you."

"No," he snapped. "And whether she's going to be happy *without* me is entirely her lookout. Rowan and Thorn, John, I'm tired of her. And if you're not careful, I'll be tired of you, too."

I looked down at his scornful face, and remembered Lisa's: pale, red-eyed. I described Willy Silver, aloud, with words my father had forbidden in his house.

He unfolded from the step, his eyes narrowed. "Explain to me, before I paint the back of the building with you. I've always been nice to you. Isn't that enough?" He said "nice" through his teeth.

"Why are you nice to me?"

"You're the only one who wants something important from me."

"Music?"

"Of course, music."

The rug fuzz had been blown from my head by his anger and mine. "Is that why you sing that way?"

"What the devil is wrong with the way I sing?"

"Nothing. Except you don't sound as if any of the songs ever happened to you."

"Of course they haven't." He was turning stiff and cold, withdrawing. That seemed worse than when he was threatening me.

The poster for the protest march still fluttered in the doorway. I grabbed it and held it out. "See her?" I asked, jabbing a finger at the picture of the woman kneeling over the student's body. "Maybe she knew that guy. Maybe she didn't. But she cares that he's dead. And I look at this picture, and *I* care about *her*. And all those people who marched past you in the street tonight? They did it because they care about a lot of people that they're never even going to see."

He looked fascinated and horrified at once. "Don't you all suffer enough as it is?"

"Huh?"

"Why would you take someone else's suffering on yourself?"

I didn't know how to answer that. I said finally, "We take on each other's happiness, too."

He shook his head, slowly. He was gathering the pieces of himself together, putting all his emotional armour back on. "This is too strange even for me. And among my people, I'm notoriously fond of strange things." He turned and walked away, as if I'd ceased to exist.

"What about tonight?" I said. He'd taken about a half-dozen steps. "Why did you bother to scare off those guys who were beating me up?"

He stopped. After a long moment he half-turned and looked at me, wild-eyed and . . . frightened? Then he went on, stiffly, across the parking lot, and disappeared into the dark.

The next night, when I came in, Willy's guitar and fiddle were gone. But Steve said he hadn't seen him.

Lisa was clearing tables at closing, her hair falling across her face and hiding it. From behind that veil, she said, "I think you should give up. He's not coming."

I jumped. "Was I that obvious?"

"Yeah." She swept the hair back and showed a wry little smile. "You looked just like me."

"I feel lousy," I told her. "I helped drive him away, I think."

She sat down next to me. "I wanted to jump off the bridge last night. But the whole time I was saying, 'Then he'll be sorry, the rat.' "

"He wouldn't have been."

"Nope, not a bit," she said.

"But I would have."

She raised her grey cat-eyes to my face. "I'm not going to fall in love with you, John."

"I know. It's okay. I still would have been sorry if you jumped off the bridge."

"Me, too," Lisa said. "Hey, let's make a pact. We won't talk about The Rat to anybody but each other."

"Why?"

"Well . . ." She frowned at the empty lighted space of the stage. "I don't think anybody else would understand."

So we shared each other's suffering, as he put it. And maybe that's why we wouldn't have called it that.

I did see him again, though.

State Street had been gentrified, and Orpheus, the building, even the parking lot, had fallen to a downtown mall where there was no place for shabbiness or magic—any of the kinds of magic that were made that Fourth of July. These things happen in twice seven long years. But there are lots more places like that, if you care to look.

I was playing at the Greenbriar Bluegrass Festival in Pocohontas County, West Virginia. Or rather, my band was. A columnist in *Folk Roots* magazine described us so:

> Bird That Whistles drives traditional bluegrass fans crazy. They have the right instrumentation, the right licks—and they're likely to apply them to Glenn Miller's 'In the Mood,' or the Who's 'Magic Bus'. If you go to see them, leave your preconceptions at home.

I was sitting in the cookhouse tent that served as the musicians' green room, drinking coffee and watching the chaos that is thirty-some traditional musicians all tuning and talking and eating at once. Then I saw, over the heads, a raven's-wing black one with a white streak.

In a few minutes, he stood in front of me. He didn't look five minutes older than he had at Orpheus. He wasn't nervous, exactly, but he wasn't at ease, either.

"Hi," I said. "How'd you find me?"

"With this," he answered, smiling a little. He held out an article clipped from a Richmond, Virginia paper. It was about the festival, and the photo was of Bird That Whistles.

"I'm glad you did."

He glanced down suddenly. "I wanted you to know that I've been thinking over what you told me."

I knew what he was talking about. "All this time?"

Now it was the real thing, his appealing grin. "It's a damned big subject. But I thought you'd like to know . . . well, sometimes I understand it."

"Only sometimes?"

"Rowan and Thorn, John, have mercy! I'm a slow learner."

"The hell you are. Can you stick around? You could meet the band, do some tunes."

"I wish I could," he said, and I think he meant it.

"Hey, wait a minute." I pulled a paper napkin out of the holder on the table and rummaged in my banjo case for a pen.

"What's that?" he asked, as I wrote.

"My address. I'm living in Detroit now, God help me. If you ever need anything—or even if you just want to jam—let me know, will you?" And I slid the napkin across the table to him.

He reached out, hesitated, traced the edges of the paper with one long, thin finger. "Why are you giving me this?"

I studied that bent black-and-white head, the green eyes half-veiled with his lids and following the motion of his finger. "You decide," I told him.

"All right," he said softly, "I will." If there wasn't something suspiciously like a quaver in his voice, then I've never heard one. He picked up the napkin. "I won't lose this," he said, with an odd intensity. He put out his right hand, and I shook it. Then he turned and pushed through the crowd. I saw his head at the door of the tent; then he was gone.

I stared at the top of the table for a long time, where the napkin had been, where his finger had traced. Then I took the banjo out of its case and put it into mountain minor tuning.

LISA TUTTLE

The Walled Garden

Lisa Tuttle is a Texan successfully transplanted to England. She has published novels, including *Familiar Spirit* and *Gabriel*, and her short stories have appeared in *Interzone*, *F&SF*, *Zenith*, *Dark Fantasies*, *Shadows* and *Alien Sex*. She has two short story collections, *A Nest of Nightmares* and *A Spaceship Built of Stone and Other Stories* and a nonfiction book, *Encyclopedia of Feminism and Heroines*. Her short story "Jamie's Grave" was chosen for *The Year's Best Fantasy: First Annual Collection*.

In "The Walled Garden," from the British anthology *Hidden Turnings*, a young woman orders her entire life around one glimpsed scene.

—E.D.

The Walled Garden

LISA TUTTLE

When I was five years old I saw the future. My future. After that, I was unable just to wait and let it happen. I had to go looking for it.

My sister Jean is three years older than me. As children we shared a room and had the same bedtime. I can remember her complaints about being treated like a baby—like me—and put to bed while it was still light. A docile child myself, I would sleep whenever I was told, but Jean, grumbling and protesting, kept me awake as long as she could, for company. She talked to me, and she told me stories. She loved making up stories; she loved things that had not happened. She pulled me along to explore the land of What-if: what if we moved to a different house, or what if we came home from school one day and there was no one here? What if all the grown-ups disappeared? What if people came from another planet and took us away in their flying saucer? When I was very young, it's true, she confused me with her questions and her stories, so that sometimes I lost track of what was real and what only imagined. She made me want a life that didn't exist; she made me cry for the loss of things I'd never known.

One summer night when I was five and Jean was eight, as I remember, she was particularly restless. Outside, it was still as light as day, a fact the thin curtains drawn across the windows couldn't disguise. I lay there in my little bed, twin to hers, patiently waiting for Jean to begin one of her stories, when all at once my sister sat bolt upright.

"It's not fair," she said. "It's not time for bed; it's *not*. Everybody else is still out. I'll bet you the Kellermans are still playing Fox and Hounds. Let's go out."

"We're in our pyjamas," I said.

"So? In China people wear their pyjamas all the time; that's the only kind of clothes they have. Anyway, you've been out in your pyjamas before."

"They won't let us."

188

"They won't *know*," she said. "We're going to escape." She suddenly leaped up and on to my bed. I squealed, pulling in my legs to protect my stomach, but Jean had no intention of tickling me. She'd only come on to my bed to open the window. I watched, thrilled and baffled. Warm air and the scent of freshly cut grass slipped into the room.

"What are you going to *do*?"

"I told you. Escape. I'm going exploring. Do you want to come, or are you going to stay here like a baby and sleep?"

Jean and I lived with our parents in a three-bedroom, one-story house in Beverly Oaks, a suburban subdivision of Houston. It was a desirable, middle-class neighbourhood which had been built soon after the war. The houses—all single-family dwellings—had attached two-car garages and well-kept lawns and gardens. I had lived there all my life, apart from three days in a downtown hospital when I was born. I knew nothing else. But Jean had spent her first two-and-half years in a mysterious place called "the country" on the farm where our grandmother had lived. Grandmother had died, and the farm had been sold, before I was born. I envied Jean that other life I could never know, and I believed she explored the tame suburban streets around us in search of some secret way back to the country. I thought she might find it, too, and I wanted to be with her when she did.

Perched on the window-sill, Jean looked at me, still snug in my bed. She said, "Maybe you'd better not come. It could be dangerous. If somebody saw us—if you weren't careful enough—if you didn't run fast enough—"

I sat up. "I will!"

She shook her head.

"Oh, please!" I said. My sleepiness, my fears, my doubts were forgotten; all in the world I wanted was to follow my big sister. Whatever she wanted, I wanted, too.

"You'll have to do *exactly* what I say."

"Yes, yes!"

"All right, then. Come on. And keep *quiet*."

Out the window and on to the grass, cool on my bare feet. Jean gripped my shoulder and her voice buzzed in my ear: "Through the Mishners. If they see us, act normal. Don't rush, but don't stop. Just wave at them and keep on walking."

The Mishners didn't have a fence, so walking through their backyard was the quickest way to get to the alley: it was a short-cut we often took, but with the risk of being captured, for they were an elderly couple always on the lookout for someone, anyone, to interrupt their boredom.

But that evening, fortunately, they were not in sight, and we passed through in safety.

I watched Jean admiringly as I struggled to keep up with her. She was the great explorer, alert to everything, sniffing the air and looking around at familiar fences, gardens and backs of houses we passed.

When we emerged from the alley on to Warburton Drive, Jean turned left without hesitation. This way would lead us to the bigger houses, the more expensive part of the subdivision. There were a couple of houses over there with swimming-pools, and one was known as "the house with the bomb shelter." Jean had told me stories, too, and I remembered one about a fabulous playhouse, full of wonderful toys, built by a wealthy couple for grandchildren who visited them only once a year. If we could find it, we could play there undisturbed.

I grabbed Jean's arm. "Are we going to look for the playhouse?"

"What playhouse? What are you talking about? Don't you know where we are?"

Her tone of voice informed me that we were in the middle of an adventure. I shook my head meekly. "I forgot."

"We're in China. We've just crossed the Gobi Desert. Everyone else on the expedition died—we're the only survivors. Now we're looking for the Forbidden City. No Westerners have ever been allowed to enter it and live, so we shall be the first—unless they catch us—"

At that moment, rounding a bend in the road, three boys on bicycles came into view.

"The Royal Guards!" said Jean. "If they see us, we're dead! We have to split up—you go that way—meet me at the river later if you manage to lose them!"

She was off. I felt panic at being left alone, and would have disobeyed her orders and followed, but she could run so much faster than me that she was already out of sight. Meanwhile, the enemy was gaining on me. I turned and ran towards the nearest house, ducking behind a bush for shelter. My heart thudded painfully as I watched the boys cycle past—for a moment I had forgotten that they were only children, and believed they would kill me, as Jean had said. When they had gone, I emerged. Now what?

Meet me at the river, she had said, but where was the river? Like the rest of the territory, rivers were defined according to a map that only Jean could read. A river might be a swift rush of water in the gutter (but the day was dry), or a dip in a lawn, or even a street we would have to pretend to swim across. I decided to start walking in the direction I had seen Jean run, and hope that she would come back and find me.

I travelled as Jean would have wanted, as if she were watching me, moving cautiously to avoid being seen, ducking behind bushes and cars, favouring alleys over streets. Gradually I left the familiar landscape behind. The houses were bigger here, the trees shading them were older and larger than those on my street. Golden lights shone from windows. The air was blue with the deepening dusk, and I began to feel afraid. I kept walking, because I didn't know what else to do, but I wondered if every step was taking me farther from Jean and safety and home.

Then I came to a high brick wall. This was unusual. In my neighbourhood there were plenty of wooden and chain-link fences, but I had never seen such a high brick wall. Jean would have wanted to know what was hidden behind it; she would have climbed over it, I thought.

My heart beat harder. Was Jean nearby? Had she been here before me? Was she already on the other side?

I called her name, but the red brick surface before me seemed to swallow the sound of my voice, and I knew she wouldn't hear. I flung myself at the wall, then, fingers scrabbling at the rough surface. But there was nothing to hold, and so I kept falling back. I jumped straight up, but that was worse than useless. The wall was much too high. I didn't think even my father could have seen over the top of it. And yet, somehow, I had become convinced that Jean was on the other side of the wall. I probably had to believe that because the idea that I might be lost in a strange place at night without my sister was far too frightening.

"Jean," I said, whispering, since I knew shouting wouldn't be any better, and I began to walk beside the wall, trailing my fingers along the rough surface. At the end of the alley the wall curved away and I followed it across the grass, right up to the side of an imposing, two-storey, redbrick house. I ran past the front of the house to the other side, and there was the wall again.

And there, in the wall, a door.

The door was very small, made of wood, painted a glossy black. It was an absurdly small door, but at the time the unlikeliness of it did not strike me. The door was smaller even than I was: almost doll-sized rather than child-sized. I crouched down and—there was no handle—pushed it open. It swung slowly inwards.

All I could see at first was green grass, the trunks of a few trees, and a flowering bush. I moved forward, on hands and knees, determined to see more. I was a small child, but the doorway was very narrow, and it seemed for a moment that I might stick half-way. But, stubbornly determined, I put my head down and pushed, scraping my shoulders and wriggling my hips, determined, and indifferent to discomfort.

And then I was through. I was in the garden, and I had done it all by myself! Wouldn't Jean be proud of me when she knew!

I had to find her. She must be here. Maybe she had found a playhouse, or some other wonderful treasure that the high wall had been built to conceal. I ran across the velvety lawn, between spreading oaks and glossy-leaved magnolias, aware of the big house which dominated the garden although I did not look at it directly. I felt giddy with excitement. I felt as if I was in the middle of a game of hide-and-seek, but I couldn't remember if I were hider or seeker. Years later, trying to remember details, I couldn't recall anything specific that I might not have seen in a dozen other gardens. Just grass and trees and leaves and flowers, greens and darker greens glowing slightly in the twilight. And yet the air, warm on my bare skin, was charged with significance. The lengthening shadows promised mysteries within. The evening held its breath: something was about to happen.

She saw me first. She saw a child with tangled brown hair and dirty feet, wearing pink pyjamas and running in wide circles on the velvety lawn, through the gathering dusk.

The child felt her unexpected presence and froze, like a wild animal, and turned her head, and stared.

There were two of them, a man and a woman. They were standing very close to each other, but not touching. Not yet. He was looking at her. She was looking at me.

We stared at each other as if we knew each other, and yet as if we had never seen each other before. There was something about her that was like my mother—like my mother disguised as someone else. I knew her and yet I didn't. I waited for her to say my name and tell me who she was.

But instead of moving towards me, she half-turned to look at the man beside her, and she reached for his hand. Then they were gazing into each other's eyes, a unit which excluded me, and I was suddenly terrified.

I suppose I ran away then. I don't remember what happened next, or how I got home. I must have told Jean about my adventure because we spent the rest of that summer searching in vain for a high brick wall and the garden behind it. We never found it. Jean lost patience, or belief. Her interests led her in other directions. But even though I stopped talking about it, I never forgot. I was sure I would find the walled garden again someday.

I was thirteen, I think, when Jean—who was in high school by then, and dating boys—bought a hair-colouring kit and streaked my hair blonde. I can't remember exactly why: whether I had wheedled, or she had decided it was time her little sister emerged from the cocoon of childhood into a brightly-coloured adolescence. At any rate, it brought us together. We were happily intimate, perched on stools in the tiny, warm, brightly-lit room, inhaling the acrid fumes from my hair while Jean worked with her pencils and brushes and pots and sticks of make-up to redefine my face. We weren't using the mirror that covered the whole wall behind the sink; instead, we gazed solemnly and intently into each other's faces. Every now and then Jean would draw back to look at the effects of her work, and my heart would lift when she nodded with satisfaction. I imagined that she was going to make me over in her own image. At last, I was going to be like Jean—I would be grown-up!

When she was done, Jean took hold of my shoulders and turned me towards the mirror.

"There," she said. "The girl becomes a woman. What do you think?"

The face in the mirror did look like a woman's, and I knew I'd seen that woman before. I stared at eyes larger and more blue, higher cheekbones, a narrower nose, a complexion without freckles, and saw a familiar stranger. I remembered the woman in the garden, and suddenly, finally, I understood. I *knew*. That woman, of course, was me.

Was the garden real? That wasn't the question. The garden *would be* real. I had been privileged to see it, to glimpse my own future, to see myself standing with the man I would love.

I was, of course, very interested in love at that age. I longed for it, for that knowledge that would make me adult. I imagined true love striking once and lasting forever, leading to marriage and eternal bliss. The boys I knew were impossible; as for the men I did desire—actors and pop stars—impossible to imagine them wanting me. All I could do was hope that when I grew up it would be different. And now I *knew* it would be. I had seen the man I was going to love; the man who would love me. It was going to happen. I only had to wait.

The memory of the man in the garden, and the hope he represented, kept me going through the next few, dreadful years. The agonies of high school and dating—or not dating. The miseries of being unchosen. I wasn't popular like my big sister. I wasn't clever, or talented at anything in particular, and although boys did occasionally ask me out, I never had anyone in love with me; I never had a particular, devoted boyfriend the way Jean, so effortlessly, always did.

But I would have my man in the garden, someday. I was alone now, but it wouldn't always be so. I had seen the future. That made me special. That kept me going.

I met Paul in my first year of college. He was a boy in one of my classes, whom I noticed from the first day. Something about him attracted me, and when I made an excuse to talk to him afterwards, about the lecture, he seemed nice: serious and a little shy. Then one day, perhaps two weeks into the semester, I was walking across the quad on my way to the library when I quite unexpectedly caught sight of him. He was standing on the grass talking to someone I didn't know. I saw Paul for the first time at a distance, in three-quarters profile. And the way he looked—tall and fair—and the way he stood, bending his neck, stooping slightly to look at the girl beside him, went straight to my heart; a stab of recognition indistinguishable from desire. I knew him. I had always known him. I wanted him.

We were soon dating, and after a few weeks we became lovers. When we spent our first night together I told Paul that he was the man in the garden. He was enchanted. I suppose it made him feel special, maybe for the first time. And he believed me. I became his fantasy as he was mine, and he fell utterly in love with me.

It was first love for both of us, and I don't think that either of us doubted for an instant of those first two months that our love would last forever. Even so, the prospect of Christmas break was devastating. We were still too young—and poor—to consider there might be alternatives to spending the vacation apart, with our parents, at opposite ends of the country. But after seeing each other every day, and spending every night together, the prospect of a whole month apart was bleak and rather frightening. I could hardly remember what I had done, what I had thought about, before I met Paul. I told him I would write to him every day. He promised to phone as often as he could.

Although I expected to miss Paul unbearably, I couldn't help being excited about going home again. I had missed my parents, and Jean, and I wanted to trade experiences with my old school friends. Above all, I longed to talk to Jean about Paul. I wondered what she would say. At last I had a boyfriend, the way she had for so many years. It made me feel that I had done the impossible and caught up to her: we were equals at last. But I needed her acknowledgement before I could entirely believe it.

Jean's boyfriend for the past two years had been a law student named Bill, and because Jean was now in her last year of college I more than half-expected her to announce their engagement that Christmas. Instead, when I asked about Bill, she told me she was no longer seeing him. She was brisk: it was over, he was forgotten. She didn't want my pity, which was a relief. She was my grown-up big sister, who knew so much more than I did, and if she had wanted my comfort I wouldn't have known how to give it. Or maybe that's an excuse for selfishness. I was too full of my new discovery to spare a thought for anything else. I didn't want to talk about Jean's life; I wanted to tell her about Paul.

She was interested, and seemed happy for me. She was such a sympathetic, understanding listener that I told her more than I had intended. I told her why I *knew* this was true love, once and forever. I explained how I had recognised Paul as the man I was meant to be with.

At first, she didn't remember our long-ago search for the walled garden, but I persisted with details until I saw it connect, saw the flare of memory in her eyes.

She said: "But that wasn't real—not a real wall, not a real garden—"

I shook my head. "Not real in the usual sense. It wasn't just another house in the neighbourhood—it wasn't something we could find and see and visit—not then. But it was—or will be—a real place. What I saw was in the future; somehow or other I travelled in time and glimpsed my own future when I was a kid. Maybe it was a dream, but it was real."

Jean had a very odd look on her face. I didn't know what it meant, but it made me uneasy. And she kept shaking her head. "It wasn't a dream. And it certainly wasn't real."

"What do you mean? I'm not making this up."

"No, I know you're not."

"Then what are you saying? That it's impossible? That things like that can't happen? Well, they can—they do. I *know*: it happened to me. I don't know how, or why, or what it means, but it happened. I remember it; I've remembered it all my life. And now that I've met Paul, it all makes sense."

"God, I don't believe this," said Jean. Her mouth was twitching, and her eyes were shiny. I felt furious with her for treating my precious secret so lightly.

"You don't have to believe me," I said coldly. "I know what happened; I don't need you to—"

"Oh, you're so wrong!"

"What do you know about it? You always think you know so much. Just because you're always reading those old books, just because you're older than me—well, there's some things you *don't* know. This isn't anything to do with you. It happened to me. It's *mine*."

I'd been silly to think we were equals, to think she would ever accept me as her equal. We were squabbling again. I was reduced to shouting and stubbornness, while she had that horribly distant, superior look on her face that meant she was about to demolish me with facts.

"You're wrong there," she said. "It didn't happen to you, and it's not yours. It's mine. It's a story that I made up and told you one night when I couldn't sleep. I was always doing that—you remember—always making up stories. And

I found that the best way to keep you awake and listening was if I made up stories about *you*. So I told you that one day when you were out exploring you found a high wall with a little tiny door in it, just big enough for you to squeeze inside. And behind that wall was a garden, and in the garden there were a woman and a man. And the woman looked strangely familiar to you, although you didn't know why. Later, when you tried to find the walled garden again, you couldn't so eventually you thought you must have imagined it, and forgot all about it. Or nearly. Because one day, when you were grown-up and married and living in a house of your own, you went out to walk in your garden, and you saw a little girl staring at you—and it was yourself."

I wished I could wake up. "Why are you *doing* this?"

"I'm not doing anything. I'm telling you the truth."

"You're not. It's not. I don't believe you."

"Why should I lie?"

"I don't believe you could make up a story as good as that. Not when you were eight—not even now."

She laughed. "Oooh, a critic! Well, you're probably right. It probably was too sophisticated for me, then. I probably stole the idea from a comic book, or something I saw on television. Most of the stories I told you I got from somewhere else and just changed the names."

I didn't want to believe her. But her certainty was compelling. And why should she lie?

"Why do I remember it, then?" I asked. "I don't remember it like a story— I remember it happening to me."

"Maybe you dreamed about it afterwards. After all, you must have been half-asleep when I was telling it to you . . . a highly suggestible state."

Later, I thought of reasons why Jean might have lied. Jealousy, the unacknowledged desire to spoil things for me because she couldn't bear to see her little sister happy in love when she herself was so unhappy. . . . Or maybe she thought she was telling the truth. Maybe, when I was small, I had told her about the garden and because Jean was the storyteller, not me, she remembered it in retrospect as one of her own stories. Maybe she just couldn't cope with something that contradicted her rational view of the world, and had to force it into fiction.

Whatever her reasons, conscious or unconscious, she certainly spoiled any future I might have had with Paul. I didn't want to believe Jean, but old habits were too strong. She was my big sister; she knew best. How could I have believed in something as far-fetched as time-travel, or seeing the future? I felt embarrassed; it was as bad as if I'd gone on into adulthood believing in Santa Claus. And because I had told him, as well as because I had based my love on this myth, I felt ashamed to go back to Paul. I treated him very badly. I dropped him flat, treated him like a stranger when I got back to college, and never explained why, never gave him a second chance.

The man in the garden, though, was not so easily dropped. Faith doesn't have much to do with facts or logic; it's more to do with need, and I obviously needed my memory of the garden. Gradually, despite my attempts to disown it, my faith in the garden returned. I didn't think about it much; I told myself that I'd stopped believing, or I told myself that it didn't matter—but eventually it came back; it was there again, beneath the things I did and thought and felt, just as it always had been.

As the years went by I had other boyfriends, and since they didn't all resemble one another, I don't know how much any of them resembled the man in the garden, if at all. I had seen that man—*if* I had seen him—for no more than a few seconds when I was five years old, and never again since. The only thing I knew for sure was that he had been taller than me. And since I am rather small, the fact that all my boyfriends were taller than me might have been no more than coincidence.

When I was twenty-five, and she was twenty-eight, my sister got married. Her husband's name was Howard Olds, he was eight years older than she was, and he was rich. That was the most impressive thing about him. He was also a lawyer, and he dabbled in local politics, not very successfully. I thought he was boring and conceited, not particularly physically attractive, and—most surprisingly for Jean, who had always admired intellect above all—not even very bright. I wondered if Jean could have stooped so low as to marry a man for his money. I didn't know the grown-up Jean very well. Although we had both moved back to Houston after college, we seldom saw each other except at unavoidable family gatherings. This changed after Jean married Howard. Everything changed after my first visit to their house.

It was a large house in River Bend, a prestigious address in an exclusive neighbourhood. It had been built twenty or thirty years ago, a two-storey, Georgian-style, brick house set on half an acre of land, well-shaded with oaks, pines, pecans and magnolias. And at the back there was a walled garden.

I'll always remember the first time I saw it. Or perhaps I should say, the second time.

Because, of course, it was the same garden. I knew that, I think, even before I saw it. Jean had invited me for dinner. She was still busy in the kitchen when I arrived, so it was Howard who took me outside to show me around. Inside the walled garden it was very beautiful and peaceful. I could hear birds, distantly, and the wind in the pines. The air was blueing towards night. I looked around and made polite, admiring noises at whatever Howard pointed out, but I wasn't paying attention to him and hardly heard a word he said. I was far too tense, vibrating inside and out, my nerves and senses all unnaturally sharpened and focused on this moment to which, it seemed, my whole life had been leading. Only one thing mattered. What I was looking for—and praying not to see— was a little girl in pink pyjamas.

She didn't come. Yet I couldn't relax. I kept waiting. And when Howard led me back indoors, I don't know if I was more relieved or disappointed. What a joke, if the little girl I had been had seen me with my sister's husband! What a bitter joke, when I had believed I was seeing true love, if I had built my whole life around a misunderstanding.

I must have been a terrible guest that night. I felt such a sense of loss, and such undirected bitterness, that I couldn't stop brooding. And half-way through the dinner I could not taste I was suddenly struck by a new fear: did Jean know? Might she guess? Had she recognised the garden? Would she say something? I waited in torment.

But, of course, she didn't know. She had probably entirely forgotten the garden fantasy. Years had passed since that last, bitter conversation about it. It was my experience, not hers. It had never been hers. Of course she didn't remember. At least, I hoped she didn't. I couldn't be sure, because I couldn't ask her without reminding her—and I didn't want that. If it was forgotten, please let it stay forgotten. At any rate, she didn't say anything that night, or on future nights.

For there were future nights, despite such a nearly disastrous beginning. I made sure of that. I made friends with Jean and was often invited to dinner. Jean liked giving dinner parties and I became a regular guest. Sometimes I brought a boyfriend, and sometimes she would invite a man for me to meet. I encouraged that, although I never admitted how important it was to me. After the initial shock, I had my faith back again, more strongly than before. I had found the garden I had been looking for. Now, all I had to do was to wait for the right moment to come around again.

I had made a few wrong assumptions, I could see that now. I had imagined that the garden must be mine, or my lover's—but why should that be? It was just a place, after all; a place where anything might happen; a place where something special *would* happen when two times of my life overlapped. I might not meet him there for the first time, but in that garden I would recognise the man who had been meant for me.

Three years passed, and I was not unhappy. Jean and I became friends and shared many things—although I never risked telling her about the garden. She was already playing her part. I began to like Howard better, seeing how happy he made my sister. He wasn't as bad as I had thought, or maybe life with Jean had improved him. And he liked me, and flirted with me in a way I enjoyed. I flirted back, meaning nothing by it.

And then, finally, my time in the garden came around again. It was a dinner-party night: Jean and Howard, a couple of neighbours, a junior partner from Howard's firm and his wife, me and Jonathan. Jonathan was a man I had recently met, and been out with twice. We hadn't so much as kissed yet—maybe we never would. By that time I had developed quite a strong superstition about the garden, and liked to bring men there who were still basically unknown to me, before anything had happened. Howard teased me about all my boyfriends; Jean defended my right to be choosy, praised my good sense in not settling for anything less than exactly what I wanted. I had a few affairs, but I couldn't really, entirely believe in a relationship which blossomed outside the walled garden; I never expected them to last very long or affect me very deeply, and they didn't.

Jonathan was supposed to go into the garden with me. That was my plan. We were walking through the house towards the back when he was sidetracked by one of the other guests who shared some mutual interest. I kept going—the other man was smoking a cigar and I wanted to get away from the smell—

trusting Jonathan to follow. But when, in the garden a minute later, I heard someone come out of the house and walk towards me, I didn't need to look around to know that it was Howard.

And then—just then!—I saw myself, the five-year-old in pink pyjamas, running across the lawn and then freezing, staring at me, eyes wide and wild as a fawn's.

I felt a moment of disbelief, and then overwhelming despair. Why now? Why did it have to be Howard?

I turned my head to look at him. I was still hoping, I think, that I was wrong, and that it wasn't Howard beside me.

It was Howard, of course, and my glance caught him offguard. I saw how he looked at me, and—I couldn't help myself—I reached for his hand. And as our eyes met, I knew that I could have just what I'd always wanted.

But was this really what I'd always wanted?

Nothing was said. If there had been time, we might have stepped behind the sheltering magnolia and fallen into each other's arms. But we heard the smooth, gliding sound of the patio door, and moved apart. I think the motion looked casual, not furtive. I greeted Jonathan and even through the blood pounding in my ears I knew my voice betrayed nothing.

I was very aware, all through dinner, of Howard's attention. But it was Jean I looked at, searching for signs of strain, unhappiness, nerves. Nothing. She didn't know. She had no idea of what she was about to lose, and to whom.

When Jonathan and I left that evening Howard—as he sometimes did—gave me a brotherly kiss on the cheek. This time, though, his hand rested for a moment on my hip. No touch has ever excited me more, or seemed to hold a more passionate promise.

I have been awake all night, thinking. I've been wanting this for so long, and now I can see the ending. I can have what I want, what I've always wanted. Is it enough for me to know that, or does Jean have to know, too? Do I need Howard to be happy? Or can I, now, imagine a new future for myself, without the walled garden?

SCOTT BAKER

Varicose Worms

Scott Baker is a very nice man who writes some very sick stories. He's the man responsible for "The Lurking Duck," about a little girl who uses mechanical killer ducks to get rid of people who annoy her. Now we have "Varicose Worms," which is about exactly what the title says—in addition to shamans, Parisian bums, and obsession. It's from the vampirism anthology *Blood Is Not Enough*.

Mr. Baker's most recent novel is *Webs* (Tor), a very effective novel of horror set in the South. But that novel, for all its scariness, isn't as outright disgustingly horrific as the wonderfully vicious tale you're about to read. For your own sake, gentle reader, don't read this story just after eating.

—E.D.

Varicose Worms

SCOTT BAKER

Eminescu Eliade's great good luck had been his last name, that and the fact that not only had he been a cultured cosmopolitan and intelligent man when he'd arrived in Paris (named Eminescu after his country's greatest nineteenth-century poet by parents who'd seen to it that he had a thorough classical education, he'd almost completed his studies as a veterinarian when he'd been forced to flee Romania as the result of an indiscretion with a rather highly placed local official's daughter) but that he'd arrived in Paris hungry, practically penniless and desperate. So desperate that when he'd seen a copy of Mircea Eliade's *Le Chamanisme et les techniques archaïques de l'extase* in a bookstore window on the rue St. Jacques, where it had been accompanied by a notice explaining that Professor Eliade had returned to Paris for a limited time to give a series of lectures at the Musée de l'Homme under the auspices of the Bollingen Foundation, he'd gone to the post office and spent what were almost the last of his few coins for two phone tokens. He called the museum with the first and somehow, despite his halting French and the implausibility of his story, convinced the woman who answered the phone to give him the phone number of the apartment in Montmartre where the professor was staying, then used the other token to call the professor himself and pretend to a family relationship that had as far as he knew no basis in fact.

His meeting with the professor a few days later resulted in nothing but an excellent hot meal and the chance to discuss his namesake's poetry in Romanian with a fellow exile, but the fact that he'd found a copy of the other's book on shamanism in a library and had read it carefully in preparation for the interview changed his life.

Because when, some weeks later, he found himself panhandling in back of the Marché St. Germain with all his clothes worn in thick layers to keep him warm and the rest of his few possessions in two plastic bags he kept tied to his waist with some twine he'd found, or sleeping huddled over the ventilation grating at the corner of the boulevard St. Germain and the rue de l'Ancienne Comédie where the hot dry air from the métro station underneath kept him warm, or under the Pont Neuf (the oldest bridge in Paris despite its name) on nights when it was raining and he couldn't get past the police who sometimes made sure no one got into the Odéon métro station without a ticket—in the weeks and months he spent standing with his fellow *clochards* sheltered from the wind against the urine-stained stone of the Église St. Sulpice, yelling and singing things at the passersby, or in alleyways passing the cheap red wine in the yellow-tinged green bottles with the fat stars standing out in bas-relief on their necks back and forth—he slowly came to realize that certain of his companions were not at all what they seemed, were in fact shamans—urban shamans—every bit as powerful, as fearsome and as wild as the long-dead Tungu shamans whose Siberian descendents still remembered them with such awe. Remembered them only, because long ago all the truly powerful shamans had left the frozen north with its starvation and poverty for the cities where they could put their abilities to better use, leaving only those whose powers were comparatively feeble or totally faked to carry on their visible tradition and be studied by scholars such as Professor Eliade.

And from his first realization of what he'd found and what it meant, it hadn't taken him all that long to put the knowledge to use and become what he'd been now for more than fifteen years: an internationally known French psychiatrist with a lucrative private practice in which the two younger psychiatrists with whom he shared his offices on avenue Victor Hugo were not his partners but his salaried employees. The diplomas hanging framed on his wall were all genuine despite the fact that the name on them—Julien de Saint-Hilaire—was false and that the universities in Paris and Geneva and Los Angeles that had issued them would have been appalled to learn just what he'd actually done to earn them. He had a twenty-two-room apartment in a private hotel overlooking the Parc Monceau that even the other tenants now thought had been in his family since the early sixteen hundreds, maids who were each and every one of them country girls from small villages in the provinces as maids were traditionally supposed to be, and a very beautiful blond-haired American wife, Liz, in her early twenties, who'd been a model for Cacharel before he'd married her and convinced her to give up her career.

He took two, and sometimes three, month-long business trips every year, leaving the routine care of his patients during his absences to Jean-Luc and Michel, both of whom were talented minor shamans though neither of them was as yet aware of just what it was that they did when they dealt with patients.

Last fall, for example, he'd left them with the practice while he attended a psychiatric congress in San Francisco where he and his fellow psychiatrists—or at least that sizable minority among them who were, like himself, practicing shamans—had gotten together in a very carefully locked and guarded auditorium, there to put on their shamanizing costumes so they could steal people's souls and introduce malefic objects into their bodies, thus assuring themselves and their less aware colleagues of an adequate supply of patients for the coming year. He'd learned quite a bit about the proper use of quartz crystals from two young aboriginal shamans attending their first international congress, but had done as poorly as usual in the competitions: The very gifts that made him so good at recovering souls no matter how well his colleagues hid them made it difficult for him to recognize those hiding places where they in turn would be unable to discover the souls *he* hid. But he'd had a good time drinking Ripple and Thunderbird and Boone's Farm Apple Wine from stained paper bags on street corners and in Golden Gate Park, where he and most of the other psychiatrists attending the congress had slept when the weather permitted, and by the time he'd returned to Paris Liz had lost all the weight she'd put on since the trip before.

But it was almost the end of March now, time to start readying himself for his next month-long separation from her and from his comfortable life as Julien de Saint-Hilaire. He had to retrieve the lost, strayed, and stolen souls of those he intended to cure, and damage or find new hiding places for the souls of those patients he intended to retain for further treatment.

And besides, Liz was starting to get fat again. It was a vicious circle: They both loved to eat but she couldn't keep up with him without putting on weight, and the fatter she got the more insecure she felt about her appearance, so the more she ate to comfort herself. She was already back to the stage where she was sneaking out to eat napoleons and lemon tarts and exotic ice creams and sherbets in three or four different tea salons every afternoon, doing it all so surreptitiously that if he didn't know beforehand where she was planning to go, it could take him a whole afternoon of searching to catch up with her; in another month or so she'd be getting worried enough to start looking to other men for reassurance again.

And that was something he couldn't, and wouldn't, allow. He had very precise plans for his heir, a boy whose soul was even now undergoing its third year of prenatal preparation in one of the invisible eagle's nests high up on the Eiffel Tower where since the turn of the century the most powerful French politicians and generals had received the training and charisma and made the contacts necessary to ready them for their subsequent roles. And after all the years he'd spent readying Liz to bear his son he wasn't going to let her negate his efforts with another man's seed. She had her pastries, her wines, cognacs, and sleeping pills, her clothing and her restaurants, her money and her social position, and she'd have to stay content with them for at least the next four years, until his son was born.

On the way to his office he stopped off at his second apartment. It was a one-room windowless garret on the rue de Condé that had obviously been somebody's attic at one time. It now boasted a tiny brick fireplace and chimney that he'd fitted with an elaborate and deadly labyrinth which enabled him to enter and leave as a bird without permitting entrance by any other shamans. He picked up some of the pills he kept for Liz. His supply was almost exhausted: He'd have to write the old Indian in Arizona (John Henry Two Feathers Thomas Thompson, whose father had toured with Buffalo Bill's Wild West Show before starting his own medicine show with a white barker for a front) again and get some more.

He put on his two caps—for something as trivial as what he was about to do he didn't really need the power the rest of his costume would have provided him with—and became a pigeon with orange eyes and naked pink legs. He negotiated the chimney maze, making sure the spirits who guarded it recognized him in the form he'd adopted, to emerge on the roof and fly back to his apartment overlooking the Parc Monceau. He and Liz had been up very late making love the night before, with only a brief pause at two in the morning for the cold buffet he'd had his catering service prepare them, and she was still asleep, even snoring slightly in the way she did when she'd had too much to drink or had taken too many sleeping pills the night before, all of which made things easier for him. As did the fact that he'd left the cage with the two mynah birds in it covered when he'd left the apartment. Liz had bought the birds at the Sunday bird market on the Île de la Cité while he'd been away on his last trip and the birds had never learned to tolerate his presence in any of the forms he took. But though they were alert enough to detect the fact that he wasn't what he seemed to be as either a bird or a man, they were too stupid to realize that despite their dark cage the night was over. So he didn't have to worry about the birds making enough noise to awaken Liz.

He slipped in through the window he'd left open in the master bedroom, plucked Liz's sleeping soul from her body and bruised it with his beak in a way he knew from experience would do her no lasting harm but which would give her migraines for the next few weeks. Then he returned her still-sleeping soul to her body and flew back to his garret, where he took off his caps and locked them away in the sky-blue steel steamer trunk he kept them in. He sprayed his hair with a kerosene-smelling children's delousing spray, to take care of the head-lice that made their home in the inner cap, then used a dry shampoo to get rid of both the spray and the smell from the cap itself. He finally locked the door behind him, making sure when he did so that the spirits guarding the apartment would continue to deny entry to anyone but himself, then went back down the five flights of stairs as Julien de Saint-Hilaire, checked with the concierge a moment, and caught a taxi to his office.

He checked with Jean-Luc and Michel when he arrived, but found that except for a matter concerning a long-time patient who was now more than a year behind on his bills and who showed no signs of being ready to pay (which wasn't their responsibility, anyway), they had everything more or less under control. Too much under control, even: Jean-Luc especially was doing those patients he worked with more good than Eminescu wanted them done, but there was no way to get the younger psychiatrist to stop curing them without explaining to him the true nature of his profession and just what it was he was really doing to get the results he was getting, and that was something Eminescu was not yet ready to let him know; perhaps in another twenty or twenty-five years, when he himself would have to begin thinking about conserving his force.

He sat down behind his desk, pretended to busy himself with one patient's case history while he thought about what to do to that patient who was refusing to pay and waited for Liz to phone him.

The call came perhaps half an hour later. She said she'd just awakened and all she could think about was how soon he was going to be going away, and did he know yet exactly when he was going to have to leave for Japan? He told her he'd received confirmation on his flights, and that he'd be leaving in another six days, on a Monday, very early in the morning. She told him that she had an awful headache; it had started as soon as she'd awakened and realized he was going to be leaving, and she asked him to bring her something for the pain, since it was obviously his fault she had the headache because he was going away and she always felt sick and tired and alone and unhappy whenever he left her for more than a few days. He said he'd bring her some of the painkillers he'd given her the last time, the ones that didn't leave her too groggy, and she said, fine, but try to make them a little stronger this time, Julien, even if they do make me a bit groggy. He said he would, but that if she was really feeling that bad perhaps it would be better if he came home early, he could cancel all his afternoon appointments. She said, no, that wouldn't be necessary, but if he'd meet her for lunch he could give her the pills then, she'd pick out the restaurant and make the reservations, come by to pick him up when it was time. About one o'clock?

He said that one o'clock would be perfect. When she arrived he gave her the first two of the old Indian's pills, and on the way to the restaurant soothed her headache. For that he didn't even need his caps, he had enough power left over from just having worn them earlier.

It was an excellent restaurant near the Comédie Française, on rue Richelieu, and he was enormously hungry—flying demanded a great deal of energy; the iron with which his bones had been reinforced and tied together after his initiatory dismemberment was heavy and hard to lift when he was a bird, for all that the iron-wrapped bones gave him the vitality and endurance of a much younger man when in human form—and both he and Liz enjoyed their meal. Afterward he dropped her off outside Notre Dame (where she had to meet some friends of her aunt's whom she'd been unable to get out of promising to show around), then went back to his apartment on the rue de Condé and put on his entire costume: the raccoon-skin cap with the snap-on tail that John Henry had given him and which he kept hidden under the over-large shapeless felt hat, the greasy false beard and hair (though in one sense they weren't really false at all, since they and the skin to which they were still attached had both been at one time his: more of the old Indian's work), the multiple layers of thermal underwear he wore under the faded work blues that were in turn covered by the old brown leather military trench coat with the missing buttons and half the left sleeve gone, the three pink plastic shopping bags from Monoprix filled with what looked like rags, but weren't, and the two pairs of crusted blue socks he wore under his seven-league work shoes (the ones he had specially made for him in Austria to look as though they were coming apart), so he could trace the pills' progress through Liz's system, and help them along when and if necessary.

It was raining by the time he'd completed his preparations and had begun beating his tambourine and hopping up and down, but he didn't feel like doing anything major about the weather even though he'd planned to go home as a pigeon again. So by the time he arrived back at the apartment he was very wet.

But that gave him an excuse to remain perched there on the bedroom windowsill, ignoring the nasty looks the mynah birds were giving him while he ruffled his feathers and looked indignant.

Liz had already gotten rid of her aunt's friends, as he'd been sure she would; she was on the phone again, trying to find someone to go tea-salon hopping with her for the rest of the afternoon. She was having trouble: Very few of her woman friends could keep up with her pastry and sweets consumption and still look the way that Liz demanded the people she was seen with look, while Eminescu had for several years now made a practice of discouraging any and all of her male friends, even the homosexuals, who showed any tendency to spend too much, or even too attentive, time with her.

Not, of course, that he'd ever done so in any way that either Liz or her admirers could have ever realized had anything to do with her husband. The men in question just always had something go horribly wrong when they were with her—sudden, near fatal attacks of choking or vomiting; running into old wives or girlfriends they'd abandoned pregnant; being mistaken for notorious Armenian terrorists or Cypriot neo-nazi bombers by the CRS and so ending up clubbed unconscious and jailed incommunicado; other things of the same sort —with the result that Liz never had any *fun* with them, and began avoiding even those few hyper-persistent or genuinely lovestruck victims who kept trying to see her anyway.

Which reminded him: It was time for her to get her headache back. As a former veterinary student he was quite familiar with Pavlovian conditioning— had, in fact, been writing his thesis on the ways it had been used to train the attack dogs used by the government in quelling the then-recent Polish workers' insurrection when he'd been forced to flee Romania—and his spiritual experience in later years had proven to him how useful a correct application of its basic principles could be to a shaman like himself. Thus, whenever Liz did something he approved of he rewarded her for it, whenever she did something he disapproved of he punished her, but always in ways that would seem to her to be in some way the direct result of her behavior, and not of any interference or judgment on his part. And that, finally, was the rationale for the use of the pills he gave her whenever he went away: Not only did they keep her properly subdued in his absence and insure that she'd have taken off her excess weight by the time he returned and restored her to normal, but they made her so miserable that when he did return she equated his presence—the secondary stimulus—with the primary stimulus of her renewed health and vitality in the same way she'd learned to equate his absence with her misery.

It was all very rational and scientific, a fact on which he prided himself. Too many of his colleagues were little better than witch-doctors.

"You're my whole happiness," Liz had told him once. "My only reason for staying alive." And that, to be sure, was how he wanted things.

It had taken her five phone calls but she'd finally found someone: Marie-Claude had agreed to accompany her, and they were going to meet at the tea room they liked on the Île St. Louis where the ice cream was so good. And the sun was coming out again. He flew there to wait for them.

From his perch in the tree across the street from the tea salon he could see them easily enough as they entered together, though when they sat down away from the window he had to cock his head just right to watch them through the walls. They both ordered ice cream—Bertillon chocolate, coffee, and chestnut for Liz, the same for Marie-Claude but with coconut in place of the coffee—and while they were waiting for the waitress to bring it convinced each other that it would be all right to have some sherbets with their coffee afterward.

Eminescu waited until Liz's first few swallows of chocolate were reaching her stomach to cock his head at the angle that let him see what was going on inside her.

Her stomach acids and digestive enzymes had already dissolved the pills and liberated the encysted bladder worms, and these in turn were reacting to the acids and enzymes by evaginating—turning themselves inside out, as though they'd been one-finger gloves with the fingers pushed in, but with the fingers now popping out again. Once the young tapeworms (as he'd learned to call them at UCLA, and it was a better name for them than the French *vers solitaires*, because these worms at least were far from solitary) had their scolexes, head-sections, free they could use the suckers and hooks on them to attach themselves to the walls of Liz's intestines, there to begin growing by pushing out new anterior segments—though he'd be back to deal with them before any of the worms was more than five or so meters long, and thus before any of the worms had reached its full sexual maturity.

Three specimens each of three kinds of tapeworm—*Taenia solium*, *Taenia saginata*, and *Diphyllobothrium latum*, the pork, beef, and fish tapeworms, respectively—he allowed to hook and sucker themselves to Liz's intestinal walls, though not without first ensuring that the individuals he favored would all be fairly slow-growing, as well as unlikely to excrete excessive amounts of those toxic waste products peculiar to their respective species. The myriad other worms whose encysted forms the pills had contained he killed, reaching out from his perch in the tree to pluck them from her intestinal walls with his beak, pinch off and kill their voracious little souls. It was all very well controlled, all very scientific, with nothing left to chance.

He watched her the rest of the afternoon, at that and three other tea salons, to make sure the nine worms he'd selected for her would do her no more damage than he'd planned for them to do, and that none of the other worms the pills had contained had escaped his attention and survived.

When at last he returned to the apartment on the rue de Condé he was weak with hunger. He took a quick shower and ate a choucroute at a nearby brasserie before going back to his office to make sure nothing unexpected had come up in his absence.

And every day until the time came for him to leave, he checked Liz two or three times, to make sure the worms now growing so rapidly inside her would do no lasting harm. He valued Liz a great deal, enjoyed her youth and spontaneity fully as much as he valued the son she was going to bear him, and he had no desire to be unnecessarily cruel to her.

On the morning he'd chosen to leave he went to his second apartment and checked on her one last time as she showered—thinner already and beautiful for all the fatigue on her face and in her posture—then returned to the windowless room and resumed his human form. He was hungry, but for the next month he was Eminescu Eliade again, and there was no way he could use Julien de Saint-Hilaire's money to pay for as much as a merguez-and-fries sandwich from one of the window-front Tunisian restaurants on the rue St. André des Arts without destroying much of his costume's power.

The rat he was to follow was waiting for him as arranged at the bottom of the stairs, behind the trash cans. He put it in one of his plastic bags, where it promptly made a nest for itself out of the rags that weren't really rags. Then he went out to beg the money for the three things he'd need to get started: the bottles of wine he'd have to share with his fellow shamans as long as he remained aboveground, the first-class métro ticket he'd need to enter the labyrinths coexistent with the Parisian métro system, and the *terrine de foie de volailles au poivre vert* from Coesnon's which the rat demanded he feed it each time it guided him through the city's subway labyrinths.

There were a lot of clochards he didn't recognize behind the Marché and on the streets nearby, even a blond-haired threesome—two bearded young men and a girl with her hair in braids—who looked more like hitch-hiking German or Scandinavian students temporarily short of money than like real clochards, for all that they seemed to know most of the others and be on good terms with them. What it added up to was an unwelcome reminder that he'd been spending too much time either abroad or as Julien de Saint-Hilaire, and not nearly enough staying in touch with his city and its spirit world—and that was an error that could well prove fatal to him unless he took steps to correct it. He'd have to stay in Paris that October after all, and miss the Australian congress that had had him so excited ever since he'd begun to learn the kinds of things one could do with quartz crystals.

It took him five days to get the money he needed: He was out of practice at begging and every few hours, of course, he had to put most of what he'd earned toward the wine he shared with the others. And Coesnon's had tripled their prices during the last year alone. But by the fifth evening he had what he needed, so he walked down the rue de l'Ancienne Comédie to the rue Dauphine, where he bought the four-hundred-and-fifty-franc terrine despite the staff's and other customers' horrified disapproval when he squeezed himself and his bulging sacks into the narrow charcuterie, knocking a platter of blood sausage with apples to the floor in the process, then spent another four hours listening to the mutterings and arguments of the future shamans awaiting birth in the hundreds of tiers of invisible pigeons' nests that completely covered the green bronze statue of Henri IV astride his horse, there on its pedestal atop the little fenced-off step pyramid on the Pont Neuf. But there was nothing useful to be heard—Tabarin and his pompous master Mondor arguing as usual in the nest they shared, Napoleon pleading to be rescued from the tiny statuette of himself that the overly zealous Bonapartist who'd been commissioned to cast Henri's statue had hidden in the king's right arm, thus inadvertently imprisoning his hero's spirit there until such time as someone should destroy the statuette or rescue him—and so after listening a while he proceeded on diagonally across the Île de la Cité to Chatelet where he entered the métro system.

He bought himself a first-class ticket and pretended to drop it as he went to insert it in the machine so he could release the rat. It scurried away from him through the thick crowds and he had to run after it as soon as the machine disgorged his enigmatically stamped ticket, plastic bags, rags and leather overcoat flapping as he ran. Four or five times he lost sight of the rat—once because some fifteen- or sixteen-year-olds thought it would be fun to trip him and see how long they could keep him from getting back to his feet before somebody stopped them—but each time he found the rat again and at last it led him in through one of the urinals to the first of the labyrinth's inner turnings. There he fed it the first half of the terrine and the stamped métro ticket.

The corridors were less crowded when he emerged from the urinal, the light dimmer and pinker, and with each subsequent turning away from the public corridors into the secret ways which led through the land of the dead there were more and more of the German shepherds whose powerful bodies housed the souls of those few dead who'd been granted leave of the Undercity for a day and a night in return for guarding Paris itself, fewer and fewer people, and those few only the dying and mentally ill, the North African blacks who worked as maintenance men and cleaners in the métro system, and shamans like himself—plus once a politician whose name he couldn't recall but to whom he'd made the proper ritual obeisances anyway.

When he regained his feet and wiped the filth from his forehead he found the corridor around him had changed yet again. The murky and polluted bottom waters of the Seine flowed sluggishly past and around him without touching him, and his guide now wore the baggy bright-red shorts with the two big gold buttons on the front that told him he'd finally escaped the outer world entirely and entered the land of the dead.

He fed the rat the rest of the terrine and began retracing the route he knew should take him back to the place where he'd hidden the soul of the first of those patients whom he intended to have make a miraculous recovery upon his return, a retired general suffering from the delusion that he was a young and bearded bouquiniste making his living selling subversive literature and antique pornographic postcards from a bookstall by the Seine.

But Hell had changed, changed radically and inexplicably in the year he'd spent away from it, and it took him almost seven weeks before he was able to escape it again by a route that led up and out through the sewer system. Because someone, somehow, had found his patients' souls where he'd buried them in the river mud and filth, had dug them up and left in their place small, vicious but somehow indistinct, creatures that had attacked him and tried to devour his soul. He'd been strong enough to fight them off, though they'd vanished before the mud cloud they'd stirred up had settled and he'd had a chance to get a closer look at them. But though he'd found his patients' souls and recovered them from their new hiding places without overmuch trouble, none of his usual contacts among the dead had been willing or able to tell him who his enemy was, or what the things that had attacked him had been.

He'd planned to stay Eminescu Eliade for a while after his return to the surface so he could try to locate his enemy where he knew the man had to be hiding, among the clochards who had not yet achieved professional recognition in a second identity (because while professional ethics allowed stealing other psychiatrists' patients' souls, even encouraged it as tending to keep everyone alert and doing their best, leaving creatures such as the things that had attacked him to devour a fellow psychiatrist's soul was specifically forbidden by the Ordre des médecins)—but when he took the form of a pigeon and returned to the apartment he shared with Liz to see how she was doing and make sure the tapeworms in her intestines hadn't done her any real harm in the extra weeks, ready to perhaps even kill one or two of them if they were getting a little too long, he saw that something further had gone wrong, horribly wrong.

Liz was in the kitchen in her striped robe, spooning chestnut purée from a one-kilo can frantically into her mouth as though she were starving, and his first impression was that he'd never before seen her looking so disgustingly fat and sloppy. But then he realized that though her belly was distended and she looked as though she'd neither slept nor washed in a few days she was if anything skinnier than she'd been when he'd seen her last. Much skinnier. And that the swollen puffiness that so disfigured her face came from the fact that she was crying, and that her legs—her legs that had always been so long and smooth and beautiful, so tawny despite her naturally ash-blond hair that she'd always refused to wear any sort of tinted or patterned stockings, even when her refusal had cost her work—her legs were streaked with long, twitching fat blue veins. Varicose veins, as though she were a fat and flaccid woman in her sixties.

He cocked his pigeon's head to the right and looked in through her abdominal walls to see what was happening within her intestines, in through the skin and muscles of her legs to understand what was going on there.

Only to find that the tapeworms had reached sexual maturity despite all the careful checking he'd done on them before his departure, and that not only had their intertwined ten-meter bodies almost completely choked her swollen and distended intestines, but that their hermaphroditic anterior segments had already begun producing eggs. And those eggs—instead of having been excreted as they should have been, to hatch only when and if stimulated by the distinctive digestive juices of the pigs, cows, or fish whose particular constellation of acids and enzymes alone could provide their species of worm with its necessary stimuli—those eggs were hatching almost immediately, while they were still within Liz's digestive tract, and the minute spherical embryos were anchoring themselves to the intestinal walls with the six long hooks they each sported, then boring through the walls to enter her bloodstream, through which they then let themselves be carried down into her legs. There, in the smaller vessels in her calves and thighs, they were anchoring themselves and beginning to grow, not encysting as normal tapeworm embryos would have done, but instead developing into myriads of long, filament-thin worms that were slowly climbing their way from their anchor points up through her circulatory system toward her heart as they lengthened.

His enemy, whoever his enemy was, had planned the whole farce with his patients' stolen but easily recoverable souls and the things that had been lying in wait for him in their place just to keep him occupied while *he* played around with the worms in Liz, modified them for his own purposes. He must have had her under observation long enough to have known about the fear of all other doctors but himself that Eminescu had long ago conditioned into her, known that he'd have a free hand with her until Eminescu got back. And if Eminescu'd stayed trapped in the secret ways even a few days longer she might well have lost her feet, perhaps even her legs, to gangrene and so been ruined as the potential mother of his son. A week or two beyond that and she could have been dead.

She was constantly moving her legs, twitching them as she gorged herself on the purée, kneading her calves and thighs. Keeping the circulation going as best she could despite the filament worms waving like strands of hungry kelp in her veins, the worms that had so far only impeded, and not yet blocked, the flow of blood through her legs.

It was all very scientific and precise, masterfully devised. Whoever'd done it could have easily killed her, done so with far less effort and imagination than he'd expended on producing her present condition. The whole thing was a challenge, could only be a challenge, traditional in intent for all that the way it had been done was new to him. And what the challenge said was, I want your practice and your position and everything else you have, and I can take it away from you, I've already proved that anything you can do I can do better, and I'm going to go ahead and do it unless you can stop me before I kill you. The challenge was undoubtedly on file with the Ordre des médecins, though there'd be no way for Eminescu to get a look at the records and learn who his challenger was: The relevant laws were older than France or Rome, and were zealously enforced.

But what he could do was take care of Liz and keep her from being damaged any further while he tried to learn more about his opponent. He reached out with his beak, twisted the souls of the filament worms in Liz's legs dead. They were much tougher than he'd anticipated, surprisingly hard to kill, but when at last they were all dead he pulled them carefully free of the blood vessels in which they'd anchored themselves, pulled them out through Liz's muscles and skin without doing her any further damage, then patched the damaged veins and arteries with tissues he yanked from the legs of a group of Catholic schoolgirls who happened to be passing in the street. They were young: They'd recover soon enough. The stagnant and polluted blood, slimy with the worms' waste products, began to flow freely through her system again.

He watched Liz closely for a while to make sure the waste products weren't concentrated or toxic enough to be dangerous to her in the time it would take her liver or other organs to filter them from her blood. When he was sure that any harm they might do her would be trivial enough to be ignored he reached out to take and squeeze the souls of the tapeworms knotted together and clogging her intestines, snatched himself back just in time to save himself when he recognized them: the creatures that had attacked him in the land of the dead.

But fearsome though they were on the spiritual plane—and now that he had a chance to examine them better he saw that their souls were not those of tapeworms but of some sort of lampreys, those long eel-like parasitic vertebrates whose round sucking mouths contain circular rows of rasping teeth with which they bore their way in through the scales of the fish they've attached themselves to, so as to suck out the fish's insides and eventually kill it in the process— physically they were still only tapeworms despite their modified reproductive systems. And that meant that he could destroy them by physical—medical— means. Quinacrine hydrochloride and aspidium oleoresin should be more than sufficient, if there hadn't been something better developed recently that he wasn't aware of yet. But to make use of any kind of medicine he'd have to resume his identity as Julien de Saint-Hilaire, if only long enough to return home, soothe Liz and prescribe for her, then make sure she was following the treatment he suggested and that it was working for her.

But before he did that he had to try to learn a little more about his challenger, so he returned to his apartment on the rue de Condé and resumed his human form. His efforts in the Undercity and just now as a bird had totally depleted his body's reserves of fat and energy; he was gaunt and trembling, so that those passersby he approached after making his way down the back stairs to the street who weren't frightened away by his diseased look were unusually generous. After he'd made the phone call that confirmed that, yes, an official challenge had been registered against Julien de Saint-Hilaire, he was able to buy not only the wine he needed to approach his fellow clochards but some food from the soup kitchen behind the Marché as well.

He slept that night in the métro, curled up on the benches with three other clochards, one of whom was a woman, though as much a shaman as himself or the other two. The woman had a bottle of cheap rosé; they passed it back and forth while they talked, and he listened to them while saying as little himself as possible, trying to find out if they knew anything about his enemy without revealing what he was doing, but either they knew nothing about his opponent or they were siding with him against Eminescu and keeping their knowledge hidden. Which was quite possible: He'd seen it happen that way a few times before, with older shamans who were particularly arrogant and disliked, though he'd never imagined it could happen to him.

The next day he spent sitting on a bench on the Pont Neuf, panhandling just enough to justify his presence there while he tried to learn something from the spirits in their nests on the statue of Henri IV. He even promised to free Napoleon from the statuette in which the former Emperor was trapped and promised him a place in one of the highest eagle's nests on the Eiffel Tower from which he'd be able to make a triumphant return to politics, if only he'd tell Eminescu his enemy's name or something that would help him find him. But Napoleon had been imprisoned there in the statuette in King Henri's statue's right arm pleading with and ranting at the shamans who refused to so much as acknowledge his existence for too many years and he'd become completely insane: He refused to reply to Eminescu's questions, continued his habitual pleas and promises even after Eminescu had begun hurting him and threatening to silence his voice forever unless he responded rationally.

Eminescu finally left him there, still ranting and pleading: It would have been pointless to waste any more of his forces in carrying out the threats he'd made. He had enough money to pay his entry to the Eiffel Tower, so he flew there as a pigeon, cursing the unaccustomed heaviness of his iron-wrapped bones, then transformed himself back into a clochard in the bushes and went up to the observation deck in the elevator, there found his son and General de Gaulle in their respective nests and asked their advice. De Gaulle—perhaps because the nest in which he was preparing his triumphal return was next to Eminescu's son's nest and the two had come to know each other fairly well—was always polite to Eminescu, wherein the other politicians and military men, able to sense the fact that he wasn't truly French and themselves chauvinistic to the core, refused to even speak to him.

But neither de Gaulle nor his son knew anything useful, and his son seemed weaker and less coherent than the last time Eminescu had spoken to him, as though the forces conspiring against his birth were already beginning to make him fade. Still, at least he was safe from any sort of direct attack: The invisible eagles that guarded his nest allowed no one not of their own kind to approach the tower in anything but human form, and would have detected and killed any mere shaman like Eminescu or his enemy who'd attempted to put on an eagle's form to gain entry.

He returned to the rue de Condé so he could beat his tambourine and sing and dance without danger of interruption, and thus summon the maximum possible power. It was night by the time he felt ready, so he took the form of an owl and returned to the apartment overlooking the Parc Monceau, perched outside the bedroom window, terrifying the mynah birds, and killed the tapeworm embryos that had made their way into Liz's bloodstream again. It was easier this time: He had a lot more strength available to him as an owl, though it was harder to hold the form and he paid for that strength later on, when he regained his humanity.

He examined the worms in Liz's intestines with the owl's sharper eyes to see if there was some way he could destroy them without harming Liz or risking his own safety, saw that even as an owl he didn't have enough concentrated spiritual strength at his disposal to destroy all the worms together. There would have been a way to do it with quartz crystals, replacing those sections of her intestines to which the tapeworms had anchored themselves with smooth crystal so they'd lose their purchase and be eliminated from her body, but he was far from skillful enough yet to carry out the operation without killing her, since loose quartz crystals in her body would be like just so many obsidian knives, and he lacked the experience needed to mold the quartz to her flesh and infuse it with her spirit so as to make it a living part of her.

He could have done it if he'd had a chance to go to that Australian convention he'd planned to attend in the fall. As it was he'd have to try to find another way.

That night he slept under the Pont Neuf on some sheets of cardboard a previous sleeper had left behind him, satisfying the tremendous hunger his efforts as an owl had awakened in him as best he could from the garbage cans behind Coes-non's and some of the other gourmet boutiques on the rue Dauphine.

The next morning he flew to his offices on Avenue Victor Hugo as a pigeon and spent a long time watching Jean-Luc and Michel. It had been months since he'd last been there as anything but Julien de Saint-Hilaire and he wanted to make sure that neither of them had developed the kind of power his challenger so obviously had. They were, after all, the two persons most likely to covet his position and the two most prepared to fill it when he was gone, despite the fact that a challenge from either of them would have been a clear violation of medical ethics and that his challenger had registered his challenge with the Ordre des médecins in thoroughly proper fashion.

He watched them working, soothing souls in pain, coaxing lost or strayed souls back to the bodies they'd left. They were both small, slim and dark, both immensely sincere, and they were both fumbling around blindly in the spirit realm for souls that they could have recovered in instants if they'd known what it was they were really doing. No, their instincts were good, but they were still just what he'd always thought them to be, talented amateurs with no idea of the true nature of their talents, even though those talents seemed to be growing, in Jean-Luc's case in particular.

Since he was there Eminescu used the opportunity to undo some of the good Michel had done a young schizophrenic he had no intention of seeing recover, then returned to the rue de Condé, and from there, as Julien de Saint-Hilaire, to his apartment overlooking the park, stopping only briefly on the way to buy and eat seven hundred and fifty grams of dark chocolates.

Liz was asleep, passed out half dressed on the living room sofa with a partially eaten meal cold on a tray on the table beside her. The kitchen was littered with empty and half-empty cans and bottles.

The servants were all gone and he knew Liz well enough to be sure she'd sent them away, unable to bear the idea of having anyone who knew her see what had happened to her legs, just as she would have been unable to face being examined by another doctor.

She twitched in her sleep, shifting the position of her legs on the sofa, then moved them back the way they'd been. The blue veins in her thighs and calves looked perhaps a little less fat and swollen than they'd seemed when he'd first found out what'd happened to her, but only slightly so: Even though he'd gotten rid of the worms in the veins themselves and replaced a tiny fraction of the damaged vessels it would take a long time for the rest to regain their elasticity. He might even have to replace them altogether.

He'd stopped at a pharmacy run by a minor shaman he knew on the way over to order the various medicines he'd need to deal with the tapeworms as well as a comprehensive selection of those sleeping and pain pills which Liz had a tendency to abuse when he failed to keep her under close enough supervision but which would serve now to keep her more or less anesthetized and incapable of worrying too much for the next few weeks, until his present troubles were over one way or another. And there was at least the consolation of knowing that if he did succeed in discovering his opponent's identity and destroying him, the other's attack on Liz would have served to further reinforce the way Eminescu'd conditioned her to associate his every absence with unhappiness and physical misery, his return with health and pleasure.

He picked up the phone, intending to awaken her with a faked call to the pharmacy so as to make it seem as though he'd just entered, taken one look at her lying there with her legs all swollen and marbled with twitching blue veins and had immediately and accurately diagnosed her condition and so known exactly what he'd have to do without needing to subject her to the indignity of further examinations or tests. It was what she expected of him: Liz had always had a childlike faith in doctors and medicine for all her fear of them. But at the last moment he put the phone down again and went back into the bedroom to take a careful look at the two mynah birds in their cage.

His presence alarmed them: They started hopping nervously back and forth between their perches, making little hushed cries of alarm as if afraid that if they were any louder they'd draw his attention to them. But hushed as their cries were they were still making more noise than he wanted them to, so he closed the heavy door behind him to cut off the sound and keep them from awakening Liz. Without his cap and costume he couldn't examine them to find out if they were just the rather stupid birds they appeared to be or if one or even both of them were spies for his enemy, perhaps that enemy himself in bird-form. (But could two shamans together challenge a third? He had the impression it was forbidden, but that there was perhaps a way for a challenger to make use of a second shaman's aid.) In any case, the mynah birds were living creatures over whom he exercised no control and which had been introduced into his home with neither his knowledge nor his permission at a time when he'd been away, and he couldn't trust them.

He opened the cage door, reached in quickly with both hands and grabbed the birds before they could escape or make more than one startled squeak apiece, then wrung their necks and threw them out the window, aiming the bodies far enough to the right so that Liz wouldn't see them if she just took a casual look out the window. He could retrieve them later and take them back with him to examine more closely at his other apartment before Liz'd had a chance to leave the house and discover them dead.

He left the cage door open and opened the window slightly, to provide an explanation for their absence when Liz noticed they were gone, then covered the cage to keep her from noticing it immediately.

He went back into the living room. Liz had turned over again and was scratching her right calf in her sleep, leaving angry red scratches all up and down it. He played out the scene he'd planned beforehand with the faked call to the pharmacy, reassured her as soon as the sound of his voice awakened her: He was back, he'd known what had happened to her as soon as he took one look at her, it was a side-effect of certain illegal hormones that people had been injecting dairy cows with recently and which had been showing up, for some as yet unexplained reason, in high concentrations only in certain crèmes pâtis-sières used in such things as napoleons and eclairs, and he knew how to cure her condition, it wasn't even really anything to worry about, she wouldn't need surgery and in a few weeks she'd be completely cured, there wouldn't be any scars or anything else to show for the episode but some unpleasant memories, her legs would be as beautiful as before and she shouldn't worry, she should just trust him.

She'd burst into tears as soon as she'd seen him there, was holding on to him and crying with relief by the time he'd finished telling her not to worry, that everything was going to be all right.

The bell rang: the pharmacy, one of the few in Paris willing to deliver, with the medicines he'd ordered. He paid the delivery man, tipping him extravagantly as always, then went back into the bedroom where Liz'd run to hide herself when she heard the bell and gave her two sleeping pills and a pain pill. Only when she was completely groggy and he'd tucked her into bed did he explain his absence, telling her about the two weeks he'd spent completely isolated in a tiny village in the mountains where the Japanese government was carrying out an experimental mental health program and from which it had been impossible to phone her, though he didn't understand how she could have failed to receive the long, long telegram he'd sent her from Tokyo after he'd tried so many times to get her on the phone without once succeeding.

She started nodding out near the end of the explanation, as he'd intended: She'd never remember exactly what it was that he'd told her but only that he'd explained things, and he could always modify his story later and then tell her that the modified story was exactly the same as the one he'd told her before. Though that was probably just an unnecessary precaution: She always believed even the most implausible stories he told her, just as she seemed to have believed his story about the hormones.

He got her to take the various pills, powders, and liquids he'd obtained to treat the tapeworms with—there'd been a number of new medicines he'd been totally unaware of on the market, yet another reminder of how out of touch he'd been allowing himself to become—then gave her two more sleeping pills to make sure she'd stay unconscious for a while. He waited until she was asleep and snoring raggedly, then left.

He retrieved the two mynah birds from the bushes, put them in a plastic sack and caught a taxi to his other apartment, where he put on his costume to examine them.

But the birds were just mynah birds, as far as he could tell when he took them apart, and when he returned once again to his other apartment as a pigeon and flew in through the bathroom window he'd left open for himself he saw that the medicines he'd used were having no effect whatsoever on the tapeworms—no effect, that is, except to stimulate them to a frantically accelerated production of new eggs.

Once again his enemy had anticipated him, known what his next move would be long before he himself had done so and had arranged to use it against him. He was being laughed at, played for a fool, a clown.

But for all the anger that knowledge awakened in him there was nothing he could do about it yet. He had to stay there beside Liz on the bed for hours, stalking nervously back and forth on his obscenely pink legs as he plucked embryo after embryo from her bloodstream and destroyed them, until he was so hungry and exhausted he could barely keep himself conscious. Then he had no choice but to return to his other apartment—resting every two or three blocks in a tree or on a window ledge—so he could resume his identity as Julien de Saint-Hilaire long enough to pay for a large meal in a restaurant.

He ate an immense meal at an Italian restaurant a few blocks away, followed it with a second, equally large, meal at a bad Chinese restaurant he usually avoided and felt better.

He tried telephoning John Henry Two Feathers Thomas Thompson but was told that the old Indian's number was no longer in service and that there was no new listing for him. Eminescu didn't know if that meant he was dead, or had moved, or had just obtained an unlisted number. But there was no one Eminescu could trust who lived near enough to his former teacher to contact him, and he didn't have the time to fly to America and try to find him himself, either as a bird or by taking a plane as Julien de Saint-Hilaire. So he sent the old Indian a long telegram, and hoped that he'd not only get it, but that he'd have something to say that would help Eminescu.

He bought a sandwich from a sidewalk stand and ate it on the way back to the rue de Condé apartment, then resumed his caps and costume and returned to the Parc Monceau apartment yet one more time as a pigeon to try to deal with the embryos, yet despite the huge meals he'd eaten and the hours he'd spent in his other identity he was still too hungry and too exhausted to keep it up for more than a few hours before the embryos started getting past him despite everything he could do. And the worms in Liz's intestines seemed to be producing their eggs ever faster now, as though the process he'd begun when he gave her the medicines was still accelerating.

Defeated and furious, he returned to his other apartment, passed out as soon as he regained his human form. When he reawakened he barely had enough strength to crawl over to the sink where he'd left the two dismembered mynah birds and strip the meat from their bones and devour it.

There was no way he could hope to save Liz if he continued the way he was going. All he was really doing was destroying himself, using up all the forces which he'd need to protect himself from his opponent when it finally came to a direct attack on him. For a moment he was tempted to just abandon Liz, give up his identity as Julien de Saint-Hilaire and let her die or be taken over by the challenger when he moved into the Julien de Saint-Hilaire role in Eminescu's place. But he'd come too far, was too close to the true power and security he knew his son would provide him with, the assurance that he himself would be born in one of the Eiffel Tower's eagles' nests, to abandon everything now. Besides, Liz still pleased him, though it wasn't just that, just the kind of sentimental weakness that he knew would destroy him if he ever let it get the upper hand. No, what mattered was that Liz was *his*, his to dispose of and no one else's, and his pride was such that he could never allow anyone else to take her away from him. That pride he knew for his strength, as all sentimentality was weakness: Without his pride he was nothing.

He had to save her life, but he couldn't do it as a pigeon, nor even as an owl. Yet they were in the heart of Paris; the only other animal forms he could put on safely—cats, perhaps ducks or other small birds, insects, rats, and mice— would be equally ineffectual. If he tried to put on an eagle's form the invisible eagles atop the Eiffel Tower would detect him and destroy him for his presumption, for all that he had a son they were raising as one of their own; if he put on a wolf's or a dog's form the dead who patrolled the city as German shepherds would bring him down, for only they were allowed to use canine form, and Paris had for centuries been forbidden to wolves. And if he tried to put on a bear's body—a bear's form would be ideal, as far as he knew he was the only shaman in France who knew how to adopt it and there'd be no way his enemy could have been prepared to deal with it, but there was also no way he could shamble the huge, conspicuous body across Paris undetected, nor anyone he could trust to transport it for him, and for all the force that being a bear would give him, the dogs would still be able to bring him down if they attacked as a pack, and he'd be vulnerable as well to humans with guns.

Unless he was willing to give up the complete separation of his two identities which he'd always maintained for his own protection, and took his costume and tambourine with him to the other apartment, and made the transformation there. The problem wasn't just the basically trivial difficulty of explaining his clochard-self's presence to Liz and the domestics (and that, anyway, would be no problem at all with the servants gone and Liz full of pills) but that the more people who knew he was both Eminescu Eliade and Julien de Saint-Hilaire, the less safe he was. Both identities were, of course, registered with the Ordre des médecins and there were a very few of his French psychiatric colleagues who knew him as both, though most knew only that he was both shaman and psychiatrist, but those few who did know were all men to whom he'd chosen to reveal himself because he was satisfied they posed no real threat to him, while at the same time they knew he in turn would never threaten them, thus rendering mutual trust possible. The clochards with whom he spent his time as Eminescu Eliade, of course, knew that he was a shaman, just as he knew which among them were also shamans, but though they knew that he had to have some sort of second identity, none of them, as far as he was aware, knew that that second identity was that of Julien de Saint-Hilaire. Thus none of them could attack him while he was in his psychiatrist's role, far from his caps, costume and drum, and so virtually defenseless.

It was Julien de Saint-Hilaire, and not Eminescu Eliade, who'd been challenged and who was under attack. Yet even so he knew that as long as he kept his unknown enemy from learning that the two were one and the same (and his opponent *couldn't* know that yet, or Eminescu would have already been dead) Eminescu Eliade would remain, if not safe, at least always free to escape to safety and anonymity. All of which would be lost if the other caught him taking his costume and drum to the other apartment.

Lost, unless he could destroy the worms in Liz and get his shamanizing aids back to the rue de Condé before the other realized what Eminescu was doing.

Or unless he managed to kill the other before he'd had a chance to make use of the information he'd gained, and before he'd had a chance to reveal it to anyone else.

And Eminescu was tired of having to defend himself, of worrying about his safety, tired and very angry. He wanted to hurt his enemy, not just avoid him or survive his attacks. The other had to have a lot of his power—and that meant a lot of his soul—in the worms: If Eminescu could destroy them he might well cripple his enemy so that he could finish him off later, at his leisure. And too, this was the only way he could save Liz, and his unborn son.

He took his father's skull from the silver hatbox in the trunk, held it out at arm's length with both hands and asked it whether or not he'd succeed in saving Liz without betraying himself to his enemy. There was no reply, the skull became neither lighter nor heavier, but that proved nothing: His father rarely responded and those few times that the skull's weight had seemed to change Eminescu had been unable to rule out the possibility that the brief alteration in its heaviness he'd felt had been no more than the result of unconscious suggestion, like the messages he'd seen Liz seem to receive when she played with her Ouija board.

He put the skull and the rest of his shamanizing equipment back in the trunk and locked it, then went downstairs as Julien de Saint-Hilaire. He ate yet another two meals at nearby restaurants, then found the concierge's husband and got him to help move the heavy steamer trunk downstairs. Back at the other apartment he tipped the taxi driver who'd brought him there substantially extra to help carry the trunk up the rear stairs. When the driver left he dragged it into the apartment and locked it in the unused spare bedroom at the far end of the apartment, where Liz was least likely to be disturbed by the noise he'd make beating his tambourine and chanting, and where she was least likely to realize that a door to which she'd never had the key was now locked against her.

She was still in the bedroom, asleep. He called his catering service and asked them to deliver cold cuts for a party of fifteen in an hour, then went downstairs and bought a side of beef and a half dozen chickens from his butcher. The butcher and his two assistants helped him up the stairs and into the kitchen with the meat. When they were gone he dragged the beef into the spare bedroom, followed it with the chickens.

The caterers managed to deliver the cold cuts without waking Liz. He ate some of them, laid the others out where he'd be able to get at them easily when he made the transformation back to human, though since he wouldn't be flying he at least wouldn't have to waste the kinds of energy it took to get his iron-weighted body airborne. Then he locked all the doors and windows carefully and turned off the phone and doorbell, so as to make sure that nothing disturbed or awakened Liz before he was finished with her.

It was good to put his caps and costume on in the Parc Monceau apartment for the first time, good to beat his tambourine there in the spare room with the late-afternoon sun coming in through the curtains screening the window. Good to put on the bear's form after so many years of forcing himself to stay content with being no more than a pigeon or owl or rat. It had been fifteen—no, seventeen—years since he'd last been a bear, there in that box canyon in Arizona with John Henry Two Feathers Thomas Thompson, and he'd forgotten what joy it was to be huge and shaggy and powerful, forgotten the bear's keen intelligence and cunning, the enormous reserves of strength its anger gave it.

Forgotten too the danger of losing himself in the bear, of letting the seeming inexhaustibility of the forces at his disposal seduce him into going too far beyond his limits, so that when the time came for him to resume his human form he'd lack the energy to animate his body and so die.

Outside a dog began to bark, and then another. He couldn't tell if they were just dogs barking, or some of the dead who'd detected his transformation, but even if they were just dogs they were a reminder that the longer he stayed a bear the more chance there was that his enemy would detect him, realize what he was doing and counterattack.

More dogs, a growing number of them living animals now, howling all around his building and even within it: He recognized the excited voices of the thirteen whippets the film distributor on the first floor kept, the sharp yapping of the old lady on the second floor's gray poodle and the deeper and stupider baying of her middle-aged daughter's obnoxious Irish setter. Lights were beginning to go on in other buildings. Which meant he had to hurry, leave the meat and chickens he'd planned to eat before he began for later, so he could get to Liz and soothe her immediately, before even drugged as she was the noise woke her.

Soothe her and then destroy the worms before the disturbance the dead were making brought his enemy. If he wasn't already here, or coming.

He'd left the door to the room he was using slightly ajar. Now he pushed it open with his snout, squeezed through the narrow doorway and shambled down the long hall toward the master bedroom. He was already hungry, though he still had some margin before he'd be in danger.

Halfway down the hall to the bedroom he knocked a tall glass lamp from a table. It hit the parquet floor and shattered loudly, and for a moment he was sure that the noise would be enough to awaken Liz after all: She metabolized her sleeping pills very rapidly and would already be beginning to get over the effects of the ones he'd given her. But when he reached the bedroom and poked his head in to check on her she was still asleep, though the howling outside and within the building was still getting louder and louder. There had to be fifty or sixty dogs out there by now, perhaps even more.

He shambled the rest of the way into the room, reared up and balanced himself on his hind legs at the foot of the bed, then reached out and plucked Liz's soul from her body, locked it away from all pain and sensation in her head. As though her skull were a mother's womb inside which she lay curled like a haggard but voluptuous foetus, her whole adult body there within her head, filling it and overflowing it slightly, one hand dangling from her right ear, a foot and ankle and short length of calf protruding from her half-open mouth.

He turned her over with his paws and made a quick incision in her belly with his long claws, pulled the flesh apart so he could reach in and flip her intestines free of her abdomen. He ripped them open and seized the worms in his teeth, ripped them free of her intestinal walls and then tore them apart, killing the scolexes and each and every segment before he swallowed them. It was easy, amazingly easy, like the time John Henry Two Feathers Thomas Thompson had taught him to flip trout from a stream with his paws, and though the tapeworms were lampreys as well as worms they couldn't get a grasp on his shaggy body with their sucking mouths, their concentric circles of razor-sharp rasping teeth, so it was only a matter of moments before he'd killed them all and devoured their dead bodies.

All eight of them, where there should have been nine.

He cursed himself for the way he'd let the noise the dogs were making outside the apartment rush him into beginning without examining Liz very, very carefully again first, realized that at no time since he'd returned from the Undercity had he thought to count the worms in her belly, that he'd just assumed that all nine were still there.

But there was no time now to try to solve the problem of the ninth worm's escape or disappearance; he had to try to get Liz's intestines back together and inside her and functioning before she bled to death, and before the hunger growing ever more insistent within him reached the point where it could be fatal.

He licked the insides of her intestines clean with his long tongue, making sure he got each and every egg and embryo and crushed the life out of them between his teeth before he swallowed them. Then he pushed the ripped intestines back into shape with his nose and tongue, licked them until they'd stopped bleeding and begun to heal, licked them a little more and then nosed them back into place in her abdominal cavity, licked the incision in her belly until it closed and healed, continued to lick it until no further trace of its presence remained.

Then he reached into her legs and bloodstream, pulled the embryos and filament worms he found there from her body, killed and devoured them.

And it had been easy, almost too easy. He would have thought the whole thing another diversion, only a means of luring him here in his shaman's self, had it not been for the fact that there was no one else in France who knew he was able to take on the form of a bear. There were very few people left anywhere in Europe who knew how to do so, and those few were all far to the North, in the Scandinavian countries.

Besides, there was still the missing tapeworm to consider.

Liz's soul still filled her head. He very carefully checked her body to make sure it was now free of worms, eggs, embryos, and toxins before he released her soul, let it begin slowly filtering down out of her head into the rest of her body.

The veins in her legs were still blue and fat, undoubtedly painful: The filament worms had damaged all the tiny valves in the vessels that kept the blood from pooling there. But all that was, now that the worms had been removed, was ordinary varicose veins; he should be able to heal them easily enough, and if they proved for some reason more difficult to deal with than he expected them to be he could always steal healthy veins from other people's legs for her. From that patient who was so late paying his bills, if his blood type was right and his circulatory system in good condition.

His hunger had passed the danger point, especially with his human form weakened as it was by his previous efforts, but he forced himself to go over the bedroom and both the attached bathrooms meticulously, looking for the ninth worm. It wasn't there. Perhaps the medicines he'd given Liz had destroyed it; perhaps the first worm's death had been the signal which had stimulated the other worms to their accelerated egg production. In any case, the worm was gone.

Liz was sleeping soundly now, would remain asleep for another five or six hours while her soul reintegrated itself with her body. More than long enough for him to change the bloodstained sheets and blankets and mattress cover.

He fell once on his way back through the corridor to the spare bedroom, got a good look at himself in the hall mirror as he was getting back up. He looked almost dead of starvation, a bit like a weasel or wolverine, but with neither the sleekness nor the grace.

He made it back into the spare bedroom and pushed the door closed behind him, though he had no way to lock it before he regained his human form. He devoured the cold cuts on their platter, ate the chickens and began ripping chunks of meat from the side of beef.

And when he'd cracked open the last bone and licked it clean of the last of the marrow it had contained he triggered his transformation.

He lay there, Eminescu Eliade, too tired to move or do anything else, just letting the strength begin flowing gently back into him from his caps and costume. There'd been enough energy in the food he'd eaten to keep him alive, just barely enough, but it would be a while before he'd be strong enough to pull his tambourine to him, tap out the rhythms on it he could use to summon the strength he'd need to get to his feet and change back into Julien de Saint-Hilaire, then get something more to eat from the kitchen and finally clean up Liz and the bed.

Everything was silent, completely silent, both within the apartment and outside. He had a throbbing pain in his head and he felt dizzy and a little nauseated and very hungry. The floor was too hard for him now that he'd lost the flesh that had formerly cushioned his bones and it hurt him even through his many layers of swaddling clothing. He'd have to find a way to explain to Liz the twenty kilos or more he'd lost so suddenly.

He lay there, half-dozing, letting the strength return to him.

And then he must have passed out, because when he opened his eyes again Liz was kneeling over him, still covered with dry blood but dressed now, her robe wrapped around her. He tried to tell her something, he wasn't sure quite what, but she shook her head and put her fingers to her lips. She was smiling, but it was a strange, tight-lipped smile and he felt confused.

The door opened behind him, letting in a current of cold air. Jean-Luc and Michel came in together, holding hands.

Liz snatched Eminescu's two caps from his head and put them on her own before he'd had a chance to realize what she was doing, and by then it was too late to even try to change himself back into a bear, or into anything else.

She motioned to Jean-Luc and Michel. They bent down to kiss her on both cheeks in greeting while she did the same to them, then took up their positions, Jean-Luc kneeling across from her on the opposite side of Eminescu's body,

Michel down by his feet. Jean-Luc helped her strip Eminescu's leather coat from him while Michel took his seven-league shoes and his socks from his feet. Without his caps he had no strength with which to even try to resist them, and with each article and layer of clothing they stripped from him he was weaker still, until at the end he no longer had the strength to so much as lift his head.

When he was naked and shivering in the cold air Liz took off her robe and gave it to Jean-Luc to hold while she dressed herself in Eminescu's many layers of rags. Then together she and Jean-Luc wrapped him in her discarded robe while Michel picked up Eminescu's tambourine and began to beat it.

Naked and weakened as he was, he could sense nothing of the power they were summoning and using. He had never felt it, not even in the end, never detected in any of them the slightest sign of the power that had defeated and destroyed him, and in a way that was almost as bad as the fact of the defeat itself, that he would never know if Liz or one of the other two had been his true enemy, keeping his or her powers hidden from Eminescu in some way he would never now get the chance to understand, or if all three of them together had been only the instrument for some challenger whose identity he would never know.

Liz knelt down beside him again, pulled the beard from his face and put it on her own. She leaned over him then, began nuzzling his cheek and then kissing him on the mouth.

Without ceasing to kiss him she brought her hands up, jammed her fingers into his mouth and pried it wide, held his jaw open despite his feeble efforts to close it while she stuck her tongue in his mouth.

Her tongue explored his mouth, then uncoiled its flat, twelve-meter body and slid slowly down his throat into its new home.

LESZEK KOLAKOWSKI
The War with Things

Leszek Kolakowski is best known in this country for his three volume *Mainstreams of Marxism* and other scholarly works, but he is also the author of short satirical fantasy stories published in Poland in the late 1950s. This year, *Tales from the Kingdom of Lailonia* has been translated into English for the first time and published together with a reprint of *The Key to Heaven* (containing satirical Biblical tales) in a volume from The University of Chicago Press.

Tales is a collection of thirteen quirky fables from the mythical country of Lailonia, bearing titles such as "How Gyom Became an Elderly Gentleman," "How the Problem of Longevity Was Solved," and "A Tale of Great Shame." In his charming introduction, Kolakowski relates how the stories came to him in a package bearing a Lailonia postmark but, alas, no return address. He and his brother devoted many years to discovering the whereabouts of Lailonia, asking friends and strangers and throwing out all the furniture in their apartment to make room for globes, atlases and maps.

"There was nothing more we could do," Kolakowski writes; "all avenues were closed. We no longer had even the heart to search through our maps. We could only sit in our apartment, weeping softly.

"Now we are very old, and we will surely never find out where Lailonia is. We know we shall never see it. But perhaps one of you will be more fortunate; perhaps one day someone will find his way to Lailonia. When you do go there, please present the queen of Lailonia with a larkspur flower in our name, and tell her how very much we wanted to come, and how we failed."

—T.W.

The War with Things

LESZEK KOLAKOWSKI

(Translated from the Polish by Agnieszka Kolakowska)

Pancakes with syrup tend to have vicious natures. Their behavior is at once cowardly and sly, and they have no understanding of deeper things. They often weep (and everyone knows that there is nothing worse than a weeping pancake), and as soon as you turn your back they cackle maliciously. They also play many unexpected pranks that often ruffle one's serenity.

So it was with a certain relief that Ditto watched as the pancakes, offended by the scowl of reluctance on his face, one by one slithered off the plate and left the room. A moment later, however, Lina entered it, and when she saw the empty plate her face wore an expression of ill-humored surprise.

"Ditto," she said, "why did you eat all the pancakes without leaving any for me?"

"I didn't eat a single one," Ditto replied.

"So what happened to them? I suppose you mean to tell me that they just went for a walk?"

"Yes, that is precisely what I mean to tell you."

"They just upped off the plate and left?"

"Yes, they just took themselves off the plate and left."

"You're a despicable greedy pig, Ditto," said Lina tearfully. "Because of you I won't get any dinner."

"But, Lina, listen, I didn't get any dinner either!"

"No dinner! You didn't get any dinner? And where are the pancakes, pray?"

"They left, I keep telling you!"

"Well then, go and bring them back!"

Ditto rushed out of the house in pursuit of the pancakes. The chase was not a long one, for pancakes, as we know, are not quick walkers: thus Ditto was able to catch up with them not too far from home. He fell upon them, panting, intending to gather them up and take them home. But the pancakes slipped out of his hands, squealing, and scattered in all directions, and Ditto couldn't decide which of them he should chase. After half an hour of dashing about Ditto finally succeeded in catching most of the pancakes, which were dripping with syrup; he stuffed them into his pockets as well as he could and triumphantly set off for home, where the offended Lina was waiting.

"Well," she said with a pout, "I suppose you've caught them?"

"Indeed I have," said Ditto. "A few of them got away, but I caught most of them."

Thus saying he began to extract the shreds of pancakes from his pockets: they were all mangled and sticky and squealing horribly, and Ditto's whole suit was liberally stained with syrup. Lina gazed at him in horror.

"Ditto," she cried, "your suit! It's ruined!"

"Well, you wanted me to go after the pancakes, so here they are. But at least don't go on about my suit."

"You're a liar, Ditto," Lina cried. "You bought the pancakes in a shop and now you want me to believe they're the same ones that supposedly went for a walk."

"But, Lina, why don't you ask the pancakes, they'll tell you themselves what happened."

So Lina asked one of the pancakes whether it was true that they'd been there on the plate and had gone off for a walk. But the pancake, which had seen the point of the question, answered spitefully that it had done nothing of the kind, that it had never been there before and that Ditto had only bought it at a baker's shop a minute ago. Each pancake in turn proceeded to tell the same story, and Ditto sat there, furious, listening to their lies and knowing that now Lina would never believe him. When Lina started to say something he quickly interrupted her and cried, "But Lina, surely you're not going to believe these despicable pancakes rather than me? You know pancakes are liars!"

"You're a liar!" Lina shouted. "How could the pancakes have made up a story like that?!"

Ditto sighed and went out, leaving Lina to the pancakes, which she set about eating with a sour expression. He went to the bathroom and there, in his indignation at the shabby way in which the pancakes had behaved, he decided to form some sort of alliance that might be helpful to him in life. He thought of toothpaste, which in his experience was of a gentle and kind disposition. He tried to enter into a conversation with it, but as soon as he opened the tube the toothpaste spewed out of it, hissing and foaming lightly. Ditto was horrified, and when Lina entered the bathroom and saw the squeezed-out toothpaste, the set of her face was grim.

"So, Ditto," she said, "you're up to your tricks again?"

"Not at all, the toothpaste squeezed itself out of the tube."

"Ditto, you're incorrigible," said Lina sadly. "Perhaps I should ask the toothpaste who squeezed it out."

But the toothpaste hissed out at once and without waiting to be asked that it was precisely Ditto who had squeezed it out. All Ditto's explanations were to no avail: he took the blame, and the toothpaste's petty spitefulness left him weary of life.

From that day on, however, all things seemed to be conspiring against Ditto and trying to compromise him. When he was lying in bed his pillow would rip itself at the seams with a crack, letting fly clouds of feathers, which descended on the jam Lina had just finished making. Afterwards the pillow would complain shamelessly that Ditto had ripped it apart on purpose. A nail would jump out of the wall, leaving a huge gaping hole that couldn't be plastered over, and then claim that Ditto had pulled it out. The pane of glass in the window, untouched by so much as a finger, would shatter into fragments and, clattering shrilly, tell Lina that Ditto had smashed it with his elbow. Coat and trouser buttons began creeping away and secreting themselves in mysterious places, and if one of them stayed behind it was only in order to inform Lina that Ditto had torn off the others and lost them playing tiddlywinks. Shoes made a point of acquiring holes in all places, handkerchiefs were constantly losing themselves out of spite, shirts purposely stained themselves with great globs of grease that were impossible to wash out, and the ink bounded with a splash off the table, making black pools on the floor.

Ditto understood then that life was one hard struggle with things; but at the same time he knew the struggle to be a hopeless one, for Lina would never believe him, she would always believe the things. And indeed Lina, for her part, believed them blindly, and Ditto was defenseless. They argued, but in the end neither was ever able to convince the other. For Ditto could see the spitefulness of things, he saw them playing their tricks, while Lina was persuaded that Ditto was doing his best to lose and ruin things on purpose. Yet nothing of the kind ever happened in her presence; on the contrary, things behaved calmly and quietly, as if they considered Lina their friend.

Moreover, even those things which were in some way a part of Ditto himself began to play stupid tricks on him. His hair fell out, and Lina claimed he was going bald on purpose. The beating of his heart became progressively weaker, and Ditto failed in his efforts to reach an understanding with it. One of his ears grew large and shapeless, and Lina accused him of having had it remodeled himself, just to spite her.

Having learnt the perfidious ways of things, Ditto saw that two final options were open to him: he could pretend to be a thing himself, or he could free himself of things entirely. This last, after some reflection, he rejected as impractical, for he didn't see how he could free himself, for instance, of things that were his directly, such as his legs, arms, or head. "If, on the other hand," he mused, "I were to change myself into a thing, then I could either show Lina how nasty things really are or, perhaps, train and educate the other things to stop their practical jokes."

Accordingly Ditto dressed up as a pancake with syrup, because pancakes had been the nastiest of the lot to him at the start. The disguise wasn't easy to keep up, but one can get used to anything in time. And when Lina was making pancakes with syrup he hopped onto the plate in his disguise. At first he tried to talk to them, make them see that their tricks were mean and nasty, shame them into compliance. But the pancakes knew at once that they were dealing with an impostor and not a real pancake and would have none of it. So Ditto adopted the second tactic, and began goading the pancakes to action, urging them to jump off the plate and splash Lina's dress with syrup. He thought that in this way he would at least succeed in convincing Lina of the viciousness of things. But the pancakes had no intention of following his advice. They allowed themselves to be eaten without a struggle and it was only at the last moment that Ditto managed to slip off the plate unnoticed.

Undaunted by the failure of his plan, Ditto tried his luck in another field. He disguised himself as one of the buttons on Lina's coat. And again the same thing happened: he was instantly unmasked by the other buttons as an impostor masquerading as a button and failed to persuade the other buttons to play any pranks on Lina. He tried to tear himself off the coat and lose himself maliciously, but as he had no practice in these things he achieved no results.

Finally Ditto realized that it was hopeless. Things just fought him, and they simply refused to fight Lina. They were friendly toward her and allowed her to do anything she wanted with them. But to him they were perversely vicious and no urgings, pleas or educational measures produced any results.

So Ditto reverted to his ordinary guise. He knew now that things could be neither educated nor changed; you had to be harsh and unyielding with them, force them into submission. But how? Ditto began by indiscriminately combating things: to Lina's indignation he sliced pancakes into little bits and threw them into the garbage, squeezed the toothpaste down the drain, violently ripped buttons off clothes and flung them into corners, poured ink out into the street and smashed glasses on the stairs. Lina screamed and wept and stamped her foot. Ditto went on like this for some time, but he could see that the things—smashed and stained, crumpled, torn and bent—submitted to all this with indifference, as if they were dead. They didn't react at all. He also realized that he would never be able to deal with all of them and that the struggle was hopeless and futile.

He concluded at that point that the battle was lost. He simply surrendered and declared himself vanquished. All his efforts had turned out to be vain, and every battle must end somehow—in victory, in defeat, or in a truce. This battle, then, ended in defeat for Ditto and there was nothing else to be said. And in accordance with the custom of those barbaric times when the vanquished were taken into slavery by the victors, Ditto became a slave to things.

And this is why, when Lina brought the pancakes with syrup to the table and went out for a moment to the kitchen, Ditto watched motionless as one pancake after another slithered slowly off the plate and crept with a malicious smile toward the door.

JANE YOLEN
The Faery Flag

Jane Yolen is America's most distinguished writer of original fairy tales, as well as a teacher, editor, ballad singer and storyteller. She is the author of over one hundred books: novels, story collections, picture books and nonfiction for adults, teenagers and children. She is also the editor of Jane Yolen Books, an imprint of Harcourt Brace Jovanovich publishing fantasy and science fiction books for children.

Of particular interest to adult fantasy readers, Yolen's work includes the adult novels *Sister Light, Sister Dark, White Jenna*, and *Cards of Grief;* the "Pit Dragon" series, for young adults; the story collections *Tales of Wonder, Merlin's Booke, Neptune Rising,* and *Dragonfields;* and *Touch Magic,* essays on fantasy and fairy tales. She has won the World Fantasy Award, the Golden Kite Award, and her picture book *Owl Moon* was honored with the Caldecott Medal. Her most recent picture book, *Dove Isabeau,* is a lovely fantasy tale based on a British folk ballad, gorgeously illustrated by Dennis Nolan. The following story comes from her latest collection of children's stories, *The Faery Flag: Stories and Poems of Fantasy and the Supernatural.*

Yolen and her husband, David Stemple, and the youngest of their three children, live on Phoenix Farm in western Massachusetts.

—T.W.

The Faery Flag

JANE YOLEN

Long ago, when the wind blew from one corner of Skye to another without ever encountering a house higher than a tree, the faery folk lived on the land and they were called the *Daoine Sithe*, the Men of Peace. They loved the land well and shepherded its flocks, and never a building did they build that could not be dismantled in a single night or put up again in a single day.

But then human folk set foot upon the isles and scoured them with their rough shoeing. And before long both rock and tree were in the employ of men; the land filled with forts and houses, byres and pens. Boats plowed the seas and netted the fish. Stones were piled up for fences between neighbors.

The *Daoine Sithe* were not pleased, not pleased at all. An edict went out from the faery chief: *Have nothing to do with this humankind.*

And for year upon year it was so.

Now one day, the young laird of the MacLeod clan—Jamie was his name— walked out beyond his manor seeking a brachet hound lost outside in the night. It was his favorite hound, as old as he, which—since he was just past fifteen years—was quite old indeed.

He called its name. "Leoid. Leeeeeeoid." The wind sent back the name against his face but the dog never answered.

The day was chill, the wind was cold, and a white mist swirled about the young laird. But many days on Skye are thus, and he thought no more about the chill and cold than that he must find his old hound lest it die.

Jamie paid no heed to where his feet led him, through the bogs and over the hummocks. This was his land, after all, and he knew it well. He could not see the towering crags of the Black Cuillins, though he knew they were there. He could not hear the seals calling from the bay. Leoid was all he cared about. A MacLeod takes care of his own.

So without knowing it, he crossed over a strange, low, stone *drochit*, a bridge the likes of which he would never have found on a sunny day, for it was the bridge into Faerie.

No sooner had he crossed over than he heard his old dog barking. He would have known that sound were there a hundred howling hounds.

"Leoid!" he called. And the dog ran up to him, its hind end wagging, eager as a pup, so happy it was to see him. It had been made young again in the land of Faerie.

Jamie gathered the dog in his arms and was just turning to go home when he heard a girl calling from behind him.

"Leoid. Leoid." Her voice was as full of longing as his own had been just moments before.

He turned back, the dog still in his arms, and the fog lifted. Running toward him was the most beautiful girl he had ever seen. Her dark hair was wild with curls, her black eyes wide, her mouth generous and smiling.

"Boy, you have found my dog. Give it me."

Now that was surely no way to speak to the young laird of the MacLeods, he who would someday be the chief. But the girl did not seem to know him. And surely he did not know the girl, though he knew everyone under his father's rule.

"This is my dog," said Jamie.

The girl came closer and put out her hand. She touched him on his bare arm. Where her hand touched, he felt such a shock, he thought he would die, but of love not of fear. Yet he did not.

"It is my dog now, Jamie MacLeod," she said. "It has crossed over the bridge. It has eaten the food of the *Daoine Sithe* and drunk our honey wine. If you bring it back to your world it will die at once and crumble into dust."

The young laird set the dog down and it frolicked about his feet. He put his hand into the girl's but was not shocked again.

"I will give it back to you for your name—and a kiss," he said.

"Be warned," answered the girl.

"I know about faery kisses," said Jamie, "but I am not afraid. And as you know my name, it is only fair that I should know yours."

"What we consider fair, you do not, young laird," she said. But she stood on tiptoe and kissed him on the brow. "Do not come back across the bridge, or you will break your parents' hearts."

He handed her the sprig of juniper from his bonnet.

She kissed the sprig as well and put it in her hair. "My name is Aizel and, like the red hot cinder, I burn what I touch." Then she whistled for the dog and they disappeared at once into the mist.

Jamie put his hand to his brow where Aizel had kissed him, and indeed she had burned him, it was still warm and sweet to his touch.

Despite the faery girl's warning, Jamie MacLeod looked for the bridge not once but many times. He left off fishing to search for it, and interrupted his hunting to search for it; and often he left his bed when the mist was thick to seek it. But even in the mist and the rain and the fog he could not find it. Yet he never stopped longing for the bridge to the girl.

His mother and father grew worried. They guessed by the mark on his brow what had occurred. So they gave great parties and threw magnificent balls that in this way the young laird might meet a human girl and forget the girl of the *Daoine Sithe*.

But never was there a girl he danced with that he danced with again. Never a girl he held that he held for long. Never a girl he kissed that he did not remember Aizel at the bridge. As time went on, his mother and father grew so desperate for him to give the MacLeods an heir, that they would have let him marry any young woman at all, even a faery maid.

On the eve of Jamie's twenty-first birthday, there was a great gathering of the clan at Dunvegan Castle. All the lights were set out along the castle wall and they twinned themselves down in the bay below.

Jamie walked the ramparts and stared out across the bogs and drums. "Oh Aizel," he said with a great sigh, "if I could but see you one more time. One more time and I'd be content."

And then he thought he heard the barking of a dog.

Now there were hounds in the castle and hounds in the town and hounds who ran every day under his horse's hooves. But he knew that particular call.

"Leoid!" he whispered to himself. He raced down the stairs and out the great doors with a torch in his hand, following the barking across the bog.

It was a misty, moisty evening, but he seemed to know the way. And he came quite soon to the cobbled bridge that he had so long sought. For a moment he hesitated, then went on.

There, in the middle, not looking a day older than when he had seen her six years before, stood Aizel in her green gown. Leoid was by her side.

"Into your majority, young laird," said Aizel. "I called to wish you the best."

"It is the best, now that I can see you," Jamie said. He smiled. "And my old dog."

Aizel smiled back. "No older than when last you saw us."

"I have thought of you every day since you kissed me," said Jamie. "And longed for you every night. Your brand still burns on my brow."

"I warned you of faery kisses," said Aizel.

He lifted his bonnet and pushed away his fair hair to show her the mark.

"I have thought of you, too, young laird," said Aizel. "And how the MacLeods have kept the peace in this unpeaceful land. My chief says I may bide with you for a while."

"How long a while?" asked Jamie.

"A faery while," replied Aizel. "A year or an heir, whichever comes first."

"A year is such a short time," Jamie said.

"I can make it be forever," Aizel answered.

With that riddle Jamie was content. And they walked back to Dunvegan Castle hand in hand, though they left the dog behind.

If Aizel seemed less fey in the starlight, Jamie did not mind. If he was only human, she did not seem to care. Nothing really mattered but his hand in hers, her hand in his, all the way back to his home.

The chief of the MacLeods was not pleased and his wife was not happy with the match. But that Jamie smiled and was content made them hold their tongues. So the young laird and the faery maid were married that night and bedded before day.

And in the evening Aizel came to them and said, "The MacLeods shall have their heir."

The days went fast and slow, warm and cold, and longer than a human it took for the faery girl to bear a child. But on the last day of the year she had lived with them, Aizel was brought to labor till with a great happy sigh she birthed a beautiful babe.

"A boy!" the midwife cried out, standing on a chair and showing the child so that all the MacLeods might see.

A great cheer ran around the castle then. "An heir. An heir to the MacLeods!"

Jamie was happy for that, but happier still that his faery wife was well. He bent to kiss her brow.

"A year or an heir, that was all I could promise. But I have given you forever," she said. "The MacLeods shall prosper and Dunvegan will never fall."

Before he could say a word in return, she had vanished and the bed was bare, though her outline could be seen on the linens for a moment more.

The cheer was still echoing along the stone passageways as the midwife carried the babe from room to room to show him to all the clan. But the young laird of the MacLeods put his head in his hands and wept.

Later that night, when the fires were high in every hearth and blaeberry wine filled every cup; when the harp and fiddle rang throughout Dunvegan with their tunes; when the bards' mouths swilled with whisky and swelled with the old songs; and even the nurse was dancing with her man, the young laird Jamie MacLeod walked the castle ramparts seven times round, mourning for his lost faery wife.

The youngest laird of the MacLeods lay in his cradle all alone.

So great was the celebration that no one was watching him. And in the deepest part of the night, he kicked off his blankets as babies often do, and he cried out with the cold.

But no one came to cover him. Not the nurse dancing with her man, nor his grandam listening to the tunes, nor his grandfather drinking with his men, nor his father on the castle walk. No one heard the poor wee babe crying with the cold.

It was a tiny cry, a thin bit of sound threaded out into the dark. It went over hillock and hill, over barrow and bog, crossed the cobbled *drochit*, and wound its way into Faerie itself.

Now they were celebrating in the faery world as well, not for the birth of the child but for the return of their own. There was feasting and dancing and the singing of tunes. There was honey wine and faery pipes and the high, sweet laughter of the *Daoine Sithe*.

But in all that fine company, Aizel alone did not sing and dance. She sat in her great chair with her arms around her brachet hound. If there were tears in her eyes, you would not have known it, for the *Daoine Sithe* do not cry, and besides the hound had licked away every one. But she heard that tiny sound as any mother would. Distracted, she stood.

"What is it, my daughter?" asked the great chief of the *Daoine Sithe* when he saw her stand, when he saw a single tear that Leoid had not had time to lick away.

But before any of the fey could tell her no, Aizel ran from the faery hall, the dog at her heels. She raced across the bridge, herself as insubstantial as the mist. And behind her came the faery troops. And the dog.

The company of fey stopped at the edge of the bridge and watched Aizel go. Leoid followed right after. But no sooner had the dog's legs touched the earth on the other side than it crumbled into dust.

Aizel hesitated not a moment, but followed that thread of sound, winding her back into the world of men. She walked over bog and barrow, over hill and hillock, through the great wooden doors and up the castle stairs.

When she entered the baby's room, he was between one breath and another. "There, there," Aizel said, leaning over the cradle and covering him with her shawl, "thy Mama's here." She rocked him till he fell back asleep, warm and content. Then she kissed him on the brow, leaving a tiny mark there for all to see, and vanished in the morning light.

The nurse found the babe sleeping soundly well into the day. He was wrapped in a cloth of stranger's weave. His thumb was in his mouth, along with a piece of the shawl. She did not know how the cloth got there, nor did his grandfather, the Great MacLeod. If his grandmother guessed, she did not say.

But the young laird Jamie knew. He knew that Aizel had been drawn back across the bridge by her son's crying, as surely as he had first been led to her by the barking of his hound.

"Love calls to love," he whispered softly to his infant son as he held him close. "And the fey, like the MacLeods, take care of their own."

The faery shawl still hangs on the wall at Dunvegan Castle on the Isle of Skye. Only now it is called a Faery Flag and the MacLeods carry it foremost into battle. I have seen it there. Like this story, it is a tattered remnant of stranger's weave and as true and warming as you let it be.

ZHAXI DAWA

Souls Tied to the Knots on a
Leather Cord

Zhaxi Dawa, an ethnic Tibetan, was born in 1959 in the Sichuan province of China, and spent his childhood in various parts of Sichuan and Tibet. He worked in the Tibetan National Theater in Lhasa as an apprentice set designer and as a playwright before turning to fiction writing. He has had several collections of his short fiction published in China, and has had one of his stories adapted for television.

The following story comes from *Spring Bamboo: A Collection of Contemporary Chinese Short Stories*. Editor and translator Jeanne Tai notes that young Chinese writers are rediscovering the wealth of myth and folklore their culture has to offer—long disdained as "feudal remnants to be eradicated." She points out that many of these writers spent a considerable portion of their youth in remote regions of China, where the folklore tradition remains the strongest, due to the Cultural Revolution movement which sent educated youths into the countryside. Also, she says, they have been inspired by the writings from South America, particularly those of Gabriel García Márquez, whose *One Hundred Years of Solitude* "served almost as a model for the possibilities of combining myth with reality. For instance, in Zhaxi Dawa's story, the fictional world is also a carefully wrought metaphor for the search for the mythic past. . . ."

Young American writers—particularly fantasy writers of the "magic realist" school—have also been strongly influenced by Márquez and other South American authors as they search for the mythic past among the many cultures that make up our own country. Thus, the following story fits easily among the others collected for this volume.

—T.W.

Souls Tied to the Knots on a Leather Cord

ZHAXI DAWA

These days you don't much hear "El Condor Pasa" anymore, that Peruvian folk tune sung with such slow and simple charm. But I have preserved it on my own cassette tape. Whenever I play it, I can see right before my eyes those valleys in the highlands. Flocks of sheep scampering among the jumbled rocks. Cultivated areas divided into little plots at the foot of the mountains. Scraggly crops. A mill by the side of a stream. Stone farmhouses hugging the ground. Heavily laden mountain folk. Brass bells tied around the cattle's necks. A lonely little eddy of wind. Dazzling sunshine.

This scenery does not belong to the central plateau in the Peruvian Andes but to the Pabu Naigang range in southern Tibet. I'm not sure if I once saw it in a dream or if I have actually been there. I can't remember anymore. I've been to too many places.

It was not until later, on a day when I finally got to the Pabu Naigang range, that I realized what was stored in my memory was no more than a beautiful nineteenth-century pastoral landscape by Constable.

Although this is still a peaceful mountain region, the people here are already quietly enjoying the comforts of modern life. There is a small airfield here with five helicopter flights each week to the city. Nearby is a solar energy power plant. In the little eatery right next to the gas station on the edge of the village of Jelu, a man with a big beard sits at my table, talking nonstop all the while. He is the chairman of the board of the famous Himalayan Transportation Company, the first in all of Tibet to own a fleet of tractor trailers imported from Germany. When I visit a local carpet factory, I find the technicians using a computer to produce their designs. The ground satellite station broadcasts on five frequencies, supplying viewers with a total of thirty-eight hours of television programming every day.

But no matter how strongly the modern world forces its inhabitants to break away from traditional ways of thinking, for the people of the Pabu Naigang mountain region some old mannerisms die hard. Whenever the village chief—who has a Ph.D. in agricultural science—talks to me, he would every now and then inhale loudly through his lips and make subservient ululating noises with his tongue. When people have a favor to ask, they stick out their thumb and wriggle it around while they blurt out a string of importuning clucks. When a visitor comes from the big city far away, some of the old folks still take off their hats and hold them against their chests as they step to one side, to show their heartfelt respect. Although a uniform system of measurements was established nationwide many years ago, when the people here want to describe a certain length they still extend one arm and chop at it with the flat of the other hand, across the wrist, or forearm, or elbow, all the way up to the shoulder.

The Living Buddha Sangjie Dapu was about to die. He had reached the ripe old age of ninety-eight, this twenty-third reincarnated Living Buddha of the Zhatuo Monastery. After he dies, there will be no more reincarnates to succeed him. I had met Sangjie Dapu before, and I wanted to write an article about him and his religion. When Tibetan Lamaism (and its various sects) loses the system of succession by reincarnates, and therefore no longer has religious leaders of greater or lesser importance, one of the world's most profound and mystical religions may be nearing the end of its days. To a certain extent outward form determines inner consciousness, I argued.

The Living Buddha Sangjie Dapu of Zhatuo shook his head in disagreement. His pupils were slowly dilating.

"Shambhala," his lips quavered, "the war has begun."

According to the ancient scriptures, there is a Pure Land in the north, a paradise on earth called Shambhala. It is said that the Heavenly Yogic Tantrism originated here, and that this was where Sakyamuni instructed the first king Sochad Napu, who later went on to propagate the secret doctrine of Way of the Wheel. The scriptures also say that one day there will be a war in Shambhala, in this land surrounded by snow-capped mountains. "You command twelve celestial legions, amidst heavenly hosts you gallop onward, never looking back. You throw your lance at Halutaman's chest, at the leader of the evil gods who defy Shambhala, and all of them shall be annihilated." This is the account in "The Oath of Shambhala" extolling the last king, the Heavenly Warrior King of the Wheel. Sangjie Dapu of Zhatuo once told me about this war. He said that after hundreds of years of terrible fighting, when the monsters and devils have all been destroyed, the Tsongkaba grave in the Gandan Monastery will open by itself and the teachings of Sakyamuni will once again be propagated for a thousand years. After that there will be windstorms and fires, and finally the whole world will be inundated by a great flood. When the end comes, there will inevitably be a few lucky ones whom the gods will rescue into heaven. And then, when the world once again takes shape, religion will also be reborn.

Sangjie Dapu of Zhatuo was lying on the bed. He was hallucinating, talking to some invisible person by his side: "When you climb over the snow-covered Kalong mountains and find yourself standing among the lines of the Lotus-Born Guru's palm, do not pursue, do not seek. In prayer you will see the light, through enlightenment you will receive the Vision. Of all the crisscrossing palm lines, only one is the road of life, the one that leads to the Pure Land on earth."

It seems to me I had watched as the Lotus-Born Guru departed from this world. A chariot descended from the heavens, and in the company of two celestial maidens he climbed into the chariot and drove away into the southern skies.

"Two young people from the Kampa district, they've gone to look for the road to Shambhala," the Living Buddha mumbled.

I looked at him wearily.

"You're saying . . . in the year 1984, two Kampa people—a man and a woman—came here?" I asked.

He nodded.

"And the man got into an accident here?" I asked again.

"You know about this too," said the Living Buddha.

Sangjie Dapu of Zhatuo closed his eyes and, by fits and starts, began to reminisce about the arrival of the two young people in the Pabu Naigang mountain region and what they told him of their experiences along the way. I recognized his narration: It was a story I had made up. As soon as I finished writing it I had locked it up in a box without showing it to anyone. Now he was telling it almost word for word. The time was 1984. The setting was on the road to a village called Jia in the Pabu Naigang mountains. The cast consisted of a man and a woman. The reason I didn't show this work to anyone was because at the end even I had no idea where the two protagonists were going. Now that the Living Buddha had enlightened me, I knew. There was only one difference between the two versions. At the end of my story, the characters were sitting in a wine shop when an old man showed them the way. But according to the Living Buddha of Zhatuo, it was right here in his room that he had pointed out the road for them. Even so, there was yet another coincidence: Both the old man and the Living Buddha talked about the lines on the Lotus-Born Guru's palm.

Eventually, other people came into the room and surrounded the Living Buddha. Eyes half open, he gradually entered a state of unconsciousness.

They began preparations for his funeral. The Living Buddha of Zhatuo was to be cremated. I knew that someone hoped to find his *sheli** among the ashes as an everlasting keepsake and collectible.

When I got home, I unlocked a box labeled "The Beloved Castaways." Arranged neatly within were almost a hundred brown envelopes containing all my unpublished works, including those I didn't want published. I picked up one marked "840720," inside which was an as yet untitled short story about how two Kampa people came to Pabu Naigang. The following is what I had written:

Chiong is herding her flock of twenty-some sheep down the mountainside when she pauses on the slope halfway. She sees a tiny figure the size of an ant, way down at the bottom of the mountain, moving slowly across the dry pebbly

* *Sheli*: a fragment of bone or tooth found in the ashes after a cremation and imbued with mystical and ritual significance in Tibetan Buddhism.

expanses of the meandering riverbed. She can tell it is a man, and he is heading right in the direction of her home. With a crack of her whip Chiong quickly drives the sheep down the hill.

She figures it will take the man roughly until nightfall to reach her home. There is no shelter in the surrounding wilderness except for the bungalows here—several small huts built of rounded stones on top of this little hump of a hill. Right behind the living quarters are pens for the sheep. There are only two households: Chiong and her father, and a mute woman in her fifties. Father is a balladeer who sings the *Gesar*, and he is often invited to perform in villages dozens of kilometers away, sometimes farther. He would be gone for several days at least, even months at a time. Always, a messenger on horseback would ride up the hill with another horse in tow, and Father, his long-necked mandolin slung across his back, would mount the second horse. Then would come the clattering of hooves mingled with the tinkling of bells, a rhythmic duet reverberating on and on through the silence of the wilderness. Standing on top of the hill, Chiong would caress the big black dog squatting at her side and watch the two horsemen until they disappeared around the next mountain.

Chiong had grown up to this monotonous cadence of hoofbeats and horsebells. Sitting alone on a rock as she watches her sheep, she would fall into a reverie, and then the ringing would turn into a wordless song wafting by from some faraway valley—a song imbued with the enduring life force of the wilderness, yet tinged with a melancholy desire that seeps through the loneliness.

The mute woman works at her loom all day long making felt. Every morning she would stand at the top of the little knoll and cry out to the Boddhisatva Guanyin as she throws a handful of *tsampa** flour into the air. Then, turning to face south, she would twirl a grease-stained prayer wheel and intone her prayers. Once in a while Father would get up in the middle of the night and go into the woman's shack, reemerging just before daybreak, with his long fur robe tossed loosely over his head, to snuggle back into his sheepskin cot. At dawn Chiong would get up to milk the sheep and make tea, then gulp down her breakfast of tsampa gruel. Next she would pack a day's provisions into a small sheepskin pouch and hoist it onto her back, along with a little black cooking pot. Then she would let the sheep out of the pen and drive them up the mountain with the help of her whip. And that is what life has been like.

Chiong prepares some food and hot tea, then stretches out on the rug to wait for the visitor. Outside the dog begins to bark. She rushes out. The moon is just rising. She grabs the dog's leash, but there is no one in sight. In a little while, though, a head pops up over the slope at her feet.

"Come up, it's alright, I'm holding onto the dog," Chiong says.

The fellow is a fine specimen of manhood.

"You must be tired, brother," Chiong says as she leads him inside the house. Under his wide-brimmed felt hat a shock of bright red tassels dangles along the side of his face. Father is away singing the *Gesar*. The banging of the loom as

---

* *tsampa*: roasted barley, a staple in the Tibetan diet.

the mute woman works on her felt can be heard from next door. The exhausted fellow finishes his dinner, thanks Chiong and falls asleep immediately in Father's bed.

Chiong stands outside the door for a little while. The night sky is studded with countless stars. The broad valley stretching out at her feet takes on a pale shimmery glow in the moonlight, and all around her is a silence unbroken by any sounds of nature. The big black dog, confined by its chain, is turning around and around on the same spot. Chiong goes over to it, bends down and puts her arms around its neck. She begins to think about the childhood and adolescence she has spent on this lonely, desolate little hilltop, about those people—always silent and expressionless—who come to fetch her father, about the traveler sound asleep inside the house, who has come from afar and will leave for some distant place the next day. And she weeps. Falling onto the ground with her face buried in her hands, she mutely begs Father's forgiveness. Then, wiping her tears away on the dog's furry hide, she stands up and goes back into the house.

In the darkness, trembling all over like a person stricken with the ague, she crawls silently under the man's blanket.

As soon as the morning star appears in the east, Chiong rolls up her thin blanket in the flickering light of a tallow lamp. Into a cloth sack she stuffs some beef jerky, a chunk of yak butter, some coarse salt, and the leather pouch she uses for kneading tsampa. Then she heaves it all onto her back, together with the little black pot she has used for making tea every day up in the mountains with her sheep. Everything that a young woman should have with her is on her back. Finally she takes one last look around the dim little hut.

"Alright," she says.

The fellow finishes his last pinch of snuff, dusts off his hands and stands up. He pats the top of her head and puts his arm around her shoulder as they duck their heads under the low doorway of the cottage. Then they set out in the direction of the west, still pitch dark at that hour. Chiong is heavily ladened with her belongings, which bang and rattle with every step she takes. She has no interest in finding out where this man would take her. It is enough to know that she is about to leave this lifeless place forever. The only thing the man carries with him is a string of sandalwood prayer beads. Striding along with his head held high, he seems full of confidence about the long journey ahead.

"Why do you have that leather cord tied around your waist?" Tabei asks. "You look like a puppy without a master at the other end of the leash."

"It's for counting the days. Can't you see the five knots on here? I've been gone from home five days already," Chiong answers.

"What's five days? I was born without a home."

And so they travel along, always on foot, she following Tabei. Sometimes they would spend the night on the threshing ground of a village or in a sheep pen, other times they would find shelter among the ruins of some temple or in a cave. And once in a while, when they were lucky, they would sleep in some farmer's outbuilding or a shepherd's tent.

Every time they entered a temple, they would stop in front of each bodhisattva statue and strike their foreheads against the altar several times, performing the ritual bow. Whenever they come across a *mani** pile, whether by the side of the road or on a riverbank, or in a mountain pass, they never fail to add a few white pebbles on top. Along the way they also pass some people performing the long kowtow: Lying spread-eagled, these devout Buddhists would knock their heads against the ground, rise, walk up to where their foreheads had hit the earth, and once more prostrate themselves, repeating the entire sequence for every step of their journey. The thick canvas aprons they tie around themselves have been patched again and again; nevertheless these would be worn down to tatters over their chests and knees. Every protrusion on their faces would be covered with grime, and on their foreheads are swellings the size of a chicken egg, bloody and caked with mud. Their hands are sheathed in tin-sheeted wooden gauntlets, which scuff the ground on each side of their prostrate bodies and leave behind a pair of telltale streaks. Because Tabei and Chiong are walking, they would always overtake the people doing the long kowtows.

Many are the mountains on the Tibetan Plateau, and they rise, range after range, all the way to the horizon. Human settlements are few and far between. One could walk for days without seeing another person, let alone a village. A cold wind whooshes through the canyons. The sun beats down mercilessly, and the earth is scorching hot. To look up at the blue skies for even a few moments is to feel lightheaded, to experience a sensation of levitating. The mountains, sound asleep in broad daylight, seem eternal and infinite in their serenity.

Strong and agile, Tabei climbs the mountain with ease, stepping nimbly from one teetering rock to another as he scampers upward. When he reaches a smooth boulder he would sit down to wait for Chiong, who is always far behind. They never exchange a word when they are on the move. Sometimes in the unbearable silence Chiong would burst into song, sounding like some she-animal in a canyon howling at the sky. Tabei would keep on walking without even turning to look at her. After a while Chiong would stop, and everything would again become deathly quiet. Head bowed, she would follow behind, breaking the silence only when they stop to rest.

"Has it stopped bleeding?"

"It doesn't hurt anymore."

"Let me see."

"Go catch me a few spiders. I'll mash them up and smear them over this so it'll heal faster."

"There are no spiders here."

"Go look in the cracks under the rocks."

One after another Chiong turns over half-buried rocks and stones as she hunts earnestly for spiders, and in a little while she has caught five or six. Cupping them in her hands, she brings them back to Tabei and presses them into his palm. One by one he crushes them and dabs them onto the wound in his leg.

"That dog was vicious! I ran and ran and ran and ran. The pot on my back was banging against my head the whole way and I was beginning to see stars."

mani: a pile of stones with mystical and ritual significance in Tibetan Buddhism.

"I should have pulled out my knife right at the beginning and killed it."

"That woman gave us this." Chiong mimics an obscene gesture, one of the most insulting. "I was so scared."

Tabei grabs another handful of dirt and spreads it on his wound, letting it bask in the sun.

"Where did she keep the money?"

"In the big cupboard in the wineshop. A stack of bills this thick," he motions with his hands. "I only took ten or twelve of them."

"What do you want to buy with them?"

"What do I want to buy? Listen, I'm going to make an offering to Buddha in the Tsigu Temple, down at the foot of the next mountain. I'm also going to keep some of it."

"That's good. Are you better now? It doesn't hurt anymore, does it?"

"No. Hey, my mouth is so dry smoke's coming out of it."

"Can't you see I've already set up the pot? I'm going right now to find some dry bramble."

Chewing on a stalk of dried grass, Tabei stretches out lazily on the rock, his broad-brimmed hat pulled over his eyes to shield them from the sun. Chiong gets down on her hands and knees in front of some rocks she has stacked into a hearth, her face rubbing in the dirt as she puffs away at the kindling. All of a sudden the fire roars to life. She jumps back and rubs her eyes, which are seared and stinging from the smoke. When she pulls down one of her forelocks for a look, she sees that it too has been singed.

On the peak of a lofty mountain in the distance are two tiny dark figures, one tall and one short. They are probably shepherds, but they look like eagles perched in a rocky aerie on top of the mountain. They are motionless.

Chiong sees them and waves, swinging her right arm around and around. Yonder the two people begin to stir as well, returning her greeting with the same whirling gestures. But they are too far away from Chiong for their voices to carry, not even if they shouted themselves hoarse.

"I thought we were the only ones around here," Chiong says to Tabei.

He closes his eyes. "I'm still waiting for your tea."

Suddenly Chiong remembers something. From the folds of her tunic she pulls out an object and shows it to Tabei with a triumphant flourish. It is a book she had palmed from the back pocket of a none-too-well-behaved young man as he murmured sweet nothings in her ear last night, in the village where they had found shelter. Tabei takes the book and examines it, but he does not understand either the language it is written in or the diagrams of machines in the book. The only thing he recognizes is the picture of a tractor on the cover.

"This thing isn't worth a straw," he says, tossing it back to her.

Chiong is crestfallen. The next time she makes tea she tears up the book and uses the pages as tinder for the fire.

As they come around a mountain at sundown, they see in the distance a village enfolded by trees. Chiong's spirits lift and she begins to sing again. Swinging her walking stick in the air, she breaks into a giddy little dance on a patch of *malan* grass nearby. Then she points the stick at Tabei and gingerly pokes him under the arms and around his middle to tickle him. Tabei grabs the stick impatiently and flings it away from him, throwing her off balance so that she totters and falls on the ground.

When they reach the village, Tabei goes off by himself to drink or to do whatever. They plan to rendezvous at the place where they would spend the night: next to the village elementary school, in the vacant building that has just been finished and is still without windows or doors. On the village common, a screen is being set up between some wooden poles for the movie about to be shown that evening.

Chiong goes into a grove of trees to gather firewood, but finds herself surrounded by a gang of children who have climbed on top of some walls nearby and are now pelting her with stones. One of the missiles hits her on the shoulder, but she does not turn around. After a while a young fellow wearing a yellow hat chases the kids away.

"They threw eight stones, and one of them hit you," Yellow Hat says as he grins at her. He thrusts his hand in front of her face to show her the electronic calculator he is holding. On its screen is the Arabic numeral 8. "Where are you from?"

Chiong stares at him.

"Do you remember how many days you've been walking?"

"No, I don't remember," Chiong says as she picks up her leather sash, "but I can find out. Come and help me count."

"Does each one of these knots mean one day?" he asks as he bends down in front of her. "How interesting . . . there, ninety-two days."

"Really?"

"Haven't you ever counted them?"

Chiong shakes her head.

"Ninety-two days, at twenty kilometers a day," he mutters, jabbing the calculator keys, "that's one thousand eight hundred and forty kilometers."

Chiong has no concept of arithmetic.

"I'm the accountant around here," the young fellow says. "Whatever problems I run into I solve them with this thing."

"What is it?" Chiong asks.

"An electronic calculator. It's a lot of fun. See here, it knows how old you are." He presses a number and shows it to Chiong.

"How old?"

"Nineteen."

"Am I nineteen?"

"You tell me."

"I don't know."

"We Tibetans never used to keep track of our age. But this thing knows. Look, that's what it says on here, nineteen."

"Doesn't look like it."

"Really? Let me see. Oh, it just takes some getting used to. The numbers on here are shaped kind of funny."

"Does it know my name?"

"Of course."

"Well, what is it?"

He punches out an eight-digit number, which fills the entire screen.

"What did I tell you? It knows."

"What's my name?"

"Can't you even read your own name? Dummy."

"How do I read it?"

"Like this." He holds it upright for her to look at.

"Does that say Chiong?"

"Of course it says Chiong, C-h-i-o-n-g."

"Hah!" she cries excitedly.

"Hah nothing, they've been doing this for years in other countries. You know, I've been thinking about this problem. In the old days we used to work from can't see in the morning to can't see at night. Well, in economic terms, the labor expended should be directly proportional to the value created." His tongue loosening, he begins to talk through his hat, sounding off about everything from the value of labor to the cash value of a workpoint to the values of commodities, with a discussion of time and arithmetic thrown in for good measure. Then he flashes another figure on his calculator. "Look, after all this calculating it comes out to be a negative number. And at the end of the year we don't even have enough to feed ourselves, we have to ask the government for surplus grain. That goes against the laws of economics. . . . Hey, why are you staring at me like that? You want to gobble me up?"

"If you have nothing to eat for dinner, you can share some of mine. As soon as I get some firewood I'll make tea."

"Damn, did you just walk out of the Middle Ages? Or are you one of those whatchamacallit extraterrestrials?"

"I came from a place very far away, and I've been walking . . ." Again she picks up the leather cord. "How many did you say just now?"

"Let me think, eighty-five days."

"I've been walking eighty-five days. No, that's not right. Just now you said ninety-two days. You tricked me!" Chiong begins to giggle.

"Oh-oh-oh! Buddha have mercy, I think I'm getting drunk," he mutters as he closes his eyes.

"Will you eat here with me? I still have some jerky."

"Young lady, how about going out with me instead? We'll go someplace with lots of happy young people, and music, beer, even disco dancing. Now get rid of those rotten twigs in your hands!"

Tabei squeezes his way out of the dark mass of people watching the movie. He is not drunk, but his head is spinning from all those brightly colored images flashing about on the screen, now close up, now far away—people, scenery, everything. They have completely worn him out. Wearily he trudges back to the vacant building. Inside, he finds the little black pot set on top of a pile of stones, all cold to the touch. Chiong's things are lying in a corner nearby. He picks up the pot and drinks a few mouthfuls of ice-cold water, then leans back against a wall to look up at the sky. He is soon lost in thought. The farther they travel, the noisier and more boisterous the villages they come across, so full of engines roaring and people singing and shouting that even the nocturnal calm of nature has been dissipated. He has no desire to travel along a road that leads to ever more frenzied and cacophonous cities. He wants to go where . . .

Lurching and swaying, Chiong stumbles in and steadies herself against the adobe wall next to the doorless portal. Even from a distance Tabei could smell the liquor on her breath, which is somewhat better smelling than his own.

"It was so much fun, they're such happy people," Chiong half sobs, half giggles. "They're as happy as the immortals. Let's leave day after tomorrow . . . no, the day after that."

"No." He never stays more than one night in the same village.

"I'm tired, I feel exhausted," Chiong shakes her head leadenly.

"What do you know about being tired? Look at those thick legs of yours, even stronger than a yak's. It's not in your nature to know what tired means."

"No, I don't mean my body." Chiong points to her heart.

"You're drunk. Go to sleep." He holds Chiong by the shoulders and presses her down onto the grimy floor. Afterwards he ties a knot for her on the leather cord.

Chiong becomes more and more tired. Whenever they stop to rest, she would lie down and refuse to get up.

"Stand up, don't lie there like a lazy cur," Tabei says.

"I don't want to go on anymore." She stretches out in the sun and squints up at him.

"What did you say?"

"You go on by yourself, I don't want to follow you anymore, walking and walking and walking all the time. Even you don't know where you're going, that's why we just wander around day after day."

But he does know which way they should go. "Woman, you don't understand anything."

"You're right, I don't understand." Chiong closes her eyes and draws herself up into a ball.

"Get on your feet!" Tabei kicks her a couple of times in the buttocks, then lifts his hand high as if ready to bring it down on her. "Otherwise I'll smack you."

"You're an ogre!" Chiong whimpers as she struggles onto her feet. Leaning on her walking stick she sets out after Tabei, who has gone on ahead.

At a seemingly opportune moment Chiong runs away. They are sleeping in a cave when she gets up in the middle of the night and slips out, taking care to bring her little black pot with her. By the light of the moon and stars she runs downhill, going back in the direction whence they came. She feels free as a bird that has just escaped from its cage. Around noon the next day, while she is resting near a cliff which drops off into a deep canyon, she sees a black speck appearing over the ridge of the next mountain, just like the one she saw that day when she was driving her flock home. Tabei has intercepted her and is now walking toward her. Trembling with anger, she grabs her pot and swings desperately at his head, ferociously enough to splatter the brains of a wild bull. Startled, Tabei manages to step aside deftly and block her arm with a counterblow. The black pot flies out of her hands and goes noisily down the side of the cliff. For quite some time they look at each other while the clattering continues to resound from the canyon. In the end Chiong has to climb down into the chasm, whimpering and sniffling the whole way. It is several hours before she reappears with the pot, which is gouged and dented all over.

"You make up for my pot," Chiong demands.

"Let me see it." She hands it to him, and together they examine it thoroughly. "Just a little crack here, I can fix it."

Tabei walks away, and a dejected Chiong follows behind.

"Aaaayyyy—" she starts to sing, so loudly she sets the whole canyon ringing.

Then one day Tabei too begins to grow tired of Chiong. He thinks to himself: "It is only because I led a virtuous life in my previous incarnation, renouncing evil and engaging in kind deeds, that I accumulated enough good karma to be born into the Middle Earth as a human being in this life, and not as some lost soul or hungry demon in the netherworld. But on the road to our final deliverance from suffering and sorrow, women and money are both extraneous things, they are stumbling blocks."

Not long after that they come to a village known as Jia. By this time the leather sash around Chiong's waist is densely braided with many little knots. To their surprise, they find the Jia villagers standing at the village gate banging gongs and drums in welcome. On each side of the entrance is an honor guard made up of members of the militia, complete with semiautomatic rifles that have been plugged with red cloth to prevent any accidents. Four villagers masquerading as yaks are dancing on the path between the guards. Greeting them at the front of the parade are the village chief and several young women, some carrying the ceremonial sashes called *hadars* and others holding silver pitchers whose spouts have been moistened with droplets of yak butter.

It turns out there has been a long drought in these parts. Not long ago a soothsayer predicted that on this very day, at sunset, two people coming from the east would arrive at the village and bring with them a propitious rainfall as wondrous as ambrosia, which would turn the parched crops into a bountiful harvest. So when Tabei and Chiong appear as presaged, the people take it as a good omen and joyfully hoist the two of them onto a tractor festooned with hadars. Then the whole jubilant procession enters the village. Men and women, young and old alike are dressed in their finest, and the five-colored prayer flags fluttering from every rooftop have been freshly changed. Somebody claims to have detected in Chiong's features, in the way she speaks and how she carries herself, the traits of the incarnated Goddess of Mercy. And so Tabei is forgotten and left to himself. But he knows Chiong is no goddess incarnate, because he has seen how hideous she looks when she is fast asleep: Her cheeks become quite jowly then, and ropey saliva oozes from the corners of her half-open mouth.

Sullenly he enters a wineshop for a drink. He is itching to start some trouble. If only someone would pick a quarrel with him, someone who doesn't like the look of his face maybe, or who just wants to give him a hard time. Then he could have a real brawl. And if the guy dares to go for a knife fight, so much the better.

But there is only an old man inside the shop, drinking by himself while flies buzz around his head. Tabei walks over and sits down across from him with a defiant look. A peasant girl wearing a colorful kerchief brings him a glass and fills it with wine.

"This stuff tastes like horse piss," he bellows after taking a swig.

No one answers him.

"Well, doesn't it?" he challenges the old man.

"Now if you're talking about horse piss, I drank quite a bit of that when I was young, and, believe me, straight from the you-know-what on a stallion's underbelly."

Tabei begins to laugh with glee.

"To get my cattle back from Amilier the Archbandit, I had to chase them from Gatsar all the way into the Taklimakhan Desert."

"Who's this Amilier?"

"Hah, don't you know, she was the leader of a gang of bandits who came from Xinjiang about thirty-some years ago, a Kazakh, notorious up and down the Ali region and all through northern Tibet. One time a chieftain had all his livestock rustled overnight. Heaven knows how many yaks and sheep there were, but they were gone from the pasture just like that. When he looked out of his yurt the next morning, all he saw were countless hoofprints on the empty white plain. Even the soldiers sent by the Kesha authorities couldn't handle her."

"And then?"

"You were talking about horse piss just now. Yes, that's right, I grabbed my musket, jumped on a horse and went after my cattle. Out there in that enormous desert, it was those mouthfuls of horse piss that saved my life."

"And then?"

"And then, the leader of the bandits wanted to keep me, wanted me to stay and be her—"

"Husband?"

"—herdsman. After all, I was the chieftain's son! She was damned good-looking too. She was just like the sun, nobody dared look her right in the eye. But I escaped and came back here. Now you tell me, is there any place I haven't been other than heaven and hell?"

"The place where I am going," Tabei says.

"Where's that?" asks the old man.

"I—I don't know." For the first time Tabei feels unsure about the destination ahead. He no longer knows which road to take.

But the old man seems to understand. Pointing to a mountain behind him, he says to Tabei: "No one has ever gone there. The village of Jia used to be a stage post, and travelers came and went in all directions, but nobody ever went there. Back in 1964," he begins to reminisce, "we set up a commune here, and everyone was talking about taking the communist road. At the time few people could rightly say what communism was, we only knew it was one of the heavens.

But nobody knew where it was. We'd ask travelers who came from the south, from the east, from the north, but none of them had ever seen it. That left only the Kalong mountains. So a few people sold all their belongings, slung their tsampa bags across their shoulders and set out to cross the Kalongs. They said they were going to Communism. But they never came back. After that, not a single person from the village ever headed out there again, no matter how hard the times got."

Clenching the rim of the glass between his teeth, Tabei cocks his eyes upward at the old man.

"But I know a little secret about the bottom of the snow-covered Kalong mountains," the old man says, winking at Tabei.

"Go ahead."

"Are you planning to go that way?"

"Maybe."

"Well, when you climb to the top you will hear a strange weeping, like the cries of a misbegotten child who has been abandoned. But that's alright, it's only the sound of the wind coming from a crevice in the rocks. Then after you've been climbing for seven days, you will reach the peak just at daybreak, but don't be in a hurry to go down the other side. Wait till after dark, because in broad daylight the glare off the snow will make you blind."

"That is no secret," Tabei says.

"You're right, that's not a secret. What I really want to tell you is, after you've been going downhill for two days and can see the foot of the mountain, you will find countless gullies down at the bottom, some shallow, others deep, all zigzagging every which way for as far as the eye can see. Going into these gullies is like entering a labyrinth. True, this is no secret either, but don't interrupt me. Now, do you know why there are so many more gullies at the bottom of this mountain than any other place? Because these gullies are the lines on the palm of the Lotus-Born Guru's right hand. Once upon a time he fought a life-and-death duel on this spot with the demon Shivamairu. For one hundred and eight days they battled, and even though the Guru used one after another of his magic powers he could not subdue the demon. Then Shivamairu turned himself into a tiny flea, thinking that he would become invisible to his archenemy. Whereupon the Lotus-Born Guru raised his magical right hand and, thundering out a terrible curse, slapped his palm onto the earth. In one fell swoop Shivamairu was banished into the netherworld. Ever since then the ground over the spot has been marked with the lines and furrows of the Guru's palm. Any ordinary mortal who stumbles into the countless cracks and crevices would inevitably lose his way in the labyrinth. It is said there is only one way out, but there are no clues or signs marking the trail."

Tabei stares intently at the old man.

"Well, this is only a legend, and even I don't know what lies beyond the maze," the old man mutters, shaking his head.

Tabei decides to go to that place. The old man then asks Tabei for a favor: Would he leave Chiong with them in the village? The old man's son has just bought a tractor. Nowadays every family wants to have one of these things. The age-old crowing of the rooster at daybreak is now drowned out by the rumbling of engines. Horse-drawn carts and donkeys are being pushed to the side of the road. Even the pure, crystal-clear water in the streams that tumble down from the snowy mountains is beginning to smell faintly of diesel. The old man runs a power-operated mill and his wife of many years farms a dozen or so hectares. Not long ago, the old man made a trip to the big city to attend something called the "Assembly of Outstanding Representatives in the Campaign to End Poverty and Achieve Prosperity," at which he was given an award as well as a prize. The newspaper even published his picture—a four-inch-square photograph, no less. Never in all the generations of their family have they ever been so well off, never in all those generations have they ever been so busy. Now they need a daughter-in-law to take care of the housework.

While the old man is talking his son comes into the shop. Trying to impress the visitor, the young man pulls out a wad of bills in various denominations and flashes it around. On his wrist is a digital watch. A sleek little cassette player hangs from his belt, a pair of earphones sits on his head, and he is bopping to the beat of music only he can hear. All the moves of a cool city dude, he has them down pat. But Tabei is not at all impressed by any of this—except for the tractor parked just outside the door with its engine still running. The put-put-put of the motor seems to have struck a chord in him. He gets up and walks over to the tractor.

Caressing the handlebars, Tabei says: "Alright, I'll leave Chiong with you."

The young fellow grins absently—most likely he has just gotten a little something from Chiong.

"May I take a ride in this thing?" Tabei asks.

"Of course. Here, let me show you. You'll get the hang of it in no time." The young fellow gives Tabei a quick lesson in driving the tractor—how to press down on the accelerator, how to shift gears, work the clutch, how to start up and how to brake.

Slowly Tabei gets the tractor moving and begins to drive down the dirt road in the twilight. Chiong watches him from the side, tears of happiness streaming down her cheeks. She is about to stay behind, at last! Just then another tractor comes hurtling down the road trailing a wagon behind it. It is one of those big powerful combines nicknamed "Iron Oxen." Tabei doesn't know what to do. There is a shallow trench on one side, and the young fellow shouts at him to drive off the road into the ditch. Tabei jumps off the driver's seat into the middle of the road while the tractor rolls slowly into the trench, but the Iron Ox could not brake in time and its wagon knocks Tabei onto the ground. Everyone runs over and crowds around as Tabei gets back on his feet and dusts himself off. Although he has been hit in the side, he insists it is nothing, that he is fine, and they all breathe a sigh of relief.

The time has come for Tabei to leave—his first attempt to operate a machine, and he gets chewed up by it instead. He puts his arms around Chiong and touches his forehead to hers in a bow of farewell, then sets out on the road to the Kalong mountains. That night the rains come at last, and the villagers all dance and sing for joy. By then Tabei has left the village of Jia far behind and entered the mountains. Along the way he spits out a mouthful of blood. He is hemorrhaging internally from the injury.

My story ended here.

I decided to return to Pabu Naigang and climb up over the Kalong mountains. I wanted to look for the hero of my story among the lines and furrows of the Lotus-Born Guru's palm.

It was a long way from the village of Jia across the mountains to the Place of the Palm Lines—much longer than I expected. The pack mule I had hired for the journey collapsed halfway through. It lay on the ground, foaming at the mouth and giving me one of those pitiful dying looks. I had no choice but to unload the bags it had been carrying and pile them onto my own back. Then I crumbled a few pieces of dehydrated bread and left them on the ground next to its muzzle before continuing on my way.

The first thing I heard when I climbed over the snow-covered peak of the Kalong mountains was a thunderous roar like that of a tidal wave. Down at the bottom snowdrifts rolled and billowed like clouds, while the grains of snow beneath my feet swept along like a rushing stream. But the air was as cold and still as on a windless winter's night, and I never felt even the slightest touch of a breeze over any part of my body. I began to go down the mountain without waiting for nightfall because I knew the goggles I was wearing would protect me from snow blindness. The thick blanket of snow had turned the entire mountainside into a huge glassy slope, so smooth it seemed there could not have been any rocks or hollows underneath. I began zigzagging downhill, slowly. But the heavy packs soon slithered from my shoulders until they were halfway down my back, and finally I had to stop to adjust them. Tucking in my stomach and pushing out my chest, I lifted them back onto my shoulders and was just trying to straighten up when the sudden shift in weight made me lose my balance and sent me hurtling downward. I knew I could no longer stop of my own accord, so I drew myself up into a ball and rolled down the mountain as heaven and earth spun around and around me.

Wonder of wonders, I did not end up plunging into some crevasse. When I came to I found myself lying in soft powdery snow on a patch of level ground at the bottom of the mountain. Above me the white slope had been slashed with a long trail running all the way up into the mist-enshrouded heights.

Up at the top of the mountain I had looked at my watch, and it had read 9:46. But now when I looked at it again, it read 8:03. I descended below the snow line and entered, in succession, a lichen zone, prairie, scrubland, a small thicket of trees, and finally a large forested area. When I emerged from the other side of the forest, the vegetation once again grew sparse, and the desolate landscape was dotted with rocky outcroppings and barren hillocks.

All along the way I kept looking at my watch, constantly comparing the time it showed with the time according to my own estimation. I finally came to the conclusion that after I climbed over the top of Mount Kalong, time had begun to run in reverse. That was why the calendar displays on my Seiko watch—this fully automatic, solar-powered electronic timepiece I was wearing—were all going backwards, and that was why its minute- and hour-hands were turning counterclockwise, at a speed five times normal.

The further I went, the more the scenery appeared deformed, or perhaps transformed. Before my eyes passed a parade of pipal trees with egg-shaped leaves and brown, wizened limbs, filing by slowly and methodically like a forest sprung from a moving conveyor belt. Yonder lay the ruins of an ancient temple. Ambling across a broad expanse of tableland was a huge elephant with legs as long as celestial ladders. The scene reminded me of Salvador Dali's "The Temptation of Saint Anthony." Warily I quickened my step and made a detour around all of this, careful not to cast a single look behind me. I did not stop to rest until I reached some hot springs that were giving off big clouds of vapor. But I dared not go to sleep then even though I was absolutely exhausted by then, because I knew that once I closed my eyes I would never again wake up in this life.

Then, through the steam, I glimpsed what appeared to be relics from some long-forgotten era: gold saddles, bow and arrows, lances, suits of armor, prayer wheels, horns, even some tattered yellow banners—quite possibly the site of an ancient battle, I thought to myself. If I hadn't been so tired I would have walked over to look at them more closely. Perhaps I would have been able to verify this spot as one of the battlefields described in the epic poem *Gesar*. But at the moment I could only sit and gaze upon all of it from a distance. Prolonged exposure to the heat of the springs had softened the metal objects so that they were no more than a flaccid heap of anomalous shapes, oozing amorphously into one another until they had rearranged themselves into hieroglyphs as abstruse as Mayan scripts. At first I suspected I was seeing a mirage, that my extended isolation had caused me to hallucinate about these strange transmutations. But right away I rejected this notion, because my mind was functioning quite logically, and my memory and analytical faculties were all sound. As always the sun journeyed from east to west, and the universe, after all, still existed and turned in accordance with its own laws. Yet although day and night continued to follow one upon the other, the hands on my watch were speeding counterclockwise and the calendar displays kept reeling backward. This, I surmised, was what had confounded my biological clock and led to the sensation of disembodiment.

And then one dawn I wake up to find myself lying at the foot of an enormous red boulder, at a point where countless gullies converge and radiate outward again. It must have been the cold damp air that roused me, and my teeth chatter in the chilly wind gusting from the depths of the surrounding canyons. Hurriedly I clamber up the rocky face of a nearby ravine and look out over the top. I can see clear to the horizon. The earth all around me is carved with countless black gullies extending in every direction like the talons of some monster's claw, or like cracks in soil parched by a millenium of drought. Some of the gullies are so deep they seem bottomless. I have reached the Place of the Palm Lines. There is not a tree in sight, nor a blade of grass. Nothing but desolation. It reminds me of the last scene in a movie about nuclear war I once saw: In a wide-angled shot, the hero and the heroine are silhouetted against a background of charred earth, after the holocaust. One in the east, the other in the west, they slowly lift their heads and crawl arduously toward each other. At last the only two survivors on earth come together and embrace. Their eyes tell of the suffering they have endured. Freeze frame. They will become the new Adam and Eve.

The body of Sangjie Dapu of Zhatuo has long since been cremated. Afterward somebody probably poked around in the still-smoldering ashes and found the precious pieces of sheli. But the hero of my story is nowhere to be seen.

"Taaa—beiiii! Where—are—yooooouuu?" I shout at the top of my lungs. I am sure he could not have found his way out of this place. The sound of my voice echoes far and wide, but there is no reply.

Before long, however, I see a miracle: A black dot appears in the distance, about one or two kilometers away. Calling out the name of my protagonist, I tear along the ridges toward the tiny figure. But when I draw close enough to see clearly, I am so stunned that I stop dead in my tracks: It is Chiong! Never in a million years would I have guessed this.

"Tabei is going to die soon," Chiong sobs as she runs toward me.

"Where is he?"

She takes me down into a gully nearby. Tabei is lying on the ground at the bottom, his face pale and haggard, his breathing labored. A steady trickle of water drips down a mossy crevice in the wall of the ravine and collects in a little pool on the ground. From time to time Chiong would dip one end of her sash in this puddle and squeeze drops of water into Tabei's half-open mouth.

His eyes upon my face, he says, "Prophet, I am waiting, I see the light, the Lord will enlighten me."

"He's very badly hurt, he must have water constantly," Chiong whispers into my ear.

"Why didn't you stay in Jia?" I ask her.

"Why should I stay in Jia?" she retorts. "The thought never crossed my mind. He never promised to stay in any one place. He plucked my heart and tied it onto the cord around his waist. I cannot survive away from him."

"Now don't be so sure," I said.

"All this time he's been wanting to know what this is." Chiong points to something behind me. Turning my head, I find that we are at the bottom of a deep ravine that runs in a perfectly straight line, all the way back to the gigantic red boulder where I had spent the night. It is only now that I see the snow-white " 𝄞 " carved into the heart of the sanguineous rock, but invisible to anyone looking up from the foot of the rock. " 𝄞 " is the note intoned by a lama after he has chanted the "om-ma-ni-pad-mah-hom" mantra one hundred times. As far as I know, there can be only two reasons why it would have been carved on this boulder: Either this is a place frequented by spirits and demons, or a great hero lies buried here. By the banks of the Chumishingu River on the way from Jiangzi to Pali, there is a rock which is also carved with a " 𝄞 ," to commemorate the spot where Bunlading the Second, commander of the Tibetan army, fell in battle against the British invaders in the year 1904. But I see no point in explaining any of this to Tabei.

Not until this very moment do I discover, belatedly, the truth about my "beloved castaways": They have all been endowed with life and will. Once characters are created, their every move becomes an objective fact. In letting Tabei and Chiong come out of that numbered manila envelope, I have clearly made an irreparable mistake. And why is it that to this day I have not been able to give shape to "people of a new type"? This is yet another mistake. If someone demands to know why, in this great and heroic era, I still allow characters like Tabei and Chiong to exist, how shall I answer?

Hoping against hope, I bend down and whisper into Tabei's ear every argument I can think of that would be comprehensible to him, trying to convince him that the place he is looking for does not exist, just as Thomas More's Utopia did not exist. It doesn't exist, that's all.

But, alas, it is too late! In these final moments of his life, it is just not possible to make him give up the faith forged through the years. He turns himself over and lays his head against the ground.

"Tabei," I stammer, "you will get better. Just wait here a while, I left all my things over there, I've got some first-aid medicine in my bag and . . ."

"Hush!" Tabei stops me, his ear pressed against the cold, soggy ground. "Listen to this! Listen!"

For the longest time all I can hear is a faint murmur in the intervals between my heartbeats.

"Help me up! I want to get up there!" Tabei cries as he sits up, waving his arms about.

I have no choice but to help him onto his feet. Chiong climbs up ahead while I prop Tabei up from below, planting my feet on the rocky ledges along the wall of the ravine. To my surprise he is quite heavy. I hold him gingerly, careful to guard with one hand the spot where he had been hit by the tractor. With my other hand I grope for the rocks in the cliff face, pulling Tabei up little by little. A sharp, jagged rock cuts my hand, leaving it numb at first, then stinging as the warm blood streams out of the wound, runs along my arm and down into my sleeve. At the top of the ravine, Chiong lies on her stomach and reaches down to grab Tabei under his arms. While she tugs and pulls from above, I heave and hoist from below until we finally lift him out of the ravine onto the ground at the top.

The eastern sky is aglow with light from the sun, which is just about to appear over the horizon. Tabei takes a deep, hungry sniff of the morning air and looks all around, his eyes alert and searching.

"What is it saying, Prophet? I can't understand it. Please tell me, quickly, you must have understood it, I beg of you." He turns around and prostrates himself at my feet.

His ears catch the signals long before mine do. It is not until several minutes later that Chiong and I hear a sound, a very real sound, coming from the sky. We listen intently.

"It's brass bells ringing on a temple roof!" Chiong cries excitedly.

"It's the chiming of church bells," I correct her.

"It's an avalanche! It's frightening!"

"No, this is the majestic sound of horns and drums and a multitude of voices singing," I correct her again. Chiong gives me a bewildered look.

"God is beginning to speak," Tabei proclaims solemnly.

This time I dare not correct anyone, even though the sound is the amplified voice of a man speaking in English. How can I tell Tabei that this is the grand opening ceremony of the Twenty-third Olympics being held in Los Angeles, U.S.A., and that, by means of satellites in space, television and radio networks are beaming their live coverage of this historic occasion to every corner of the earth?

I finally get a sense of time. My watch has stopped completely. From the motionless hands and calendar displays on the dial I learn that it is now 7:30 A.M., Beijing time, on the twenty-ninth day of July, in the year A.D. 1984.

"This is not a sign from God, my child. It is the sound of chimes and trumpets and a vast choir, signifying mankind's challenge to the world." It is the only thing I can think of to tell him.

I don't know if he hears me. Perhaps he already understands everything. Curling up as if he were cold, he closes his eyes and seems to go to sleep.

I lay him down on the ground again and kneel beside him, trying to straighten his tattered clothes. But I end up staining them with blood from the gash on my hand, and suddenly I am filled with remorse. It is I who have brought Tabei to this. And my other protagonists before him—how many of them, too, have I led to their deaths? It is time for some rigorous soul-searching.

"Now I am left all alone," Chiong murmurs piteously.

"You are not going to die, Chiong. You have made it through the difficult journey, and now little by little I will mold you into a new human being," I say to Chiong, lifting my eyes to look at her. Her innocent face brightens with hope.

The leather cord around her waist sways in front of my eyes. Curious to know how long it has been since she left home, I pick up one end of the cord and begin to count the knots carefully:

". . . five . . . eight . . . twenty-five . . . fifty-seven . . . ninety-six . . ."

The last knot is number one hundred and eight, which is exactly how many prayer beads there are on the string draped around Tabei's hands.

By this time the sun has begun its majestic and stately ascent, bathing earth and sky in the same golden splendor.

I take Tabei's place. Chiong follows behind me, and we set out on the journey back. Time begins again, from the beginning.

STEVEN MILLHAUSER
The Illusionist

Steven Millhauser is a literary mainstream writer whose dark fantasy story, "The Illusionist" was published by *Esquire* magazine, one of the few remaining newsstand magazine venues for fiction in this country.

This is a story *about* fantasy, about what is real and what is not and the ability of gifted artists to blur the line between the two.

—T.W.

The Illusionist

STEVEN MILLHAUSER

In the last years of the nineteenth century, when the Empire of the Hapsburgs was nearing the end of its long dissolution, the art of magic flourished as never before. In obscure villages of Moravia and Galicia, from the Istrian peninsula to the mists of Bukovina, bearded and black-caped magicians in market squares astonished townspeople by drawing streams of dazzling silk handkerchiefs from empty paper cones, removing billiard balls from children's ears, and throwing into the air decks of cards that assumed the shapes of fountains, snakes, and angels before returning to the hand. In cities and larger towns, from Zagreb to Lvov, from Budapest to Vienna, on the stages of opera houses, town halls, and magic theaters, traveling conjurers equipped with the latest apparatus enchanted sophisticated audiences with elaborate stage illusions. It was the age of levitations and decapitations, of ghostly apparitions and sudden vanishings, as if the tottering Empire were revealing through the medium of its magicians its secret desire for annihilation. Among the remarkable conjurers of that time, none achieved the heights of illusion attained by Eisenheim, whose enigmatic final performance was viewed by some as a triumph of the magician's art, by others as a fateful sign.

Eisenheim, né Eduard Abramowitz, was born in Bratislava in 1859 or 1860. Little is known of his early years, or indeed of his entire life outside the realm of illusion. For the scant facts we are obliged to rely on the dubious memoirs of magicians, on comments in contemporary newspaper stories and trade periodicals, on promotional material and brochures for magic acts; here and there the diary entry of a countess or ambassador records attendance at a performance in Paris, Cracow, Vienna. Eisenheim's father was a highly respected cabinet-maker, whose ornamental gilt cupboards and skillfully carved lowboys with lion-paw feet and brass handles shaped like snarling lions graced the halls of the gentry of Bratislava. The boy was the eldest of four children; like many Bratislavan

Jews, the family spoke German and called their city Pressburg, although they understood as much Slovak and Magyar as was necessary for the proper conduct of business. Eduard went to work early in his father's shop. For the rest of his life he would retain a fondness for smooth pieces of wood joined seamlessly by mortise and tenon. By the age of seventeen he was himself a skilled cabinetmaker, a fact noted more than once by fellow magicians who admired Eisenheim's skill in constructing trick cabinets of breathtaking ingenuity. The young craftsman was already a passionate amateur magician, who is said to have entertained family and friends with card sleights and a disappearing-ring trick that required a small beechwood box of his own construction. He would place a borrowed ring inside, fasten the box tightly with twine, and quietly remove the ring as he handed the box to a spectator. The beechwood box, with its secret panel, was able to withstand the most minute examination.

A chance encounter with a traveling magician is said to have been the cause of Eisenheim's lifelong passion for magic. The story goes that one day, returning from school, the boy saw a man in black sitting under a plane tree. The man called him over and lazily, indifferently, removed from the boy's ear first one coin and then another, and then a third, coin after coin, a whole handful of coins, which suddenly turned into a bunch of red roses. From the roses the man in black drew out a white billiard ball, which turned into a wooden flute that suddenly vanished. One version of the story adds that the man himself then vanished, along with the plane tree.

Eduard had once seen a magic shop, without much interest; he now returned with passion. On dark winter mornings on the way to school he would remove his gloves to practice manipulating balls and coins, with chilled fingers, in the pockets of his coat. He enchanted his three sisters with intricate shadowgraphs representing Rumpelstiltskin and Rapunzel, American buffaloes and Indians, the golem of Prague. Later a local conjurer called Ignazc Molnar taught him juggling for the sake of coordinating movements of the eye and hand. Once, on a dare, the thirteen-year-old boy carried an egg on a soda straw all the way to Bratislava Castle and back. Much later, when all this was far behind him, the Master would be sitting gloomily in the corner of a Viennese apartment where a party was being held in his honor, and reaching up wearily he would startle his hostess by producing from the air five billiard balls that he proceeded to juggle flawlessly.

But who can unravel the mystery of the passion that infects an entire life, bending it away from its former course in one irrevocable swerve? Abramowitz seems to have accepted his fate slowly. It was as if he kept trying to evade the disturbing knowledge of his difference. At the age of twenty-four he was still an expert cabinetmaker who did occasional parlor tricks.

As if suddenly, Eisenheim appeared at a theater in Vienna and began his exhilarating and fatal career. The brilliant newcomer was twenty-eight years old. In fact, contemporary records show that the cabinetmaker from Bratislava had appeared in private performances for at least a year before moving to the Austrian capital. Although the years preceding the first private performances remain mysterious, it is clear that Abramowitz gradually shifted his attention more and more to magic, by way of the trick chests and cabinets that he had begun to supply to local magicians. Eisenheim's nature was like that: he proceeded slowly and cautiously, step by step, and then, as if he had earned the right to be daring, he would take a sudden leap.

The first public performances were noted less for their daring than for their subtle mastery of the stage illusions of the day, although even then there were artful twists and variations. One of Eisenheim's early successes was The Mysterious Orange Tree, a feat made famous by Robert-Houdin. A borrowed handkerchief was placed in a small box and handed to a member of the audience. An assistant strode onto the stage, bearing in his arms a small green orange tree in a box. He placed the box on the magician's table and stepped away. At a word from Eisenheim, accompanied by a pass of his wand, blossoms began to appear on the tree. A moment later, oranges began to emerge; Eisenheim plucked several and handed them to members of the audience. Suddenly two butterflies rose from the leaves, carrying a handkerchief. The spectator, opening his box, discovered that his handkerchief had disappeared; somehow the butterflies had found it in the tree. The illusion depended on two separate deceptions: the mechanical tree itself, which produced real flowers, real fruit, and mechanical butterflies by means of concealed mechanisms; and the removal of the handkerchief from the trick box as it was handed to the spectator. Eisenheim quickly developed a variation that proved popular: the tree grew larger each time he covered it with a red silk cloth, the branches produced oranges, apples, pears, and plums, at the end a whole flock of colorful, real butterflies rose up and fluttered over the audience, where children screamed with delight as they reached up to snatch the delicate silken shapes, and at last, under a black velvet cloth that was suddenly lifted, the tree was transformed into a birdcage containing the missing handkerchief.

At this period, Eisenheim wore the traditional silk hat, frock coat, and cape, and performed with an ebony wand tipped with ivory. The one distinctive note was his pair of black gloves. He began each performance by stepping swiftly through the closed curtains onto the stage apron, removing the gloves, and tossing them into the air, where they turned into a pair of sleek ravens.

Early critics were quick to note the young magician's interest in uncanny effects, as in his popular Phantom Portrait. On a darkened stage, a large blank canvas was illuminated by limelight. As Eisenheim made passes with his right hand, the white canvas gradually and mysteriously gave birth to a brighter and brighter painting. Now, it is well known among magicians and mediums that a canvas of unbleached muslin may be painted with chemical solutions that appear invisible when dry; if sulphate of iron is used for blue, nitrate of bismuth for yellow, and copper sulphate for brown, the picture will appear if sprayed with a weak solution of prussiate of potash. An atomizer, concealed in the conjurer's sleeve, gradually brings out the invisible portrait.

Eisenheim increased the mysterious effect by producing full-length portraits that began to exhibit lifelike movements of the eyes and lips. The fiendish portrait of an archduke, or a devil, or Eisenheim himself, would then read the contents of sealed envelopes, before vanishing at a pass of the magician's wand.

However skillful, a conjurer cannot earn and sustain a major reputation without producing original feats of his own devising. It was clear that the restless young magician would not be content with producing clever variations of familiar tricks, and by 1890 his performances regularly concluded with an illusion of striking originality. A large mirror in a carved frame stood on the stage, facing the audience. A spectator was invited onto the stage, where he was asked to walk around the mirror and examine it to his satisfaction. Eisenheim then asked the spectator to don a hooded red robe and positioned him some ten feet from the mirror, where the vivid red reflection was clearly visible to the audience; the theater was darkened, except for a brightening light that came from within the mirror itself. As the spectator waved his robed arms about, and bowed to his bowing reflection, and leaned from side to side, his reflection began to show signs of disobedience—it crossed its arms over its chest instead of waving them about, it refused to bow. Suddenly the reflection grimaced, removed a knife, and stabbed itself in the chest. The reflection collapsed onto the reflected floor. Now a ghostlike white form rose from the dead reflection and hovered in the mirror. All at once the ghost emerged from the glass, floated toward the startled and sometimes terrified spectator, and at the bidding of Eisenheim rose into the dark and vanished. This masterful illusion mystified even professional magicians, who agreed only that the mirror was a trick cabinet with black-lined doors at the rear and a hidden assistant. The lights were probably concealed in the frame between the glass and the lightly silvered back; as the lights grew brighter the mirror became transparent and a red-robed assistant showed himself in the glass. The ghost was more difficult to explain, despite a long tradition of stage ghosts; it was said that concealed magic lanterns produced the phantom, but no other magician was able to imitate the effect. Even in these early years, before Eisenheim achieved disturbing effects unheard of in the history of stage magic, there was a touch of the uncanny about his illusions; and some said even then that Eisenheim was not a showman at all, but a wizard who had sold his soul to the Devil in return for unholy powers.

Eisenheim was a man of medium height, with broad shoulders and large, long-fingered hands. His most striking feature was his powerful head: the black, intense eyes in the strikingly pale face, the broad black beard, the thrusting forehead with its receding hairline, all lent an appearance of unusual mental force. The newspaper accounts mention a minor trait that must have been highly effective: when he leaned his head forward, in intense concentration, there appeared over his right eyebrow a large vein shaped like an inverted Y.

As the last decade of the old century wore on, Eisenheim gradually came to be acknowledged as the foremost magician of his day. These were the years of the great European tours, which brought him to Egyptian Hall in London and the Théâtre Robert-Houdin in Paris, to royal courts and ducal palaces, to halls in Berlin and Milan, Zurich and Salamanca. Although his repertoire continued to include perfected variations of popular illusions like The Vanishing Lady, The Blue Room, The Flying Watch, The Spirit Cabinet (or Specters of the Inner Sanctum), The Enchanted House, The Magic Kettle, and The Arabian Sack Mystery, he appeared to grow increasingly impatient with known effects and began rapidly replacing them with striking inventions of his own. Among the most notable illusions of those years were The Tower of Babel, in which a small black cone mysteriously grew until it filled the entire stage; The Satanic Crystal Ball, in which a ghostly form summoned from hell smashed through the glass globe and rushed out onto the stage with unearthly cries; and The Book of Demons, in which black smoke rose from an ancient book which suddenly burst into flames that released hideous dwarfs in hairy jerkins who ran howling across the stage. In 1898 he opened his own theater in Vienna, called simply Eisenheimhaus, or The House of Eisenheim, as if that were his real home and all other dwellings illusory. It was here that he presented The Pied Piper of Hamelin. Holding his wand like a flute, Eisenheim led children from the audience into a misty hill with a cavelike opening and then, with a pass of his wand, caused the entire hill to vanish into thin air. Moments later a black chest materialized, from which the children emerged and looked around in bewilderment before running back to their parents. The children told their parents that they had been in a wondrous mountain, with golden tables and chairs and white angels flying in the air; they had no idea how they had gotten into the box, or what had happened to them. A few complaints were made; and when, in another performance, a frightened child told his mother that he had been in hell and seen the Devil, who was green and breathed fire, the chief of the Viennese police, one Walther Uhl, paid Eisenheim a visit. The Pied Piper of Hamelin never appeared again, but two results had emerged: a certain disturbing quality in Eisenheim's art was now officially acknowledged, and it was rumored that the stern Master was being closely watched by Franz Josef's secret police. This last was unlikely, for the Emperor, unlike his notorious grandfather, took little interest in police espionage; but the rumor surrounded Eisenheim like a mist, blurring his sharp outline, darkening his features, and enhancing his formidable reputation.

Eisenheim was not without rivals, whose challenges he invariably met with a decisiveness, some would say ferocity, that left no doubt of his self-esteem. Two incidents of the last years of the century left a deep impression among contemporaries. In Vienna in 1898 a magician called Benedetti had appeared. Benedetti, whose real name was Paul Henri Cortot, of Lyon, was a master illusionist of extraordinary smoothness and skill; his mistake was to challenge Eisenheim by presenting imitations of original Eisenheim illusions, with clever variations, much as Eisenheim had once alluded to his predecessors in order to outdo them. Eisenheim learned of his rival's presumption and let it be known through the speaking portrait of a devil that ruin awaits the proud. The very next night, on Benedetti's stage, a speaking portrait of Eisenheim intoned in comic accents that ruin awaits the proud. Eisenheim, a proud and brooding man, did not allude to the insult during his Sunday-night performance. On Monday night, Benedetti's act went awry: the wand leaped from his fingers and rolled across the stage; two fishbowls with watertight lids came crashing to the floor from beneath Benedetti's cloak; the speaking portrait remained mute; the levitating lady was seen to be resting on black wires. The excitable Benedetti, vowing revenge, accused Eisenheim of criminal tampering; two nights later, before a packed house, Benedetti stepped into a black cabinet, drew a curtain, and was never seen again. The investigation by Herr Uhl failed to produce a trace of foul play. Some said the unfortunate Benedetti had simply chosen the most convenient way of escaping to another city, under a new name, far from the scene of his notorious debacle; others were convinced that Eisenheim had somehow spirited him off, perhaps to hell. Viennese society was enchanted by the scandal, which made the rounds of the cafés; and Herr Uhl was seen more than once in a stall of the theater, nodding his head appreciatively at some particularly striking effect.

If Benedetti proved too easy a rival, a far more formidable challenge was posed by the mysterious Passauer. Ernst Passauer was said to be a Bavarian; his first Viennese performance was watched closely by the Austrians, who were forced to admit that the German was a master of striking originality. Passauer took the city by storm; and for the first time there was talk that Eisenheim had met his match, perhaps even—was it possible?—his master. Unlike the impetuous and foolhardy Benedetti, Passauer made no allusion to the Viennese wizard; some saw in this less a sign of professional decorum than an assertion of arrogant indifference, as if the German refused to acknowledge the possibility of a rival. But the pattern of their performances, that autumn, was the very rhythm of rivalry: Eisenheim played on Sunday, Wednesday, and Friday nights, and Passauer on Tuesday, Thursday, and Saturday nights. It was noted that as his rival presented illusions of bold originality, Eisenheim's own illusions became more daring and dangerous; it was as if the two of them had outsoared the confines of the magician's art and existed in some new realm of dexterous wonder, of sinister beauty. In this high but by no means innocent realm, the two masters vied for supremacy before audiences that were increasingly the same. Some said that Eisenheim appeared to be struggling or straining against the relentless pressure of his brilliant rival; others argued that Eisenheim had never displayed such mastery; and as the heavy century lumbered to its close, all awaited the decisive event that would release them from the tension of an unresolved battle.

And it came: one night in mid-December, after a particularly daring illusion, in which Passauer caused first his right arm to vanish, then his left arm, then his feet, until nothing was left of him but his disembodied head floating before a black velvet curtain, the head permitted itself to wonder whether Herr "Eisenzeit," or Iron Age, had ever seen a trick of that kind. The mocking allusion caused the audience to gasp. The limelight went out; when it came on, the stage contained nothing but a heap of black cloth, which began to flutter and billow until it gradually assumed the shape of Passauer, who bowed coolly to tumultuous applause; but the ring of a quiet challenge was not lost in the general uproar. The following night Eisenheim played to a packed, expectant house. He ignored the challenge while performing a series of new illusions that in no way resembled Passauer's act. As he took his final bow, he remarked casually that Passauer's hour had passed. The fate of the unfortunate Benedetti had not been forgotten, and it was said that if the demand for Passauer's next performance had been met, the entire city of Vienna would have become a magic theater.

Passauer's final performance was one of frightening brilliance; it was well attended by professional magicians, who agreed later that as a single performance it outshone the greatest of Eisenheim's evenings. Passauer began by flinging into the air a handful of coins that assumed the shape of a bird and flew out over the heads of the audience, flapping its jingling wings of coins; from a silver thimble held in the flat of his hand he removed a tablecloth, a small mahogany table, and a silver salver on which sat a steaming roast duck. At the climax of the evening, he caused the the properties of the stage to vanish one by one: the magician's table, the beautiful assistant, the far wall, the curtain. Standing alone in a vanished world, he looked at the audience with an expression that grew more and more fierce. Suddenly he burst into a demonic laugh, and reaching up to his face he tore off a rubber mask and revealed himself to be Eisenheim. The collective gasp sounded like a great furnace igniting; someone burst into hysterical sobs. The audience, understanding at last, rose to its feet and cheered the great master of illusion, who himself had been his own greatest rival and had at the end unmasked himself. In his box, Herr Uhl rose to his feet and joined in the applause. He had enjoyed the performance immensely.

Perhaps it was the strain of that sustained deception, perhaps it was the sense of being alone, utterly alone, in any case Eisenheim did not give another performance in the last weeks of the fading century. As the new century came in with a fireworks display in the Prater and a one-hundred-gun salute from the grounds of the Imperial Palace, Eisenheim remained in his Vienna apartment, with its distant view of the same river that flowed through his childhood city. The unexplained period of rest continued, developing into a temporary withdrawal from performance, some said a retirement; Eisenheim himself said nothing. In late January he returned to Bratislava to attend to details of his father's business; a week later he was in Linz; within a month he had purchased a three-story villa in the famous wooded hills on the outskirts of Vienna. He was forty or forty-one, an age when a man takes a hard look at his life. He had never married, although romantic rumors occasionally united him with one or another of his assistants; he was handsome in a stern way, wealthy, and said to be so strong that he could do thirty knee bends on a single leg. Not long after his move to the Wienerwald he began to court Sophie Ritter, the twenty-six-year-old daughter of a local landowner who disapproved of Eisenheim's profession and was a staunch supporter of Lueger's anti-Semitic Christian Social Party; the girl appears to have been in love with Eisenheim, but at the last moment something went wrong, she withdrew abruptly, and a month later married a grain merchant from Graz. For a year Eisenheim lived like a reclusive country squire. He took riding lessons in the mornings, in the afternoons practiced with pistols at his private shooting range, planted a spring garden, stocked his ponds, designed a new orchard. In a meadow at the back of his house he supervised the building of a long low shedlike structure that became known as the Teufelsfabrik, or Devil's Factory, for it housed his collection of trick cabinets, deceptive mirrors, haunted portraits, and magic caskets. The walls were lined with cupboards that had sliding glass doors and held Eisenheim's formidable collection of magical apparatus: vanishing birdcages, inexhaustible punch bowls, Devil's targets, Schiller's bells, watch-spring flowers, trick bouquets, and an array of secret devices used in sleight-of-hand feats: ball shells, coin droppers, elastic handkerchief-pulls for making handerchiefs vanish, dummy cigars, color-changing tubes for handkerchief tricks, hollow thumb-tips, miniature spirit lamps for the magical lighting of candles, false fingers, black silk ball-tubes. In the basement of the factory was a large room in which he conducted chemical and electrical experiments, and a curtained darkroom; Eisenheim was a close student of photography and the new art of cinematography. Often he was seen working late at night, and some said that ghostly forms appeared in the dim-lit windows.

On the first of January, 1901, Eisenheim suddenly returned to his city apartment, with its view of the Danube and the Vienna hills. Three days later he reappeared onstage. A local wit remarked that the master of illusion had simply omitted the year 1900, which with its two zeros no doubt struck him as illusory. The yearlong absence of the Master had sharpened expectations, and the standing-room-only crowd was tensely quiet as the curtains parted on a stage strikingly bare except for a plain wooden chair behind a small glass table. For some in that audience, the table already signaled a revolution; others were puzzled or disappointed. From the right wing Eisenheim strode onto the stage. A flurry of whispers was quickly hushed. The Master wore a plain dark suit and had shaved off his beard. Without a word he sat down on the wooden chair behind the table and faced the audience. He placed his hands lightly on the tabletop, where they remained during the entire performance. He stared directly before him, leaning forward slightly and appearing to concentrate with terrific force.

In the middle of the eighteenth century the magician's table was a large table draped to the floor; beneath the cloth an assistant reached through a hole in the tabletop to remove objects concealed by a large cone. The modern table of Eisenheim's day had a short cloth that exposed the table legs, but the disappearance of the hidden assistant and the general simplification of design in no sense changed the nature of the table, which remained an ingenious machine equipped with innumerable contrivances to aid the magician in the art of deception: hidden receptacles, or *servantes*, into which disappearing objects secretly dropped, invisible wells and traps, concealed pistons, built-in spring pulls for effecting the disappearance of silk handkerchiefs. Eisenheim's transparent glass table announced the end of the magician's table as it had been known throughout the history of stage magic. This radical simplification was not only aesthetic: it meant the refusal of certain kinds of mechanical aid, the elimination of certain effects.

And the audience grew restless: nothing much appeared to be happening. A balding man in a business suit sat at a table, frowning. After fifteen minutes a slight disturbance or darkening in the air was noticeable near the surface of the table. Eisenheim concentrated fiercely; over his right eyebrow the famous vein, shaped like an inverted Y, pressed through the skin of his forehead. The air seemed to tremble and thicken—and before him, on the glass table, a dark shape slowly formed. It appeared to be a small box, about the size of a jewel box. For a while its edges quivered slightly, as if it were made of black smoke. Suddenly Eisenheim raised his eyes, which one witness described as black mirrors that reflected nothing; he looked drained and weary. A moment later he pushed back his chair, stood up, and bowed. The applause was uncertain; people did not know what they had seen.

Eisenheim next invited spectators to come onto the stage and examine the box on the table. One woman, reaching for the box and feeling nothing, nothing at all, stepped back and raised a hand to her throat. A girl of sixteen, sweeping her hand through the black box, cried out as if in pain.

The rest of the performance consisted of two more "materializations": a sphere and a wand. After members of the audience had satisfied themselves of the immaterial nature of the objects, Eisenheim picked up the wand and waved it over the box. He next lifted the lid of the box, placed the sphere inside, and closed the lid. When he invited spectators onto the stage, their hands passed through empty air. Eisenheim opened the box, removed the sphere, and laid it on the table between the box and the wand. He bowed, and the curtain closed.

Despite a hesitant, perplexed, and somewhat disappointed response from that first audience, the reviews were enthusiastic; one critic called it a major event in the history of stage illusions. He connected Eisenheim's phantom objects with the larger tradition of stage ghosts, which he traced back to Robertson's Phantasmagoria at the end of the eighteenth century. From concealed magic lanterns Robertson had projected images onto smoke rising from braziers to create eerie effects. By the middle of the nineteenth century magicians were terrifying spectators with a far more striking technique: a hidden assistant, dressed like a ghost and standing in a pit between the stage and the auditorium, was reflected onto the stage through a tilted sheet of glass invisible to the audience. Modern ghosts were based on the technique of the black velvet backdrop: over-head lights were directed toward the front of the stage, and black-covered white objects appeared to materialize when the covers were pulled away by invisible blackhooded assistants dressed in black. But Eisenheim's phantoms, those im-material materializations, made use of no machinery at all—they appeared to emerge from the mind of the magician. The effect was startling, the unknown device ingenious. The writer considered and rejected the possibility of hidden magic lanterns and mirrors; discussed the properties of the cinematograph re-cently developed by the Lumière brothers and used by contemporary magicians to produce unusual effects of a different kind; and speculated on possible scientific techniques whereby Eisenheim might have caused the air literally to thicken and darken. Was it possible that one of the Lumière machines, directed onto slightly misted air above the table, might have produced the phantom objects? But no one had detected any mist, no one had seen the necessary beam of light. However Eisenheim had accomplished the illusion, the effect was incomparable; it appeared that he was summoning objects into existence by the sheer effort of his mind. In this the master illusionist was rejecting the modern conjurer's increasing reliance on machinery and returning the spectator to the troubled heart of magic, which yearned beyond the constricting world of ingenuity and artifice toward the dark realm of transgression.

The long review, heavy with fin-de-siècle portentousness and shot through with a secret restlessness or longing, was the first of several that placed Eisenheim beyond the world of conjuring and saw in him an expression of spiritual striving, as if his art could no longer be talked about in the old way.

During the next performance Eisenheim sat for thirty-five minutes at his glass table in front of a respectful but increasingly restless audience before the darkening was observed. When he sat back, evidently spent from his exertions, there stood on the table the head and shoulders of a young woman. The details of witnesses differ, but all reports agree that the head was of a young woman of perhaps eighteen or twenty, with short dark hair and heavy-lidded eyes. She faced the audience calmly, a little dreamily, as if she had just wakened from sleep, and spoke her name: Greta. Fräulein Greta answered questions from the audience. She said she came from Brünn; she was seventeen years old; her father was a lens grinder; she did not know how she had come here. Behind her, Eisenheim sat slumped in his seat, his broad face pale as marble, his eyes staring as if sightlessly. After a while Fräulein Greta appeared to grow tired. Eisenheim gathered himself up and fixed her with his stare; gradually she wavered and grew dim, and slowly vanished.

With Fräulein Greta, Eisenheim triumphed over the doubters. As word of the new illusion spread, and audiences waited with a kind of fearful patience for the darkening of the air above the glass table, it became clear that Eisenheim had touched a nerve. Greta fever was in the air. It was said that Fräulein Greta was really Marie Vetsera, who had died with Crown Prince Rudolf in the bedroom of his hunting lodge at Mayerling; it was said that Fräulein Greta, with her dark, sad eyes, was the girlhood spirit of the Empress Elizabeth, who at the age of sixty had been stabbed to death in Geneva by an Italian anarchist. It was said that Fräulein Greta knew things, all sorts of things, and could tell secrets about the other world. For a while Eisenheim was taken up by the spiritualists, who claimed him as one of their own: here at last was absolute proof of the materialization of spirit forms. A society of disaffected Blavatskyites called the Daughters of Dawn elected Eisenheim to an honorary membership, and three bearded members of a Salzburg Institute for Psychic Research began attending performances with black notebooks in hand. Magicians heaped scorn on the mediumistic confraternity but could not explain or duplicate the illusion; a shrewd group of mediums, realizing they could not reproduce the Eisenheim phenomena, accused him of fraud while defending themselves against the magicians' charges. Eisenheim's rigorous silence was taken by all sides as a sign of approval. The "manifestations," as they began to be called, soon included the head of a dark-haired man of about thirty, who called himself Frankel and demonstrated conventional tricks of mind reading and telepathy before fading away. What puzzled the professionals was not the mind reading but the production of Frankel himself. The possibility of exerting a physical influence on air was repeatedly argued; it was suggested in some quarters that Eisenheim had prepared the air in advance with a thickening agent and treated it with invisible chemical solutions, but this allusion to the timeworn trick of the muslin canvas convinced no one.

In late March Eisenheim left Vienna on an Imperial tour that included

bookings in Ljubljana, Prague, Teplitz, Budapest, Kolozsvar, Czernowitz, Tar-
nopol, Uzghorod. In Vienna, the return of the Master was awaited with an
impatience bordering on frenzy. A much-publicized case was that of Anna
Scherer, the dark-eyed sixteen-year-old daughter of a Vienna banker, who declared that she felt a deep spiritual bond with Greta and could not bear life
without her. The troubled girl ran away from home and was discovered by the
police two days later wandering disheveled in the wooded hills northeast of the
city; when she returned home she shut herself in her room and wept violently
and uncontrollably for six hours a day. An eighteen-year-old youth was arrested
at night on the grounds of Eisenheim's villa and later confessed that he had
planned to break into the Devil's Factory and learn the secret of raising the dead.
Devotees of Greta and Frankel met in small groups to discuss the Master, and
it was rumored that in a remote village in Carinthia he had demonstrated magical
powers of a still more thrilling and disturbing kind.

And the Master returned, and the curtains opened, and fingers tightened on
the blue velvet chair arms. On a bare stage stood nothing but a simple chair.
Eisenheim, looking pale and tired, with shadowy hollows in his temples, walked
to the chair and sat down with his large, long hands resting on his knees. He
fixed his stare at the air and sat rigidly for forty minutes, while rivulets of sweat
trickled along his high-boned cheeks and a thick vein pressed through the skin
of his forehead. Gradually a darkening of the air was discernible and a shape
slowly emerged. At first it seemed a wavering and indistinct form, like shimmers
above a radiator on a wintry day, but soon there was a thickening, and before
the slumped form of Eisenheim stood a beautiful boy. His large brown eyes,
fringed with dark lashes, looked out trustingly, if a little dreamily; he had a
profusion of thick hay-colored curls and wore a school uniform with dark-green
shorts and gray socks. He seemed surprised and shy, uncomfortable before the
audience, but as he began to walk about he became more animated and told
his name: Elis. Many commented on the striking contrast between the angelic
boy and the dark, brooding magician. The sweetness of the creature cast a spell
over the audience, broken only when a woman was invited onto the stage. As
she bent over to run her fingers through Elis's hair, her hand passed through
empty air. She gave a cry that sounded like a moan and hurried from the stage
in confusion. Later she said that the air had felt cold, very cold.

Greta and Frankel were forgotten in an outbreak of Elis fever. The immaterial
boy was said to be the most enchanting illusion ever created by a magician; the
spiritualist camp maintained that Elis was the spirit of a boy who had died in
Helgoland in 1787. Elis fever grew to such a pitch that often sobs and screams
would erupt from tense, constricted throats as the air before Eisenheim slowly
began to darken and the beautiful boy took shape. Elis did not engage in the
conventions of magic, but simply walked about on the stage, answering questions
put to him by the audience or asking questions of his own. He said that his
parents were dead; he seemed uncertain of many things and grew confused when
asked how he had come to be there. Sometimes he left the stage and walked
slowly along the aisle, while hands reached out and grasped empty air. After
half an hour Eisenheim would cause him to waver and grow dim, and Elis

would vanish away. Screams often accompanied the disappearance of the beautiful boy; and after a particularly troubling episode, in which a young woman leaped onto the stage and began clawing the vanishing form, Herr Uhl was once again seen in attendance at the theater, watching with an expression of keen interest.

He was in attendance when Eisenheim stunned the house by producing a companion for Elis, a girl who called herself Rosa. She had long dark hair and black, dreamy eyes and Slavic cheekbones; she spoke slowly and seriously, often pausing to think of the exact word. Elis seemed shy of her and at first refused to speak in her presence. Rosa said she was twelve years old; she said she knew the secrets of the past and future, and offered to predict the death of anyone present. A young man with thin cheeks, evidently a student, raised his hand. Rosa stepped to the edge of the stage and stared at him for a long while with her earnest eyes; when she turned away she said that he would cough up blood in November and would die of tuberculosis before the end of the following summer. Pale, visibly shaken, the young man began to protest angrily, then sat down suddenly and covered his face with his hands.

Rosa and Elis were soon fast friends. It was touching to observe Elis's gradual overcoming of shyness and the growth of his intense attachment to her. Immediately after his appearance he would begin to look around sweetly, with his large, anxious eyes, as if searching for his Rosa. As Eisenheim stared with rigid intensity, Elis would play by himself but steal secret glances at the air in front of the magician. The boy would grow more and more agitated as the air began to darken; and a look of almost painful rapture would glow on his face as Rosa appeared with her high cheekbones and her black, dreamy eyes.

Often the children would play by themselves onstage, as if oblivious of an audience. They would hold hands and walk along imaginary paths, swinging their arms back and forth, or they would water invisible flowers with an invisible watering can; and the exquisite charm of their gestures was noted by more than one witness. During these games Rosa would sing songs of haunting, melancholy beauty in an unfamiliar Low German dialect.

It remains unclear precisely when the rumors arose that Eisenheim would be arrested and his theater closed. Some said that Uhl had intended it from the beginning and had simply been waiting for the opportune moment; others pointed to particular incidents. One such incident occurred in late summer, when a disturbance took place in the audience not long after the appearance of Elis and Rosa. At first there were sharp whispers, and angry shushes, and suddenly a woman began to rise and then leaned violently away as a child rose from the aisle seat beside her. The child, a boy of about six, walked down the aisle and climbed the stairs to the stage, where he stood smiling at the audience, who immediately recognized that he was of the race of Elis and Rosa. Although the mysterious child never appeared again, spectators now began to look nervously at their neighbors; and it was in this charged atmosphere that the rumor of impending arrest sprang up and would not go away. The mere sight of Herr Uhl in his box each night caused tense whispers. It began to seem as if the policeman and the magician were engaged in a secret battle: it was said that

Herr Uhl was planning a dramatic arrest, and Eisenheim a brilliant escape. Eisenheim, for his part, ignored the whispers and did nothing to modify the disturbing effects that Elis and Rosa had on his audience; and as if to defy the forces gathering against him, one evening he brought forth another figure, an ugly old woman in a black dress who frightened Elis and Rosa and caused fearful cries from the audience before she melted away.

The official reason given for the arrest of the Master, and the seizure of his theater, was the disturbance of public order; the police reports, in preparation for more than a year, listed more than one hundred incidents. But Herr Uhl's private papers reveal a deeper cause. The chief of police was an intelligent and well-read man who was himself an amateur conjurer, and he was not unduly troubled by the occasional extreme public responses to Eisenheim's illusions, although he recorded each instance scrupulously and asked himself whether such effects were consonant with public safety and decorum. No, what disturbed Herr Uhl was something else, something for which he had difficulty finding a name. The phrase "crossing of boundaries" occurs pejoratively more than once in his notebooks; by it he appears to mean that certain distinctions must be strictly maintained. Art and life constituted one such distinction; illusion and reality, another. Eisenheim deliberately crossed boundaries and therefore disturbed the essence of things. In effect, Herr Uhl was accusing Eisenheim of shaking the foundations of the universe, of undermining reality, and in consequence, of doing something far worse: subverting the Empire. For where would the Empire be, once the idea of boundaries became blurred and uncertain?

On the night of February 14, 1902—a cold, clear night, when horseshoes rang sharply on the avenues, and fashionable women in chin-high black boas plunged their forearms into heavy, furry muffs—twelve uniformed policemen took their seats in the audience of Eisenheimhaus. The decision to arrest the Master during a performance was later disputed; the public arrest was apparently intended to send a warning to devotees of Eisenheim, and perhaps to other magicians as well. Immediately after the appearance of Rosa, Herr Uhl left his box. Moments later he strode through a side door onto the stage and announced the arrest of Eisenheim in the name of His Imperial Majesty and the City of Vienna. Twelve officers stepped into the aisles and stood at attention. Eisenheim turned his head wearily toward the intruding figure and did not move. Elis and Rosa, who had been standing at the edge of the stage, began to look about fearfully: the lovely boy shook his head and murmured "No" in his angelic voice, while Rosa hugged herself tightly and began to hum a low melody that sounded like a drawn-out moan or keen. Herr Uhl, who had paused some ten feet from Eisenheim in order to permit the grave Master to rise unaided, saw at once that things were getting out of hand—someone in the audience began murmuring "No" and the chant was taken up. Swiftly Uhl strode to the seated magician and placed a hand on his shoulder. That was when it happened: his hand fell through Eisenheim's shoulder, he appeared to stumble, and in a fury he began striking at the magician, who remained seated, calmly through the paroxysm of meaningless blows. At last the officer drew his sword and sliced through Eisenheim, who at this point rose with great dignity and turned to Elis and Rosa.

They looked at him imploringly as they wavered and grew dim. The Master then turned to the audience; and slowly, gravely, he bowed. The applause began in scattered sections and grew louder and wilder until the curtains were seen to tremble. Six officers leaped onto the stage and attempted to seize Eisenheim, who looked at them with an expression of such melancholy that one policeman felt a shadow pass over his heart. And now a nervousness rippled through the crowd as the Master seemed to gather himself for some final effort: his face became rigid with concentration, the famous vein pressed through his forehead, the unseeing eyes were dark autumn nights when the wind picks up and branches creak. A shudder was seen to pass along his arms. It spread to his legs, and from the crowd rose the sound of a great inrush of breath as Eisenheim began his unthinkable final act: bending the black flame of his gaze inward, locked in savage concentration, he began to unknit the threads of his being. Wavering, slowly fading, he stood dark and unmoving there. In the Master's face some claimed to see, as he dissolved before their eyes, a look of fearful exaltation. Others said that at the end he raised his face and uttered a cry of icy desolation. When it was over the audience rose to its feet. Herr Uhl promptly arrested a young man in the front row, and a precarious order was maintained. On a drab stage, empty except for a single wooden chair, policemen in uniform looked tensely about.

Later that night the police ransacked the apartment with a distant view of the Danube, but Eisenheim was not there. The failed arrest was in one respect highly successful: the Master was never seen again. In the Devil's Factory trick mirrors were found, exquisite cabinets with secret panels, ingenious chests and boxes representing high instances of the art of deception, but not a clue about the famous illusions, not one, nothing. Some said that Eisenheim had created an illusory Eisenheim from the first day of the new century; others said that the Master had gradually grown illusory from trafficking with illusions. Someone suggested that Herr Uhl was himself an illusion, a carefully staged part of the final performance. Arguments arose over whether it was all done with lenses and mirrors, or whether the Jew from Bratislava had sold his soul to the Devil for the dark gift of magic. All agreed that it was a sign of the times; and as precise memories faded, and the everyday world of coffee cups, doctors' visits, and war rumors returned, a secret relief penetrated the souls of the faithful, who knew that the Master had passed safely out of the crumbling order of history into the indestructible realm of mystery and dream.

CHARLES DE LINT

Timeskip

Canadian author Charles de Lint is a versatile and original writer who has immersed himself in the worlds of fantasy as an author, critic, scholar, publisher, and musician specializing in traditional folk material. He is a pioneer of "urban fantasy" which brings folklore motifs into a modern context, using myth and dream as a way of exploring the modern world. Work in this vein includes his newest novel, *Ghostwood*, as well as *Moonheart, Mulengro, Yarrow, Greenmantle,* and *Jack the Giant-killer: The Jack of Kinrowan.*

"Timeskip" is a tender and magical story set in modern Canada that uses some of the same characters to be found in two other de Lint stories published this year: "Romano Drom" (*Pulphouse Issue 5*) and "The Stone Drum" (privately printed by Triskell Press). Were it not for space limitations, all three could be included in this volume, for they are all among the year's best stories—and the best work yet from this talented young author.

De Lint lives in Ottawa with his wife, MaryAnn Harris, a soft-sculpture artist.

—T.W.

Timeskip

CHARLES DE LINT

Every time it rains a ghost comes walking.

He goes up by the stately old houses that line Stanton Street, down Henratty Lane to where it leads into the narrow streets and crowded back alleys of Crowsea, and then back up Stanton again in an unvarying routine.

He wears a worn tweed suit—mostly browns and grays with a faint rosy touch of heather. A shapeless cap presses down his brown curls. His features give no true indication of his age, while his eyes are both innocent and wise. His face gleams in the rain, slick and wet as that of a living person. When he reaches the streetlamp in front of the old Hamill estate, he wipes his eyes with a brown hand. Then he fades away.

Samantha Rey knew it was true because she'd seen him.

More than once.

She saw him every time it rained.

"So have you asked her out yet?" Jilly wanted to know.

We were sitting on a park bench, feeding pigeons the leftover crusts from our lunches. Jilly had worked with me at the post office that Christmas they hired outside staff instead of letting the regular employees work the overtime, and we'd been friends ever since. These days she worked three nights a week as a waitress, while I made what I could busking on the Market with my father's old Czech fiddle.

Jilly was slender, with a thick tangle of brown hair and pale blue eyes, electric as sapphires. She had a penchant for loose clothing and fingerless gloves when she wasn't waitressing. There were times, when I met her on the streets in the evening, that I mistook her for a bag lady: skulking in an alleyway, gaze alternating between the sketchbook held in one hand and the faces of the people on the streets as they walked by. She had more sketches of me playing my fiddle than had any right to exist.

"She's never going to know how you feel until you talk to her about it," Jilly went on when I didn't answer.

"I know."

I'll make no bones about it: I was putting the make on Sam Rey and had been ever since she'd started to work at Gypsy Records half a year ago. I never much went in for the blond California beach girl type, but Sam had a look all her own. She had some indefinable quality that went beyond her basic cheerleader appearance. Right. I can hear you already. Rationalizations of the North American libido. But it was true. I didn't just want Sam in my bed; I wanted to know we were going to have a future together. I wanted to grow old with her. I wanted to build up a lifetime of shared memories.

About the most Sam knew about all this was that I hung around and talked to her a lot at the record store.

"Look," Jilly said. "Just because she's pretty doesn't mean she's having a perfect life or anything. Most guys look at someone like her and they won't even approach her because they're sure she's got men coming out of her ears. Well, it doesn't always work that way. For instance"—she touched her breastbone with a narrow hand and smiled—"consider yours truly."

I looked at her long fingers. Paint had dried under her nails.

"You've started a new canvas," I said.

"And you're changing the subject," she replied. "Come on, Geordie. What's the big deal? The most she can say is no."

"Well, yeah. But—"

"She intimidates you, doesn't she?"

I shook my head. "I talk to her all the time."

"Right. And that's why I've got to listen to your constant mooning over her." She gave me a sudden considering look, then grinned. "I'll tell you what, Geordie, me lad. Here's the bottom line: I'll give you twenty-four hours to ask her out. If you haven't gotten it together by then, I'll talk to her myself."

"Don't even joke about it."

"Twenty-four hours," Jilly said firmly. She looked at the chocolate chip cookie in my hand. "Are you eating that?" she added in that certain tone of voice of hers that plainly said: "All previous topics of conversation have been dealt with and completed. We are now changing topics."

So we did. But all the while we talked, I thought about going into the record store and asking Sam out, because if I didn't, Jilly would do it for me. Whatever else she might be, Jilly wasn't shy. Having her go in to plead my case would be as bad as having my mother do it for me. I'd never be able to show my face in there again.

Gypsy Records is on Williamson Street, one of the city's main arteries. The street begins as Highway 14 outside the city, lined with a sprawl of fast food outlets, malls, and warehouses. The commercial properties give way to ever-increasing handfuls of residential blocks until it reaches the downtown core, where shops and low-rise apartments mingle in gossiping crowds.

The store gets its name from John Butler, a short, round-bellied man without a smidgin of Romany blood, who began his business out of the back of a hand-drawn cart that gypsied its way through the city's streets for years, always keeping just one step ahead of the municipal licensing board's agents. While it carries the usual best-sellers, the lifeblood of its sales are more obscure titles—imports and albums published by independent record labels. Albums, singles and compact discs of punk, traditional folk, jazz, heavy metal, and alternative music line its shelves. Barring Sam, most of those who work there would look at home in the fashion pages of the most current British alternative fashion magazines.

Sam was wearing a blue cotton dress today, embroidered with silver threads. Her blond hair was cut in a short shag on the top, hanging down past her shoulders at the back and sides. She was dealing with a defect when I came in. I don't know if the record in question worked or not, but the man returning it was definitely defective.

"It sounds like there's a radio broadcast right in the middle of the song," he was saying as he tapped the cover of the Pink Floyd album on the counter between them.

"It's supposed to be there," Sam explained. "It's *part* of the song." The tone of her voice told me that this conversation was going into its twelfth round or so.

"Well, I don't like it," the man told her. "When I buy an album of music, I expect to get just music on it."

"You still can't return it."

I worked in a record shop one Christmas—two years before the post office job. The best defect I got was from someone returning an in-concert album by Marcel Marceau. Each side had thirty minutes of silence, with applause at the end—I kid you not.

I browsed through the Celtic records while I waited for Sam to finish with her customer. I couldn't afford any of them, but I liked to see what was new. Blasting out of the store's speakers was the new Beastie Boys album. It sounded like a cross between heavy metal and bad rap and was about as appealing as being hit by a car. You couldn't deny its energy, though.

By the time Sam was free, I'd located five records I would have bought in more flush times. Leaving them in the bin, I drifted over to the front cash register just as the Beastie Boys' last cut ended. Sam replaced them with a tape of New Age piano music.

"What's the new Oyster Band like?" I asked.

Sam smiled. "It's terrific. My favorite cut's 'The Old Dance.' It's sort of an allegory based on Adam and Eve and the serpent that's got a great hook in the chorus. Telfer's fiddling just sort of skips ahead, pulling the rest of the song along."

That's what I like about alternative record stores like Gypsy's—the people working in them actually know something about what they're selling.

"Have you got an open copy?" I asked.

She nodded and turned to the bin of opened records behind her to find it. With her back to me, I couldn't get lost in those deep blue eyes of hers. I seized my opportunity and plunged ahead.

"Are you working tonight, would you like to go out with me somewhere?"

I'd meant to be cool about it, but the words all blurred together as they left my throat. I could feel the flush start up the back of my neck as she turned and looked back at me with those baby blues.

"Say what?" she asked.

Before my throat closed up on me completely, I tried again, keeping it short. "Do you want to go out with me tonight?"

Standing there with the Oyster Band album in her hand, she'd never looked better. Especially when she said, "I thought you'd never ask."

I put in a couple of hours of busking that afternoon, down in Crowsea's Market, the fiddle humming under my chin to the jingling rhythm of the coins that passersby threw into the case lying open in front of me. I came away with twenty-six dollars and change—not the best of days, but enough to buy a halfway decent dinner and a few beers.

I picked up Sam after she finished work, and we ate at The Monkey Woman's Nest, a Mexican restaurant on Williamson just a couple of blocks down from Gypsy's. I still don't know how the place got its name. Ernestina Verdad, the Mexican woman who owns the place, looks like a showgirl, and not one of her waitresses is even vaguely simian in appearance.

It started to rain as we were finishing our second beer, turning Williamson Street slick with neon reflections. Sam got a funny look on her face as she watched the rain through the window. Then she turned to me.

"Do you believe in ghosts?" she asked.

The serious look in her eyes stopped the half-assed joke that two beers were brewing in the carbonated swirl of my mind. I never could hold my alcohol. I wasn't drunk, but I had a buzz on.

"I don't think so," I said carefully. "At least I've never seriously stopped to think about it."

"Come on," she said, getting up from the table. "I want to show you something."

I let her lead me out into the rain, though I didn't let her pay anything toward the meal. Tonight was my treat. Next time I'd be happy to let her do the honors.

"Every time it rains," she said, "a ghost comes walking down my street. . . ."

She told me the story as we walked down into Crowsea. The rain was light and I was enjoying it, swinging my fiddle case in my right hand, Sam hanging onto my left as though she'd always walked there. I felt like I was on top of the world, listening to her talk, feeling the pressure of her arm, the bump of her hip against mine.

She had an apartment on the third floor of an old brick and frame building on Stanton Street. It had a front porch that ran the length of the house, dormer windows—two in the front and back, one on each side—and a mansard roof. We stood on the porch, out of the rain, which was coming down harder now.

An orange-and-white tom was sleeping on the cushion of a white wicker chair by the door. He twitched a torn ear as we shared his shelter, but didn't bother to open his eyes. I could smell the mint that was growing up alongside the porch steps, sharp in the wet air.

Sam pointed down the street to where the yellow glare of a streetlamp glistened on the rain-slicked cobblestone walk leading to the Hamill estate. The Hamill house itself was separated from the street by a low wall and a dark expanse of lawn, bordered by the spreading boughs of huge oak trees.

"Watch the street," she said. "Just under the streetlight."

I looked, but I didn't see anything. The wind gusted suddenly, driving the rain in hard sheets along Stanton Street, and for a moment we lost all visibility. When it cleared, he was standing there, Sam's ghost, just as she'd told me. As he started down the street, Sam gave my arm a tug. I stowed my fiddle case under the tom's wicker chair, and we followed the ghost down Henratty Lane.

By the time he returned to the streetlight in front of the Hamill estate, I was ready to argue that Sam was mistaken. There was nothing the least bit ghostly about the man we were following. When he returned up Henratty Lane, we had to duck into a doorway to let him pass. He never looked at us, but I could see the rain hitting him. I could hear the sound of his shoes on the pavement. He had to have come out of the walk that led up to the estate's house, at the same time as that sudden gust of wind-driven rain. It had been a simple coincidence, nothing more. But when he returned to the streetlight, he lifted a hand to wipe his face, and then he was gone. He just winked out of existence. There was no wind. No gust of rain. No place he could have gone. A ghost.

"Jesus," I said softly as I walked over to the pool of light cast by the streetlamp. There was nothing to see. But there had been a man there. I was sure of that much.

"We're soaked," Sam said. "Come on up to my place and I'll make us some coffee."

The coffee was great and the company was better. Sam had a small clothes dryer in her kitchen. I sat in the living room in an oversize housecoat while my clothes tumbled and turned, the machine creating a vibration in the floorboards that I'm sure Sam's downstairs neighbors must have just loved. Sam had changed into a dark blue sweat suit—she looked best in blue, I decided—and dried her hair while she was making the coffee. I prowled around her living room while she did, admiring her books, her huge record collection, her sound system, and the mantel crammed with knickknacks above a working fireplace.

All her furniture was the kind made for comfort—it crouched like sleeping animals about the room. Fat sofa in front of the fireplace, an old pair of matching easy chairs by the window. The bookcases, record cabinet, side tables, and trim were all natural wood, polished to a shine with furniture oil.

We talked about a lot of things, sitting on the sofa, drinking our coffee, but mostly we talked about the ghost.

"Have you ever approached him?" I asked at one point.

Sam shook her head. "No. I just watch him walk. I've never even talked about him to anybody else." That made me feel good. "You know, I can't help but feel that he's waiting for something, or someone. Isn't that the way it usually works in ghost stories?"

"This isn't a ghost story," I said.

"But we didn't imagine it, did we? Not both of us at the same time?"

"I don't know."

But I knew someone who probably did. Jilly. She was into every sort of strange happening, taking all kinds of odd things seriously. I could remember her telling me that one of her professors in Boston was a wizard who had a brown-skinned goblin for a valet, but the thing I remembered most was her talking about that scene in Disney's *101 Dalmations*, where the dogs are all howling to send a message across town, one dog sending it out, another picking it up and passing it along, all the way across town and out into the country. "That's how they do it," Jilly had said. "Just like that."

And if you walked with her at night and a dog started to howl—if no other dog picked it up, then she'd pass it on. She could mimic any dog's bark or howl so perfectly it was uncanny. It could also be embarrassing, because she didn't care who was around or what kinds of looks she got. It was the message that was important.

When I told Sam about Jilly, she smiled, but there wasn't any mockery in her smile. Emboldened, I related the ultimatum that Jilly had given me that afternoon.

Sam laughed aloud. "Jilly sounds like my kind of person," she said. "I'd like to meet her."

When it started to get late, I collected my clothes and changed in the bathroom. I didn't want to start anything, not yet, not this soon, and I knew that Sam felt the same way, though neither of us had spoken of it. She kissed me at the door, a long, warm kiss that had me buzzing again.

"Come see me tomorrow?" she asked. "At the store?"

"Just try to keep me away," I replied.

I gave the old tom on the porch a pat and whistled all the way home to my own place on the other side of Crowsea.

Jilly's studio was its usual organized mess. It was an open loft-like affair that occupied half of the second floor of a four-story brown brick building on Yoors Street, where Foxville's low rentals mingle with Crowsea's shops and older houses. One half of the studio was taken up with a Murphy bed that was never folded back into the wall, a pair of battered sofas, a small kitchenette, storage cabinets, and a tiny boxlike bathroom obviously designed with dwarfs in mind.

Her easel stood in the other half of the studio, by the window where it could catch the morning sun. All around it were stacks of sketchbooks, newspapers, unused canvases, and art books. Finished canvases leaned face front, five to ten deep, against the back wall. Tubes of paint covered the tops of old wooden orange crates—the new ones lying in neat piles like logs by a fireplace, the used ones in a haphazard scatter, closer to hand. Brushes sat waiting to be used in Mason jars. Others were in liquid waiting to be cleaned. Still more, their bristles stiff with dried paint, lay here and there on the floor like discarded pick-up sticks.

The room smelled of oil paint and turpentine. In the corner farthest from the window was a life-size fabric mache sculpture of an artist at work that bore an uncanny likeness to Jilly herself, complete with Walkman, one paintbrush in hand, another sticking out of its mouth. When I got there that morning, Jilly was at her new canvas, face scrunched up as she concentrated. There was already paint in her hair. On the windowsill behind her a small ghetto blaster was playing a Bach fugue, the piano notes spilling across the room like a light rain. Jilly looked up as I came in, a frown changing liquidly into a smile as she took in the foolish look on my face.

"I should have thought of this weeks ago," she said. "You look like the cat who finally caught the mouse. Did you have a good time?"

"The best."

Leaving my fiddle by the door, I moved around behind her so that I could see what she was working on. Sketched out on the white canvas was a Crowsea street scene. I recognized the corner—McKennitt and Lee. I'd played there from time to time, mostly in the spring. Lately a rockabilly band called the Broken Hearts had taken over the spot.

"Well?" Jilly prompted.

"Well what?"

"Aren't you going to give me all the lovely sordid details?"

I nodded at the painting. She'd already started to work in the background with oils.

"Are you putting in the Hearts?" I asked.

Jilly jabbed at me with her paintbrush, leaving a smudge the color of a Crowsea red brick tenement on my jean jacket.

"I'll thump you if you don't spill it all, Geordie, me lad. Just watch if I don't."

She was liable to do just that, so I sat down on the ledge behind her and talked while she painted. We shared a pot of cowboy coffee, which was what Jilly called the foul brew she made from used coffee grounds. I took two spoons of sugar to my usual one, just to cut back on the bitter taste it left in my throat. Still, beggars couldn't be choosers. That morning I didn't even have used coffee grounds at my own place.

"I like ghost stories," she said when I had finished telling her about my evening. She'd finished roughing out the buildings by now and bent closer to the canvas to start working on some of the finer details before she lost the last of the morning light.

"Was it real?" I asked.

"That depends. Bramley said—"

"I know, I know," I said, breaking in.

Bramley, if you can believe it, was the name of her wizard professor in Boston. Bramley Dapple. According to Jilly, one of his favorite topics of conversation was consensual reality, the idea that things exist *because* we agree that they exist.

"But think about it," Jilly went on. "Sam sees a ghost—maybe because she expects to see one—and you see the same ghost because you care about her, so you're willing to agree that there's one there where she says it will be."

"Say it's not that, then what could it be?"

"Any number of things. A timeslip—a bit of the past slipping into the present. It could be a restless spirit with unfinished business. From what you say Sam's told you, though, I'd guess that it's a case of a timeskip."

She turned to grin at me, which let me know that the word was one of her own coining. I gave her a dutifully admiring look, then asked, "A what?"

"A timeskip. It's like a broken record, you know? It just keeps playing the same bit over and over again, only unlike the record it needs something specific to cue it in."

"Like rain."

"Exactly." She gave me a sudden sharp look. "This isn't for one of your brother's stories, is it?"

My brother Christy collects odd tales just as Jilly does, only he writes them down. I've heard some grand arguments between the two of them, comparing the superior qualities of the oral versus written traditions.

"I haven't seen Christy in weeks," I said.

"All right, then."

"So how do you go about handling this sort of thing?" I asked. "Sam thinks he's waiting for something."

Jilly nodded. "For someone to lift the tone arm of time." At the pained look on my face, she added, "Well, have you got a better analogy?"

I admitted that I didn't. "But how do you do that? Do you just go over and talk to him, or grab him, or what?"

"Any and all might work. But you have to be careful about that kind of thing."

"How so?"

"Well," Jilly said, turning from the canvas to give me a serious look, "sometimes a ghost like that can drag you back to whenever it is that he's from and you'll be trapped in his time. Or you might end up taking his place in the timeskip."

"Lovely."

"Isn't it?" She went back to the painting. "What color's that sign Duffy has over his shop on McKennitt?" she asked.

I closed my eyes, trying to picture it, but all I could see was the face of last night's ghost, wet with rain.

It didn't rain again for a couple of weeks. They were good weeks. Sam and I spent the evenings and weekends together. We went out a few times, twice with Jilly, once with a couple of Sam's friends. Jilly and Sam got along just as well as I'd thought they would—and why shouldn't they? They were both special people. I should know.

The morning it did rain it was Sam's day off from Gypsy's. The previous night was the first I'd stayed over all night. The first we made love. Waking up in the morning with her warm beside me was everything I'd thought it would be. She was sleepy-eyed and smiling, more than willing to nestle deep under the comforter while I saw about getting some coffee together.

When the rain started, we took our mugs into the living room and watched the street in front of the Hamill estate. A woman came by, walking one of those fat white bull terriers that look more pig than dog. The terrier didn't seem to mind the rain, but the woman at the other end of the leash was less than pleased. She alternated between frowning at the clouds and tugging him along. About five minutes after the pair had rounded the corner, our ghost showed up, just winking into existence out of nowhere. Or out of a slip in time. One of Jilly's timeskips.

We watched him go through his routine. When he reached the streetlight and vanished again, Sam leaned her head against my shoulder. We were cozied up together in one of the big comfy chairs, feet on the windowsill.

"We should do something for him," she said.

"Remember what Jilly said," I reminded her.

Sam nodded. "But I don't think he's out to hurt anybody. It's not as if he were calling out to us or anything. He's just there, going through the same moves, time after time. The next time it rains—"

"What're we going to do?"

Sam shrugged. "Talk to him maybe?"

I didn't see how that could cause any harm. Truth to tell, I was feeling sorry for the poor bugger myself.

"Why not?" I said.

About then Sam's hands got busy, and I quickly lost interest in the ghost. I started to get up, but Sam held me down in the chair.

"Where you going?" she asked.

"Well, I thought the bed would be—"

"We've never done it in a chair before."

"There's a lot of places we haven't done it yet," I said.

Those deep blue eyes of hers, about five inches from my own, just about swallowed me.

"We've got all the time in the world," she said.

It's funny how you remember things like that later.

The next time it rained, Jilly was with us. The three of us were walking home from Your Second Home, a sleazy bar on the other side of Foxville, where the band of a friend of Sam's was playing. None of us looked quite right for the bar when we walked in. Sam was still the perennial California beach girl, all blond and curves in a pair of tight jeans and a white T-shirt, with a faded jean jacket on top. Jilly and I looked like the scruffs we were.

The bar was a place for serious drinking during the day, serving mostly un-employed blue-collar workers spending their welfare checks on a few hours of forgetfulness. By the time the band started around nine, thought, the clientele underwent a drastic transformation. Scattered here and there through the crowd was the odd individual who still dressed for volume—all the colors turned up loud—but mostly we were outnumbered thirty to one by spike-haired punks in their black leathers and blue jeans. It was like being on the inside of a bruise.

The band was called the Wang Boys and ended up being pretty good—especially on their original numbers—if a bit loud. My ears were ringing when we finally left the place sometime after midnight. We were having a good time on the walk home. Jilly was in rare form, half-dancing on the street around us, singing the band's closing number, making up the words, turning the piece into a punk gospel number. She kept bouncing around in front of us, skipping backward as she tried to get us to sing along.

The rain started as a thin drizzle as we were making our way through Crowsea's narrow streets. Sam's fingers tightened on my arm and Jilly stopped fooling around as we stepped into Henratty Lane, the rain coming down in earnest now. The ghost was just turning in the far end of the lane.

"Geordie," Sam said, her fingers tightening more.

I nodded. We brushed by Jilly and stepped up our pace, aiming to connect with the ghost before he made his turn and started back toward Stanton Street.

"This is not a good idea," Jilly warned us, hurrying to catch up. But by then it was too late.

We were right in front of the ghost. I could tell he didn't see Sam or me, and I wanted to get out of his way before he walked right through us—I didn't relish the thought of having a ghost or a timeskip or whatever he was going through me. But Sam wouldn't move. She put out her hand, and as her fingers brushed the wet tweed of his jacket, everything changed.

The sense of vertigo was strong. Henratty Lane blurred. I had the feeling of time flipping by like the pages of a calendar in an old movie, except each page was a year, not a day. The sounds of the city around us—sounds we weren't normally aware of—were noticeable by their sudden absence. The ghost jumped at Sam's touch. There was a bewildered look in his eyes and he backed away. That sensation of vertigo and blurring returned until Sam caught him by the arm and everything settled down again. Quiet, except for the rain and a far-off voice that seemed to be calling my name.

"Don't be frightened," Sam said, keeping her grip on the ghost's arm. "We want to help you."

"You should not be here," he replied. His voice was stiff and a little formal. "You were only a dream—nothing more. Dreams are to be savored and re-membered, not walking the streets."

Underlying their voices I could still hear the faint sound of my own name being called. I tried to ignore it, concentrating on the ghost and our surroundings. The lane was cleaner than I remembered it—no trash littered against the walls, no graffiti scrawled across the bricks. It seemed darker, too. It was almost possible to believe that we'd been pulled back into the past by the touch of the ghost.

I started to get nervous then, remembering what Jilly had told us. Into the past. What if we *were* in the past and we couldn't get out again? What if we got trapped in the same timeskip as the ghost and were doomed to follow his routine each time it rained?

Sam and the ghost were still talking, but I could hardly hear what they were saying. I was thinking of Jilly. We'd brushed by her to reach the ghost, but she'd been right behind us. Yet when I looked back, there was no one there. I remembered that sound of my name, calling faintly across some great distance. I listened now, but heard only a vague, unrecognizable sound. It took me long moments to realize that it was a dog barking.

I turned to Sam, tried to concentrate on what she was saying to the ghost. She was starting to pull away from him, but now it was his hand that held her arm. As I reached forward to pull her loose, the barking suddenly grew in volume—not one dog's voice, but those of hundreds, echoing across the years that separated us from our own time. Each year caught and sent on its own dog's voice, the sound building into a caphonic brouhaha of yelps and barks and howls.

The ghost gave Sam's arm a sharp tug and I lost my grip on her, stumbling as the vertigo hit me again. I fell through the sound of all those barking dogs, through the blurring years, until I dropped to my knees on the wet cobblestones, my hands reaching for Sam. But Sam wasn't there.

"Geordie?"

It was Jilly, kneeling by my side, hand on my shoulder. She took my chin and turned my face to hers, but I pulled free.

"Sam!" I cried.

A gust of wind drove rain into my face, blinding me, but not before I saw that the lane was truly empty except for Jilly and me. Jilly, who'd mimicked the barking dogs to draw us back through time. But only I'd returned. Sam and the ghost were both gone.

"Oh, Geordie," Jilly murmured as she held me close. "I'm so sorry."

I don't know if the ghost was ever seen again, but I saw Sam one more time after that night. I was with Jilly in Moore's Antiques in Lower Crowsea, flipping through a stack of old sepia-toned photographs, when a group shot of a family on their front porch stopped me cold. There, among the somber faces, was Sam. She looked different. Her hair was drawn back in a tight bun and she wore a plain, unbecoming dark dress, but it was Sam all right. I turned the photograph over and read the photographer's date on the back: 1912.

Something of what I was feeling must have shown on my face, for Jilly came over from a basket of old earrings that she was looking through.

"What's the matter, Geordie, me lad?" she asked.

Then she saw the photograph in my hand. She had no trouble recognizing Sam either. I didn't have any money that day, but Jilly bought the picture and gave it to me. I keep it in my fiddle case.

I grow older each year, building up a lifetime of memories, only I've no Sam to share them with. But every time it rains, I go down to Stanton Street and stand under the streetlight in front of the old Hamill estate. One day I know she'll be waiting there for me.

ROBERT R. McCAMMON

Something Passed By

"Something Passed By" is another of the stories in this volume with a science fiction premise that generates horror. It's from Robert R. McCammon's excellent collection *Blue World*, and is only one of a number of excellent short stories he had out in 1989. I was torn between "Something Passed By" and "Eat Me" from *Book of the Dead*, but felt the former was chillier. "Black Boots," from *Razored Saddles* and "Lizardman," from *Stalkers* were also exceptional short works by McCammon.

—E.D.

Something Passed By

ROBERT R. McCAMMON

ONE

Johnny James was sitting on the front porch, sipping from a glass of gasoline in the December heat, when the doomscreamer came. Of course doomscreamers were nothing new; these days they were as common as blue moons. This one was of the usual variety: skinny-framed, with haunted dark eyes and a long black beard full of dust and filth. He wore dirty khaki trousers and a faded green Izod shirt, and on his feet were sandals made from tyres with the emblem still showing: Michelin. Johnny sipped his Exxon Super Unleaded and pondered that the doomscreamer's outfit must be the Yuppie version of sackcloth-and-ashes.

"Prepare for the end! Prepare to meet your Maker!" The doomscreamer had a loud, booming voice that echoed in the stillness over the town that stood on the edge of Nebraska cornfields. It floated over Grant Street, where the statues of town fathers stood, past the Victorian houses at the end of King's Lane that had burned with such beautiful flames, past the empty playground at the silent Bloch school, over Bradbury park where paint flaked off the grinning carousel horses, down Koontz Street where the businesses used to thrive, over Ellison Field where no bat would ever smack another softball. The doomscreamer's voice filled the town, and ignited the ears of all who remained: "No refuge for the wicked! Prepare for the end! Prepare! Prepare!"

Johnny heard a screened-door slam. His neighbour in the white house across the way stood on his own porch loading a rifle. Johnny called, "Hey! Gordon! What're you doin', man?"

Gordon Mayfield continued to push bullets into his rifle. Between Johnny and Gordon the air shimmered with hazy heat. "Target practice!" Gordon shouted; his voice cracked, and his hands were shaking. He was a big, fleshy man with a shaved head, and he wore only blue jeans, his bare chest and shoulders glistening with sweat. "Gonna do me some target practice!" he said, as he pushed the last shell into the rifle's magazine and clicked the safety off.

Johnny swallowed gasoline and rocked in his chair. "Prepare! Prepare!" the doomscreamer hollered, as he approached his end. The man was standing in front of the empty house next to Gordon's, where the Carmichael family had lived before they fled with a wandering evangelist and his flock on his way to California. "Prepare!" The doomscreamer lifted his arms, sweat stains on his Izod, and shouted to the sky. "Oh ye sinners, prepare to—"

His voice faltered. He looked down at his Michelins, which had begun to sink into the street.

The doomscreamer made a small, terrified squeak. He was not prepared. His ankles had sunk into the grey concrete, which sparkled like quicksilver in a circle around him. Swiftly, he sank to his waist in the mire, his mouth open in a righteous oh.

Gordon had lifted the rifle to put a bullet through the doomscreamer's skull. Now he realized a pull of the trigger would be wasted energy, and might even increase his own risk of spontaneous combustion. He released the trigger, and slowly lowered his gun.

"Help me!" The doomscreamer saw Johnny, and lifted his hands in supplication. "Help me, brother!" He was up to his alligator in the shimmering, hungry concrete. His eyes begged, like those of a lost puppy. "Please . . . help me!"

Johnny was on his feet, though he didn't remember standing. He had set the glass of gasoline aside, and he was about to walk down the porch steps, across the scorched yard and offer his hand to the sinking doomscreamer. But he paused, because he knew he'd never get there in time, and when the concrete pooled like that you never knew how firm the dirt would be either.

"Help me!" The doomscreamer had gone down to his chin. He stretched, trying to claw his way out but quicksilver offers no handholds. "For God's sake, he—" His face went under. His head slid down, and the concrete swirled through his hair. Then—perhaps two seconds later—his clawing hands were all that was left of him, and as they slid down after him the street suddenly solidified again in a ripple of hardening silver. Concrete locked around the ex-doomscreamer's wrists, and his hands looked like white plants growing out of the centre of the street. The fingers twitched a few times, then went rigid.

Gordon went down his steps and walked carefully to the upthrust hands, prodding his path with the rifle's barrel. When he was certain, or as certain as he could be, that the street wouldn't suck him under too, he knelt beside the hands and just sat there staring.

"What is it? What's going on?" Brenda James had come out of the house, her light brown hair damp with sweat. Johnny pointed at the hands, and his wife whispered, "Oh my God."

"Got on a nice wristwatch," Gordon said after another moment. He leaned closer, squinting at the dial. "It's a Rolex. You want it, Johnny?"

"No," Johnny said. "I don't think so."

"Brenda? You want it? Looks like it tells good time."

She shook her head, and grasped Johnny's arm.

"It'd be a waste to leave it out here. First car that comes along, no more watch." Gordon glanced up and down the street. It had been a long time since a car had passed this way, but you never knew. He decided, and took the Rolex off the dead man's wrist. The crystal was cracked and there were flecks of dried concrete on it, but it was a nice, shiny watch. He put it on and stood up. "Happened too fast to do anythin' about. Didn't it, Johnny?"

"Yeah. Way too fast." His throat was dry. He took the last sip of gasoline from the glass. His breath smelled like the pumps at Lansdale's Exxon Station on deLint Street.

Gordon started to walk away. Brenda said, "Are you . . . are you just going to *leave* him there?"

Gordon stopped. He looked down at the hands, wiped his brow with his forearm and returned his gaze to Brenda and Johnny. "I've got an axe in my garage."

"Just leave him there," Johnny said, and Gordon nodded and walked up his porch steps, still testing the earth with the rifle's barrel. He sighed with relief when he reached the porch's sturdy floor.

"Poker game at Ray's tonight," Gordon reminded them. "You gonna make it?"

"Yeah. We'd planned on it."

"Good." His gaze slid towards the white hands, then quickly away again. "Nothin' like winnin' a little cash to take your mind off your troubles, right?"

"Right," Johnny agreed. "Except you're the one who usually wins all the money."

"Hey, what can I say?" Gordon shrugged. "I'm a lucky dude."

"I thought I'd bring J.J. tonight," Brenda offered in a high, merry voice. Both Johnny and Gordon flinched a little. "J.J. needs to get out of the house," Brenda went on. "He likes to be around people."

"Uh . . . sure." Gordon glanced quickly at Johnny. "Sure, Brenda. Ray won't mind. See you folks later, then." He darted another look at the white hands sticking out of the street, and then he went into his house and the screened door slammed behind him.

Brenda began to sing softly as Johnny followed her into their house. An old nursery song, one she'd sung to J.J. when he was just an infant: *"Go to sleep, little baby, when you wake I'll give you some cake and you can ride the pretty little poneeee . . ."*

"Brenda? I don't think it's a good idea."

"What?" She turned towards him, smiling, her blue eyes without lustre. "What's not a good idea, hon?"

"Taking J.J. out of his room. You know he likes it in there."

Brenda's smile fractured. 'That's what *you* say! You're always trying to hurt me, and keep me from being with J.J. Why can't I take J.J. outside? Why can't I sit on the porch with my baby like other mothers do? Why can't I? Answer me, Johnny?' Her face had reddened with anger. *"Why?"*

Johnny's expression remained calm. They'd been over this territory many times. "Go ask J.J. why," he suggested, and he saw her eyes lose their focus, like ice forming over blue pools.

Brenda turned away from him and strode purposefully down the corridor. She stopped before the closed door of J.J.'s room. Hanging on a wall hook next to the door was a small orange oxygen tank on a backpack, connected to a clear plastic oxygen mask. Brenda had had much practice in slipping the tank on, and she did it with little difficulty. Then she turned on the airflow and strapped the hissing oxygen mask over her nose and mouth. She picked up a crowbar, inserting it into a scarred furrow in the doorjamb of J.J.'s room. She pushed against it, but the door wouldn't budge.

"I'll help you," Johnny said, and started towards her.

"No! No, I'll do it!" Brenda strained against the crowbar with desperate strength, her oxygen mask fogging up. And then there was a small cracking noise followed by a *whoosh* that never failed to remind Johnny of a poptop coming off a vacuum-sealed pack of tennis balls. Air shrilled for a few seconds in the hallway, the suction staggering Johnny and Brenda off balance, and then the door to J.J.'s room was unsealed. Brenda went in, and lodged the crowbar between the doorjamb and the door so it wouldn't trap her when the air started to leak away again, which would be in less than two minutes.

Brenda sat down on Johnny Junior's bed. The room's wallpaper had aeroplanes on it, but the glue was cracking in the dry, airless heat and the paper sagged, the aeroplanes falling to earth. "J.J.?" Brenda said. "J.J.? Wake up, J.J." She reached out and touched the boy's shoulder. He lay nestled under the sheet, having a good long sleep. "J.J. it's Momma," Brenda said, and stroked the limp dark hair back from the mummified, gasping face.

Johnny waited in the corridor. He could hear Brenda talking to the dead boy, her voice rising and falling, her words muffled by the oxygen mask. Johnny's heart ached. He knew the routine. She would pick up the dry husk and hold him—carefully, because even in her madness she knew how fragile J.J. was—and maybe sing him that nursery rhyme a few times. But it would dawn on her that time was short, and the air was being sucked out of that room into a vacuum-sealed unknown dimension. The longer the door was left open, the harder the oxygen was pulled into the walls. If you stayed in there over two or three minutes, you could feel the walls pulling at you, as if they were trying to suck you right through the seams. The scientists had a name for it: the "pharaoh effect." The scientists had a name for everything, like "concrete quicksand" and "gravity howitzers" and "hutomic blast," among others. Oh, those scientists were a real smart bunch, weren't they? Johnny heard Brenda begin to sing, in an oddly-disconnected, wispy voice: "*Go to sleep, little baby, when you wake I'll give you some cake . . .*"

It had happened almost two months ago. J.J. was four years old. Of course things were crazy by then, and Johnny and Brenda had heard about the "pharaoh effect" on the tv news but you never thought such a thing could ever happen in your own house. J.J. had gone to bed, like any other night, and sometime before morning all the air had been sucked out of his room. Just like that. All gone. Air was the room's enemy; the walls hated oxygen, and sucked it all into that unknown dimension before it could collect. They both had been too shocked to bury J.J., and it was Johnny who'd realized that J.J.'s body was rapidly mummifying in the airless heat. So they let the body stay in that room, though they could never bring J.J. out because the corpse would surely fall apart after a few hours of exposure to oxygen.

Johnny felt the air swirling past him, being drawn into J.J.'s room. "Brenda?" he called. "You'd better come on out now."

Brenda's singing died. He heard her sob quietly. The air was beginning to whistle around the crowbar, a dangerous sound. Inside the room, Brenda's hair danced and her clothes were plucked by invisible fingers. A storm of air whirled around her, being drawn into the walls. She was transfixed by the sight of J.J.'s white baby teeth in his brown, wrinkled face: the face of an Egyptian prince. "Brenda!" Johnny's voice was firm now. "Come on!"

She drew the sheet back up to J.J.'s chin; the sheet crackled like a dead leaf. Then she smoothed his dried-out hair and backed towards the door with insane winds battering at her body.

They both had to strain to dislodge the crowbar. As soon as it came loose, Johnny grasped the door's edge to keep it from slamming shut. He held it, his strength in jeopardy as Brenda squeezed through. Then he let the door go. It slammed with a force that shook the house. Along the door's edge was a quick *whoooosh* as it was sealed tight. Then silence.

Brenda stood in the dim light, her shoulders bowed. Johnny lifted the oxygen tank and backpack off her, then took the mask from her face. He checked the oxygen gauge; have to fill it up again pretty soon. He hung the equipment back on its hook. There was a shrill little steampipe whistle of air being drawn through the crack at the bottom of the door, and Johnny pressed a towel into it. The whistle ceased.

Brenda's back straightened. "J.J. says he's fine," she told him. She was smiling again, and her eyes glinted with a false, horrible happiness. "He says he doesn't want to go to Ray's tonight. But he doesn't mind that we go. Not one little bit."

"That's good," Johnny said, and he walked to the front room. When he glanced at his wife, he saw Brenda still standing before the door to the room that ate oxygen. "Want to watch some TV?" he asked her.

"TV. Oh. Yes. Let's watch some TV." She turned away from the door, and came back to him.

Brenda sat down on the den's sofa, and Johnny turned on the Sony. Most of the channels showed static, but a few of them still worked: on them you could see the negative images of old shows like *Hawaiian Eye*, *My Mother The Car*, *Checkmate*, and *Amos Burke Secret Agent*. The networks had gone off the air a month or so ago, and Johnny figured these shows were just bouncing around in space, maybe hurled to Earth out of the unknown dimension. Their eyes were used to the negative images by now. It beat listening to the radio, because on the only station they could get, Beatles songs were played backwards at half speed, over and over again.

Between *Checkmate* and a commercial for Brylcreme Hair Dressing—"A Little Dab'll Do Ya!"—Brenda began to cry. Johnny put his arm around her, and she leaned her head against his shoulder. He smelled J.J. on her: the odour of dry corn husks, burning in the midsummer heat. Except it was almost Christmas time, ho ho ho.

Something passed by, Johnny thought. That's what the scientists had said, almost six months ago. *Something passed by*. That was the headline in the newspapers, and on the cover of every magazine that used to be sold over at Sarrantonio's newsstand on Gresham Street. And what it was that passed by, the scientists didn't know. They took some guesses, though: magnetic storm, black hole, time warp, gas cloud, a comet of some material that kinked the very fabric of physics. A scientist up in Oregon said he thought the universe had just stopped expanding, and was now crushing inward on itself. Somebody else said he believed the cosmos was dying of old age. Galactic cancer. A tumour in the brain of Creation. Cosmic AIDS. Whatever. The fact was that things were not what they'd been six months ago, and nobody was saying it was going to get better. Or that six months from now there'd be an Earth, or a universe where it used to hang.

Something passed by. Three words. A death sentence.

On this asylum planet called Earth, the molecules of matter had warped. Water had a disturbing tendency to explode like nitroglycerine, which had rearranged the intestines of a few hundred thousand people before the scientists figured it out. Gasoline, on the contrary, was now safe to drink, as well as engine oil, furniture polish, hydrochloric acid and rat poison. Concrete melted into pools of quicksand, the clouds rained stones, and . . . well, there were other things too terrible to contemplate, like the day Johnny had been with Marty Chesley and Bo Duggan, finishing off a few bottles at one of the bars on Monteleone Street. Bo had complained of a headache, and the next minute his brains had spewed out of his ears like grey soup.

Something passed by. And because of that, anything could happen.

We made somebody mad, Johnny thought; he watched the negative images of Doug McClure and Sebastian Cabot. We screwed it up, somehow. Walked where we shouldn't have. Done what we didn't need to do. We picked a fruit off a tree we had no business picking, and . . .

God help us, he thought. Brenda made a small sobbing sound.

Sometime later, red-bellied clouds came in from the prairie, their shadows sliding over the straight and empty highways. There was no thunder or lightning, just a slow, thick drizzle. The windows of the James house streamed crimson, and blood ran in the gutters. Pieces of raw flesh and entrails thunked down onto the roofs, fell onto the streets, lay steaming in the heat-scorched yards. A blizzard of flies followed the clouds, and buzzards followed the flies.

TWO

"Read 'em and weep, gents," Gordon said, showing his royal flush. He swept the pot of dimes and quarters towards him, and the other men at the round table moaned and muttered. "Like I say, I'm a lucky dude."

"Too lucky." Howard Carnes slapped his cards down—a measly aces and fours—and reached for the pitcher. He poured himself a glassful of high octane.

"So I was sayin' to Danny," Ray Barnett went on, speaking to the group as he waited for Gordon to shuffle and deal. "What's the use of leavin' town? I mean, it's not like there's gonna be anyplace different, right? Everything's screwed up." He pushed a plug of chewing tobacco into his mouth, and offered the pack to Johnny.

Johnny shook his head. Nick Gleason said, "I heard there's a place in South America that's normal. A place in Brazil. The water's still all right."

"Aw, that's bullshit." Ike McCord picked up his newly dealt cards and examined them, keeping a true poker face on his hard, flinty features. "The whole damn Amazon River blew up. Bastard's still on fire. That's what I heard, before the networks went off. It was on CBS." He rearranged a couple of cards. "Nowhere's any different from here. The whole world's the same."

"You don't know everything!" Nick shot back. A little red had begun to glow in his fat cheeks. "I'll bet there's someplace where things are normal! Maybe at the north pole or somewhere like that!"

"The north pole!" Ray laughed. "Who the hell wants to live at the damned north pole?"

"I could live there," Nick went on. "Me and Terri could. Get us some tents and warm clothes, we'd be all right."

"I don't think Terri would want to wake up with an icicle on her nose," Johnny said, looking at a hand full of nothing.

Gordon laughed. "Yeah! It'd be ol' Nick who'd have an icicle hangin' off somethin', and it wouldn't be his nose!" The other men chortled, but Nick remained silent, his cheeks reddening; he stared fixedly at his cards, which were just as bad as Johnny's.

There was a peal of high, false, forced laughter from the front room, where Brenda sat with Terri Gleason, Jane McCord and her two kids, Rhonda Carnes and their fifteen-year-old daughter, Kathy, who lay on the floor listening to Bon Jovi tapes on her Walkman. Elderly Mrs. McCord, Ike's mother, was needlepointing, her glasses perched on the end of her nose and her wrinkled fingers diligent.

"So Danny says he and Paula want to go west," Ray said. "I'll open for a quarter." He tossed it on to the pot. "Danny says he's never seen San Francisco, so that's where they want to go."

"I wouldn't go west if you paid me." Howard threw a quarter in. "I'd get on a boat and go to an island. Like Tahiti. One of those places where women dance with their stomachs."

"Yeah, I could see Rhonda in a grass skirt! I'll raise you a quarter, gents." Gordon put his money into the pot. "Couldn't you guys see Howard drinkin' out of a damn coconut? Man, he'd make a monkey look like a prince char—"

From the distance came a hollow *boom* that echoed over town and cut Gordon's jaunty voice off. The talking and forced laughter ceased in the front room. Mrs. McCord missed a stitch, and Kathy Carnes sat up and took the Walkman's earphones off.

There was another *boom*, closer this time. The house's floor trembled. The men sat staring desperately at their cards. A third blast, further away. Then silence, in which hearts pounded and Gordon's new Rolex ticked off the seconds.

"It's over," old Mrs. McCord announced. She was back in her rhythm again. "Wasn't even close."

"I wouldn't go west if you paid me," Howard repeated. His voice trembled. "Gimme three cards."

"Three cards it is." Gordon gave everybody what they needed, then said, "One for the dealer." His hands were shaking.

Johnny glanced out the window. Far away, over the rotting cornfields, there was a flash of jagged red. The percussion came within seconds: a muffled, powerful *boom*.

"I'm bumpin' everybody fifty cents," Gordon announced. "Come on, come on! Let's play cards!"

Ike McCord folded. Johnny had nothing, so he folded too. "Turn 'em over!" Gordon said. Howard grinned and showed his kings and jacks. He started to rake in the pot, but Gordon said, "Hold on, Howie," as he turned over his hand and showed his four tens and a deuce. "Sorry, gents. Read 'em and weep." He pulled the coins towards himself.

Howard's face had gone chalky. Another blast echoed through the night. The floor trembled. Howard said, "You're cheatin', you sonofabitch."

Gordon stared at him, his mouth open. Sweat glistened on his face.

"Hold on, now, Howard," Ike said. "You don't want to say things like—"

"You must be helpin' him, damn it!" Howard's voice was louder, more strident, and it stopped the voices of the women. "Hell, it's plain as day he's cheatin'! Ain't nobody's luck can be as good as his!"

"I'm not a cheater." Gordon stood up; his chair fell over backwards. "I don't take that kind of talk from any man."

"Come on, everybody!" Johnny said. "Let's settle down and—"

"I'm not a cheater!" Gordon shouted. "I play 'em honest!" A blast made the walls moan, and a red glow jumped at the window.

"You always win the big pots!" Howard stood up, trembling. "How come you always win the big pots, Gordon?"

Rhonda Carnes, Jane McCord and Brenda were peering into the room, eyes wide and fearful. "Hush up in there!" old Mrs. McCord hollered. "Shut your traps, children!"

"Nobody calls me a cheater, damn you!" Gordon flinched as a blast pounded the earth. He stared at Howard, his fists clenched. "I deal 'em honest and I play 'em honest, and by God I ought to—" He reached out, his hand grasping for Howard's shirt collar.

Before his hand could get there, Gordon Mayfield burst into flame.

"Jesus!" Ray shrieked, leaping back. The table upset, and cards and coins flew through the air. Jane McCord screamed, and so did her husband. Johnny staggered backwards, tripped and fell against the wall. Gordon's flesh was aflame from bald skull to the bottom of his feet, and as his plaid shirt caught fire Gordon thrashed and writhed. Two burning deuces spun from the inside of his shirt, and snapped at Howard's face. Gordon was screaming for help, the flesh running off him as incandescent heat built inside his body. He tore at his skin, trying to put out the fire that would not be extinguished. "Help him!" Brenda shouted. "Somebody help him!" But Gordon staggered back against the wall, scorching it. The ceiling above his head was charred and smoking. His Rolex exploded with a small *pop*. Johnny was on his knees in the protection of the overturned table, and as he raised up he felt Gordon's heat pucker his own face. Gordon was flailing, a mass of yellow flames, and Johnny leapt up and grasped Brenda's hand, pulling her with him towards the front door. "Get out!" he yelled. "Everybody get out!"

Johnny didn't wait for them; he pulled Brenda out the door, and they ran through the night, south on Silva Street. He looked back, saw a few more figures fleeing the house but he couldn't tell who they were. And then there was a white flare that dazzled his eyes and Ray Barnett's house exploded, timbers and roof tiles flying through the sultry air. The shockwave knocked Brenda and Johnny to the pavement. She was screaming, and Johnny clasped his hand over her mouth because he knew that if he started to scream it was all over for him. Fragments of the house rained down around them, along with burning clumps of human flesh. Johnny and Brenda got up and ran, their knees bleeding.

They ran through the centre of town along the straight thoroughfare of Straub Street, past the Spector Theatre and the Skipp Religious Bookstore. Other shouts and screams echoed through the night, and red lightning danced in the cornfields. Johnny had no thought but to get them home, and hope that the earth wouldn't suck them under before they got there.

They fled past the cemetery on McDowell Hill, and there was a crash and *boom* that dropped Johnny and Brenda to their knees again. Red lightning arched overhead, a sickly-sweet smell in the air. When Johnny looked at the cemetery again, he saw there was no longer a hill; the entire rise had been mashed flat, as if by a tremendous crushing fist. And then, three seconds later, broken tombstones and bits of coffins slammed down on the plain where a hill had stood for two hundred years. *Gravity howitzer*, Johnny thought; he hauled Brenda to her feet, and they staggered on across Olson Lane and past the broken remnants of the Baptist church at the intersection of Daniels and Saul Streets.

A brick house on Wright Street was crushed to the ground as they fled past it, slammed into the boiling dust by the invisible power of gravity gone mad. Johnny gripped Brenda's hand and pulled her on, through the deserted streets. Gravity howitzers boomed all across town, from Schow Street on the west to Barker Promenade on the east. The red lightning cracked overhead, snapping through the air like cats-o'-nine-tails. And then Johnny and Brenda staggered on to Strieber Circle, right at the edge of town, where you had a full view of the fields and the stars and kids used to watch, wishfully, for UFOs.

There would be no UFOs tonight, and no deliverance from this Earth. Gravity howitzers smashed into the fields, making the stars shimmer. The ground shook, and in the glare of the red lightning Johnny and Brenda could see the effect of the gravity howitzers, the cornstalks mashed flat to the ground in circles twelve or fifteen feet around. The fist of God, Johnny thought. Another house was smashed to rubble on the street behind them; there was no pattern or reason for the gravity howitzers, but Johnny had seen what was left of Stan Haines after the man was hit by one on a sunny Sunday afternoon. Stan had been a mass of bloody tissue jammed into his crumpled shoes, like a dripping mushroom.

The howitzers marched back and forth across the fields. Two or three more houses were hit, over on the north edge of town. And then, quite abruptly, it was all over. There was the noise of people shouting and dogs barking; the sounds seemed to combine, until you couldn't tell one from the other.

Johnny and Brenda sat on the kerb, gripping hands and trembling. The long night went on.

THREE

The sun turned violet. Even at mid-day, the sun was a purple ball in a white, featureless sky. The air was always hot, but the sun itself no longer seemed warm. The first of a new year passed, and burning winter drifted towards spring-time.

Johnny noticed them in Brenda's hands first. Brown freckles. Age spots, he realized they were. Her skin was changing. It was becoming leathery, and deep wrinkles began to line her face. At twenty-seven years of age, her hair began to go grey.

And sometime later, as he was shaving with gasoline, he noticed his own face: the lines around his eyes were going away. His face was softening. And his clothes: his clothes just didn't fit right anymore. They were getting baggy, his shirts beginning to swallow him up.

Of course Brenda noticed it too. How could she not, though she tried her best to deny it. Her bones ached. Her spine was starting to bow over. Her fingers hurt, and the worst was when she lost control of her hands and dropped J.J. and a piece of him cracked off like brittle clay. One day in March it became clear to her, when she looked in the mirror and saw the wrinkled, age-freckled face of an old woman staring back. And then she looked at Johnny, and saw a nineteen-year-old boy where a thirty-year-old man used to be.

They sat on the porch together, Johnny fidgety and nervous, as young folks are when they're around the grey-haired elderly. Brenda was stooped and silent, staring straight ahead with watery, faded blue eyes.

"We're goin' in different directions," Johnny said, in a voice that was getting higher pitched by the day. "I don't know what happened, or why. But . . . it just did." He reached out, took one of her wrinkled hands. Her bones felt fragile, bird-like. "I love you," he said.

She smiled. "I love you," she answered, in her old woman's quaver.

They sat for a while in the purple glare. And then Johnny went down to the street and pitched stones at the side of Gordon Mayfield's empty house while Brenda nodded and slept.

Something passed by, she thought, in her cage of dreams. She remembered her wedding day, and she oozed a dribble of saliva as she smiled. *Something passed by.* What had it been, and where had it gone?

Johnny made friends with a dog, but Brenda wouldn't let him keep it in the house. Johnny promised he'd clean up after it, and feed it, and all the other stuff you were supposed to do. Brenda said certainly not, that she wouldn't have it shedding all over her furniture. Johnny cried some, but he got over it. He found a baseball and bat in an empty house, and he spent most of his time swatting the ball up and down the street. Brenda tried to take up needlepoint, but her fingers just weren't up to it.

These are the final days, she thought as she sat on the porch and watched his small body as he chased the ball. She kept her Bible in her lap, and read it constantly though her eyes burned and watered. The final days were here at last, and no man could stop the passage of their hours.

The day came when Johnny couldn't crawl into her lap, and it hurt her shoulders to lift him but she wanted him nestled against her. Johnny played with his fingers, and Brenda told him about paradise and the world yet to be. Johnny asked her what kind of toys they had there, and Brenda smiled a toothless grin and stroked his hair.

Something passed by, and Brenda knew what it was: time. Old clocks ticking down. Old planets slowing in their orbits. Old hearts, labouring. The huge machine was winding to a finish now, and who could say that was a bad thing?

She held him in her arms, as she rocked slowly on the front porch. She sang to him, an old, sweet song: "*Go to sleep, little baby, when you wake—*"

She stopped, and squinted at the fields.

A huge wave of iridescent green and violet was undulating across the earth. It came on silently, almost . . . yes, Brenda decided. It came on with a lovely grace. The wave rolled slowly across the fields, and in its wake it left a grey blankness, like the wiping clean of a schoolboy's slate. It would soon reach the town, their street, their house, their front porch. And then she and her beautiful child would know the puzzle's answer.

It came on, with relentless power.

She had time to finish her song. "*. . . I'll give you some cake and you can ride the pretty little poneeee.*"

The wave reached them. It sang of distant shores. The infant in her arms looked up at her, eyes glowing, and the old woman smiled at him and stood up to meet the mystery.

DAN DALY

Self-Portrait Mixed-Media on Pavement, 1988

"Self-Portrait Mixed-Media on Pavement, 1988" is a wry fantasy tale set in a bizarre and fantastical world: the current art scene in New York City, a place capable of being so preposterous (witness self-promotion master Kostobi, et al.) that this story takes only a few steps from plausibility into fantasy.

   Like the best of contemporary magic realism, Daly uses fantasy to illuminate reality, and does it with black humor and style. The story comes from the final issue of *Pulpsmith*, a small literary magazine published in New York.

—T.W.

That the New York art scene is trendy, not to mention vicious, is a given. In this lovely piece of ironic horror, both these aspects are pushed to the limit. I think the story is pretty funny.

—E.D.

Self-Portrait Mixed-Media on Pavement, 1988

DAN DALY

What do you say to someone who wants to jump out your window? Jeannette resisted her first instinct to show him the door, deciding instead to treat their meeting as she would any other artist interview. "Have a drink, then," she gestured toward her makeshift bar. "Tell me a little about yourself and your project."

His name was Martin. Just Martin. He had bluffed his way past the new receptionist by convincing her he had an appointment with Armando, the curator. And with Armando in Milan, Jeannette had him now. Martin wanted to hurl himself out her fifth floor window into a six-foot-square frame painted on the sidewalk. He wanted to donate his self-portrait to the gallery.

Framed by the window, Martin blocked Jeannette's usual view—the reflection of her building in the glass one across 57th Street.

"It will be my most important work," he was saying.

"Better be. It will also be your last." He didn't smile, just bit at the cuticles on his fingers. Maybe he's for real, she thought, stranger things had happened in New York. Usually below 14th Street, though.

Martin set a vodka-rocks down on Jeannette's desk. "Well, as you know, ours is a violent society. Violence is essential in our lives today. I plan to carry that to the extreme, to fuse with the violence and anger within myself. I see it as a self-portrait of what I have become. What we've all become, really."

Jeannette sipped at her drink. "And what made you come to us Mr., uh, Martin?"

"Just Martin." He slowly shifted his weight. "Simple. Yours is the highest gallery in the city."

First she thought he meant it was a compliment, then realized he meant it was the highest altitude in the city. Was he serious?

"I don't know," she said. "I'll need a little time to think this over."

He looked down at the sidewalk. "I don't have much time."

Armando would be in Europe for another month. She could use that time to determine if Martin was just trying to make a point, or crazy enough to go through with this. "I'll call you," she said. "Who represents you?"

"No one represents me." He said, stuffing his hands into his back pockets. "Think it over, Miss Olsen. Opportunity knocks."

After he left, she punched out Willy's extension. "Willy! Are we the highest gallery in the city?" Against her better judgment, she explained the situation to him.

"Is he crazy?" Willy asked. "Are you crazy? Tell him Armando doesn't handle performance art."

"See what you can find out on him, Willy. As soon as possible, please." Willy knew everything about everybody in the art world, or at least where it could be found.

Jeannette called Peter, her ex, at *Artmag*. His secretary hesitated briefly before putting Jeannette through.

"Jeannette?" Peter's voice sounded a little brusque.

She explained about Martin, and asked if he had anything on him in his files. "Let's meet for lunch tomorrow," she said, listening to him tap away at his PC. "But keep it under your hat till then."

"Wait one second! You never return my calls. I don't hear from you for six months. Now I'm supposed to drop everything to research some guy who wants to decorate your doorstep?"

"I know, Hon." Jeannette knew he would help her when he didn't say no right away, and pushed aside any guilt for calling him out of the blue. Peter was the only one in town who knew more dirt then Willy. "This is important, Pete. You know I wouldn't call otherwise."

"Yeah, yeah. OK, I'll see what I can dig up from the morgue."

"I wish you wouldn't put it that way."

"Meet me at my place after work Thursday. You kept a key, right?"

Peter didn't seem to think it was strange that she had gone along with Martin so far. But, covering all the weird trends at *Artmag*, nothing fazed him anymore.

One thing was certain: Martin had upset her, and she wouldn't be upset if she didn't believe he would go through with it. If not her window, then someone else's.

"Armando's on two!" Charlene's voice jumped out at her from the phone. She picked up the receiver, and the crackle of long distance was broken by Armando trying to project his voice five thousand miles.

"Zhu-net-ta!" Armando's accent, smooth as his silk suits, used to make her knees weak. Now it disgusted her. Sleeping with him was probably the biggest mistake she had made in ten years.

"Armando!" He was still her boss, though. "How's Europe?"

"Lonely. I miss you and I'm coming home early."

Her throat went dry. "Oh? When?"

"Next week. I'm flying into Newark. Shall I take the limo directly to your place?"

"Oh, no, don't do that." She couldn't have him coming to her place. "Tell you what, you just relax, and I'll see you bright and early the next morning."

"I see." He paused and the line crackled again. "Until next week then. Oh, and Jeannette? Willy left an urgent message with the desk. See what it's all about and take care of it, please. Thank you."

Time to start looking for a new job, she thought, hanging up. She tried to imagine life without the gallery. After six years, why even consider tossing it all for some Performance Nut? Then again, if Martin did jump, she'd be holding one of the hottest properties in town. She'd start her own gallery.

Willy! That little shit had already tried to warn Armando about the acquisition. She began dialing his extension, and thought better of it.

Jeannette carried her Chinese take-out dinner to the little park along the East River. There, she could see the Triboro Bridge uptown, and downtown, the 59th Street Bridge. The strings of lights on the two spans resembled competing pearl necklaces. Jeannette was one of those people who loved bridges; she didn't know why. She would probably write a sixty-page catalogue on the inevitable statements within Martin's work, but, at gunpoint, she wouldn't be able to explain why she found those bridges so beautiful.

Thursday afternoon was dark and cool. Layers of clouds banded the sky with varying shades of gray, in the Late Romantic style. Jeannette had to look closely to see where the gray buildings ended and the gray sky began. She took a cab down to Spring Street and rode the service elevator up to Peter's loft. True to form, he was late.

Everything was as she remembered, except for the dozen paintings lined up against the long back wall.

They were lined up chronologically, "MG" and dates scrawled in the lower left corner of each. At first, she noticed the intensity of the brushstrokes. As she moved along the wall, the later paintings seemed to be details of the earlier ones. In the corner of the loft she stopped at the last one. A dark figure huddled in an oddly shaped doorway. "MG 83." Five years ago. Anything since then, she wondered?

Jeannette was still admiring the last painting, and thinking of a solo show for Martin, when Peter's keys rattled at the lock.

"Hello in there!" he called. "Anybody home?"

"In here."

There was a bit more gray in his beard, but he looked as handsome as the day she'd met him at *Artmag*. He kissed her cheek. "I see you've found the treasure."

"They're wonderful! But why do they stop at 1983? And where did you get them? Are there others?"

"Just relax one second." Peter loosened his tie and wandered into the kitchen. "I found out Harry Kantor handles him. Or used to, anyway. Harry was a little suspicious, but he was only too happy to sell me all of them. Not much of a market for Mr. Martin's work, I guess."

"You bought all of them?"

Peter nodded. "I have a hunch they're going to appreciate soon."

"What happened to this guy? He paints beautifully! Next thing you know, he's leaping off buildings."

"How much do you know about his 'events,' anyway?" Peter ticked them off on his fingers. "Let's see, he chained himself to a police station. Tried to take a gun made of flowers onto an airplane. I love it."

"Some group shows, early eighties." Jeannette read from Willy's notes. "Pulled out of his first solo show a week before the opening. Then the performance art." She looked up. "I still don't get it. The man can paint."

Peter shrugged. "Harry told me he stopped painting in '83. 'Paint is deader than the novel,' I think was the quote. Needless to say, Harry did not approve of this career move."

"Peter, I think you're enjoying this."

"Immensely." He brought her a soda, in a glass, but drank his out of a coffee cup, one of his most annoying habits. "I hear you and Armando have been seeing a lot of each other."

"Where you'd hear that? Willy?"

"Not directly. But I wouldn't be surprised if he started the rumors."

"Yeah, well. Let's just stick to the paintings, OK? How much did you pay for these?"

"Harry gave me a volume discount. Who knows what they'll be worth once gravity gets through with our Mr. Martin?"

Her stomach tightened. "You think he's for real, then?"

"Jeannette, this is a guy who went into a biker bar in drag just to *prove* they'd beat him up. And while I may not wear Armando's twelve-hundred-dollar suits, I'm not stupid."

"Stop it."

"One more thing. You realize, of course, *Artmag* gets the exclusive on this."

She turned toward him.

"Hey, business is business."

When she hadn't heard from Martin in a few days, Jeannette considered calling his old agent, Harry Kantor. She was alternating between relief and disappointment, thinking Martin had changed his mind.

Did she want to be known as the curator who sent her artists to their deaths? She shivered. But did she want anyone else to get this piece? It would be one of most talked-about works of the 20th Century, the start of a new era. She didn't have a choice any longer. He had come to her; she would just wait and see what happened.

On the other hand, you never knew with these guys. Maybe the 'event' was meeting with her in the first place. She might never see him again.

*   *   *

"Jeannette, Mr. Martin to see you."

"Just Martin," she heard in the background.

"He says he has an appointment, but I don't see it in the—"

"That's OK, Charlene, send him in."

He appeared a bit thinner, though she'd only seen him a few days earlier. "Have you lost weight?"

"Eight pounds. It has to do with terminal velocity."

Terminal velocity, right. He *was* crazy. "So you're determined," she asked, "to go through with this?"

"Of course."

"My crack research staff informs me we're not the highest gallery in New York. Cameron's, in Soho, is on the eighth floor." She was testing him, would he break out in a smile and reveal the whole thing was a hoax?

"Too high." His expression did not change. "Besides, I want 57th Street. To be honest, I want you."

"Me?" A flash of determination in his blue eyes startled her. He really did have this planned out. She had tensed every time he walked near the window. But if he had truly thought this through, he wouldn't do anything without warning. "What do *I* have to do with this?"

"Everything," He pulled some papers from a portfolio he had brought. "Didn't you say, 'Today's artists must kick and scream and bite and turn the current art scene on its post-modern ear?' That, 'The artist must erase the line between his life and his art. He must become the art'?"

Jesus. She had written that when she was still at *Artmag*. They thrived on stuff like that. She felt violated. He had no right to drag up things she had written back then.

" 'The future of art is Inter-Active,' " he continued, " 'the juxtaposition of the art and the artist. Civilization is falling down around our ears. We can no longer hide behind arbitrary barriers such as canvas, brass and marble if we are to remain a civilized people.' "

"Stop it! I was referring to media! I didn't say artists should jump out windows."

"In a way you did. To me, at least."

He was twisting everything she had ever said or felt into nonsense. Looking down at her desk, she pressed her fingers to her temples. "But you paint so beautifully."

"You've seen my paintings?" He glared at her. "I haven't used paint in years."

"I know, I know, 'paint is deader than the novel.' "

His mouth tightened into a thin line. So, he didn't like having his words used against him. "No matter," he said.

Jeannette needed him out of there. "I think you should go now," she said.

"I thought you were committed to the sacrifice of creativity?" Martin headed for the door, then stopped. "Look, all I need from you is a window and a sidewalk. And an assurance that my piece will be preserved. I don't want to be hosed off by some maintenance man." The dull brass doorknob twisted in his delicate hand.

Jeannette called his bluff. "Go ahead, then. Jump. Make your point."

"Great!" He smiled for the first time. "Excellent. See you tomorrow."

"Tomorrow!" What? Was he serious? She couldn't possibly get the men and materials she needed in time.

"The winds are low tomorrow. It's perfect."

"Right," she said. No time to back down now. "I can have you dug up and moved inside within minutes." Jeannette ran the logistics through her mind, chilled by the realization of how well managing a gallery had prepared her for such a project.

"OK, then," he said. "Three o'clock?"

"Better make it four. I'll have to meet with our lawyer."

The office window was open just a crack. A crack she imagined sliding through. In her imagination, she didn't fall. Instead, she floated out over 57th Street like smoke, spiraling up toward the open blue sky.

Later that afternoon she dialed her home number to check messages on her answering machine. The machine clicked on. Two salesmen, then the gravelly voice of Harry Kantor.

"Yeah, Jeannette. Harry Kantor here. What the fuck's going on with Martin Gibbons? I don't hear from the schmuck for five years, then—bam!—everyone in town wants a piece of him. What gives? I'll tell you, I ever get my hands on the little sonofabitch, I'll—"

The machine cut off, preventing her from knowing what Harry Kantor had planned for Martin. Not to worry, Harry, not to worry.

The phone still in her hand, she tapped out Peter's number. Did she still have some clothes at his place?

"Pete?"

"What's wrong, Hon?" he asked.

"It's tomorrow." She paused. "Mind if I stay at the loft tonight?"

"Tomorrow, huh?" He whistled softly into the phone. "Sure, sure. Of course."

She waited until the next afternoon to explain the situation to Willy, leaving him no time to call Armando. "I'm not sure I want to be a part of this," Willy said. "Have you even consulted with Armando, Jeannette?"

"No. And I know he's not taking your calls, either."

Willy looked pale, paler even than Martin, who would be doing the jumping.

Ralph Murphy, the gallery's chief counsel, arrived fifteen minutes early. He shook his head without greeting, the sign he had something legally pertinent to announce. "I think it essential," he began, "that anyone here tomorrow in relation to this acquisition, be here, officially, on unrelated business." He cleared his throat to punctuate his sentences, as if there were legal nuggets caught in his chest. "The gallery's official position in this matter must be one of professional ambivalence. No official assistance may be rendered Mr. Martin in his perpetration of an illegal act." He spoke as if he were reading prepared remarks, though he had taken nothing out of his briefcase.

"That's why you're here, Ralph," Jeannette said, hoping to convince everyone it was just another business meeting. "To cover our ass." She slapped the conference table for effect. "This guy's a goner. If not my window, someone else's. I don't see the sin in it. But I do see the sin in letting this work slip through our fingers." This was beginning to sound logical to her.

Ralph frowned. "Miss Olsen, I am the gallery's legal counsel. I do not purport to discourse on sin. I merely render legal advice." He began pulling papers from his briefcase. "At the very least we will have to obtain a signed release from damages from Mr. Martin."

Willy leaned forward. "Ralph, I think—"

But Ralph waved him off. "I will defer to Miss Olsen for the duration of Armando's absence." He nodded at Willy, who must have called Ralph and told him he couldn't get through to Armando in Europe. "Once Armando returns, he may find that Miss Olsen has gained a certain notoriety and position of her own." He lowered his voice to Jeannette. "Do keep that in mind if you find yourself in need of counsel, Miss Olsen."

"Does he have to sign all those?" Jeannette asked when she saw the armload of documents.

"Most. They release the trustees, the gallery as a whole, its employees—and advisors—from legal responsibility. The gallery's responsibility lies in ensuring the safety of its patrons and personnel, as well as passersby. It stops short of an artist trespassing on gallery premises with the intent to commit a crime. One thing though," he pulled a single sheet from his jacket pocket. "Mr. Martin must leave a suicide note."

They all nodded.

"I have taken the liberty," Ralph waved the paper at them, "of drawing up a document for him to sign."

"What does it say?" Jeannette tried to imagine a suicide note written by an attorney.

" 'Good-bye cruel world,' basically. It will suit our purposes."

It was then that Ralph took Jeannette aside and launched into a discussion on behalf of Dr. and Mrs. Byrne, his biggest clients and the gallery's biggest benefactors. "In consulting with my clients last night, they expressed an interest in purchasing the piece from the gallery. He whispered, "What's it worth?"

It was the first time that Jeannette thought of the work in terms of money, rather than career. How much was it worth? A lot more than she would admit to Ralph Murphy. "Fifty thousand, maybe. For the novelty factor," she added.

"However," Ralph interrupted, "should major collectors such as the Byrnes express an interest . . ."

Jeannette shrugged. "The sky's the limit."

"Of course, they couldn't touch it for several years. These documents allow for the donation of the piece to the gallery—or whatever employment you may be holding once Armando returns—provided events occur in the manner we have anticipated. If he should land on someone, for instance, my clients will not be in a position to handle the piece. All bets are off."

Oh God, she thought, *Still Life with Pedestrian.*

*   *   *

At four-fifteen Jeannette began to worry about Martin, hoping he hadn't lost his nerve, or come to his senses. It was too late to be sensible now. She paced nervously to the window and saw him kneeling on the sidewalk. Pedestrians stepped around his rather elaborate frame without breaking stride.

"He's here," she announced. Ralph gave her the stack of papers. Willy left to organize the maintenance men who would remove the concrete panels from the sidewalk.

"Miss Olsen?" Ralph said.

She gripped the doorknob, half-in, half-out of the office. "Yes?"

"What if he does hit someone? That is unacceptable, you know."

"All bets are off," she echoed.

Martin signed the papers without asking what they were. She didn't offer.

Jeannette returned from the street. "He promises not to hit anyone," she said. "It would ruin the piece." Turning to Willy, "I asked the maintenance men to cordon off the sidewalk."

"Since when does it take eight men with jackhammers and a cement mixer to repaint a doorway?" Willy asked.

"When it might be splattered with blood."

Finally, at four forty-five, Martin entered. Get moving, she thought, the nine-to-fivers wil be out pretty soon.

Ralph stepped away from the window. "All set on our end, Mr. Martin."

Jeannette felt she had to say something. "Good luck."

"Fuck you," he said. Famous last words. She would have to remember those.

Gently, Martin opened the window, then put a hand to either side. He rocked back and forth before leaping out like a paratrooper.

Martin's exit created a wind current within the office which carried some loose papers off Jeannette's desk and sent them fluttering toward the open window. Not knowing how important they might be, she stepped up to grab them before they flew out, being careful not to step too close to the window. She wouldn't allow herself to be drawn too close, lest she be carried out in his wake, only to slam down on top of him as the pedestrians stepped impatiently around them.

MICHAEL DE LARRABEITI
The Plane Tree and the Fountain

Michael de Larrabeiti is best known to fantasy readers as the author of the three *Borrible* books—offbeat fantasies about feral, magical children in the backstreets of London. He is also a writer of mystery, western and suspense novels. De Larrabeiti has been a cameraman for documentary films; a travel guide in France, Spain, and Morocco; and a photographer on the Marco Polo expedition—traveling four months overland to Afghanistan and India on a motorcycle. De Larrabeiti currently lives in Oxfordshire with his wife and three daughters.

"The Plane Tree and the Fountain" comes from a remarkable book: de Larrabeiti's *Provençal Tales*. In 1959, while living in the French countryside, de Larrabeiti accompanied a group of Provençal shepherds on their annual *transhumance*, a trek of about two hundred kilometers to bring three thousand sheep from the coast to their summer pasture in the Basses Alps. The shepherds, like modern day troubadours, were full of stories about the country they passed through—not only contemporary stories of day-to-day life but also the old tales and legends of the region. "An on-going, everlasting discourse that, I suppose, had been kept up for generations . . . spoken in low murmurs all the way down the long road." De Larrabeiti recounts his journey, and the tales he learned along the way, in a straight-forward prose that is both wry and romantic, as seen in the following story.

—T.W.

The Plane Tree and the Fountain

MICHAEL DE LARRABEITI

"What the populace would like to see," said the steward, "is a fountain and a plane tree in the centre of the town square. Then, so they argue, they would not be obliged to fetch water from the stream below the hillside and, in addition the ladies of Bargemon, and the gentlemen of course, would have somewhere agreeable to congregate in the cool of the evening. Well, my lord, I have given this matter a great deal of thought but have come to the conclusion that it would be too costly . . . therefore, sire, I have delayed my decision."

The Lord of Bargemon, the Baron de Barjaude, looked from his window and sighed. It was not worth his while answering the steward for the man was used to ordering the estates on his own authority. He would go on prattling, quite unperturbed, through the whole of that morning's business; it made no difference whether his master intervened or not.

The Baron sighed again. He would have to abandon this dreary servant and his droning voice. Instead of standing there trying not to yawn he would command his groom to bring his best horse from the stable and take himself off to the hillsides. He would go into the wild forest and wander at will along the deserted tracks, hiding from the sun under the green shade of the green leaves, absenting himself for a month or more.

The castle which the Baron desired to quit so eagerly was in fact a delight to look upon. It stood halfway up a range of wooded hills and stared southwards over the curved roof-tiles of a town where scores of houses clambered carelessly onto each other's backs. It was an enchanting castle, built for pleasure rather than conflict, and it was furnished with fine carpets and soft couches. Without realizing it the courtiers of Bargemon had been born into one of the most easeful places on earth. Minstrels played to them: troubadours told stories of distant lands and the ladies of the court listened and embroidered those same stories into tapestries. In Bargemon everyone was happy. Everyone, that was, save the Lord of Bargemon himself.

As the long years had passed over him the Baron had found himself increasingly possessed by a powerful melancholy. At first it had puzzled him; his peasants worked hard and provided all that he needed; his courtiers sought enjoyment and found it readily and Bargemon flourished almost without supervision. Indeed his lands were so well-regulated it appeared that all the Baron had to do to secure the continuation of his own and his subjects' happiness was to play his part and do nothing. It was only gradually therefore that he came to understand how it was this very feeling of indolence, winding into his heart like a worm, that made him sad.

To counter this sadness he had thought, once or twice, of marriage but the idea of sharing his life with another frightened him. Besides he had left it too late and was too set in his ways. At fifty years of age, as he now was, what woman young enough to bear children would take him as a husband? His neck was wrinkled and his back was stooped. In any event the problem of the succession did not worry him. There was the son of a cousin somewhere beyond Fayence who would be only too pleased to step into his shoes when the time came. "No," said the Baron to himself on the frequent occasions when he pondered the subject, "there is nothing to be done."

So it happened that, despairing of ever being as content in age as he had been in youth, the Baron took to riding alone in the savage country towards Brovès, roaming even as far as la Bastide and idling along by the banks of the Artuby. He came to admire this country with its abrupt hillsides and fierce sunsets. He respected too the rugged people he found there. He did not know them or they him but he was accepted without affectation and always given shelter for the night when he needed it. Somehow these people, their solidity and simplicity, seemed to help the Baron retain his hold on life; sometimes he even thought that it was only their existence that reassured him and kept him alive.

In the beginning these absences of the Baron had worried his courtiers and several of them had gone for advice to the astrologer who lived in Bargemon, near the main square, in a dwelling that was half house and half cave. According to common rumour this man, who was dark-skinned, had come originally from the East. It was also said that he was ageless, knew all things and was master of great magic. The learned scoffed at this foolishness and pointed out that no one had ever seen the old man do anything more amazing than mend an arm or set a leg; all the rest was idle gossip.

So much then was in doubt but it was known for certain that the astrologer was very short-tempered and disliked being disturbed at his books. "You are idiots!" he cried at those courtiers who had come to seek his opinion. "You lead a perfect life in an earthly paradise and yet you cannot let things be. As long as the Baron is content let him wander as he will . . . perhaps he finds your company as tiresome as I do. Now leave me to my solitude and my studies or I shall turn you all into snakes."

With this answer the courtiers were obliged to be content and they left the astrologer's house with great speed, trampling on each others' heels in their eagerness, and after that one attempt to understand the Baron's melancholy they made no more. It seemed, on reflection, wiser to leave things as they were.

In this way did life go by at Bargemon and on the day that the steward had talked to his lord about the plane tree and the fountain the Baron left his subjects, mounted his horse and rode northwards, not pausing until he had reached the banks of the River Artuby. There he allowed his mount to drink and, as the animal quenched its thirst, the Baron noticed a young man lying in the flowered grass on the far side of the water.

There was something about the young man that caught the interest of the Baron and he studied him closely. Obviously a troubadour he wore a loose tunic embroidered all over with blooms as bright as those he lay among, and so colourful were they, and so cunningly fashioned, that it was impossible at first glance to tell where the tunic ended and the meadow began. By his side was a lute and a large goatskin bag containing his few possessions and his songs and poems. With his eyes closed this wanderer lay flat on his back, protected from the heat of the day by the shade of the low branches above him. His legs were crossed at the ankle and both arms were flung out from the body as far as they would go. Round his shoulders curled his long black hair and his breathing was light and even. He was a man who looked perfectly at peace with himself and in total harmony with the spinning planet at his back.

The Baron dismounted and, the Artuby being little more than a stream at this point, he crossed it and stared down into the sleeping troubadour's face. Such was the beauty and contentment of what he saw that, although he kept his voice low, he could not refrain from speaking to himself aloud. "Ah," he said, "this man sleeps as innocently as a child. Here indeed is a happy mortal. He has no cares and he goes where he will, blowing where the wind listeth. There is no melancholy for him."

A voice answered the Baron immediately and he started in surprise, realizing in the same second that the troubadour was speaking although he hadn't moved and nor had he bothered to open his eyes.

"What I do," he said, "any man can do. It may be certain that not everyone on earth has the talent of the troubadour, but anyone can learn to love the poems of others and learn to sing a song well enough. That will cast melancholy aside. What do you need in life but sufficient food and a rough roof for the winter?"

"As for that," answered the Baron, squatting down on his haunches, "I have more than I need. There are servants to do my bidding, peasants to grow my crops and courtiers to serve and amuse me. Even so, I am not happy as you are happy. Happiness is a gift and it is a gift I have not been given."

Here at last the troubadour opened his eyes and sat up, his face flushed with the anger of argument. "Since when," he demanded, "has happiness been a gift? Do you think it comes to you out of the sky, like rain? Have I not searched for years? Did I not follow other troubadours and listen to their every word? Did I not seek out remarkable men and sit at their feet? Happiness! I tell you, stranger, a life is like a work of art and must be fashioned as a poem is fashioned—throw away all that is dross and keep only that which you need. For all your fine clothes I can see that you have wasted your life on the wrong things and you know nothing. Well, know this, fool, you will never turn a bend in the road and find happiness waiting for you at the end of the journey as if it were a city . . . happiness is the road itself and you must walk it."

The Baron sprang to his feet, enraged at being admonished in such a forthright manner by a mere troubadour. "Hold your tongue," he cried. "Why, I am the Baron de Barjaude, Lord of Bargemon, and I could have you whipped for this."

To the Baron's astonishment the troubadour laughed, long and loud, rolling over in the grass, helpless with mirth. "In this wilderness you are lord of nothing," he replied as soon as he had recovered himself, "and if your life compared to mine in its wisdom and pleasure you would know it, and you would not be threatening me with talk of whippings. I suspect, my Lord of Bargemon, that in this life there has been no love for you and that even your courtiers only serve you out of custom. You are their master and you keep them in idleness —that is the only tie between you."

The Baron bit his lip and remained silent. He knew that the troubadour had spoken no more than the truth. Though much younger than the Baron his experience of life was wider and deeper, and he did indeed seem to carry wisdom and pleasure about him in equal proportions. The Baron swallowed. He meant to be angry but could not. There was something in the troubadour's words that eased the melancholy around the Baron's heart. He smiled. "Perhaps what you say is correct," he said, "but it is too late for me to learn your wisdom now."

The troubadour rose to his feet and brushed the grass from his embroidered jerkin. "Wisdom has no date," he said, and then: "Only a mile or so from here, on the road to Jabron, there lies a woodcutter's shanty. I have half a loaf in my sack, you no doubt have something better in your saddle-bag, and I know the generous woodcutter will give us a cup of wine or two and the loan of his shed to sleep in. Let us spend the night there and if you wish it you may journey a little of my way with me and we will talk together until the path divides. What do you say, you Lord of Bargemon?"

The Baron laughed at the troubadour's impertinence as he had not laughed for many a year. "I agree," he said, "wholeheartedly, but tell me your name for you know mine."

The troubadour bent for his lute and struck a chord on it, afterwards making a reverence like a courtier. "My name," he said, "is Mariu de Montepezet, and there will be a time when my songs are known by all those who speak or hear the golden words of Provençal."

The Baron was transformed by the troubadour's company and the two men spent more than a month wandering the roads together.

The nobleman's melancholy disappeared so completely that he could hardly remember it. He slept in the meanest huts and ate the roughest fare, even selling his horse and saddle to keep himself in funds. His clothes became worn and dusty and he laughed at it. His hair and his beard grew tangled and he combed them with his fingers. Never had the Baron felt so fulfilled or so attached to life. He learnt the songs and poems of the troubadours just as quickly as Mariu would teach them and he and his companion talked endlessly as they journeyed. At night they sang ballads to shepherds for food and told stories to peasants for wine.

For the Baron such a way of life was a revelation and he never wanted to leave it, but it could not be. One day Mariu halted on the banks of a great river and, staring across it, he laid his hand gently on the Baron's shoulder and spoke, his voice trembling with affection.

"Lord of Bargemon, my friend," he said, "this is where our roads part. This is the Durance, beyond it is Manosque and now I must go on alone."

The sadness of this announcement struck the Baron like a blow but he had learnt enough about the calling to realize that a troubadour was obliged to follow his own path through life; it was in the nature of things. In spite of this the Baron allowed his feelings to show and a tear moistened his eye. "It is like death to leave you, Mariu," he said, "but I am grateful. You taught me much and cured me of my grieving."

Mariu nodded and both men rested on a rock and shared a last meal. "I am content for you," said the troubadour, "but it was not really I who taught you . . . you learnt to be yourself, that is all. For years you did not know what you wanted and were disgusted by what you had. From the chasm that lay between rose your melancholy."

"Can I be happy and wise now, if I am myself?"

"Perhaps," said Mariu, "but be on your guard. You are still the Lord of Bargemon. To lead the simple life is not simple. Every day you will have to open your eyes and ask why you are alive, and every day you must also ask, "If my life is a poem am I writing it well?" Think of your time on earth as a wine which is already leaking out of the pitcher drop by drop. It is a wine beyond price. Do not spill it carelessly and do not pour it out before fools."

Here the two men finished their meal and put away what remained of their provisions, then they stood and embraced in farewell.

"Adieu, my friend," said Mariu. "Remember that the lion and the goat must live side by side. You must keep the lion tranquil while at the same time you graze and milk the goat. Once more, adieu—we shall never meet again," and so the troubadour turned from the Baron, waded into the shallow river and then struck out for the distant shore. Not once did he look back.

On his arrival at Bargemon the Baron went directly to his castle and, without changing his clothes, washing his body or combing his beard, he commanded that all his subjects—courtiers, men-at-arms and servants—should attend him without delay in the great hall. There, in straightforward terms, he explained his long absence and told his people that from that moment on he was determined to lead a simpler life, one that was closer to nature and one that he hoped would lead him, in his last years, along the philosopher's road of self-perfection.

On the other hand, insisted the Baron, his decision would alter nothing in respect of his subjects. Those who lived in the castle, or elsewhere for that matter, should continue exactly as before. Anyone who wanted might use the

Baron's private apartments. His horses were at everyone's disposal, as were the contents of his cellars and the produce of the valley. "Share all there is amongst you," he cried.

As for the Baron himself he would not be far away but he made a point of ordering his vassals, under pain of his utmost displeasure, not to interrupt him in his new life. There was an old and abandoned farmhouse in the hills towards Montferrat and there, accompanied only by the servant who had been his companion and friend since childhood, he would live.

The people of Bargemon who, to be truthful, had hardly missed their lord during his travels, watched with equanimity as he and his servant left the castle. Over recent years they had become quite used to the Baron's moods and changing whims. This, they considered, was just another example, a little more extreme but that was all. To their minds it was obvious that he was going mad; tramping the countryside with common troubadours; sleeping in ditches and eating with shepherds, now he was going to live as one. Well, it did not matter, nothing would change. From the very day of the Baron's inheritance they had always directed their own affairs. The Lord of Bargemon had thought to govern them, especially at the beginning, but that had never been the case and certainly not since the onset of his melancholy. So let him go into the hills towards Montferrat, and let him stay there till he died.

In this manner were things arranged and for many months the life of Bargemon hardly seemed any different. The peasants toiled in the dust of the fields and the nobles took their dues. The sun shone, the wind bent the trees and the birds sang, but all was not well—jealousy and hatred began to grow in people's hearts. Great quarrels arose amongst the courtiers. First one and then another moved into the Baron's apartments, for to occupy them and issue orders became the desire of every petty noble in the castle. They squabbled over the horses and they fought over the wines. From day to day the situation worsened, blows were struck and swords were drawn. No one was content and everyone took sides; cabals were formed until at last one of the most powerful of all the courtiers died under mysterious circumstances—suffocation said some, poison said others. Whatever the truth of the matter life in Bargemon had become not only unpleasant but dangerous also, and that was not the end of it.

The peasants, seeing that the courtiers fought amongst themselves, began to fail in their duties. They neglected to pay their taxes and they refused to bring their produce to the castle, keeping everything for themselves and selling what they did not need in the markets, hiding their money away in secret places.

Alarmed, the courtiers tried to forget their differences, banding together to threaten the peasants with the soldiery but the threat was an empty one. Most of the Baron's soldiers had wandered away to serve other lords and those that had not were peasants themselves and had returned to their families and their farms. It was not long before the courtiers grew ill-fed and unkempt and the peasants mocked them, nor would they bow when they went by or raise their hats. The castle itself fell into disrepair. Piles of dust rose in the corners of every room. Rats nested in the rafters and the tapestries fell from the walls. Bargemon was dying and it seemed that nothing could be done. Fortunately not everyone still living in the castle surrendered to despair. The man who had once been the Baron's steward gathered together a few like-minded courtiers and, after a long and violent discussion it was decided that the Lord of Bargemon had, by default, relinquished all his rights to sovereignty. In consequence a messenger was sent to the Baron's cousin at Fayence, telling him what had happened and begging him to present himself at the castle without delay so that he might claim his inheritance and become the rightful lord of all.

The cousin received these tidings with delight. For many years, though he was still a young man, he had been waiting to seize Bargemon and its domain. Now his waiting was over. Gathering about him his friends and sycophants, and as many armed men as he could pay for, he set out across country and within a very short time was riding into the courtyard of the castle. Here he was welcomed with great warmth and, dismounting, he quickly inspected every room and chamber of his new residence.

He was very much dismayed by what he saw and, with oaths and blows, he set the servants to scrubbing the castle clean and re-hanging the tapestries, and as for the courtiers, he told them to prepare for a great ball that very evening.

"A ball," cried the steward, hardly able to believe his ears. "But there is no food in the castle, no wine."

The new Lord of Bargemon sneered. "Let that be my care," he said. "While you make ready I shall take my soldiers to visit the peasants . . . just to show them that times have changed." And with a laugh he strode to the courtyard and leapt into his saddle.

That day the peasants did indeed learn that the times had changed for the soldiers burst into their farmhouses and took everything they wanted. Fruit, meat and wines were loaded into stolen wagons until the axles almost snapped under the weight, and anyone who dared dissent was tied to a wheel and whipped until the blood ran down into the dust. "This is no more than you deserve," said their lord, "for months you have not paid what you owe . . . now the time has come to make it good."

The ball was a great success and the courtiers were overwhelmed by the alteration in their fortunes. The castle shone in its cleanliness and there was more food and wine to be had than ever before. Everyone agreed that inviting the cousin to be their lord was the best thing they could have done. They smiled and danced and raised their goblets, praising each other all night long and not one of them felt weary until many many hours after the sun had climbed into the sky.

The peasants woke to a very different day. For them the world had changed also but not one jot for the better. In the briefest of moments all the provisions they had laid by and all their wealth had been stolen from them. And, as if to mock their predicament, down from the castle floated sweet music and the shouting of the revellers as they drank and danced. There was worse to come. Over the next few months, to make sure that the peasants had truly learnt their lesson, the new lord sent his soldiers everywhere through the estates, giving them full license to behave like the troops of a conquering army and to beat senseless anyone who offered resistance.

The peasants and the farmers had no way of defending themselves against this onslaught. They were ignorant people and had little experience in the ways of the world, but, in spite of this, some of them began to meet in secret, coming together at night so they could discuss their troubles and attempt to find a way out of them. It was not an easy undertaking and, finally, after several meetings and many hours of talking, they could think of nothing better than to go to the astrologer and ask him for the benefit of his wisdom and erudition.

The astrologer was as angry with the peasants as he had once been with the courtiers, perhaps even angrier. "I might expect such foolishness from flunkeys and parasites," he said, "but from good peasant stock I at least look for some degree of mother-wit. Isn't that what living close to nature is supposed to teach a man . . . isn't such a life meant to lead directly to common sense? Had you but kept your so-called masters happy in their castle, supplied with as much food and wine as they needed, you could have lived your lives as you wished and would not be suffering today from the outrages of this upstart lord and his soldiers. I do not even pity you in your stupidity . . . you wallow in it. I can think of nothing for you to do save one thing only . . . persuade your rightful lord to return to his duty. Now begone, all of you. If you bother me again I shall turn you all into the oxen you already resemble." And with this threat the astrologer drove the peasants from his door with a heavy stick.

It did not take long for the peasants to implement the advice they had received and within a day or two a few of their number set off to present themselves before the Baron. These men found that their one-time lord had established himself, and his servant, in a sturdy, stone-built farmhouse. It was a beautiful place and well sheltered from the bite of the mistral: there was a deep well in the hillside that never ran dry; shade from the sun in summer and a huge stock of sawn wood for the fire in winter. On every side, and in amongst the trees, a small flock of sheep and goats grazed and their bells sounded now and then, drowsily, as they moved. Keeping watch over the animals was a girl, a shepherdess who went barefoot across the grass and wore a simple dress.

The Baron was simply dressed also and his subjects found him sitting in a comfortable chair on the shady side of the house, a book in his hands. He looked well, both in body and spirit and, although jealous of his contentment and seclusion, he received the peasants well enough for he had always been kind to his bondsmen. His solitary wanderings, as well as the time he had spent in the hills with the troubadour, had only served to strengthen what in him was a natural inclination.

His pleasure was short-lived. On hearing what had happened at the castle during his absence, especially in regard to his cousin's behaviour, he flew into a mighty rage. He rose from his chair and threw down his book. "Why is it," he exclaimed, "that men cannot live together? It is such a simple thing. You have done wrong in not sharing your produce with those who live in the castle, but they have done worse by ill-treating those whom they should protect. As for this kinsman of mine, this heir, he overreaches himself and he shall find that he has roused a sleeping lion. My courtiers should have had wisdom enough to govern themselves—now they deserve punishment. You are simpler and will receive my help. What is more I am angry and touched in my pride . . . leave me to ponder my revenge . . . I shall stand by you."

The peasants were delighted by the Baron's response to their petition. They thanked him and bowed and went on their way. As soon as he was alone the Baron dressed in the best clothes that remained to him, girded on his sword, mounted his horse and set out for the castle. Once there he rode to the door of the great hall, swung from his saddle and strode directly through the throng of courtiers and soldiers until he came to his cousin who sat, lounging, in a huge chair which stood raised a step or two on a wide dais like a throne. Silence fell and every face turned towards the centre. The Baron, impressive in his anger, raised an arm and pointed at his cousin.

"Usurper," he cried. "You have come here without my command and against my wish, you have taken my castle and my lands like a robber in the night. You oppress my subjects and steal their goods, you wrong their women and whip those who dare deny you. Never have the people of Bargemon suffered so and they will suffer so no longer. Get you gone and wait your appointed time, you imposter. Crawl away to your hovel and take your men with you." And here the Baron drew his sword.

Immediately after this speech there came another silence, extremely short, broken as it was by the cousin's sneering laughter. After a moment's hesitation the courtiers laughed too and the soldiers and the servants followed suit. They realized that, brave though the Baron was, there was nothing he could do. The cousin clicked his fingers above his head and his soldiers advanced; lowering their pikes, they ringed the Baron with sharp steel. One word of command and he would have been slain.

"You buffoon," said the cousin. "What foolishness brings you here? You abandoned your inheritance and you deserted your courtiers . . . there has already been bloodshed. Had it not been for me your peasants would have starved the inhabitants of this castle to death, they would have taken our lands and our wealth. Who could live in such a world? Not these people, not I, not even your peasants. You are an old man now, so go back to your garden and your goats, live in Arcadia and live in peace. Go sing songs with your shepherdess and let her stroke your grey hair." And the cousin laughed again, uncontrollably this time, and the whole assembly laughed with him.

The Baron was struck dumb. Not for a moment had he imagined that he might be treated in this manner. Rather would he have died fighting, but even that escape was not allowed him. Instead the soldiers moved forward, striking the sword from his hand, and they beat him about the shoulders and hustled him from the great hall, out to the very gates of the castle where the servants heaped dust and kitchen refuse on his head. And when they had done, and still laughing, they bound him backwards on his horse and led him down into the town. There they left him for the townsfolk to see but the townsfolk turned away from the man who had once been their master and the peasants, who had been waiting to discover the outcome of the Baron's encounter with his cousin, turned away also, realizing that they, in the end, would have to accept their lot and make the best of what life brought them.

Only the shepherdess, who loved the Baron and had followed him to the castle, did not flinch but went to him and cut his bonds and wiped his face. "Be wise," she said as she helped him from his saddle. "Do not be angry. Remember the happiness we have together. Come, let us return to our home. Forget your people, you can do nothing for them. Come."

But a great anger had now arisen in the Baron's heart and although he knew the truth of what his shepherdess had said his pride was too strong and he pushed her away.

"I will have revenge," he cried, "and I will not rest until I see this cousin's blood running into the castle drains and every courtier who laughed at me today will kneel in the mire and kiss my shoe."

"But how," questioned the shepherdess, "will you accomplish this? You have no soldiers, you have no riches."

"I will go to the Count of Provence," said the Baron, his eyes flashing madly, as if anger had robbed him of reason. "He will give me soldiers, and then there's my astrologer," added the Baron suddenly. "I have kept him in idleness for years, as did my father before me, and his debt to my house is great. Never have I asked him the smallest service. He will know what I should do. He can read the future and he has the magic. Let him turn my cousin into a pig to eat the swill that lies below the castle walls . . ."

By now the Baron, who had been walking this way and that in his excitement, found himself at the astrologer's door and, without pausing to reflect, he knocked and strode into the house like one who owned it. The astrologer was at his books and as irritable as always.

"Well Baron," he said, hardly looking up, "here you are in a sad muddle of your own making, and, by the stars, you smell very like the pig you desire that I would turn your cousin into."

"You heard . . . ?"

"Humph," snorted the astrologer. "It would be a sorry state of affairs if I had studied magic all these years without being able to do something occasionally."

"That's it exactly," said the Baron. "I know your powers, I know you can read the future . . . tell me what I must do . . . and tell me what will be best for my subjects also."

The astrologer folded his arms, hiding his hands in the wide sleeves of his gown. "Do as your shepherdess tells you," he said. "Return to your garden, your flocks and your books. Your peasants will be no worse with your cousin than they were with you . . . not in the long term they won't."

"If you do not help me," retorted the Baron, "I shall go to the Count of Provence and he will give me a great army. I promise you there will be bloodshed and men will die, though I also promise you that there shall be a peace and contentment afterwards that my peasants have never dreamt of. Bargemon shall be blessed."

"Humph," said the astrologer again. "You seem to be looking into a future that bears no resemblance to the one I see. I tell you, Baron, I have seen many a war and though I once thought them amusing I do not now want one on my doorstep with both sides disturbing my solitude."

"This is ridiculous," cried the Baron, "with your gifts you can do anything, even alter the course of events if you wish. You could help me save the peasants."

The astrologer shook his head. "It is a bad idea to interfere with the natural order."

"Natural order," shouted the Baron, shaking with rage. "There is no such thing as a natural order when you may change it at will. Listen to me. When my parents gave you this house to live in did you not promise that you would assist their child in every way? I am that child. Help me in this war. Help me to punish my courtiers and kill my cousin."

Again the astrologer shook his head. "Your courtiers are too ignorant to change and your peasants do not understand what you offer them. I can tell you that even if you have your war it will all come back to the same thing in the end, so you might as well save yourself, and me, the trouble. Go home, back to your life of contemplation."

"You charlatan," hissed the Baron between his clenched teeth. "If you have the gift of second sight, if you possess the magic then why did you not warn me that all this was going to happen? Why did you let me suffer the melancholy? Why allow me to fall under the spell of the troubadour? Why bring me to this fall and why set my cousin up to make a mock of me, covering me with offal from the kitchen. Why did you not help me?" And the Baron sobbed from his heart and hid his face in his hands.

The astrologer sighed and closed the book he held in his hand. "My son," he said, his voice strained, "how you would curse me if I made magic all the time and did not allow you to direct your life. You would hate me even more than you hate me now." Here the astrologer rose from his seat and a bitter smile flitted across his lips. "I too would like to live the tranquil life but I know I never shall. Very well, Baron, this once, and this once only, I shall go against my own laws and aid you."

The Baron uncovered his face and stared at the astrologer. "You are truly as kind as my parents told me," he said, "and I swear to you that as soon as I have righted these terrible wrongs I shall desire nothing more than to live as the troubadour taught me to live, never wasting my energies in vain pursuits but simply to live and to love."

The astrologer half-turned his head and studied the features of the shepherdess. He raised an eyebrow. "That is a wisdom given to few," he said. "Now come with me and bring the girl." And the astrologer smiled his bitter smile once more and, with his robes flowing behind him, he led the Baron and the shepherdess out of the house and into the open square that stood at the centre of the town. There he halted.

"See Baron," he said, "how calm and quiet everything is. Your courtiers have accepted your cousin, as have the townsfolk and the peasants too. Bargemon is as near perfection as your subjects deserve. It is pointless to struggle further. I know."

"Help me as you promised," said the Baron, "and restore me to my rightful place."

"I will," said the astrologer and, closing his eyes, he began to chant in a strange and incomprehensible language, first raising his hands in the air and then laying them on the Baron's head.

To begin with the Baron smiled, as if he were convinced that he was about to see the realization of all his dreams. He was perhaps, but not in a way he expected. Slowly his body grew taller and taller, his feet spread and sprouted into the ground and became great gnarled roots and his arms rose gracefully above his head and multiplied and became long branches, heavy with wide green leaves.

A terrible moan broke from the Baron's lips. "No," he cried, "this is not what I meant, I beg you, release me."

The astrologer ignored this entreaty and moved his hands through the air again. More branches sprang from the Baron's body and his skin turned mottled and hard, like bark, thickening until it was bark and the Baron had disappeared altogether, and in his place stood a lofty plane tree giving a cool shade where before there had been none.

The astrologer was pleased with his work and although several white faces looked out from neighbouring windows no one came to challenge him. There was silence and only a light breeze stirred in the leaves of the tree until, all at once, there came a loud scream and the astrologer turned, surprised. He had forgotten the shepherdess and she, distracted at seeing the man she loved transformed like this, shrieked again and fell to her knees, sobbing like a wild thing.

The astrologer wrinkled his nose in distaste at this outburst of emotion. "Come woman," he said. "I thought you wiser than that. He has found the tranquility he said he sought for, and his people will be as happy as any alive. Take your own advice and return to your flocks and be content, as he is content."

The shepherdess lifted her stained and reddened face and, between sobs, answered the astrologer. "Love is not philosophy," she said, "have you not learnt that, you who know everything? I wanted to spend my life with him and would have followed him to war if that had been the only way."

The astrologer stamped the ground in irritation. "How I forget things," he said, "even that love is foolish. Would you follow the Baron now?"

Through her tears the shepherdess smiled. "I would," she said, "I would."

The astrologer shook his head in disbelief but at the same time he spoke once more in the strange tongue and moved his hands over the girl's head. Now it was her body that altered and grew taller, and her flesh solidified and becme stone and in the same second she was transformed into a fluted pillar of marble and from it poured clear water to form a fountain at her feet, a fountain that was bound in by a solid coping, high enough to sit upon.

"It is done," said the astrologer when his task was complete, "there may you weep for your love, little shepherdess," and, throwing his gown across his shoulder, the astrologer made his way back to his house and the comfort of his study. With a sigh of relief he settled into his chair and opened his book. "And now," he said, "perhaps we shall all be happy."

Outside on the square there was, at first, no movement, but gradually the more adventurous of the inhabitants of Bargemon emerged from their houses and, their faces blank with wonder, they came to the tree and the fountain and touched them with their hands, unwilling as yet to believe the evidence of their own senses. They looked up also and saw where the branches of the tree swooped down as if to embrace the fountain, and they were amazed and frightened.

And to this day in Bargemon, just as the shepherdess had wept for the Baron in life, so from time to time the waters of the fountain overflow and moisten the roots of the plane tree as if in love and pity. There is also a second tree which stands nearby—it gives a smaller shade than the first—and some say this is the Baron's servant who loved his master and grew so lonely without him that he too went to the astrologer, and the astrologer, angrier than ever at being disturbed now that he had convinced himself at last that all disturbances were at an end, changed the servant into a tree even before the poor wretch could give a reason for his visit.

Luckily the transformation was exactly what the servant had desired and if, as it was said, the astrologer had the gift of second sight then he was only anticipating what he had no doubt foreseen. But of course we should beware of stories that tell of astrologers who know all and see all; such tales are suspect, often being nothing more than the light-hearted inventions of a vagabond minstrel singing for his supper. There is certainly no record in Bargemon itself of such happenings and if, by chance, you should stop someone in the street there and ask for the truth of the matter, they will look at you in a strange way and tell you what they believe—that the trees of Bargemon are merely trees and the fountain just a fountain—and then they will hurry away, not in the least eager to prolong such a conversation with a stranger.

TANITH LEE

White as Sin, Now

Tanith Lee's fantasy work often treads the border between horror and fantasy and—like Angela Carter—she is a master of adult fairy tales that are sensual, evocative, and often deeply disturbing—like the following story.

Lee is a British writer of fantasy, science fiction, and children's novels and stories, with over forty books to her credit. She has also written for radio and television, and is a talented artist. She has won both the World Fantasy Award and the British Fantasy Award.

The Forests of the Night, from which "White as Sin, Now" is drawn, is a collection of twenty superb stories published in an attractive edition by British publisher Unwin Hyman. Along with Lee's previous collection *Red as Blood,* it is must reading for lovers of dark fantasy and fairy tales.

"Most of my obsessions have crowded into it," Lee writes of the following story, "including queens and dwarves, wolves and virgins and priests, deep snow, flowery meadows, ruins. The omnipresent forest appears again, also, in person, and in two distinct guises. A last excursion then, into the wood. . . ."

—T.W.

For my part, "White as Sin, Now," is an elegant, lush, and surreal tapestry of the fairy-tale landscape in all its dark sensual glory.

—E.D.

White as Sin, Now

TANITH LEE

THE DWARF (THE RED QUEEN)

The dwarf Heracty balances on the rim of a frozen fountain, drawing pictures with his nails in the ice. His handsome face is set into the frame of a great leonine head applicable to a muscular man six feet tall. Heracty's form is that of an elf. But he has, too, an elf's eyes, long, aslant, and crystal-green.

Engaged on the scales of a mermaid, Heracty pauses, listening. His hearing is so acute, his ears sometimes hear noises that do not exist. He must decide now whether this sound physically belongs to the world, is a phantom, or a memory. Presently Heracty becomes sure that two narrow feet in shoes are descending a flight of cold stones.

He turns a little, looking sideways from his slanting eyes.

Held high in an archway over the stair are towers resembling a crown of thorns, on a half-disc of twilight. From that point, the Upper Palace drops like a cliff into a riverbed.

And from those heights she has again come down.

It is always at this hour, just as the sun goes away. In the ghostly 'tweentime, when all pale things pulse and stare . . . the white beasts of the fountain, the roses of snow across the gardens.

When she comes out suddenly from the arch at the bottom of the stair, she also is glimmering as if luminous.

She only looks straight ahead, beyond the fountain and the winter lawn, to a second arch, a second falling staircase. She does not see Heracty, has never seen him there, as she passes by like a sleepwalker.

The wide eyes of the Queen are so astute, Heracty knows, she sometimes glimpses things that do not exist.

As before, he slides from the fountain's rim, and silently follows her.

They then descend twenty flights of steps one after another, and the nineteen terraces between.

THE DWARF'S FIRST INTERVIEW WITH HIS GRANDMOTHER

On a bitter morning in spring, mother and son went to visit the grandmother in her marble house.

The woman was hardly more than thirty-five years of age, but with old, terrible, unhuman, alligator eyes.

To begin with she did not upbraid Heracty's mother, but only questioned her on domestic matters. The boy sat motionless and dumb on the rugs. He was very much aware of himself and of his mother's tense and trembling awareness of him. But his grandmother, by a slight flexing of her colossal will, had shut him out, so that he was not in the chamber at all. Until finally:

"It's a curse that struck you," announced the grandmother to her daughter. "I don't begin to guess who you wronged, to incur it. If I had my way, such things would be smothered as soon as their nature was evident." Every syllable referred, of course, to Heracty.

The mother whispered, as she had done on many occasions, "His father was normal. Straight, well-made—"

"Yes, yes," said the grandmother, "and between you, you managed this. A monster." Now she bent her awful glance on the boy. "I have come to a decision," said Heracty's grandmother. His mother waited in abjection, and he in fear. "The Prince collects freaks. He has got into his possession, so I hear, a two-headed dog, a unicorn, a gulon. And besides, six of *this* kind, half-men—though a pair are reckoned to be females, so I'm told."

"You mean my son is to go up into the court of the Prince?" asked Heracty's mother, astonished.

"No. Into the Prince's menagerie."

THE HUNTER (THE YOUNG GIRL)

While the vampire lies sleeping, its soul, or what passes for it, roams the night, dreaming it is a wolf.

The season is winter, therefore snow covers the forests, hills and plains, and far away the mountains blackly glow upon a blacker sky where all the stars are out. Between the black and the white, the black wolf runs.

Presently there is a small stone house on the dark, with one lit pane.

The wolf runs among the fir trees. He raises himself up, something now between man and creature. His eyes of colourless mercury meet the image of a poor room, where a girl sits sewing by the hearth.

The wolf-soul does not see a girl. What it sees is a stream of living holy light far brighter than the dying wood on the fire, and an icon burning in it, as if in a cathedral window. There is a white hand containing red blood, plying the silver needle, a bending throat like the stem of a goblet of glass.

She puts her hair back from her cheek, and in that moment hears a noise outside, which is like the murmur of the trees, internalised, the rhythm of the sea in a shell.

Rising, the girl leaves her task. She has been stitching an altar-cloth for the church in the valley. But her eyes and hands, her shoulders, her very brain, are tired now. It is a relief for her to walk to the window of the room, to look out.

There is no moon. The forest stands against the door, and the wall of the dark. She beholds her own face reflected on the pane, transparent as a spirit. The strange noise comes again.

The girl lifts the latch of the door, and going out on the snow which so far is unmarked, prints it with the signature of her own bare feet. Forgotten, the door is left open behind her.

She thinks she sees for an instant a tall male figure against the fir trees, but it has the head of a wolf. Then there is also a pale-faced man, and two eyes of iron.

She moves forward, leaving her last message on the snow.

And abruptly the darkness engulfs her. She vanishes. Without a cry, she is gone for ever.

THE RED QUEEN (THE LOST CHILD)

Innocin, the Queen, has become conscious only gradually that something follows her. At first, she believes it to be a cat, then, later, a child. But the presence is subtly more imminent. Crossing through the deep shadows of pillared gullies, the Lower Palace, she realises that what is mysteriously on her track is nothing less—or more—than one of her stepson's pet dwarfs.

She wonders if the Prince himself has sent this spy. But surmise fades. Such matters have no interest.

In the shadows, the blood-red mantle of the Queen, limned with white ermine, her hair like red-bronze surrounding an ivory face, are elements of a female.

She enters a long corridor with a low ceiling, intricately carved. For all the hundreds of times she has traversed this thoroughfare, Innocin has never properly regarded the carving. She does not know what it represents although she has seen it over and over.

There was a day when she looked into her mirror. The light cut sharply as broken porcelain against one side of her face. She saw that she had lost her youth. It was then that she thought of a young girl, dressed in purest palest white, the sin of her husband, the dead King. Somewhere within the enormous labyrinth of the Palace, between the topmost towers and the deepest basements, the girl must have secreted herself. The afternoon had passed, and the sun gone down. But that sunset the Queen became, like a star, certain of her course.

She descended then the stairways to the terrace with the lawn and the great fountain. It had been autumn still, and sallow leaves lay adrift on the water of the basin.

Nothing disturbed the preoccupation of Innocin. She had crossed the terrace of the lawn and progressed down twenty further flights. She searched night after night, among decayed architecture, and neglected rooms, for the unmistakable, beautiful young girl.

So far, she has not found her.

Sometimes there is a glimpse or a clue—the white flicker of a skirt between two columns, a sigh that circles an upper gallery where no one seems to be and, on ascending, where no one is. Or a rose moulded from snow, poised in a hollow vase of ice.

THE HUNTER'S PREY (THE DARK PRIEST)

As a small child she had played about the cottage, a darling of the entire family. The truth was, the child did not belong to them at all. At midnight once, going out to make water, the man of the house had found an infant huddled in his doorway. It was late in summer, the nights not yet cold, but the child shivered and moaned. Conversely, although she could form noises, she had never apparently been taught human language. She could tell them nothing.

The woman had lost her baby some months before. This seemed the returns of heaven. Her husband was a woodcutter, quite prosperous, having three men in his employ, besides two strapping sons.

The household took in the girl-child, and gave her a village name.

Her origins she forgot instantly, except sometimes in nervous dreams. Then the woman would comfort her. "Here is your mother," the woman would confide, "you're safe, my baby." The man and the two boys brought her dolls and baubles from the town. Her childhood was happy and carefree.

However, about nine years old, by some arcane law, she had become a woman, and all was changed. She had work to do at which first she laboured diligently. But, as there was never respite when she grew bored or exhausted, her duties soon turned to drudgery. It did not occur to any of them, perhaps she had been born for something else.

While years sprang in flowers on the turf beyond the house, or fell in sculpted cones from the branches of the fir trees, the woodcutter's daughter also unremembered she had ever been a happy, carefree child. She was the maidservant of her father and two brothers, and her mother's nurse, for the woman waxed sickly. The evening before the girl's fourteenth birthday—that is, the night-day of her discovery in the door of the stone house—her stepmother died.

"She shan't marry now," said neighbours, down the valley in the village street. "She must tend her own. She's got men enough to care for."

A new priest had taken up his office at the church not long before. He was tall and slender, with a broad low brow, and his hair—untonsured, for this was a wild place—was black as the wing of a crow.

The young girl, seeing him stand above the coffin of her stepmother's corpse, dreamed a waking dream which that night was translated. She believed she was a nun, gowned and coifed in snowy white. She served a dim altar where a tall crucifix gleamed, a man's pale body hammered on to it.

She would go to church every holy day, and often visited her stepmother's grave. She never approached the priest directly, but when he requested of his flock various attentions to the church, the young girl, though burdened by duties to home and kindred, gave her service.

The other women free to do so were mostly old, or else fat, sullen widows. The young girl felt herself shine strangely among them, a clear lily in withered reeds.

That was a terrible winter for wolves. They preyed on the sheepfolds and the byres, and several children were taken, or so it was supposed. One lean black wolf was seen frequently, but though the men scoured the forests round about, and laid snares, this animal was never trapped or killed.

THE DARK PRIEST (THE WOLFSHEAD)

The priest elevates the Host, an offering and invitation to God. It is a moment of supreme sanctity, of supreme savagery even. Less substantially, he senses the consciousness of those persons who fill up the building, trailing from his lifted hands. A vast light, without tint or radiance, enspheres the church. And he is the arrow-head of the flight, fired out toward the celestial target of the omnipresent, awful, eternal, invisible, and actual, centre of all things. A ray of the sinking sun, unearthly and lemon-green, pierces through the window, penetrates the body of the priest—And at that instant the door of the church crashes wide.

The priest's awareness is smashed in pieces.

He turns, slowly lowering the sacred element. His black eyes give to him a scene of the sudden and the inappropriate. Whatever it may be proved to be— the onslaught of a local calamity, death, plague, or war, this interruption is to him only an unforgivable sacrilege.

A body of men stands in the nave, staring from side to side, in their hands some makeshift weapons. They are the inhabitants of outlying parts. They seldom enter the village save to get their ration of beer. Now it is not beer they want. The woodcutter's second son thrusts forward. He bellows insanely into the church: "Out! Out! Demon! Out!" And swings up his axe.

"The Devil's hiding in your flock, shepherd," says another man roughly, to the priest. "It went by night and murdered his sister."

The congregation starts to its feet, becomes a beast of many limbs and eyes and voices. The church is no longer a special place. The priest does not remonstrate. He sets down the precious Host, and feels keenly how it goes back into dust. The last of the vivid sunset is perishing round the feet of trampling peasants. There is nothing to be done, or said.

Arrogantly the priest watches from his altar as the mob, not finding after all the one suspected, blunders forth on to the greenly embered snow, bolts and plunges up an incline, collides with darkness at the entry of a hovel near the village cess-pit. Great blows shake the flimsy hut. Even from the church-door the priest hears them. He is very cold.

Shortly, a half-wit man who subsists in the hovel, the tender of the midden, is brought out on to the snow. The villagers search him, looking for marks of the Devil, tufts of feral hair, claws, certain lupine deformities of jaw, teeth and forehead. Presumably they uncover them all. While this goes on, the half-wit smiles courteously, and moves himself this way and that, in order to be helpful.

Next, still smiling and assisting them, he goes up the hill with the men, and the brother of the young girl—fifteen years of age, who, the night before, was found lying among the fir trees by her father's cottage, her throat torn open like a winter rose.

The crowd vanishes over the hill. Presently a scream sounds, shrill and sheer from the forest's edge above.

The priest does not make any gesture, except that, going back into the empty church, now closed already by shadow, he shuts and bars God's door.

HERACTY'S SECOND INTERVIEW WITH HIS GRANDMOTHER

Having reached the age of sixteen Heracty, the Prince's seventh dwarf, decided once again to visit his grandmother. This time he imagined he could do so on his own terms.

He dressed in a suit of clothes of wan green satin, a mulberry-red cloak, and wore in his ear a large pearl. He rode a most charming dappled pony, another of the Prince's gifts, and took with him for escort his little page not yet eight years old. Over the saddle of the pony, too, had been placed a couple of embroidered bags containing delicacies.

The gardens of the enormous eccentric Palace were equally vast and varied. Downhill lay the grandmother's marble box, a house given her decades before by an admirer (Heracty's unintentional grandfather), when she frequented the court. To get there first Heracty, the pony and page, must navigate an ornamental river. Then came a number of high floral steppes. Next they entered a mock forest, densely planted with pine, fir, rhododendron and cedar trees. Even at noon it was dusk in this forest, and here and there clockwork animals prowled and howled. At the turn of the track, a grey wolf pounced out on them, and the small page had hysterics.

"Hush," said Heracty, who had been in the forest before. And he threw the clockwork wolf a peach from the bags, which it greedily and realistically ate, trotting off afterwards to bury the stone.

Beyond the forest lay an acre or two of modest meadows, and here the grandmother had her abode. As they got on to the path, the dwarf could see, across the shoulder of the landscape, the blurred valleys below where his mother had lived. But by this time she was dead.

The grandmother of Heracty was now not much over forty. Her complexion was nearly flawless as a girl's, her eyes had advanced from alligator to dragon.

"Well," she said, looking her grandson over, satin, pearl, pony, page, and bags.

Heracty had the page distribute his presents. The grandmother fingered some of them and set them aside. The food and flasks of fine wine caused her short fits of harsh laughter.

"What a splendid fellow!" she jeered.

Heracty sat down, although, in her chairs, his feet hung in limbo far above the rugs.

"You did me a good turn, Granny," said the dwarf, "when you persuaded my mamma to send me into the Prince's service."

"My idea was merely to get you out of the way and out of my sight."

"Yet here I am again. What a sad nuisance."

"Your tongue," she said, "has grown longer, if nothing else of you has. Or is it," she amended, "true? That which is said of the loins of your sort."

The dwarf blushed, could not help it. But he had been well seasoned at the court, and he replied, "Those few among the Prince's eldest servants who remember you always remark you had less manners than a pig. Naturally, I defend you, and only confess the sin of lying on holy days."

The grandmother took one candied nut from the gifts and bit it in two. She then dropped both bites in the fireplace.

"What do you want, monster?"

"Tell me," said Heracty immediately, "about Innocin, the Red Queen."

"When you hear so many remarks, how is it you never heard that?"

Heracty sat and waited. He made his face quite blank and his elf's body immobile. At last, the grandmother shifted.

"She was a slut in the kitchen, or something of that kind. He saw her, raised her, bedded her, became besotted, so married her. She's now Queen, but she was his second wife. The first died. When the King died himself, and his lechery with him, the Prince took power. It remains to be seen if he will ever get himself properly recognised, become King like his father. But for her, she's gone mad. So she wanders about, looking for a vanished daughter she had by the King."

"A lost child?" said Heracty. He considered. "Did it die at birth? Was the matter hidden?"

"How should I tell you?" asked the grandmother, "What do I know?"

"Granny," said the dwarf, "in the basket of sugar-plums—I understand you're fond of them—is one sweet containing a potent and unpleasing purgative. Without harming you, it will cause you extreme discomfort."

"Nasty little beast," said his grandmother, bright-eyed. "I'll eat none of them."

"What a waste, and your favourites, too. The particular plum," he added, "is easy to identify, once I describe it."

"Perhaps you are lying again. And perhaps any way, you'd indicate the wrong plum."

"Perhaps. Or not."

They sat then in silence some minutes, the dwarf a small elegant statue, she a lizard in a girl's skin.

Finally she said this:

"In the position I had at court, I learned that the Queen was to be thought of as barren. But it was not possibly the case. One infant, a girl, had certainly been born, but a portent made the Queen afraid of it, or her own shame at her low beginnings and bad blood. She sent it away into the forests, to be brought up among ignorant strangers."

The dwarf sighed. "Her lost child is," he murmured, "her own youth."

Granny threw all the sugar-plums in the fire.

THE MENAGERIE (THE COURT)

Indeed, they live close to the Prince's menagerie. On calm nights, when the music from the Upper Palace is not too lively, they may hear the gulon catawaul and screech at the full moon, or the unicorn clicketing up and down on its gemmed hoofs, though the dog of two heads is generally reticent.

The dwarfs had been given their own town at the foot of the Palace. Each house is a doll's mansion, equipped with furnishings all the proper size, and with intelligent child servants always replaced in their tenth year. Rose gardens and knot gardens and gardens of topiary and water gardens, and so forth, make wondrous chessboard squares around the mansions. Everything is enclosed by a stout wall, whose gates are guarded at night by specially bred miniature mastiffs, who, introduced to the dwarfs as puppies, threaten to maul anyone who disturbs them. Only the prince himself, and his selected courtiers, can invade the sanctum whenever desired. But that is not often.

Heracty quickly became accustomed to the dwarfs' estate. He grasped how they were patronised, yet simultaneously, how could he dislike anything that so suited, and that rendered him so comfortable.

The four fellow male dwarfs were comely and alert, two with high boyish voices which, in one case, flowed out into a clear alto instrument for song, seemingly much prized by the Prince. The two dwarfesses were remarkable for their charms and accomplishments, one blonde, one dusky. The latter had wed her dwarf suitor—the wedding had been a fête at the Palace; the Prince gave the bride away—and it was said the union produced a child. But as the baby evinced every sign of growing up into an ordinary woman, it too was taken off, as a potential cause of future grief to the parents.

Heracty, sent among the dwarf community when it was established, expanding it into an uneven number: seven, though never made unwelcome, stayed an outsider. He became instead a student of men, the other species. When summoned to delight the Prince by his presence, handsomeness and wit, Heracty on his side narrowly observed everyone about him. He definitely supposed that he came of another race, human, but unadulterated. What he saw of fully formed human behavior confirmed this opinion.

It was at a banquet that, initially, Heracty beheld the Red Queen, the dead King's widow.

She entered late, and the Prince rose graciously, and with ill-concealed boredom, to greet her. Seating herself, she stared about as if not knowing where she was, thinking it a dream. Occasionally she would take up some morsel from her plate, or begin to lift her goblet—but sustenance never reached her mouth, for obviously she forgot its purpose half-way. She wore a gown the shade of dying autumn, not a single jewel.

The Prince, demanding antics constantly that evening from Heracty, interrupted the dwarf's study a hundred times. Courteous and wise, Heracty never once displayed his annoyance.

The Queen left the feast before midnight. Heracty was not permitted to leave until the men lay drunken in their chairs, or over the tables.

When dawn breaks, Heracty frequently goes into the menagerie. Adjacent to the dwarfs' enclosure, it is simple of access.

More often than not the unicorn falls asleep at dawn, its muzzle laid on its flank, the curving horn, more swarthy than its hide, like the sinking crescent of the moon. The two-headed dog sits sadly, one head deep in thought and the other slumbering with the tongue hanging out.

But the gulon stalks its prettified pen, disdaining the luxury of its kennel. A fox-cat, it looks now most feline, but next second mostly canine, having strong features of both types. It is the colour of Queen Innocin's banquet gown, and her hair, and Heracty has been told that combings of its long damascined fur are sometimes woven to trim her mantles.

The eyes of the gulon are rather like Heracty's own, but lack any trace either of courtly politeness or civilisation.

The gulon has been known to savage its keepers, one of whom lost an arm as the result. It is dissatisfied with its life and does not appreciate its uniqueness.

Heracty is wondering if Innocin the Queen has ever looked on the gulon.

When he witnessed her descent through the palace, sensed the wild, inane search, it fitted her like a costly necklace. It is a perfection. She could do no other thing.

He values it in her.

THE LOST CHILD (THE PALACE)

The girl Idrel wakes like an early crocus.

She lifts her head, and all about her lies the snow. Snow is her coverlet in a four-poster bed of ice. Slight wonder she dreamed she lay in a coffin, but the coffin was of glass. . . .

The girl gets to her feet. She does not feel the cold, only a deep desire to lie down again and sleep again—and this she believes is to be resisted. She is garbed only in a shift, and not, she guesses, her own. It covers her decently from neck to foot and even drags a little behind her as she walks. But for a shield against the winter it is useless. However, she is under protection, feels it must be so. All the ways of the forest look alike to her. She consents to walk forward, in the direction she faced on waking, rising.

A stealthy umbra permeates the woods, it might be any time of day, though not of night. The snow is packed very hard and does not take an impression of the bare soles of Idrel. She expects wild animals lair among the firs and cedars, and perhaps will run out at her. Twice she catches a glimpse of some sinuous thing, the colour itself of the forest dusk—but this does not approach.

Sometimes a branch or bough cracks under the snow's weight, startling, like a whiplash. There are no other sounds but for the glacial ringing of silence itself.

How long the girl walks, in distance or time, she is unsure. But suddenly, the trees have thinned, and there ahead is a thick sky of grey nacre, and the terraces of a snow-hill cut into it.

Ghostly winds run on the hill, and blow the snow like white steam along the ground. Idrel climbs with three winds taking up her hair and throwing it to each other, and then down, clutching at her ankles, slapping her cheeks, and her eyes fill with slow tears. Then, at the summit, she discovers an odd road made all of solid ice.

Idrel steps on to the road of ice. Dimly, a reflection tapers from under her feet, and also there are objects caught there, mostly abstractions, though she begins to fancy statuary or frozen people are trapped in the glass coffin of it.

In a brief while, she perceives herself to have come in, almost unawares in the sameness of the snow, to a colossal ruin, maybe of a city. Tiles and parts of walls, doorways, roof-beams, arches, the skeletons of windows, have stolen round her, and high above a briary of knife-like cruel towers hangs abandoned in heaven.

The sight of this abnormal edifice, or what there is left of it, causes Idrel, lost and alone, to question for the first time where she has come from, and who she is, and why she has travelled to such a place.

After an appreciable time, she mutters aloud, "I shall remember, soon."

And then she goes on, walking through the eroded architecture, down into dark avenues where pillars have collapsed and become static rollers of snow, and up stairways innumerable to her. And on her journey she passes only once something which touches her poignantly. This is an enormous flower, portionally of stone but mostly of opaque, bluish ice. The shape of the flower is a rose, but this the lost girl fails to ascertain. Perhaps she never saw a rose before, in whatever spot she has come from.

At last—the sky is stained with a more foreboding twilight—the girl Idrel reaches a wide platform against a door that seems to be of iron. Icicles drip down it, with edges that are like razors. She is afraid to put her hand to the door.

She sits before it. Night now must find her here.

The desire to sleep returns, and there in the leaden sunset she shuts her eyes and knows no more.

THE KING (THE QUEEN'S FIRST SIN)

It was not true, she had not been a slut of the kitchen, not even a scullery maid, Innocin—but neither had she been called, then, Innocin.

On a day in late spring, returning from a hunt, the King had passed across the rough meadows below the Palace. A few good houses stood about, with formal small gardens, and orchards. But on the meadowland the first poppies were blooming, and a girl was there, plucking them like the strings of the day-harp, gathering armfuls of fire. Her hair was like a soft fire, also, but not much in evidence, scraped back from her yellow-white face and confined in a long rat's tail of braid.

She was dressed like a servant and doubtless that was what she was.

The King, having glanced at her—attention caught by the blot of red among the redness of the poppies—rode on. Half a mile further, he reined in. He called someone, his steward, or some aristocratic companion. "I spied a damsel in that last field. Have her got."

This King had whims, now and then, and his court was not unaccustomed to them. An envoy was sent—but the girl had vanished from the meadow, perhaps frightened away by her vision of loud horsemen and the carcasses of deer.

He went back behind the great iron doors of his house, the King. He brooded. He was used to getting that which he chose to want. A dark man, big and bear-like, he began to think of delicate things, waist-chains of slender gold, satin stockings, tortoise-shell combs which, taken forth, let fall a light flood of hair . . .

Another whim came over him, and inside two days he had had made a slim dress of poppy-red velvet, and red-gold slippers with buckles printed by rubies. He had judged her measures; for the footwear, if it did not fit, he supposed she would make the best of things, the shoes being what they were.

He had the garments transported around the peripheries of the Palace, and out to the marble houses on the meadows. He did not go so far as to accompany the party in disguise. His only instruction was: "Red hair, white face. And if these bits go on to her, then you have the proper animal."

But the hunt did not turn up anything of the right looks, let alone the correct build to fill garments and slippers.

The King began to fret. He was not used to this, to not getting his way.

They said afterwards the management of temporal affairs suffered at that time, but in fact, by now, the King was no longer necessary in the manner of a ruler. The direction of such lands as were postulated to be his was under the sway of councils, assemblies and ministers. What matter if a scatter of minor papers went unsigned, or a town or two was spared a royal progress?

Months presented themselves and were spent.

Came a morning, sportively pretending to simplicity the King went out, on foot, with ten men and some dogs. He had almost forgotten the girl among the poppies, she was fading from him as the flowers had already had the grace to do. He would refer to how he had been cheated, occasionally, since he had stubbornly retained his dissatisfaction, the whiff of baulked romance, lose his temper then, or frown and call for music. This daybreak, it was quite out of his head.

There was a mist, mild and sweet, and in the mist suddenly he saw the girl, walking along, russet-cloaked, a basket on her arm.

She was going towards the ornamental woods out of which, further down, the King and his company had just emerged. In the mist, she seemed not to note eleven hunters and seven dogs. Perhaps her eyesight was poor, as others came later to believe.

Because she was slipping away into the shadows of the forest, the King motioned his men to silent stasis. He alone went back into the wood after her.

She had committed a kind of heresy against him. She had kept him waiting, and worse, vexed. He felt an entitlement now to do what he liked, although he would have done what he liked in any event.

THE BLONDE DWARFESS
(THE BEAST IN THE WOOD)

Heracty has been told that the flaxen dwarfess once had an adventure in the mock forest below the Palace.

He does not know whether to credit this. She herself has never told him anything of it, though she is far from reticent.

Apparently, she had gone down the floral steppes, and wandered, astray, among the trees. She was gathering flowers, and carried a basket. But she wore courtly finery, and a scarlet snood sewn with brilliants, a gift of the Prince's. No one had warned her of the clockwork animals in the forest. Or, if they ever had, she misunderstood. She had left her maid, a canny brat of six years, behind.

When something howled, the dwarfess took the noise for that of one of the Prince's hounds, which were sometimes exercised in a large enclosure at the other side of the steppes. It was a still afternoon, and sounds might travel.

Then, as she bent towards a clump of pale hyacinths, the dwarfess saw, in the midst of a bush, two narrow, gleaming and carnivorous eyes.

Next moment, a grey wolf slunk from the thicket.

The dwarfess curtsied to the wolf. Though she had not been informed, or had unremembered, clockwork, the etiquette of the Palace was by now ingrained in her. And at her curtsy, indeed, the wolf smiled, and prancing forward, capered all about her with expressions of amiability, so she was not in the least alarmed at it.

Presently the two walked on together. The wolf was helpful, nosing out for her absolute treasuries of flowers, aiding her in uprooting them. The dwarfess became fond of the smiling wolf, and on impulse placed her hand on his grey head.

No sooner had she done so than the wolf sprang and dashed her full-length on the ground. That done, it jumped on her, muddying her skirts and tearing them with its claws. It gave off bear-like roars, drooled and licked her, and

sometimes bit her with excitement. Though these toothings were no more dangerous than the nips of an eager puppy, the lady in her terror imagined herself
about to be devoured, eaten alive. She fainted.

On reviving, she found the wolf stretched heavily across her, using her pliant
body and hair for a couch, fast asleep or certainly in the attitude of one grossly
sleeping.

Not until the wolf awoke did she dare to stir. To her amazed relief, at her
first cautious movement the beast quickly leapt away from her and darted into
the forest.

The dwarfess, weeping, gathered up her slobbered skirts, and abandoning the
spilled, crushed flowers, limped home.

At length, the gruesome tale was whispered to her consoeur, who pertly replied,
"Why, you should have thrown the brute an apple or a sweetmeat. That's all it
wants."

But the blonde dwarfess wished aloud, or so it was reported, that men might
go and axe down the dreadful wood.

THE PRIEST'S DARKNESS (THE BEAUTY)

Comfortless, the vampire dreams, while that which passes for its soul, a beast,
lies snarling on the snow, pinned by hafts and staves. The cold is like a wound,
felt all through the tangled blackness of the pelt, through to the scald of the
blood, and snow burns on the lashes of the fiery eyes, which are not composed
of pure ferocity but of questions, and lit by bewildered distress and pain. It cannot
comprehend, this thing, why it has been pursued, brought down, is tortured
now, solely for being, for living as what it is.

The speech of the hunters is a blur of successful hatred and successful fear.
They are recalling an idiot, tender of a midden, whom in error they did to death
for these crimes. Yet here is the culprit, caught in the act, the milk-white lamb
in its jaws—

"But the other shape—!" one cries out now, frantic.

"That perishes too. See—what's done here, we'll go back and search the
houses to find."

"Somewhere the devil will be weltered in his own blood."

They laugh. It is a laugh of utter fright.

And the black wolf writhes, grinning, also afraid.

Until it beholds an axe, glinting silver in the torchlight, the rays struck upward
from the fevered snow, an axe of silver iron raised over all their heads.

The axe flashes and crashes down.

He experiences the impact, the *blow*, and starts up choking, blind and mad-
dened, calling out to God, in the turmoil of a hard, thin bed.

But he is not killed, can breathe and see. And if he shouted aloud, beyond
the walls his frozen village lies submissive enough, under the sterile quarter
moon.

He has had this dream before, the priest. This dream, others. Once he would dream always that he led them, his flock, over the cliff of night into a valley of shadow, and there, as they entered the defile, he, the shepherd, seized them and sank his fangs into their throats. His dark priestly robe is a black pelt. He puts it on. Beware of me, he whispers, setting the wafer between their lips, giving them their sip of God's blood, as he aches for the beauty of their wine. He stalks them and can pull them down with pitiable ease. He has had so many. Is it only hundreds?

Now he sobs, kneeling before the window, which has no glass, only a broken shutter. There are no riches here. Only the love of God and the blessing of the Devil.

What is to be done?

He looks round wildly, but there is nothing to hand. Even the razor for shaving is blunt in its dish.

Besides, it is just an evil dream. Of course, he is so tired. This terrible place, when he had once thought of lofty cathedrals, of purity, dedication, and bliss.

The priest lies down again on the bony bed. He stares with open eyes at the beams in the roof, and disciplines himself to think of . . . beauty.

Now he stares with open, inner eyes. He sees an altar-cloth, a white dove ascending on gold; this becomes a window in a church which touches the sky. But then it is a white girl painted against flames, and in her hands is a poisoned apple, like red flesh, which she throws to him. There is the choice, to catch the apple, to allow it to go by. If it does so, another will catch it. The apple fills his hand. He senses its fragrance. He longs to shut his inner eyes, but to do so must open again the outer ones. The moon is in the window now. His lids are wet. He is ashamed.

BEAUTY IN THE PALACE (THE VAMPIRE'S DREAM)

Somehow, perhaps by magic, the door has been opened. Icicles lie around Idrel on her platform. Within the doorway, a stair mounts into darkness. This is not inviting, yet seemingly it is an invitation, as sure as if a dark figure waited at the darkness' heart, calmly beckoning. Getting to her feet, the girl enters the doorway and climbs the stair.

The ruin is intent with strangeness, and the loud silence of snow and settled night.

Far beneath, in the blue ice-rose of a paralysed fountain, a mermaid had been trapped. Or, possibly, only drawn there with a dagger. And here, all at once, there are candelabra, with snow or wax heaped down their stems, but in their cups flames are beginning to burn up, like blossoms breaking too soon.

And then Idrel emerges high on the mountain of the wrecked enormous edifice, among its circlet of thorny towers. She is in a great hall, which has no roof and into which the towers seem to be gazing from huge eyes of dimly tinted glass. On the roofless walls hang lamps. As Idrel looks at them, they are being ignited, two or three at a time, by invisible tapers carried in unseen hands.

A cavern of pillared hearth has already flowered into fire. Instinctively, the young girl goes to it and stretches out her arms, flexes her fingers. The fire gives off heat. It warms her. It shows the crimson under her skin. Behind a curtain she finds a little closed chamber of some opulence, nested there in the ruin, and prepared for her, obviously for her.

A bath stands on silver feet, and from it rises scented steam, and a silver-framed table of vanities, mirrors, cosmetics, curling-tongs, and with jewellery littered about as if a princess had only just got up from it. Tall chests will offer her clothing. The unseen invisibles are pulling wide all the drawers and doors and trays, to demonstrate. While under its canopy, a bed has been aired with hot stones. It is a broad couch, the virgin notices, a marriage-bed, such as her foster parents shared. She senses, without nervousness or embarrassment, that someone may be watching her.

Idrel allows the sprites of the ruin to remove the shift of her village burial, steps into the soothing bath, and is laved so gently with unguents and water she cannot for an instant misinterpret the supernatural familiarities as anything human. She is made, and becomes, a beauty.

As she eats the dainty supper they have laid for her, the girl accepts the solution of her prior death, for this must be heaven and she is receiving her reward. As to the means of death, she cannot conjure any.

She inhabited one world, and now is here. She does not insult her condition by thinking she is dreaming. Perhaps, however, she is part of the dream of another.

That in mind, she ponders her pale hand with its new cuff of black, over both of which a coil of hair has poured itself, in the firelight hectically coloured. A dramatic concoction for herself or any watcher: Black as ebony, red as blood, white as snow.

THE QUEEN'S SECOND SIN (THE DEAD KING)

After he was done with her, the King lumbered to his feet, regarded her, and made as if to help her in turn to rise. Tumbled, her very downfall appealed to and enticed him. Provisions from her basket—she had been taking loaves and cakes to someone, somewhere—lay all over the turf. Candied cherries had bruised on her gown. Cherries, fulvous hair, maiden blood, a foam of petticoats. He was pleased by the artistic chaos he had created from her.

But she seemed to have lost her memory. He found that out when he had dragged her up. She had forgotten where she was going, where she had come from, even who she was. Her very name. He took it for a gambit, and guffawed. "But you know who I am?" She thought, and shook her fragile head. "Your King," he told her, not without pride. She looked at him in complete belief and pure uninterest. He felt then he could not leave such a simpleton at large. He would have her at home a day or so more. He ate her pastries like a hearty ploughboy as they went, having summoned the abortive hunt with a yell. They had only been waiting out of sight. "A fine quarry, eh?" said the King, jostling his lackwit doll.

In the Palace, he soon grew used to her amnesia. It was rather novel. He gave her things instead, rooms, clothes. Even the dress and shoes he had bandied about. The slippers were in fact too small, and did not fit.

He had had a royal wife, once, who produced a viperish son, now being tutored, as was the vogue, elsewhere. The queen-mother next contracted a fatal plague during a pilgrimage she insisted on making, so it served her right. For himself the King did not foresee an era when he too, poisoned more slowly by various indulgences, would be gone, becoming in popular parlance "Dead."

What began as a clumsy snatch in a wood progressed to a merry hole-in-corner adventure, involving the game of secret passages and similar artifice.

Eventually, by accident, the King learned who it was probable he had abducted. An elderly aristocrat, living in a remote nook of the Palace grounds, which were considerable even in those days, had lost a child, a young, not quite legitimate daughter, fifteen years of age. It was suggested jealous older sisters of less beauty, the product of another union, had got rid of her. The description of the lost girl tallied sufficiently with that of the amnesiac now haunting the apartment of the King's favourite doxy.

Certain gifts were instigated. Vows of unspeaking were fashioned. The lady, garbed in her autumnal camouflage, was brought out and discovered to be, first, a duchess, and next, a queen. The ulcerous foot, and some other heralding ailments, had by now taken charge of the King. Virtue did not alleviate them.

Something else atrocious had meanwhile happened.

The Red Queen had ceased to be a girl, was not fifteen, not seventeen, not twenty, not thirty, any longer. Flourished in the harsh illumination of the public court, far from her shady room and fireglims, she revealed her decay into a woman.

There was a story she had conceived but not borne to term. If one had asked this Queen, to her face, she would not have dissembled, for she did not seem to know, even now, anything valid about herself.

She could not truly be said to know, even, what she might be assumed to have realised—that she had been leapt on and vampirised, buried, dug out, thrust into the violent glare of an empty mirror which leered at, and insolently answered her, saying, Now you are old.

The King's bleared eyes, certainly, saw the etching of her bleak, icy face, as if it had been drawn on by a nail. It was unforgivable of her.

By the night of his summer death, he had, though, both forgiven and forgotten.

The son, fattened from viper to python, coming back, treated the madwoman Innocin with urbanity. He found it amusing so to do. After the amused period, it was established custom. Being very young, he thought her an antique. Such articles might keep their place, come and go as they wanted, wandering like a lost soul if no longer a lost child. Sometimes he would point her out to visitors, as another curio of his collection.

THE DWARF'S THIRD INTERVIEW WITH HIS GRANDMOTHER

"Go away," stridently commands Heracty's relative, as she sees him through her ice-locked window. In winter the marble houses are difficult to warm and tend to promote rheumatism. But the handsome dwarf, ignoring all temper of weather or woman, is already in, and standing by the hearth.

"What did I say to you?" snarls the grandmother.

"You welcomed me with tender cries," says Heracty. "And look at what I've brought you. A mantle trimmed by damascined fur combed from the Prince's gulon."

The grandmother examines the item unkindly.

"There is no such animal as a gulon," she remarks.

"The Red Queen," says Heracty, musingly, "has all her winter cloaks enhanced with gulon-fur, when not by ermine."

"An ermine is only a weasel."

"And what is a ghost?"

"The demon of a sickly stunted brain."

"Wrong once more," says Heracty. "I'll tell you." He seats himself by the fire, and props his boots on a stool. He notices today the grandmother looks ninety, and she that his legs seem to have grown longer. That is impossible. "The Queen," says Heracty, "has visualised and hunted her lost youth so determinedly, it has taken on a shape. It has become a girl, lovely, clad in black velvet. But daylight or a lamp shine through her. She isn't substantial. And I believe, from the manner in which she gazes about, the Palace is just as unreal, in its way, to her. A ruin maybe is all she sees. Or else she exists in a previous or later time. Other dwarfs have met her. They say she lies down on their beds, with her feet and hair, both spangled, hanging over the ends. They say she wears slippers made of ice, or glass. The mastiffs fawn on her. The unicorn offers her rides. Even the two-headed dog turns one head. The gulon, naturally, spits and makes water. It's peevish. Have a honeyed almond? No? The gulon is very partial to them."

"To hell with you, sir, your ghosts and gulons and honey and *legs*."

"And here's a rose I found, after the phantom passed me on a stair." Heracty extends it. "A flower blooming in the snow."

But, though exactly formed, the rose also is made of ice. Grandmother burns her fingers on it, and thrown at a wall, it smashes.

THE BEAST (THE BRIDE)

The sumptuous bed, entombed by its curtains on which are sewn bizarre animals and birds, has invented a separate breathing. It had, of course, not been there when she lay down to sleep—but is now so close to her that, as she wakes, she partly believes the rhythm of breath is her own. Not, however, the smooth planes of flesh, the cool hands which take her face between them, the lips which press her mouth.

She is not afraid. It was so inevitable, this. Surely she has known these caresses before. She yields without a word, with all her self. And since this place is heaven, love too is unalloyed. She is spun away as if through a starry sky. She falls to earth uninjured, but completely changed.

The man who has shared with her the bed of the act of love, invisible to her in the dark as any of the magical servants, is held in her arms. She ventures only now to question him, because now it does not matter.

"You ask me for my name," he responds. His voice is musical and low. "Call me Lucander. He, Lucander, will be with you here, at night. But you will never see him."

"But will I see you?"

"At these times, he and I are the same. Never."

"Never?"

It is a ritual. It neither frightens nor convinces her, though she is prepared to honour its outer show. In the same way, in her former life, she would have cast spilt salt across one shoulder.

"Not once, Idrel. Never. Never attempt to see my face."

"Why not? Why?"

"Light, and my face, can't agree together. Even the moon's my enemy. Especially that. Without doubt the sun."

"But a single candle," she says.

"Don't try to discover me. The revelation would drive you mad."

"But why?"

"The beast stays to be found in man. The hunter which preys on the trusting sheep."

"A beast."

"The bestial joke of God. Monstrous."

In the blinded blackness, the bride describes the face of her husband. Her fingertips learn only the mask of a human male, the brows and lashes, the lips and earlobes, the jaw with its masculine roughening. And the taste of him, of the fruits of the darkness.

"But by night you will be here with me?" She employs his name, "Lucander."

She is already, in his second embrace, planning for his future slumber, a tinder struck and the surprising candleflame.

INNOCIN'S ASCENT (THE QUEEN'S LAST SIN)

Can it be her stepson's dwarf is continuing to follow her? No, surely, it is just her shadow compressed and thrown behind. For a new idea has occurred to Innocin. Not to descend in the twilight, but instead to seek higher, into the diadem of the Upper Palace, its tallest towers.

They are remote and neglected, and in the vast attics there perhaps a white skirt has often gone up and down, and pale feet have all this while been stepping.

As she ascends, the Queen considers the sin of her husband, a black sticky sin, or spotted red, the murder of her past amounting to an utter death. This sin it was that gave her to conceive the child clad in clement white.

The stairs are craning, spindly, thick with webs and dust. Yet far above in the air, a pastel eye beams on her, a window made encouraging by a lamp. Or only the moon in a cloud.

She crosses a passage, her cloak industriously sweeping up the dirt and old nests—once doves brooded here. The stars glint in broken bricks. The towers are very ancient. They belong to other, earlier, histories.

On a threshold, the Queen hesitates. It is now too dark for her to see anything, and the guiding light has vanished. Nevertheless, a sweet, slight voice is singing, the words indistinguishable, like a faint zephyr tingling through the bones of the tower.

Innocin sighs.

The voice she hears is like that of a child, but not a child lost and alone, bleeding or crying in the bitter cold. This is a found child, braiding her hair and playing with a rope of pearls. Roses unseasonably grow about her, a fire dances. There is food and wine. Slaves to serve, not to exact service. There is love.

Suddenly Innocin can see a cave of golden light, and a shining young woman going by through the yellow heart of it.

"Oh," whispers the Red Queen. "There she is."

She smiles at the glamour and riches, all the nights and mornings, guessing the beloved is due to return. Not for the found daughter a wild beast in a forest, rending and blight.

The Queen smiles, and lets her soul go out of her.

The soul is gone.

Like an amber dove she falls from the tower-top, her mantle bearing her on its wing. She falls at Heracty's feet, where he stands in a court below.

Though her skeletal structure is dislodged at the impact, her body settles, resting her pristine on her back, her hands folded on her breast, her long lids closed, and her mouth still blossoming its flame of smile. Oh, she is yet saying, there she is. And the mirror has cracked, and set her free, at last.

THE WOLF'S HEAD (THE AWAKENING)

There have been many nights and days. In the day, sometimes, led by the unseen slaves, Idrel explored the ruin, discovering its secret wonders. The labyrinth is full of ghosts. Frequently, the girl has witnessed, tiny in the telescoped lens of distant corridors, or courtyards five flights of stairs beneath, frantic scenes of another world, which plainly do not otherwise have substance. Idrel observes impartially games and feasts, courtings and quarrellings, aristocrats and unicorns and dwarfs.

But the nights are better for exploring.

In the snow-field of white sheets, her night-husband draws her away into the forest of desire—and abruptly the darkness engulfs her.

To these delights, the lingering tension of Idrel's plan has subtly been added. Tonight she will carry it out.

Slipping from the bed, she fetches a candle. As she does this, a sigh seems to flutter round the chamber. The ruin is crammed with phantoms, and Idrel pays no heed.

Light is absent, the fire long-smothered and all the lamps doused before her lover's arrival. Carefully returning through screens and panes of blackness to the bed, she puts the candle down, strikes the tinder, lets the fire-bud drop on to the waxen branch where, like a canary, it beats its wings. When the flame steadies, holding it high, Idrel pulls aside a fold of the bed-curtain. She stares down at what lies sleeping on the white drift of the sheet.

Shadows and sheen combine to describe. Here are the lines of a man's body, which at the shoulders culminate in the head of a black wolf.

As soon as she sees it, she remembers, everything.

In that moment, too, perhaps alerted by the light and its flickering, or solely by the intensity of the watcher, the creature wakes. It growls softly, or, the muzzle of the wolf does so. Feral, human, lupine eyes glare up at the young girl standing there, pinning it with a stave of light, and clothed herself in her white nakedness, save where the same light blushes her apple-red.

"I look and I see," says Idrel.

Her eyes say clearly: I knew all the time it was there, your black wolf. To live is to die. I'm dead, and here with you. You made me holy, taking my blood.

And leaning down, she kisses the wolf face, over and over, with quiet still kisses. And as she does this, the candle tilts and the burning hot wax sears and seals his skin, but he does not flinch at it. When Idrel lifts her head, she finds a man, with a man's skull and features, a broad low brow, hair black as crow's feathers, black-water eyes that regard her.

"There will be another bed," he murmurs, "with a dead wolf in it, or a living man—but not this one."

"But you are Lucander. You are with me, here."

The vampire, or supernatural spirit, whatever it is, has now fully recognised the soul, or ghost, of Idrel. That is, if Idrel ever existed beyond the brain of a red-haired queen.

They contemplate each other in the melting honey of the candle-gloom. When the candle finishes, who can say if they remain in the black night, or if they too have gone away.

Even the serene susurrous of their voices, which is yet to be distinguished, may not be real. Although more so, perhaps, than the stairs and galleries and towers of the preposterous Palace.

THE BLACK QUEEN (THE SEVEN DWARFS)

Because he thinks of himself as an innovator, the Prince has had a strange new mausoleum built, on a hill three or four miles from the Palace. In the mausoleum lies the body of his stepmother, the dead Queen.

The view from the mausoleum is eloquent. Above, uncut meadows, woodland tapering to park, the mountain of the royal domicile. Below, the sapphire basins of the valleys, the faraway forests which are not fakes, a thunder-cloud of trees, redolent and rowdy with every animal applicable to the clime.

The corpse of Innocin was come on at daybreak in a yard of the Upper Palace by some sozzled young nobles, who were startled but not astounded. It was decided she had toppled from a tower. The sin of suicide was not mentioned. Nevertheless the location of the new tomb was fortuitous, it did not require sacred ground. It could be erected as a monument. Somewhat to that end, the Prince had organised rather a peculiar funeral rite, which, repeated on and off in subsequent years, became known as the Masque of the Black Queen.

The title role was undertaken by the dusky dwarfess. Attired like midnight, with sables, and jets in her hair, she was drawn in a carriage by a team of plumed black greyhounds. The other six dwarfs, each got up allegorically, came behind, mounted or on foot as their character advised. Heracty had the part of Worldly Fame, his pony, a suit of cloth-of-gold, and the obligation of lugging on leash two ill-mannered peacocks. His brother dwarfs represented Modesty, Sloth, Rage and Joy. The blonde dwarfess, in butterfly costume, was asked to suggest Unearthly Apprehension. The dusky dwarfess, the Black Queen, was unarguably Lady Death.

Additional pets of the Prince's had work in the procession. The unicorn appeared wreathed in thorns as the Pardon of Heaven. The gulon and dual-headed dog were excluded, however, as untrustworthy.

All this display, with the snuffling, labouring court plodding after, toiled out through heavy snow to the mausoleum, where dirges were sung, and flowers dyed black, or gilded, tossed on the ice. The mausoleum steps had gone to mirror, and the miraculous dome was topped again by a scoop of snow.

Months on, when the thaws of spring had manhandled the land and flung down the rime and snow from the slopes, the court would voluntarily visit the area, also the dwarfs. They would sit on the tomb-steps, and look pensively out into the valleys. Their reasons for doing so, particularly the reasons of the dwarfs, were banal. They liked the vista, thought it prudent to pretend respect, or relished the proof of the high brought low.

Heracty attends the tomb seldom. When giving the gulon exercise, as he now sometimes does, he will tend that way.

For its part, the fox-cat sniffs all about the mausoleum, trotting up the steps to peer with peridot eyes in at the transparent dome. Does the gulon recognise the bleached trimmings in which Innocin has been laid to rest? More likely, being fed on carrion, its interest is of that order.

THE TOMB (THE SPRING)

The priest walks to the summit of a hill on an evening of late spring—and sees in front of him a curious monument.

The ordeal which he endured in a backward, superstitious village is over with.

He has been recalled to the towns and cities of his earliest dreaming. Conversely, he has sloughed those dark nightmares that haunted his beginnings. The inner outcry for flesh, the carnal ravening, like hunger, these impediments are surpassed. He has wrestled with the subterranean angel, and triumphed.

Birds sing in the warm avenues of sky. The westering sun flies against a dome of glass, piercing it with a brilliant nail.

Having space, and peace, the young priest makes a detour and climbs the steps, and so concludes the monument is a tomb. Marble and granite, like a fist it grips an egg of sheer transparency. And in this oval mirror a woman lies composed, robed in creamy white, coifed like a nun, a circlet of gold binding her forehead. There is not a mark on her face. She would seem to be a girl. This aspect will be eternal. The sarcophagus has shut her fast in a vacuum, where no atmosphere can enter to corrupt. She will, therefore, never grow old. She will never decay. Always her bones will be decently clad, until the Final Judgment.

The young man gazes in at the dead, seemingly sleeping girl. A kiss might awaken her.

It comes to him, how the Devil left him in the likeness of a black wolf, running off briskly along the roads of slumber. Of what is this dead girl dreaming, this white queen, as she lies in her shell of crystal for ever?

On the other side of the tomb, a blonde dwarf lady is seated at an aesthetic angle, but she too has gone to sleep. In a basket at her side are apples and peaches, one with a chunk bitten out of it.

Above, beyond, meadows, hillside, the winking of water, a wood where rhododendrons are flowering, some hint of towers or roofs.

A nonsensical beast like a large brown cat, or possibly a tabby fox, is eating poppies in the meadow-grass.

The priest walks on, leaving the tomb of glass for the sunset and the night.

HERACTY'S OMISSION OF A FURTHER INTERVIEW WITH HIS GRANDMOTHER

On the rim of the fountain, the seventh dwarf balances in the afterglow of summer sunfall, diving his hand into the water, making believe it is a fish. Then, removing his hand and knowing it again as the hand of an elf.

The creatures of the fountain loom over him, still tanned with pink day; great heat stays cosy in the stone. Roses have burst across the lawn.

Although she will never any more glide down the stair, cross this terrace, go by him sightlessly, sinking through the Palace, even so, sometimes he waits for her.

Heracty does not anticipate Innocin's ghost. A ghost cannot *become* a ghost. When a ghost dies, it springs to life.

It is years now since he went to call on his grandmother, but Heracty does think of her, for that old witch is waiting for him with malicious hope, but he will never go near her again. Her vigil is accordingly as pointless as this one he keeps on the fountain terrace.

Something stirs among the roses, and a shower of petals snows the dusk.

The moon is rising like a coin of breath, and the gulon, early, starts to yowl. The heart or soul of the gulon is rushing at liberty through a forest. And somewhere else, Heracty is a man with lion's hair, over six feet tall, his shoulders filling a doorway. Heracty knows this other life of his goes on. It is just there, or *there*—beneath an arch, behind a door. It takes only the brush of a feather to dislodge the barrier of iron between. He believes this, and knows this, and how simple it would be to do it. Heracty is puzzled, less dismayed than nonplussed, that he has never found the way.

PAT CADIGAN

The Power and the Passion

What kind of person would be the best for the job of vampire killer? Cadigan answers this by creating the memorable narrator of "The Power and the Passion." I hope we'll see more of him in the future.

Pat Cadigan, featured in last year's volume with "It Was the Heat," has demonstrated a sharp ear for dialogue in several dozen short fictions published in a variety of venues over the last few years. This story first appeared in her recent story collection, *Patterns*.

Cadigan's first novel, *Mindplayers* (Bantam) was published in 1988. Her second, *Synners*, will be published in 1991.

—E.D.

The Power and the Passion

PAT CADIGAN

The voice on the phone says, "We need to talk to you, Mr. Soames," so I know to pick the place up. Company coming. I don't like for company to come into no pigsty, but one of the reasons the place is such a mess all the time is, it's so small, I got nowhere to keep shit except around, you know. But I shove both the dirty laundry and the dirty dishes in the oven—my mattress is right on the floor so I can't shove stuff under the bed, and what won't fit in the oven I put in the tub and just before I pull the curtain, I think, well, shit, I shoulda just put it all in the tub and filled it and got it all washed at once. Or, well, just the dishes, because I can take the clothes over to the laundromat easier than washing them in the tub.

So, hell, I just pull the shower curtain, stack the newspapers and the magazines—newspapers on top of the magazines, because most people don't take too well to my taste in magazines, and they wouldn't like a lot of the newspapers much either, but I got the Sunday paper to stick on top and hide it all, so it's okay. Company'll damned well know what's under those Sunday funnies because they know *me*, but as long as they don't have to have it staring them in the face, it's like they can pretend it don't exist.

I'm still puttering and fussing around when the knock on the door comes and I'm crossing the room (the only room unless you count the bathroom, which I do when I'm in it) when it comes to me I ain't done dick about myself. I'm still in my undershirt and shorts, for chrissakes.

"Hold on," I call out, "I ain't decent, quite," and I drag a pair of pants outa the closet. But all my shirts are either in the oven or the tub and company'll get fanny-antsy standing in the hall—this is not the watchamacallit, the place where Lennon bought it, the Dakota, yeah. Anyway, I answer the door in my one hundred percent cotton undershirt, but at least I got my fly zipped.

Company's a little different this time. The two guys as usual, but today they got a woman with them. Not a broad, not a bitch, not a bimbo. She's standing between and a little behind them, looking at me the way women always look at me when I happen to cross their path—chin lifted up a little, one hand holding her coat together at the neck in a fist, eyes real cold, like, "Touch me and die horribly, I wish," standing straight fuckin' up, like they're Superman, and the fear coming off them like heat waves from an open furnace.

They all come in and stand around and I wish I'd straightened the sheets out on the mattress so it wouldn't look so messy, but then they'd see the sheets ain't clean, so six of one, you know. And I got nothing for anyone to sit on, except that mattress, so they just keep standing around.

The one guy, Steener, says, "Are you feeling all right, Mr. Soames?" looking around like there's puke and snot all over the floor. Steener don't bother me. He's a pretty man who probably was a pretty boy and a pretty baby before that, and thinks the world oughta be a pretty place. Or he wants to prove pretty guys are really tougher and better and more man than guys like me, because he's afraid it's vice versa, you know. Maybe even both, depending on how he got up this morning.

The other guy, Villanueva, I could almost respect him. He didn't put on no face to look at me, and he didn't have no power fantasies about who he was to me or vice versa. I think Villanueva probably knows me better than anyone in the world. But then, he was the one took my statement when they caught up with me. He was a cop then. If he'd still been a cop, I'd probably respect him.

So I look right at the woman and I say, "So, what's this, you brought me a date?" I know this will get them because they know what I do to dates.

"You speak when spoken to, Mr. Soames," Steener says, kinda barking like a dog that wishes it were bigger.

"You spoke to me," I point out.

Villanueva takes a few steps in the direction of the bathroom—he knows what I got in there and how I don't want company to see it, so this is supposed to distract me, and it does a little. The woman steps back, clutching her light coat tighter around her throat, not sure who to hide behind. Villanueva's the better bet, but she doesn't want to get any further into my stinky little apartment, so she edges toward Steener.

And it comes to me in a two-second flash-movie just how to do it. Steener'd be easy to take out. He's a rusher, don't know dick about fighting. He'd just go for me and I'd just whip my hand up between his arms and crunch goes the windpipe. Villanueva'd be trouble, but I'd probably end up doing him, too. Villanueva's smart enough to know that. First, though, I'd bop the woman, just bop her to keep her right there—punch in the stomach does it for most people, man or woman—and then I'd do Villanueva, break his neck.

Then the woman. I'd do it all, pound one end, pound the other, switching off before either one of us got too used to one thing or the other. Most people, man or woman, blank out about then. Can't face it, you know, so after that, it's free-for-fuckin'-all. You can do just any old thing you want to a person in shock, they just don't believe it's happening by then. This one I would rip up sloppy, I would send her to hell and then kill her. I can see how it would look, the way her body would be moving, how her flesh would jounce flabby—

But I won't. I can't look at a woman without the flash-movie kicking in, but it's only a movie, you know. This is company, they got something else for me.

"Do you feel like working?" Villanueva asks. He's caught it just now, what I was thinking about, he knows, because I told him how it was when I gave him my statement after I got caught.

"Sure," I say, "what else have I got to do?"

He nods to Steener, who passes me a little slip of paper. The name and address. "It's nothing you haven't done before," he says. "There are two of them. You do as you like, but you *must* follow the procedure as it has been described to you—"

I give a great big nod. "I know how to do it. I've studied on it, got it all right up here." I tap my head. "Second nature to me now."

"I don't want to hear the word 'nature' out of *you*," Steener sneers. "You've got nothing to do with nature."

"That's right," I agree. I'm mild mannered because it's just come to me what is Steener's problem here. It is that he is like me. He enjoys doing to me what he does the way I enjoy doing what I do, and the fact that he's wearing a white hat and I'm not is just a watchamacallit, a technicality. Deep down at heart, it's the same fuckin' feeling and he's going between loving it and refusing to admit he's like me, boing-boing, boing-boing. And if he ever gets stuck on the loving-it side, well, son of a bitch will there be trouble.

I look over at Villaneuva and point at the woman, raising my eyebrows. I don't know exactly what words to use for a question about her and anything I say is gonna upset everybody.

"This person is with us as an observer," Villanueva says quietly, which means I can just mind my own fuckin' business and don't ask questions unless it's about the job. I look back at the woman and she looks me right in the face. The hand clenched high up on her coat relaxes just a little and I see the purple-black bruises on the side of her neck before she clutches up again real fast. She's still holding herself the same way, but it's like she spoke to me. The lines of communication, like the shrinks say, are open, which is not the safest thing to do with me. She's gotta be a nurse or a teacher or a social worker, I think, because those are the ones that can't help opening up to someone. It's what they're trained to do, reach out. Or hell, maybe she's just somebody's mother. She don't look too motherly, but that don't mean dick these days.

"When?" I say to Steener.

"As soon as you can pack your stuff and get to the airport. There's a cab downstairs and your ticket is waiting at the airline counter, in your name."

"You mean the Soames name," I say, because Soames is not my name for real.

"Just get ready, get going, get it done, and get back here," Steener says. "No side trips, or it's finished. Don't even *attempt* a side trip or it's finished." He starts to turn toward the door and then stops. "And you know that if you're caught in or after the act—"

"Yeah, yeah, I'm on my own and you don't know dick about squat, and nobody ever hearda me, case closed." I keep myself from smiling; he watched too much *Mission Impossible* when he was a kid. Like everyone else in his outfit. I think it's where they got the idea, kind of, some of it anyway.

Villanueva tosses me a fat roll of bills in a rubber band just as he's following Steener and the woman out the door. "Expenses," he says. "You have a rental car on the other end, which you'll have to use cash for. You can only carry cash, so don't get mugged and robbed. You know the drill."

"Drill?" I say, acting perked up, like I'm thinking, *Wow, what a good idea.*

Villanueva refuses to turn green for me, but he shuts the door behind him a little too hard.

I don't waste no time; I go to the closet and pull out my traveling bag. Everything's in it, but I always take a little inventory anyway, just to be on the safe side. Helluva thing to come up empty handed at the wrong moment, you know. Really, though, I just like to handle the stuff: hacksaw, mallet, boning blade, iodized salt, lighter fluid, matches, spray bottle of holy water, four pieces of wood pointed sharp on one end, half a dozen rosaries, all blessed, and two full place settings of silverware, not stainless, mind you, but real silver. And the shirts I don't never put in the tub. What do they make of this at airport security? Not a fuckin' thing. Ain't no gun. Guns don't work for this. Anyway, this bag's always checked.

The flight is fine. It's always fine because they always put me in first class and nobody next to me if possible. On the night flights, it's generally possible and tonight, I have the whole first-class section to myself, hot and cold running stews, who are (I can tell) forcing themselves to be nice to me. I don't know what it is, and I don't mind it, but it makes me wonder all the same: is it a smell, or just the way my eyes look? Villanueva told me once, it's just something about me gives everyone the creeps. I lean back, watch the flash-movies, don't bother nobody, and everybody's happy to see me go when the plane finally lands.

I get my car, nice midsize job with a phone, and head right into the city. I know this city real good, I been here before for them, but it ain't the only one they send me to when they need to TCB.

Do an easy fifty-five into the city and go to the address on the paper. Midtown, two blocks east of dead center, medium-size Victorian. I can see the area's starting to get a watchamacallit, like a facelift, the rich ones coming in and fixing up the houses because the magazines and the TV told them it's time to love old houses and fix them up.

I think about the other houses all up and down the street of the one I gotta go to, what's in them, what I could do. I sure feel like it, and it would be a lot less trouble, but I made me a deal of my own free will and I will stick to it as long as they do, Steener and Villanueva and the people behind them. But if they bust it up somehow, if they fuck me, that will be real different, and they will be real sorry.

I call the house; nobody home. That's about right. I got to wait, which don't bother me none, because there's the flash-movies to watch. I can think on what

I want to do after I get through what I have to do, and those things are not so different from each other. What Steener calls the procedure I just call a new way to play. Only not so new, because I thought of some of those things all on my own when I was watchamacallit, freelance so to say, and done some of them, kind of, which I guess is what made them take me for this stuff, instead of letting me take a quick shot in a quiet room and no funeral after.

So, it gets to be four in the morning and here we come. Somehow, I know as soon as I see the figure coming up the sidewalk across the street that this is the one in the house. I can always tell them, and I don't know what it is, except maybe it takes a human monster to know an inhuman monster. And I don't feel nothing except a little nervous about getting into the house, which is always easier than you'd think it would be, but I get nervous on it anyway.

Figure comes into the light and I see it's a man, and I see it's not alone, and then I get pissed, because that fucking Steener, that fucking Villaneuva, they didn't say nothing about no kid. And then I settle some, because I can tell the kid is one, too. Ten, maybe twelve from the way he walks. I take the razor and I give myself a little one just inside my hairline, squeeze the blood out to get it running down my face, and then I get out of the car just as they put their feet on the first step up to the house.

"Please, you gotta help me," I call, not too loud, just so they can hear, "they robbed me, they took everything but my clothes, all my ID, my credit cards, my cash—"

They stop and look at me running across the street at them and the first thing they see is the blood, of course. This would scare anybody but them (or me, naturally). I trip myself on the curb and collapse practically at their feet. "Can I use your phone? Please? I'm scared to stay out here, my car won't start, they might be still around—"

The man leans down and pulls me up under my arm. "Of course. Come in, we'll call the police. I'm a doctor."

I have to bite my lip to keep from laughing at that one. He's an operator maybe but no fucking doctor. Then I taste blood, so I let it run out of my mouth and the two of them, the man and the kid get so hot they can't get me in the house fast enough.

Nice house. All the Victorian shit restored, even the fuzzy stuff on the wallpaper, watchamacallit, flocked wallpaper. I get a glimpse of the living room before the guy's rushing me upstairs, saying he's got his medical bag up there. I just bet he does, and I got mine right in my hand, which they do not bother wondering about what with all this blood and this guy with no ID and out at four in the morning, must be a criminal anyway. I used to ask Villanueva, don't they ever get full, like they can't drink another drop, but Villaneuva told me no, they always had room for one more, it was time they were pressed for. Dawn. I'd be through long before then, but even if I wasn't, dawn would take care of the rest of it for me.

They're getting so excited it's getting me even more excited. I look at the kid and man, if I'd been anyone else, I woulda started screaming and trying to get away, because he's all gone. I mean, the kid part is all gone and just this fucking hungry thing from hell. So I stop feeling funny about there being a kid, because like I said, there ain't no kid, just a short one along with the tall one.

And shit if he don't twig, right there on the stairs. I musta looked like I recognized him.

"We're burned! We're burned!" he yells and tries to elbow me in the face. I dip and he goes right the fuck over my head and down, ka-boom, ka-boom. Guess what, they can't fly. It don't do him, but they can feel pain, and if you break their legs, they can't walk for awhile until they can get extra blood to heal them up. The kid's fucking neck is broke, you can see it plain as anything.

But I don't get no chance to study on it because the big one growls like a fucking attack dog and grabs me up from behind around the waist. They really are stronger than normal and you better believe it hurt like a motherfucker. He squeezes and there go two ribs and the soft drinks I had on the plane, like a fucking fountain.

"You'll go slow for that," he says, "you'll go for days, and you'll beg to die."

Obviously, he don't know me. I'm hurting all right, but it takes a lot more than a couple of ribs to put me down and I never had to beg for nothing, but these guys get all their dialogue off the late show anyway and they ain't thinking of nothing except sticking it to you and drinking you dry. Fucking undead got a, a watchamacallit, a narrow perspective and they think everyone's scared of them.

That's why they send me, because I don't see no undead and I don't see no human being, I just see something to play with. I gotta narrow perspective, too, I guess.

But then everything is not so good because he tears the bag outa my hand and flings it away up in the hallway. Then he carries me the rest of the way upstairs and down the opposite end and tosses me into a dark room and slams the door and locks it.

I hold still until I can figure out how to move and cause myself the least pain, and I start taking off my shirts. I'm wearing a corduroy shirt with a pure linen lining sewn into the front and two heavy one-hundred-percent cotton T shirts underneath. I have to tear one of the T shirts off, biting through the neck, and I bite through the neck of the other one but leave it on (thinking about the guy biting through necks while I do it), and put the corduroy shirt back on, keeping it open. Ready to go.

The guy has gone downstairs. I hear the kid scream and then muffle it, and I hear footsteps coming back up the stairs. There's a pause, and then I see his feet at the bottom of the door in the light, and he unlocks the door and opens it.

"Whoever you think you are," he says, "you're about to find out what you really are."

I give a little whimper, which makes him sure enough to grab me by one leg and start dragging me out into the hallway, where the kid is lying on his back. When we're out in the light, he stops and stands over me, one leg on each side, and looks down at my crotch. I know what he's thinking, because I'm looking up at his and thinking something not too different.

He squats on my thighs, and I rip my shirts open.

It's like an invisible giant hand hit him in the face; he goes backwards with a scream, still bent at the knees, on top of my legs. I heave him off quick. He's so fucked I have time to get to him, roll him over on his back and give him a nice full frontal while I sit on his stomach.

It is a truly def tattoo. This is not like bragging, because I didn't do it, though I did name it: The Power and the Passion. A madwoman with a mean needle in Coney did it, one-handed with her hair standing on end, fingering her rosary beads with the other hand, and when I saw it finished, with the name I had given it on a banner above it, I knew she was the best tattoo artist in the whole world and so I did not do her, I did *not*. It was some very ignorant asshole who musta come in after I did that split her open and nailed her to the wall with a stud gun, but I caught the beef on it, and the tattoo that saved her from me saved me from the quick shot and gave me to Steener's people, courtesy of Villanueva who is, I should mention, also Catholic.

So it's a tattoo that means a lot to me in many ways, you see, but mostly I love it because it is so perfect. It runs from just below where my shirt collars are to my navel, and full across my chest, and if you saw it, you would swear it had been done by someone who had been there to see what happened.

The cross is not just two boards, but a tree trunk and a crossbar, and the spikes are driven into the wrists where the two bones make a natural holder for that kind of thing—you couldn't hang on a cross from spikes driven through your palms like a lot of people think. They'd rip through. The crown of thorns has driven into the flesh to the bone, and the blood drips from the matted beard *distinctly*—the madwoman was careful and skilled so that the different shades of red didn't muddy up. Nothing muddied up; you can see the face clear as you can see where the whips came down, as clear as the wound in his side, (which is not some wimpy slit but the best watchamacallit, rendering of a stab wound I have seen outside of real life), as clear as you can see how the arms have pulled out of the sockets, and how the legs are broken.

You just can't find no better picture of slow murder. I know; I seen photos of all kinds, I seen some righteous private art, and I seen the inside of plenty of churches, and ain't nobody done justice to nothing anybody ever done to someone, including the Crucifixion. Especially the Crucifixion, I guess.

Because, you see, you cannot take a vamp out with a cross, that don't mean dick to them, a fucking plus-sign, that's all. It's the Crucifixion that gets them, you gotta have a good crucifix, or some other representation of the Crucifixion, and it has to be sacred in some way, to inflict the agony of the real thing on them. Mine is sacred—that madwoman mumbling her rosary all the way through the work, don't it just figure that she was a runaway nun? I wouldn'ta thought it would matter, but I guess when you take them vows, you can't give them back. Sorta like a tattoo.

Well, that's what that madwoman believed, anyway, and I believe it, too, because I like believing that picture happened, and the vamp I'm sitting on, it don't mean shit if he believes or not, because I got him and he don't understand how I could even get close to him. So while I go get my bag (giving a good flash to the kid, who goes into shock), I explain about pure fibers found in nature like the linen they say they wrapped that man on the cross in (I think that's horseshit myself, but it's all in it being natural and not watchamacallit, synthetic, so that don't matter), and how it keeps the power from getting out till I need it to.

And then it's showtime.

I have a little fun with the silver for a while, just laying it against his skin here and there, and it crosses my mind not for the first time how a doctor could do some interesting research on burns, before I start getting serious. Like a hot knife through butter, you can put it that way and be dead on. Or undead on, ha, ha.

You know what they got for insides? Me neither, but it's as bad for them as anyone. And I wouldn't call *that* a heart, but if you drive a pure wood stake through it, it's lights out.

It lasts forever for him, but not half long enough for me. Come dawn, it's pretty much over. Them watchamacallits, UV rays, they're all over the place. Skin cancer on fast forward, you can put it that way. I leave myself half an hour for the kid, who is not really a kid because if he was, he'd be the first kid I ever killed, and I ain't no fucking kid killer, because I seen what *they* get in prison and I said, whoa, not *my* ass.

I stake both hearts at the same time, a stake in each hand, sending them to hell together. Call me sentimental. Set their two heads to burning in the cellar and hang in just long enough to make sure we got a good fire going before I'm outa there. House all closed up the way it is, it'll be a while before it's time to call the fire department.

I'm halfway to the airport when I realize my ribs ain't bothered me for a long time. Healed up, just like that.

Hallelujah, gimme that old-time religion.

"As usual," Steener says, snotty as all get-out, "the bulk of the fee has been divided up among your victims' families, with a percentage to the mission downtown. Your share this time is three hundred." Nasty grin. "The check's in the mail."

"Yeah," I say, "you're from the government and you're here to help me. Well, don't worry, Steener, I won't come in your *mouth*."

He actually cocks a fist and Villanueva steps in front of him. The woman with them gives Steener a really sharp look, like she's gonna come to my defense, which don't make sense. Villanueva starts to rag my ass about pushing Steener's hot button but I'm feeling important enough to wave a hand at him.

"Fuck that," I say, "it's time to tell me who *she* is."

Villanueva looks to the woman like he's asking her permission, but she steps forward and lets go of her coat, and I see the marks on her neck are all gone. "I'm the mother. And the wife. They tried to—" she bites her lips together and makes a stiff little motion at her throat. "I got away. I tried to go to church, but I was . . . tainted." She takes a breath. "The priest told me about—" she dips

her head at Villanueva and Steener, who still wants a piece of me. "You really
. . . put them away?"

The way she says it, it's like she's talking about a couple of rabid dogs. "Yeah,"
I tell her, smiling. "They're all gone."

"I want to see the picture," she says, and for a moment, I can't figure out
what she's talking about. And then I get it.

"Sure," I say, and start to raise my undershirt.

Villanueva starts up. "I don't think you *really* want—"

"Yeah, she does," I say. "It's the only way she can tell she's all right now."

"The marks disappeared," Villanueva snaps. "She's fine. You're fine," he
adds to her, almost polite.

She feels the side of her neck. "No, he's right. It *is* the only way I'll know
for sure."

I'm shaking my head as I raise the shirt slowly. "You guys didn't think to
sprinkle any holy water on her or nothing?"

"I wouldn't take the chance," she says, "it might have—"

But that's as far as she gets, because she's looking at my chest now and her
face—oh, man, I start thinking I'm in love, because that's the look, that's the
look you oughta have when you see The Power and the Passion. I know, because
it's the look on my own face when I stand before the mirror and stare, and stare,
and stare. It's so fucking *there*.

Villanueva and Steener are looking off in the opposite direction. I give it a
full two-minute count before I lower my shirt. The look on her face goes away
and she's just another character for a flash-movie again. Easy come, easy go.
But now I know why she was so scared when she was here before. Guess they
didn't think to tell her about pure natural fibers.

"You're perfect," she says and turns to Steener and Villanueva. "He's perfect,
isn't he? They can't tempt him into joining them, because he can't. He couldn't
if he wanted to."

"Fuckin' A," I tell her.

Villanueva says, "Shut up," to me and looks at her like he's kinda sick.
"You don't know what you're talking to. You don't know what's standing in
this room with us. I couldn't bring myself to tell you, and I was a cop for
sixteen years—"

"You told me what would have to be done with my husband and son," she
says, looking him straight in the eye and I start thinking maybe I'm in love after
all. "You spelled that out easily enough. The agony of the Crucifixion, the
burning and the cutting open of the bodies with silver knives, the stakes through
the hearts, the beheadings, the fire. That didn't bother you, telling me what
was going to happen to my family—"

"That's because they're the white hats," I say to her, and I can't help smiling,
smiling, smiling. "If they had to do it, they'd do it because they're on the side
of Good and Right."

Suddenly Steener and Villanueva are falling all over each other to hustle her
out and she don't resist, but she don't cooperate, either. The last thing I see

before the door closes is her face looking at me, and what I see in that face is not understanding, because she couldn't go that far, but acceptance. Which is one fucking hell of a lot more than I'll ever get from Steener or Villanueva or anybody-the-fuck-else.

And Steener and Villanueva, they don't even get it, I know it just went right by them, what I told her. They'd do it because they're on the side of Good and Right.

I do it because I like to.

And I don't pretend like I ain't no monster, not for Good and Right, and not for Bad and Wrong. I know what I am, and the madwoman who put The Power and the Passion on my chest, she knew, too, and I think now she did it so the vamps would never get me, because God help you all if they had.

Just a coincidence, I guess, that it's my kind of picture.

MIDORI SNYDER
Jack Straw

Midori Snyder is one of the finest new writers to enter the fantasy field. She is the author of *Soul String* and *New Moon*, with two more adult fantasy novels forthcoming. She has also written urban fantasy for teenagers in the *Borderland* series, and is at work on other stories for teenagers and children. In addition to writing, Snyder is a scholar of African languages and literature, a brown belt in karate, a musician specializing in Irish folk ballads, and the publisher of Leaping Hart Press. The daughter of a French poet and an American scholar of East Asian cultures, she grew up in the U.S. and Africa and now lives in Milwaukee with her husband Steven, a teacher, and her two children.

"Jack Straw" is a perfect gem of a story, told with elegant simplicity. It was written for Jane Yolen and published in her children's story collection *Things That Go Bump in the Night* (co-edited with Martin H. Greenberg).

—T.W.

Jack Straw

MIDORI SNYDER

The first time I saw Jack Straw was in the winter. I was sick. Very sick. Mama
had kept me home from school, just hoping the fever I'd caught would take care
of itself. That week there was a blizzard, and the snow piled up in huge, white
drifts beneath my window. The thermometer outside kept dropping, while the
one in my mouth just went higher. Mama wasn't sure which way to go, keep
me dry at home and hope for the best, or take me out in the damp cold and
risk the long drive from our farm to the hospital. I heard her talking late one
night to Daddy and Granny Frank. "Just wait a little longer," Daddy had said,
"just wait a little longer." So they waited, one after another in my bedroom,
sitting in the old rocking chair and watching for hopeful signs. Granny Frank's
knitting needles clicked and clicked like a worried bug caught on the window-
pane.

Funny thing about being sick. The worse off you are, the less you're able to
tell folks. *I knew* I wasn't doing good at all. Beneath the blankets they'd piled
on me for warmth, my bones rattled with the chills. I couldn't breathe too well
either—each time I drew in air it felt sticky, and each time I let air out, it sort
of oozed up my throat and wheezed. I couldn't tell Mama that nothing in the
room looked the same. The petals on the wallpaper daisies were turning brown,
and I could see them peeling off the wall and floating down to the floor. The
hollow sounds of the wind against the pane made me see big white dogs, their
hairy faces crowding my bed, steaming up the room with their breath.

Only thing that seemed to hold me firm in the bed was my quilt. Mama
made it for me when I was little out of all the pieces left over in Granny Frank's
rag-bag. It was beautiful, and I knew where each piece had come from. The
blue polka dot was Aunt Anna's dress that she wore to meet Uncle George when
he came back from the war. The red-and-white-striped bit was from Granny
Frank's confirmation dress, and the green silk triangles were Great-Grandma

Jenny's riding dress, made from imported fabric. There was a yellow-flowered calico that was Mama's summer dress when she was a teenager, and there was a square of white-and-pink apples that was mine when I was a baby. I liked to think about all those women in my family saving those bits and pieces of themselves, never wasting a thing if they could turn it to another purpose. After Mama had pieced it all together, Granny Frank sewed fancy stitches around each piece, setting each one off with its own frame of embroidery.

I was holding tight to my quilt, just praying that the blue polka dots would stop rolling off the fabric, when Jack Straw came up to the bed. I looked up feeling the cold draft and saw him step out of a mist into the moonlight that fell across the room.

He had his hands stuck in the pockets of a pair of old overalls, and a battered hat with a torn brim was pulled low over his face.

"Who are you?" I asked.

"Jack. Jack Straw," he answered, and I felt the chill creep over my spine at the dry sound.

He looked liked a scarecrow, old corn stalks tied together and dressed like a man. When he moved he rustled, and the mist sort of followed after him, rising off his hunched shoulders.

"I don't know you," I said weakly, struggling to sit up, and all the while pulling my quilt higher to my chin.

"Everyone knows me," he said, and pushed back his hat to show me his face.

Thin it was, with a nose that hooked down sharply trying to reach his chin. He smiled, and the creases in his cheeks folded with a scratchy sound.

He was right. Soon as I saw those white eyes, with shining black stones for a center, I knew him. Granny Frank told me once about old Jack Straw, shuffling through the fields on his way to harvest. But it wasn't crops he raked in, it was people. Right then I knew I was dying, even though my heart pounded like a bass drum and blood heated up my face like a furnace fire.

He pulled a hand from his pocket and reached out to me. Fingers of bundled sticks went to pluck the quilt from me, but I clutched it tighter, refusing to let go.

"I ain't going with you," I said angrily.

"No point in your refusing," he answered, and stepped closer to take a firmer hold of the quilt. The cold mist swirled toward me, and I felt its icy touch on my forehead.

"No!" I yelled, and then, "Mama!" I called for her where she was sitting in the chair, still sleeping. She didn't stir, and for an awful moment I feared Jack Straw had already taken me.

"Now wait here, Jack Straw," I said, yanking my quilt back from his spindly fingers. In my panicked thinking I had remembered something Granny Frank told me about Jack Straw. "I'll make you a bargain."

He frowned at me, and his eyes narrowed. Ever so slowly, he slipped his hand back into his pocket and stood, rocking on his heels. Thinking, I guessed.

"What sort of bargain?"

"I'll riddle you one, and if you can't guess, then I get to keep my life."

"Forever?" he asked with a sneer, and I noticed now that his teeth were sharp and jagged.

"No," I answered, shaking my head. "Just the usual span of time."

He laughed as if I'd said something really funny. "There ain't no season in which I can't harvest, ain't no span of time that's usual."

"Not for you maybe, but for me there is. I got things I want to do," I argued. "I still got a life I want to live."

Jack Straw sat on the bed with a whispery noise like the wind shaking the stooks in the field.

"All right," he said. "Give me your riddle."

All the while I had been trying to convince Jack Straw to bargain, I'd been desperately trying to think on a good riddle. I figured he'd probably already heard every one ever given out, so I knew it had to be a riddle that only I knew, that only I had cause to make happen right then. I stared down at that old quilt, Granny Frank's stitches like silver ribbons in the moonlight, and tried to think.

"Give me your riddle," he said again, and this time I heard the spreading coldness in his voice.

It came to me all of a moment, and in that same moment I felt the fear go out of me. I looked up from the quilt and stared straight into his dry, crackling face. "I'll riddle it to you," I started, just like Granny Frank did in the story, and I saw him straighten his back in expectation. "I died in pieces and was reborn whole. I followed the road over ridges and valleys but never moved."

I held my breath as I watched him figure the riddle. He didn't move, but stayed there black eyed and rigid. The cold mist was settling around the bed, and a drop of it trickled down the side of my face. But I couldn't move, couldn't take my eyes from him.

Then with a snarl he sprang up from my bed. The wind howled outside and rattled the panes as if to break them. Hands upraised over his head, Jack Straw called to the howling wind. The mist thickened in the room, and the white dogs were there beside him, snapping and baying. Hoarfrost cobwebbed across my quilt as Jack Straw shook his raggedy arms at me in fury. I screamed then, fearing he meant to take me, though he'd not given me my answer.

But the scream was scarce from my mouth when he disappeared, and it was Mama who reached out to take me, her arms sleep warm and soft.

"Hush now, hush," she whispered in my ear. "You're dreaming, Katie," she said. "You're dreaming. Mama's right here." She held me tight, and after a bit I felt my fear thaw and stopped shaking.

And even though I knew she was wrong, that I hadn't been dreaming, I let her lay me back on the pillows and tuck in the blankets around me again. She bent over and kissed me, one hand pushing back the wet hair from my forehead.

"My quilt," I whispered to her proudly, and saw her look of confusion.

"Your quilt's here, honey," she said to soothe me.

"No," I said. "That's the answer to the riddle."

"Sure it is," she murmured. She thought I was talking in my sleep, still dreaming. But it didn't matter. The truth was I was still alive because I had beaten Jack Straw.

Just before I fell back to sleep, I heard her talking in low whispers to Daddy. "She's gonna be fine," I heard her say. "Looks like the fever's breaking." Daddy mumbled something. Mama answered. "No, just dreaming, I guess. She's sleeping good now. I think the worst's over."

And in my bed, half asleep, I thought so, too.

But it wasn't. Somehow the worst had only begun.

I stayed in bed another five days and then went back to school. I had five days of lying in my bed to think over what had happened. Oh, I was happy to be alive, to be waking up each day and watching the sun shine through my windows, lighting up the white daisies on my wallpaper. Everything was just as it had been before I got sick. And that scared me. I had sent Jack Straw on his way. But I got to thinking that I was going to spend the rest of my life looking over my shoulder, waiting for him to sneak up on me. And the thought of that dry face, those long spindly arms reaching out to grab me when I wasn't looking, made my victory seem cold.

"Look at your face," Granny Frank said on the morning I got up to eat breakfast before going to school.

"What's the matter with it?" I asked.

"It's screwed tight. Grim as a soldier's. Where's that smile of yours, child?"

"It's there," I snapped, and then felt bad for being cross with her. "I just don't feel like smiling," I said more softly.

"Worried about school?"

"Uh-huh," I answered, because it was easier than telling her the truth.

"It'll be fine," she said, picking up her knitting. "You'll be caught up in no time."

But school wasn't fine. It was terrible. Things had changed while I was out sick. They had painted the halls a new white with a blue stripe down the middle to hide where everybody's hand sort of naturally drags and leaves a dirty smear. The posters on my classroom wall had all been changed, the map showed a new continent, and the desks had been rearranged. People had changed too. My best friend, Mary Beth, came up to me as soon I got into school and gave me a big hug. I didn't recognize her at first because she'd gone and cut off her beautiful long red braids and curled her hair. So instead of being happy to see her, I was mad.

"Why'd you cut your hair?" I yelled.

"Looks better this way," she said, tossing back the short curls. "More grown-up."

"What's so good about growing up?" I said angrily. "You just die anyway."

Mary Beth opened her mouth and then shut it again without saying anything. She waited a few moments, maybe to see if I'd come to my senses and say something nice. But I didn't, so she turned on her heel and left me standing there in that new-painted hallway.

Everything new made me feel scared, made me tremble. Change was an enemy that stole away my hard-won victory and left me open to the next coming of Jack Straw. I wanted time just to stop, for everything and everyone around me to stay safe in its place. But the world isn't like that, is it? It just keeps on going, and I knew that sooner or later Jack Straw would come around again to me. So every day when I left for school, I felt the fear draw tighter and tighter around me as I tried to shut my eyes and ears to the changes. Granny Frank was right in calling me a grim soldier, because I faced each new thing like a battle. Even my own riddle came back to haunt me, for like Granny Frank's stitches, I followed a road over hills and valleys, but never moved.

Whatever illness it was that took me came again and caught Daddy. I found him one day in the barn, just leaning his head against the old cow, too sick with fever to stand. His breathing was harsh, and his eyes burned a fiery red. I helped him to the house and into bed. For two weeks after school and at night, I stood guard over him, waiting lest Jack Straw come to take him. Daddy thrashed with fevered dreams, and his cries wrenched me from the rocking chair to my feet in terror. But the fever broke, and except for a terrible cough that lingered, he mended.

Mama got it next, and for a second time I stood my guard, certain that this time Jack Straw was playing with me. Punishing me for beating him. I sat next to her bed, put cool cloths on her head, and held her hand while she struggled with the fever. When Granny Frank tried to get me to leave and have a rest of my own, I refused. I was so scared that if I moved one foot from that room while Mama was sick, Jack Straw would come for sure and take her behind my back. The first thing Mama did when she felt the fever come down was order me to bed. Only then did I leave her side.

I hardly noticed when winter changed and became wet spring. I had spent so much time worrying and fretting about things out of my hands that I walked around as ragged and worn as Jack Straw himself. The face I saw in the mirror was haggard, my eyes dark gray with purple smudges beneath. My hair had lost its shine, and my mouth was a sour frown. No wonder my friends shied away from me at school, talking in whispers when I passed like some spook down the halls.

They couldn't know how heavy my burden felt, for with the spring Granny Frank took sick with the fever. And with each day that she got weaker and weaker, my burden grew until I felt I could no longer lift my head with the weight of so much dread. Granny Frank would smile at me, pat my hand, and tell me it was all right. "Everything's got a season," she would say. I didn't understand her then and thought she meant the coming spring. Then one night I heard her singing in a tiny, sweet voice a song about spooning in the moonlight. She seemed so happy I thought maybe she'd been spared after all. But when I come closer and touched her head, I knew it wasn't so. Her forehead was hot and dry. Her eyes stared out, not seeing me, but set on some happier memory. I took her hand and clutched it tight.

A cold draft swept through the room. Looking up, I saw Jack Straw standing in the corner, just as before, with his hat pulled down and his hands stuck in his pockets.

"No," I shouted at him. "You can't have her!"

He pushed back his hat, and his face was wrinkled with sadness. "You mean to keep this one from me, too?" he asked.

"Yes," I said.

"Is that what she wants, or what you want?"

"Makes no difference." I stamped my foot like a child.

"Ask her then," he said.

I turned to look down at Granny Frank and bit back a cry. She had stopped singing and was lying quietly, peaceful as a sleeper. By the light of a small lamp I saw suddenly how tiny and frail she had become in the last few days. And how old. Her skin had lost its color, growing pale and yellow like the husk of the corn dollies she used to make. Her white hair was tangled as dried corn silk.

"Do you still want to riddle me, Katie?" Jack Straw asked, his voice no louder than the rustle of leaves.

I didn't answer. There was nothing to say. I realized then that just as I couldn't stop things from changing in life, I couldn't keep Granny Frank from her appointed death. I bowed my head, eyes squeezed shut, and clung to Granny Frank's hand. She squeezed back once, her grip firm for a moment as if to give me strength. And then her hand went limp. I shuddered as the cold draft circled my shoulders. When the room grew warm again, I knew she was gone with Jack Straw. And then I cried, cried hard, grief breaking like a branch within me.

We buried Granny Frank on a beautiful spring morning. From cemetery hill I could see down into the pockets of fields newly plowed, the mist rising like steam from the earth. The air was soft and warm, full of promise, as crocus and daffodil buds swelled and burst open with color.

I was done crying, though I wore the sadness of Granny Frank's death like a long-needed relief. I had been so long frozen that Granny Frank's passing took me like a field set to by the plow blade. I was wounded, cut open, and yet, in the furrow left by her death, I also felt released. I looked up across the open grave into which they lowered Granny Frank's casket and saw Jack Straw one more time. He was standing between the preacher, who was saying the words, and Mrs. Johnson, who jiggled her new baby to keep him from fussing. He didn't look so frightening to me anymore now that I knew him. He looked over and gave me a sad, weathered smile, like he was satisfied with what he had done and sorry at the pain it had caused me.

Then he tipped me his hat in farewell and started ambling off toward the fields. I watched him as he went, like a freed scarecrow with his long, lanky body of dried yellowed stalks. And just before the morning mist swallowed him, I caught a glimpse of faint shimmering green: the new rye grass resurrecting in the fields around him.

J. N. WILLIAMSON
The Sudd

J. N. Williamson has edited three volumes of *Masques,* and written more than thirty novels and one hundred short stories. He lives in Indiana.

In this nightmare journey down the exotic Nile, the Sudd, "a moveable swamp," according to one character, is more than just a physical entity—it is a state of mind. "The Sudd" first appeared in *Pulphouse.*

—E.D.

The Sudd

J. N. WILLIAMSON

Peter had told him to go to Cairo, and Price Sterling nodded as if he were a minister and God had told him to go to hell. He was only thirty; he'd heard that a lot already in the movie business. What he hadn't heard was an order that put him on his own, thousands of miles away, with little said about expenses. And while he expected Egypt to be considerably different from hell, the origins of command had seemed similar to a new second unit director.

What Peter hadn't thought to tell him in his customary mercurial manner was *how* Price should go to Cairo, or hell.

Which was why he opted for getting there from Kenya by way of a steamer up the Nile.

After all, Price had reasoned, they'd blow enough film for four new versions of *The African Queen* without approaching Huston anyway, and he knew at least two scenes that would play better aboard ship. With a little location work out of the way, he'd know what to recommend and might even wind up a hero.

Besides, Price had yearned to take this cruise since Hollywood High. Generations late for believing Tarzan implicitly, he'd been stuck watching PBS one night. The girl's name was long forgotten, now, but she had turned on a travelogue that bored him, first, then galvanized him to action, ultimately motivated him to pursue his career in film. His realization that it was possible not only to travel on a river that ran four thousand miles and be paid for it, but to record for posterity—and for other teenage boys with uncooperative dates—sights ordinary folks would never see, had overwhelmed him.

It hadn't occurred to Price until he sat sweating profusely in a deck chair aboard the *Willem Rotter*—making notes about the eland and beisa seething silkily up the river bank without noticing him or the steamer—that he could be as ordinary as the girl-with-no-name who had prodded him into watching public television.

Part of the diminution of ego he experienced was linked to the rich mix of nationalities he'd encountered after two days on the steamer. Ahmed Firouk, returning to Alexandria after weeks of undisclosed business, smiled as if taking a screen test. Krapf, no Christian name volunteered, a Durban resident with lips that would've looked great in blackface. Aging Mrs. Marxe from Leopoldville, citing the "e" in her name like an academic credential. Originally British Bruce Smallesmith, from Capetown now. One Carlos Brazza of vague origins by any judgment, destination north of the Sudan. (Price would have doubted the day of the week from that man.) Emma Vanderblatt, a scintillating fifty, asea on revivified charm and her birthday. Stanley Sidney Odney, an Australian who liked enunciating his own name; he had been on holiday in Mozambique and mentioned a spot of biz at Lake No.

The girl.

Further reasons for Price's modified ego had to do with his certain hunch that each of them was exceptionally rich. None of them treated him an iota different, or better, when he told them what he did.

Especially the girl, and that was all the intercourse he'd had with any of them up to now.

And the peculiar likelihood that none of the people he had met knew anybody else on ship. Even before he introduced himself to them, he saw that they were already playing specific parts, enacting them as if it was insignificant whether they were good at it, important that they pleased themselves.

That variety of pretense or individuation impressed Price, reminded him he had come this far, partly, in the hope of recalling the way he had been before encountering culture on PBS. People he ran with went nowhere except *en masse*, *en suite*; whether they were gaffers or best boys, second unit directors, screen-writers or the odd featured player who got off on slumming, it was central to each that the rest perceive the point of his private little drama. True leadership in Hollywood appeared to amount to how many others agreed to be spear wielders in one's extemporaneous and open-ended soap. Price thought the reason orgies and drug parties had succeeded was that no one had the foggiest notion of how to be alone. Someone else was always around, and the mere thought of loneliness was literally a fear of the unknown.

Making notes and blocking scenes, Price studied the foreigners playing, reading, drinking on the steamer deck and wondered if he had booked a passage on one of those old movie boats headed for hell. It wasn't difficult to imagine, even if such films usually lost big bucks. Because it was hot enough for the Styx. Barely twilight, Price's third evening aboard, and the perpetuity of the pounding waves of heat began to seem Kismetic as cancer. For a lean, serene, imperturbable man like he was, the relentless rising temperatures were like some ridiculous wild girl from Kansas who'd do anything to impress him. He started trying to envision either Khartoum or Cairo as paradise.

Most of the ego sloughing away that afternoon, and now, involved what Price Sterling had been observing on the banks of the Nile.

They had been following that part of the world's second longest river which was called the *Bahr el Abyed*, or White Nile. As a buff, Price knew that at roughly the time the Nile received the waters of the Giraffe River their direction would veer slightly, indiscernibly, until his long-planned cruise wound up in the Sudan, at Khartoum. He'd fly from there to Cairo if he had any intention left to arrive before Peter and the rest. There were hands of the Egyptian hierarchy to shake, tribute paid before the clasps were broken. Always, it was that way on location, whether the official with anticipatory eyes wore a turban, or a name-tag marked Mayor.

The steamer sizzled along like some smouldering insect on the unchanging Nile, the incomparable river flowing with almost sentient deliberation into channels beyond a cartographer's skills, and Price wondered about skipping both heaven and hell. He thought about purposes or their absence, the girl in the swimming pool, the way meandering waters with an elevation of sixteen hundred feet, here, narrowed to the width of Hollywood Boulevard due west, now, of Ethiopia . . .

One hour ago it had been broad, searing daylight and he'd caught glimpses of crocodile as long as cleared banquet tables lolling in readiness between the boat and people on the banks. He saw weavers; old women with stooped backs, at work; bare brown children whose bellies looked seven months pregnant; young males who ran in razorish Zeekoevlei grass like suicides' shadows haunting a heap of broken green bottles. "The Bantu" was the collective term Krapf from Durban used for the people, speaking full voice. Chin lowered and guttural when he drank illegal *skokiaan* opposite Brazza, the Afrikaaner also called the people "kaffir." Price grunted. He knew the American equivalent of the word.

More minutes later, stars out like teeth in a necklace, he saw the Bantu had left the bank. *Do they have a dinner hour or are they too smart to schedule pleasure?* Price wondered. When he rose and went to the rail through surges of heat like passionate breath, he could not see the crocs, either. But a pale ibis, sacred still to some human beings dependent upon the *Bahr el Abyed*, rocketed over the waters as if gusted there by jaws snapped shut a lifetime late.

And when he rested against the railing a yard or two from Smallesmith, the Brit, Price studied the girl in the pool, thinking she might turn into a fish. A pandodont, maybe, or a shiny bichir. Not a mormyrid, or elephant fish. These steamers had been outfitted, Price mused, for the maximum delight of their passengers. While the *Willem Rotter* had never been an æsthetically enticing craft unboarded, it sported every modern convenience—if by modern, Price thought, one meant 1949 or so. The pool was situated at the center of the main deck in order for tourists to watch the bathers, and for the latter to know it was happening.

When at last the swimming girl surfaced in her one-piece suit that was strangely out of date to the Californian, her abrupt exit made him think of seals leaving the water. She virtually squeaked, bare- and flat-footed across the deck in what could be a direct line toward Price Sterling. The swimsuit made him think of new car tires. The bathing cap was brushed by stars hanging low as lanterns at a Beverly Hills pool party, turning her outerspace baldish until she was close. When she was as near him as she was going to be, the cap was peeled away and hair red as Kenyan *tamaties* rained in torrents.

Merle Oberon eyes, Price thought, saw her gaze touch his tanned face without seeing him at all. Then the eyes and her naked knees dipped the swimmer into a chair beside Mrs. Marxe from Leopoldville. What shocked him was both the way the girl totally did not see him, the incivility of that, and a new awareness that no passenger had glanced for even an instant at the astonishing sights along the river. Not once, he believed, in two days, three evenings.

"She's beautiful," Bruce Smallesmith acknowledged, at his side. He didn't lower his voice despite the proximity of the two women in shadows at the table. The hum-and-shudder of the steamer was such a constant that it was easily ignored but, if it hadn't been, the weight of the African night pressed upon them like a murderer's pillow, muffling sound. Recently, Price recalled, a lion had roared and its impact was no more immediate than MGM's Leo. "But not exceptional."

"Everybody is beautiful, in Hollywood," Price said, putting most of his hands in the slits of his tight white slacks. "It's the law."

Smallesmith had cultivated an image of impeccability with such fidelity that he looked innocent as an infant; like a dead man, he no longer aged, just crisped. "You didn't comment about laws obliging Californians to be exceptional."

Price presented a sincere grin. Probably the Brit wanted something, everybody did, but this moment broke the spell of apartness troubling Price. "Well, this happens after you've signed a contract," he explained. "You're exceptional as long as it's been paid."

"I see," Smallesmith chuckled. His gaze, slightly veiled by tinted lenses in his glasses and his own private purposes, had returned to the swimming girl. Each man noticed she had dried her red hair but not her body, nor had she donned a robe. "That must be what happened in television."

"I don't . . ."

"When residuals went in," the Englishman explained, "it was like born-again exceptionability."

Price laughed. He wondered, suddenly, if Bruce Smallesmith was also trying to figure out a way to sit at the table with Mrs. Marxe and the unexceptional swimmer. He wondered how the Brit kept from sweating, or from showing it, why Mrs. Marxe didn't seem to have spoken to the redhead and went on reading a novel with a title in a language he didn't recognize; why the girl sat down there or, finally had come out of the pool at all. He wondered a lot.

"Why don't . . . these people . . . mingle?" He was half-startled he'd asked it. Yet there were probably two dozen men and women, no kids Price had seen, to whom he hadn't introduced himself, and all were alone. Or, like the women nearby, individually preoccupied. "Why don't they wish to meet one another?"

Smallesmith's brows rose above his tinted spectacles. "But we do know each other, dear boy," he said. "For the most part. The majority of us have met many times, at many places."

So you don't like each other, Price thought without speaking.

The older man went on as if he had. "It's the Nile, you see, Sterling. We're a smidge more sociable when on land."

"It's like commuting, then," Price said, excited as he understood. "Now I get it! People taking the same train to New York every day must get pretty bored, too." He laughed nervously. "I feel like such a damned tourist now."

The pause before Smallesmith answered was long enough for Price to turn toward him. The *Willem Rotter* was rounding a bend and all the American detected of the other's face were the colored lenses.

"You don't get it, at all." The eyes were those of a blinded owl. "All any of us will ever be on this benighted river is tourists."

Involuntarily, Price jumped. "Pardon me?"

"It's sheer mesmerism, one's first time out here," the Englishman said. "When one does not live in Africa." He had lowered his pitch now and it was sporadically as if his voice merged with the neighboring sounds of purring civets, the squeal of the earth pig, the conversations of lemur families. A stork like snow vaulted into the moon, vanished. "You'll see the lily of the Nile growing wild, Sterling, with exquisite azure flowers—and stalks large enough to encompass a man's fist. Your destination, the Sudan, has grass that reaches a height of ten feet." His features swam into focus, the lips scarcely moving. "The Nile basin extends from 4° South latitude to 31° North. There are alpine flora in the Ruwenzori Range, for God's sake!"

"You're saying . . . ?"

"It's too much, boy, it's too vast." Smallesmith looked incredulous. "Price—they didn't even discover the headwaters of this damned river until 1862!" Slim hand slipped into jacket pocket, he made ready to leave. "We are afraid, dear chap." His free hand found Price Sterling's bicep, squeezed and released it. "None of us really wish to be here, you see; but there's no other way."

"No, I don't see!" Price declared. "What—"

"Here, look at this." Smallesmith withdrew his hand carefully, turned it palm up. Something brown and gross, bloated, clung. "It's called a Kenopus."

"A what?" Price said impatiently. He edged a step off before prodding at the creature with a ring finger. "Damn, man, it's *dead*."

"It's not." Smallesmith flexed his fingers. Eyes far too big for it popped; then the creature leaped, cleared the railing, was swallowed by the river. Sweat streaked one of the Englishman's colored lenses. "It is a toad without any tongue," he said. "Fancy that." His gaze swiveled to the bank, back. "From Ethiopia."

"Bruce, I don't get the drift," said Price. But Smallesmith was at the table with the disaffected women. "I don't see at all."

The man stopped without looking at either woman, or anything on the steamer. "It's *the sudd*, old boy. You may assume that's why we're afraid."

The girl in the one-piece swimsuit looked expressionlessly toward Price. It was the first time he thought she'd seen him. The coal brows of the old woman formed the letter V and dripped perspiration on her open book. An elderly man across the deck gripped a shuffleboard stick like a crutch. Smallesmith was gone, and Price remembered dinosaurs fast frozen in the act of masticating, ships of fame sinking.

"Nearer," he whispered not quite sardonically as he turned back to the railing and the river bank, "my God, to Thee."

Uncountable eyes regarded him.

When the lids closed, the African night was impermeable.

It didn't occur to Price until morning, after several solitary hours of muttering imprecations at the inadequate air conditioning in the state rooms, that he hadn't seen "a Black" among the *Willem Rotter* passengers. Some were employees. Stewards, waiters, a grinning middle-aged man with a tiny boy who accepted the letters Price had written. But the bad part was that he hadn't been conscious of their absence whatsoever until seeing that the paying customers of the steamship line constituted a miniscule minority. And he wondered, even before he saw the red-haired woman was back in the pool, how it stayed possible for a people in such overwhelming numbers to be invisible.

Price was in trunks and perched on the apron of the swimming pool, dangling tanned legs and perceiving for the first time how pasty, how unrelievedly white, he looked, in contrast to the others on board.

Except the swimmer in her one-piece suit.

She said, shockingly, "Get me something cool to drink, quickly." Her Martian head and shoulders had sprung from the water at Price's feet. She was addressing him. She either added the word "please" or he expected it enough to imagine she said it.

"Okay, all right." He was standing by the time he answered her, questing for a waiter, hoping he didn't have to leave to obey. The young woman was beginning to assume for him the properties of a mermaid and, if she again submerged, she might disappear into a river cave forever.

But he was overeager, had one side turned when a waiter materialized with a tray, and the swimmer slithered up beside him and accepted a glass when the waiter stooped to her. *"Hamba gahle,"* she murmured—and Price realized she had a drink, as well, for him.

"What did that mean?" He wanted to pay for the drinks but that, too, had been done somehow. Maybe she was keeping a tab.

She showed him perfect teeth, a moist red curl fleeing from the bathing cap, and cleavage that was exceptional enough, enroute to the Sudan and a world of veils. "Go in peace," she said. She hadn't told him her name and had yet to look at him, really, a second time. Perhaps she truly looked at no one.

"In what tongue?" asked Price.

"In Swahili," the girl retorted. Her upper lip on the rim of the glass was thin; determined. "He'd have preferred Twi-Fante, but one can't spend all her time learning the Sudanese dialects."

"I think it's marvelous you know Swahili," Price said. His drink, principally, was gin; he was relieved it wasn't *skokiaan*, which he'd learned was moonshine. She smiled and he caught it. "What's funny?"

"Tourists. The world. One form or another of Sudanese is spoken by fifty million of them. If you don't speak a bit of their chatter, you're positively at their mercy." Those Merle Oberon eyes contrived to look covert and put-upon. "There's Dinka, Yoruba, Twi-Fante—I mentioned that one—Fulani, Hausa —that's useful in trading." She stared down at the bottom of her glass, sighed. "God knows what the Tallensi, Mangbetu or Wolof are chattering away in these days." Her nose wrinkled. "Too much outside influence."

"Where are you going?"

For an instant she didn't understand the question. Then, startlingly, she laughed. "To the end of the trolley ride."

He laughed with her as best he could. "Then what?"

"Then," she said, yanking the suit up snugly over her bosom, "then I'll catch another trolley back."

"What did Bruce Smallesmith mean when he said you were all afraid, out here?" He realized she'd started to slip back into the pool and put out his fingers to touch her arm. Skin not nearly as tanned as his felt remarkably cool. "Of what?"

For a moment he thought she wouldn't answer him. She did, expressionlessly once more. "Bruce Smallesmith is *English*." She hissed the curse.

"But what's 'the sudd'?" he called after her, getting to his knees like a perplexed boy attempting to follow a mermaid trail. "Why are you terrified by it?"

She showed her cheek and one Oberon eye to him from a third the length of the pool away, not even pretending she hadn't heard.

Obviously, she had given him her answer. She had also stayed in the swimming pool.

Before noon, the *Willem Rotter* wended its methodical way into another of the interminable branches of the river, passage seemed to narrow to the width of a two-lane highway and Price found himself at the railing between Stanley Sidney Odney, the lanky ex-Aussie in outback shorts that reached the knee, and Krapf, from Durban. All three started at a number of tribesmen laden with pots and carefully wrapped packages which they pulled behind them on sleds Price Sterling found ingenious.

"Nomadic herders, mate," Odney answered his question, "prob'ly from the Dongola provinces. Off to swap beer and unleavened bread—dates, too, and whatnot—for camels or horses. They're called Kababish."

"Kababish?" Price repeated. "That doesn't sound—"

"They speak a Semitic tongue," Krapf interjected, pursing thick lips. "Aside from that, they're industrious, at least."

"The girl in the pool," Price began, addressing Odney, "she said the blacks on this tub were probably Twi-Fante. How could she tell?"

Odney, to his amazement, broke into laughter. The Afrikaaner crimsoned, glared at Price as if he'd enjoy killing him, and wandered off in the general direction of the man named Brazza.

"What did I say wrong?" Price demanded of the Australian, spreading his hands. "Is there something wrong with the Twi-Fante?"

"Wrong?" Stan Odney repeated, grinning. "Nothin' about the ol' Twi-Fante a well-placed *kisu-ki-kali* wouldn't fix right up!" Odney came closer. "They're Akan people, do a bit of arts and crafts and brass-castin' for their tea and cakes." He cast a discreet but amused glance around. "Y'see, sport, there's only one way the lydy could be sure these kaffir are Twi-Fante so I doubts she knew about the waiter for sure." Whispering, "They's one of the tribes in these immediate parts what's downright opposed to circumcision!"

Late in the afternoon, Price asked Smallesmith what *kisu-ki-kali* meant in Swahili and the exact translation was "knife-sharp."

After that, it got hot on the Nile.

Price had spent his life in California, rarely seeing any winter except when he went into the mountains to ski. He liked everything hot. But the temperature on the *Willem Rotter* was exceeding anything he'd even imagined. Definitely, he thought while going down to the lounge with the rest, this was not paradise—somehow, even demons would flee from such a hell.

Sagging at a table with Ahmed Firouk, the customarily self-irradiated Mrs. Vanderblatt and Brazza—unasked—Price was stunned to think that a man might perish quite easily there. The Sudan, his stop, lay just south of the Sahara, encysted by the tropical forests of Guinea and the Congo. He remembered reading that Ethiopia had been dead in the path of innumerable fortune-seeking types from the east, had been a superior culture-carrier, strategically, to Egypt. All around those people were fortunes, indeed, found and forged and taken; plentiful game had roamed wild around them with nothing but the shoebill heron of the furtive Nile to return, to enlighten them.

"It's warming up," Firouk declared with the flashing smile of a manic weather man.

Mrs. Vanderblatt, ravishing and golden at fifty, looked away. She hadn't touched the drink she ordered and the wonders of her cosmetic base were proving as man-made and feckless as her dietary conquests.

Carlos Brazza, doe-eyed and massive of torso, made a snorting sound and moved his feet heavily under the table. "You'd like them to keep records here, yes? To know if it's near one for this time of year?"

Ahmed was incorrigibly cheerful. "That would be truly interesting." He wafted immaculate shoulders and Price had a glimpse of a Russian word on his suitcoat lapel. "If we must have the heat, an element of sport would be nice, yes?"

"Please." Emma Vanderblatt, hesitant about departing but clearly thinking of standing. Her alto was a tiny mouse fleeing across the checkered tablecloth. *"Please."*

Brazza sniffed, swallowed his beer, gestured at a waiter. Price asked if he could help Emma, and Brazza, lumbering to his feet, seemed entertained. "You can't help. Señora heard the captain's report of ambatch, *Umel Suf*, and papyrus." His soft mole's eyes looked amused but he turned to the Twi-Fante rushing with his drink and snatched it from the small, dapper waiter. The latter ducked his head as if awaiting a blow, winking his eyes shut as if doing so might save him and resurrect something. Brazza put a hand on the waiter's neck but looked at Price. "It's never confined to one channel, and she knows it."

Emma stared not at Brazza but at the Twi-Fante, forming soundless words with lips that cracked. Then she hurled herself from the table, lurched out of the lounge.

Price thought she had whispered, *kill him*. When he started to question Brazza, the burly man was stomping toward the lavatories. Ahmed Firouk also stood, drawing a newspaper from his pocket, smiling pleasantly. He discerned Price's bewildered look, and paused.

"There is always much water loss, due to high temperature, sir." A shrug. "As a rule, there's no conjunction of a perilously reduced water level—and the *sudd*." An index finger that resembled the Kenopus cautioned the American. "As a rule."

Price sought a nap, couldn't find sleep. Sitting up drenched, he had a mental image of something satin with sequins in it, and needed instantly to know the time. His wrist showed him white where his watch ought to have been. In a dimly lit corridor outside his room, he saw the small, wincing waiter from the lounge and followed him to the deck for no reason he could grasp. But Smallesmith was the only man he saw through a blistering haze and the Brit crossed toward him with motions that made Price think of swimming. Smallesmith's body showed skeletally through his soaked clothing, but he halted before going below, a born explainer.

"The *sudd*," he said without preamble, "is Nile garbage, old boy. Floating vegetation." He managed to seem chipper. "It's rather like . . . a movable swamp." He squinted above Price's head. "To put things into perspective, I should say the *sudd* is Africa's equivalent of . . . an *iceberg*."

"But the boat—"

"Is designed to carve straight through. Quite." His brows lifted, perspiration ran unimpeded. "All our vehicles are built to get us from point A, to B—even C, or X. The alphabet isn't that reliable, in the jungle."

"Papyrus," Price recalled, aloud, "ambatch . . ."

"Bordered by a remarkably dense growth of rushes and reeds. You remember them from Bible class, don't you?" He stepped through the door but hesitated. "If the old hulk won't go through, the trick is to avoid running her aground. That is messy."

Then he left and Price, obedient to ancient needs, turned toward the yawning swimming pool. The girl he didn't know was gone; he'd see her one other time. Behind him, Krapf came to the doorway smacking his lips over a dish called *mabela* which tasted remotely like hot chocolate pudding. A woman of Color whom Price hadn't met stood beside but not with Krapf. Neither addressed Price and he never saw her again.

He gazed across the deck and the water, and it was twilight but he scarcely noticed even after he had gone to the railing. He did see how narrow this channel was, then for a second doubted his senses and clung to the rail simply to regain every kind of balance.

The banks on either side of the steamer appeared so near he might have thrown a beach-ball anywhere and struck dry land. To his left, forest, to his right, forest, each inhospitable and sealed like the gates to heaven or hell. Nothing Price could see whispered, muttered low in its collective throat, and said nothing he was able to understand. He quit striving to penetrate the jungle of night, wetness scorching his eyes, incapable of distinguishing between perspiration and tears.

Which was when the Blacks on board left the *Willem Rotter* although none of the Whites or Coloreds knew it for two hours, including Price. But they learned of the exodus when the steamer ran aground.

Then came the mosquitoes, the tse-tse flies, that summer bug called a miggie. Next, midnight; but their time pieces were slow . . .

Smallesmith, it was, who told them the radio was out now, and he said nothing when Krapf swore, said it had happened intentionally. Ahmed observed that it didn't matter, considering the temp, the limited water and food, the distance (as he put it good-humoredly) "to any place." Emma Vanderblatt remained in her cabin, and Stan Odney wondered if she was bloody alive in there, but did not go to see. Some old man Price had dimly noticed did.

Brazza pretended to get drunk just inside the mess, holstered revolver brandished on a meaty leg. Aging Mrs. Marxe finished reading the novel in a language Price didn't recognize and began another, sanguine and solitary.

Someone shot himself. The report was its own news bulletin and a few of the rest, Price believed, were envious. Nobody was wounded or ill, no one was hungry, no one was especially thirsty, and they were going to die there.

Alone, Price felt himself start to panic and went back on deck where he saw the girl in the swimming suit reclining on a rubber mat beside the pool. He thought she was dead. He heard her humming, the fragile sound as distant as breathless anticipation on the surrounding river banks. He stripped off his shirt, mopped his eyes to look at the *sudd* on which the steamer was grounded, dimly conscious of the captain manfully trying to ram through the colorful floe, the "Nile garbage." The air was redolent with a pleasing, woodsy scent like a cologne he'd brought. Vivid but small, a passerine stood at one of the young woman's outflung arms, but the bird was no longer singing. When Price had drawn close enough, he perceived that she was propping it up with her lolling fingers. Its neck had been wrung.

"*Ham-ba gahle,*" she sang, off-key, looking beautiful, desirable. The Merle Oberon eyes were glassy. She was wet from head to toe, red hair like a fountain of blood, the rest of her sensual with perspiration. "*Ham-ba gahhhhh-lee.*"

He bent, dizzy, to see what was the matter with her and recognized the familiar clear-plastic packet of *dagga*, the Sudanese drug of preference.

Price stripped down completely enroute to the railing and the Nile. It looked like an easy swim to either shore, if the crocodiles had fed. Nude, knees bent on the railing, he stared right, then left, into thickets of unblinking, watchful eyes. They stretched to unguessable horizons without malice. He was turned black by night, but that mightn't be enough.

"*Kwakheri,*" called the young swimmer. "*Niii-ight.*"

Price nodded, dove off the railing.

Every pair of eyelids closed.

JONATHAN CARROLL

Mr. Fiddlehead

This dark fantasy tale falls, like so much of Carroll's work, into the shadowy area between fantasy and horror. Carroll won the World Fantasy Award for "Friend's Best Man" and has written several strange and marvelous novels. Devotees of *The Land of Laughs*, *Voice of Shadows*, *Bones of the Moon* and the excellent "Rumplestiltskin" novel *Sleeping in Flames* will find Carroll at his wry best in the following story from the pages of *Omni* magazine. Carroll lives in Vienna, Austria.

—T.W.

Carroll is an expert at insinuating the awful things that lurk in the shadows of human consciousness, and he writes the kind of horror that sneaks up on you. "Mr. Fiddlehead" plays a small part in his novel *A Child Across the Sky*. All of his novels and stories move with a subtle shift from the everyday world to the slightly off-kilter. This tale is no exception.

—E.D.

Mr. Fiddlehead

JONATHAN CARROLL

On my fortieth birthday Lenna Rhodes invited me over for lunch. That's the tradition—when one of us has a birthday, there's lunch, a nice present, and a laughing afternoon to cover the fact we've move one more step down the staircase. We met years ago when we happened to marry into the same family: Six months after I said yes to Eric Rhodes, she said it to his brother Michael.

Lenna got the better end of *that* wishbone: She and Michael are still delighted with each other, while Eric and I fought about everything and nothing and then got divorced.

But to my surprise and relief, they were a great help to me during the divorce, even though there were obvious difficulties climbing over some of the thorn-bushes of family and blood allegiance.

She and Michael live in a big apartment on One-hundredth Street with long halls and not much light. But the gloom of the place is offset by their kids' toys everywhere, colorful jackets stacked on top of each other, and coffee cups with WORLD'S GREATEST MOM and DARTMOUTH written on the side. Theirs is a home full of love and hurry, children's drawings on the fridge alongside reminders to buy *La Stampa*. Michael owns a very elegant vintage fountain pen store, while Lenna freelances for *Newsweek*. Their apartment is like their life: high-ceilinged, thought-out, overflowing with interesting combinations and possibilities. It is always nice to go there and share it a while.

I felt pretty good about being forty years old. Finally there was some money in the bank and someone I liked, talking about a trip together to Egypt in the spring. Forty was a milestone but one that didn't mean much at the moment. I already thought of myself as being slightly middle-aged anyway, but I was healthy and had good prospects, so *so what!* to the beginning of my fifth decade.

"You cut your hair!"

"Do you like it?"

"You look very French."

"Yes, but do you *like* it?"

"I think so. I have to get used to it. Come on in."

We sat in the living room and ate. Elbow, their bull terrier, rested his head on my knee and never took his eyes off the table. After the meal was over we cleared the plates, and she handed me a small red box.

"I really hope you like them. I made them myself."

Inside the box were a pair of the most beautiful gold earrings I have ever seen.

"My God, Lenna. They're *exquisite*! You *made* these? I didn't know that you made jewelry."

She looked happily embarrassed. "You like them? They're real gold, believe it or not."

"I believe it. They're art! You *made* them, Lenna? I can't get over it. They're really works of art; they look like something by Klimt." I took them carefully out of the box and put them on.

She clapped her hands like a girl. "Oh, Juliet, they really do look good!"

Our friendship *is* important and goes back a long way, but this was a lifetime present—one you gave a spouse or someone who'd saved your life.

Before I could say that (or anything else), the lights went out. Her two young sons brought in the birthday cake, forty candles strong.

A few days later I was walking down Madison Avenue and, caught by something there, looked in a jewelry store window. There they were—my birthday earrings. The exact ones. Looking closer, open-mouthed, I saw the price tag. Five thousand dollars! I stood and gaped for what must have been minutes. I was shocked. Had she lied about making them? Or spent five thousand dollars for my birthday present? Lenna wasn't a liar, and she wasn't rich. All right, so she had them copied in brass or something and just *said* they were gold to make me feel good. That wasn't her way either. What the hell was going on?

The confusion emboldened me to walk right into the store. Or rather to walk right up and press the buzzer. Someone rang me in. The salesgirl who appeared from behind a curtain looked like she had graduated from Radcliffe with a degree in bluestocking. Maybe you had to to work in this place.

"Can I help you?"

"Yes. I'd like to see the pair of these earrings you have in the window."

Looking at my ears, she suddenly realized I had a very familiar five thousand dollars hanging from my earlobes. It changed everything: Her expression said she would be my slave—or friend—for life. "Of course, the Dixies."

"The what?" She smiled, like I was being very funny. It quickly dawned on me that she must have thought I knew very well what "Dixies" were, since I was wearing some.

She took them out of the window and put them carefully down in front of me on a blue velvet card. They were beautiful, and admiring them, I entirely forgot for a while I had some on.

"I'm so surprised you have a pair. They only came in a week ago."

Thinking fast, I said, "My husband bought them for me, and I like them so much I'm thinking of getting a pair for my sister. Tell me about the designer. What's his name, Dixie?"

"I don't know much, madam. Only that the owner knows who Dixie is, where they come from . . . and that whoever it is is a real genius. Apparently both Bulgari and people from the Memphis group have already been in, asking who it is and how they can contact him."

"How do you know it's a man?"

I put the earrings down and looked directly at her.

"Oh, I don't. It's just that the work is so masculine that I assumed it. Maybe you're right; maybe it *is* a woman." She picked one up and held it to the light. "Did you notice how they don't really reflect light so much as enhance it? Golden light you can own. I've never seen that. I envy you."

They were real. I went to a jeweler on Forty-seventh Street to have them appraised, then to the only other two stores in the city that sold "Dixies." No one knew anything about the creator or weren't talking if they did. Both dealers were very respectful and pleasant, but mum's the word when I asked about the jewelry's origin.

"The gentleman asked us not to give out information, madam. We must respect his wishes."

"But it *is* a man?"

A professional smile. "Yes."

"Could I contact him through you?"

"Yes, I'm sure that would be possible. Can I help with anything else, madam?"

"What other pieces did he design?"

"As far as I know, only the earrings, the fountain pen, and this key ring." He'd shown me the pen, which was nothing special. Now he brought out a small golden key ring shaped in a woman's profile. Lenna Rhodes's profile.

The doorbell tinkled when I walked into the store. Michael was with a customer and, smiling hello, gave me the sign he'd be over as soon as he was finished. He had started INK almost as soon as he got out of college, and from the beginning it was a success. Fountain pens are cranky, unforgiving things that demand full attention and patience. But they are also a handful of flash and old-world elegance: gratifying slowness that offers no reward other than the sight of shiny ink flowing wetly across a dry page. INK's customers were both rich and not so, but all of them had the same collector's fiery glint in their eyes and addict's desire for more.

A couple of times a month I'd work there when Michael needed an extra hand. It taught me to be cheered by old pieces of Bakelite and gold plate, as well as other people's passion for unimportant but lovely objects.

"Juliet, hi! Roger Peyton was in this morning and bought that yellow Parker Duofold. The one he's been looking at for months!"

"Finally. Did he pay full price?"

Michael grinned and looked away. "Rog can never afford full price. I let him do it in installments. What's up with you?"

"Did you ever hear of a Dixie pen? Looks a little like the Cartier Santos?"

"Dixie? No. It looks like the Santos?" The expression on his face said he was telling the truth.

I bought out the brochure from the jewelry store and, opening it to the pen photograph, handed it to him. His reaction was immediate.

"Why, that bastard! How much do I have to put up with?"

"You know him?"

Michael looked up from the photo, anger and confusion competing for first place on his face. "Do I know him? Sure I know him. He lives in my goddamned *house*, I know him so well! Dixie, huh? Cute name. Cute man."

"Wait. I'll show you something, Juliet. Just stay there. Don't move! That shit."

There's a mirror behind the front counter at INK. When Michael motored off to the back of the store, I looked at my reflection and said, *"Now* you did it."

He was back in no time. "Look at this. You want to see something beautiful? Look at this." He handed me something in a blue velvet case. I opened it and saw . . . the Dixie fountain pen.

"But you told me that you'd never heard of them."

His voice was hurt and loud. "It is *not* a Dixie fountain pen. It's a Sinbad. An original, solid-gold Sinbad made at the Benjamin Swire Fountain Pen Works in Konstanz, Germany, around 1915. There's a rumor the Italian futurist Antonio Sant'Elia did the design, but that's never been proven. Nice, isn't it?"

It was nice, but he was so angry I wouldn't have dared say it wasn't. I nodded eagerly. He took it back. "I've been selling pens twenty years, but I've only seen two of these in all that time. One of them was owned by Walt Disney, and I have the other. Collector's value? About seven thousand dollars."

"Won't the Dixie people get in trouble for copying it?"

"No, because I'm sure they either bought the design or there are small differences between the original and this one. Let me see that brochure again."

"But you have an original, Michael. It still holds its value."

"That's not the point. It's not the value that matters. I'd never sell this.

"You know the classic 'bathtub' Porsche? One of the strangest, greatest-looking cars of our time. Some smart, cynical person realized that and is now making fiberglass copies of the thing.

"But it's a lie car, Juliet; sniff it and it smells only of today—little plastic things and cleverly cut corners you can't see. Not important to the car but essential to the real *object*.

"The wonder of the thing was Porsche designed it so well and thoughtfully so long ago. That's art. But the art is in its original everything, not just the look or the convincing copy.

"I can guarantee you that your Dixie pen has too much plastic inside where you can't see and a gold point that probably has about a third as much gold on it as the original. It looks good, but they always miss the whole point with their cut corners.

"Look, you're going to find out sooner or later, so I think you better know now."

"What are you talking about?"

He brought a telephone up from beneath the counter and gestured for me to wait a bit. He called Lenna and in a few words told her about the Dixies, my discovery of them. . . .

Michael was looking at me when he asked. "Did he tell you he was doing that, Lenna?"

Whatever her long answer was, it left his expression deadpan. "Well, I'm going to bring Juliet home. I want her to meet him. What? Because we've got to do something about it, Lenna! Maybe she'll have an idea of what to do. Do you think this is normal? Oh, you do? That's interesting. Do you think it's normal for *me*?" A dab of saliva popped off his lip and flew across the store.

When Michael opened the door, Lenna stood right on the other side, arms crossed tight over her chest. Her soft face was squinched into a tight challenge. "Whatever he told you probably isn't true, Juliet."

I put up both hands in surrender. "He didn't tell me anything, Lenna. I don't even want to *be* here. I just showed him a picture of a pen."

Which wasn't strictly true. I showed him a picture of a pen because I wanted to know more about Dixie and maybe my five-thousand-dollar earrings. Yes, sometimes I am nosy.

Both of the Rhodeses were calm and sound people. I don't think I'd ever seen them really disagree on anything important or raise their voices at each other.

Michael growled, "Where is he? Eating again?"

"Maybe. So what? You don't like what he eats anyway."

He turned to me. "Our guest is a vegetarian. His favorite food is plum pits."

"Oh, that's *mean*, Michael. That's really mean." She turned and left the room.

"So he is in the kitchen? Good. Come on, Juliet." He took my hand and pulled me behind on his stalk to their visitor.

Before we got to him I heard music. Ragtime piano. Scott Joplin?

A man sat at the table with his back to us. He had long red hair down over the collar of his sport jacket. One freckled hand was fiddling with the dial on a radio nearby.

"Mr. Fiddlehead? I'd like you to meet Lenna's bestfriend, Juliet Skotchdopole."

He turned, but even before he was all the way around, I knew I was sunk. What a face! Ethereally thin, with high cheekbones and deep-set green eyes that were both merry and profound. Those storybook eyes, the carroty hair, and freckles everywhere. How could freckles suddenly be so damned sexy? They were for children and cute advertisements. I wanted to touch every one on him.

"Hello, Juliet! Skotchdopole, is it? That's a good name. I wouldn't mind havin' it myself. It's a lot better than Fiddlehead, you know."

His deep voice lay in a hammock of a very strong Irish accent.

I put out a hand, and we shook. Looking down, I ran my thumb once quickly, softly across the top of his hand. I felt hot and dizzy, as if someone I wanted had put his hand gently between my legs for the first time.

He smiled. Maybe he sensed it. There was a plate of something on the table next to the radio.

To stop staring so embarrassingly at him, I focused on it and realized the plate was full of plum pits.

"Do you like them? They're delicious." He picked one off the shiny orange-brown pile and, putting the stony thing in his mouth, bit down on it. Something cracked loud, like he'd broken a tooth, but he kept his angel's smile on while crunching away on the plum pit.

I looked at Michael, who only shook his head. Lenna came into the kitchen and gave Mr. Fiddlehead a big hug and kiss. He only smiled and went on eating . . . pits.

"Juliet, the first thing you have to know is I lied about your birthday present. I didn't make those earrings—Mr. Fiddlehead did. But since he's me, I wasn't *really* lying. " She smiled as if she was sure I understood what she was talking about. I looked at Michael for help, but he was poking around in the refrigerator. Beautiful Mr. Fiddlehead was still eating.

"What do you mean, he's 'you'?"

Michael took out a carton of milk and, at the same time, a plum, which he exaggeratedly offered his wife. She made a face at him and snatched it out of his hand. Biting it, she said, "Remember I told you I was an only child? Well, like a lot of lonely kids, I solved my problem the best way I could—by making up an imaginary friend."

My eyes widened. I looked at the red-headed man. He winked at me.

Lenna went on. "I made up Mr. Fiddlehead. I read and dreamed so much then that one day I put it all together into my idea of the perfect friend: First, his name would be Mr. Fiddlehead because I thought that was the funniest name in the world—something that would always make me laugh when I was sad. Then he had to come from Ireland because that was the home of all the leprechauns and fairies. In fact, I wanted a kind of life-size human leprechaun. He'd have red hair and green eyes and, whenever I wanted, the magical ability to make gold bracelets and jewelry for me out of thin air."

"Which explains the Dixie jewelry in the stores?"

Michael nodded. "He said he got bored just hanging around, so I suggested he do something useful. Everything was fine so long as it was just the earrings and key chain." He slammed the glass down on the counter. "But I didn't know about the fountain pen until today. What's with *that*, Fiddlehead?"

"Because I wanted to try me hand at it. I loved the one you showed me, so I thought I'd use that as my model. Why not? You can't improve on perfection. The only thing I did was put some more gold in it here and there."

I put my hand up like a student with a question. "But who's Dixie?"

Lenna smiled and said, "I am. That was the secret name I made up for myself when I was little. The only other person who knew it was my secret friend." She stuck her thumb in his direction.

"Wonderful! So now Dixie fountain pens, which are lousy rip-offs of Sinbads, will be bought by every asshole in New York who can afford to buy a Piaget watch or a Hermes briefcase. It makes me sick." Michael glared at the other man and waited belligerently for a reply.

Mr. Fiddlehead's reply was to laugh like Woody Woodpecker. Which cracked both Lenna and me up.

Which sent her husband storming out of the kitchen.

"Is it true?"

They both nodded.

"But I had an imaginary friend, too, when I was little! The Bimbergooner. But I've never seen him for real."

"Maybe you didn't make him real enough. Maybe you just cooked him up when you were sad or needed someone to talk to. In Lenna's case, the more she needed me, the more real I became. She needed me a lot. One day I was just there for good."

I looked at Lenna. "You mean he's been here since you were a girl? Living with you?"

She laughed. "No. As I grew up I needed him less. I was happier and had more friends. My life got fuller. So he was around less." She reached over and touched his shoulder.

He smiled, but it was a sad one, full of memories. "I can give her pots of gold and do great tricks. I've even been practicing ventriloquism and can throw my voice a little. But you'd be surprised how few women love ventriloquists.

"If you two'll excuse me, I think I'll go in the other room and watch TV with the boys. It's about time for *The Three Stooges*. Remember how much we loved that show, Lenna? I think we saw one episode at least ten times. The one where they open up the hairdressing salon down in Mexico?"

"I remember. You loved Moe, and I loved Curly."

They beamed at each other through the shared memory.

"But wait, if he's . . . what you say, how come he came back now?"

"You didn't know it, but Michael and I went through a *very* bad period a little while ago. He even moved out for two weeks, and we both thought that was it: no more marriage. One night I got into bed crying like a fool and wishing to hell Mr. Fiddlehead was around again to help me. And then suddenly there he was, standing in the bathroom door smiling at me." She squeezed his shoulder again. He covered her hand with his own.

"God, Lenna, what did you do?"

"Screamed! I didn't recognize him."

"What do you mean?"

"I mean he grew up! The Mr. Fiddlehead I imagined when I was a child was exactly my age. I guess as I got older, so did he. It makes sense."

"I'm going to sit down now. I have to sit down because this has been the strangest afternoon of my life." Mr. Fiddlehead jumped up and gave me his seat. I took it. He left the room for television with the boys. I watched him go. Without thinking, I picked up Michael's half-empty glass of milk and finished it. "Everything that you told me is true?"

She put up her right hand. "I swear on our friendship."

"That beautiful man out there is an old dream of yours?"

Her head recoiled. "Ooh, do you think he's beautiful? Really? I think he's kind of funny looking, to tell the truth. I love him as a friend, but"—she looked guiltily at the door— "I'd never want to go *out* with him or anything."

But *I* did, so we did. After the first few dates I would have gone and hunted rats with him in the South Bronx if that's what he liked. I was completely gone for him. The line of a man's neck can change your life. The way he digs in his pockets for change can make the heart squawk and hands grow cold. How he touches your elbow or the button that is not closed on the cuff of his shirt are demons he's loosed without ever knowing it. They own us immediately. He was a thoroughly compelling man. I wanted to rise to the occasion of his presence in my life and become something more than I'd previously thought myself capable of.

I think he began to love me, too, but he didn't say things like that. Only that he was happy or that he wanted to share things he'd held in reserve all his life.

Because he knew sooner or later he'd have to go away (*where* he never said, and I stopped asking), he seemed to have thrown all caution to the wind. But before him, I'd never thrown anything away, caution included. I'd been a careful reader of timetables, made the bed tight and straight first thing every morning, and hated dishes in the sink. My life at forty was comfortably narrow and ordered. Going haywire or off the deep end wasn't in my repertoire, and normally people who did made me squint.

I realized I was in love *and* haywire the day I taught him to play racketball. After we'd batted it around an hour, we were sitting in the gallery drinking Coke. He flicked sweat from his forehead with two fingers. A hot, intimate drop fell on my wrist. I put my hand over it quickly and rubbed it into my skin. He didn't see. I knew then I'd have to learn to put whatever expectations I had aside and just live purely in his jet stream, no matter where it took me.

That day I realized I'd sacrifice anything for him, and for a few hours I went around feeling like some kind of holy person, a zealot, love made flesh.

"Why does Michael let you stay?"

He took a cigarette from my pack. He'd begun smoking a week before and loved it. Almost as much as he liked to drink, he said. The perfect Irishman.

"Don't forget he was the one who left Lenna. Not vice versa. When he came back he was pretty much on his knees to her. He had to be. There wasn't a lot he could say about me being there. Especially after he found out who I was. Do you have any plum pits around?"

"Question two: Why in God's name do you eat those things?"

"That's easy: because plums are Lenna's favorite fruit. When she was a little girl, she'd have tea parties for just us two. Scott Joplin music, imaginary tea, and real plums. She'd eat the fruit, then put the pit on my plate to eat. Makes perfect sense."

I ran my hand through his red hair, loving the way my fingers got caught in all the thick curls. "That's disgusting. It's just like slavery! Why am I getting to the point where I don't like my best friend so much anymore?"

"If you like me, you should like her, Juliet—she made me."

I kissed his fingers. "*That* part I like. Would you consider moving in with me?"

He kissed my hand. "I would love to consider that, but I have to tell you I don't think I'll be around very much longer. But if you'd like, I'll stay with you until I, uh, have to go."

I sat up. "What are you talking about?"

He put his hand close to my face. "Look hard and you'll see."

It took a moment, but then there it was; from certain angles I was able to see right through the hand. It had become vaguely transparent.

"Lenna's happy again. It's the old story—when she's down she needs me and calls." He shrugged. "When she's happy again, I'm not needed, so she sends me away. Not consciously, but . . . look, we all know I'm her little Frankenstein monster. She can do what she wants with me. Even dream up that I like to eat fucking plum pits."

"It's so wrong!"

Sighing, he sat up and started pulling on his shirt. "It's wrong, but it's life, sweet girl. Not much we can do about it, you know."

"Yes, we can. We can do something."

His back was to me. I remember the first time I'd ever seen him. His back was to me then, too. The long red hair falling over his collar. When I didn't say anything more, he turned and looked at me over his shoulder, smiling.

"We can do something? What can we do?"

His eyes were gentle and loving, eyes I wanted to see for the rest of my life.

"We can make her sad. We can make her need you."

"What do you mean?"

"Just what I said, Fiddy. When she's sad she needs you. We have to decide what would make her sad a long time. Maybe something to do with Michael. Or the children."

His fingers had stopped moving over the buttons. Thin, artistic fingers. Freckles.

DAN SIMMONS
Shave and a Haircut, Two Bites

Dan Simmons is the author of the World Fantasy Award-winning novel *Song of Kali* and the epic novel of vampirism, *Carrion Comfort*. He has also written the mainstream novel *Phases of Gravity* and the science fiction novels *Hyperion* and *The Fall of Hyperion*. His short fiction has appeared in *Omni*, *Twilight Zone*, and *Asimov's*.

Have you ever wondered what the barber pole signifies? Obviously, Simmons has, and in this finely structured narrative from *Masques III*, he gives his own unique interpretation.

—E.D.

Shave and a Haircut,
Two Bites

DAN SIMMONS

Outside, the blood spirals down.

I pause at the entrance to the barbershop. There is nothing unique about it. Almost certainly there is one similar to it in your community; its function is proclaimed by the pole outside, the red spiraling down, and by the name painted on the broad window, the letters grown scabrous as the gold paint ages and flakes away. While the most expensive hair salons now bear the names of their owners, and the shopping-mall franchises offer sickening cutenesses—Hairport, Hair Today: Gone Tomorrow, Hair We Are, Headlines, Shear Masters, The Head Hunter, In-Hair-itance, and so forth, ad infinitum, ad nauseam—the name of this shop is eminently forgettable. It is meant to be so. This shop offers neither styling nor unisex cuts. If you hair is dirty when you enter, it will be cut dirty; there are no shampoos given here. While the franchises demand fifteen to thirty dollars for a basic haircut, the cost here has not changed for a decade or more. It occurs to the potential new customer immediately upon entering that no one could live on an income based upon such low rates. No one does. The potential customer usually beats a hasty retreat, put off by the too-low prices, by the darkness of the place, by the air of dusty decrepitude exuded from both the establishment itself and from its few waiting customers, invariably silent and staring, and by a strange sense of tension bordering upon threat which hangs in the stale air.

Before entering, I pause a final moment to stare in the window of the barbershop. For a second I can see only a reflection of the street and the silhouette of a man more shadow than substance—me. To see inside, one has to step closer to the glass and perhaps cup hands to one's temples to reduce the glare. The blinds are drawn but I find a crack in the slats. Even then there is not much to see. A dusty window ledge holds three desiccated cacti and an assortment of dead flies. Two barber chairs are just visible through the gloom; they are of a sort no longer made: black leather, white enamel, a high headrest. Along one wall, half a dozen uncomfortable-looking chairs sit empty and two low tables show a litter of magazines with covers torn or missing entirely. There are mirrors on two of the three interior walls, but rather than add light to the long, narrow room, the infinitely receding reflections seem to make the space appear as if the barbershop itself were a dark reflection in an age-dimmed glass.

A man is standing there in the gloom, his form hardly more substantial than my silhouette on the window. He stands next to the first barber chair as if he were waiting for me.

He is waiting for me.

I leave the sunlight of the street and enter the shop.

"Vampires," said Kevin. "They're both vampires."

"Who're vampires?" I asked between bites on my apple. Kevin and I were twenty feet up in a tree in his backyard. We'd built a rough platform there that passed as a tree house. Kevin was ten, I was nine.

"Mr. Innis and Mr. Denofrio," said Kevin. "They're both vampires."

I lowered the *Superman* comic I'd been reading. "They're not vampires," I said. "They're *barbers*."

"Yeah," said Kevin, "but they're vampires too. I just figured it out."

I sighed and sat back against the bole of the tree. It was late autumn and the branches were almost empty of leaves. Another week or two and we wouldn't be using the tree house again until next spring. Usually when Kevin announced that he'd just figured something out, it meant trouble. Kevin O'Toole was almost my age, but sometimes it seemed that he was five years older and five years younger than I at the same time. He read a lot. And he had a weird imagination. "Tell me," I said.

"You know what the red means, Tommy?"

"What red?"

"On the barber pole. The red stripes that curl down."

I shrugged. "It means it's a barbershop."

It was Kevin's turn to sigh. "Yeah, sure, Tommy, but why *red*? And why have it curling down like that for a barber?"

I didn't say anything. When Kevin was in one of his moods, it was better to wait him out. ⟩

"Because it's blood," he said dramatically, almost whispering. "Blood spiraling down. Blood dripping and spilling. That's been the sign for barbers for almost six hundred years."

He'd caught my interest. I set the *Superman* comic aside on the platform. "Okay," I said, "I believe you. Why is it their sign?"

"Because it was their *guild sign*," said Kevin. "Back in the Middle Ages, all the guys who did important work belonged to guilds, sort of like the union our dads belong to down at the brewery, and . . ."

"Yeah, yeah," I said. "But why *blood*?" Guys as smart as Kevin had a hard time sticking to the point.

"I was getting to that," said Kevin. "According to this stuff I read, way back in the Middle Ages, barbers used to be surgeons. About all they could do to help sick people was to bleed them, and . . ."

"*Bleed* them?"

"Yeah. They didn't have any real medicines or anything, so if somebody got sick with a disease or broke a leg or something, all the surgeon . . . the barber . . . could do was bleed them. Sometimes they'd use the same razor they shaved people with. Sometimes they'd bring bottles of leeches and let them suck some blood out of the sick person."

"Gross."

"Yeah, but it sort of worked. Sometimes. I guess when you lose blood, your blood pressure goes down and that can lower a fever and stuff. But most of the time, the people they bled just died sooner. They probably needed a transfusion more than a bunch of leeches stuck on them."

I sat and thought about this for a moment. Kevin knew some really weird stuff. I used to think he was lying about a lot of it, but after I saw him correct the teachers in fourth and fifth grade a few times . . . and get away with it . . . I realized he wasn't making things up. Kevin was weird, but he wasn't a liar.

A breeze rustled the few remaining leaves. It was a sad and brittle sound to a kid who loved summer. "All right," I said. "But what's all this got to do with vampires? You think 'cause barbers used to stick leeches on people a couple of hundred years ago that Mr. Innis and Mr. Denofrio are *vampires*? Jeez, Kev, that's nuts."

"The Middle Ages were more than five hundred years ago, Niles," said Kevin, calling me by my last name in the voice that always made me want to punch him. "But the guild sign was just what got me thinking about it all. I mean, what other business has kept its guild sign?"

I shrugged and tied a broken shoelace. "Blood on their sign doesn't make them vampires."

When Kevin was excited, his green eyes seemed to get even greener than usual. They were really green now. He leaned forward. "Just think about it, Tommy," he said. "When did vampires start to disappear?"

"Disappear? You mean you think they were *real*? Cripes, Kev, my mom says you're the only gifted kid she's ever met, but sometimes I think you're just plain looney tunes."

Kevin ignored me. He had a long, thin face—made even thinner-looking by the crew cut he wore—and his skin was so pale that the freckles stood out like spots of gold. He had the same full lips that people said made his two sisters look pretty, but now those lips were quivering. "I read a lot about vampires," he said. "A *lot*. Most of the serious stuff agrees that the vampire legends were fading in Europe by the seventeenth century. People still *believed* in them, but they weren't so afraid of them anymore. A few hundred years earlier, suspected vampires were being tracked down and killed all the time. It's like they'd gone underground or something."

"Or people got smarter," I said.

"No, *think*," said Kevin and grabbed my arm. "Maybe the vampires were being wiped out. People knew they were there and how to fight them."

"Like a stake through the heart?"

"Maybe. Anyway, they've got to hide, pretend they're gone, and still get blood. What'd be the easiest way to do it?"

I thought of a wise-acre comment, but one look at Kevin made me realize that he was dead serious about all this. And we were best friends. I shook my head.

"Join the barbers' guild!" Kevin's voice was triumphant. "Instead of having to break into people's houses at night and then risk others' finding the body all drained of blood, they *invite* you in. They don't even struggle while you open their veins with a knife or put the leeches on. Then they . . . or the family of the dead guy . . . *pay* you. No wonder they're the only group to keep their guild sign. They're vampires, Tommy!"

I licked my lips, tasted blood, and realized that I'd been chewing on my lower lip while Kevin talked. "All of them?" I said. "Every barber?"

Kevin frowned and released my arm. "I'm not sure. Maybe not all."

"But you think Innis and Denofrio are?"

Kevin's eyes got greener again and he grinned. "There's one way to find out."

I closed my eyes a second before asking the fatal question. "How, Kev?"

"By watching them," said Kevin. "Following them. Checking them out. *Seeing* if they're vampires."

"And if they are?"

Kevin shrugged. He was still grinning. "We'll think of something."

I enter the familiar shop, my eyes adjusting quickly to the dim light. The air smells of talcum and rose oil and tonic. The floor is clean and instruments are laid out on white linen atop the counter. Light glints dully from the surface of scissors and shears and the pearl handles of more than one straight razor.

I approach the man who stands silently by his chair. He wears a white shirt and tie under a white smock. "Good morning," I say.

"Good morning, Mr. Niles." He pulls a striped cloth from its shelf, snaps it open with a practiced hand, and stands waiting like a toreador.

I take my place in the chair. He sweeps the cloth around me and snaps it shut behind my neck in a single fluid motion. "A trim this morning, perhaps?"

"I think not. Just a shave, please."

He nods and turns away to heat the towels and prepare the razor. Waiting, I look into the mirrored depths and see multitudes.

Kevin and I had made our pact while sitting in our tree on Sunday. By Thursday we'd done quite a bit of snooping. Kev had followed Innis and I'd watched Denofrio.

We met in Kevin's room after school. You could hardly see his bed for all the heaps of books and comics and half-built Heath Kits and vacuum tubes and plastic models and scattered clothes. Kevin's mother was still alive then, but she had been ill for years and rarely paid attention to little things like her son's bedroom. Or her son.

Kevin shoved aside some junk and we sat on his bed, comparing notes. Mine were scrawled on scraps of paper and the back of my paper-route collection form.

"Okay," said Kevin, "what'd you find out?"

"They're not vampires," I said. "At least my guy isn't."

Kevin frowned. "It's too early to tell, Tommy."

"Nuts. You gave me this list of ways to tell a vampire, and Denofrio flunks *all* of them."

"Explain."

"Okay. Look at Number One on your stupid list. 'Vampires are rarely seen in daylight.' Heck, Denofrio and Innis are both in the shop all day. We both checked, right?"

Kevin sat on his knees and rubbed his chin. "Yeah, but the barbershop is *dark*, Tommy. I told you that it's only in the movies that the vampires burst into flame or something if the daylight hits them. According to the old books, they just don't *like* it. They can get around in the daylight if they have to."

"Sure," I said, "but these guys work all day just like our dads. They close up at five and walk home before it gets dark."

Kevin pawed through his own notes and interrupted. "They both live alone, Tommy. That suggests something."

"Yeah. It suggests that neither one of them makes enough money to get married or have a family. My dad says that their barbershop hasn't raised its prices in years."

"Exactly!" cried Kevin. "Then how come almost no one goes there?"

"They give lousy haircuts," I said. I looked back at my list, trying to decipher the smeared lines of penciled scrawl. "Okay, Number Five on your list. 'Vampires will not cross running water.' Denofrio lives across the *river*, Kev. I watched him cross it all three days I was following him."

Kevin was sitting up on his knees. Now he slumped slightly. "I told you that I wasn't sure of that one. Stoker put it in *Dracula*, but I didn't find it in too many other places."

I went on quickly. "Number Three—'Vampires hate garlic.' I watched Mr. Denofrio eat dinner at Luigi's Tuesday night, Kev. I could smell the garlic from twenty feet away when he came out."

"Three wasn't an essential one."

"All right," I said, moving in for the kill, "tell me *this* one wasn't essential. Number Eight—'All vampires hate and fear crosses and will avoid them at all cost.' " I paused dramatically. Kevin knew what was coming and slumped lower. "Kev, Mr. Denofrio goes to St. Mary's. *Your church*, Kev. Every morning before he goes down to open up the shop."

"Yeah. Innis goes to First Prez on Sundays. My dad told me about Denofrio being in the parish. I never see him because he only goes to early Mass."

I tossed the notes on the bed. "How could a vampire go to your church? He not only doesn't run away from a cross, he sits there and stares at about a hundred of them each day of the week for about an hour a day!"

"Dad says he's never seen him take Communion," said Kevin, a hopeful note in his voice.

I made a face. "Great. Next you'll be telling me that anyone who's not a priest has to be a vampire. Brilliant, Kev."

He sat up and crumpled his own notes into a ball. I'd already seen them at school. I knew that Innis didn't follow Kevin's Vampire Rules either. Kevin said, "The cross thing doesn't prove . . . or disprove . . . anything, Tommy. I've been thinking about it. These things joined the barber's guild to get some protective coloration. It makes sense that they'd try to blend into the religious community, too. Maybe they can train themselves to build up a tolerance to crosses, the way we take shots to build up a tolerance to things like smallpox and polio."

I didn't sneer, but I was tempted. "Do they build up a tolerance to mirrors, too?"

"What do you mean?"

"I mean I know something about vampires too, Kev, and even though it wasn't in your stupid list of rules, it's a fact that vampires don't like mirrors. They don't throw a reflection."

"That's not right," said Kevin in that rushy, teacherish voice he used. "In the movies they don't throw a reflection. The old books say that they avoided mirrors because they saw their *true* reflection there . . . what they looked like being old or undead or whatever."

"Yeah, whatever," I said. "But *whatever* spooks them, there isn't any place worse for mirrors than a barbershop. Unless they hang out in one of those carnival fun-house mirror places. Do *they* have guild signs, too, Kev?"

Kevin threw himself backward on the bed as if I'd shot him. A second later he was pawing through his notes and back up on his knees. "There was one weird thing," he said.

"Yeah, what?"

"They were closed Monday."

"Real weird. Of course, every darn barbershop in the entire *universe* is closed on Mondays, but I guess you're right. They're closed on Mondays. They've got to be vampires. 'QED,' as Mrs. Double Butt likes to say in geometry class. Gosh, I wish *I* was smart like you, Kevin."

"Mrs. Doubet," he said, still looking at his notes. He was the only kid in our class who liked her. "It's not that they're closed on Monday that's weird, Tommy. It's what they do. Or at least Innis."

"How do you know? You were home sick on Monday."

Kevin smiled. "No, I wasn't. I typed the excuse and signed Mom's name. They never check. I followed Innis around. Lucky he has that old car and drives slow, I was able to keep up with him on my bike. Or at least catch up."

I rolled to the floor and looked at some kit Kevin'd given up on before finishing. It looked like some sort of radio crossed with an adding machine. I managed to fake disinterest in what he was saying even though he'd hooked me again, just as he always did. "So where did he go?" I said.

"The Mear place. Old Man Everett's estate. Miss Plankmen's house out on 28. That mansion on the main road, the one the rich guy from New York bought last year."

"So?" I said. "They're all rich. Innis probably cuts their hair at home." I was proud that I had seen a connection that Kevin had missed.

"Uh-huh," said Kevin, "the richest people in the county, and the one thing they have in common is that they get their haircuts from the lousiest barber in the state. Lousiest *barbers*, I should say. I saw Denofrio drive off, too. They met at the shop before they went on their rounds. I'm pretty sure Denofrio was at the Wilkes estate along the river that day. I asked Rudy, the caretaker, and he said either Denofrio or Innis comes there most Mondays."

I shrugged. "So rich people stay rich by paying the least they can for haircuts."

"Sure," said Kevin. "But that's not the weird part. The weird part was that both of the old guys loaded their car trunks with small bottles. When Innis came out of Mear and Everett's and Plankmen's places, he was carrying *big* bottles, two-gallon jars at least, and they were *heavy*, Tommy. Filled with liquid. I'm pretty sure the smaller jars they'd loaded at the shop were full too."

"Full of what?" I said. "Blood?"

"Why not?" said Kevin.

"Vampires are supposed to take blood *away*," I said, laughing. "Not *deliver* it."

"Maybe it was blood in the big bottles," said Kevin. "And they brought something to trade from the barbershop."

"Sure," I said, still laughing, "hair tonic!"

"It's not funny, Tom."

"The heck it isn't!" I made myself laugh even harder. "The best part is that your barber vampires are biting just the rich folks. They only drink premium!" I rolled on the floor, scattering comic books and trying not to crush any vacuum tubes.

Kevin walked to the window and looked out at the fading light. We both hated it when the days got shorter. "Well, I'm not convinced," he said. "But it'll be decided tonight."

"Tonight?" I said, lying on my side and no longer laughing. "What happens tonight?"

Kevin looked over his shoulder at me. "The back entrance to the barbershop has one of those old-style locks that I can get past in about two seconds with my Houdini Kit. After dinner, I'm going down to check the place out."

I said, "It's dark after dinner."

Kevin shrugged and looked outside.

"Are you going alone?"

Kevin paused and then stared at me over his shoulder. "That's up to you."

I stared back.

There is no sound quite the same as a straight razor being sharpened on a leather strop. I relax under the wrap of hot towels on my face, hearing but not seeing the barber prepare his blade. Receiving a professional shave is a pleasure which modern man has all but abandoned, but one in which I indulge myself every day.

The barber pulls away the towels, dries my upper cheeks and temples with a dab of a dry cloth, and turns back to the strop for a few final strokes of the razor.

I feel my cheeks and throat tingling from the hot towels, the blood pulsing in my neck. "When I was a boy," I say, "a friend of mine convinced me that barbers were vampires."

The barber smiles but says nothing. He has heard my story before.

"He was wrong," I say, too relaxed to keep talking.

The barber's smile fades slightly as he leans forward, his face a study in concentration. Using a brush and lather whipped in a cup he quickly applies the shaving soap. Then he sets aside the cup, lifts the straight razor, and with a delicate touch of only his thumb and little finger, tilts my head so that my throat is arched and exposed to the blade.

I close my eyes as the cold steel rasps across the warmed flesh.

"You said two seconds!" I whispered urgently. "You've been messing with that darned lock for *five minutes!*" Kevin and I were crouched in the alley behind Fourth Street, huddled in the back doorway of the barbershop. The night air was cold and smelled of garbage. Street sounds seemed to come to us from a million miles away. *"Come on!"* I whispered.

The lock clunked, clicked, and the door swung open into blackness. *"Voilà,"* said Kevin. He stuck his wires, picks, and other tools back into his imitation-leather Houdini Kit bag. Grinning, he reached over and rapped "Shave and a Haircut" on the door.

"Shut up," I hissed, but Kevin was gone, feeling his way into the darkness. I shook my head and followed him in.

Once inside with the door closed, Kevin clicked on a penlight and held it between his teeth the way we'd seen a spy do in a movie. I grabbed on to the tail of his windbreaker and followed him down a short hallway into the single, long room of the barbershop.

It didn't take long to look around. The blinds were closed on both the large window and the smaller one on the front door, so Kevin figured it was safe to use the penlight. It was weird moving across that dark space with Kevin, the penlight throwing images of itself into the mirrors and illuminating one thing at a time—a counter here, the two chairs in the center of the room, a few chairs and magazines for customers, two sinks, a tiny little lavatory, no bigger than a closet, its door right inside the short hallway. All the clippers and things had been put away in drawers. Kevin opened the drawers, peered into the shelves. There were bottles of hair tonic, towels, all the barber tools set neatly into top drawers, both sets arranged the same. Kevin took out a razor and opened it, holding the blade up so it reflected the light into the mirrors.

"Cut it out," I whispered. "Let's get out of here."

Kevin set the thing away, making sure it was lined up exactly the way it had been, and we turned to go. His penlight beam moved across the back wall, illuminating a raincoat we'd already seen, and something else.

"There's a door here," whispered Kevin, moving the coat to show a doorknob. He tried it. "Drat. It's locked."

"Let's *go!*" I whispered. I hadn't heard a car pass in what felt like hours. It was like the whole town was holding its breath.

Kevin began opening drawers again. "There has to be a key," he said too loudly. "It must lead to a basement; there's no second floor on this place."

I grabbed him by his jacket. "Come on," I hissed. "Let's get out of here. We're going to get *arrested*."

"Just another minute . . ." began Kevin and froze. I felt my heart stop at the same instant.

A key rasped in the lock of the front door. There was a tall shadow thrown against the blind.

I turned to run, to escape, anything to get out of there, but Kevin clicked off the penlight, grabbed my sweatshirt, and pulled me with him as he crawled under one of the high sinks. There was just enough room for both of us there. A dark curtain hung down over the space and Kevin pulled it shut just as the door creaked open and footsteps entered the room.

For a second I could hear nothing but the pounding of blood in my ears, but then I realized that there were *two* people walking in the room, men by the sounds of their heavy tread. My mouth hung open and I panted, but I was unable to get a breath of air. I was sure that any sound at all would give us away.

One set of footsteps stopped at the first chair while the other went to the rear hall. A second door rasped shut, water ran, and there came the sound of the toilet flushing. Kevin nudged me, and I could have belted him then, but we were so crowded together in fetal positions that any movement by me would have made a noise. I held my breath and waited while the second set of footsteps returned from the lavatory and moved toward the front door. *They hadn't even turned on the lights*. There'd been no gleam of a flashlight beam through our curtain, so I didn't think it was the cops checking things out. Kevin nudged me again and I knew he was telling me that it had to be Innis and Denofrio.

Both pairs of footsteps moved toward the front, there was the sound of the door opening and slamming, and I tried to breathe again before I passed out.

A rush of noise. A hand reached down and parted the curtain. Other hands grabbed me and pulled me up and out, into the dark. Kevin shouted as another figure dragged him to his feet.

I was on my tiptoes, being held by my shirtfront. The man holding me seemed eight feet tall in the blackness, his fist the size of my head. I could smell garlic on his breath and assumed it was Denofrio.

"Let us go!" shouted Kevin. There was the sound of a slap, flat and clear as a rifle shot, and Kevin was silent.

I was shoved into a barber chair. I heard Kevin being pushed into the other one. My eyes were so well adjusted to the darkness that now I could make out the features of the two men. Innis and Denofrio. Dark suits blended into black, but I could see the pale, angular faces that I'd been sure had made Kevin think they were vampires. Eyes too deep and dark, cheekbones too sharp, mouths too cruel, and something about them that said *old* despite their middle-aged looks.

"What are you doing here?" Innis asked Kevin. The man spoke softly, without evident emotion, but his voice made me shiver in the dark.

"Scavenger hunt!" cried Kevin. "We have to steal a barber's clippers to get in the big kids' club. We're sorry. Honest!"

There came the rifle shot of a slap again. "You're lying," said Innis. "You followed me on Monday. Your friend here followed Mr. Denofrio in the evening. Both of you have been watching the shop. Tell me the truth. *Now!*"

"We think you're vampires," said Kevin. "Tommy and I came to find out."

My mouth dropped open in shock at what Kevin had said. The two men took a half-step back and looked at each other. I couldn't tell if they were smiling in the dark.

"Mr. Denofrio?" said Innis.

"Mr. Innis," said Denofrio.

"Can we go now?" said Kevin.

Innis stepped forward and did something to the barber chair Kevin was in. The leather armrests flipped up and out, making sort of white gutters. The leather strops on either side went up and over, attaching to something out of sight to make restraining straps around Kevin's arms. The headrest split apart, came down and around, and encircled Kevin's neck. It looked like one of those trays the dentists puts near you to spit into.

Kevin made no noise. I expected Denofrio to do the same thing to my chair, but he only laid a large hand on my shoulder.

"We're not vampires, boy," said Mr. Innis. He went to the counter, opened a drawer, and returned with the straight razor Kevin had been fooling with earlier. He opened it carefully. "Mr. Denofrio?"

The shadow by my chair grabbed me, lifted me out of the chair, and dragged me to the basement door. He held me easily with one hand while he unlocked it. As he pulled me into the darkness, I looked back and caught a glimpse of my friend staring in silent horror as Innis drew the edge of the straight razor slowly across Kevin's inner arm. Blood welled, flowed, and gurgled into the white enamel gutter of the armrest.

Denofrio dragged me downstairs.

The barber finishes the shave, trims my sideburns, and turns the chair so that I can look into the closer mirror.

I run my hand across my cheeks and chin. The shave was perfect, very close but with not a single nick. Because of the sharpness of the blade and the skill of the barber, my skin tingles but feels no irritation whatsoever.

I nod. The barber smiles ever so slightly and removes the striped protective apron.

I stand and remove my suitcoat. The barber hangs it on a hook while I take my seat again and roll up my left sleeve. While he is near the rear of the shop, the barber turns on a small radio. The music of Mozart fills the room.

The basement was lighted with candles set in small jars. The dancing red light reminded me of the time Kevin took me to his church. He said the small red flames were votive candles. You paid money, lit one, and said a prayer. He wasn't sure if the money was necessary for the prayer to be heard.

The basement was narrow and unfinished and almost filled by the twelve-foot slab of stone in its center. The thing on the stone was almost as long as the slab. The thing must have weighed a thousand pounds, easy. I could see folds of slick, gray flesh rising and falling as it breathed.

If there were arms, I couldn't see them. The legs were suggested by folds in slick fat. The tubes and pipes and rusting funnel led my gaze to the head.

Imagine a thousand-pound leech, nine or ten feet long and five or six feet thick through the middle as it lies on its back, no surface really, just layers of gray-green slime and wattles of what might be skin. Things, organs maybe, could be seen moving and sloshing through flesh as transparent as dirty plastic. The room was filled with the sound of its breathing and the stench of its breath. Imagine a huge sea creature, a small whale, maybe, dead and rotting on the beach for a week, and you've got an idea of what the thing itself smelled like.

The mass of flesh made a noise and the small eyes turned in my direction. Its eyes were covered with layers of yellow film or mucus and I was sure it was blind. The thing's head was no more defined than the end of a leech, but in the folds of slick fat were lines which showed a face that might have once been human. Its mouth was very large. Imagine a lamprey smiling.

"No, it was never human," said Mr. Denofrio. His hand was still firm on my shoulder. "By the time they came to our guild, they had already passed beyond hope of hiding amongst us. But they brought an offer which we could not refuse. Nor can our customers. Have you ever heard of symbiosis, boy? Hush!"

Upstairs, Kevin screamed. There was a gurgle, as of old pipes being tried.

The creature on the slab turned its blind gaze back to the ceiling. Its mouth pulsed hungrily. Pipes rattled and the funnel overflowed.

Blood spiraled down.

The barber returns and taps at my arm as I make a fist. There is a broad welt across the inner crook of my arm, as of an old scar poorly healed. It is an old scar.

The barber unlocks the lowest drawer and withdraws a razor. The handle is made of gold and is set about with small gems. He raises the object in both hands, holds it above his head, and the blade catches the dim light.

He takes three steps closer and draws the blade across my arm, opening the scar tissue like a puparium hatching. There is no pain. I watch as the barber rinses the blade and returns it to its special place. He goes down the basement stairs and I can hear the gurgling in the small drain tubes of the armrest as his footsteps recede. I close my eyes.

I remember Kevin's screams from upstairs and the red flicker of candlelight on the stone walls. I remember the red flow through the funnel and the gurgle of the thing feeding, lamprey mouth extended wide and reaching high, trying to encompass the funnel the way an infant seeks its mother's nipple.

I remember Mr. Denofrio taking a large hammer from its place at the base of the slab, then a thing part spike and part spigot. I remember standing alone and watching as he pounded it in, realizing even as I watched that the flesh beneath the gray-green slime was a mass of old scars.

I remember watching as the red liquid flowed from the spigot into the crystal glass, the chalice. There is no red in the universe as deeply red, as purely red as what I saw that night.

I remember drinking. I remember carrying the chalice—carefully, so carefully—upstairs to Kevin. I remember sitting in the chair myself.

The barber returns with the chalice. I check that the scar has closed, fold down my sleeve, and drink deeply.

By the time I have donned my own white smock and returned, the barber is sitting in the chair.

"A trim this morning, perhaps?" I ask.

"I think not," he says. "Just a shave, please."

I shave him carefully. When I am finished, he runs his hands across his cheeks and chins and nods his approval. I perform the ritual and go below.

In the candlelight hush of the Master's vault, I wait for the Purification and think about immortality. Not about the true eon-spanning immortality of the Master . . . of all the Masters . . . but of the portion He deigns to share with us. It is enough.

After my colleague drinks and I have returned the chalice to its place, I come up to find the blinds raised, the shop open for business.

Kevin has taken his place beside his chair. I take my place beside mine. The music has ended and silence fills the room.

Outside, the blood spirals down.

ANDREW STEPHENSON
Cinema Altéré

Andrew Stephenson was born in Maracaibo, Venezuela, and now lives in the U.K. His first short story was published by *Analog* in 1971 and he is the author of two novels, *Nightwatch* (1977) and *The Wall of Years* (1979).

"Cinema Altéré," from the British anthology *Zenith*, is a time travel story. There is a sub-genre of time travel stories in which visitors from the future visit the past for vicarious thrills—this horrific story takes that idea one step further.

—E.D.

Cinema Altéré

ANDREW STEPHENSON

Roll titles.

High summer, high noon, high temperature.

The overheated city teems with lunchbreak life: along congested streets the war of foot and wheel is fought with sullen resolution, each faction gaining ground by turns, as traffic lights wink through idiot rounds of stop and go.

Seen from this Olympian perspective, the pulsing corpuscular flow mimics that of living blood. Thus the great square, where arterial ways converge to mix their contents, surely is the pump and heart of this metropolis.

Pan across the square. Ordinary folk throng shop-lined outer pavements. Most prefer not to linger out of doors; but a few sit on benches beneath shady trees, nibbling sandwiches, tolerating the heat for the sake of daylight and open air. Overhead, on branch and cornice, starlings and pigeons hold mute parliaments, too torpid to beg for crumbs. Higher still, lofty façades glitter in the sun.

Fed and drained by side streets, a sluggish triple stream of motorized traffic processes around the square. Isolated within this cordon of metal and fumes is a tranquil scrap of green.

These are the ornamental gardens. At their hub, like a pivot for the entire city, the statue of a bygone king gazes blindly out from a high pedestal fringed by pink roses that slowly wilt in the heat.

Hold on gardens. Zoom in slowly on a bench, near the road, occupied by a well-dressed, balding, somewhat overweight man. He seems strangely alone amid so much human activity. Close-up: sagging face, eyes masked by lowered lids, big nose squashed down above pouting lips twisted into a semblance of distaste.

Distaste for what? There is no clue.

He might be dozing. But no, his mouth twitches. One eye opens, studies the large digital clock on the entablature above the portico of the Central Library, opposite. Black on white, the numerals show 11:55.

The other eye opens. Casually he turns in his seat, towards the statue behind him, as though to contemplate the stone monarch. No, not the statue. Rather, the intersection beyond, where the lights have just changed to green.

The unmarked black tanker truck eases into the square and commences the long circuit around to where the man sits. He turns away, trying to ignore it.

Sam Sensharra does not relish what will happen so soon.

He is finding it hard to wait for voluntary death, hoping this will be one of those times that never were, reflecting on how there must always be the consciousness of watching eyes and the dread of that ultimate finality that would ensue, should the scheme misfire.

He distracts himself by plucking a rose and sniffing at it.

On the table between the three men, sheets of plans and schedules rustled as Samuel Sensharra rearranged them. Several rooms away a clock chimed, tinkling sweetly in the quiet studio offices. A door slammed.

"This business stinks," Sensharra conceded, "but I try to be artistic, to give it meaning."

Cody Lewis and Piotr de Veet made no comment. Lewis did not care to argue further. De Veet had known Sensharra too long to bother disagreeing. Both waited while he stared unseeing at the top sheet, a blown-up photomap of the new location. Abruptly he shoved it aside, disordering the pile once more.

"But who understands?" he demanded. "Do the guys who grab at my work —the fat cat network bosses and the fat slob viewers—do they even make the effort? I try to shock, to teach them. They watch unmoved; and there they do me a wrongness, because I say gratuitous violence isn't art. It's obscenity."

De Veet shook his head. "What matter, Sam?" he said. "We get top rating. We get paid. We get to eat."

Sensharra stared at him. "Pete, you been listening to me? It matters because nobody thinks it matters. Today's screen violence is a circus of pictures and noises. And that's what's screwed up with the world: at heart, nobody gives a damn. They sit at home in comfy armchairs and watch puppets on TV doing their hurting for them. That's what I've fought all my life, ever since it was still a thrill to see a guy shot in the movies and the real thing was unthinkable. God's truth, Pete, when those shmucks turn on one of my movies, I'd like for them to feel a real gut-searching panic. To *identify*."

"Still, you're right. We don't get to choose, do we? The Joe Show sponsors want their pound of flesh raw, blood and all. But mark me, Pete: this time, when I collar the man in the street and I yell in his face, *Joe Public, this is your life; and smile 'cause you're on camera, boy!* by God I want him to *believe* it! When the viewers realize this is the Big Scene, where the world shatters and the blood runs in rivers, I want strong men to faint dead away, on account of how it *hits* them. You hear me?"

"For sure, Sam, I hear you."

Out in the frosty parking lot a diesel engine coughed and grumbled. Sensharra inspected his watch. "That's our cue. Cody, any late doubts? The location's right, no question?"

Cody Lewis, two metres of suntanned muscle garbed in khaki trousers and bush jacket, nodded slowly, then settled his stetson more firmly on his head. He met Sensharra's earnest stare with his own steady gaze, before the other looked away to de Veet.

"Pete, those cameras spotted where I wanted them?"

"Eight, near enough. The other two . . ." De Veet sucked his yellowed teeth. "They got to be mobile. Headband jobs. So N'gabe goes with me, instead of with Cody. Sorry, Sam, I know you say to keep the kid out of it, but . . ." His wrinkled face creased along its worry lines like an old shoe retreading familiar steps. His shoulders seemed more stooped than usual.

"It happens." Sensharra passed a hand through the remnants of his hair, and sighed. "Time he learned the dirty side of our business. Okay, but double-check his gear. We can't afford to lose any footage on this scene. The budget won't allow for a retake, and God alone knows what the Civil Liberties Board would say to a reapplication. So let's go."

The tanker dominates the traffic lane nearest the gardens. So close to the edge of the road is it, its tyres skim the kerb. It reeks of oil and diesel. And of something else.

Beyond the tinted glass of its cab is the rigid face of Wolfgang Brock, the stunt man, inching his charge towards its ordained position. Brock glances in Sensharra's direction. His lips are barely parted by a cigarette hanging loosely, unlit and dry, between them. The knuckles of his hands show white with the strength of their grip on the wheel.

Brock is the top suicide in the business. Sensharra reassures himself with this thought as he savours the rose. He regrets that he will not live to see the man's full performance at first hand. Also he wishes Brock had removed that cigarette: details matter.

He wonders whether his own simulated *sangfroid* should be hailed as a masterpiece, under the circumstances.

The Library clock shows 11:58.

In the shadows of a deserted and inconspicuous alley a blue haze bloomed. Swelling rapidly to a diffuse cloud, it abruptly collapsed and darkened, coalescing into an apparently normal trader's van: dirty, green, undistinguished. On the van's flanks peeling signs in white paint claimed, *Deliveries Made, Anywhere, Anytime*—a feeble joke?

After a few moments, Sensharra and de Veet emerged from the front. Then the back doors creaked open and a youth joined them. The latter was rubbing his forehead to dispel the nausea that accompanied time travel. Sensharra looked at him.

"You okay, Woru?" he asked.

Worunga N'gabe nodded, but shivered despite the heat. His voice was unsteady.

"Uh, I guess. Is this the first or second time through?"

De Veet, tinkering with his headband camera, eyes masked by dark glasses which were really viewfinders, allowed his mouth to smile. "Always the second time, unless . . ." The smile faded.

Sensharra frowned at him. "Cut that, Pete. No call to rattle the kid. Save the ad-libs for when we're checking the rushes. Woru, don't you fret. Cody'll come through."

Locking the van, together they moved towards the mouth of the alley. In the bright sunshine ahead dense traffic crept by: cars, buses, people afoot and cycling, all unaware of the deadly threat the three men posed. Sensharra studied his watch, said to de Veet, "What time have you got? Local, that is."

Both de Veet and N'gabe looked at their wrists. De Veet hesitated, preparing to say something, thought better of it, answered flatly, "Ten before twelve."

N'gabe's breathing deepened. De Veet's momentary misinterpretation of Sensharra's question had not escaped him. They might have all too little time.

At the main road, Sensharra halted and covertly peered along it. "Stand by," he said. "Brock's coming."

It had been agreed at the studios that it would be left to the stunt man to make contact. So the three stayed put, acting like innocent tourists. When the black tanker finally came level it braked noisily; only then did they pretend to notice it.

Brock jumped down from the cab.

"Hey, I got a load for the library," he shouted. "You folks direct me?" He joined them. A nearby policeman scowled, first at Brock, then at the tanker which was now impeding the traffic. He advanced on the group, reaching for his notepad. In a hurried undertone, Brock demanded:

"Okay, what do I do?"

"You there!" yelled the policeman.

Brock looked around.

"Be moving it in a moment," he called. Slightly appeased, the policeman nodded and retired to the shade of a shop front, where he made notes.

Sensharra gesticulated, in the manner of one directing a stranger, but kept his voice low, watching the policeman all the while. "Take this road. Go to the square at the end. Circle halfway around, staying close to the middle. You'll see me. Get as near as you can. When I nod, do it."

Brock drew a cigarette from a squashed pack and stuck it between his lips. "Suits me," he said, his words slurred by the cigarette. "Do I survive?" The cigarette bobbed as he spoke.

"No chance."

"Good. Better get on with it then." He pulled a lighter from his pocket and put the flame close to the cigarette. Before it caught, Sensharra said:

"I want this to be as good as the shopping mall you did for us. The critics liked you in that."

Brock paused. "How jolly for them," he remarked. He put away his lighter, forgetting the cigarette was still unlit. "Me, I never watch your flicks." Returning to the tanker, he climbed in, smiling ingratiatingly at the policeman.

"So it's the first time," N'gabe said. "No sign of Cody."

"Looks like it," agreed de Veet.

Sensharra said nothing. Brock's remark had stung.

The tanker passed them slowly, belching sooty exhaust.

There is dust on the rose, Sensharra observes. But then, why should there not be? A busy public place like this, with so much traffic. A spell of dry weather. The dust will soon rise. Yet the scent remains sweet, evoking for him a lost time of innocence, when beauty was a pleasure, not an industry.

He has made many films, or—as he calls them, being a traditionalist—movies. Techniques have come and gone, to be exploited as fashion and expediency dictate. This is but one of many: the folding of a life upon itself, the pinching-off of a segment and its preservation in the timeless limbo of the camera stacks. This is simply one facet of his art, as he calls it.

The process inherently has obviated earlier subjective proofs. Now his eyes are being opened. He never suspected how intense, how mystical, could be these seconds before the rock plunges into his private pool of tranquillity. At last he can be satisfied that his other self, the one who survives, has not been wrong all along. He is pleased. The thrill of participation is truly overwhelming and increases by the second. Indeed, he is intrigued to discover that it verges on being erotic. No more the remote director, the lofty overseer, now he knows what it is to be the person on the other side of the little screen, the one who will perish alongside the cyphers with whom he chooses to share his dissolution. To be Joe Public.

Oh, Sam Sensharra loves his trade. He feels honoured to give himself to it, literally. He imagines he has principles.

He makes a point of appearing in the Big Scene in all his productions. Thus he preserves his objectivity, his humility and his self respect. Or so he tells those in whom he confides. "Otherwise," he often adds, seriously, "I might forget I'm just a human movie-maker with a duty to my characters, and start imagining myself as God." Here he laughs. "I mean, hell, only gods direct real lives without suffering the consequences."

This, then, is his excuse, which he believes.

The three had reached the outer edge of the busy square and were preparing to go to their marks when an urgent shout made them pause. It was Lewis: he was running drunkenly, obviously still dizzy from his jump through time.

"Thank you, oh Lord," whispered N'gabe, eying the heavens. By their expressions, the others shared his relief.

They stopped to let Lewis catch up and gathered round him while he recovered some of his composure. A small audience of curious onlookers gradually drifted away.

"Problems with the equipment," he panted, before gulping several deep breaths. "I set the coordinates right, but it put me down here late."

"Good that you come no later," commented de Veet. "I think then we all have been in trouble. For always. You also."

Lewis rounded on him. "Look, I said what happened. So keep the lecture. Just because you were panicking like some old—"

"We were starting to worry," Sensharra interjected mildly. Abruptly his manner changed. "My God: the tanker! If Brock decides to let rip without the signal we'll have a real disaster. Woru, stop him—*run!*"

And N'gabe ran. Already the tanker waited at the lights, on the point of entering the square, too far away to see what Brock was making of their meeting, or whether he had even spotted them in the crowd. N'gabe raced towards it, dodging most obstructions with reckless swerves, bowling over anyone who got in his way. Just as the light changed to green, he leapt forward and managed to bang a fist against the driver's door.

By the Library clock, the time was 11:55.

Watching the tanker creep closer, Sensharra tries to stay calm. He fails. One minute ago he used the remote control in his pocket to start all the cameras, so this has to be the first time through.

Big and messy, that's the bomb inside the tanker. Three hundred kilos of explosive act as trigger and dispersal agent. The remainder of the load is naphthenate palmitate. Napalm. About one hundred thousand litres of it.

The Special Effects Department have promised Sensharra excellent results. They anticipate thorough coverage of the square and of the seven major roads radiating from it. The napalm includes a new fluidizer, to make it flow faster and further, leaving its combustion properties unaffected. Adhesion is not of paramount importance in this application. The script merely specifies 'a terrorist outrage', and Sensharra is talented enough to compensate for any lack of descriptive detail. He sees no reason to doubt the Department's estimates. He also trusts Lewis, who claims to have found the most inflammable city centre available under the terms of the relevant laws.

The clock stands at 11:59.

Somewhere recent—even Sensharra does not know where or when—Lewis will have been waiting in a time-travelling van, alone . . .

Cut to interior of van. An oblong box pierced by a row of slots looms over a workbench in front of Lewis. On the bench is a picture stack viewer. He presses a switch on the box. The slots flare blue, one by one; suddenly each encloses a camera. Methodically, he reviews what images every camera contains. If none holds what is wanted, he has the strictest orders: to take the van back to the studios and conduct the rest of his life as though he never heard of Sam Sensharra or the current project.

But always the cameras seem to have recorded the required scenes. That is the wonder of the process, which some take as conclusive proof that the Creator has a sense of humour.

Sam Sensharra loses no sleep over the question. It works for him.

He tries to pick out the eight fixed cameras in various positions around the square. There are five which include him in their field of view. He knows this and where they are situated but cannot see them. Instead his imagination lets him hear their scan circuits whistling, shuttling images into solid-state stacks as the countdown proceeds.

The clock trembles on the edge of noon. The tanker is very close.

*   *   *

Brock spun the wheel to full lock and gunned the engine. Turning ponderously into the alley, where two vans now waited, the tanker squeezed between opposing pavements with no room to spare. The rear wheels mounted the kerb, then dropped onto the tarmac. Engine rumbling, the truck moved up to the nearer van and stopped. Brock killed the power. The fog of exhaust fumes began to dissipate. Sensharra and the others watched him dismount.

"What a bitch," Brock breathed. "Hell, I done some stunts, but naping a rush-hour crowd beats all. What kind of flick is this, Sam? Sado-porn?"

"You know better than to ask," said Sensharra. "Just take your money."

Lewis proffered a plastic card. Brock accepted it and ran his pocket reader across it.

"What's the bonus for?" he asked.

Lewis answered, noncommittally: "Results."

Brock raised an eyebrow and put the card in his breast pocket, sealing the flap carefully. He hooked a thumb at the tanker. "And her?"

"I'll take it back," said Lewis. "You can go. We'll be in touch about the next job."

"Which is . . . ? No, I don't suppose you'd care to predict." The stunt man grimaced and stepped clear, adjusting the studs on his ornate belt. "Close-mouthed bunch, aren't we?" he remarked, dissolving into a blue mist that soon dispersed.

"We need to be," murmured Sensharra, as though to himself. "My public wouldn't understand." To Lewis he said, "What about those results you mentioned?"

"It's a ratings-buster."

"So tell me."

"Sam, I don't know where to start. Just one glance and I felt sick. Me, Iron-Guts Lewis, I almost puked. Such footage! The slow motion, for instance: there's a mother and her child—"

"Is that it? Only suffering?"

Lewis dropped his eyes. "What else did you expect?"

"I'd hoped for something to give it a purpose. Heroism. Dignity, perhaps. Proof that people can be human, even today."

"There was an old blind guy knocked his dog unconscious with his white cane."

"That'll have to do, I guess. And the spectacle?"

Lewis perked up, eager to gloss over his embarrassment. "Fantastic. Best disaster footage we've staged since we switched to paradox production. It goes on from where *Quo Vadis* left off. You never saw a city burn like this: two square klicks ablaze, with a smoky column of roaring flame as the firestorm catches hold; half a million casualties at least; flames washing across the streets; melted fat running in the gutters; buses like islands in the fires, their paint bubbling—"

"That's *enough!*" Sensharra had paled: whether in shock, or in fury, it was hard to know; but one hand trembled, as though on the point of striking Lewis.

"While your wages come from me, Cody, there's one thing you don't forget, ever: those were real people we killed." Suddenly the trembling hand relaxed, waving Lewis away; and tiredly Sensharra said, "Take the tanker back."

Without a further word, Lewis hauled himself into the cab. The tanker shimmered and vanished, to reappear five months later in the snow and ice of the studio parking lot.

"Pete," said Sensharra, "you take Lewis' van. Woru and I will travel in the other."

But even after de Veet had gone, N'gabe stayed where he was, head tilted slightly backwards, surveying the narrow confines of the alley. His face showed puzzlement and disbelief. "Mister Sensharra," he asked in a small voice, "did I really die here?"

Sensharra came and stood next to him, and he too regarded the crumbling eaves of the dilapidated buildings, and the pale strip of sky beyond. "We all did," he replied at last.

"Don't seem possible. How'd we make a film when nothing happened?"

"It did happen." Sensharra laid a reassuring hand on N'gabe's shoulder. "And we made a movie of it. Or we would have, except Cody stopped us, because the camera stacks he received held the right images."

"But if he stopped us, where'd the images come from?"

"They were there to start with."

N'gabe squinted dubiously at the pudgy hand resting on his shoulder. "That sounds crazy."

"Not at all. The logic is perfect. Suppose the factory makes a stack, a chunk of crystal doped with bits of this and that, a random mix. Nobody plays it, so it could hold anything. Anything, not just white noise. Among the anythings that stack might hold are pictures. So we push it through the process and get a sequence of movie footage. The universe doesn't care. That footage is one of the possible random mixes. Paradox production makes sure that mix suits our own purposes; the events the movie shows never actually took place, that's all."

"Then why do I feel so dirty?" asked N'gabe, bitterly. He shook off the reassuring hand and faced the other man. "Why, Mister Sensharra? What did you almost make me do?"

"I wish I knew," said Sensharra. "I really do."

Shortly thereafter, in their turn, van and men faded into the future; and moments later the clocks of the city began to chime the noonday hour.

The tanker's engine is clearly audible above the general traffic noise. To Sensharra its growl is the only sound in the whole world. The front wheels are drawing level. Brock awaits the signal, one hand down out of sight, resting on the trigger.

Sensharra crumbles the rose between his blunt fingers. Petals flutter to the ground, a shower of purest pink against dusty grey. He offers a short prayer to his private gods before raising his eyes and gazing around the square at where he knows the cameras are.

Look at me, he thinks. Look at us. See how we die. Wallowing in comfort, in safety, will you contemptible swine understand what chances at heroism I am granting these little people here? Will you learn by their example? If not, try at least to enjoy the spectacle: some of you have earned that right; some of you are here with me. Find yourselves—if you think to look.

Standing, he meets Brock's staring, frightened eyes.

Angle: medium long shot, on Sensharra's back, such that the Central Library clock is visible, defocused, beyond him. Hold to establish, then smoothly refocus on clock. Numerals change: 11:59 becomes 12:00.

Fade down street sounds into silence. Cut to front view of Sensharra, and fade in first chimes of city clocks: cascades of metal-throated belfry song, joyful carillon and sonorous tocsin, all the famous tunes beloved of rhyme and legend—.

Sensharra nods.

Cut clocks. Freeze action. Catch the mask of ecstasy upon his face; trap the shame of it, forever. Swell Sensharra to full screen, revealing loathsome rapture. Then zoom out, skyward, framing bench and gardens, the square and its traffic stilled an instant before extinction, buildings a heartbeat from destruction, the radiating streets, the crowds, the surrounding blocks and their networks of human life, and—in the mind alone—on out to the limits of sympathy for prey and predator alike.

GARY A. BRAUNBECK

Matters of Family

Gary A. Braunbeck is from Columbus, Ohio and is a bartender. Previously he was a dog groomer. He has been publishing fiction in small press markets for three to four years and for the last nine years he has written the film column for *Eldritch Tales*.

"Matters of Family" is from the small press publication *Not One of Us*. It's about familial duty, perhaps the strongest "ties that bind."

—E.D.

Matters of Family

GARY A. BRAUNBECK

"Man has places in his heart which do not yet exist, and into them enters suffering, in order that they may have existence."—Leon Bloy

Albert stared out the window and watched the world melt under the weight of rain. Small sections of tree bark slid off a stump and sank into the mud, all of it flowing toward the fence where it picked up a few thin branches of shrubbery that looked like twisted arms reaching, a form too much like the misshapen thing on the bed behind him; silent, unmoving, his responsibility now.

"Did she give you any . . . trouble?" he asked.

"None," replied Fran. He turned toward her voice, searching through the gloom for some echo he expected to take form over his head. Beyond the bed, down near the corner of the door, a small blue nightlight glowed. It was shaped like an annoying cartoon character from Saturday morning television. He almost thought the voice had come from its mouth.

"Will you . . . um, is there anything you need?" said Fran.

"Not that I can think of. Has she been . . . did she go to the bathroom?" He blinked, cursing himself for phrasing it that way. *Of course she didn't go to the bathroom, you idiot. In order to do that, she'd have to be able to stand, know where it was, and walk there on her own power. What you really want to know is did she pee or shit herself, and did Fran change the diaper?*

"Yes," replied Fran. "She's all taken care of for the night." He lit a cigarette, took a deep drag, watched as the blue-tinted smoke curled toward the ceiling. He remembered the way his mother had always gotten angry at having to change the diaper twice, sometimes three times an hour; she always rolled her eyes toward the ceiling, as if expecting something to drift down and spare her the task. Of course, that was always the way around the house, at least when he lived here; there was really nothing wrong with Suzanne, she was just a VERY ILL little girl, a girl who would someday GET BETTER, a SICKLY child who, with time, patience, and caring, would be UP an AT'EM in no time, just you watch.

"I hope you don't mind my asking," said Fran, "but, well . . . how was . . ."

"The turnout? A lot of people came. I hadn't realized that Mom and Dad had so many friends." Something shifted within the blue cartoon glow, blocking the tail of his smoke snake. He took another drag as the rain drummed impatient fingers along the metal gutter. Small strands of smoke twisted before his face: he'd just walked into a spider's web, and Fran, with a wave of her hand, swept the web up toward the ceiling before he became entangled.

"May I fix you some coffee?" she said. "Maybe something to eat?"

"Some hot tea might be nice." His eyes were fixed on the bed and the thing lying upon it. He remembered that he'd known it. It was his sister. It had a name. Suzanne, wasn't it?

Her eyes were glossy, blank, open.

Staring toward the ceiling like Mother so often did. *Had.*

Somewhere heavy streams of water and mud were pulsing toward the open graves, pouring over the edges, slipping down, pools slowly rising, drowning the caskets. But, then, Mom and Dad were used to that; they'd drowned once already. Dad and his little boat. Mom hadn't wanted to go out with him that day, the weather looked too—

"Come on," said Fran, taking his hand. Before he left he turned once more toward his sister. She, also, was tinted in cartoon blue. Had he not known better, he would have thought she was suffocating. And what if she were? Would she even realize it? What could he do?

He could close the door, pretending not to notice.

Which is what he did.

The brightness of the kitchen's overhead light was too much for him; he flipped the switch and dropped the room into a greyness like the brief flashes one might see behind closed eyes.

Fran prepared the tea, then sat across from him as he sipped. She'd made it too hot.

"What are you going to do with her?" she said.

"Hell if I know. Maybe put her in some kind of home. I don't know the first thing about how to take care of a . . . of her." He set his cup down and looked at Fran. "She always scared me, even when I was a kid."

"You mean she's . . . older than you?"

"She's thirty-one. She stopped growing by the time I was eleven. All the doctors expected her to die before she turned eighteen. Mom never wanted to put her away; she thought it was cruel."

"And your father?"

"He never talked about it much. I never saw him go into her room, ever, except for this one night. I got up, it was about, oh, three in the morning, and I saw him at the foot of the stairs. He was standing at her door, staring in. Then he looked around, took this real deep breath, and went in so . . . quickly. Like he'd been doing it for a long time and hadn't gotten caught. I remember I tiptoed down and stood by the door, listening.

"He *read* to her, as if he couldn't believe that she couldn't . . .

"It was pretty strange. I tried, I really tried to love her. I knew that I should've because she was my sister; she came from the same part of Mom and Dad that I did, so we were both kind of . . . *the same* in that way, you know? No one ever mentioned putting her away when there were other people around. It was one of our private things, one of those matters of family that never left the house under any circumstances." He sipped his tea again; the temperature was just right.

"I even tried reading to her one night, but it got to the point where my voice sounded like it was being sucked into the walls. She never so much as blinked. All I ever wanted from her was just some kind of *reaction*, something that would tell me I was getting through. And I remember that night when I listened to Dad reading to her, I *swear* she giggled. I dunno, though; maybe it was just wishful thinking."

"Would you like me to hang around for a while? I can, you know. Jim's with the kids and he's not expecting me home at any certain time."

He looked through the greyness at Fran's eyes. Kind eyes. He wondered why he hadn't snatched her up when he had the chance.

"Probably wouldn't be the best idea," he said. "I make no guarantees that I'd behave myself." There was a brief glint of something that might have been mischief in her eyes, and he wondered if she really loved her husband and children or if—like him—she'd awakened one morning and found her body wrapped so tightly in family matters that backing out was impossible. As he reached over and took her hand he wondered if love within a family—or between a man and a woman, for that matter—took a back seat to necessity, a nagging feeling that you didn't love so much because you *wanted* to, but because you felt *obligated* to. And what then? Easy: the happiness and welfare of those you loved, things you once vowed to hold sacred, became less a loving task and more a burden you no longer wished to bear, draping its arms around your neck like a child wanting to ride piggy-back, pulling in, slowly cutting off your breath. But you couldn't just cast it away, this burdensome child, because you were all it had, like it or not. Everything became secondary to the burden of that obligation. Even love.

"Little Miss Muffet," he said.

"*What?*" said Fran, the word a half laugh.

"Little Miss Muffet. Dad was reading that to her. I remember I heard her giggle at the part about the spider." He watched the thin streams of steam rise from the tea a vanish into the greyness, taking on no certain shape before it dissolved.

A sound came from the back of the house. A child-sound. Fran didn't seem to notice.

"I don't know what made me think of that," he said, lighting another cigarette, wondering if Fran would wave her hand before the strings of smoke entangled his neck and choked him to death. He wondered how blue his face would get before he lost consciousness—or did suffocation victims die that way, their features twisted and discolored forever?

He glanced at Fran through the sputtering flame of his lighter. She was looking at the ceiling.

Fran kissed him when she left, a kiss that was a little too friendly and went on a little too long. She promised to call him in the morning and come over to help him with Suzanne if he wanted. He held her hand for a moment, gently brushing his fingertips over her palm once so soft and now showing signs of hardness, dryness brought on from washing too many dishes, mending too many socks, changing too many diapers. As he watched her dash out toward her car, he saw—through the droplets of rain that seemed to shimmer from within like a candle flame—what would become of her, what became of all women he'd known who chose the life of wife and mother: a young woman so vibrant and trim and lovely, going happily away, promising to return home one day a woman of the world, waving with hands that always became calloused, running on legs that always grew too heavy, smiling a smile that always grew tired, uncertain, and finally false—all this he saw ignite around her in brief shimmerings of the spattering downpour. She'd kissed him as a young woman, smiled at him from the steps middle-aged, and climbed into her car an overweight, dreamless matron, driving off toward a marriage that would one day seem futile, trap-like, if not outright parasitic.

He closed the door on this image and shook his head.

Get a drink. Something stronger than tea.

Four drinks and six cigarettes later, he opened the door to his sister's room and stared at her. She was still breathing; Cartoon Blue hadn't done her in yet. He walked in, closed the door, and pulled up a chair. He downed what was left in the glass, sat next to her. "Why didn't you ever giggle for me?" he said, watching the ash of his cigarette grow long. "Why couldn't you have given me just one lousy little response?" He watched as the ash fell off, just missing the covers.

An idea came to him.

"I could do it, you know? Just blow on the cherry until it's real hot, lay it next to your pillow and leave, drink a little more. I might go to court, but I'd never do any time. A young man—well, not old, anyway—his parents not ten hours in their graves, saddled with the responsibility of caring for a . . . his sister, drinks a bit too much to ease the day, falls asleep with the cigarette, and—"

The holes in that story began presenting themselves to him with loud and annoying fanfare.

It wasn't in him.

But Suzanne frightened him; worse than anything he'd ever known.

He winced, knowing how ashamed his father would be were he still alive and knew the horrid thoughts his son had been having.

"Do you miss them?" he whispered to the still form. "Were you ever even aware they were here?"

The smoke danced about the ceiling, jumping around like water on a hot griddle. Then it once again began to take form.

"Little Miss Muffet sat on her tuffet," he said.

—*wagon wheel the smoke looks like a wagon wheel don't it Sis?*"

". . . eating her curds and whey . . ."

—*what the hell is whey I never ate that crap and goddam boy no son of mine would ever think something like that you ought to be ashamed she knews that you're around she's your sister and she loves you just like your mother and me*—

". . . along came a spider . . ."

A sound from within the pillow. No. *On* the pillow.

He leaned in close.

Her breathing, soft, smooth, constant, broken by a slight sound like a plump bug being squashed—

A tiny, almost imperceptible giggle.

He crushed the cigarette out in his hand, grinding in the hot ash.

"I feel so much better," he said, then leaned in and kissed her on the forehead. Her face felt funny to him, wider than he remembered. Although Cartoon Blue gave off some light, it was not enough to make out her features. He cupped both his hands on the sides of her face, gently pushing back her hair. His fingers felt where her left ear *should have* been, only there was something *hard* there, something sticking out. He took a breath, slowly turning her head so as not to put a strain on her throat—*God knows we don't want anything to happen to her breathing*—and bent down, blinking his eyes until he was sure his vision was clear. He ran his fingers down her cheek to where the side of her neck *should have* been, but there were pink, wet lips there. He stook back to look. It seemed so natural to him that the two of them should be together like this, and which, *you might ask yourself*, is the real face and which is the Halloween mask that has slid to one side?

A small laugh escaped him.

Suzanne's face lay toward Cartoon Blue.

His mother's face lay staring up at him.

"I wondered how long it would take," he said to her.

"You have to be good," said his mother from the side of Suzanne's head. "You have to help us, Albert. Take care of us."

"I always did, Mom."

"Yes, honey, that you did." Her eyes darted up to a string of Suzanne's hair. "Please cover me back up. I don't want to frighten Fran when she comes back."

"I will. It's good to see you again, Mom."

"Goodnight, Albert."

He brushed the hair down, taking one last look into his mother's eyes, now only the briefest of glimmering stars behind the nightclouds of Suzanne's hair. "Goodnight, Mom."

He then turned his sister's face back around and again kissed her on the forehead. "They never could let go of you," he said, He rose, went to the kitchen, poured another drink, stared at the clock.

It was almost ten p.m.

He checked her again at midnight, his chest burning from booze and cigarettes.

Dad was back now, a second mask on the other side of Suzanne's head, but he was sleeping; Albert knew that one did not disturb his father's sleep for any reason. They'd talk in the morning, like they always had. *Did.*

Back to the kitchen now where his parents sat waiting for him, their faces gone and in their place a smooth sheet of sallow flesh. They reminded him of those "Any Face You Want" dolls he'd had as a child, dolls that were dressed like soldiers or policemen and had nothing for a face, but that was all right because they came with a pen that could draw in four erasable colors so you could draw whatever face you wanted with whatever expression you chose.

He looked at how they sat.

Dad-doll sat at the kitchen table, hands folded together as if in prayer, a cup of cold coffee before him. Albert remembered many nights of seeing his father this way; alone, sitting in the dark, lost in deep concern over his family, finances, or where his younger dreams had gone once the marriage vows had been taken.

That's how I remember you Dad. So quiet, so serious. You never once smiled, not that I saw. I always meant to ask you why.

Mom-doll was over in the living room, sitting in her favorite chair with a cup of tea and a sandwich on her lap, waiting for a late night re-run of a once popular hospital drama that had a cute young doctor. It was always the high point of her day. Albert waited for her to turn toward him and ask if he'd like to join her, she had no company at night and watching the show was so much better if you—

But she had no mouth to speak with. Or eyes to see. Still she waited for the show to start.

And Albert had no four color pen with erasable ink.

Why these? he thought.

Why, of all the memories you could have left me, did you choose these? I remember these so well, Mom and Dad, because, to me, they *were* you. If all images and memories of you were to be sucked out of my brain, these would be the ones too powerful ever to leave me.

And they were also the worst. Because he'd know at these times his parents gave everything second place to obligation. And were alone and lonely because of it. Helpless and entangled and choking and nailed down to a life and family, neither of which had turned out as they'd hoped.

He turned away, grabbed the bottle of scotch and a fresh pack of cigarettes, and went to his old bedroom in the back. It was just as he'd left it—sparse. A bed, a dresser, a chair, a desk, and nothing more. He kept a makeshift work space here, just in case his own apartment grew too quiet some night. He could always come back here.

Back to the family.

And matters of.

The burning in his chest grew worse over the next four hours, but he kept smoking one cigarette after another, at one point discovering that he had five going at the same time.

Around four-thirty in the morning he heard another child-sound from Suzanne's room. He crept slowly toward the door, pressed his ear against it.

She was giggling.

". . . and frightened Miss Muffet away," came the dull echo of his father's voice, speaking in rhythm with the drumming fingers of rain on the roof. A silent flash of lightning, raindrops into candle flames, and Dad began reciting another, different verse.

"You never read stories to me," whispered Albert to the door. "I always wanted you to, but you never did."

He turned and went back to his drink, to his cigarettes. He tried to fall asleep, but the constant murmuring of their voices kept him around. At five he picked up the phone. Dialed. Listened as the phone buzzed, buzzed buzzed into a click and then a hiss and then—

". . . lo?" The voice was soft, thick with sleep.

"Fran?"

The voice coughed, cleared its throat. "Albert? That you?"

"Yeah, Jim. Sorry to wake you." There was the sound of sheets rustling. Whispering. He closed his eyes, imagining what Jim had been doing to Fran before sleep took them away to a false safety and security. The things. Warm and moist.

Fran, at last.

"Albert? Is everything all right?"

I should've snatched you up when I had the chance. "I didn't mean to wake you, Fran. I'm sorry."

"Don't apologize. What is it? You okay?"

You'd never have let me come back here. "Could you . . . come back?"

"Is there something wrong with Suzanne?"

"Sort of. She won't stop giggling."

". . . what?"

I never would have felt so goddamn responsible. "It's not so much . . . so much her, though." The smoke of his new cigarette blew up, scattered, pulled back, webbing, webbing, coming toward him—"It's Mom and Dad; they're keeping her awake."

Silence from the other end; the web kept coming and Fran wasn't here to wave it away . .

". . . drunk?"

"Maybe a little," said Albert.

"I knew I should've stayed."

Would you have let me be warm and moist with you like Jim? "I think they're mad at me. They didn't give me any pen to draw . . . their faces with."

"I'll be over in a few minutes. You just stay put and don't drink any more, all right?"

". . . sucked it all out, all of them but those two . . . don't know why . . ."

He felt weak, as if his limbs were wrapped in rope.

The smoke-web widened.

The giggling grew louder.

He didn't even hear Fran hang up. He kept talking into the receiver.

". . . always wanted to help them out, you know . . . but I never counted on having to run their whole lives . . . poor little thing, I should've been more . . . love her, really I did because maybe she understands love, maybe, and . . ."

Click, Squeak.

Suzanne's door opened.

Giggling.

He kept talking.

"Was never really a part of things . . . wanted to be, though. The thing is that I never really tried. I just worried about it too much. . . ." He didn't realize that he'd begun weeping. He took another drag, another drink. The burning grew worse, snaking through him. He looked up at the ceiling. Saw. Something dangled there; thin, vein-like, rough-looking . . . maybe . . . hairy . . . ?"

" . . . never read to me. I always wondered why. He always worried so much about things . . ."

Giggling. A brushing of something against his leg.

He leaned back, closed his eyes, let the receiver drop.

Weight shifted around him; he felt arms, legs, lips touching against his cheek, words whispered, embraces, warm, so many hands, long, thin, weak, bumpy, strong, twisted . . .

. . . he opened his eyes and saw the web descend toward him.

Pounding, pounding . . . he thought maybe in his head.

No, the door.

Fran. She'd wave it away, save him from being strangled by Cartoon Blue.

He started to move from the chair, found that he was already standing.

Looking back where he sat, the Albert-doll, no face, no tears, only the cigarette ash on his pant leg, the cherry growing brighter, falling off, flames licking at his clothes like the tongue of a lover . . .

He moved toward the door as his father spoke.

"Your sister wants you to read to her, Albert. Would you like that? I'll read to you, too, if you'd like. Seems the least I can do."

"Let's *all* read to her," said Mom.

"Yeah," said Albert. "That would be nice."

Suzanne giggled.

It was good for them to be together like this.

Behind him, the Albert-doll was sitting there, holding hands with Mom-doll and Dad-doll, all of them seeming so happy, burning away as the smoke-web wrapped around them, arms twisting together, legs sticking out like—

Mother's voice: *"Little Miss Muffet sat on her tuffet . . ."*

Flash of lightning, and Albert saw their reflection in the mirror, so clear, turning a full circle so each could get a good look at the face—

Father now: ". . . *eating her curds and whey . . .*"

The flames spit up higher and Albert knew he'd let the cigarette drop for a reason, because they needed the web, yes they did, there was no other way for them to entangle, and entanglement was the only action left them . . .

. . . *poundpoundpoundpound. . .*

"Albert!" Fran's voice. She sounded so worried. No need to worry now, Fran, everything's fine, we've settled our private family matters.

". . . *along came a spider,*" said Albert, reaching for the door, turning the knob.

. . . *and sat down beside her* . . ." said all of them.

Freed, the door swung open.

Pleased, Suzanne giggled.

Completed, the web offered shelter.

Scuttling around on the arms and legs, twisting and smiling, Albert and his family looked up.

Given a clear look by the pouring firedrops, Fran began screaming.

JANE YOLEN

Beauty and the Beast:
An Anniversary

In addition to owning a formidable reputation as a writer of original fantasy stories, Jane Yolen is also a fairy- and folk-tale scholar. She edits collections such as *Folktales from Around the World* (for which she won the World Fantasy Award) and is known in academic circles for her important essay tracing the development of the Tattercoats (Cinderella) story from ancient times to our own.

She has worked with fairy-tale themes and retellings in picture books and short stories, and in lovely poems like the one on the following page. Currently she is at work on a novel retelling the Briar Rose (Sleeping Beauty) story for the Tor Books/Endicott Studio "Adult Fairy Tales" series.

"Beauty and the Beast: An Anniversary"—like the story published elsewhere in this volume—comes from her most recent collection, *The Faery Flag*.

—T.W.

Beauty and the Beast: An Anniversary

JANE YOLEN

It is winter now,
and the roses are blooming again,
their petals bright against the snow.
My father died last April;
my sisters no longer write,
except at the turning of the year,
content with their fine houses
and their grandchildren.
Beast and I
putter in the gardens
and walk slowly on the forest paths.
He is graying
around the muzzle
and I have silver combs
to match my hair.
I have no regrets.
None.
Though sometimes I do wonder
what sounds children
might have made
running across the marble halls,
swinging from the birches
over the roses
in the snow.

JOAN AIKEN
Find Me

British author Joan Aiken is one of the most distinguished names in children's literature on both sides of the Atlantic, as well as a renowned author of adult mysteries. She has written more than a dozen novels, story collections, and picture books for children, including *A Whisper in the Night*, *The Shadow Guest*, *Bridle the Wind*, *The Moon's Revenge*, and *The Last Slice of Rainbow*. Her suspenseful and irreverent "Dido Twite" books are favorites with both children and adults; the most recent of these, *Dido and Pa*, I heartily recommend. Ms. Aiken has won the Lewis Carroll Award, the Carnegie Medal, the Guardian Award for Children's Fiction, and the Edgar Allan Poe Award. She currently divides her time between homes in Sussex, England and New York City.

The following is a brief but haunting little tale that lingers in the heart long after it is done. It comes from the pages of her collection *Give Yourself a Fright: Thirteen Stories of the Supernatural*.

—T.W.

Find Me

JOAN AIKEN

After the funeral Prince Tom managed to escape from his attendants and slip away. This was not hard, for he was small, and everybody was crying, they had handkerchiefs to their eyes and did not see him go.

A footman had once told him about the house in Kettle Street, where you go when you have lost something. The house is old, and empty, probably haunted. It has been empty for years. In one of the bedrooms is a mirror, and if you are brave enough to go upstairs and look in that mirror, you will see the thing you lost, lying in the place where you lost it.

Tom thought he was brave enough. He felt so sad that he did not think *anything* could frighten him.

Kettle Street lay a long way off, in a poor run-down part of the city, miles from the palace. Nobody paid any heed to Prince Tom, hurrying, head down, in his black coat, sometimes studying a street map he held in his hand.

Number Thirteen Kettle Street was a tall, shabby house, no different from its neighbors, with blank windows and broken steps leading to a scabbed and peeling door.

Tom tried the handle. Suppose it was locked? But no, it was not. He opened the door and walked in, closing the door again gently behind him, waiting a moment, for it was dusky inside, with his heart going bang-bang-bang among his ribs.

Then he started up the stairs he saw straight ahead. The stairs did not feel at all safe: they creaked and sank as he made his careful way. At the top were three doors. He chose the middle one, but that led to a room with a great hole in the floor, so he tried the right-hand one. There was the mirror! tilted on a stand, throwing an oblong of silver light across the dirty ceiling.

Tom stole across to the mirror, avoiding holes and rotten spots in the floorboards. All his mind was on what he had lost, as he gazed down at the slanted glass.

Part of the mirror surface was worn away, and, under the glass, there were black patches. But, as Tom gazed, he found that he could see a long distance, as if through a telescope. Rooms he could see, and houses, streets, and gardens; they slid and blurred and moved on, changing all the time, but all familiar, places where Tom had lived and played, eaten and slept. And in all those places were things he had lost. Oh! he thought. There's that spotted wooden dog!—it must have fallen into the pool—and my red scarf—and the little book Nan gave me—

Better not think about Nan. If he had not lost his lucky piece of string, perhaps Nan would not have caught pneumonia and died.

There was the string! Caught, with a grubby handkerchief, under a root of the big walnut tree in the palace garden.

If only he had known before. . . . Drawing a deep shaky breath, rubbing his nose on his sleeve, Tom turned to go. What a lot of things I've lost, he thought. Suppose an old, old person, Nan, for instance, came? Why, it would take weeks to find all the lost things! He paused for a last look in the mirror, to thank it, perhaps. The glass was calm now, nothing in it. But yes, there was! Another face, a girl's, thin, rather sad, older than Tom, almost grown up—but nothing like so old as Nan had been. Stepping forward, she gave Tom a little nod, then studied the glass.

"You lost something too?" he whispered.

"My job," she whispered back. "The factory closed. . . ."

Leaving her to her search, Tom went downstairs. But he sat down abruptly on the bottom step. Inside, he felt as if something had snapped, a long, long thread.

After all, Nan had looked after him ever since he was born.

He laid his head down on his knees.

By and by, steps came down behind him. Tom stood, and looked at the girl. At first her shape slid about, blurred, like the pictures in the mirror. Then it steadied.

"Did you find what you were looking for?" he asked.

"I—think so. Did you?"

"My string? Yes. Now I know where it is."

"Then," she said, "hadn't we better get you home, so you can find it?"

And she took his hand in hers, where it fitted comfortably.

JAMES P. BLAYLOCK
Unidentified Objects

James P. Blaylock is one of the most interesting and talented writers to grace the fantasy field, with such quirky, wry, fantastical novels as *The Digging Leviathan*, *The Last Coin*, *The Land of Dreams*, and the humorous fantasy books: *The Elfin Ship*, *The Disappearing Dwarves*, and *The Stone Giant*. He has written a number of memorable short stories, and has won a World Fantasy Award for his work.

"Unidentified Objects" is a beautifully written, wistful tale of magic realism. Originally published in *Omni* magazine, it has been selected for the *Prize Stories 1990: The O. Henry Awards* volume, honoring the best American short stories of the year, by the Society of Arts and Sciences—which is still (regrettably) an unusual distinction for a fantasy story, and well-deserved in the case of this excellent piece.

Blaylock lives with his wife and children in southern California.

—T.W.

Unidentified Objects

JAMES P. BLAYLOCK

In 1956 the downtown square mile of the city of Orange was a collection of old houses: craftsman bungalows and tile-roofed Spanish, and here and there an old Queen Anne or a gingerbread Victorian with geminate windows and steep gables, and sometimes a carriage house alongside, too small by half to house the lumbering automobiles that the second fifty years of the century had produced. There were Studebakers at the curbs and Hudsons and Buicks with balloon tires like the illustrations of moon-aimed rockets on the covers of the pulp magazines.

Times were changing. Science was still a professor with wild hair and a lab coat and with bubbling apparatus in a cellar; but in a few short years he would walk on the moon—one last ivory and silver hurrah—and then, as if in an instant, he would grow faceless and featureless and unpronounceable. There would come the sudden knowledge that Moon Valley wasn't so very far away after all, and neither was extinction; that the nation that controlled magnetism, as Diet Smith would have it, controlled almost nothing at all; and that a score of throbbing bulldozers could reduce the jungled wilds around Opar and El Dorado to desert sand in a few short, sad years. The modern automobile suddenly was slick and strange, stretched out and low and with enormous fins that swept back at the rear above banks of superfluous taillights. They seemed otherworldly at the time and were alien reminders, it seems to me now, of how provincial we had been, balanced on the back edge of an age.

The pace of things seemed to be accelerating, and already I could too easily anticipate stepping out onto my tilted front porch some signifying morning, the wind out of the east, and seeing stretched out before me not a shaded avenue of overarching trees and root-cracked sidewalks but the sleek, desertlike technology of a new age, a new suburbia, with robots in vinyl trousers sweeping fallen leaves into their own open mouths.

418

*   *   *

There is a plaza in the center of town, with a fountain, and in the autumn
—the season when all of this came to my attention—red brown leaves from
flowering pear trees drift down onto the sluggish, gurgling water and float there
like a centerpiece for a Thanksgiving table. On a starry evening, one November
late in the Seventies, I was out walking in the plaza, thinking, I remember, that
it had already become an artifact, with its quaint benches and granite curbs and
rose garden. Then, shattering the mood of latenight nostalgia, there shone in
the sky an immense shooting star, followed by the appearance of a glowing
object, which hovered and darted, sailing earthward until I could make out its
shadow against the edge of the moon and then disappearing in a blink. I shouted
and pointed, mostly out of surprise. Strange lights in the sky were nothing
particularly novel; I had been seeing them for almost twenty years. But nothing
that happens at night among the stars can ever become commonplace. At that
late hour, though, there was almost certainly no one around to hear me; or so
I thought.

So when she stood up, dropping papers and pencils and a wooden drawing
board onto the concrete walk, I nearly shouted again. She had been sitting in
the dim lamplight, hidden to me beyond the fountain. Dark hair fell across her
shoulders in a rush of curl and hid her right eye, and with a practiced sweep of
her hand she pulled it back in a shock and tucked it behind her ear, where it
stayed obediently for about three quarters of a second and then fell seductively
into her face again. Now, years later, for reasons I can't at all define, the sight
of a dark-haired woman brushing wayward hair out of her eyes recalls without
fail that warm autumn night by the fountain.

She had that natural, arty, blue-jeans-and-floppy-sweater look of a college girl
majoring in fine arts: embroidered handbag, rhinestone-emerald costume
brooch, and translucent plastic shoes the color of root beer. I remember thinking
right off that she had languorous eyes, and the sight of them reflecting the soft
lamplight of the fountain jolted me. But the startled look on her face implied
that she hadn't admired my shouting like that, not at eleven o'clock at night in
the otherwise deserted plaza.

There was the dark, pouting beauty in her eyes and lips of a woman in a Pre-
Raphaelite painting, a painting that I had stumbled into in my clodlike way,
grinning, I thought, like a half-wit. I too hastily explained the shooting star to
her, gesturing too widely at the sky and mumbling that it hadn't been an ordinary
shooting star. But there was nothing in the sky now besides the low-hanging
moon and a ragtag cloud, and she said offhandedly, not taking any notice of
my discomfort, just what I had been thinking, that there was never anything
ordinary about a shooting star.

I learned that her name was Jane and that she had sketched that fountain a
dozen times during the day, with the blooming flowers behind it and the changing
backdrop of people and cars and weather. I almost asked her whether she hadn't
ever been able to get it quite right, but then, I could see that that wasn't the
point.

Now she had been sketching it at night, its blue and green and pink lights illuminating the umbrella of falling water against night-shaded rosebushes and camphor trees and boxwood hedges.

It was perfect—straight out of a romantic old film. The hero stumbles out of the rain into an almost deserted library, and at the desk, with her hair up and spectacles on her nose, is the librarian who doesn't know that if she'd just take the glasses off for a moment . . .

I scrabbled around to pick up fallen pencils while she protested that she could just as easily do it herself. It was surely only the magic of that shooting star that prevented her from gathering up her papers and going home. As it was, she stayed for a moment to talk, assuming, although she never said so, that there was something safe and maybe interesting in a fancier of shooting stars. I felt the same about her and her drawings and her root beer shoes.

She was distracted, never really looking at me. Maybe the image of the fountain was still sketched across the back of her eyes and she couldn't see me clearly. It was just a little irritating, and I would discover later that it was a habit of hers, being distracted was, but on that night there was something in the air and it didn't matter. Any number of things don't matter at first. We talked, conversation dying and starting and with my mind mostly on going somewhere—my place, her place—for a drink, for what? There was something, an atmosphere that surrounded her, a musky sort of sweater and lilacs scent. But she was distant; her work had been interrupted and she was still half lost in the dream of it. She dragged her hand in the water of the fountain, her face half in shadow. She was tired out, she said. She didn't need to be walked home. She could find her way alone.

But I've got ahead of myself. It's important that I keep it all straight—all the details; without the details it amounts to nothing. I grew up on Olive Street, southwest of the plaza, and when I was six, and wearing my Davy Crockett hat and Red Rider shirt, and it was nearly dusk in late October, I heard the ding-a-linging of an ice cream truck from some distant reach of the neighborhood. The grass was covered with leaves, I remember, that had been rained on and were limp and heavy. I was digging for earthworms and dropping them one by one into a corral built of upright sticks and twigs that was the wall of the native village on Kong Island. The sky was cloudy, the street empty. There was smoke from a chimney across the way and the cloud-muted hum of a distant airplane lost to view. Light through the living room window shone out across the dusky lawn.

The jangling of the ice cream bell drew near, and the truck rounded the distant corner, the bell cutting off and the truck accelerating as if the driver, anticipating dinner, had given up for the day and was steering a course for home. It slowed, though, when he saw me, and angled in toward the curb where I stood holding a handful of gutter-washed earthworms. Clearly he thought I'd signaled him. There were pictures of frozen concoctions painted on the gloss-white sides of the panel truck: coconut-covered Neapolitan bars and grape Popsicles, nut and chocolate drumsticks, and strawberry-swirled vanilla in paper cups with flat paper lids. He laboriously climbed out of the cab, came around the street side to the back, and confronted me there on the curb. He smiled and winked and wore a silver foil hat with an astonishing bill, and when he yanked open the hinged, chrome door there was such a whirling of steam off the dry ice inside that he utterly vanished behind it, and I caught a quick glimpse of cardboard bins farther back in the cold fog, stacked one on top of another and dusted with ice crystals.

I didn't have a dime and wouldn't be allowed to eat ice cream so close to dinnertime anyway, and I said so, apologizing for having made him stop for nothing. He studied my earthworms and said that out in space there were planets where earthworms spoke and wore silk shirts, and that I could fly to those planets in the right sort of ship.

Then he bent into the freezer and after a lot of scraping and peering into boxes found a paper-wrapped ice cream bar—a FLYING SAUCER BAR, the wrapper said. It was as big around as a coffee cup saucer and was domed on top and fat with vanilla ice cream coated in chocolate. He tipped his hat, slammed his door, and drove off. I ate the thing guiltily while sitting beneath camellia bushes at the side of the house and lobbing sodden pink blooms out onto the front yard, laying siege to the earthworm fortress and watching the lamps blink on one by one along the street.

There are those incidents from our past that years later seem to us to be the stuff of dreams: the wash of shooting stars seen through the rear window of the family car at night in the Utah desert; the mottled, multilegged sun star, as big as a cartwheel, inching across the sand in the shallows of a northern California bay; the whale's eyeball floating in alcohol and encased in a glass fishing float in a junk store near the waterfront; the remembered but unrecoverable hollow sensation of new love. The stars vanish in an instant; the starfish slips away into deep water and is gone; the shop with its fishing float is a misty dream, torn down in some unnumbered year to make room for a hotel built of steel and smoked glass. Love evaporates into the passing years like dry ice; you don't know where it's gone. The mistake is to think that the details don't signify—the flying saucer bars and camellia blooms, rainy autumn streets and lamplight through evening windows and colored lights playing across the waters of a fountain on a warm November evening.

All the collected pieces of our imagistic memory seem sometimes to be trivial knickknacks when seen against the roaring of passing time. But without those little water-paint sketches, awash in remembered color and detail, none of us, despite our airy dreams, amount to more than an impatient ghost wandering through the revolving years and into an increasingly strange and alien future.

I came to know the driver of the ice cream truck. We became acquaintances. He no longer sold ice cream; there was no living to be made at it. He had got a penny a Popsicle, he said, and he produced a slip of paper covered with numbers—elaborate calculations of the millions of Popsicles he'd have to sell over the years just to stay solvent. Taken altogether like that it was impossible.

He had been new to the area then and hadn't got established yet. All talk of money aside, he had grown tired of it, of the very idea of driving an ice cream truck—something that wouldn't have seemed possible to me on the rainy evening of the flying saucer bar, but which I understand well enough now.

He had appeared on our front porch, I remembered, when I was ten or eleven, selling wonderful tin toys door-to-door. My mother bought a rocket propelled by compressed air. It was painted with bright, circus colors, complete with flames swirling around the cylindrical base of the thing. Looking competent and serious and very much like my ice cream man was a helmeted pilot painted into a bubblelike vehicle on the top of the rocket, which would pop off, like a second stage, when the rocket attained the stupendous height of thirty or forty feet. I immediately lost the bubble craft with its painted astronaut. It shot off, just like it was supposed to, and never came down. I have to suppose that it's rusting in the branches of a tree somewhere, but I have a hazy memory of it simply shooting into the air and disappearing in a blink, hurtling up through the thin atmosphere toward deep space. Wasted money, my mother said.

Our third meeting was at the Palm Street Market, where I went to buy penny candy that was a nickel by then. I was thirteen, I suppose, or something near it, which would have made it early in the Sixties. The clerk being busy, I had strayed over to the magazine shelves and found a copy of *Fate*, which I read for the saucer stories, and which, on that afternoon, was the excuse for my being close enough to the "men's" magazines to thumb through a couple while the clerk had his back turned. I had the *Fate* open to the account of Captain Hooton's discovery of an airship near Texarkana, and a copy of something called *Slick* or *Trick* or *Flick* propped open on the rack behind. I read the saucer article out of apologetic shame in between thumbing through the pages of photographs, as if my reading it would balance out the rest, but remembering nothing of what I read until, with a shock of horror that I can still recall as clearly as anything else in my life, I became aware that the ice cream man, the tin toy salesman, was standing behind me, reading over my shoulder.

What I read, very slowly and carefully as three fourths of my blood rose into my head, was Captain Hooton's contempt for airship design: "There was no bell or bell rope about the ship that I could discover, like I should think every well-regulated air locomotive should have." At the precise moment of my reading that sentence, the clerk's voice whacked out of the silence: "Hey, kid!" was what he said. I'd heard it before. It was a weirdly effective phrase and had such a freezing effect on me that Captain Hooton's bit of mechanical outrage has come along through the years with me uninvited, pegged into my memory by the manufactured shame of that single moment.

Both of us bought a copy of *Fate*. I had to, of course, although it cost me forty cents that I couldn't afford. I remember the ice cream man winking broadly at me there on the sidewalk, and me being deadly certain that I had become as transparent as a ghost fish. Everyone on Earth had been on to my little game with the magazine. I couldn't set foot in that market without a disguise for a solid five years. And then, blessedly, he was gone, off down the street, and me in the opposite direction. I stayed clear of the market for a couple of months and then discovered, passing on the sidewalk, that the witnessing clerk was gone, and that went a long way toward putting things right, although Captain Hooton, as I said, has stayed with me. In fact, I began from that day to think of the ice cream man as Captain Hooton, since I had no idea what his name was, and years later the name would prove strangely appropriate.

It was in the autumn, then, that I first met Jane on that November night in the plaza, and weeks later when I introduced her to him, to Captain Hooton. She said in her artistic way that he had a "good face," although she didn't mean to make any sort of moral judgment, and truthfully his face was almost inhumanly long and angular. She said this after the three of us had chatted for a moment and he had gone on his way. It was as if there were nothing much more she could say about him that made any difference at all, as if she were distracted.

I remember that it irritated me, although why it should have I don't know, except that he had already begun to mean something, to signify, as if our chance meetings over the years, if I could pluck them out of time and arrange them just so, would make a pattern.

"He dresses pretty awful, doesn't he?" That's what she said after he'd gone along and she could think of nothing more to say about his face.

I hadn't noticed, and I said so, being friendly about it.

"He's smelly. What was that, do you think?"

"Tobacco, I guess. I don't know. Pipe tobacco." She wasn't keen on tobacco, or liquor either. So I didn't put too fine a point on it because I didn't want to set her off, to have to defend his smoking a pipe. It was true that his coat could have used a cleaning, but that hadn't occurred to me, actually, until she mentioned it, wrinkling up her nose in that rabbit way of hers.

"I keep thinking that he's got a fish in his pocket."

I smiled at her, suddenly feeling as if I were betraying a friend.

"Well . . ." I said, trying to affect a dropping-the-subject tone.

She shuddered. "People get like that, especially old people. They forget to take baths and wash their hair."

I shrugged, pretending to think that she was merely trying to be amusing.

"He's not that old," I said. But she immediately agreed. That was the problem, wasn't it? You wouldn't think . . . She looked at my own hair very briefly and then set out down the sidewalk with me following and studying my shadow in the afternoon sun and keeping my hands away from my hair. It looked neat enough there in the shadow on the sidewalk, but I knew that shadows couldn't be trusted, and I was another five minutes worrying about it before something else happened, it doesn't matter what, and I forgot about my hair and my vanity.

Her own hair had a sort of flyaway look to it, but perfect, if you understand me, and it shone as if she'd given it the standard hundred strokes that morning. A dark-red ribbon held a random clutch of it behind her ear, and there was something in the ribbon and in the way she put her hand on my arm to call my attention to some house or other that made me think of anything but houses. She had a way of touching you, almost as if accidentally, like a cat sliding past your leg, rubbing against you, and arching just a little and then continuing on, having abandoned any interest in you. She stood too close, maybe, for comfort—although *comfort* is the wrong word because the sensation was almost ultimately comfortable—and all the while that we were standing there talking about the lines of the roof, I was conscious only of the static charge of her presence, her shoulder just grazing my arm, her hip brushing against my thigh, the heavy presence of her sex suddenly washing away whatever was on the surface of my mind and settling there musky and soft. There hasn't been another man in history more indifferent to the lines of a roof.

In the downtown circular plaza each Christmas, there was an enormous Santa Claus built from wire and twisted paper, lit from within by a spiral of pin lights, and at Halloween, beneath overcast skies and pending rain, there were parades of schoolchildren dressed as witches and clowns and bed-sheet ghosts. Then in spring there was a May festival, with city dignitaries riding in convertible Edsels and waving to people sitting in lawn chairs along the boulevard. One year the parade was led by a tame ape followed by fezzed Shriners in Mr. Toad cars.

Twice during the two years that Jane studied art, while the town shrank for her and grew cramped, we watched the parade from a sidewalk table in front of Felix's Café, laughing at the ape and smiling at the solemn drumming of the marching bands. The second year one of the little cars caught fire and the parade fizzled out and waited while a half-dozen capering Shriners beat the fire out with their jackets. It was easy to laugh then, at the ape and the Edsels and the tiny cars, except that even then I suspected that her laughter was half cynical. Mine wasn't, and this difference between us troubled me.

In the summer there was a street fair, and the smoky aroma of sausages and beer and the sticky-sweet smell of cotton candy. We pushed through the milling crowds and sat for hours under an ancient tree in the plaza, watching the world revolve around us.

It seems now that I was always wary then that the world in its spinning might tumble me off, and there was something about the exposed roots of that tree that made you want to touch them, to sit among them just to see how immovable they were. But the world couldn't spin half fast enough for her. You'd have thought that if she could get a dozen paintings out of that fountain, then there would be enough, even in a provincial little town like this one, to amuse her forever.

Captain Hooton always seemed to be turning up. One year he put on a Santa costume and wandered through the shops startling children. The following year at Halloween he appeared out of the doorway of a disused shop, wearing a fright wig and carrying an enormous flashlight like a lighthouse beacon, on the lens of which was glued a witch cut out of black construction paper. He climbed into a sycamore tree in front of Watson's Drugs and shined the witch for a half hour onto the white stone facade of the bank, and then, refusing to come down unless he was made to, was finally led away by the police. Jane ought to have admired the trick with the flashlight, but she had by then developed a permanent dislike for him because, I think, he didn't seem to take her seriously, her or her paintings, and she took both of those things very seriously indeed, while pretending to care for almost nothing at all.

He ate pretty regularly for a time at Rudy's counter, at the drugstore. It was a place where milk shakes were still served in enormous metal cylinders and where shopkeepers sat on red Naugahyde and ate hot turkey sandwiches and mashed potatoes and talked platitudes and weather and sports, squinting and nodding. Captain Hooton wasn't much on conversation. He sat alone usually, smoking and wearing one of those caps that sports car enthusiasts wear, looking as if he were pondering something, breaking into silent laughter now and then as he watched the autumn rain fall and the red-brown sycamore leaves scattering along the street in the gusting breeze.

There was something awful about his skin—an odd color, perhaps, too pink and blue and never any hint of a beard, even in the afternoon.

A balding man from Fergy's television repair referred to him jokingly as Doctor Loomis, apparently the name of an alien visitor in a cheap, old science-fiction thriller. I chatted with him three or four times when Jane wasn't along, coming to think of him finally as a product of "the old school," which, as Dickens said, is no school that ever existed on Earth.

There were more sightings of things in the sky—almost always at night, and almost always they were described in slightly ludicrous terms by astonished citizens, as if each of them had mugged up those old issues of *Fate*. The things were egg-shaped, wingless, smooth silver; they beamed people up through spiraling doors and motored them around the galaxy and then dropped them off again, in a vacant lot or behind an apartment complex or bowling alley and with an inexplicable lapse of memory. The *City News* was full of it.

Once, at the height of the sightings, men in uniforms came from the East and the sightings mysteriously stopped. Something landed in the upper reaches of my avocado tree one night and glowed there. Next morning I found a cardboard milk carton smelling of chemicals, the inside stained the green of a sunlit ocean, lying in the leaves and humus below. It had little wings fastened with silver duct tape. The bottom of it had been cut out and replaced with a carved square of pumice, a bored-out carburetor jet glued into the center of it.

It happened that Captain Hooton lived on Pine Street by that time, and so did I. I rented half of a little bungalow and took walks in the evening when I wasn't with Jane. His house was deceptively large. From the street it seemed to be a narrow, gabled Victorian with a three-story turret in the right front corner, and with maybe a living room, parlor, and kitchen downstairs. Upstairs there might have been room for a pair of large bedrooms and a library midway up in the turret. There was a lot of split clinker brick mortared onto the front in an attempt to make the house look indefinably European, and shutters with shooting stars cut into them that had been added along the way. Old newspapers piled up regularly on the front porch and walk as if he were letting them ripen, and the brush-choked flower beds were so overgrown that none of the downstairs windows could have admitted any sunlight.

Jane seemed to see it as being a shame—the mess of weeds and brush, the cobbled-together house, the yellowing papers. Somehow I held out hope that it would strike her as—what?—original. Eccentric, maybe. At first I thought that they were too much alike in their eccentricities. I considered her root beer shoes and her costume jewelry and her very fashionable and practiced disregard for fashion and her perfectly disarranged hair, and it occurred to me that she was art, so to speak—artifice, theater. And although she talked about spontaneity, she was a marvel of regimentation and control, and never more so than when she was being spontaneous. The two of them couldn't have been more unalike.

He was vaguely alarming, though. You couldn't tell what he was thinking; his past and his future were misty and dim, giving you the sort of feeling you get on cheap haunted-house thrill rides at carnivals, where you're never quite sure what colorful, grimacing thing will leap out at you from behind a plywood partition.

I could see the rear of his house from my backyard, and from there it appeared far larger. It ran back across the deep lot and was a wonder of dormers, gables, and lean-to closets, all of it overshadowed by walnut trees and trumpet flower vines on sagging trellises and arbors. Underneath was a sprawling basement, which at night glowed with lamplight through aboveground transom windows. The muted ring of small hammers and the hum of lathes sounded from the cellar at unwholesomely late hours.

The double doors of his garage were fastened with a rusted iron lock as big as a man's hand, and he must have had a means by which to enter and leave the garage—and perhaps the house itself—without using any of the visible doors. I rarely saw him out and about. When I did, he sometimes seemed hardly to know me, as if distracted, his mind on mysteries.

Once, while I was out walking, I came across him spading up a strip of earth beneath his kitchen window, breaking the clods apart and pulling iron filings out of them with an enormous magnet. I recalled our distant meeting behind the ice cream truck, but by now he seemed to remember it only vaguely. I took him to be the sort of eccentric genius too caught up in his own meanderings to pay any attention to the mundane world.

He'd started a winter garden there along the side of his house, and a dozen loose heads of red-leaf lettuce grew in the half-shade of the eaves. We chatted amiably enough, about the weather, about gardens. He gave me a sidewise squint and asked if I'd seen any of the alleged "saucers" reported in the newspaper, and I said that I had, or at least that I had seen some saucer or another months ago. He nodded and frowned as if he'd rather hoped I hadn't, as if the two of us might have sneered at the notion of it together.

A spotted butterfly hovered over the lettuce, alighting now and then and finally settling in "to eat the lettuce alive," as he put it. He wouldn't stand for it, he said, and very quietly he plucked up a wire-mesh flyswatter that hung from a nail on the side porch, and he flailed away at the butterfly until the head of lettuce it had rested on was shredded. He seemed to think it was funny, particularly so because the butterfly itself had got entirely away, had fluttered off at the first sign of trouble. It was a joke, an irony, a metaphor of something that I didn't quite catch.

He gave me a paper sack full of black-eyed peas and disappeared into the house, asking after the "young lady" but not waiting for an answer, and then shoving back out through the door to tell me to return the sack when I was through with it, and then laughing and winking and closing the door, and winking again through the kitchen window so that it was impossible to say what, entirely, he meant by the display.

There wasn't much I could have told him about the "young lady." Much of what I might have said would already be a reminiscence. The thing that mattered, I suppose, was that she made me weak in the knees, but I couldn't say so. And she was entirely without that clinging, dependent nature that feeds a man's vanity at first but soon grows tiresome. Jane always talked as if she had places to go to, people to meet. There was something in the tone of her voice that made such talk sound like a warning, as if I weren't invited along, or weren't up to it, or were a momentary amusement, like the May parade, perhaps, and would have to suffice while she was stuck there in that little farflung corner of the globe.

She wanted to travel to the Orient, to Paris. I wanted to travel, too. It turned out that her plans didn't exclude me. I would go along—quit work and go, just like that, spontaneously, wearing a beret and a knapsack. And that's just what I did, finally, although without the beret; I'm not the sort of a man who can wear a hat. I'm too likely to affect the carefree attitude and then regret the hat, or whatever it is I'm wearing, and then whatever it is I'm not wearing but should have. It's a world of regrets, isn't it? Jane didn't think so. She hadn't any regrets, and said so, and for a while I was foolish enough to admire her saying so. I don't believe that Captain Hooton would have understood her saying such a thing, let alone have admired it.

I brought around his paper sack, right enough, two days later, and he took it from me solemnly, nodding and frowning. At once he blew it up like a balloon—inflated it until it was almost spherical—and then, waving a finger in order to show me, I suppose, that I hadn't seen anything yet, he pulled a slip of silver ribbon out of his vest pocket, looped it around the bunched paper at the bottom, and tied it off. He lit a kitchen match with his fingernail and held it to the tails of the ribbon. Immediately the inflated sack began to glow and rocketed away through the curb trees like a blowfish, the ribbons trailing streams of blue sparks. It angled skyward in a rush and vanished.

I must have looked astonished, thinking of the milk carton beneath my tree. He pretended to smoke his pipe with his ear. Then he sighted along the stem as if it were a periscope, and made whirring and clicking sorts of submarine noises with his tongue. Then waggling his shoulder as if generally loosening his joints, he blew softly across the reeking pipe bowl, dispersing the smoke and making a sound uncannily like Peruvian pan-pipes. He was full of tricks. He suddenly looked very old—certainly above seventy. His hair, which must have been a transplant, grew in patterns like hedgerows, and in the sunlight that shone between the racing clouds, his skin was almost translucent, as if he were a laminated see-through illustration in a modern encyclopedia.

And so one evening late I knocked on the cellar window next to his kitchen door, then stood back on the dewy lawn and waited for him. He was working down there, tinkering with something; I could see his head wagging over the bench.

In a moment he opened the door, having come upstairs. He didn't seem at all surprised to see me skulking in the yard like that but waved me in impatiently as if he had been waiting for my arrival, maybe for years, and now I'd finally come and there was no time to waste.

The cellar was impossibly vast, stretching away room after room, a sort of labyrinth of low-ceilinged, concrete-floored rooms. I couldn't be certain of my bearings any longer, but it seemed that the rooms must have been dug beneath the driveway alongside his house as well as under the house itself—maybe under the house next door; and once I allowed for such a thing, it occurred to me that his cellars might as easily stretch beneath my own house. I remembered nights when I had been awakened by noises, by strange creaks and clanks and rattles of the sort that startle you awake, and you listen, your heart going like sixty, while you tell yourself that it's the house "settling," but you don't believe it. And all this time it might have been him, muffled beneath the floor and perhaps a few feet of earth, tapping away at a workbench like a dwarf in his mine.

All of this filled my head when I stood on the edge of his stairs, breathing the musty cellar air. It was late, after all, and a couple of closets with lights casting the shadows of doorways and shelves might have accounted for the illusion of vast size. We wandered away through the clutter, with me in my astonishment only half-listening to him, and despite all the magical debris, what I remember most, like an inessential but vivid element in a dream, was his head ducking and ducking under low, rough-sawn ceiling joists that were almost black with age.

I have a confused recollection of partly built contrivances, some of them moving due to hidden, clockwork mechanisms, some of them sighing and gurgling, hooked up to water pipes curling out of the walls or to steam pipes running in copper arteries toward a boiler that I can't remember seeing but could hear sighing and wheezing somewhere nearby. There were pendulums and delicate hydraulic gizmos, and on the corner of one bench a gyroscope spun in a little depression, motivated, apparently, by nothing at all. The walls were strewn with charts and drawings and shelves of books, and once, when we bent through a doorway and into a room inhabited by the hovering, slowly rotating hologram of a space vehicle, we surprised a family of mice at work on the remains of a stale sandwich. What did they make, I wonder, of the ghost of the spacecraft? Had they tried to inhabit it, to build a nest in it? Would it have mattered to them that they were inhabiting a dream?

What did I make of it? *Here's Captain Hooton's airship*, I remember thinking. *Where's the bell rope?* But it wasn't his airship, not exactly; the ship itself was in an adjacent room.

The whole thing was a certainty in an instant—the lights in the sky, the odd debris beneath the avocado tree, even the weird pallor of his see-through skin. It had all been his doing all these years. That's no surprise, I suppose, when it's taken altogether like this. When all the details are compressed, the patterns are clear.

He had come from somewhere and was going back again. With the lumber of mechanical trash spread interminably across bench tops, and the cluttered walls and the mice, and him with his pipe and hat, he seemed so settled in, so permanent. And yet the continual tinkering and the lights on at all hours made it clear that he was on the edge of leaving—maybe in a week, maybe in the morning, maybe right now; that's what I thought as I stood there looking at the ship.

It was nearly spherical, with four curved appendages that were a hybrid of wings and legs and that held the craft up off the concrete floor. Circular hatches ringed the ship, each covered with lapped plates that looked as if they'd spiral open to expose a door or a glassed-over window. The metal of the thing was polished to the silver shine of a perfect mirror that stretched our reflections like taffy as I stood listening to him tell me how we were directly under the backyard, and how he would detonate a charge, and one foggy night the ship would sail up out of the ground in a rush of smoke and dirt and be gone, affording the city newspapers their last legitimate saucer story.

I didn't tell Jane about it. There were a lot of things I couldn't or wouldn't tell her. I wanted some little world of my own, which was removed from the world we had together, but which, of course, could be implied now and then for effect, but never revealed lest it seem to her to be amusing. One day soon the papers would be full of it anyway—the noise in the night, the scattered sightings of the heaven-bound craft, the backyard crater. There would be something then in being the only one who knew.

And he no doubt wasn't anxious that the spaceship became general knowledge. There was no law against it, strictly speaking, but if they'd jailed him for the trick with the flashlight and the paper witch, or rather for refusing to come down out of a tree, then who could say what they might do if they got wind of a flying saucer buried in a cellar?

Then there was the chance that I might be aboard. He was willing to take me along. We talked about it all that night, about the places I'd see and the people I'd meet—a completely different sort of crowd than Jane and I would run into in our European travels.

It was then, about two years after I'd met Jane, that I gave up the house on Pine Street and moved in with her. She was free of school at last and was in an expansive, generous mood, which I'll admit I took advantage of shamelessly, and when, in early July, she received money from home and bought a one-way ticket to Rome, I bought one, too, only mine was a round-trip ticket with a negotiable return date. That should have bothered her, my having doubts, but it didn't. She didn't remark on it at all. From the start it had been my business—another aspect of her modern attitude toward things, an attitude I could neither share nor condemn out loud.

The rest is inevitable. I returned and she didn't. Captain Hooton was gone, and there was a crater with scorched grass around the perimeter of it in the backyard of his empty house. I might have gone along with him. But I didn't, and what I get to keep is the memory of it all—the hologram, so to speak, of the ship and of faded desire, having given up the one for the already fading dream of the other.

There's the image in my mind of a card house built of picture postcards pulled from a rusting wire rack of memories—the sort of thing that even a mouse wouldn't live in, preferring something more permanent and substantial. But then, nothing is quite as solid as we'd like it to be, and the map of our lives, sketched out across our memory, is of a provincial little neighborhood, criss-crossed with regret and circumscribed by a couple of impassable roads and by splashes of bright color that have begun to fade even before we have them fixed in our memory.

RAMSEY CAMPBELL

Meeting the Author

Ramsey Campbell has been a full-time writer since 1973. His first novel was *The Doll Who Ate His Mother* and his most recent is *Ancient Images*. His collection, *Dark Feasts*, was published in England last year. This is his third consecutive appearance in *The Year's Best Fantasy and Horror*. "Meeting the Author" is reprinted from the British SF and fantasy magazine *Interzone*.

There has long been debate concerning the effect of fantastic literature on its readership, particularly on children. Besides critics, psychologists, and sociologists also endlessly agonize over whether dark fantasy exorcises demons or encourages them to surface in the impressionable minds of young readers. In the following story the reading experience is taken one step further: the normally benign or beneficial experience of author-reader contact becomes a strange, darkly obsessive episode. Only Ramsey Campbell could have turned this trick.

—E.D.

Meeting the Author

RAMSEY CAMPBELL

I was young then. I was eight years old. I thought adults knew the truth about most things and would own up when they didn't. I thought my parents stood between me and anything about the world that might harm me. I thought I could keep my nightmares away by myself, because I hadn't had one for years —not since I'd first read about the little match girl being left alone in the dark by the things she saw and the emperor realizing in front of everyone that he wasn't wearing any clothes. My parents had taken me to a doctor who asked me so many questions I think they were what put me to sleep. I used to repeat his questions in my head whenever I felt in danger of staying awake in the dark.

As I said, I was eight when Harold Mealing came to town. All my parents knew about him was what his publisher told the paper where they worked. My mother brought home the letter she'd been sent at the features desk. "A celebrity's coming to town," she said, or at least that's what I remember her saying, and surely that's what counts.

My father held up the letter with one hand while he cut up his meat with his fork. " 'Harold Mealing's first book *Beware of the Smile* takes its place among the classics of children's fiction,' " he read. "Well, that was quick. Still, if his publishers say so that's damn near enough by itself to get him on the front page in this town."

"I've already said I'll interview him."

"Robbed of a scoop by my own family." My father struck himself across the forehead with the letter and passed it to me. "Maybe you should see what you think of him too, Timmy. He'll be signing at the bookshop."

"You might think of reviewing his book now we have children writing the children's page," my mother added. "Get some use of that imagination of yours."

The letter said Harold Mealing had written "a return to the old-fashioned moral tale for children—a story which excites for a purpose." Meeting an author

432

seemed an adventure, though since both my parents were journalists, you could say I already had. By the time he was due in town I was so worked up I had to bore myself to sleep.

In the morning there was an accident on the motorway that had taken the traffic away from the town, and my father went off to cover the story. Me and my mother drove into town in her car that was really only big enough for two. In some of the streets the shops were mostly boarded up, and people with spray paint who always made my father angry had been writing on them. Most of the town worked at the toy factory, and dozens of their children were queuing outside Books & Things. "Shows it pays to advertise in our paper," my mother said.

Mrs. Trend, who ran the shop, hurried to the door to let my mother in. I'd always been a bit afraid of her, with her pins bristling like antennae in her buns of hair that was black as the paint around her eyes, but her waiting on us like this made me feel grown up and superior. She led us past the toys and stationery and posters of pop stars to the bookshop part of the shop, and there was Harold Mealing in an armchair behind a table full of his book.

He was wearing a white suit and bow tie, but I thought he looked like a king on his throne, a bit petulant and bored. Then he saw us. His big loose face that was spidery with veins started smiling so hard it puffed his cheeks out, and even his grey hair that looked as if he never combed it seemed to stand up to greet us. "This is Mary Duncan from the *Beacon*," Mrs. Trend said, "and her son Timothy who wants to review your book."

"A pleasure, I'm sure." Harold Mealing reached across the table and shook us both by the hand at once, squeezing hard as if he didn't want us to feel how soft his hands were. Then he let go of my mother's and held onto mine. "Has this young man no copy of my book? He shall have one with my inscription and my blessing."

He leaned his elbow on the nearest book to keep it open and wrote "To Timothy Duncan, who looks as if he knows how to behave himself: best wishes from the author." The next moment he was smiling past me at Mrs. Trend. "Is it time for me to meet the little treasures? Let my public at me and the register shall peal."

I sat on the ladder people used to reach the top shelves and started reading his book while he signed copies, but I couldn't concentrate. The book was about a smiling man who went from place to place trying to tempt children to be naughty and then punished them in horrible ways if they were. After a while I sat and watched Harold Mealing smiling over all the smiles on the covers of the books. One of the children waiting to have a book bought for him knocked a plastic letter-rack off a shelf and broke it, and got smacked by his mother and dragged out while nearly everyone turned to watch. But I saw Harold Mealing's face, and his smile was wider than ever.

When the queue was dealt with, my mother interviewed him. "A writer has to sell himself. I'll go wherever my paying public is. I want every child who will enjoy my book to be able to go into the nearest bookshop and buy one," he said, as well as how he'd sent the book to twenty publishers before this one had bought it and how we should all be grateful to his publisher. "Now I've given up teaching I'll be telling all the stories I've been saving up," he said.

The only time he stopped smiling was when Mrs. Trend wouldn't let him sign all his books that were left, just some in case she couldn't sell the rest. He started again when I said goodbye to him as my mother got ready to leave. "I'll look forward to reading what you write about my little tale," he said to me. "I saw you were enjoying it. I'm sure you'll say you did."

"Whoever reviews your book won't do so under any coercion," my mother told him, and steered me out of the shop.

That evening at dinner my father said "So how did it feel to meet a real writer?"

"I don't think he likes children very much," I said.

"I believe Timmy's right," my mother said. "I'll want to read this book before I decide what kind of publicity to give him. Maybe I'll just review the book."

I finished it before I went to bed. I didn't much like the ending, when Mr. Smiler led all the children who hadn't learned to be good away to his land where it was always dark. I woke in the middle of the night, screaming because I thought he'd taken me there. No wonder my mother disliked the book and stopped just short of saying in her review that it shouldn't have been published. I admired her for saying what she thought, but I wondered what Harold Mealing might do when he read what she'd written. "He isn't entitled to do anything, Timmy," my father said. "He has to learn the rules like the rest of us if he wants to be a pro."

The week after the paper printed the review we went on holiday to Spain, and I forgot about the book. When we came home I wrote about the parts of Spain we'd been to that most visitors didn't bother with, and the children's page published what I'd written, more or less. I might have written other things, except I was too busy worrying what the teacher I'd have when I went back to school might be like and trying not to let my parents see I was. I took to stuffing a handkerchief in my mouth before I went to sleep so they wouldn't hear me if a nightmare woke me up.

At the end of the week before I went back to school, my mother got the first phone call. The three of us were doing a jigsaw on the dining-table, because that was the only place big enough, when the phone rang. As soon as my mother said who she was, the voice at the other end got so loud and sharp I could hear it across the room. "My publishers have just sent me a copy of your review. What do you mean by saying that you wouldn't give my book to a child?"

"Exactly that, Mr. Mealing. I've seen the nightmares it can cause."

"Don't be so sure," he said, and then his voice went from crafty to pompous. "Since all they seem to want these days are horrors, I've invented one that will do some good. I suggest you give some thought to what children need before you presume to start shaping their ideas."

My mother laughed so hard it must have made his earpiece buzz. "I must say I'm glad you aren't in charge of children any longer. How did you get our home number, by the way?"

"You'd be surprised what I can do when I put my mind to it."

"Then try writing something more acceptable," my mother said, and cut him off.

She'd hardly sat down at the table when the phone rang again. It must have been my imagination that made it sound as sharp as Harold Mealing's voice. This time he started threatening to tell the paper and my school who he was convinced had really written the review. "Go ahead if you want to make yourself look more of a fool," my mother said.

The third time the phone rang, my father picked it up. "I'm warning you to stop troubling my family," he said, and Harold Mealing started wheedling: "They shouldn't have attacked me after I gave them my time. You don't know what it's like to be a writer. I put myself into that book."

"God help you, then," my father said, and warned him again before cutting him off. "All writers are mad," he told us, "but professionals use it instead of letting it use them."

After I'd gone to bed I heard the phone again, and after my parents were in bed. I thought of Harold Mealing lying awake in the middle of the night and deciding we shouldn't sleep either, letting the phone ring and ring until one of my parents had to pick it up, though when they did nobody would answer.

Next day my father rang up Harold Mealing's publishers. They wouldn't tell him where Harold Mealing had got to on his tour, but his editor promised to have a word with him. He must have, because the phone calls stopped, and then there was nothing for days until the publisher sent me a parcel.

My mother watched over my shoulder while I opened the padded bag. Inside was a book called *Mr. Smiler's Pop-Up Surprise Book* and a letter addressed to nobody in particular. "We hope you are as excited by this book as we are to publish it, sure to introduce Harold Mealing's already famous character Mr. Smiler to many new readers and a state-of-the-art example of pop-up design" was some of what it said. I gave the letter to my mother while I looked inside the book.

At first I couldn't see Mr. Smiler. The pictures stood to attention as I opened the pages, pictures of children up to mischief, climbing on each other's shoulders to steal apples or spraying their names on a wall or making faces behind their teacher's back. The harder I had to look for Mr. Smiler, the more nervous I became of seeing him. I turned back to the first pages and spread the book flat on the table, and he jumped up from behind the hedge under the apple tree, shaking his long arms. On every two pages he was waiting for someone to be curious enough to open the book that little bit further. My mother watched me, and then she said "You don't have to accept it, you know. We can send it back."

I thought she wanted me to be grown-up enough not to be frightened by the book. I also thought that if I kept it Harold Mealing would be satisfied, because he'd meant it as an apology for waking us in the night. "I want to keep it. It's good," I said. "Shall I write and say thank you?"

"I shouldn't bother." She seemed disappointed that I was keeping it. "We don't even know who sent it," she said.

Despite the letter, I hoped Harold Mealing might have. Hoped! Once I was by myself I kept turning the pages as if I would find a sign if I looked hard enough. Mr. Smiler jumped up behind a hedge and a wall and a desk, and every time his face reminded me more of Harold Mealing's. I didn't like that much, and I put the book away in the middle of a pile in my room. After my parents had tucked me up and kissed me good night, early because I was starting school in the morning, I wondered if it might give me nightmares, but I slept soundly enough. I remember thinking Mr. Smiler wouldn't be able to move with all those books on top of him.

My first day at school made me forget him. The teacher asked about my parents, who she knew worked on the paper, and wanted to know if I was a writer too. When I said I'd written some things she asked me to bring one in to read to the class. I remember wishing Harold Mealing could know, and when I got home I pulled out the pop-up book as if that would let me tell him.

At first I couldn't find Mr. Smiler at all. I felt as if he was hiding to give me time to be scared of him. I had to open the book still wider before he came up from behind the hedge with a kind of shivery wriggle that reminded me of a dying insect. Once was enough. I pushed the book under the bottom of the pile and looked for something to read to the class.

There wasn't anything I thought was good enough, so I wrote about meeting Harold Mealing and how he'd kept phoning, pretty well as I've written it now. I finished it just before bedtime. When the light was off and the room began to take shape out of the dark, I thought I hadn't closed the pop-up book properly, because I could see darkness inside it that made me think of a lid, especially when I thought I could see a pale object poking out of it. I didn't dare get up to look. After a while I got so tired of being frightened I must have fallen asleep.

In the morning I was sure I'd imagined all that, because the book was shut flat on the shelf. At school I read out what I'd written. The children who'd been at Books & Things laughed as if they agreed with me, and the teacher said I wrote like someone older than I was. Only I didn't feel older, I felt as I used to feel when I had nightmares about books, because the moment I started reading aloud I wished I hadn't written about Harold Mealing. I was afraid he might find out, though I didn't see how he could.

When I got home I realized I was nervous of going to my room, and yet I felt I had to go there and open the pop-up book. Once I'd finished convincing my mother that I'd enjoyed my day at school I made myself go upstairs and pull it from under the pile. I thought I'd have to flatten it even more to make Mr. Smiler pop up. I put it on the quilt and started leaning on it, but it wasn't even open flat when he squirmed up from behind the hedge, flapping his arms, as if he'd been waiting all day for me. Only now his face was Harold Mealing's face.

It looked as if part of Mr. Smiler's face had fallen off to show what was underneath, Harold Mealing's face gone grey and blotchy but smiling harder than ever, straight at me. I wanted to scream and rip him out of the book, but all I could do was fling the book across my bed and run to my mother.

She was sorting out the topics she'd be covering for next week's paper, but she dropped her notes when she saw me. "What's up?"

"In the book. Go and see," I said in a voice like a scream that was stuck in my throat, and then I was afraid of what the book might do to her. I went up again, though only fast enough that she would be just behind me. I had to wait until she was in the room before I could touch the book.

It was leaning against the pillow, gaping as if something was holding it open from inside. I leaned on the corners to open it, and then I made myself pick it up and bend it back until I heard the spine creak. I did that with the first two pages and all the other pairs. By the time I'd finished I was nearly sobbing, because I couldn't find Mr. Smiler or whatever he looked like now. "He's got out," I cried.

"I knew we shouldn't have let you keep that book," my mother said. "You've enough of an imagination without being fed nonsense like that. I don't care how he tries to get at me, but I'm damned if I'll have him upsetting any child of mine."

My father came home just then, and joined in. "We'll get you a better book, Timmy, to make up for this old rubbish," he said, and put the book where I couldn't reach it, on top of the wardrobe in their bedroom.

That didn't help. The more my mother tried to persuade me that the pop-up was broken and so I shouldn't care about not having the book, the more I thought about Mr. Smiler's face that had stopped pretending. While we were having dinner I heard scratchy sounds walking about upstairs, and my father had to tell me it was a bird on the roof. While we were watching one of the programmes my parents let me watch on television a puffy white thing came and pressed itself against the window, and I almost wasn't quick enough at the window to see an old bin-liner blowing away down the road. My mother read to me in bed to try and calm me down, but when I saw a figure creeping upstairs beyond her that looked as if it hadn't much more to it than the dimness on the landing, I screamed before I realized it was my father coming to see if I was nearly asleep. "Oh dear," he said, and went down to get me some of the medicine the doctor had prescribed to help me sleep.

My mother had been keeping it in the refrigerator. It must have been years old. Maybe that was why, when I drifted off to sleep although I was afraid to in case anything came into my room, I kept jerking awake as if something had wakened me, something that had just ducked out of sight at the end of the bed. Once I was sure I saw a blotchy forehead disappearing as I forced my eyes open, and another time I saw hair like cobwebs being pulled out of sight over the footboard. I was too afraid to scream, and even more afraid of going to my parents, in case I hadn't really seen anything in the room and it was waiting outside for me to open the door.

I was still jerking awake when the dawn came. It made my room even more threatening, because now everything looked flat as the hiding-places in the pop-up book. I was frightened to look at anything. I lay with my eyes squeezed shut until I heard movements outside my door and my father's voice convinced me it was him. When he inched the door open I pretended to be asleep so that he wouldn't think I needed more medicine. I actually managed to sleep for a couple of hours before the smell of breakfast woke me up.

*   *   *

It was Saturday, and my father took me fishing in the canal. Usually fishing made me feel as if I'd had a rest, though we never caught any fish, but that day I was too worried about leaving my mother alone in the house or rather, not as alone as she thought she was. I kept asking my father when we were going home, until he got so irritable that we did.

As soon as he was in his chair he stuck the evening paper up in front of himself. He was meaning to show that I'd spoiled his day, but suddenly he looked over the top of the paper at me. "Here's something that may cheer you up, Timmy," he said. "Harold Mealing's in the paper."

I thought he meant the little smiling man was waiting in there to jump out at me, and I nearly grabbed the paper to tear it up. "Good God, son, no need to look so timid about it," my father said. "He's dead, that's why he's in. Died yesterday of too much dashing about in search of publicity. Poor old twerp, after all his self-promotion he wasn't considered important enough to put in the same day's news."

I heard what he was saying, but all I could think was that if Harold Mealing was dead he could be anywhere—and then I realized he already had been. He must have died just about the time I'd seen his face in the pop-up book. Before my parents could stop me, I grabbed a chair from the dining suite and struggled upstairs with it, and climbed on it to get the book down from the wardrobe.

I was bending it open as I jumped off the chair. I jerked it so hard as I landed that it shook the little man out from behind the hedge. I shut my eyes so as not to see his face, and closed my hand around him, though my skin felt as if it was trying to crawl away from him. I'd just got hold of him to tear him up as he wriggled like an insect when my father came in and took hold of my fingers to make me let go before I could do more than crumple the little man. He closed the book and squeezed it under his arm as if he was as angry with it as he was with me. "I thought you knew better than to damage books," he said. "You know I can't stand vandalism. I'm afraid you're going straight to bed, and think yourself lucky I'm keeping my temper."

That wasn't what I was afraid of. "What are you going to do with the book?"

"Put it somewhere you won't find it. Now, not another word or you'll be sorry. Bed."

I turned to my mother, but she frowned and put her finger to her lips. "You heard your father."

When I tried to stay until I could see where my father hid the book, she pushed me into the bathroom and stood outside the door and told me to get ready for bed. By the time I came out, my father and the book had gone. My mother tucked me into bed and frowned at me, and gave my forehead a kiss so quick it felt papery. "Just go to sleep now and we'll have forgotten all about it in the morning," she said.

I lay and watched the bedroom furniture begin to go flat and thin as cardboard as it got dark. When either of my parents came to see if I was asleep I tried to make them think I was, but before it was completely dark I was shaking too much. My mother brought me some of the medicine and wouldn't go away until I'd swallowed it, and then I lay there fighting to stay awake.

I heard my parents talking, too low for me to understand. I heard one of them go out to the dustbin, and eventually I smelled burning. I couldn't tell if that was in our yard or a neighbour's, and I was too afraid to get up in the dark and look. I lay feeling as if I couldn't move, as if the medicine had made the bedclothes heavier or me weaker, and before I could stop myself I was asleep.

When I jerked awake I didn't know what time it was. I held myself still and tried to hear my parents so that I'd know they hadn't gone to sleep and left me alone. Then I heard my father snoring in their room, and I knew they had, because he always went to bed last. His snores broke off, probably because my mother had nudged him in her sleep, and for a while I couldn't hear anything except my own breathing, so loud it made me feel I was suffocating. And then I heard another sound in my room.

It was a creaking as if something was trying to straighten itself. It might have been cardboard, but I wasn't sure, because I couldn't tell how far away from me it was. I dug my fingers into the mattress to stop myself shaking, and held my breath until I was almost sure the sound was ahead of me, between me and the door. I listened until I couldn't hold my breath any longer, and it came out in a gasp. And then I dug my fingers into the mattress so hard my nails bent, and banged my head against the wall behind the pillow, because Harold Mealing had risen up in front of me.

I could only really see his face. There was less of it than last time I'd seen it, and maybe that was why it was smiling even harder, both wider and taller than a mouth ought to be able to go. His body was a dark shape he was struggling to raise, whether because it was stiff or crippled I couldn't tell. I could still hear it creaking. It might have been cardboard or a corpse, because I couldn't make out how close he was, at the end of the bed and big as life or standing on the quilt in front of my face, the size he'd been in the book. All I could do was bruise my head as I shoved the back of it against the wall, the furthest I could get away from him.

He shivered upright until his face was above mine, and his hands came flapping towards me. I was almost sure he was no bigger than he'd been in the book, but that didn't help me, because I could feel myself shrinking until I was small enough for him to carry away into the dark, all of me that mattered. He leaned toward me as if he was toppling over, and I started to scream.

I heard my parents waken, far away. I heard one of them stumble out of bed. I was afraid they would be too late, because now I'd started screaming I couldn't stop, and the figure that was smaller than my head was leaning down as if it meant to crawl into my mouth and hide there or drag what it wanted out of me. Somehow I managed to let go of the mattress and flail my hands at him. I hardly knew what I was doing, but I felt my fist close around something that broke and wriggled, just as the light came on.

Both my parents ran in. "It's all right, Timmy, we're here," my mother said, and to my father "It must be that medicine. We won't give him any more."

I clenched my fist harder and stared around the room. "I've got him," I babbled. "Where's the book?"

They knew which one I meant, because they exchanged a glance. At first I couldn't understand why they looked almost guilty. "You're to remember what I said, Timmy," my father said. "We should always respect books. But listen, son, that one was bothering you so much I made an exception. You can forget about it. I put it in the bin and burnt it before we came to bed."

I stared at him as if that could make him take back what he'd said. "But that means I can't put him back," I cried.

"What've you got there, Timmy? Let me see," my mother said, and watched until I had to open my fist. There was nothing in it except a smear of red that she eventually convinced me was ink.

When she saw I was afraid to be left alone she stayed with me all night. After a while I fell asleep because I couldn't stay awake, though I knew Harold Mealing was still hiding somewhere. He'd slipped out of my fist when I wasn't looking, and now I'd lost my chance to trap him and get rid of him.

My mother took me to the doctor in the morning and got me some new medicine that made me sleep even when I was afraid to. It couldn't stop me being afraid of books, even when my parents sent *Beware of the Smile* back to the publisher and found out that the publisher had gone bankrupt from gambling too much money on Harold Mealing's books. I thought that would only make Harold Mealing more spiteful. I had to read at school, but I never enjoyed a book again. I'd get my friends to shake them open to make sure there was nothing inside them before I would touch them, only before long I didn't have many friends. Sometimes I thought I felt something squirming under the page I was reading, and I'd throw the book on the floor.

I thought I'd grown out of all this when I went to college. Writing what I've written shows I'm not afraid of things just because they're written down. I worked so hard at college I almost forgot to be afraid of books. Maybe that's why he kept wakening me at night with his smile half the height of his face and his hands that feel like insects on my cheeks. Yes, I set fire to the library, but I didn't know what else to do. I thought he might be hiding in one of those books.

Now I know that was a mistake. Now you and my parents and the rest of them smile at me and say I'll be better for writing it down, only you don't realize how much it's helped me see things clear. I don't know yet which of you smilers Harold Mealing is pretending to be, but I will when I've stopped the rest of you smiling. And then I'll tear him up to prove it to all of you. I'll tear him up just as I'm going to tear up this paragraph.

GWYNETH JONES

The Lovers

Gwyneth Jones was born and raised in Manchester, England, but lived in Singapore and traveled extensively in Southeast Asia before settling on the southern coast of England. She is the author of three adult science fiction novels—*Divine Endurance, Escape Plans,* and *Kairos*—in addition to articles, reviews, short stories, and books for children under the pseudonym Ann Hallam. She is particularly interested in "the continuity of the human imagination: the striking identities between stories written today, and those known for thousands of years," an interest which is evident in the following tale.

"The Lovers" mixes symbolism from classical mythology and fairy tales such as "East of the Sun, West of the Moon" with imagery both modern and ancient. The result is a beautifully written modern fairy tale from an author who excels in this area of fantasy.

—T.W.

The Lovers

GWYNETH JONES

The radiance of the candle flame lay only for a moment across his face, only for a moment its light shone on the lips and eyelids that she had so often kissed; and her long held breath was released in a soft sigh of relief. This was a human face, a lovely face, the rumour that she was married to a monster had all been lies.

Then the light went out. The little wind that had snuffed the candle flame grew fierce and strong. It roared in her ears. Suddenly frightened she reached for her lover's warm body. He wasn't there. Her hands clutched on nothing, there was nothingness all around her . . . Gradually she became aware that she was in a new place, still all alone. She was standing barefoot on some rough rocky surface, shivering in her thin nightgown. The air was cold and dank. Somehow she was aware that this place was buried deep underground.

Then the voice came. She couldn't tell from where, it might be only in her mind. It was a woman's voice, rich and strong and calm; it spoke with stern regret of the consequences of her folly. She had betrayed her lover, she had failed him. She had lost the right forever to be his bride.

Psyche was terrified of the dark. "Oh please," she sobbed, "please, I'll do anything. Only let me have my chance to win him back."

The voice was kind.

"Trust me, Psyche. If you perform the tasks I set you honestly and well, in the end I promise you will be free to return to your lover, completely free."

Something dropped from the darkness.

"Your first task. My son's nightshirt is badly marked with smoky tallow drips, because a silly girl held a candle to his face last night; as if she could not recognize without such crude assistance the wonder and beauty that she held in her arms. Wash my son's shirt, Psyche. You will find water close by."

She groped on the floor, picked up the shirt and began to stumble around in the utter darkness, listening for the sound of water. It was a long time, it might have been hours or weeks or years, before she found her way to the underground stream. The water was numbing cold, when she thrust the shirt into it the linen folds immediately became heavy as lead, and a strong biting current dragged against the frail strength of her arms.

"But how will I know?" she cried.

"Know what, Psyche?"

"It is so dark. I can't see my own hands. How will I know when the shirt is clean?"

The voice was noble and gentle as ever; Psyche felt guilty at her suspicion that somebody was laughing unkindly.

"My son's shirts are very fine linen and need long and careful washing. You must scrub on faithfully, like a good washerwoman, until the whiteness of that shirt illumines the whole cavern. So it will be easy for you to tell when your work is done. You see, I am doing all I can to help you, Psyche. Don't you think you should thank me?"

She wanted to scream that the task was impossible, that this wasn't justice, it was vengeance—but she wanted her lover more. Psyche learned her first lesson. "Thank you, Lady," she said quietly; and began to scrub.

How many years? There were no days, no nights, no seasons, there was nothing but the work. Her hands were raw and she hauled the heavy, slimy linen out of the water, slept beside it like the dead; woke and scrubbed again and again until her fingers were covered in weeping sores. She grew old learning how much cold and darkness and pain and back-breaking toil she was able to bear; and at last the shirt was white and, blind as a worm, she was released from darkness by its light. Then there was—what was there? The terrible gleaning of the battle fields. The water of youth to be carried out of the desert (and the sun devoured the water out of her cupped hands when she'd taken three steps away from the fountain. How many times did that happen?—before she learned to protect it with her own shadow, walking backwards over the knife-sharp burning rocks). And then the rose of knowledge had to be plucked from its savage briars. And then, in an oven fired by the flames of that rose, with the water of youth and the flour ground from death's cold stone, Psyche must bake the Lady's bread, which must be lighter than a feather and sweeter than breath. Over and over the harvest was gathered but the rose's petals fell before they could be kindled; the fire was kindled but the bread was soured with tears and would not rise . . .

But there came an hour, a day, a season when the tasks were all done, and nothing remained but for Psyche to take the roads behind the sun and before the moon, out of the Other World and back into the light of common day.

And finally she was once more alone in the dark, cold rough stone underfoot. She heard voices. She walked towards them (quite indifferent to darkness now), and in a very short time found herself in a broad well-lit passageway full of shuffling bodies. She slipped through them, not sure whether these brightly clothed figures were real or more of the Lady's phantasms. No one seemed to notice her. She came to the cavern's mouth and stepped out into harsh sunlight.

She held her head, she rubbed her arms, she looked down at her own body in amazement. There were air-conditioned coaches in the car park; and an artistic modern pavilion serving light refreshments: coffee, *chai*, local cakes stuffed with nuts and honey. Signboards explained in several different languages that these caves had once been believed to lead down to Hades. There were guided tours through them three times a day, as far as the banks of the Dark River.

No further. Psyche had been much further; but it seemed, miraculously, that she had been allowed to return.

Psyche had always known that the country ruled by her lover's mother was old and mysterious and magical, filled with ancient ruins and the shadows of forgotten mysteries. It was very strange to return to it (after how long?) and find that she had become the ancient one. Standing in that brash modern car park she felt like a whisper from a world of ghosts, a word in a lost language; she felt as if she had been dead for thousands of years. She walked through the blaring of motor horns and the wail of music from the tourists' distant countries, picked her way out to the road; stood with the local people and climbed on the next bus into town. She was going to have to tell the driver she had no money. She hoped he would have pity on her—poor, ragged, calloused, twisted old crone. She sat on the bus preparing herself to beg (she could do anything now). But when the driver came she looked down and found a purse on her lap, a small shoulder bag at her feet. She opened the purse and gave him money.

Her hands were not the crone's hands. They didn't look so very different from Psyche's hands of long ago.

She looked at herself in shop windows. She was dressed in summer clothes, a little too light for the chill that set in towards sunset. She had scarcely aged at all, except for her hair which was more silver now than fair. Sandals on her feet, money and papers in her purse. It was as if she had gone out to take that tourist excursion on a whim, closed her eyes for a moment and dreamed everything: her love, her loss, her trial and her punishment.

She found herself in a small hotel in the tourist town, and since it was late in the season she had no trouble booking a modest room. She sat on her small white covered bed, the pillows and coverlet embroidered crustily with the Lady's emblems (as was still the custom in remote places); and tried to grasp the fact of her triumph. She had won the prize and passed the test and paid the penalty. She was free. She was even still young.

All she had to do now was to rejoin her lover. Unless things had changed very much—and it seemed as if nothing at all had changed—she knew where to find him. He would be living as before not in the capital where the mundane government of his people was carried on, but in his mother's palace in the Old City, which was buried deep in these ruin-haunted mountains. It was not even far to travel: a few hours' journey at the most over those hair-raising roads, to the other side of the spectacular, glacier-riven peak they called the Glass Mountain. She could be with him before dawn.

At that thought Psyche jumped up and hurried out into the street, wondering why she had delayed at all. She would hire a car. She passed the phone, the only phone the place possessed, in the hotel lobby; glanced at it, remembered 'phone calls' for the first time but couldn't wait.

She ran around the streets, deserted now in the cold of the evening, into the lobby of a big hotel and ran to the reception desk.

"I need to hire a car—

"Can I hire a car here? Is the office still open?"

Two young women and a boy, attractively dressed in a homogenized version of the mountain costume, went on with what they were doing, placidly.

"Excuse me!!" shouted Psyche, in English. She had been speaking the language of the country; perhaps these servants only answered to foreigners. She banged on the desk. The women and the boy didn't even glance up. A sheaf of loose papers under her hand did not stir.

Psyche left the hotel grounds, slowly, frowning. She went to the bus station next, and there failed to buy a ticket. She tried to climb on the night bus without one—and, as in a dream, a nightmare, her hand grasped nothing, her foot stepped on nothing. She went back to her hotel and tried to place a call to the Old Palace, using the lobby phone. Her hand went through the handset as if one of the two wasn't there.

In the morning she discovered that there was an airport now, with light planes carrying on a regular service in the season to a small strip outside the Old City. She knew that it would be no good but she had learned to be thorough so she tried anyway. She was a ghost in the airline office, too. She could not buy a plane ticket.

She packed her small bag, she paid her bill. With a smiling face and a feeling almost that the world had returned to normal after a brief spell of madness, she set out in her thin clothes and summer sandals to climb the mountain road. The modern town ended. She walked through a stand of pines and beside a row of pretty peasant cottages, their steep roofs weighed down with boulders in the old style. A car engine started up behind her. The engine roared closer. Psyche turned . . . and the road had become the street where she had found her little hotel, just getting noisy with its morning traffic.

She tried again.

She tried again.

No majestic voice spoke from the sky, or in her mind. But Psyche understood. The trails were not over yet, after all. She was still exiled from the human race though they seemed to be all around her. No human hand had been joined with hers, rubbing and scrubbing in the dark stream long ago. She had been living in another world, and she was trapped there still. No one could follow where she must go—not even now, so near the end. She must scale the Glass Mountain as she had wrung that shirt: all alone, and still, it seemed, wrapped in a kind of darkness.

Meanwhile, in the Old City, preparations were being made for the marriage of Madame's son. He was to marry the beauty, the singer who was called La Sensuala, who was famous far outside her own country and a scandal within it. But La Sensuala was a licensed scandal, and not half such a rebel or so dangerous as the name they gave her suggested. People wondered if this time, Madame la

Présidente might really let the young man take a wife. She had been for so long the only woman who ruled in this man's world, in this ancient country; nobody believed she would tolerate a rival. But apparently La Sensuala had somehow won her approval.

On the icy cliffs of silence Psyche wandered—she who had not even considered this possibility. She thought of her lover waiting, of his years of loneliness. She wanted to smooth his soft rough hair, to hold him in the hollow of her shoulder; kiss and tell him this was the end of their suffering and the beginning of all delight. Her body was sore, her vision shaken by the cold waste's glassy shining. But though her eyes were blinded and her feet were broken she never faltered, and never for a moment dreamed of turning back.

She was sitting on a heap of stones by a hill track, tying up her battered feet again after bathing them in a little stream, when a dirty old truck stopped beside her, and she knew that she had returned again from the world outside time. The driver told her that the Présidente's son was getting married.

"Again?" murmured Psyche, showing no sign of horror.

He laughed heartily. "Not really. There was no proper wedding the other time, you see. It was just a little bit of a secret affair. La Sensuala has forgiven him, I'm sure."

"I'm sure you're right," said Psyche. "A woman in love will forgive anything."

She still knew that all she had to do was to reach her lover. This other bride was one of the Lady's cruelties, nothing more. She had kept her side of the bargain. The prize must be hers as long as she never faltered. La Sensuala's house was an inward-turned, old-fashioned building, with late roses still blooming in the courtyards inside its blind walls. Psyche asked her way there and persuaded the cook to take her on as a kitchenmaid; they needed extra staff because the bride-to-be was doing a lot of entertaining. She really was dressed in rags now, but nobody minded that. La Sensuala travelled round the world in jet planes but in the back rooms of her house time had been standing still for a thousand years. The new kitchenmaid slept on the scullery floor, and they called her 'little mutton fat' because she couldn't get the smell of the washing up out of her hair. She was safe. Her lover's mother would never expect to find her here, never know her if she did.

Once, when she was carrying a pile of dirty table linen across a courtyard, she saw the Présidente's son. He was older, but not much older. He didn't look at her. She didn't want him to; not until the moment came when the abyss of years healed over and everything was made right. Several times as she went about her business she saw La Sensuala—a tall woman always wrapped in bright-coloured shawls, with a sheaf of tawny hair. Psyche wasn't in the least jealous. She didn't give the other woman a second thought, not even to feel sorry for her.

On a chain around her neck she wore, as she had always worn since the night her lover first came to her, a golden key. It was the key, he had told her, to every secret door in the Old Palace. In fact it was a tiny thing, just a love token, incised all over with little doves, one of the Lady's favourite emblems. But not all Madame's powers, or her vindictive jealousy, had managed to part Psyche from this charm. It had become a symbol to her of the truth of her love and his.

One night when she was helping (behind the scenes) to serve one of the cook's elaborate and wonderful meals, she managed to drop the golden key into what she thought was her lover's dish.

She washed her face, she changed her rags, she tried to comb her hair. None of it mattered. The major-domo, a magnificent creature in a portly white waistcoat and scarlet cummerbund, appeared at the back scullery door.

"Did any person here," he asked, "drop a foreign body into one of Cook's dishes?"

"It was me," confessed Psyche.

"La Sensuala wishes to see you," he told her, as if he could hardly believe it.

Psyche went running to meet her lover. She pushed through clouds of silk curtains, stumbled over gorgeous rugs, tripped over cushions; and was ushered, rather brusquely, into a small glowing room. The woman with the tawny hair turned from a curvaceous window that looked inward into one of the rose-garden courts, and held up Psyche's key in one hand; in the other, one exactly similar.

"You," she said.

She was a very wise woman. She wasn't confused by the rags or the grease at all. She burst into a storm of passionate tears.

La Sensuala insisted that Psyche must be bathed, dressed, combed, fed. She stayed by her rival all the while; holding her hand, stroking her silver-fair hair, biting her lip and exclaiming over the state of Psyche's worn body and her hard-working hands. It was as if at last someone had seen through the veil of glamour thrown by the Lady between her victim and the rest of humanity; and poor worn and weary Psyche was pitied and cradled in loving arms. La Sensuala said, "I know all about you. He never speaks of you, but I know he has never forgotten you. Sometimes I wake in the night and he is not beside me. He is only across the room maybe, or else he comes back in an hour and says he was restless and went for a stroll . . . But I think of you then, Psyche. And I am afraid he is still searching for you, though he himself believes that he gave up hope long ago."

Of course he is still searching, thought Psyche. And you are merely another of his mother's tricks. But she said nothing, she didn't want to be unkind.

Then, in La Sensuala's little glowing parlour, they bargained like two market women.

"Give me one night," said Psyche.

"Take three—"

"One night, when I will take your place and be smuggled into his private rooms in the Old Palace for a love tryst."

"Does everybody in the kitchen know about our meetings?"

"Of course we do. And so does the Lady, without a doubt. And approves of the arrangement, or at least allows it."

"I can arrange for him to come here. I mean, privately, at night, apart from the public times. Meet him in my house, Psyche. It will be safer for you."

"La Sensuala, you are too generous."

Poor golden singer, she thought. I am so much stronger than she is. I have so much more to offer.

La Sensuala wiped her eyes and smiled. "Don't you see? I love him, too. I would rather know, even the worst. I want to be sure."

"So it's agreed. One night."

"Three. And here."

"If you insist, three. But in the palace."

"Agreed."

They clasped hands: the silver hair and the sheaves of gold mingled. Outside in the rose court a flight of doves rose clattering and wheeled across the narrow sky. It was only three nights now to the wedding. But for three nights more, Madame ruled alone.

It was dark inside the Old Palace. It had always been dark in here. How cold it was, too—and what a dank strange smell the air had, like somewhere underground. Still she groped her way onward, following the light carried by the servant who would lead her to her lover's chamber. How very cold this passage was. Here was the door, however: massive and ancient like all the palace furniture. And her guide had discreetly vanished.

She saw a large dim shape, she hopped, skipped over the icy floor, and dropping La Sensuala's shawls sat down, as she thought, on the bed.

It was not a bed. She sat on a cold smooth stone in pitch darkness; and knew she had been tricked.

"Where am I?"

"In my son's bedchamber, child, as you wished to be; where he will surely come to sleep at last."

"I am in a tomb."

"The family vault, no less."

"La Sensuala—!"

"No, she is innocent. What does she know of our world, Psyche? Unless I chose to teach her, that is; but that's no concern of yours. The passages above you have been sealed for many years. They are still sealed now, and will remain so until the next royal funeral. Sleep well, Psyche."

"But I have paid! I did everything you asked!"

"Then you are safe, Psyche. In *this* world no one breaks the law or goes back on a bargain. If you have kept faith with your quest, you will find a way out."

Then there was silence. When she was sure she was alone, Psyche began to laugh. She unfastened the fine chain from her neck and held in her hand the trinket that La Sensuala had returned to her. The key, the key to all his mother's secrets. She passed her hand, holding it, over the surface and sides of the coffin table, and at last there came a tiny chink of metal on metal.

In another moment the stone door was open, Psyche was running sure-footed in the cold darkness down and down a spiral staircase. At the foot of the stair she found a level passage where the air smelled fresh. The passage twisted and turned, it split into two. Psyche stumbled over long smooth staves, and round things that rolled and rattled. But she was not afraid of the dead or the dark or even of being buried alive. Elated by her own calm and coolness she followed the breath of freshness still; and at last came scrambling out from underground. Strange shapes loomed around her: she was in the old cemetery outside the city walls. The sky was grey and dim. Psyche ran like the wind: through the ancient royal gateway, up the wide avenue between rows of time-blurred guardian statues, up to the palace walls; and just as she touched them a pitiless finger of warm light struck her on the shoulder.

And that was one night gone.

La Sensuala had not explained to her bridegroom why she was letting him spend these last bachelor nights alone. But strangely enough, he, too, was thinking of Psyche. The first night he spent alone, brooding and dreaming. On the second night he left the palace and walked the city streets. He was trying to remember what it had been like to be young, to love so absolutely; to be so helpless. He had learned how to live with his mother now. La Sensuala was safe because she threatened no one. He knew that in time the Lady would give him all the power any man could desire; and this marriage was the first instalment. She was not unwilling, she wanted him to have his share of the world she ruled. It was only Psyche who had caused the trouble between them.

"Psyche—"

He spoke her name in the chill silvery dawn, and a woman's figure wrapped in glowing shawls crossed the street ahead of him. She was coming away from the palace, bowed as if under a heavy burden. He cried again "Psyche!"— though it was Sensuala he thought he saw. The woman turned her face.

The Lady's son felt a shock almost like terror. For a moment his first love stood in front of him, absolutely young and pure and beautiful. The light changed, the shadows vanished: an old crone pulled her shawl around her sunken cheeks and scurried away.

And that was two nights gone.

La Sensuala was frightened. "Supposing she tricks you again?" she wailed. "Oh Psyche, promise me one thing. Let me bring you together in daylight, in some ordinary way, if you don't meet tonight. Or else how will I ever know, how will I ever be sure?"

"It would do you no good," Psyche told her. "You can't ever be sure of his love, not the way you long to be. Only of your own."

"But will you promise?"

"No, I will not. Would you want me to come back from the dead, and try and see if I could make your husband follow me to my grave? Don't be scared—I only meant you to understand how dangerous a promise can be if you make it when the Lady is listening. And she is always listening, naturally. I know the rules, you see. I know how the wheels go round. I have felt them, going over me."

"Anyway—" Psyche smiled: it was like a flash of edged steel in the soft, richly coloured room. "There'll be no more tricks. He and I must meet tonight. The sun won't rise before I am in his arms, the stars won't move until that moment comes."

* * *

It was dark again. When she heard his step she meant to light a candle, but just for a while she would sit without light and taste for the last time how it felt to be alone in the dark. Here was their bed. Here she sat, and soon her lover would come through the door . . .

What would she say to him? Would she tell him about washing a shirt in darkness, and how the cold of the water burned? Would she tell him how long and strange and cruel it all was? Would she tell him, lying in his warm arms, how it felt to walk alone on the cliffs of ice . . .

La Sensuala, thought Psyche, would have wept and created on the bank of the Dark River, and complained she had a hangnail and she was catching cold. And maybe, who knows, the Lady would have been forced to give in. Strength isn't what you need, not always, to win human happiness. Strength is the reward of suffering, not a defence against it.

Slowly, as if spellbound once more, she got to her feet. She had been sitting here for a long time.

She crept through the gloomy old-fashioned halls of Madame's palace, wondering where her lover had been delayed. She crept by the kitchens, and heard two young servants talking to each other.

"He came down here looking for a girl, can you imagine?"

"That didn't take long! So where's he off to now?"

"To La Sensuala's. He reckons if it wasn't here it was there he saw the kitchenmaid he fancies!"

The two boys roared with laughter.

Psyche ran.

She ran, and she knew that within the silent houses as she passed life paused between a breath and a breath, the fingers of all the clocks had ceased to move; and above the hunched ancient roofs and towers the dance of the sky was still.

And there they were in La Sensuala's parlour, clinging close in candlelight, the lovers. They were both of them in tears.

Psyche stood in the doorway, transfixed. Her beloved, her dear one turned and stood, and took one step away from La Sensuala.

"I saw your face," he whispered. "Yesterday, in the grey dawn, I saw you. I would never have believed I would know you again unless I had you in my arms. It was only for a moment, wasn't it, and only by candlelight. You vanished—again—but then I knew you were somewhere near, I just had to remember where. Oh Psyche—"

La Sensuala stood up too, but didn't try to get between them.

"Husband," she said, in a sad little voice. "You lost the key to your treasure chest and made yourself a new one. But now the first key is found. Which are you going to keep?"

Psyche's beloved took one more step. He held out his arms. She heard him calling, "Psyche? Psyche?" But what was happening? She could see him there, and yet there was a mist between them. It was the same as in that town at the foot of the Glass Mountain. She could not touch or be touched, she was wrapped in invisible darkness.

"Lady, you can't do this!" she cried. "The price is paid and he is mine, he is mine. If you break your promise you will stop the stars in their courses. I *know you cannot* break your promises . . ."

Psyche felt herself becoming crystal and diamond. In the caverns, in the desert and the wilderness of her longing, she had been washed and burned and scoured into perfection. She tried to run forward, offering her dear one all these riches . . . but even as she moved, she understood; she saw what the lovers saw.

La Sensuala was sobbing bitterly. Her beloved was being carried off by a monster: a burning, impossible thing of ice and fire . . . not human at all. Once again the Lady had found a way to destroy the happiness of her son and the woman he loved.

Psyche understood then how devious and invincible the Lady's law could be. And yet she felt sure that the choice was real. Nothing that she had gained on her quest could be carried back into her first world; but to reach her lover she had only to become his bride again. If she could only fall weeping into his arms, there would be no more shining mist and invisible darkness, and La Sensuala would be forgotten. Psyche was free, quite free; just as the Lady had promised.

She sighed.

"Psyche?" she repeated, as if puzzled. La Sensuala was crying, the young man torn between past and present looking bewildered and miserable. "Psyche? No, I don't think so. In fact, I'm sure you must be thinking of someone else— someone who died a long time ago."

Outside in the chilly sky of sunrise the doves rose and rattled across the sky like gunfire.

"Quickly!" cried Psyche. "You'd better go, the two of you. Hurry, she must not catch you here together. She'll come around; but give her time, don't provoke her. . . ."

The lovers fled.

Psyche was left alone.

She blew out the candles and waited. The room grew cold.

She lifted her head, smiling.

"Ah, there you are, my Lady. Welcome back. And what is the next task to be? Something quite impossible, I hope. I want work."

CHET WILLIAMSON

Yore Skin's Jes's Soft 'n Purty . . . He Said. (Page 243)

A perfectly horrific love story about a naif infatuated with the American West—or his fantasy of it. Chet Williamson, who has quickly gained a reputation for effective horror with novels like *Lowland Rider* and *Ash Wednesday*, disabuses his protagonist of his illusions in an unfortunately swift, merciless, and—to be succinct—gruesome fashion.

"Yore Skin's . . . " first appeared in the western horror/fantasy anthology *Razored Saddles*.

—E.D.

Yore Skin's Jes's Soft 'n Purty ... He Said. (Page 243)

CHET WILLIAMSON

It was a land where a man could be himself, where none of the feebly voiced restrictions of society were to say him nay. The mountains, the winding trails, the arching blue sky alone were the only judges of a man's mettle. Here in the west a man could be a man, and a woman a woman. She knew that now, knew it with all the implacable truth of nature and of the west.

He turned his face toward her as his horse galloped into the dawn.

Eustace P. Saunders shut *The Desperado* with a delighted shudder, sat for a moment, his languid eyes closed, then opened the book again and looked at his illustrations, finding the smooth plates easily, sweet oases of images between the chunks of text. But dear God, what *wonderful* text. Here was romance, here was adventure, here was balm for the soul jaded by the tired and stolid fictions of society life. His gaze hung upon the frontispiece, wherein Jack Binns, the desperado, sat by the midnight campfire with Maria Prescott, the eastern heiress, touching her hand with wonder. Eustace didn't need to read the caption below—

"Yore skin's jes's soft 'n purty . . ." he said.

—and below, the page number on which the illustrated scene appeared.

Again he blessed Arthur Hampton at Harper's for giving him the assignment. Not that he had needed it from a financial standpoint, for he was far busier than he had ever been, regularly doing illustrations for *McClure's, Leslie's Weekly, The Century,* and *The Red Book,* as well as books. Indeed, even though pictures bearing the signature of E.P. Saunders had appeared in the popular magazines since 1883, these first few years of the new century had been more rewarding than ever, artistically as well as financially. The black and white washes he had done for last year's new Robert Chambers novel had been among his best, as was the gouache work he had done for the F. Marion Crawford short story collection. And then . . . *The Desperado!*

Arthur, God bless him, had seen something in Eustace's work that he felt might complement M. Taggart Westover's first book. It still amazed Eustace that Arthur had not gone after an artist who had already proven himself competent with western themes, like Keller, whose work for *The Virginian* had been so fine. Still, Arthur had thrown down the gauntlet, and Eustace, welcoming a change from the crinolines and frock coats of contemporary city novels, took it up, but with more than a touch of hesitancy.

Still, the final results were admirable. Arthur called them Eustace's best work ever, and Eustace had to agree. It was because he worked them in oils, he felt, and also because he gave them his soul.

He had originally intended to do them in gouache, but, upon reading the book and falling utterly in love with it, decided to work in oils instead, even though the reproductions would be monochromatic. There was more *color* in this book, he thought, than any other he had illustrated, indeed, than any other he had ever read. Then too, the fact that they were done in oils made them easier to repaint when they came back from Harper's.

For repaint them he did, placing his own face and form over that of one of the main characters. It was not Jack Binns, the desperado, whose visage vanished beneath layers of paint, but Maria Prescott, the heroine, for Eustace P. Saunders was a mental practitioner of what he considered a Secret Vice, referred to, when it was done so at all by people of breeding, as The Love That Dares Not Speak Its Name. Only in the case of Eustace P. Saunders, it was so secret that Eustace had never practiced it save in the darkened boudoirs of his imagination. It was not that he had never had the opportunity, for he suspected that a number of his colleagues shared the same predilection, and had even received a proposal of an illicit, illegal, and societally perverse nature from one of the younger illustrators who was as open with his brush as he seemed to be with his longings. Eustace, out of fear of exposure, had tactfully refused. Indeed, Eustace had been chaste with both sexes for all of his forty-three years, and had intended to remain thus until *The Desperado* seduced his mind and turned his fancies to outdoor love of a most healthful and manly nature.

He placed the book down upon his reading table with a sigh of regret that he had finished it once again, then brightened as he realized that its grand adventure could *begin* again as well. All he need do was turn to page one. Dear God, what a place—the west, where a man could act as he pleased without fear of polite society's repercussions, where his fancies could come to blazing, lusty life, a land where the pseudo-life of his paintings could exist in total reality.

Eustace stood, sipped another few drops of sherry, and climbed the steps to his studio, where he turned on the lights, illuminating a number of paintings and other works sitting neatly on easels or drawing tables. He walked to the closed door at the end of the long room, withdrew a key from the pocket of his lounging jacket, and unlocked the door. Inside was a small chamber ten feet by eight, with paintings and drawings both framed and unframed leaning against the walls. Eustace drew a white sheet from half a dozen large, unframed canvases, wrapped his spindly arms about them, and carried them into the studio, where he leaned them against a table, drew up a chair, and sat down.

The effort had made him a trifle breathless, but he grew more breathless still when he looked at the first painting. There he was, Eustace P. Saunders, seated next to Jack Binns, who was holding his hand and gazing lovingly into his eyes, which gleamed orange in the firelight. He could almost hear the words, spoken in a soft, gentle drawl—"Yore skin's jes's soft 'n purty . . ."

Eustace looked for a long time, until he could hear not only his lover's voice, but the crackle of logs burning in the fire, smell the biscuits and coffee he had cooked for Jack and himself, feel the soft wind blowing across the Badlands.

After a time, the vision faded, as it always did, and he turned to the next picture, and the next, and the next, until at length he arrived at the end of the book, in which Maria, at first held for ransom, eventually wins the love of the wild outlaw, reforms him, marries him, and stays with him in his vast and honest land. In the final illustration, she stands outside their modest cabin, built with their own toil, and waves to her husband and lover as he rides off to begin his day's work on the range—

"He turned his face toward her as his horse galloped into the dawn."

But now, instead of Maria, a plain white blouse, a long leather skirt, and a bandanna replacing her eastern finery, this painting, like all the others, bore the image of Eustace P. Saunders, dressed in western garb, waving goodbye to Jack.

"Why can't it be that way?" said Eustace, tears forming in his eyes for his lost love, his love never found. "*Why?*"

Then it came to him. It could. In the west, land of promise and dreams, anything was possible. He didn't have to go on painting his desires, for in the west he could live them. *The Desperado* had told him that, and he believed it as he had never believed the tales of the Christ he had learned at his mother's knees. With all his heart, he believed in this primitive kingdom where none would say him nay.

He did not go into the west, however, with the stated nor even the conscious intention of seeking love. He went, as he put it to Arthur Hampton and others, in order to breathe in the heart of the west, to immerse himself therein in the hopes that his art could faithfully portray the country's sights and sounds and spirit. To this end, Eustace took along a great many supplies: innumerable sketch books, rolls of canvas, oils, watercolors, and more. His baggage totalled a dozen large trunks, for, since he did not truly intend to return east, he thought it prudent to bring as many of his possessions as possible, all the fewer that would need to be sent for later.

His destination, chosen after only brief deliberation, was Deadwood, South Dakota, the same area in which *The Desperado* was set. Eustace travelled alone, beginning on a bright April day a series of train rides that brought him to Deadwood four days later than had been scheduled, an hiatus that, rather than discouraging him, only further whetted his appetite for his final destination. A transfer from the St. Paul Railway to the Northwestern in Rapid City proved to be the final stumbling block, but, after receiving assurances from the conductor that all his trunks were safely aboard the baggage car, Eustace P. Saunders arrived in Deadwood late on a Friday afternoon.

He had no time to drink in the aroma of the west, which, to his way of thinking, was rather soured by the smell of horse droppings which carpeted the dirt street next to the ramshackle railroad station, for he had to immediately attend to his trunks, which had been unceremoniously dumped onto the platform by the baggage car man, who, without a wave of regret, pulled the massive door closed as the train rattled out of the station toward its next stop. Eustace sought and obtained the attention of a noble young scion of the west, and gave him a quarter dollar to go to the hotel and inform the manager that Mister Saunders had arrived and needed a cab for his luggage. When a half hour passed and the loiterer did not return, Eustace asked the man at the ticket window for directions to the hotel, and if he would be kind enough to watch Eustace's trunks while he fetched a cabman.

The man replied through a mist of tobacco spittle that he was closing up and had no leisure to observe luggage, but that he would stop at the hotel and inform the proprietor that a guest was in need of teamster service.

After another half hour, a rickety wagon drawn by two horses dropped anchor in the Sargasso of horse dung. Painted in faded letters on two of the remaining side boards was the legend *Barkley Hotel, Deadwood*. The coachman, a living embodiment, Eustace thought, of the old west, jumped down from his box, entirely oblivious to the way his boots sank into the equestrian mire. "You Sanders?" he said through a broken picket fence of yellow teeth, making Eustace think that perhaps the art of dentistry had not penetrated this far west.

"That's Saunders," Eustace replied. "I have some trunks." And he gestured to the small mountain on the platform.

"Holy jacksh_t," the man expostulated. "Never seen so g_dd_m many in my f__in' life!"

Muttering vociferously, the rustic nonetheless carried them one at a time from platform to wagon, dropping only one in the reeking miasma. Eustace opened his mouth to protest, but a harsh glare from the man made him slap his mouth shut. When the trunks were loaded, the frontier coachman climbed onto his box and fixed Eustace with a withering stare. "You comin' or ain'tcha?"

Eustace glanced tremulously at the surface he had to cross to arrive at the coach, then said to himself, "I am, after all, in the west, where a man's character is not diminished by the presence of honest soil on his boots," and stepped boldly into the muck, wincing only once when part of the gelid mass crept over the edge of his shoe.

Despite the presence of horse manure in his heel, Deadwood struck Eustace P. Saunders as a veritable fairyland. This then was the west, and these bold men and women who lined the wooden sidewalks were the pioneers of their age. He felt a tingle of hormonal as well as intellectual excitement as he recalled the second plate of *The Desperado*:

"It was a new world to her, and one she feared to enter."

He wished he could open the trunk that contained the *Desperado* oils and gaze at it right now (they were the only finished works that he had brought with him, for how could he have his maid discover them when she prepared his other work for delivery to the west!). But he could see it in his mind's eye well enough—Eustace P. Saunders riding into the town in a stagecoach, looking out from its windows at the rough men lining the street in front of the saloon, leering at him with unnameable desires in their head beneath their ten-gallon hats.

And God, yes! there was a saloon now, and, glory of glories, on the other half of the building that housed it was the Barkley Hotel. It had been everything he had dreamed it would be, a rough-hewn, clapboard edifice of three stories, with loungers out front waiting no doubt for the sun to go down. But none of them, he noticed, wore a gunbelt. It was a bit of a disappointment.

As Eustace walked into the hotel, the imprecations of the teamster dying away behind him, the idlers eyed him, but Eustace felt that it was more out of curiosity than from any interest in a lasting bond of manly friendship. Ah well, he thought, Maria Prescott too had been looked on with mere curiosity upon her arrival in the west, as primitives are apt to gaze upon a rare and lovely flower without understanding its potential for pollination.

The manager of the hotel, Mr. Owen Barkley, was rather more solicitous than had been the grizzled coachman, and Eustace was relieved to find that he had indeed been expected, even though Barkley addressed him as Mr. Sanders, perpetuating the error the coachman had made. Barkley himself showed Eustace to his room on the second floor, a clean if Spartan chamber boasting the scant amenities that most third class eastern hotels would have offered.

"And what brings you to our little town?" asked Barkley, a fat and florid man in his early sixties.

"Art, really," Eustace replied.

"Art?"

Eustace then spoke of the magazines and books he had illustrated, and Barkley's eyes glowed. "I've got that Chambers book—my sister back east sent it to me last Christmas. And we've got lots of your magazines in the lobby—*Country Gentleman, Harper's*, lots of them—d_mn good pictures in them too. An artist, eh? My, that's really something."

They chatted all during the time it took for the coachman to bring up all twelve trunks, and it took only until trunk number three for Eustace to inquire about outlaws.

"Outlaws?" Barkley said, as though the word was foreign to him. "I'll tell you, Mr. Sanders, there sure aren't many outlaws these days. We're pretty d_n civilized now out here. But when I was a youngster, well, things were mighty different then . . ."

It took until trunk number five for Eustace to persuade Barkley to end his reminiscences of gunfights past. "Please do try and think of some in the present day," Eustace pleaded. "You see, the reason I came out here was to sketch and paint some of the more, shall we say, adventuresome of your denizens, in order to add as much verisimilitude as possible to my work."

"Uh-huh." Barkley nodded. "Uh-huh. So you're lookin' for some bad men.

Well, I'll tell you, anybody commits crimes nowadays our country sheriff—
that's Zed Dorwart—arrests them pretty d_mn quick, so they're either behind
bars or hung."

"But isn't there anyone," Eustace persevered as trunk number six arrived,
"who has eluded the law, who is secreted in some hole-in-the-wall, as it were?"

Barkley thought for a moment. "Nope," he said.

Then the coachman *cum* teamster *cum* porter spoke up. "Them Brogger
brothers are mean sonsab_tches." This uninvited comment earned the menial
a glance from his employer sharp enough to send him out of the room with
more haste than was his wont.

"The Brogger brothers?" Eustace repeated. "Now who are they?"

Barkley shook his head grimly. "You don't want to get mixed up with the
Brogger boys," he cautioned. "They're not outlaws, they're just crazy."

It took until trunk number eleven for Eustace to wheedle the full story of
Olaf and Frederick Brogger from Barkley. They were two brothers in their early
thirties. Born of a Norwegian father and a Scotch-Irish mother, they were hated
by the god-fearing Norwegians in the county because they gave Norwegians a
bad name. Rejecting the farm life of their father, they had purchased a small
spread where they raised enough stock to get by, though many said that it was
not their skinny herd of cattle, but thievery around the Deadwood area that
brought them the little money they had. Nothing had ever been proven, however,
though it was felt that the Broggers had more luck than skill or intelligence.

"Mean as coyotes but a lot dumber," was Barkley's studied opinion. "Used
to come to the saloon, bother people. Zed told 'em not to come back no more,
so they went down to Terry, but even the women there won't have nothin' to
do with them. Cause fights, sometimes people been found beaten, but they
won't say who 'twas done it. One time a few years back Zed found a feller beat
somethin' awful—died without comin' to. He'd been in an argument with Fred
Brogger a few days before."

"Fred—is he the worse?" Eustace inquired.

"You could say. Olaf's quieter, but still waters run deep. Fred's the loud one,
and Olaf does what he says."

The poor lad, thought Eustace. No doubt influenced by his evil older brother
to follow a life of crime. And he thought of the illustration on page 362, of Jack
Binns placing a protective left arm around Maria's (now Eustace's) shoulder,
while his right hand pointed a pistol at his former partner in crime, Texas Bill
Wyatt—

"So,' Wyatt sneered, 'throwin' over yer old pard fer a skirt!' "

Jack Binns had seen the light. Love had made him do so. And Eustace had
read time and again that love was capable of a great many such things.

"I'd like to meet them," he told Barkley.

The hotelier's eyes grew wide, and his face even more pink than before. "No
sir. You stay away from them two. Bad medicine, both of 'em. Some of the
other things you hear said about them, why, I wouldn't even repeat to a Christian
gentleman."

Through the door came box number twelve, and its bearer let it drop onto the straw mat floor with a weary sigh. "That's all of 'em," he said, extended his hand for the silver dollar that Eustace deposited therein, and left the room.

"Hope you have a good stay," said Barkley. "We got a fine restaurant down-stairs, and the saloon is open till midnight. You need anything, just pull that cord on the wall."

"Now that you mention it," Eustace said, wiggling his toes, "do you have a bootblack in town?"

Rather than go through his trunks to find another pair of the several he had brought, he waited until his shoes came back, and in the meantime removed his soiled socks and washed his feet in the basin. Freshly shod, he descended to the restaurant, a surprisingly comfortable room that could have been uprooted from New York's west side, had it not been for the more rowdy clientele. Eustace ordered a steak with potatoes, and watched the people, some of them cowboys surely, finish their meals and pass through the swinging doors into the saloon side of the building, from whence came the strains of ragtime music and frequent hearty shouts.

His meal finished, Eustace joined the throng, sitting at a table well away from the bar, where the most active customers sat and from which the loudest yells (often good-natured curses) emanated. He suspected that the sherry he nursed had been sitting on some dusty under-shelf for many years, as it seemed to have turned to a syrupy vinegar.

He had just made up his mind to take a chance on the beer, when he heard a familiar voice behind him. "You're askin' about the Buggers."

Eustace turned and saw the wizened old gentleman who had carried his trunks. "I beg your pardon?"

"The *Buggers*. The ones you'se talkin' about with Barkley."

"Do you mean the Broggers?"

"I calls 'em as I sees 'em." Without being invited, the man sat across the small table from Eustace. His aroma, as before, told Eustace that he was less than fastidious in his toilet habits. "You wanta see 'em?"

A thrill ran through Eustace. "Olaf and Frederick?" he said breathlessly, and the man made a face. "Yes, I would like very much to meet them."

"I can take ya there. Fer a price."

"Where?"

"Terry Peak. They place is north o' there."

Eustace nodded sagely. "Yes, Mr. Barkley mentioned Terry."

The old man shook his head disgustedly. "Not Terry, not that little sh_thole in the wall. I'm talkin' Terry *Peak*. You wanta go there?"

"Yes. Yes, I do."

"How much it worth to ya?"

"Well, I, I—"

"Ten dollars?"

"Well, yes, of course, I'd be willing to pay ten dollars."

"All right then, you be in back of the hotel at five o'clock tomorrow morning."

"Five o'clock?" It was a bit early. Eustace seldom broke his fast before nine.

"It's near 'bout eight miles to there, and I start workin' for Barkley at seven. It's then or never."

"Well . . ." Eustace thought about the cold and darkness of five o'clock in the morning, then thought about a land "where none of the feebly voiced restrictions of society were to say him nay," of handsome young rogues living under a sky as blue as an outlaw's eyes, of high cheekbones sculpted by the western wind, of taut muscles roiling beneath skin bronzed by the western sun, of Olaf and Frederick.

Only they wouldn't be called that, would they? No, they would be Oley and Fred, the Brogger Boys, scourge of the west, with passions as fierce as the country that bred them—passion for the land, for adventure, and for other, more secret cravings that they might never have suspected, but that could be awakened . . .

" 'Yore skin's jes's soft'n purty—' "

"Whut?" The old man grimaced. "Whut you say?"

Eustace cleared his throat. "Five o'clock will be just fine."

He was unable to sleep at all that night, since he could not find the alarm clock that he was sure he had packed, and he did not want to inform the front desk that he was to be awakened so early, as that might have aroused Barkley's interest. Even had he been able to find the alarm clock, his excitement was too great to permit slumber. He was, however, able to uncover the clothing that he had purchased in New York especially for this occasion. The outfit consisted of a checkered shirt, a leather vest, a pair of hand-tooled boots (not overly ostentatious), and rugged dungarees, to be held up by a belt that matched the subtle pattern etched on the boots. He sponge-bathed thoroughly before dressing, and made certain to wear his softest underclothing.

Just before five o'clock he added the final touch—a large, white, soft-brimmed hat with a leather band. He tilted it on his head until he fancied the look was jaunty enough, then took a deep breath and walked down the back stairs and out into the biting morning cold.

He had expected to find the old man there with the hotel wagon, so was quite surprised to find instead his cicerone astride one horse and holding a second by the reins. "Whutcha starin' at?" the man asked. "Mount up 'n let's go."

"You want me to . . . ride that?"

The man stared at him for a moment. "Whut you *want* to do? F__k it?"

"But . . . what about the wagon?" said Eustace, stammering both from fear and the cold.

"Can't take a d__mn wagon where we're goin'. Now mount up and stop funnin' me."

"But I can't ride!" Eustace admitted.

The old man shook his head. "Sh__t," he muttered, and spat in the dust.

A brief lesson in equestrianism ensued, and in another five minutes Eustace was seated astride the horse, one white-knuckled hand gripping the saddlehorn, the other holding tightly to the reins. "Jes' hold on to the b__st__rd," the old man said, "and he'll follow me—and keep that d__mn foot in the stirrup!"

Once Eustace learned the folly of bouncing upward while the horse was sinking earthward, the comfort of the ride increased, and within a few miles he found that he was actually enjoying the motion, although the area of his anatomy that straddled the saddle was beginning to feel a marked tenderness. After five miles of riding, however, the tenderness became undeniable soreness as the old man turned off the main road onto a stony trail on which the speed of the mounts was not reduced to compensate for the increased irregularity of their route's surface. In short, Eustace ached unbearably in his manly parts, and it was only by keeping the beauties and glories of what lay before him in his mind that he was able to curb his whimpering as his horse's foot slipped once again, jostling him painfully.

After what seemed an interminable ride through spindly trees and over an infinity of boulders, they came out upon a small plain between the trees and what looked to Eustace like a tall mountain. "See 'at cabin up air?" the man called back to him.

Eustace squinted through the morning haze and was able to distinguish a small building nestled amidst the trees at the base of the mountain, which he rightly assumed was the aforementioned Terry Peak.

"'At's it," said the man, and turned his mount so that it came back to Eustace's. "Got my ten bucks?"

Eustace nodded, took ten dollars from the change purse in his vest pocket, and handed it to the man. "Aren't you going to take me up and introduce me?"

"Innerduce ya? Yer funnin' me agin."

"But you'll wait here, won't you?"

"Wait? Wait fer whut?"

"Why, for me, of course! How will I get back?"

"You *come*, didn't ya? You get back the way you *come*."

"But I . . . well, I really wasn't paying attention."

"Sweet J—s—s Chr—st in a g—dd—mn wh—rehouse!" his guide ejaculated. "F——kin'h—ll, ain't you got the f——kin' sense God give a f——kin' goat? Just follow the f——kin' *trail*, fer cr—ssakes! The horse'll getcha back. G—dd—mn dudes . . ."

The man dug his heels into his horse's sides and started to pick his way back down the trail. Eustace watched him go, feeling suddenly lost and alone. What if the Brogger brothers were not at home? He sincerely doubted that they would have a menial with whom he could leave a card.

Still and all, it was rather early, and he wondered if they had even risen yet. Perhaps it might be better, he considered, to wait for a short time until he observed signs of stirring within the brothers' humble home. Finding such a course sensible, he attempted to urge his steed onward toward the cabin, but no matter how he tried to persuade it, it refused to stir, and he decided his only recourse was to dismount and walk the remaining distance.

The dismounting, however, was more easily said than done. Unable to recall how he had come to be sitting on the horse in the first place, Eustace was able to disentangle himself from the Laocoon-like web of harness and stirrups by disengaging both feet and pushing himself slowly backward until he slipped off the rear of the mount. Reaching the earth, he attempted to keep his footing, but was unable to, and the seat of his dungarees came into oblique contact with the steaming pile of droppings the weary steed had evacuated but a short time before. Wiping himself as clean as possible with leaves, Eustace took the bridle and led the horse to a nearby tree, where he tied it with a square knot, and then started to walk toward the cabin.

As he drew nearer the modest abode, the picture came strongly to his memory of himself, dressed very similarly, walking toward the hole-in-the-wall of Jack Binns, for, after having escaped the lustful clutches of Texas Bill Wyatt, Maria, instead of returning to Deadwood to inform the law of all she has suffered, returns instead to Jack's hideout:

"Her heart pounded as she neared the cabin, knowing that her own true love, dangerous as he might be to the rest of the world, was within." (Page 414)

And Eustace's heart pounded now, pounded with excited anticipation as the cabin grew nearer. There was no smoke rising from its stone chimney, and no noise from within. Though he was tempted to look through one of the uncurtained windows, his eastern gentility restrained him from doing so, so he merely sat on the natural stone stoop that served this Romulus and Remus of the range as a front porch, readjusted his trousers so that he ached only mildly, and waited.

It was not until he sat down on an unmoving surface that he realized just how tired he was. A night without sleep and eight miles of hard riding had exhausted him, and he allowed his head to droop, his eyes to close, and he slept and dreamed.

He dreamed of a vast prairie, of Olaf Brogger or Jack Binns (they were of course identical) standing at his side, their arms around each other's waists, of looking into Olaf/Jack's clear, honest eyes, of Jack/Olaf's leathery but soft lips opening to speak, of the words coming out like the scent of wild roses on the free wind—

"Vat the h_ll is *this?*"

When Eustace opened his eyes he knew he must have slept for more than a few minutes, for the sky was far brighter and the sun further up in the sky. He blinked several times to adjust his eyes to the additional illumination, and realized that the voice he had heard had not been in his dream.

"Who're *you?*" The words were harsh and guttural, spoken with a hooting accent Eustace had never heard before. He looked up and saw, glaring down at him, a pale-bodied man wearing only a pair of red flannel drawers. A mop of tousled blond hair capped a stubbled face deeply fissured with pockmarks.

"Olaf?" came another voice from inside.

"Some stranger out here," Olaf called to the one inside, and examined Eustace quickly with his eyes. "No gun, though. Vat you here for?"

Eustace stumbled to his feet, stepped off the stoop, doffed his hat, and made a short bow with his head. "You're Olaf Brogger?"

"Who vants to know?" The man was shorter than Eustace had expected, but had a chest like a barrel.

"My name is Eustace P. Saunders. I'm an illustrator from New York City."

The door slammed open, and another man whom Eustace took to be Frederick Brogger came outside. His hair had a reddish tint, his face was as scarred as his brother's, and he wore a night shirt, from beneath whose hem could be glimpsed the end of his dangling member. Eustace glanced away quickly. "Who's this?" Frederick asked.

Eustace reintroduced himself, trying to keep his gaze only on the men's faces.

"Vat you mean an illusdrader?" asked Frederick.

"I draw pictures. For magazines and books."

"I saw a book vunce," Olaf said. "Our mother had a book."

"Shut up, Olaf," Frederick said, punctuating the command with a blow to the arm.

Eustace noticed that Olaf did not even wince. Oh noble and brave lad, Eustace thought, it is as I had thought—an artistic temperament restrained by a crude and unfeeling sibling. A rough Esau to your kindly Jacob.

"So vat you vant here?" asked Frederick.

"I thought I might . . . draw your pictures."

"Vhy?"

"I had heard . . . that is to say, in Deadwood . . . that you were, um, rather rustic and free individuals."

"They vould say anything about us in Deadwood," Frederick said, splitting a morning gobbet of phlegm into the dust. Then a look of shrewdness came into his cratered face. "You pay us to draw our pictures?"

"Well, yes, I'd be happy to."

"You haf money?" Olaf asked.

Eustace smiled tenderly at the lad. "Yes, of course."

"Who come out here with you?"

Why let them think he had been guided? Much more romantic, after all, for him to have sought them on his own. Besides, he didn't even know his old guide's name. "No one," he prevaricated. "I came alone."

The two brothers nodded in unison. "So," said Frederick. "You vant to draw now?"

"Well, actually I haven't brought any materials along. I really wanted to meet you first, get acquainted. I think it's very important to know one's subject before beginning work. I mean to say, I do a great deal of research before I—"

"Research?" Olaf said, his bushy eyebrows furrowed.

"Yes, research, uh, gathering background information, um . . ." My, Eustace thought, this was not going smoothly at all. Then the image came to him, and he smiled. "Scouting the trail, so to speak."

"Scouting the trail," Frederick repeated, and nodded. "Come inside, Mister Illusdrader. Ve haf coffee."

Eustace followed the two brothers into the cabin, the furnishings of which consisted of a small table, two chairs, and, near the fireplace, a bed with a mattress of straw ticking on which blankets were tossed at random. Pegs on the wall held a modest assortment of clothing, as well as several rifles, and rough hewn shelves contained a few dishes and some cans of food. Piles of gear whose purpose Eustace could not guess lay in the corners. "Sit down," Frederick said, gesturing to the bed while he and Olaf each took a chair.

At first fearful that his smeared dungarees might stain their bed, Eustace hesitated, but when he observed the condition of the bed, he felt that the traces of horse dung remaining on his trousers could do no further harm, and sat. For a long time the men only looked at each other without speaking, and although Eustace was uncomfortable in the silence, it at least gave him leisure to observe the Brogger brothers.

Olaf was by far the more attractive of the pair, stout and well muscled, and although his face was pitted by smallpox scars, there was a regular handsomeness about his features, and the brightness of his hair, even in its uncombed and unwashed state, was stunning. The same blond shade was evident in the hair of his chest, particularly in the tufts about his nipples. Eustace glanced at Frederick, who was apparently oblivious to the nakedness of his nether parts, his legs spread in seeming unconcern of his lack of modesty.

"Olaf," Frederick said finally, "get us some coffee."

The lad obediently went to the fireplace, removed a blue enamel pot from a hook, and poured the steaming liquid into three chipped and cracked cups. The first he gave to Frederick, and the second he took to Eustace, who made sure to touch the dirty but strong fingers that gave him the cup. Whatever message of masculine friendship was sent was also received, as Olaf paused, and looked deeply into Eustace's eyes, a look that thrilled him to the marrow of his bones. Things seemed, he thought, to be going rather nicely after all.

Olaf sat down, and they drank their coffee and continued to look at one another. Finally Frederick spoke again. "Vat you looking at Olaf for?"

Eustace snapped his head around toward the older brother. "I beg your pardon?"

"You're looking at Olaf. You're looking at him as if he were a *vooman*."

"Oh . . . oh no. I'm sure you're mistaken."

But Eustace was wrong. Frederick was not mistaken. Frederick knew the look because he had felt it on his own countenance many times before. Unbeknownst to Eustace, but hinted at among the denizens of Deadwood and Terry, Frederick and Olaf, unable to find solace of a romantic nature among the looser women of either town, had for a long time resorted to comforting each other by the very homoerotic means of which Eustace had only dreamed.

Frederick's eyes narrowed. "You know, Mister Illusdrader, maybe you're right. Maybe vith your pretty clothes and your pretty smell, it's *you* who vants to be the vooman."

There was a way to come to this, Eustace thought, but surely not so bluntly. It made it all seem so very cheap, so utterly sordid. "I'm awfully sorry, but I have no idea of what it is you're talking about."

"How much money you got, Mister Illusdrader?" Frederick asked.

Eustace looked to Olaf for help, but the lad's keen, brave eyes were fixed on the dirt floor. "I . . . well, perhaps fifty dollars or so. With me. Why?"

"Because I think ve maybe take it from you vithout you drawing our picture. And then maybe ve shoot you and put you in the voots for the bears to eat, yah?"

Ice seemed to surge through every one of Eustace's limbs, and his mouth was suddenly too dry to protest. Fear held every muscle as he watched Frederick stand and take a rifle from the wall.

"No, Frederick," came Olaf's voice. "Don't kill him."

Yes! Exhilaration shot through Eustace, melting the ice, replacing it with the fire of love. He had seen the young man's eyes when their fingers had touched, and now was the moment of truth, the moment when Jack Binns would save Maria from Texas Bill. In another second, Eustace was sure of it, Frederick would say the Norwegian equivalent of, "So! Throwin' over yer old pard fer a skirt!" and the battle would begin in earnest, a battle with only one possible ending—happiness, love, eternal devotion!

Olaf looked at him and smiled. "Don't kill him, Frederick." He stood up, walked to the bed, and sat next to Eustace, then took his hand. "Your skin is just as soft and pretty as a vooman's."

Oh yes! As if it was destined! All fear left Eustace's heart as he looked into Olaf's bright blue eyes, felt the warmth of his hand.

"You vant to *be* a vooman . . ."

Olaf, still holding Eustace's hand, began nodding, and the smile on his face twisted to something that terrified Eustace even more than had the prospect of death.

"Ve can *make* you a vooman . . ."

The old man arrived a half hour late for work that morning at the Barkley Hotel. Owen Barkley, having noticed that his new guest was absent from breakfast, and recalling his conversation of the day before concerning the Brogger brothers, was quick to formulate an hypothesis, and the old man was quick to ascertain it upon fear of losing his position.

Two hours later, Sheriff Zedediah Dorwart, the town doctor, and three deputies armed with Parker double-barreled shotguns and Winchester .30-30's rode into the clearing that housed the Brogger brothers' cabin. When the sheriff had been told by Owen Barkley that Wiley Andrews had taken an eastern guest out to the cabin on Terry Peak, he had left town immediately with his deputies, fearing for the easterner's welfare, and, with a premonition of violence, had asked the doctor to accompany them. The five horsemen tethered their mounts at the edge of the clearing near a horse they recognized as belonging to Owen Barkley, and the sheriff and deputies walked stealthily toward the cabin. Not until they were within a few yards of the front door did they hear the moans.

Sheriff Dorwart then pulled his Colt Army .45 from its holster, ran to the door, kicked it off its hinges, and followed it swiftly into the single room, where Frederick Brogger leapt from the bed, dashed to the opposite wall, and from it yanked a rifle which he attempted to turn upon the sheriff. The sheriff shot him directly in the chest, and the charge thrust him backward against the wall, down which he proceeded to slide like a sack of lime. He was quite dead when his bare posterior struck the floor.

Olaf Brogger, in the meantime, was trying to dislodge a Colt Dragoon pistol from somewhere within the folds of a red and heaving mass upon the bed, but stopped when two of the deputies pressed the muzzles of their shotguns against his head and upper back. It was not until he stood up, stark naked and smeared with blood, that the lawmen ascertained where it was the gun was lodged. Then two of the men, who had witnessed many gunshot wounds of various and violent types, turned pale, and the sheriff's arm went up to point his pistol directly into Olaf Brogger's face.

"Take it out of him and then drop it," the sheriff said. "And may g—d d—mn your soul, you be gentle."

Olaf did as he was directed, careful to keep his fingers on the grip alone, and not to allow them anywhere near the trigger. The barrel, which had refused to disengage before when forced now slid out smoothly, and Olaf, the shotguns still prodding his skin, dropped the weapon on the floor.

"Doc!" the sheriff called, then said, "Tie his hands." He coughed up and spat out the bile that had risen to his throat. "Chr—st," he said softly of the thing moaning on the bed. "Oh dear Chr—st."

Eustace P. Saunders's toothless mouth was horribly bruised; the flesh of his chest had been severed so that large flaps of skin hung down in a hideous parody of a woman's dugs, and his organs of regeneration had been detached from his body and lay on the dirt floor amid his scattered teeth. His heart's blood was everywhere.

"Is there any way he's gonna live?" one of the older deputies asked the doctor, who shook his craggy head.

"He's lost too much already. Best I can do is make him comfortable," and he drew from his bag a vial and a needle.

"He vanted to be a vooman," Olaf began to say, but the youngest deputy brought up the butt of his shotgun and broke the Norwegian's jaw, knocking him to the floor.

"Sorry, Sheriff, Doc, but d—mn it . . ."

"Never mind," said the sheriff. "Take him outside. And keep him naked."

"And get Mr. Sanders some water," said the doctor, who pulled a blanket over Eustace while the deputies conveyed Olaf outside, where two remained with him while the third got water from a bucket that stood next to the stone stoop. The doctor trickled water into Eustace's mouth until he regained enough consciousness to begin screaming.

"All right, son, all right," said the doctor, jabbing him with the needle. "This'll make you feel better." The doctor shook his head, looked at Olaf, then at the sheriff as the screaming subsided. "I can't believe you're gonna waste a trial on that son of a b—tch. I sure as h—ll don't want to testify about this."

Sheriff Dorwart nodded sagely and examined the lined and leathered face of his eldest deputy. "What do you think?"

"If the doc don't say nuthin', I never will."

The sheriff looked again at Eustace lying on the bed. "Any man does that to another doesn't deserve a trial. I can't be party to it, neither can the deputies, we took oaths. But nobody's to stop you, Doc, from swattin' a horse's —ss."

The doctor smiled grimly. "I'm game for it."

"What about Hippocrates?" the sheriff asked.

"Hippocrates would've cut the b_st_rd's throat himself and laughed about it," the doctor said.

The sheriff sat rapt in contemplation for a long time before he spoke. "Get him ready, Dan." The deputy left the cabin.

"Whe . . . where . . ." Eustace called from the bed. His eyes were open, and he was attempting to raise his head as if to look about the room.

"Just take it easy now," the doctor cautioned.

"Where . . ." said Eustace through his toothless gums. "Where . . . Olaf?"

"He's outside," said the doctor. "He won't hurt you again. He's going for a little ride in a minute."

"Take me," Eustace said through bloody froth. "Want to . . . see."

The doctor looked at the sheriff. "Why not?" Sheriff Dorwart said. "He deserves to see it if any man does." Then he whispered to the doctor. "Will he ever tell?" The doctor shook his head.

When the deputies hauled out the bed on which Eustace lay, Olaf Brogger was saddled naked upon his horse, and a rope trailed from around his neck over the branch of a large tree down to the trunk, where it was firmly tied. The deputies put their strong hands beneath Eustace's shoulders, raising him gently so that he might more easily see the tree, the rump of the horse, Olaf's bare back.

The doctor walked up to the horse and gave it a resounding blow upon the left flank. It whinnied, reared, and bolted, its involuntary rider remaining in the space it had just deserted, his legs jerking, shoulders twitching, the rope twisting so that his choking, swollen face turned toward Eustace, who remembered:

"He turned his face toward her as his horse galloped into the dawn."

Eustace found just enough strength to raise an arm, and, like Maria Prescott, like the Eustace of the painting, wave farewell to his handsome, western lover.

There is nothing that dies so hard as romance.

BRUCE STERLING
Dori Bangs

Bruce Sterling is a writer usually associated with the "cyberpunk" movement in contemporary science fiction, exploring the impact of new computer technologies on future arts, style, and society. His best known novels are *Schismatrix* and *Islands in the Net*, and he is the editor of the anthology *Mirrorshades*, containing fiction by the leading cyberpunk authors such as William Gibson, Pat Cadigan, Lewis Shiner, and others.

In "Dori Bangs" Sterling tells a contemporary tale of magic realism—the imaginary biography of two real people; a history that never was, but should have been. It's a lovingly written work of short fiction, and a strong contender for the best story of the year. It comes from the pages of *Isaac Asimov's Science Fiction Magazine*.

Sterling currently lives in Austin, Texas.

—T.W.

Dori Bangs

BRUCE STERLING

"The following story is a work of fantasy. It is not reportage, and it does not pretend to be objective, fair, balanced, accurate, or even sane. The stuff that 'actually happened' in the story was mostly invented by the two main characters, who were Artists, and therefore cram-full of distortion, legend, and chest-banging poetic license. Don't believe anything they say about anyone, including themselves! And the author himself clearly has an artistic axe to grind—so don't take his word at face value, either." —Bruce Sterling

True facts, mostly: Lester Bangs was born in California in 1948. He published his first article in 1969. It came in over the transom at *Rolling Stone*. It was a frenzied review of the MC5's "Kick Out the Jams."

Without much meaning to, Lester Bangs slowly changed from a Romilar-guzzling college kid into a "professional rock critic." There wasn't much precedent for this job in 1969, so Lester kinda had to make it up as he went along. Kind of *smell* his way into the role, as it were. But Lester had a fine set of cultural antennae. For instance, Lester invented the tag "punk rock." This is posterity's primary debt to the Bangs oeuvre.

Lester's not as famous now as he used to be, because he's been dead for some time, but in the 70s Lester wrote a million record reviews, for *Creem* and the *Village Voice* and *NME* and *Who Put The Bomp*. He liked to crouch over his old manual typewriter, and slam out wild Beat-influenced copy, while the Velvet Underground or Stooges were on the box. This made life a hideous trial for the neighborhood, but in Lester's opinion the neighborhood pretty much had it coming. *Epater les bourgeois*, man!

Lester was a party animal. It was a professional obligation, actually. Lester was great fun to hang with, because he usually had a jagged speed-edge, which made him smart and bold and rude and crazy. Lester was a one-man band, until he got drunk. Nutmeg, Romilar, belladonna, crank, those substances Lester could handle. But booze seemed to crack him open, and an unexpected black dreck of rage and pain would come dripping out, like oil from a broken crankcase.

Toward the end—but Lester had no notion that the end was nigh. He'd given up the booze, more or less. Even a single beer often triggered frenzies of self-contempt. Lester was thirty-three, and sick of being groovy; he was restless, and the stuff he'd been writing lately no longer meshed with the surroundings that had made him what he was. Lester told his friends that he was gonna leave New

York and go to Mexico and work on a deep, serious novel, about deep serious issues, man. The real thing, this time. He was really gonna pin it down, get into the guts of Western Culture, what it really was, how it really felt.

But then, in April '82, Lester happened to catch the flu. Lester was living alone at the time, his mom, the Jehovah's Witness, having died recently. He had no one to make him chicken soup, and the flu really took him down. Tricky stuff, flu; it has a way of getting on top of you.

Lester ate some Darvon, but instead of giving him that buzzed-out float it usually did, the pills made him feel foggy and dull and desperate. He was too sick to leave his room, or hassle with doctors or ambulances, so instead he just did more Darvon. And his heart stopped.

There was nobody there to do anything about it, so he lay there for a couple of days, until a friend showed up and found him.

More true fax, pretty much: Dori Seda was born in 1951. She was a cartoonist, of the "underground" variety. Dori wasn't ever famous, certainly not in Lester's league, but then she didn't beat her chest and bend every ear in the effort to make herself a Living Legend, either. She had a lot of friends in San Francisco, anyway.

Dori did a "comic book" once, called *Lonely Nights.* An unusual "comic book" for those who haven't followed the "funnies" trade lately, as *Lonely Nights* was not particularly "funny," unless you really get a hoot from deeply revealing tales of frustrated personal relationships. Dori also did a lot of work for *WEIRDO* magazine, which emanated from the artistic circles of R. Crumb, he of "Keep On Truckin'" and "Fritz the Cat" fame.

R. Crumb once said: "Comics are words and pictures. You can do anything with words and pictures!" As a manifesto, it was a typically American declaration, and it was a truth that Dori held to be self-evident.

Dori wanted to be a True Artist in her own real-gone little 80s-esque medium. Comix, or "graphic narrative" if you want a snazzier cognomen for it, was a breaking thing, and she had to feel her way into it. You can see the struggle in her "comics"—always relentlessly autobiographical—Dori hanging around in the "Café La Boheme" trying to trade food-stamps for cigs; Dori living in drafty warehouses in the Shabby Hippie Section of San Francisco, sketching under the skylight and squabbling with her roommate's boyfriend; Dori trying to scrape up money to have her dog treated for mange.

Dori's comics are littered with dead cig-butts and toppled wine-bottles. She was, in a classic nutshell, Wild, Zany, and Self-Destructive. In 1988 Dori was in a car-wreck which cracked her pelvis and collarbone. She was laid up, bored, and in pain. To kill time, she drank and smoked and took painkillers.

She caught the flu. She had friends who loved her, but nobody realized how badly off she was; probably she didn't know it herself. She just went down hard, and couldn't get up alone. On February 26 her heart stopped. She was thirty-six.

So enough "true facts." Now for some comforting lies.

*   *   *

As it happens, even while a malignant cloud of flu virus was lying in wait for the warm hospitable lungs of Lester Bangs, the Fate, Atropos, she who weaves the things that are to be, accidentally dropped a stitch. Knit one? Purl two? What the hell does it matter, anyway? It's just human lives, right?

So Lester, instead of inhaling a cloud of invisible contagion from the exhalations of a passing junkie, is almost hit by a Yellow Cab. This mishap on his way back from the deli shocks Lester out of his dogmatic slumbers. High time, Lester concludes, to get out of this burg and down to sunny old Mexico. He's gonna tackle his great American novel: *All My Friends are Hermits*.

So true. None of Lester's groovy friends go out much any more. Always ahead of their time, Lester's Bohemian cadre are no longer rock and roll animals. They still wear black leather jackets, they still stay up all night, they still hate Ronald Reagan with fantastic virulence; but they never leave home. They pursue an unnamed lifestyle that sociologist Faith Popcorn—(and how can you doubt anyone with a name like *Faith Popcorn*)—will describe years later as "cocooning."

Lester has eight zillion rock, blues, and jazz albums, crammed into his grubby NYC apartment. Books are piled feet deep on every available surface: Wm. Burroughs, Hunter Thompson, Celine, Kerouac, Huysmans, Foucault, and dozens of unsold copies of *Blondie*, Lester's book-length band-bio.

More albums and singles come in the mail every day. People used to send Lester records in the forlorn hope he would review them. But now it's simply a tradition. Lester has transformed himself into a countercultural info-sump. People send him vinyl just because he's *Lester Bangs*, man!

Still jittery from his thrilling brush with death, Lester looks over this lifetime of loot with a surge of Sartrean nausea. He resists the urge to raid the fridge for his last desperate can of Blatz Beer. Instead, Lester snorts some speed, and calls an airline to plan his Mexican wanderjahr. After screaming in confusion at the hopeless stupid bitch of a receptionist, he gets a ticket to San Francisco, best he can do on short notice. He packs in a frenzy and splits.

Next morning finds Lester exhausted and wired and on the wrong side of the continent. He's brought nothing with him but an Army duffel-bag with his Olympia portable, some typing paper, shirts, assorted vials of dope, and a paperback copy of *Moby Dick*, which he's always meant to get around to re-reading.

Lester takes a cab out of the airport. He tells the cabbie to drive nowhere, feeling a vague compulsive urge to soak up the local vibe. San Francisco reminds him of his *Rolling Stone* days, back before Wenner fired him for being nasty to rock-stars. Fuck Wenner, he thinks. Fuck this city that was almost Avalon for a few months in '67 and has been on greased skids to Hell ever since.

The hilly half-familiar streets creep and wriggle with memories, avatars, talismans. Decadence, man, a no-kidding *death of affect*. It all ties in for Lester, in a bilious mental stew: snuff movies, discos, the cold-blooded whine of synthesizers, Pet Rocks, S&M, mindfuck self-improvement cults, Winning Through Intimidation, every aspect of the invisible war slowly eating the soul of the world.

After an hour or so he stops the cab at random. He needs coffee, white sugar, human beings, maybe a cheese Danish. Lester glimpses himself in the cab's window as he turns to pay: a chunky jobless thirty-three-year-old in a biker jacket, speed-pale dissipated New York face, Fu Manchu mustache looking pasted on. Running to fat, running for shelter. . . . no excuses, Bangs! Lester hands the driver a big tip. Chew on that, pal—you just drove the next Oswald Spengler.

Lester staggers into the cafe. It's crowded and stinks of patchouli and clove. He sees two chainsmoking punkettes hanging out at a formica table. CBGB's types, but with California suntans. The kind of women, Lester thinks, who sit crosslegged on the floor and won't fuck you but are perfectly willing to describe in detail their highly complex postexistential *weltanschauung*. Tall and skinny and crazy-looking and bad news. Exactly his type, really. Lester sits down at their table and gives them his big rubber grin.

"Been having fun?" Lester says.

They look at him like he's crazy, which he is, but he wangles their names out: "Dori" and "Krystine." Dori's wearing fishnet stockings, cowboy boots, a strapless second-hand bodice-hugger covered with peeling pink feathers. Her long brown hair's streaked blonde. Krystine's got a black knit tank-top and a leather skirt and a skull-tattoo on her stomach.

Dori and Krystine have never heard of "Lester Bangs." They don't read much. They're *artists*. They do cartoons. Underground comix. Lester's mildly interested. Manifestations of the trash aesthetic always strongly appeal to him. It seems so American, the *good* America that is: the righteous wild America of rootless European refuse picking up discarded pop-junk and making it shine like the Koh-i-noor. To make "comic books" into Art—what a hopeless fucking effort, worse than rock and roll and you don't even get heavy bread for it. Lester says as much, to see what they'll do.

Krystine wanders off for a refill. Dori, who is mildly weirded-out by this tubby red-eyed stranger with his loud come-on, gives Lester her double-barreled brush-off. Which consists of opening up this Windex-clear vision into the Vent of Hell that is her daily life. Dori lights another Camel from the butt of the last, smiles at Lester with her big gappy front teeth and says brightly:

"You like *dogs*, Lester? I have this dog, and he has eczema and disgusting open sores all over his body, and he smells *really* bad . . . I can't get friends to come over because he likes to shove his nose right into their, you know, *crotch* . . . and go Snort! Snort!"

" 'I want to scream with wild dog joy in the smoking pit of a charnel house,' " Lester says.

Dori stares at him. "Did you make that up?"

"Yeah," Lester says. "Where were you when Elvis died?"

"You taking a survey on it?" Dori says.

"No, I just wondered," Lester says. "There was talk of having Elvis's corpse dug up, and the stomach analyzed. For dope, y'know. Can you *imagine* that? I mean, the *thrill* of sticking your hand and forearm into Elvis's rotted guts and slopping around in the stomach lining and liver and kidneys and coming up out of dead Elvis's innards triumphantly clenching some crumbs off a few Percodans and Desoxyns and 'ludes . . . and then this is the *real* kick, Dori: you pop these crumbled-up bits of pills in your *own mouth* and bolt 'em down and get high on drugs that not only has Elvis Presley, the *King*, gotten high on, not the same brand mind you but the same *pills*, all slimy with little bits of his innards, so you've actually gotten to *eat* the King of Rock and Roll!"

"*Who* did you say you were?" Dori says. "A rock journalist? I thought you were putting me on. 'Lester Bangs,' that's a fucking weird name!"

Dori and Krystine have been up all night, dancing to the heroin headbanger vibes of Darby Crash and the Germs. Lester watches through hooded eyes: this Dori is a woman over thirty, but she's got this wacky airhead routine down smooth, the Big Shiny Fun of the American Pop Bohemia. "Fuck you for believing I'm this shallow." Beneath the skin of her Attitude he can sense a bracing skeleton of pure desperation. There is hollow fear and sadness in the marrow of her bones. He's been writing about a topic just like this lately.

They talk a while, about the city mostly, about their variant scenes. Sparring, but he's interested. Dori yawns with pretended disinterest and gets up to leave. Lester notes that Dori is taller than he is. It doesn't bother him. He gets her phone number.

Lester crashes in a Holiday Inn. Next day he leaves town. He spends a week in a flophouse in Tijuana with his Great American Novel, which sucks. Despondent and terrified, he writes himself little cheering notes: "Burroughs was almost fifty when he wrote *Nova Express*! Hey boy, you only thirty-three! Burnt-out! Washed-up! Finished! A bit of flotsam! And in that flotsam your salvation! In that one grain of wood. In that one bit of that irrelevance. If you can bring yourself to describe it. . . ."

It's no good. He's fucked. He knows he is, too, he's been reading over his scrapbooks lately, those clippings of yellowing newsprint, thinking: it was all a box, man! *El Cajon!* You'd think: wow, a groovy youth-rebel Rock Writer, he can talk about *anything*, can't he? Sex, dope, violence, Mazola parties with teenage Indonesian groupies, Nancy Reagan publicly fucked by a herd of clapped-out bull walruses . . . but when you actually READ a bunch of Lester Bangs Rock Reviews in a row, the whole shebang has a delicate hermetic whiff, like so many eighteenth-century sonnets. It is to dance in chains; it is to see the whole world through a little chromed window of Silva-Thin 'shades. . . .

Lester Bangs is nothing if not a consummate romantic. He is, after all, a man who *really no kidding believes* that Rock and Roll Could Change the World, and when he writes something which isn't an impromptu free lesson on what's wrong with Western Culture and how it can't survive without grabbing itself by the backbrain and turning itself inside-out, he feels like he's wasted a day. Now Lester, fretfully abandoning his typewriter to stalk and kill flophouse roaches, comes to realize that HE will have to turn himself inside out. Grow, or die. Grow into something but he has no idea what. He feels beaten.

So Lester gets drunk. Starts with Tecate, works his way up to tequila. He wakes up with a savage hangover. Life seems hideous and utterly meaningless. He abandons himself to senseless impulse. Or, in alternate terms, Lester allows himself to follow the numinous artistic promptings of his holy intuition. He returns to San Francisco and calls Dori Seda.

Dori, in the meantime, has learned from friends that there is indeed a rock journalist named "Lester Bangs" who's actually kind of *famous*. He once appeared on stage with the J. Geils Band "playing" his typewriter. He's kind of a big deal, which probably accounts for his being kind of an asshole. On a dare, Dori calls Lester Bangs in New York, gets his answering machine, and recognizes the voice. It was him, all right. Through some cosmic freak, she met Lester Bangs and he tried to pick her up! No dice, though. More Lonely Nights, Dori!

Then Lester calls. He's back in town again. Dori's so flustered she ends up being nicer to him on the phone than she means to be.

She goes out with him. To rock clubs. Lester never has to pay; he just mutters at people, and they let him in and find him a table. Strangers rush up to gladhand Lester and jostle round the table and pay court. Lester finds the music mostly boring, and it's no pretense; he actually *is* bored, he's heard it all. He sits there sipping club sodas and handing out these little chips of witty guru insight to these sleaze-ass Hollywood guys and bighaired coke-whores in black Spandex. Like it was his *job*.

Dori can't believe he's going to all this trouble just to jump her bones. It's not like he can't get women, or like their own relationship is all that tremendously scintillating. Lester's whole set-up is alien. But it *is* kind of interesting, and doesn't demand much. All Dori has to do is dress in her sluttiest Goodwill get-up, and be This Chick With Lester. Dori likes being invisible, and watching people when they don't know she's looking. She can see in their eyes that Lester's people wonder Who The Hell Is She? Dori finds this really funny, and makes sketches of his creepiest acquaintances on cocktail napkins. At night she puts them in her sketch-books and writes dialogue balloons. It's all really good material.

Lester's also very funny, in a way. He's smart, not just hustler-clever but scary-crazy smart, like he's sometimes profound without knowing it or even *wanting* it. But when he thinks he's being most amusing, is when he's actually the most incredibly depressing. It bothers her that he doesn't drink around her; it's a bad sign. He knows almost nothing about art or drawing, he dresses like a jerk, he dances like a trained bear. And she's fallen in love with him and she knows he's going to break her goddamn heart.

Lester has put his novel aside for the moment. Nothing new there; he's been working on it, in hopeless spasms, for ten years. But now juggling this affair takes all he's got.

Lester is terrified that this amazing woman is going to go to pieces on him. He's seen enough of her work now to recognize that she's possessed of some kind of genuine demented genius. He can smell it; the vibe pours off her like Everglades swamp-reek. Even in her frowsy houserobe and bunny slippers, hair a mess, no makeup, half-asleep, he can see something there like Dresden china, something fragile and precious. And the world seems like a maelstrom of jungle hate, sinking into entropy or gearing up for Armageddon, and what the hell can anybody do? How can he be happy with her and not be punished for it? How long can they break the rules before the Nova Police show?

But nothing horrible happens to them. They just go on living.

Then Lester blunders into a virulent cloud of Hollywood money. He's written a stupid and utterly commercial screenplay about the laff-a-minute fictional antics of a heavy-metal band, and without warning he gets eighty thousand dollars for it.

He's never had so much money in one piece before. He has, he realizes with dawning horror, sold out.

To mark the occasion Lester buys some freebase, six grams of crystal meth, and rents a big white Cadillac. He fast-talks Dori into joining him for a supernaturally cool Kerouac adventure into the Savage Heart of America, and they get in the car laughing like hyenas and take off for parts unknown.

Four days later they're in Kansas City. Lester's lying in the back seat in a jittery Hank Williams half-doze and Dori is driving. They have nothing left to say, as they've been arguing viciously ever since Albuquerque.

Dori, white-knuckled, sinuses scorched with crank, loses it behind the wheel. Lester's slammed from the back seat and wakes up to find Dori knocked out and drizzling blood from a scalp wound. The Caddy's wrapped messily in the buckled ruins of a sidewalk mailbox.

Lester holds the resultant nightmare together for about two hours, which is long enough to flag down help and get Dori into a Kansas City trauma room.

He sits there, watching over her, convinced he's lost it, blown it; it's over, she'll hate him forever now. My God, she could have died! As soon as she comes to, he'll have to face her. The thought of this makes something buckle inside him. He flees the hospital in headlong panic.

He ends up in a sleazy little rock dive downtown where he jumps onto a table and picks a fight with the bouncer. After he's knocked down for the third time, he gets up screaming for the manager, how he's going to *ruin that motherfucker!* and the club's owner shows up, tired and red-faced and sweating. The owner, whose own tragedy must go mostly unexpressed here, is a fat white-haired cigar-chewing third-rater who attempted, and failed, to model his life on Elvis' Colonel Parker. He hates kids, he hates rock and roll, he hates the aggravation of smart-ass doped-up hippies screaming threats and pimping off the hard work of businessmen just trying to make a living.

He has Lester hauled to his office backstage and tells him all this. Toward the end, the owner's confused, almost plaintive, because he's never seen anyone as utterly, obviously, and desperately fucked-up as Lester Bangs, but who can still be coherent about it and use phrases like "rendered to the factor of machinehood" while mopping blood from his punched nose.

And Lester, trembling and red-eyed, tells him: fuck you Jack, I could run this jerkoff place, I could do everything you do blind drunk, and make this place a fucking *legend in American culture,* you booshwah sonofabitch.

Yeah punk if you had the money, the owner says.

I've *got* the money! Let's see your papers, you evil cracker bastard! In a few minutes Lester is the owner-to-be on a handshake and an earnest-check.

Next day he brings Dori roses from the hospital shop downstairs. He sits next to the bed; they compare bruises, and Lester explains to her that he has just blown his fortune. They are now tied down and beaten in the corn-shucking heart of America. There is only one possible action left to complete this situation.

Three days later they are married in Kansas City by a justice of the peace.

Needless to say marriage does not solve any of their problems. It's a minor big deal for a while, gets mentioned in rock-mag gossip columns; they get some telegrams from friends, and Dori's mom seems pretty glad about it. They even get a nice note from Julie Burchill, the Marxist Amazon from *New Musical Express* who has quit the game to write for fashion mags, and her husband Tony Parsons the proverbial "hip young gunslinger" who now writes weird potboiler novels about racetrack gangsters. Tony & Julie seem to be making some kind of go of it. Kinda inspirational.

For a while Dori calls herself Dori Seda-Bangs, like her good friend Aline Kominsky-Crumb, but after a while she figures what's the use? and just calls herself Dori Bangs which sounds plenty weird enough on its own.

Lester can't say he's really *happy* or anything, but he's sure *busy*. He re-names the club "Waxy's Travel Lounge," for some reason known only to himself. The club loses money quickly and consistently. After the first month Lester stops playing Lou Reed's *Metal Machine Music* before sets, and that helps attendance some, but Waxy's is still a club which books a lot of tiny weird college-circuit acts that Albert Average just doesn't get yet. Pretty soon they're broke again and living on Lester's reviews.

They'd be even worse off, except Dori does a series of promo posters for Waxy's that are so amazing that they draw people in, even after they've been burned again and again on weird-ass bands only Lester can listen to.

After a couple of years they're still together, only they have shrieking crockery-throwing fights and once, when he's been drinking, Lester wrenches her arm so badly Dori's truly afraid it's broken. It isn't, luckily, but it's sure no great kick being Mrs. Lester Bangs. Dori was always afraid of this: that what he does is *work* and what she does is *cute*. How many Great Women Artists are there anyway, and what happened to 'em? They went into patching the wounded ego and picking up the dropped socks of Mr. Wonderful, that's what. No big mystery about it.

And besides, she's thirty-six and still barely scraping a living. She pedals her beat-up bike through the awful Kansas weather and sees these yuppies cruise by with these smarmy grins: hey we don't *have* to invent our lives, our lives are *invented for us* and boy does that ever save a lot of soul-searching.

But still somehow they blunder along; they have the occasional good break. Like when Lester turns over the club on Wednesdays to some black kids for (ecch!) "disco nite" and it turns out to be the beginning of a little Kansas City rap-scratch scene, which actually makes the club some money. And "Polyrock," a band Lester hates at first but later champions to global megastardom, cuts a live album in Waxy's.

And Dori gets a contract to do one of those twenty-second animated logos for MTV, and really gets into it. It's fun, so she starts doing video animation work for (fairly) big bucks and even gets a Macintosh II from a video-hack admirer in Silicon Valley. Dori had always loathed feared and despised *computers* but this thing is *different*. This is a kind of art that *nobody's ever done before* and has to be invented from leftovers, sweat, and thin air! It's wide open and way rad!

Lester's novel doesn't get anywhere, but he does write a book called A *Reasonable Guide to Horrible Noise* which becomes a hip coffeetable cult item with an admiring introduction by a trendy French semiotician. Among other things, this book introduces the term "chipster" which describes a kind of person who, well, didn't really *exist* before Lester described them but once he'd pointed 'em out it was *obvious to everybody*.

But they're still not *happy*. They both have a hard time taking the "marital fidelity" notion with anything like seriousness. They have a vicious fight once, over who gave who herpes, and Dori splits for six months and goes back to California. Where she looks up her old girlfriends and finds the survivors married with kids, and her old boyfriends are even seedier and more pathetic than Lester. What the hell, it's not happiness but it's something. She goes back to Lester. He's gratifyingly humble and appreciative for almost six weeks.

Waxy's does in fact become a cultural legend of sorts, but they don't pay you for that; and anyway it's hell to own a bar while attending sessions of Alcoholics Anonymous. So Lester gives in, and sells the club. He and Dori buy a house, which turns out to be far more hassle than it's worth, and then they go to Paris for a while, where they argue bitterly and squander all their remaining money.

When they come back Lester gets, of all the awful things, an academic gig. For a Kansas state college. Lester teaches Rock and Popular Culture. In the '70s there'd have been no room for such a hopeless skidrow weirdo in a, like, Serious Academic Environment, but it's the late '90s by now, and Lester has outlived the era of outlawhood. Because who are we kidding? Rock and Roll is a satellite-driven worldwide information industry which is worth billions and *billions*, and if they don't study *major industries* then what the hell are the taxpayers funding colleges for?

Self-destruction is awfully tiring. After a while, they just give it up. They've lost the energy to flame-out, and it hurts too much; besides it's less trouble just to live. They eat balanced meals, go to bed early, and attend faculty parties where Lester argues violently about the parking privileges.

Just after the turn of the century, Lester finally gets his novel published, but it seems quaint and dated now, and gets panned and quickly remaindered. It would be nice to say that Lester's book was rediscovered years later as a Klassic of Litratchur but the truth is that Lester's no novelist; what he is, is a cultural mutant, and what he has in the way of insight and energy has been eaten up. Subsumed by the Beast, man. What he thought and said made some kind of difference, but nowhere near as big a difference as he'd dreamed.

In the year 2015, Lester dies of a heart attack while shoveling snow off his lawn. Dori has him cremated, in one of those plasma flash-cremators that are all the mode in the 21st-cent. undertaking business. There's a nice respectful retrospective on Lester in the *New York Times Review of Books* but the truth is

Lester's pretty much a forgotten man; a colorful footnote for cultural historians who can see the twentieth century with the unflattering advantage of hindsight.

A year after Lester's death they demolish the remnants of Waxy's Travel Lounge to make room for a giant high-rise. Dori goes out to see the ruins. As she wanders among the shockingly staid and unromantic rubble, there's another of those slips in the fabric of Fate, and Dori is approached by a Vision.

Thomas Hardy used to call it the Immanent Will and in China it might have been the Tao, but we late 20th-cent. postmoderns would probably call it something soothingly pseudoscientific like the "genetic imperative." Dori, being Dori, recognizes this glowing androgynous figure as The Child They Never Had.

"Don't worry, Mrs. Bangs," the Child tells her, "I might have died young of some ghastly disease, or grown up to shoot the President and break your heart, and anyhow you two woulda been no prize as parents." Dori can see herself and Lester in this Child, there's a definite nacreous gleam in its right eye that's Lester's, and the sharp quiet left eye is hers; but behind the eyes where there should be a living breathing human being there's *nothing*, just a kind of chill galactic twinkling.

"And don't feel guilty for outliving him either," the Child tells her, "because you're going to have what we laughingly call a natural death, which means you're going to die in the company of strangers hooked up to tubes when you're old and helpless."

"But did it *mean* anything?" Dori says.

"If you mean were you Immortal Artists leaving indelible grafitti in the concrete sidewalk of Time, no. You've never walked the earth as Gods, you were just people. But it's better to have a real life than no life." The Child shrugs. "You weren't all that happy together, but you *did* suit each other, and if you'd both married other people instead, there would have been *four* people unhappy. So here's your consolation: you helped each other."

"So?" Dori says.

"So that's enough. Just to shelter each other, and help each other up. Everything else is gravy. Someday, no matter what, you go down forever. Art can't make you immortal. Art can't Change the World. Art can't even heal your soul. All it can do is maybe ease the pain a bit or make you feel more awake. And that's enough. It only matters as much as it matters, which is zilch to an ice-cold interstellar Cosmic Principle like yours truly. But if you try to live by my standards it will only kill you faster. By your own standards, you did pretty good, really."

"Well okay then," Dori says.

After this purportedly earth-shattering mystical encounter, her life simply went right on, day following day, just like always. Dori gave up computer-art; it was too hairy trying to keep up with the hotshot high-tech cutting edge, and kind of undignified, when you came right down to it. Better to leave that to hungry kids. She was idle for a while, feeling quiet inside, but finally she took up watercolors. For a while Dori played the Crazy Old Lady Artist and was kind of a mainstay of the Kansas regionalist art scene. Granted, Dori was no Georgia O'Keeffe, but she was working, and living, and she touched a few people's lives.

*   *   *

Or, at least, Dori surely would have touched those people, if she'd been there to do it. But of course she wasn't, and didn't. Dori Seda never met Lester Bangs. Two simple real-life acts of human caring, at the proper moment, might have saved them both; but when those moments came, they had no one, not even each other. And so they went down into darkness, like skaters, breaking through the hard bright shiny surface of our true-facts world.

Today I made this white paper dream to cover the holes they left.

JOE R. LANSDALE

The Steel Valentine

Equally at home in several genres, Joe R. Lansdale keeps busy editing anthologies such as *Razored Saddles* and penning novels like *The Drive-in*. He is always sharp and frequently surprising, and produces gritty, realistic stories about hard-asses who meet their match. This is one of the original stories in Lansdale's new collection, *By Bizarre Hands*, and it's a classic revenge drama with one last vicious twist. Not for the faint of heart.

—E.D.

The Steel Valentine

JOE R. LANSDALE

For Jeff Banks

Even before Morley told him, Dennis knew things were about to get ugly.

A man did not club you unconscious, bring you to his estate and tie you to a chair in an empty storage shed out back of the place if he merely intended to give you a valentine.

Morley had found out about him and Julie.

Dennis blinked his eyes several times as he came to, and each time he did, more of the dimly lit room came into view. It was the room where he and Julie had first made love. It was the only building on the estate that looked out of place; it was old, worn, and not even used for storage; it was a collector of dust, cobwebs, spiders and desiccated flies.

There was a table in front of Dennis, a kerosine lantern on it, and beyond, partially hidden in shadow, a man sitting in a chair smoking a cigarette. Dennis could see the red tip glowing in the dark and the smoke from it drifted against the lantern light and hung in the air like thin, suspended wads of cotton.

The man leaned out of shadow, and as Dennis expected, it was Morley. His shaved, bullet-shaped head was sweaty and reflected the light. He was smiling with his fine, white teeth, and the high cheek bones were round, flushed circles that looked like clown rouge. The tightness of his skin, the few wrinkles, made him look younger than his fifty-one years.

And in most ways he was younger than his age. He was a man who took care of himself. Jogged eight miles every morning before breakfast, lifted weights three times a week and had only one bad habit—cigarettes. He smoked three packs a day. Dennis knew all that and he had only met the man twice. He had learned it from Julie, Morley's wife. She told him about Morley while they lay in bed. She liked to talk and she often talked about Morley; about how much she hated him.

"Good to see you," Morley said, and blew smoke across the table into Dennis's face. "Happy Valentine's Day, my good man. I was beginning to think I hit you too hard, put you in a coma."

"What is this, Morley?" Dennis found that the mere act of speaking sent nails of pain through his skull. Morley really had lowered the boom on him.

"Spare me the innocent act, lover boy. You've been laying the pipe to Julie, and I don't like it."

"This is silly, Morley. Let me loose."

"God, they do say stupid things like that in real life. It isn't just the movies . . . You think I brought you here just to let you go, lover boy?"

Dennis didn't answer. He tried to silently work the ropes loose that held his hands to the back of the chair. If he could get free, maybe he could grab the lantern, toss it in Morley's face. There would still be the strand holding his ankles to the chair, but maybe it wouldn't take too long to undo that. And even if it did, it was at least some kind of plan.

If he got the chance to go one on one with Morley, he might take him. He was twenty-five years younger and in good shape himself. Not as good as when he was playing pro basketball, but good shape nonetheless. He had height, reach, and he still had wind. He kept the latter with plenty of jogging and tossing the special-made, sixty-five pound medicine ball around with Raul at the gym.

Still, Morley was strong. Plenty strong. Dennis could testify to that. The pulsating knot on the side of his head was there to remind him.

He remembered the voice in the parking lot, turning toward it and seeing a fist. Nothing more, just a fist hurtling toward him like a comet. Next thing he knew, he was here, the outbuilding.

Last time he was here, circumstances were different, and better. He was with Julie. He met her for the first time at the club where he worked out, and they had spoken, and ended up playing racquetball together. Eventually she brought him here and they made love on an old mattress in the corner; lay there afterward in the June heat of a Mexican summer, holding each other in a warm, sweaty embrace.

After that, there had been many other times. In the great house; in cars; hotels. Always careful to arrange a tryst when Morley was out of town. Or so they thought. But somehow he had found out.

"This is where you first had her," Morley said suddenly. "And don't look so wide-eyed. I'm not a mind reader. She told me all the other times and places too. She spat at me when I told her I knew, but I made her tell me every little detail, even when I knew them. I wanted it to come from her lips. She got so she couldn't wait to tell me. She was begging to tell me. She asked me to forgive her and take her back. She no longer wanted to leave Mexico and go back to the States with you. She just wanted to live."

"You bastard. If you've hurt her—"

"You'll what? Shit your pants? That's the best you can do, Dennis. You see, it's me that has *you* tied to the chair. Not the other way around."

Morley leaned back into the shadows again, and his hands came to rest on the table, the perfectly manicured fingertips steepling together, twitching ever so gently.

"I think it would have been inconsiderate of her to have gone back to the States with you, Dennis. Very inconsiderate. She knows I'm a wanted man there, that I can't go back. She thought she'd be rid of me. Start a new life with her ex-basketball player. That hurt my feelings, Dennis. Right to the bone." Morley smiled. "But she wouldn't have been rid of me, lover boy. Not by a long shot. I've got connections in my business. I could have followed her anywhere . . . In fact, the idea that she thought I couldn't offended my sense of pride."

"Where is she? What have you done with her, you bald-headed bastard?"

After a moment of silence, during which Morley examined Dennis's face, he said, "Let me put it this way. Do you remember her dogs?"

Of course he remembered the dogs. Seven Dobermans. Attack dogs. They always frightened him. They were big mothers, too. Except for her favorite, a reddish, undersized Doberman named Chum. He was about sixty pounds, and vicious. "Light, but quick," Julie used to say. "Light, but quick."

Oh yeah, he remembered those goddamn dogs. Sometimes when they made love in an estate bedroom, the dogs would wander in, sit down around the bed and watch. Dennis felt they were considering the soft, rolling meat of his testicles, savoring the possibility. It made him feel like a mean kid teasing them with a treat he never intended to give. The idea of them taking that treat by force made his erection soften, and he finally convinced Julie, who found his nervousness hysterically funny, that the dogs should be banned from the bedroom, the door closed.

Except for Julie, those dogs hated everyone. Morley included. They obeyed him, but they did not like him. Julie felt that under the right circumstances, they might go nuts and tear him apart. Something she hoped for, but never happened.

"Sure," Morley continued. "You remember her little pets. Especially Chum, her favorite. He'd growl at me when I tried to touch her. Can you imagine that? All I had to do was touch her, and that damn beast would growl. He was crazy about his mistress, just crazy about her."

Dennis couldn't figure what Morley was leading up to, but he knew in some way he was being baited. And it was working. He was starting to sweat.

"Been what," Morley asked, "a week since you've seen your precious sweetheart? Am I right?"

Dennis did not answer, but Morley was right. A week. He had gone back to the States for a while to settle some matters, get part of his inheritance out of legal bondage so he could come back, get Julie, and take her to the States for good. He was tired of the Mexican heat and tired of Morley owning the woman he loved.

It was Julie who had arranged for him to meet Morley in the first place, and probably even then the old bastard had suspected. She told Morley a partial truth. That she had met Dennis at the club, that they had played racquetball together, and that since he was an American, and supposedly a mean hand at chess, she thought Morley might enjoy the company. This way Julie had a chance to be with her lover, and let Dennis see exactly what kind of man Morley was.

And from the first moment Dennis met him, he knew he had to get Julie away from him. Even if he hadn't loved her and wanted her, he would have helped her leave Morley.

It wasn't that Morley was openly abusive—in fact, he was the perfect host all the while Dennis was there—but there was an obvious undercurrent of connubial dominance and menace that revealed itself like a shark fin everytime he looked at Julie.

Still, in a strange way, Dennis found Morley interesting, if not likeable. He was a bright and intriguing talker, and a wizard at chess. But when they played and Morley took a piece, he smirked over it in such a way as to make you feel he had actually vanquished an opponent.

The second and last time Dennis visited the house was the night before he left for the States. Morley had wiped him out in chess, and when finally Julie walked him to the door and called the dogs in from the yard so he could leave without being eaten, she whispered, "I can't take him much longer."

"I know," he whispered back. "See you in about a week. And it'll be all over."

Dennis looked over his shoulder, back into the house, and there was Morley leaning against the fireplace mantle drinking a martini. He lifted the glass to Dennis as if in salute and smiled. Dennis smiled back, called goodbye to Morley and went out to his car feeling uneasy. The smile Morley had given him was exactly the same one he used when he took a chess piece from the board.

"Tonight. Valentine's Day," Morley said, "that's when you two planned to meet again, wasn't it? In the parking lot of your hotel. That's sweet. Really. Lovers planning to elope on Valentine's Day. It has a sort of poetry, don't you think?"

Morley held up a huge fist. "But what you met instead of your sweetheart was this . . . I beat a man to death with this once, lover boy. Enjoyed every second of it."

Morley moved swiftly around the table, came to stand behind Dennis. He put his hands on the sides of Dennis's face. "I could twist your head until your neck broke, lover boy. You believe that, don't you? Don't you? . . . Goddamnit, answer me."

"Yes," Dennis said, and the word was soft because his mouth was so dry.

"Good. That's good. Let me show you something, Dennis."

Morley picked up the chair from behind, carried Dennis effortlessly to the center of the room, then went back for the lantern and the other chair. He sat down across from Dennis and turned the wick of the lantern up. And even before Dennis saw the dog, he heard the growl.

The dog was straining at a large leather strap attached to the wall. He was muzzled and ragged looking. At his feet lay something red and white. "Chum," Morley said. "The light bothers him. You remember ole Chum, don't you?

Julie's favorite pet . . . Ah, but I see you're wondering what that is at his feet. That sort of surprises me, Dennis. Really. As intimate as you and Julie were, I'd think you'd know her. Even without her makeup."

Now that Dennis knew what he was looking at, he could make out the white bone of her skull, a dark patch of matted hair still clinging to it. He also recognized what was left of the dress she had been wearing. It was a red and white tennis dress, the one she wore when they played racquetball. It was mostly red now. Her entire body had been gnawed savagely.

"Murderer!" Dennis rocked savagely in the chair, tried to pull free of his bonds. After a moment of useless struggle and useless epithets, he leaned forward and let the lava hot gorge in his stomach pour out.

"Oh, Dennis," Morley said. "That's going to be stinky. Just awful. Will you look at your shoes? And calling me a murderer. Now, I ask you, Dennis, is that nice? I didn't murder anyone. Chum did the dirty work. After four days without food and water he was ravenous and thirsty. Wouldn't you be? And he was a little crazy too. I burned his feet some. Not as bad as I burned Julie's, but enough to really piss him off. And I sprayed him with this."

Morley reached into his coat pocket, produced an aerosol canister and waved it at Dennis.

"This was invented by some business associate of mine. It came out of some chemical warfare research I'm conducting. I'm in, shall we say . . . espionage? I work for the highest bidder. I have plants here for arms and chemical warfare . . . If it's profitable and ugly, I'm involved. I'm a real stinker sometimes. I certainly am."

Morley was still waving the canister, as if trying to hypnotize Dennis with it. "We came up with this to train attack dogs. We found we could spray a padded up man with this and the dogs would go bonkers. Rip the pads right off of him. Sometimes the only way to stop the beggers was to shoot them. It was a failure actually. It activated the dogs, but it drove them out of their minds and they couldn't be controlled at all. And after a short time the odor faded, and the spray became quite the reverse. It made it so the dogs couldn't smell the spray at all. It made whoever was wearing it odorless. Still, I found a use for it. A very personal use.

"I let Chum go a few days without food and water while I worked on Julie . . . And she wasn't tough at all, Dennis. Not even a little bit. Spilled her guts. Now that isn't entirely correct. She didn't spill her guts until later, when Chum got hold of her . . . Anyway, she told me what I wanted to know about you two, then I sprayed that delicate thirty-six, twenty-four, thirty-six figure of hers with this. And with Chum so hungry, and me having burned his feet and done some mean things to him, he was not in the best of humor when I gave him Julie.

"It was disgusting, Dennis. Really. I had to come back when it was over and shoot Chum with a tranquilizer dart, get him tied and muzzled for your arrival."

Morley leaned forward, sprayed Dennis from head to foot with the canister. Dennis turned his head and closed his eyes, tried not to breathe the foul-smelling mist.

"He's probably not all that hungry now," Morley said, "but this will still drive him wild."

Already Chum had gotten a whiff and was leaping at his leash. Foam burst from between his lips and frothed on the leather bands of the muzzle.

"I suppose it isn't polite to lecture a captive audience, Dennis, but I thought you might like to know a few things about dogs. No need to take notes. You won't be around for a quiz later.

"But here's some things to tuck in the back of your mind while you and Chum are alone. Dogs are very strong, Dennis. Very. They look small compared to a man, even a big dog like a Doberman, but they can exert a lot of pressure with their bite. I've seen dogs like Chum here, especially when they're exposed to my little spray, bite through the thicker end of a baseball bat. And they're quick. You'd have a better chance against a black belt in karate than an attack dog."

"Morley," Dennis said softly, "you can't do this."

"I can't?" Morley seemed to consider. "No, Dennis, I believe I can. I give myself permission. But hey, Dennis, I'm going to give you a chance. This is the good part now, so listen up. You're a sporting man. Basketball. Racquetball. Chess. Another man's woman. So you'll like this. This will appeal to your sense of competition.

"Julie didn't give Chum a fight at all. She just couldn't believe her Chummy-whummy wanted to eat her. Just wouldn't. She held out her hand, trying to soothe the old boy, and he just bit it right off. Right off. Got half the palm and the fingers in one bite. That's when I left them alone. I had a feeling her Chummy-whummy might start on me next, and I wouldn't have wanted that. Oooohhh, those sharp teeth. Like nails being driven into you."

"Morley listen—"

"Shut up! You, Mr. Cock Dog and Basketball Star, just might have a chance. Not much of one, but I know you'll fight. You're not a quitter. I can tell by the way you play chess. You still lose, but you're not a quitter. You hang in there to the bitter end."

Morley took a deep breath, stood in the chair and hung the lantern on a low rafter. There was something else up there too. A coiled chain. Morley pulled it down and it clattered to the floor. At the sound of it Chum leaped against his leash and flecks of saliva flew from his mouth and Dennis felt them fall lightly on his hands and face.

Morley lifted one end of the chain toward Dennis. There was a thin, open collar attached to it.

"Once this closes it locks and can only be opened with this." Morley reached into his coat pocket and produced a key, held it up briefly and returned it. "There's a collar for Chum on the other end. Both are made out of good leather over strong, steel chain. See what I'm getting at here, Dennis?"

Morley leaned forward and snapped the collar around Dennis's neck.

"Oh, Dennis," Morley said, standing back to observe his handiwork. "It's you. Really. Great fit. And considering the day, just call this my valentine to you."

"You bastard."

"The biggest."

Morley walked over to Chum. Chum lunged at him, but with the muzzle on he was relatively harmless. Still, his weight hit Morley's legs, almost knocked him down.

Turning to smile at Dennis, Morley said, "See how strong he is? Add teeth to this little engine, some maneuverability . . . it's going to be awesome, lover boy. Awesome."

Morley slipped the collar under Chum's leash and snapped it into place even as the dog rushed against him, nearly knocking him down. But it wasn't Morley he wanted. He was trying to get at the smell. At Dennis. Dennis felt as if the fluids in his body were running out of drains at the bottoms of his feet.

"Was a little poontang worth this, Dennis? I certainly hope you think so. I hope it was the best goddamn piece you ever got. Sincerely, I do. Because death by dog is slow and ugly, lover boy. They like the throat and balls. So, you watch those spots, hear?"

"Morley, for God's sake, don't do this!"

Morley pulled a revolver from his coat pocket and walked over to Dennis. "I'm going to untie you now, stud. I want you to be real good, or I'll shoot you. If I shoot you, I'll gut shoot you, then let the dog loose. You got no chance that way. At least my way you've got a sporting chance—slim to none."

He untied Dennis. "Now stand."

Dennis stood in front of the chair, his knees quivering. He was looking at Chum and Chum was looking at him, tugging wildly at the leash, which looked ready to snap. Saliva was thick as shaving cream over the front of Chum's muzzle.

Morley held the revolver on Dennis with one hand, and with the other he reproduced the aerosol can, sprayed Dennis once more. The stench made Dennis's head float.

"Last word of advice," Morley said. "He'll go straight for you."

"Morley . . ." Dennis started, but one look at the man and he knew he was better off saving the breath. He was going to need it.

Still holding the gun on Dennis, Morley eased behind the frantic dog, took hold of the muzzle with his free hand, and with a quick ripping motion, pulled it and the leash loose.

Chum sprang.

Dennis stepped back, caught the chair between his legs, lost his balance. Chum's leap carried him into Dennis's chest, and they both went flipping over the chair.

Chum kept rolling and the chain pulled across Dennis's face as the dog tumbled to its full length; the jerk of the sixty pound weight against Dennis's neck was like a blow.

The chain went slack, and Dennis knew Chum was coming. In that same instant he heard the door open, glimpsed a wedge of moonlight that came and went, heard the door lock and Morley laugh. Then he was rolling, coming to his knees, grabbing the chair, pointing it with the legs out.

And Chum hit him.

The chair took most of the impact, but it was like trying to block a cannonball. The chair's bottom cracked and a leg broke off, went skidding across the floor.

The truncated triangle of the Doberman's head appeared over the top of the chair, straining for Dennis's face. Dennis rammed the chair forward.

Chum dipped under it, grabbed Dennis's ankle. It was like stepping into a bear trap. The agony wasn't just in the ankle, it was a sizzling web of electricity that surged through his entire body.

The dog's teeth grated bone and Dennis let forth with a noise that was too wicked to be called a scream.

Blackness waved in and out, but the thought of Julie lying there in ragged display gave him new determination.

He brought the chair down on the dog's head with all his might.

Chum let out a yelp, and the dark head darted away.

Dennis stayed low, pulled his wounded leg back, attempted to keep the chair in front of him. But Chum was a black bullet. He shot under again, hit Dennis in the same leg, higher up this time. The impact slid Dennis back a foot. Still, he felt a certain relief. The dog's teeth had missed his balls by an inch.

Oddly there was little pain this time. It was as if he were being encased in dark amber; floating in limbo. Must be like this when a shark hits, he thought. So hard and fast and clean you don't really feel it at first. Just go numb. Look down for your leg and it's gone.

The dark amber was penetrated by a bright stab of pain. But Dennis was grateful for it. It meant that his brain was working again. He swiped at Chum with the chair, broke him loose.

Swiveling on one knee, Dennis again used the chair as a shield. Chum launched forward, trying to go under it, but Dennis was ready this time and brought it down hard against the floor.

Chum hit the bottom of the chair with such an impact, his head broke through the thin slats. Teeth snapped in Dennis's face, but the dog couldn't squirm its shoulders completely through the hole and reach him.

Dennis let go of the chair with one hand, slugged the dog in the side of the head with the other. Chum twisted and the chair came loose from Dennis. The dog bounded away, leaping and whipping its body left and right, finally tossing off the wooden collar.

Grabbing the slack of the chain, Dennis used both hands to whip it into the dog's head, then swung it back and caught Chum's feet, knocking him on his side with a loud splat.

Even as Chum was scrambling to his feet, out of the corner of his eye Dennis spotted the leg that had broken off the chair. It was lying less than three feet away.

Chum rushed and Dennis dove for the leg, grabbed it, twisted and swatted at the Doberman. On the floor as he was, he couldn't get full power into the blow, but still it was a good one.

The dog skidded sideways on its belly and forelegs. When it came to a halt, it tried to raise its head, but didn't completely make it.

Dennis scrambled forward on his hands and knees, chopped the chair leg down on the Doberman's head with every ounce of muscle he could muster. The strike was solid, caught the dog right between the pointed ears and drove his head to the floor.

The dog whimpered. Dennis hit him again. And again.

Chum lay still.

Dennis took a deep breath, watched the dog and held his club cocked.

Chum did not move. He lay on the floor with his legs spread wide, his tongue sticking out of his foam-wet mouth.

Dennis was breathing heavily, and his wounded leg felt as if it were melting. He tried to stretch it out, alleviate some of the pain, but nothing helped.

He checked the dog again.

Still not moving.

He took hold of the chain and jerked it. Chum's head came up and smacked back down against the floor.

The dog was dead. He could see that.

He relaxed, closed his eyes and tried to make the spinning stop. He knew he had to bandage his leg somehow, stop the flow of blood. But at the moment he could hardly think.

And Chum, who was not dead, but stunned, lifted his head, and at the same moment, Dennis opened his eyes.

The Doberman's recovery was remarkable. It came off the floor with only the slightest wobble and jumped.

Dennis couldn't get the chair leg around in time and it deflected off of the animal's smooth back and slipped from his grasp.

He got Chum around the throat and tried to strangle him, but the collar was in the way and the dog's neck was too damn big.

Trying to get better traction, Dennis got his bad leg under him and made an effort to stand, lifting the dog with him. He used his good leg to knee Chum sharply in the chest, but the injured leg wasn't good for holding him up for another move like that. He kept trying to ease his thumbs beneath the collar and lock them behind the dog's windpipe.

Chum's hind legs were off the floor and scrambling, the toenails tearing at Dennis's lower abdomen and crotch.

Dennis couldn't believe how strong the dog was. Sixty pounds of pure muscle and energy, made more deadly by Morley's spray and tortures.

Sixty pounds of muscle.

The thought went through Dennis's head again.

Sixty pounds.

The medicine ball he tossed at the gym weighed more. It didn't have teeth, muscle and determination, but it did weigh more.

And as the realization soaked in, as his grip weakened and Chum's rancid breath coated his face, Dennis lifted his eyes to a rafter just two feet above his head; considered there was another two feet of space between the rafter and the ceiling.

He quit trying to choke Chum, eased his left hand into the dog's collar, and grabbed a hind leg with his other. Slowly, he lifted Chum over his head. Teeth snapped at Dennis's hair, pulled loose a few tufts.

Dennis spread his legs slightly. The wounded leg wobbled like an old pipe cleaner, but held. The dog seemed to weigh a hundred pounds. Even the sweat on his face and the dense, hot air in the room seemed heavy.

Sixty pounds.

A basketball weighed little to nothing, and the dog weighed less than the huge medicine ball in the gym. Somewhere between the two was a happy medium; he had the strength to lift the dog, the skill to make the shot—the most important of his life.

Grunting, cocking the wiggling dog into position, he prepared to shoot. Chum nearly twisted free, but Dennis gritted his teeth, and with a wild scream, launched the dog into space.

Chum didn't go up straight, but he did go up. He hit the top of the rafter with his back, tried to twist in the direction he had come, couldn't, and went over the other side.

Dennis grabbed the chain as high up as possible, bracing as Chum's weight came down on the other side so violently it pulled him onto his toes.

The dog made a gurgling sound, spun on the end of the chain, legs thrashing. It took a long fifteen minutes for Chum to strangle.

When Chum was dead, Dennis tried to pull him over the rafter. The dog's weight, Dennis's bad leg, and his now aching arms and back, made it a greater chore than he had anticipated. Chum's head kept slamming against the rafter. Dennis got hold of the unbroken chair, and used it as a step ladder. He managed the Doberman over, and Chum fell to the floor, his neck flopping loosely.

Dennis sat down on the floor beside the dog and patted it on the head. "Sorry," he said.

He took off his shirt, tore it into rags and bound his bad leg with it. It was still bleeding steadily, but not gushing; no major artery had been torn. His ankle wasn't bleeding as much, but in the dim lantern light he could see that Chum had bitten him to the bone. He used most of the shirt to wrap and strengthen the ankle.

When he finished, he managed to stand. The shirt binding had stopped the bleeding and the short rest had slightly rejuvenated him.

He found his eyes drawn to the mess in the corner that was Julie, and his first thought was to cover her, but there wasn't anything in the room sufficient for the job.

He closed his eyes and tried to remember how it had been before. When she was whole and the room had a mattress and they had made love all the long, sweet, Mexican afternoon. But the right images would not come. Even with his eyes closed, he could see her mauled body on the floor.

Ducking his head made some of the dizziness go away, and he was able to get Julie out of his mind by thinking of Morley. He wondered when he would come back. If he was waiting outside.

But no, that wouldn't be Morley's way. He wouldn't be anxious. He was cocksure of himself, he would go back to the estate for a drink and maybe play a game of chess against himself, gloat a long, sweet while before coming back to check on his handiwork. It would never occur to Morley to think he had survived. That would not cross his mind. Morley saw himself as Life's best chess master, and he did not make wrong moves; things went according to plan. Most likely, he wouldn't even check until morning.

The more Dennis thought about it, the madder he got and the stronger he felt. He moved the chair beneath the rafter where the lantern was hung, climbed up and got it down. He inspected the windows and doors. The door had a sound lock, but the windows were merely boarded. Barrier enough when he was busy with the dog, but not now.

He put the lantern on the floor, turned it up, found the chair leg he had used against Chum, and substituted it for a pry bar. It was hard work and by the time he had worked the boards off the window his hands were bleeding and full of splinters. His face looked demonic.

Pulling Chum to him, he tossed him out the window, climbed after him clutching the chair leg. He took up the chain's slack and hitched it around his forearm. He wondered about the other Dobermans. Wondered if Morley had killed them too, or if he was keeping them around. As he recalled, the Dobermans were usually loose on the yard at night. The rest of the time they had free run of the house, except Morley's study, his sanctuary. And hadn't Morley said that later on the spray killed a man's scent? That was worth something; it could be the edge he needed.

But it didn't really matter. Nothing mattered anymore. Six dogs. Six war elephants. He was going after Morley.

He began dragging the floppy-necked Chum toward the estate.

Morley was sitting at his desk playing a game of chess with himself, and both sides were doing quite well, he thought. He had a glass of brandy at his elbow, and from time to time he would drink from it, cock his head and consider his next move.

Outside the study door, in the hall, he could hear Julie's dogs padding nervously. They wanted out, and in the past they would have been on the yard long before now. But tonight he hadn't bothered. He hated those bastards, and just maybe he'd get rid of them. Shoot them and install a burglar alarm. Alarms didn't have to eat or be let out to shit, and they wouldn't turn on you. And he wouldn't have to listen to the sound of dog toenails clicking on the tile outside of his study door.

He considered letting the Dobermans out, but hesitated. Instead, he opened a box of special Cuban cigars, took one, rolled it between his fingers near his ear so he could hear the fresh crackle of good tobacco. He clipped the end off the cigar with a silver clipper, put it in his mouth and lit it with a desk lighter without actually putting the flame to it. He drew in a deep lungfull of smoke and relished it, let it out with a soft, contented sigh.

At the same moment he heard a sound, like something being dragged across the gravel drive. He sat motionless a moment, not batting an eye. It couldn't be lover boy, he thought. No way.

He walked across the room, pulled the curtain back from the huge glass door, unlocked it and slid it open.

A cool wind had come along and it was shaking the trees in the yard, but nothing else was moving. Morley searched the tree shadows for some tell-tale sign, but saw nothing.

Still, he was not one for imagination. He *had* heard something. He went back to the desk chair where his coat hung, reached the revolver from his pocket, turned.

And there was Dennis. Shirtless, one pants leg mostly ripped away. There were blood-stained bandages on his thigh and ankle. He had the chain partially coiled around one arm, and Chum, quite dead, was lying on the floor beside him. In his right hand Dennis held a chair leg, and at the same moment Morley noted this and raised the revolver, Dennis threw it.

The leg hit Morley squarely between the eyes, knocked him against his desk, and as he tried to right himself, Dennis took hold of the chain and used it to swing the dead dog. Chum struck Morley on the ankles and took him down like a scythe cutting fresh wheat. Morley's head slammed into the edge of the desk and blood dribbled into his eyes; everything seemed to be in a mixmaster, whirling so fast nothing was identifiable.

When the world came to rest, he saw Dennis standing over him with the revolver. Morley could not believe the man's appearance. His lips were split in a thin grin that barely showed his teeth. His face was drawn and his eyes were strange and savage. It was apparent he had found the key in the coat, because the collar was gone.

Out in the hall, bouncing against the door, Morley could hear Julie's dogs. They sensed the intruder and wanted at him. He wished now he had left the study door open, or put them out on the yard.

"I've got money," Morley said.

"Fuck your money," Dennis screamed. "I'm not selling anything here. Get up and get over here."

Morley followed the wave of the revolver to the front of his desk. Dennis swept the chess set and stuff aside with a swipe of his arm and bent Morley backwards over the desk. He put one of the collars around Morley's neck, pulled the chain around the desk a few times, pushed it under and fastened the other collar over Morley's ankles.

Tucking the revolver into the waistband of his pants, Dennis picked up Chum and tenderly placed him on the desk chair, half-curled. He tried to poke the dog's tongue back into his mouth, but that didn't work. He patted Chum on the head, said, "There, now."

Dennis went around and stood in front of Morley and looked at him, as if memorizing the moment.

At his back the Dobermans rattled the door.

"We can make a deal," Morley said. "I can give you a lot of money, and you can go away. We'll call it even."

Dennis unfastened Morley's pants, pulled them down to his knees. He pulled the underwear down. He went around and got the spray can out of Morley's coat and came back.

"This isn't sporting, Dennis. At least I gave you a fighting chance."

"I'm not a sport," Dennis said.

He sprayed Morley's testicles with the chemical. When he finished he tossed the canister aside, walked over to the door and listened to the Dobermans scuttling on the other side.

"Dennis!"

Dennis took hold of the doorknob.

"Screw you then," Morley said. "I'm not afraid. I won't scream. I won't give you the pleasure."

"You didn't even love her," Dennis said, and opened the door.

The Dobermans went straight for the stench of the spray, straight for Morley's testicles.

Dennis walked calmly out the back way, closed the glass door. And as he limped down the drive, making for the gate, he began to laugh.

Morley had lied. He did too scream. In fact, he was still screaming.

JOHN SHIRLEY
Equilibrium

John Shirley is the author of numerous novels of horror and the fantastic including *Cellars, In Darkness Waiting, Eclipse,* and *A Splendid Chaos.* "Equilibrium" is from his recently published collection *Heatseeker.*

Shirley is one of several young writers who can shift easily between science fiction, fantasy and horror. "Equilibrium," a psychological horror story, has no demons or beasties in it—except those in the mind. It is about a disturbed war veteran who decides to mete out his own brand of justice.

—E.D.

Equilibrium

JOHN SHIRLEY

He doesn't know me, but I know him. He has never seen me, but I know that he has been impotent for six months, can't shave without listening to the news on TV at the same time, and mixes bourbon with his coffee during his afternoon coffeebreak. And is proud of himself for holding off on the bourbon till the afternoon.

His wife doesn't know me, has never seen me, but I know that she regards her husband as "something to put up with, like having your period"; I know that she loves her children blindly, but just as blindly drags them through every wrong turn in their lives. I know the names and addresses of each one of her relatives, and what she does with her brother Charlie's photograph when she locks herself in the bathroom. She knows nothing of my family (I'm not admitting that I have one) but I know the birthdays and hobbies and companions of her children. The family of Marvin Ezra Hobbes. Co-starring: Lana Louise Hobbes as his wife, and introducing Bobby Hobbes and Robin Hobbes as their two sons. Play the theme music.

I know Robin Hobbes and he knows me. Robin and I were stationed together in Guatemala. We were supposed to be there for "exercises" but we were there to help train the Contras. It was a couple of years ago. The CIA wouldn't like it if I talk about the details, much.

I'm not the sort of person you'd write home about. But Robin told me a good many things, and even entrusted a letter to me. I was supposed to personally deliver it to his family (no, I never did have a family . . . really . . . I really didn't . . .) just in case anything "happened" to him. Robin always said that he wouldn't complain as long as "things turn out even." If a Sandinista shoots Robin's pecker away, Robin doesn't complain as long as a Sandinista gets *his* pecker blown away. Doesn't even have to be the same Sandinista. But the war wasn't egalitarian. It remained for me to establish equilibrium for Robin.

Robin didn't want to enlist. It was his parents' idea.

It had been raining for three days when he told me about it. The rain was like another place, a whole different part of the world, trying to assert itself over the one we were in. We had to make a third place inside the first one and the interfering one, had to get strips of tin and tire rubber and put them over our tent, because the tent fabric didn't keep out the rain after a couple of days. It steamed in there. My fingers were swollen from the humidity, and I had to take off the little platinum ring with the equal ($=$) sign on it. Robin hadn't said anything for a whole day, but then he just started talking, his voice coming out of the drone of the rain, almost the same tone, almost generated by it. " 'They're gonna start up the draft for real and earnest,' my dad said. 'You're just the right age. They'll get you sure. Thing to do is, join now. Then you can write your own ticket. Make a deal with the recruiter.' My dad wanted me out of the house. He wanted to buy a new car, and he couldn't afford it because he was supporting us all, and I was just another expense. That was what renewed my dad, gave him a sense that life had a goal and was worth living: a new car, every few years. Trade in the old one. Get a whole new debt. . . . My mom was afraid I'd be drafted too. I had an uncle was in the Marines, liked to act like he was a Big Man with the real in-the-know scuttlebutt; he wrote us and said the Defense Department was preparing for war, planning to invade Nicaragua, going to do some exercises down that way first. . . . So we thought the war was coming for real. Thought we had inside information. My mom wanted me to join to save my life, she said. So I could choose to go to someplace harmless, like Europe. But the truth is, she always was wet for soldiers. My uncle Charlie use to hang around in his dress uniform a lot. Looking like a stud. She was the only woman I ever knew who liked war movies. She didn't pay attention during the action parts; it wasn't that she was bloodthirsty. She liked to see them displaying their stripes and their braid and their spit and polish and marching in step, their guns sticking up. . . . So she sort of went all glazed when Dad suggested I join the Army and she didn't defend me when he started putting the guilt pressure on me about not getting a job and two weeks later I was recruited and the bastards lied about my assignment and here I fucking am, right here. It's raining. It's raining, man."

"Yeah," I said. "It'd be nice if it wasn't raining. But then we'd get too much sun or something. Has to balance out."

"I'm sick of you talking about balancing stuff out. I want it to stop raining."

So it did. The next day. That's when the Sandinistas started shelling the camp. Like the shells had been waiting on top of the clouds and when they pulled the clouds away, the trap door opened, and the mortar rounds fell through . . .

Immediately after something "happened" to Robin, I burned the letter he'd given me. Then I was transferred to the Fourth Army Clerical Unit. I know, deeply and intuitively, that the transfer was no accident. It placed me in an ideal position to initiate the balancing of Equilibrium and was therefore the work of the Composers. Because with the Fourth Clerical I was in charge of dispensing information to the families of the wounded or killed. I came across Robin

Hobbes's report, and promptly destroyed it. His parents never knew, till I played out my little joke. I like jokes. Jokes are always true, even when they're dirty lies.

I juggled the papers so that Robin Hobbes, twenty years old, would be sent to a certain sanitarium, where a friend of mine was a Meditech who worked admissions two days a week. The rest of the time he's what they call a Handler. A Psych Tech. My friend at the sanitarium likes the truth. He likes to see it, to smell it, particularly when it makes him gag. He took the job at the sanitarium with the eighteen-year-old autistics who bang their heads bloody if you don't tie them down and with the older men who have to be diapered and changed and rocked like babies and with the children whose faces are strapped into fencing masks to prevent them from eating the wallpaper and to keep them from pulling off their lips and noses—he took the job because he *likes* it there. He took it because he likes jokes.

And he took good care of Robin Hobbes for me until it was time. I am compelled to record an aside here, a well-done and sincere thanks to my anonymous friend for his enormous patience in spoon-feeding Robin Hobbes twice daily, changing his bedpan every night, and bathing him once a week for the entire six months' interment. He had to do it personally, because Robin was there illegally, and had to be hidden in the old wing they don't use anymore.

Meanwhile, I observed the Hobbes family.

They have one of those new bodyform cars. It's a fad thing. Marvin Hobbes got his new car. The sleek, fleshtone fiberglass body of the car is cast so that its sides are imprinted with the shape of a nude woman lying prone, her arms flung out in front of her in the diving motion of the Cannon beachtowel girl. The doors are in her ribs, the trunk opens from her ass. She's ridiculously improportional, of course. The whole thing is wildly kitsch. It was an embarrassment to Mrs. Hobbes. And Hobbes is badly in debt behind it, because he totaled his first bodyform car. Rammed a Buick Sissy Spacek into a Joe Namath pickup. Joe and Sissy's arms, tangled when their front bumpers slammed, were lovingly intertwined.

Hobbes took the loss, and bought a Miss America. He is indifferent to Mrs. Hobbes's embarrassment. To the particularly judgmental way she uses the term *tacky*.

Mr. Hobbes plays little jokes of his own. Private jokes. But I knew. Mr. Hobbes had no idea I was watching when he concealed his wife's Lady Norelco. He knew that she'd want it that night, because they were invited to a party, and she always shaved her legs before a party. Mrs. Hobbes sang a little tuneless song as she quested systematically for the shaver, bending over to look in the house's drawers and cabinets, and *behind* the drawers and cabinets, peering into all the secret nooks and burrow-places we forget a house has; her search was so thorough I came to regard it as the product of mania. I felt a sort of warmth, then: I can appreciate . . . thoroughness.

Once a week, he did it to her. He'd temporarily pocket her magnifying mirror, her makeup case. Then he'd pretend to find it. "Where any idiot can see it."

Bobby Hobbes, Robin's younger brother, was unaware that his father knew about his hidden cache of Streamline racing-striped condoms. The elder Hobbes thought he was very clever, in knowing about them. But he didn't know about me.

Marvin Hobbes would pocket his son's rubbers and make *snuck-snuck* sounds of muffled laughter in his sinuses as the red-eared teenager feverishly searched and rechecked his closet and drawers.

Hobbes would innocently saunter in and ask, "Hey—you better get goin' if you're gonna make that date, right? Whatcha lookin' for anyway? Can I help?"

"Oh . . . uh, no thanks, Dad. Just some . . . socks. Missing."

As the months passed, and Hobbes's depression over his impotence worsened, his fits of practical joking became more frequent, until he no longer took pleasure in them, but performed his practical jokes as he would some habitual household chore. Take out the trash, cut the lawn, hide Lana's razor, feed the dog.

I watched as Hobbes, driven by some undefined desperation, attempted to relate to his relatives. He'd sit them at points symmetrical (relative to him) around the posh living room; his wife thirty degrees to his left, his youngest son thirty degrees to his right. Then, he would relate a personal childhood experience as a sort of parable, describing his hopes and dreams for his little family.

"When I was a boy we would carve out tunnels in the briar bushes. The wild blackberry bushes were very dense, around our farm. It'd take hours to clip three feet into them with the gardener's shears. But after weeks of patient work, we snipped a network of crude tunnels through the half-acre filled with brambles. In this way, we learned how to cope with the world as a whole. We would crawl through the green tunnels in perfect comfort, but knowing that if we stood up, the thorns would cut us to ribbons."

He paused and sucked several times loudly on the pipe. It had gone out ten minutes before. He stared at the fireplace where there was no fire.

Finally he asked his wife, "Do you understand?" Almost whining it.

She shook her head ruefully. Annoyed, his jaws bruxating, Hobbes slipped to the floor, muttering he'd lost his tobacco pouch, searching for it under the coffee table, under the sofa. His son didn't smile, not once. His son had hidden the tobacco pouch. Hobbes went scurrying about on the rug looking for the tobacco pouch in a great dither of confusion, like a poodle searching for his rawhide bone. Growling low. Growling to himself.

Speculation as to how I came to know these intimate details of the Hobbes family life will prove as futile as Marvin's attempt to relate to his relatives.

I have my ways. I learned my techniques from other Composers.

Presumably, Composers belong to a tacit network of free agents the world over, whose sworn duty it is to establish states of interpersonal Equilibrium. No Composer has ever knowingly met another; it is impossible for them to meet, even by accident, since they carry the same charge and therefore repel from each other. I'm not sure just how the invisible Composers taught me their technique for the restoration of states of Equilibrium. To be precise, I *am* sure as to how it was done—I simply can't articulate it.

I have no concrete evidence that the Composers exist. Composers perform the same service for society that vacuum tubes used to perform for radios and amplifiers. And the fact of a vacuum tube's existence is proof that someone must have the knowledge, somewhere, needed to construct a vacuum tube. Necessity is its own evidence.

Now picture this: Picture me with a high forehead crowned by white hair and a square black graduation cap with its tassel dangling. Picture me with a drooping white mustache and wise blue eyes. In fact, I look a lot like Albert Einstein, in this picture. I am wearing a black graduation gown, and clutched in my right hand is a long wooden pointer.

I don't have a high forehead. I don't have any hair at all. No mustache. Not even eyebrows. I don't have blue eyes. (Probably, neither did Einstein.) I don't look like Einstein in the slightest. I don't own a graduation gown, and I never completed a college course.

But picture me that way. I am pointing at a home movie screen with my official pointer. On the screen is a projection of a young man who has shaved himself bald and who wears a tattered Army uniform with a Clerical Corps patch on the right shoulder, half peeled off. The young man has his back to the home movie camera. He is playing a TV-tennis game. This was one of the first video games. Each player is given a knob which controls a vertical white dash designating the 'tennis racket,' one to each half of the television screen. On a field of blank gray the two white dashes bandy between them a white blip, the 'tennis ball.' With a flick of the dial, snapping the dash/racket up or down, one knocks the blip past the other electronic paddle and scores a point. Jabbing here and there at the movie screen I indicate that the game is designed for two people. I nod my head sagely. But this mysterious young man manipulates left and right dials with both hands at once. (If you look closely at his hands, you'll note that the index finger of his left hand is missing. The index finger of his right hand is missing, too.) Being left-handed, when he first began to play himself, the left hand tended to win. But he establishes perfect equilibrium in the interactive poles of his parity. The game is designed to continue incessantly until fifteen points are scored by either side. He nurtured his skill until he could play against himself for long hours, beeping a white blip with euphoric monotony back and forth between wrist-flicks, never scoring a point for either hand.

He never wins, he never loses, he establishes perfect equilibrium.

The movie ends, the professor winks, the young man was at no time turned to face the camera.

My practical joke was programmed to compose an Equilibrium for Robin Hobbes and his family. Is it Karma? Are the Composers the agents of Karma? No. There is no such thing as Karma: that is why the Composers are necessary. To redress the negligence of God. We try. But in establishing the Equilibrium—something far more refined than vengeance—we invariably create another imbalance, for justice cannot be precisely quantified. And the new imbalance gives rise to a contradictory inversity, and so the Perfect and Mindless Dance of equilibrium proceeds. For there to be a premise there must somewhere exist its contradiction.

Hence I present my clue to the Hobbeses encrypted in a reversal of the actual situation.

In the nomenclature of the Composers, a snake symbolizes an octopus. The octopus has eight legs, the snake is legless. The octopus is the greeting, the snake is the reply; the centipede is the greeting, the worm is the reply.

And so I selected the following document, an authentic missive illicitly obtained from a certain obsessive cult, and mailed it to the Hobbeses, as my clue offered in all fairness; the inverted foreshadowing:

My dear, dear Tonto,

You recall, I assume, that Perfect and Holy Union I myself ordained, in my dominion as High Priest—the marriage of R. and D., Man and Wife in the unseeing eyes of the Order, they were obligated to seek a means of devotion and worship, in accordance with their own specialties and proclivities. I advised them to jointly undertake the art of Sensual Communion with the Animus, and this they did, and still they were unsatisfied. Having excelled in the somatic explorations that are the foundation of the Order, they were granted leave to follow the lean of their own inclinations. Thus liberated, they settled on the fifth Degree in Jolting, the mastery of self-modification. They sought out a surgeon who, for an inestimable price, fused their bodies into one. They became Siamese twins; the woman joined to his right side. They were joined at the waist through an unbreakable bridge of flesh. This grafting made sexual coupling, outside of fondling, nearly impossible. The obstacle, as we say in the Order, is the object. But R. was not content. Shorn of normal marital relations, R.'s latent homosexuality surfaced. He took male lovers and his wife was forced to lay beside the copulating men, forced to observe everything, and advised to keep her silence except in the matter of insisting on latex condoms. At first this stage left her brimming with revulsion; but she became aware that through the bridge of flesh which linked them she was receiving, faintly at first and then more strongly, her husband's impressions. In this way she was vicariously fulfilled and in the fullness of time no longer objected when he took to a homosexual bed. R.'s lovers accepted her presence, as if she were the incarnate spirit of the frustrated feminine persona which was the mainspring of their inner clockworks. But when their new complacency was established, the obstacle diminished. It became necessary to initiate new somatic obstacles. Inevitably, another woman was added to the Siamese coupling, to make it a tripling, a woman on R.'s left. Over a period of several months more were added, after the proper blood tests. Today, they are joined to six other people in a ring of exquisite Siamese multiplicity. The juncturing travels in a circle so the first is joined to the eighth, linked with someone else on both sides. All face inward. There are four men and four women, a literal wedding ring. (Is this a romantic story, Tonto?) Arrayed as they are in an unbreakable ring, they necessarily go to great lengths to overcome practical and psychological handicaps. For example, they had to practice for two days to learn how to collectively board D.'s Lear Jet. Four, usually the women, ride in the arms of the other four; they sidle into the plane, calling signals for the steps. This enforced teamwork lends a new perspective to the most mundane daily affairs. Going to the toilet becomes a yogic exercise requiring the utmost concentration. For but one man to pee, each of the joined must provide a precisely measured degree of pressure. . . . They have been surgically arranged so that each man can copulate with the woman opposite him or, in turns, the man diagonal. Homosexual relations are limited to one coupling at a time since members of the same sex are diagonal to one another. Heterosexually, the cell has sex simultaneously. The surgeons have continuated the nerve ends through the links so that the erogenous sensations of one are shared by all. I was privileged to observe one of these highly practiced acrobatic orgies. I admit to a secret yen to participate, to stand nude in the center of the circle and experience flesh-tone piston-action from every point of the compass. But this is below my Degree; only the High Priest's divine mount, the Perfect and Unscrubbed *Silver*, may know him carnally. . . . Copulating as an octuplet whole, they resemble a pink sea anemone capturing a wriggling minnow. Or perhaps interlocked fingers of arm wrestlers. Or a letter written all in one paragraph, a single unit. . . . But suppose a fight breaks out between the grafted Worshippers? Suppose one of them should die or take sick? If one contracts an illness, all ultimately come down with it. And if one should die, they would have to carry the corpse wherever they went until it rotted away—the operation is irreversible. But that is all part of the Divine Process.

> Yours very, very affectionately,
> The Lone Ranger

Mrs. Hobbes found the letter in the mailbox, and opened it. She read it with visible alarm, and brought it to her husband, who was in the backyard, preparing to barbecue the ribs of a pig. He was wearing an apron printed with the words, DON'T FORGET TO KISS THE CHEF. The word FORGET was almost obliterated by a rusty splash of sauce.

Hobbes read the letter, frowning. "I'll be goshdarned," he said. "They get crazier with this junk mail all the time. Goddamned pornographic." He lit the letter on fire and used it to start the charcoal.

Seeing this, I smiled with relief, and softly said: "Click!" A letter for a letter, equilibrium for the destruction of the letter Robin Hobbes had given me in

Guatemala. If Mr. and Mrs. Hobbes had discerned the implication of the inverted clue I would have been forced to release Robin from the sanitarium, to the custody of the Army.

When the day came for my joke, I had my friend bring Robin over to my hotel room which was conveniently two blocks from the Hobbes' residence.

It should be a harmless gesture to describe my friend, as long as I don't disclose his name. Not a Composer in face but one in spirit, my Meditech friend is pudgy and square shouldered. His legs look like they're too thin for his body. His hair is clipped close to his small skull and there is a large white scar dividing his scalp, running from the crown of his head to the bridge of his nose. The scar is a gift from one of his patients, given in an unguarded moment. My friend wears thick wire-rim glasses with an elastic band connecting them in the rear.

Over Robin's noisy protests I prepared him for the joke. To shut him up I considered cutting out his tongue. But that would require compensating with some act restoring equilibrium which I had not time to properly devise. So I settled for adhesive tape, over his mouth. And of course the other thing, stuck through a hole in the tape.

Mr. Hobbes was at home, his Miss America bodyform car filled the driveway. The front of the car was crumpled from a minor accident of the night before, and her arms were corrugated, bent unnaturally inward, one argent hand shoved whole into her open and battered mouth.

Suppressing sniggers—I admit this freely, we were like two twelve-year-olds —my friend and I brought Robin to the porch and rang the doorbell. We dashed to the nearest concealment, a holly bush undulating in the faint summer breeze.

It was shortly after sunset, eight-thirty p.m. and Mr. Hobbes had just returned from a long Tuesday at the office. He was silent and grumpy, commiserating with his abused Miss America. Two minutes after our ring, Marvin Hobbes opened the front door, newspaper in hand. My friend had to bite his lip to keep from laughing out loud. But for me, the humor had quite gone out of the moment. It was a solemn moment, one with a dignified and profound resonance.

Mrs. Hobbes peered over Marvin's shoulder, electric shaver in her right hand; Bobby, behind her, stared over the top of her wig, something hidden in his left hand. Simultaneously, the entire family screamed, their instantaneous timing perhaps confirming that they were true relatives after all.

They found Rob as we had left him on the doorstep, swaddled in baby blankets, diapered in a couple of Huggies disposable diapers, a pacifier stuck through the tape over his mouth, covered to the neck in gingham cloth (though one of his darling stumps peeked through). And equipped with a plastic baby bottle. The shreds of his arms and legs had been amputated shortly after the mortar attack on Puerto Barrios. Pinned to his chest was a note (I lettered it myself in the crude handwriting I thought would reflect the mood of a desperate mother.) The note said:

PLEASE TAKE CARE OF MY BABY

JOE HALDEMAN
Time Lapse

Hugo and Nebula awards-winner Joe Haldeman, best known for his science fiction novels, is also an award-winning SF poet. "Saul's Death," a heroic sestina, won the Rhysling Award; "DX," a poem about Vietnam, appeared in our first annual collection. His most recent novels are *Buying Time* and *The Hemingway Hoax*.

"Time Lapse" is a painful portrait of a domestic tragedy in which the trust between parent and child is violated, with long term effects. This poem first appeared in *Blood Is Not Enough*.

—E.D.

Time Lapse

JOE HALDEMAN

At first a pink whirl
there on the white square:
the girl too small to stay still.

    After a few years, though
    (less than a minute),
    her feet stay in the same place.

Her pink body vibrates with undiscipline;
her hair a blond fog. She grows now
perceptibly. Watch . . . she's seven,
eight, nine: one year each twelve seconds.

        Always, now, in the audience,
        a man clears his throat.
        Always, a man.

Almost every morning
for almost eighteen years,
she came to the small white room,
put her bare feet on the cold floor,
on the pencilled H's,
and stood with her hands palms out
while her father took four pictures:
both profiles, front, rear.

504

It was their secret. Something
they did for Mommy in heaven,
a record of the daughter
she never lived to see.

    By the time she left (rage and something
    else driving her to the arms of a woman)
    he had over twenty thousand
    eight-by-ten glossy prints of her
    growing up, locked in white boxes.

He sought out a man with a laser
who some called an artist
(some called a poseur),
with a few quartets of pictures,
various ages: baby, child, woman.
He saw the possibilities.
He paid the price.

    It took a dozen Kelly Girls
    thirty working hours apiece
    to turn those files of pretty pictures
    into digits. The artist,
    or showman,
    fed the digits into his machines,
    and out came a square
    of white where
    in more than three dimensions
    a baby girl
    grows into a woman
    in less than four minutes.

Always a man clears his throat.
The small breasts bud

    and swell in seconds. Secret
    places grow blond stubble, silk;
    each second a spot of blood.

Her stance changes
as hips push out
and suddenly
she puts her hands on her hips.
For the last four seconds,
four months;
a gesture of defiance.

The second time you see her
(no one watches only once),
concentrate on her expression.
The child's ambiguous flicker
becomes uneasy smile,
trembling thirty times a second.
The eyes, a blur at first,
stare fixedly
in obedience
and then
(as the smile hardens)
the last four seconds,
four months:

     a glare of rage

    All unwilling,
    she became the most famous
    face and figure of her age.
    Everywhere stares.
    As if Mona Lisa, shawled,
    had walked into the Seven/Eleven . . .

    No wonder she killed her father.

     The judge was sympathetic.
     The jury wept for her.
     They studied the evidence
     from every conceivable angle:

Not guilty,
by reason of insanity.

So now she spends her days
listening quietly, staring
while earnest people talk,
trying to help her grow.

     But every night she starts to scream
     and has to be restrained, sedated,
     before she'll let them take her back

    to rest

        in her small white room.

GARRY KILWORTH

White Noise

Garry Kilworth is a Briton temporarily living with his wife in Hong Kong. His most recent collection of stories, *In the Hollow of the Deep-Sea Wave* was published in Great Britain by The Bodley Head. His mainstream story, "The Blood Orange," has been selected by Ruth Rendell for a "Best Of" collection in England.

"White Noise," from *Zenith*, is one of a number of stories in this collection with a science fiction premise that generates a horrific sensibility. Sometimes uncertainty can keep a person sane.

—E.D.

White Noise

GARRY KILWORTH

I was sitting at a street table under the awning of an Arab coffee stall. Ben, my chief engineer, was drinking *mazqul*, a coffee too bitter for my palate. Having been raised in Italy, he was used to thick brown sludge. I drank orange juice.

It was evening and the sound of the muezzins calling the faithful to prayer could be heard floating over the rooftops. I suspected that like some English churches, with their tape recordings of bells, the voices came from hi-fi speakers situated at the top of minarets. Despite the fact that I was (and still am) the Regional Telecommunications Manager in an independent Arab state, I dislike this dehumanizing approach.

Ben was talking about two of our technicians who had recently been sent to check on an installation on the shores of the Red Sea.

"They didn't go in," he said. "They were scared."

My company's head office is in London, where they recruit telecommunications personnel for overseas appointments. Ben, now thirty, had joined us as a nineteen-year-old and his English was impeccable. His full name was Peter Benoni and like myself he was a telecommunications man through and through. If you get into telecomms early enough, it becomes a religion. Ben was the same. We cut our teeth on morse keys, accepted the coming of teleprinters with eagerness, hailed the introduction of satellite communications and were patiently awaiting worldwide networks of fibre optic cables. One of its attractions was that it was continually changing, progressing, and its mysteries deepened rather than were resolved.

Ben seemed angry for some reason, as if the fact that the technicians had failed to do their work was a slight on him, personally. He had recently been through a terrible ordeal and I knew I had to be patient with his apparent moodiness.

"Scared?" I said. I couldn't think why the two Arabs should be frightened to enter a cable station. There was nothing in these unmanned buildings except terminals, where the undersea cable was converted to overhead cross-country lines.

"Yes, afraid."

"What of?" I was thinking of terrorists—republicans opposed to the royalist government—but Ben's reply surprised me.

"They say it's haunted, the cable station."

"I don't understand."

A pi-dog slunk under the table looking for scraps. Ben moved it on gently with his foot. The creatures were covered in tics and fleas.

"Not much to understand. They're a superstitious lot." He flicked a dead fly from the tabletop. There was contempt in his voice. "They're terrified of ghosts. What can you expect?"

"I expect them to do their jobs. *Haunted?* The cable station? What about that old fort where they spend the night? Surely there are more ghosts in places like that than a newly-built cable station?"

Ben shrugged. We talked a little more, but the darkness had closed in around us and I wanted to be back in my rooms. I agreed with Ben that the best idea was to visit the station ourselves. At least we would get some first-hand knowledge of the situation and as manager I was expected to cover my region, checking on all installations at least once a year. Now was a good enough time as any to inspect Wadi Haalla.

Back in my quarters I began packing a few items for the trip the next day. Now that it was dark and the town was silent except for the dogs, sounds began to travel farther. I could hear Ben behind the thin walls, in his own apartment. He paced up and down for about thirty minutes, his flip-flops slapping on the tiled floors. Then he began his nightly prayers. I sat on the edge of my bed, the droning more irritating to me than the whine of a mosquito. Finally I put my hands over my ears. I had nothing but contempt for Ben's devotions. I had long since discovered that there was no God.

We set off the next morning. Apart from provisions we carried rifles in the Land Rover, since terrorist activity was reaching alarming levels. Ben had recently been kidnapped by some republican extremists and though he escaped he had to walk three days in the desert to get back to civilization. Characteristically, he maintained that it was his faith that had kept him alive. Once, when I asked him what that meant, he went into a tiresome lecture. The crux of his argument appeared to be the need for belief without conclusive proof.

"The existence of absolute proof negates the need for *faith*," he said, "and without faith we would be nothing more than automatons."

The tyres of the vehicle hummed on the hot asphalt until we had gone about fifty miles, when we left the tarmac and followed a dirt track between two mountain ranges. Ben was silent most of the way. Sullen and uncommunicative, he left me to stare at the gravel wastes as we bumped and bounced along. I tried to fight the despair that hunted me down at moments like this, but it was a persistent predator, intent on devouring me.

We camped for the night at the foot of some rocks that rose like lava tongues out of the dust. I sucked on a bottle of scotch that I'd packed the night before, and sensed Ben's disapproval. He busied himself around the campsite while I got quietly drunk.

I lay back in the stillness of the desert, staring up at the stars. I thought about Sally. Sally had died in an aircraft accident, on her way out to join me. It had taken her a long time to decide, but once her mind had been made up, she wrote to me that she was on her way. Ironically, I knew that she was already dead by the time I received the letter. They said that there was a bomb on the plane, but no one knew for sure. What I never understood was, why Sally? I know, I know, *why anyone*, but Sally—Sally bubbled with enthusiasm for life. Why not some bastard the world would be better without? Why not some suicide, bent on going anyway? I know these things are not meant to make sense, but they damn well *should* do. I felt sure, absolutely sure, that if there had been a God he would never have wiped out Sally. She had done nothing but sung His praises all her life, and actively worked on His behalf. Why would He kill one of His most ardent supporters or even allow her to die? No, it *didn't* make sense, and therefore there was no God. Ben was wasting his breath on worshipping a void. The whole thing was a blank, a mistake. There was nothing to look forward to after death. And that was the worst thing—the very worst thing about it.

I finished the bottle, throwing it out amongst the rocks and enjoying the sound of breaking glass. I still found it hard to get to sleep. Even a day in the desert gives one a kind of circular mental perspective. The tedium of mile on mile of gravel and rock *must* make some impression on the mind. I used to think, before I came to know the desert, that such a place would leave one's head uncluttered and receptive. In fact, the real experience is quite the opposite. You tend to lock into a set of thoughts that go round and round, like those of an insomniac, and if you do not take care you begin to translate particular obsessions into visual images. Mirages. Each time I go back in I am surprised by the swiftness with which an empty desolate landscape can work on an active mind. After a walk in the desert one might see an ordinary bush burning and believe it to be something miraculous.

At noon two days later, we reached our destination. Ben and I had not been speaking to each other over the last few rugged miles. Some trivial argument had left us both feeling aggrieved: a common enough problem out in the wilderness. Once we got back to town we would forget it quickly enough.

The cable station was perched on a knoll above its surroundings. Between the sea and this hill, and stretching for several miles on either side, were the coastal marshes. It was a typical river delta, which would be completely flooded in the rainy season, but at the moment the wadi was only ankle deep in brackish water, maintaining the life of the reed beds around the station.

In the noon-day sun the rushes looked crisp and brown, rippling gently in the hot onshore breezes from the Red Sea.

The place was alive with insects, which danced in clouds above the tips of the reeds: a quiet, eerie landscape which had not changed in thousands of years.

There was an alarming sense of a brooding past which hung over the region. It whispered of papyrus and reed boats, of infants abandoned in watertight cradles amongst the rushes. It murmured of fishers and hunters, and primitive tribal religions. And over the whole of the rock and dust hinterland, a throbbing heat, a moody sense of injustice over some imagined neglect.

The station on the top of the hill was the only object, natural or artificial, that anchored us in the modern world. It was the junction for the undersea telephone cable from Cairo. It was a simple square structure, built to house line checking equipment and terminals. On its land side, the incoming cable became overhead wires looped across the desert rockland on poles, and up, over the mountains, to the exchange in the nearest town.

We were making our way up the slope to the station, when Ben suddenly stopped and turned to stare out over the shimmering marshland.

"What's the matter?" I asked.

He waved a hand at me. "Listen!"

I listened but could hear only the station. Someone had left a speaker plugged into a line and white noise was hissing out.

"No wonder the technicians were scared," said Ben, after a few moments.

"What? I can't hear anything."

"That's just it—we should be hearing wildlife. These marshes are crammed with creatures—birds, frogs, cicadas. They're normally singing their heads off."

He was right. I hadn't noticed how quiet it was. Ben started off down the slope, and I followed him. If something was nagging at him, we would have to get it sorted out before going up to the station. I really could not understand what all the fuss was about. So the marshes were quite? So what?

We went into the boggy ground and Ben searched amongst the tall grasses. I was hot. Sweat had soaked the back of my shirt. My hat was uncomfortable and my scalp prickled with the heat. I just wanted to get the job done and find a cool place to rest. Pretty soon he picked something up and held it out to me. A small green frog rested on his palm.

"Well?" I snapped.

"They're here," he said, his dark brown eyes looking puzzled, "but they're not making any sounds. That isn't natural, you have to admit."

The creature's small black eyes seemed fixed on some distant horizon that was hidden from us. There was something about its position which for a moment suggested genuflection. I started to laugh. The situation was becoming ludicrous and our imaginations were running away with us. There was something quite sinister in the air, but I couldn't pin it down, and laughing helped to dispel it.

Ben's eyes were on my face at that point, but then he turned his head, very slowly, until his gaze was high above my left shoulder, and distant. He was staring at the cable station.

"It's listening to *that*," he said.

I began to get annoyed.

"The white noise? Oh, come on. What are you, a zoologist now? How can you tell what it's listening to, if anything at all. This is crazy, Ben."

I should have taken the initiative at that point. I should have left him there and marched up to the shack, disconnected the speaker, and begun the checks. If I had done that, I'm sure he would have shaken out of the mood he had suddenly fallen into. The practicalities of the work would have taken over, and he would have slipped into his routine. However, I did not do this. I simply waited, my impatience increasing with every moment, for Ben to put down the frog and get to work himself.

Finally he replaced the creature in the reeds and made his way up the slope to the station. I followed behind. There wasn't a lot of point in remonstrating with him. I'm not one of these autocratic managers anyway. I prefer reaching decisions democratically.

We unlocked the door to the building and entered the confined space. Musty, stale air hit us. The station was like an oven inside.

Sure enough, someone had left a speaker plugged into the line. There were microphone implants in the cable repeater units all along the sea bed. What we were hearing over the speaker was the noise of the ocean floor. The mikes helped us identify any interference with the cable, by sharks, or fishing nets, any external agent.

Ben disconnected the speaker and plugged a set of headphones into the same channel. Then he sat on a dusty stool and began listening intently to the white noise, the backwash of sounds from the sea bed. I stood and watched him for a while, but there was little I could do while he was sitting at the console, so I left him to it. I went outside to get some air. There were checks I had to make, too, but I wanted Ben to finish his work first, and leave me alone in the station.

I crossed the marshland, wary of snakes, to reach the beach. There, the thick black cable emerged from the ocean. Out on the Red Sea a dhow was treading slowly westwards, following an ancient road to Africa. I studied the point where the cable came out of the water like a satanic python slithering up the beach. Snakes. Satan. All my images were biblical. I couldn't even string a set of thoughts together without a religious intrusion, damn it. God and all his trappings had been invented by some sadist to torment people like me.

I must have fallen asleep, and some time later, perhaps an hour, a shadow fell over me. I woke, startled. Ben was standing there. He had a rifle in the crook of his arm and his eyes had taken on that intense look which meant he was disturbed about something.

"What's the matter?" I asked.

"Come and listen," he answered.

I followed him to the station, wondering why he had gone back to the Land Rover for the gun. Was he expecting trouble? I asked him, but got no reply. Once in the station, he motioned for me to put on the headphones. I did so and my head was immediately swamped with white noise. There was a faint rumbling thunder, like surf crashing over groynes. A kind of hollow booming. Breakers along the beach? What did it mean? I took off the headphones and looked up at Ben, inquisitively.

"Do you hear it?" he said.

"Do I hear what?"

"The *noise*. The noise of the battle. It's coming directly from the sea bed.

Cold current tapes—remember the article from Comms Monthly? I cut it out and left it on your desk."

I was wilting in the oppressive heat. The situation seemed to be a little unstable. I said, "Have you done the checks?" and he looked at me as if he were exasperated.

"The article," he insisted. "About the American submarine. Last year they were doing an oceanic survey and they picked up the noise of sea fights on the mikes they placed on the sea bed. I talked to you about it at the time."

I recalled the article now. "Yes, I do remember. They came to the conclusion that cold currents retained sound impressions . . ."

"That's it. Cold, dense water is less likely to disperse, or be infiltrated by warm streams. The circular currents weave their way intact around the ocean floor like blind worms."

"And they retain sound patterns . . ."

"Like magnetic tape. When the scientists from that survey analysed the recordings they discovered they were listening to sea battles from the First World War."

"So they say—it must have been guesswork. Anyway, you think that's what we've got here? Sounds of battle? What, from the Six Day War? Or Yom Kippur?"

Ben shook his head vigorously. "No, not that. Not so recent. Some of the cold currents in these regions have been around for thousands of years."

"And?"

"So what we're receiving from our mikes is an *ancient* fight—a retreat across the Red Sea. Listen again."

He looked very wild and I obediently put on the headphones. I wanted to say something banal, about getting the job done, doing the checks, finishing up, and *then* perhaps discussing weird phenomena, but the atmosphere was tense. I felt myself being mentally pressured into humouring his mood. My idea at that time was to listen, to agree with him that he could be right, then suggest we do the work before the day ran out on us.

So, I listened.

"Close your eyes—concentrate," said Ben.

I did as he asked. The problem with putting on a set of headphones is that you effectively lock out the rest of the world. You enter another world completely and you find that all your attention is directed towards the sounds in your head. After a while I *could* hear faint shouts and yells, under the rush and hiss of the white noise. Perhaps, perhaps the rumbling of wheels, the rattle of metal . . . ? I tried rejecting these ideas and replacing them with the thought of trawler nets snagging the cable, or predatory fish worrying the repeaters. It didn't work. These were different sounds. I had heard that sort of interference and it was nothing like the noise coming from the headphones now. These were *new* sounds, the like of which I had not heard before. I began to get excited. Surely Ben was right! I could hear it. However, I know that if you listen to something hard enough, with preconceived notions, suggestion fills any hollows. I tried to clear my head, listen objectively. Still, I could hear the shouts, the clashing of— what?—bronze swords on shields? Surely those sharp cracks were whips? I looked up at Ben. His eyes were shining strangely. I took off the headphones.

"We have to tape this," I said. "Have it analysed."

"I don't think that's a good idea." He glanced at the console and then at me again. "I don't think that's a good idea at all."

I was surprised. Ben was one of those men who are passionately in favour of finding new uses for telecomms equipment. He loved to experiment with such things. What the hell was he playing at now?

"What's wrong with it?" I asked, calmly.

"We might hear something that would destroy us."

His eyes had taken on a heavy hooded appearance and he began to fiddle with the rifle's safety catch. I did not have a clue what he was talking about, but his whole attitude made my skin prickle with apprehension.

He nodded at the headphones, which were still gushing out their sounds of battle. "What we have here," he said, slowly, "is the flight from Egypt—Moses and his people."

"Moses," I repeated.

"That's right." He paced up to the small window at the end and stared out at the sea. I was sweating heavily and I could feel the wetness trickling down my neck. Ben still seemed calm enough, holding the rifle loosely in the crook of his arm. I noticed that the safety catch was now off. My heart was racing but my brain felt leaden.

"You see," he said, "although there was a path across the Red Sea—the parting of the waters—there must have been water all around them, towering above them. A tunnel of water, recording the events that took place on the ocean bed. The crossing of the Red Sea. The flight from Egypt. You know where we are. It happened *here*."

I heard screams coming from the speakers. The sounds of water rushing into a gap. Horses whinnying in fear. Harsh calls from the mouths of men who were used to being masters. Again, the cracking of whips, the slapping of leather harnesses. The rumble of chariot wheels. Surely I was just fitting images to random noises? *Fata Morgana*. Sound mirages.

"Impressionable," I heard myself muttering. "The desert softens our brains and suggestions leave imprints. We are seduced by each other's imaginations. We must be careful of our theories, we . . . our perceptions are warped out here. Too eager. That frog, for example . . ."

"The frogs and crickets? They know. They're waiting to hear."

"Hear what?"

He turned to face me. He seemed completely in control of himself. "The voice of God," he said, simply.

I rocked back a little on my seat. Although he had spoken the words soberly, quietly, I felt as if he had shouted at me in rage. I was disorientated for a moment and had to pull my thoughts together, to regain my equilibrium.

"The voice of God," I repeated, slowly.

"God spoke to Moses, and if we're right, that what we're listening to on that speaker is the flight from Egypt, then it will not be long before we hear the voice of God."

Suddenly he strode across the room, reached over me, and pulled out the plug, so that we were in silence.

"What?—what the hell are you doing?" I cried.

He stared hard at me. "We mustn't hear it," he said. "This is not meant for our ears. If we were to hear God speak, we would *know*. We would know for sure. It would make a worthless thing of faith."

"You're crazy."

"Perhaps, but I don't want to take the chance. Maybe God didn't speak to Moses while he was making the crossing. Maybe I'm all wrong about the whole thing. But I can't risk it."

I knew his ideas on the evils of *proof absolute*, how such a thing would destroy the soul, the need for a spirit within a mortal. But what about *my* needs? Didn't I get a choice? I knew what I wanted, too. I had seen a way out of the grief that had been troubling me for so long. There was a way the nightmares could end, a way the cycle of obsessive thoughts could be broken. As far as I was concerned Ben could go to heaven or hell, so long as it could be proved that such places existed outside the human imagination.

I reached for the plug.

"Go and stuff—your ears. I want to know if I'm going to see Sally again—I want . . ." I felt a blow behind the left ear and I staggered, half falling, half crawling, to the open doorway.

"You bastard—" I began, but he pushed me through the doorway, into the dust outside. I stumbled away, thinking he was crazy enough at that moment to shoot me in the back. My guts were churning with fear. I heard him firing the rifle in the station. I guessed he was destroying the console so that I would not be able to go back and record the sounds. By the time I had it repaired, the cold current would be gone. I reached the bottom of the hill and fell on my side, panting.

The next moment there was a tremendous explosion which rocked the whole delta. A hot wind blasted my cheek and I was showered with grit and small stones. When I was brave enough to look back, I could see that the station had been gutted. Although the walls were still standing, the window had been blown out and the roof had gone. Fire engulfed the interior.

"Ben, you bastard," I screamed with rage. "I wanted to hear. I wanted to hear His voice."

Eventually I was able to approach the fire. There was an acrid smell coming from the charred ruins. Black smoke still billowed from the smouldering brickwork. I could not see any body, but then I couldn't get close enough to look inside the walls. It crossed my mind that Ben might have fired the station on purpose, from outside, and run away into the hills. Then again, he might have decided that the beginning of the end of faith was so near that he wanted to become a martyr to its cause.

The station would have to be rebuilt and by that time the cold current would have moved on. Perhaps it wouldn't pass this way again for another ten, fifty, even a hundred years or more? The old feeling of despair was on me again. Ben must have hit one of three drums of emergency fuel we kept stored under the back bench, for visiting vehicles.

Ben was one of those men like my grandfather. He needed a mystery. It might have been hi-tech electronics, or the wonders of the atom, or even American football—but it wasn't any of those. It was religion.

With the black smoke of the funeral pyre of *proof* obscuring the blue sky, I climbed back into the Land Rover and started the engine. Out in the marshes a change had taken place. The frogs were singing once again.

ROBLEY WILSON

Terrible Kisses

"Terrible Kisses" comes from a story collection of the same title by a writer who is primarily known in literary circles, but who has published short fiction in venues as diverse as *The New Yorker* and *Twilight Zone Magazine*.

It is a contemporary magic realist tale that works on both the fantastic and metaphoric levels, about the nature of love itself.

—T.W.

Terrible Kisses

ROBLEY WILSON

December. On the twenty-fourth, Harris Calder will celebrate his fortieth birthday, and Maureen, his lover, wants to do something memorable to mark the day. What her gift will be, Harris cannot imagine, and though Maureen moves through the days leading up to the birthday with a secret smile playing at the corners of her mouth, she gives him no clues.

They work in the same downtown bank, Consolidated Federal Trust, Harris as a loan officer and Maureen as a clerk in the safety deposit section, and they can just glimpse each other across the bank's broad main lobby—if Harris leans to the left to get a clear view past the frame of his cubicle, and if Maureen raises herself up a few inches to see over the sign on the counter that reads BOXHOLDERS STOP HERE.

Their colleagues are charmed by them, considering Harris and Maureen a perfect couple. In fact, the two have lived together for nearly a year, commencing the week after Harris's divorce. First he moved into Maureen's apartment, and then, because the apartment was too small, they talked to Ferdie Allerton in the mortgage section. Ferdie knew about a pending foreclosure—a nice little Cape Cod in the suburbs—and as soon as the paperwork was taken care of, the lovers moved in with two cats, a modest amount of Danish furniture, and a small German car. Such happy circumstances; they are the envy of all.

The birthday arrives. CFT closes its doors at noon for the holidays; Harris and Maureen meet in the cloakroom, where he helps her into her fake-fur jacket.

"Is it animal, vegetable, or mineral?" Harris asks, but Maureen keeps silent and puts out her lower lip in a mock pout. It is as if she knows that his ignorance makes her gift, whatever it is, more precious.

On the bus that takes them home, Harris studies Maureen's young profile—

the small, perfect nose, the ripe lower lip, the jaw that is strong but not too strong—trying to read her. Walking from the bus stop to the house, he holds her gloved left hand and hums Christmas carols, watching his breath cloud the crisp air with music. On the front step he unlocks the door and ushers Maureen into the hallway. She turns to him then, hugs him and kisses him on the mouth.

"My birthday man," she says.

He shivers. "I love your kisses," he tells her.

"I know." She repeats the kiss. Then she hangs her jacket in the hall closet and starts toward the kitchen. "Why don't you take a nice hot shower," she says, "and then I'll make us a drink?"

When he finishes his shower, Maureen is seated at the dressing table, wearing the white chenille robe she has owned since her college days. Her bare legs suggest she is wearing only the robe, and Harris feels an echo of the shiver her kisses provoked in the downstairs hall.

"How about that drink?" he says.

"In a minute."

Harris sees that she is leaning into the dressing-table mirror, putting on lipstick. He sits on the bed and towels his damp hair distractedly.

"I thought you didn't use makeup," he says.

"Not usually. A little mascara, so my eyes don't look so piggy-tiny." She blots her mouth with a pale-blue tissue and studies the imprint she has made.

"So why the lipstick?"

She shakes her head. "It's part of your surprise," she says. "But I don't know which shade to use."

"Let me help," Harris says. He prides himself on his judgment in aesthetic matters. "How many choices?"

"Just two." She holds up the lipsticks—gold-colored tubes with extended narrow tongues of pale red.

"They look the same."

"No," Maureen says. "Come over here."

He stands before her. She pushes his bathrobe aside and plants a firm kiss over his left nipple. "This one is called Bon-Bonfire," she says. She scrubs at her lips with a tissue, then watches her reflection apply color from the other tube. She presses a second kiss above his right nipple. "And this one is Coral Blaze."

He holds the lapels of the robe apart and studies the impressions of her kisses, which look like small, symmetrical wounds on his chest. No, they are more like vivid parachutes his nipples are riding down into the curly forest of his hair. Or do they seem to be curious watermarks on the parchment of his damp skin?

"They look the same," he says.

Maureen sighs. "No," she says. She touches the imprint on the left side. "This is more pink. The other is a sort of pale magenta."

"I think I prefer the magenta," Harris says.

"Good," Maureen says. "So do I." She freshens the gloss already on her lips. "Now you have to take off your bathrobe and lie down for me."

* * *

She begins at the soles of his feet, kissing the left, then the right, pausing to put on new lipstick, kissing left and right, pausing again, until Harris sees—propped on his elbows to watch—that she intends to cover him with kisses. The prints of her lips blanket his feet and ankles like a pattern as pronounced as argyle, and the pattern moves slowly up his legs—to his knees, his thighs, his groin. He thinks she will stop there, having made her affection for him visible, and that now the two of them will make love—that this is the birthday gift, symbolic and real at the same time, she has been planning all along.

"You really know how to drive a man crazy," he says.

She is kneeling beside him, refreshing the lipstick, and she smiles at his words. "It takes a lot of time," she says. "I have to reapply the color every couple of kisses, or else they won't be bright enough."

"They certainly are bright," Harris concedes. Looking down the length of his body, he feels like a freak in a sideshow, the multiplied images of Maureen's mouth opening all over his legs like tattoo-parlor roses. "Now let me put my arms around you," he says, reaching.

"Not yet," she says.

Instead, he is obliged to turn onto his stomach, and now she prints her kisses up the backs of his legs—left, right, pause, left, right—over his buttocks, along his spine, across his shoulder blades. It is like no birthday gift he could have imagined. Alicia, his ex-wife, would never have thought it up; no other woman in his life could have invented it, devised it, carried it out. His skin burns with the touch of Maureen's tender mouth. He thinks he can discriminate each individual kiss, each tiny nerve end the warmth of the lipstick balances on. He has never been so sensitized, and no lover has ever been so attentive to him.

"Now on your back," she says.

And he rolls over without question or hesitation, to let Maureen finish what she has begun. He closes his eyes. Over his stomach and chest and throat and face her kisses pour like gouts of cinnamoned honey, like overripe strawberries leaving their sticky mark wherever they touch. His very eyelids are heavy with her imprint. His shoulders, his arms and wrists, the palms of his hands— Maureen leaves her pouting mouth on his every surface, in his every fold and corner. It is a process that seems to be taking hours, but when it is done it seems to have taken no time at all.

"I had to use some of the other color," Maureen says at last. "I ran out of the Coral Blaze." And finally she lies down beside him.

By the time they finish lovemaking, the bed linens are a pattern of pale kisses, as is Maureen's white robe—and Maureen herself is mostly decorated with the faint lip-shapes her lover's weight has pressed against her skin. As for Harris, the cloak of Maureen's myriad kisses glows as brightly as at first; he is from head to toe a perfect lithograph of passion.

"I hope you never forget this birthday," Maureen says. She lies beside him, leaning on one elbow, touching one or another of her imprinted kisses randomly and lightly with her free hand.

"I'll never," Harris says. "Never in a hundred years."

* * *

The kisses do not wash off. In the morning, while Maureen sleeps and the cats eat tuna and milk, Harris stands in the shower, soaps and soaps again. Though the kisses seem at first to fade in the general glow of the hot shower, he realizes when he has toweled dry and leaned into the mirror to shave that his skin still carries the marks of Maureen's patient gift. The kisses are like a pale flush on his cheeks and throat; his brow looks feverish. The backs of his hands as he raises them to his face bear the faint rosettes of Maureen's half-parted lips.

This is a strange persistence, Harris thinks. He puts his hands under the cold-water tap and scrubs them with the harsh soap he keeps to remove grease when he has worked on the car. The coarse lather leaves his hands ruddy, but the pattern of kisses remains. On Maureen's side of the medicine chest he finds a jar of cold cream and rubs some of the goop into his hands and forearms, then he wipes it off with facial tissues. The tissues take on a greasy pink tinge, but his skin does not come clear.

"Maureen," he whispers to the mirror. "Maureen," he says out loud, and goes to the bedroom.

She rolls over to face him.

"Look," he says. He holds out his arms to her, his bathrobe open to show the rust-colored design on his body.

"I know," she says. "You're lovely."

"No," he says. "Look at me."

"I see you. You're still wearing the red birthday suit I gave you."

"It isn't funny," he says. "The kisses won't go away." His voice breaks like a teen-aged boy's.

Maureen sits up in the bed. "Come here," she says. She takes his left hand in hers and draws it into focus. She puts her fingers to her mouth and rubs saliva on the back of the hand. She purses her lips and frowns.

"You see?" Harris says plaintively.

"Look in the drawer to the right of the bathroom sink and bring me that little pumice stone. And a wet washcloth."

"This is so weird," Harris says. He brings the pumice. "This is crazy."

Maureen scours his arm with the rough stone. "Nothing's happening," she says.

"I tingle," Harris says.

"Where I rubbed with the pumice?"

"All over," he says. "I tingle all over."

And it's true. It is as if his skin is dancing under the weight of the kisses, as if the kisses are alive and sing through his pores to his listening blood. It seems his whole body has become the instrument of Maureen's impetuous and beautiful kisses.

"Dear heaven," Harris groans, "what am I going to do?" and he falls helplessly onto the bed beside Maureen.

No matter what he does, no matter what Maureen suggests, the kisses remain. Between Christmas and New Year's, while Maureen works at CFT, Harris uses vacation time to stay at home with the cats and grapple with his problem. He tries everything. He drinks liquids and buries himself under layers of blankets, hoping to sweat away the kisses as he might break a fever. He burns himself with caustics—bleaches and paint removers and drain cleaners—but gets nothing for his trouble except pain and blisters. He lies under sunlamps; his skin turns Florida-gold, and the kisses darken to bronze. He uses emery and sandpaper, he rubs his face with fish oil and gets the cats to lick him with their rough tongues, he applies lotions and dyes and stains. He scrapes at his flesh with such force that he draws blood—but when new skin appears, it bears freshened kisses to mock his labors. The tingling grows worse, deeper and hotter, until by the end of the year he cannot sit or lie or be quiet anywhere. He paces endlessly, as if he might somehow walk away from the agony of the kisses, but he wears that agony like perverse clothing. He feels like a man living in a tragedy excessively Greek. He wonders how it will all end. He wonders if he will have to kill himself in order to be free.

On the day after New Year's he goes back to the bank. Maureen spends an hour preparing him, covering the kisses on his face and neck and hands with makeup base so no one will know what has happened to him. The face he sees in the mirror is like a clever mask; the image is not Harris Calder, though it resembles him.

"They'll know," he says to Maureen. He holds out his hands as if they do not belong to him. "They'll see."

"I told them you've been ill," she says. "A rash. An allergic reaction."

To love, Harris thinks. I'm a man allergic to love.

At CFT, his colleagues seem pleased at his return, ask him how he feels, say they hope his rash is better. "All that rich Christmas food," Ferdie Allerton tells him. "Plum pudding; Tom and Jerry."

"No doubt," Harris says. All day he processes bill-payer loans while Maureen's fierce kisses burn under his clothes, under the tight mask of makeup, like a persistent guilty secret. He feels like a man on fire. It is all he can do to wait for the end of the banking day.

That night, he tells Maureen he is quitting CFT.

"I have to go away," he says. "I have to hide out until whatever is happening to me stops happening."

"Where will you go?"

"I'll find work where nobody knows me," Harris says. "I'll be an auto mechanic or a carpenter. I'll get a job in a booth on the tollway."

"What about me?" She puts her arms around Harris and holds him. The kisses on his body are like a thousand mouths that open to breathe in her embrace. "What will I do by myself?"

"I'll leave tomorrow, while you're at the bank," Harris says. Gently, he disengages himself from her arms. "When you come home, I'll be gone. After a while, you won't even miss me."

"Please stay," she whispers.

"I can't."

All night he lies on his back, staring up into the black sky of the bedroom. Maureen is beside him; sometimes she sleeps, sometimes she wakes to plead with him. Her tears on his face feel cold beside the fever of her kisses. He wishes his skin were a thin shirt he could take off and fold and put away in the drawer next to his pajamas.

Just before dawn, he drops off into crazy dreams. When he opens his eyes to the day, Maureen has left for work and it is time for him to get out of bed, to pack. Essentials, he tells himself; he will take only the essentials. He is going to shower, to shave, to rouse his sleepy senses with hot water and the sharp smell of soap; but on the bathroom mirror Maureen has left him a farewell message, scrawled in lipstick:

> *terrible kisses—*
> *indelible love*

and Harris has to think seriously about where he will go, what he will do— what curious stories he will have to invent—before he discovers that the ineradicable pattern of the kisses is like a birthmark signaling the genesis of love, and that the fever of his body is nothing more and nothing less than the relentless climate of Paradise.

GREG BEAR

Sleepside Story

In the 1980s, Greg Bear emerged as one of the most important names in contemporary science fiction with such standout books as *Blood Music*, *Eon*, and *Eternity*, as well as a number of Hugo and Nebula award-winning short stories. Known as a master of "hard" science fiction, Bear surprised many by moving from the language of science and technology to that of myth and fairy tale, proving himself equally adept in both areas. His fantasy novels *The Infinity Concerto* and *Serpent's Mage* are among the best fantasy works of the last decade, and the following story—first published by the small press Cheap Street in a limited edition chapbook—is a tour-de-force. "Sleepside Story" is a contemporary reworking of a familiar fairy tale, and an excellent example of urban fantasy. It is, to my mind, the best fantasy novella of the year.

Greg Bear lives with his wife, Astrid Anderson, and two children near Seattle, Washington.

—T.W.

Sleepside Story

GREG BEAR

Oliver Jones differed from his brothers as wheat from chaff. He didn't grudge them their blind wildness; he loaned them money until he had none, and regretted it, but not deeply. His needs were not simple, but they did not hang on the sharp signs of dollars. He worked at the jobs of youth without complaining, knowing there was something better waiting for him. Sometimes it seemed he was the only one in the family able to take cares away from his momma, now that Poppa was gone and she was lonely even with the two babies sitting on her lap, and his younger sister Yolanda gabbing about the neighbors.

The city was a puzzle to him. His older brothers Denver and Reggie believed it was a place to be conquered, but Oliver did not share their philosophy. He wanted to make the city part of him, sucked in with his breath, built into bones and brains. If he could dance with the city's music, he'd have it made, even though Denver and Reggie said the city was wide and cruel and had no end; that its four quarters ate young men alive, and spat back old people. Look at Poppa, they said; he was forty-three and he went to the fifth quarter. Darkside, a bag of wearied bones; they said, take what you can get while you can get it.

This was not what Oliver saw, though he knew the city was cruel and hungry.

His brothers and even Yolanda kidded him about his faith. It was more than just going to church that made them rag him, because they went to church, too, sitting superior beside Momma. Reggie and Denver knew there was advantage in being seen at devotions. It wasn't his music that made them laugh, for he could play the piano hard and fast as well as soft and tender, and they all liked to dance, even Momma sometimes. It was his damned sweetness. It was his taste in girls, quiet and studious; and his honesty.

On the last day of school, before Christmas vacation, Oliver made his way home in a fall of light snow, stopping in the old St. John's churchyard for a moment's reflection by his father's grave. Surrounded by the crisp, ancient slate gravestones and the newer white marble, worn by the city's acid tears, he thought he might now be considered grown up, might have to support all of his family. He left the churchyard in a somber mood and walked between the tall brick and brownstone tenements, along the dirty, wet black streets, his shadow lost in Sleepside's greater shade, eyes on the sidewalk.

Denver and Reggie could not bring in good money, money that Momma would accept; Yolanda was too young and not likely to get a job anytime soon, and that left him, the only one who would finish school. He might take in more piano students, but he'd have to move out to do that, and how could he find another place to live without losing all he made to rent? Sleepside was crowded.

Oliver heard the noise in the flat from half a block down the street. He ran up the five dark, trash-littered flights of stairs and pulled out his key to open the three locks on the door. Swinging the door wide, he stood with hand pressed to a wall, lungs too greedy to let him speak.

The flat was in an uproar. Yolanda, rail-skinny, stood in the kitchen doorway, wringing her big hands and wailing. The two babies lurched down the hall, diapers drooping and fists stuck in their mouths. The neighbor widow Mrs. Diamond Freeland bustled back and forth in a useless dither. Something was terribly wrong.

"What is it?" he asked Yolanda with his first free breath. She just moaned and shook her head. "Where's Reggie and Denver?" She shook her head less vigorously, meaning they weren't home. "Where's Momma?" This sent Yolanda into hysterics. She bumped back against the wall and clenched her fists to her mouth, tears flying. "Something happened to Momma?"

"Your momma went uptown," Mrs. Diamond Freeland said, standing flat-footed before Oliver, her flower print dress distended over her generous stomach. "What are you going to do? You're her son."

"Where uptown?" Oliver asked, trying to control his quavering voice. He wanted to slap everybody in the apartment. He was scared and they weren't being any help at all.

"She we-went sh-sh-shopping!" Yolanda wailed. "She got her check today and it's Christmas and she went to get the babies new clothes and some food."

Oliver's hands clenched. Momma had asked him what he wanted for Christmas, and he had said, "Nothing, Momma. Not really." She had chided him, saying all would be well when the check came, and what good was Christmas if she couldn't find a little something special for each of her children? "All right," he had said. "I'd like sheet music. Something I've never played before."

"She must of taken the wrong stop," Mrs. Diamond Freeland said, staring at Oliver from the corners of her wide eyes. "That's all I can figure."

"What happened?"

Yolanda pulled a letter out of her blouse and handed it to him, a fancy purple paper with a delicate flower design on the borders, the message handwritten very prettily in gold ink fountain pen and signed. He read it carefully, then read it again.

To the Joneses,

Your momma is uptown in My care. She came here lost and I tried to help her but she stole something very valuable to Me she shouldn't have. She says you'll come and get her. By you she means her youngest son Oliver Jones and if not him then Yolanda Jones her eldest daughter. I will keep one or the other here in exchange for your momma and one or the other must stay here and work for Me.

Miss Belle Parkhurst
969 33rd Street

"Who's she, and why does she have Momma?" Oliver asked.

"I'm not going!" Yolanda screamed.

"Hush up," said Mrs. Diamond Freeland. "She's that whoor. She's that uptown whoor used to run the biggest cathouse."

Oliver looked from face to face in disbelief.

"Your momma must of taken the wrong stop and got lost," Mrs. Diamond Freeland reiterated. "That's all I can figure. She went to that whoor's house and she got in trouble."

"I'm not going!" Yolanda said. She avoided Oliver's eyes. "You know what she'd make me do."

"Yeah," Oliver said softly. "But what'll she make me do?"

Reggie and Denver, he learned from Mrs. Diamond Freeland, had come home before the message had been received, leaving just as the messenger came whistling up the outside hall. Oliver sighed. His brothers were almost never home; they thought they'd pulled the wool over Momma's eyes, but they hadn't. Momma knew who would be home and come for her when she was in trouble.

Reggie and Denver fancied themselves the hottest dudes on the street. They claimed they had women all over Sleepside and Snowside; Oliver was almost too shy to ask a woman out. He was small, slender, and almost pretty, but very strong for his size. Reggie and Denver were cowards. Oliver had never run from a true and worthwhile fight in his life, but neither had he started one.

The thought of going to Miss Belle Parkhurst's establishment scared him, but he remembered what his father had told him just a week before dying. "Oliver, when I'm gone—that's soon now, you know it—Yolanda's flaky as a bowl of cereal and your brothers . . . well, I'll be kind and just say your momma, she's going to need you. You got to turn out right so as she can lean on you."

The babies hadn't been born then.

"Which train did she take?"

"Down to Snowside," Mrs. Diamond Freeland said. "But she must of gotten off in Sunside. That's near Thirty-third."

"It's getting night," Oliver said.

Yolanda sniffed and wiped her eyes. Off the hook. "You going?"

"Have to," Oliver said. "It's Momma."

Said Mrs. Diamond Freeland, "I think that whoor got something on her mind."

*   *   *

On the line between dusk and dark, down underground where it shouldn't have mattered, the Metro emptied of all the day's passengers and filled with the night's.

Sometimes day folks went in tight-packed groups on the Night Metro, but not if they could avoid it. Night Metro was for carrying the lost or human garbage. Everyone ashamed or afraid to come out during the day came out at night. Night Metro also carried the zeroes—people who lived their lives and when they died no one could look back and say they remembered them. Night Metro—especially late—was not a good way to travel, but for Oliver it was the quickest way to get from Sleepside to Sunside; he had to go as soon as possible to get Momma.

Oliver descended the four flights of concrete steps, grinding his teeth at the thought of the danger he was in. He halted at the bottom, grimacing at the frightened knots of muscle and nerves in his back, repeating over and over again, "It's Momma. It's Momma. No one can save her but me." He dropped his bronze cat-head token into the turnstile, clunk-chunking through, and crossed the empty platform. Only two indistinct figures waited trackside, heavy-coated though it was a warm evening. Oliver kept an eye on them and walked back and forth in a figure eight on the grimy foot-scrubbed concrete, peering nervously down at the wet and soot under the rails. Behind him, on the station's smudged white tile walls hung a gold mosaic trumpet and the number 7, the trumpet for folks who couldn't read to know when to get off. All Sleepside stations had musical instruments.

The Night Metro was run by a different crew than the Day Metro. His train came up, clean and silver-sleek, without a spot of graffiti or a stain of tarnish. Oliver caught a glimpse of the driver under the SLEEPSIDE/CHASTE RIVER/SUNSIDE-46TH destination sign. The driver wore or had a bull's head and carried a prominent pair of long gleaming silver scissors on his Sam Browne belt. Oliver entered the open doors and took a smooth handgrip even though the seats were mostly empty. Somebody standing was somebody quicker to run.

There were four people on his car; two women—one young, vacant, and not pretty or even very alive-looking, the other old and muddy-eyed with a plastic daisy-flowered shopping bag—and two men, both sunny blond and chunky, wearing shiny-elbowed business suits. Nobody looked at anybody else. The doors shut and the train grumbled on, gathering speed until the noise of its wheels on the tracks drowned out all other sound and almost all thought.

There were more dead stations than live and lighted ones. Night Metro made only a few stops congruent with Day Metro. Most stations were turned off, and the only people left standing there didn't show in bright lights. Oliver tried not to look, to keep his eyes on the few in the car with him, but every so often he couldn't help peering out. Beyond I-beams and barricades, single orange lamps and broken tiled walls rushed by, platforms populated by slow smudges of shadow.

Some said the dead used the Night Metro, and that after midnight it went all the way to Darkside. Oliver didn't know what to believe. As the train slowed for his station, he pulled the collar of his dark green nylon windbreaker up around his neck and rubbed his nose with one finger. Reggie and Denver would never have made it even this far. They valued their skins too much.

The train did not move on after he disembarked. He stood by the open doors for a moment, then walked past the lead car on his way to the stairs. Over his shoulder, he saw the driver standing at the head of the train in his little cabin of fluorescent coldness, the eyes in the bull's head sunk deep in shade. Oliver felt rather than saw the starlike pricks in the sockets, watching him. The driver's left hand tugged on the blades of the silver shears.

"What do you care, man?" Oliver asked softly, stopping for an instant to return the hidden stare. "Go on about your work. We all got stuff to do."

The bull's nose pointed a mere twitch away from Oliver, and the hand left the shears to return to its switch. The train doors closed. The silver side panels and windows and lights picked up speed and the train squealed around a curve into darkness. He climbed the two flights of stairs to Sunside Station.

Summer night lay heavy and warm on the lush trees and grass of a broad park. Oliver stood at the head of the Metro entrance and listened to the crickets and katydids and cicadas sing songs unheard in Sleepside, where trees and grass were sparse. All around the park rose dark-windowed walls of high marble and brick and gray stone hotels and fancy apartment buildings with gable roofs.

Oliver looked around for directions, a map, anything. Above the Night Metro, it was even possible ordinary people might be out strolling, and he could ask them if he dared. He walked toward the street and thought of Momma getting this far and of her being afraid. He loved Momma very much. Sometimes she seemed to be the only decent thing in his life, though more and more often young women distracted him as the years passed, and he experienced more and more secret fixations.

"Oliver Jones?"

A long white limousine waited by the curb. A young, slender woman in violet chauffeur's livery, with a jaunty black and silver cap sitting atop exuberant hair, cocked her head coyly, smiled at him, and beckoned with a white-leather-gloved finger. "Are you Oliver Jones, come to rescue your momma?"

He walked slowly toward the white limousine. It was bigger and more beautiful than anything he had ever seen before, with long ribbed chrome pipes snaking out from under the hood and through the fenders, stand-alone golden headlights, and a white tonneau roof made of real leather. "My name's Oliver," he affirmed.

"Then you're my man. Please get in." She winked and held the door open.

When the door closed, the woman's arm—all he could see of her through the smoky window glass—vanished. The driver's door did not open. She did not get in. The limousine drove off by itself. Oliver fell back into the lush suede and velvet interior. An electronic wet bar gleamed silver and gold and black above a cool white-lit panel on which sat a single crystal glass filled with ice cubes. A spigot rotated around and waited for instructions. When none came, it gushed fragrant gin over the ice and rotated back into place.

Oliver did not touch the glass.

Below the wet bar, the television set turned itself on. Passion and delight sang from the small, precise speakers. "No," he said. "No!"

The television shut off.

He edged closer to the smoky glass and saw dim street lights and cab headlights moving past. A huge black building trimmed with gold ornaments, windows outlined with red, loomed on the corner, all but three of its windows dark. The limousine turned smoothly and descended into a dark underground garage. Lights throwing huge golden cat's eyes, tires squealing on shiny concrete, it snaked around a slalom of walls and pillars and dusty limousines and came to a quick stop. The door opened.

Oliver stepped out. The chauffeur stood holding the door, grinning, and doffed her cap. "My pleasure," she said.

The car had parked beside a big wooden door set into hewn stone. Fossil bones and teeth were clearly visible in the matrix of each block in the walls. Glistening ferns in dark ponds flanked the door. Oliver heard the car drive away and turned to look, but he did not see whether the chauffeur drove this time or not.

He walked across a wood plank bridge and tried the black iron handle on the door. The door swung open at the suggestion of his fingers. Beyond, a narrow red-carpeted staircase with rose-bush carved maple banisters ascended to the upper floor.

The place smelled of cloves and mint and, somehow, of what Oliver imagined dogs or horses must smell like—a musty old rug sitting on a floor grate. (He had never owned a dog and never seen a horse without a policeman on it, and never so close he could smell it.) Nobody had been through here in a long time, he thought. But everybody knew about Miss Belle Parkhurst and her place. And the chauffeur had been young. He wrinkled his nose; he did not like this place.

The dark wood door at the top of the stairs swung open silently. Nobody stood there waiting; it might have opened by itself. Oliver tried to speak, but his throat itched and closed. He coughed into his fist and shrugged his shoulders in a spasm. Then, eyes damp and hot with anger and fear and something more, he moved his lips and croaked, "I'm Oliver Jones. I'm here to get my momma."

The door remained unattended. He looked back into the parking garage, dark and quiet as a cave; nothing for him there. Then he ascended quickly to get it over with and passed through the door into the ill-reputed house of Miss Belle Parkhurst.

The city extends to the far horizon, divided into quarters by roads or canals or even train tracks, above or underground; and sometimes you know those divisions and know better than to cross them, and sometimes you don't. The city is broader than any man's life, and it is worth more than your life not to understand why you are where you are and must stay there. The city encourages ignorance because it must eat.

The four quarters of the city are Snowside, Cokeside where few sane people go, Sleepside, and Sunside. Sunside is bright and rich and hazardous because that is where the swell folks live. Swell folks don't tolerate intruders. Not even the police go into Sunside without an escort. Toward the center of the city is uptown, and in the middle of uptown is where all four quarters meet at the

Pillar of the Unknown Mayor. Outward is the downtown and scattered islands of suburbs, and no one knows where it ends.

The Joneses live in downtown Sleepside. The light there even at noon is not very bright, but neither is it burning harsh as in Cokeside where it can fry your skull. Sleepside is tolerable. There are many good people in Sleepside and Snowside, and though confused, the general run is not vicious. Oliver grew up there and carries it in his bones and meat. No doubt the Night Metro driver smelled his origins and knew here was a young man crossing a border going uptown. No doubt Oliver was still alive because Miss Belle Parkhurst had protected him. That meant Miss Parkhurst had protected Momma, and perhaps lured her, as well.

The hallway was lighted by rows of candles held in gold eagle claws along each wall. At the end of the hall, Oliver stepped into a broad wood-paneled room set here and there with lush green ferns in brass spittoons. The Oriental carpet revealed a stylized Oriental garden in cream and black and red. Five empty black velvet-upholstered couches stood unoccupied, expectant, like a line of languorous women amongst the ferns. Along the walls, chairs covered by white sheets asserted their heavy wooden arms. Oliver stood, jaw open, not used to such luxury. He needed a long moment to take it all in.

Miss Belle Parkhurst was obviously a very rich woman, and not your ordinary whore. From what he had seen so far, she had power as well as money, power over cars and maybe over men and women. Maybe over Momma. "Momma?"

A tall, tenuous white-haired man in a cream-colored suit walked across the room, paying Oliver scant attention. He said nothing. Oliver watched him sit on a sheet-covered chair. He did not disturb the sheets, but sat through them. He leaned his head back reflectively, elevating a cigarette holder without a cigarette. He blew out clear air, or perhaps nothing at all, and then smiled at something just to Oliver's right. Oliver turned. They were alone. When he looked back, the man in the cream-colored suit was gone.

Oliver's arms tingled. He was in for more than he had bargained for, and he had bargained for a lot.

"This way," said a woman's deep voice, operatic, dignified, easy and friendly at once. He could not see her, but he squinted at the doorway, and she stepped between two fluted green onyx columns. He did not know at first that she was addressing him; there might be other gentlemen, or girls, equally as tenuous as the man in the cream-colored suit. But this small, imposing woman with upheld hands, dressed in gold and peach silk that clung to her smooth and silent, was watching only him with her large dark eyes. She smiled richly and warmly, but Oliver thought there was a hidden flaw in that smile, in her assurance. She was ill at ease from the instant their eyes met, though she might have been at ease before then, *thinking* of meeting him. She had had all things planned until that moment.

If he unnerved her slightly, this woman positively terrified him. She was beautiful and smooth-skinned, and he could smell the sweet roses and camellias and magnolia blossoms surrounding her like a crowd of familiar friends.

"This way," she repeated, gesturing through the doors.

"I'm looking for my momma. I'm supposed to meet Miss Belle Parkhurst."

"I'm Belle Parkhurst. You're Oliver Jones . . . aren't you?"

He nodded, face solemn, eyes wide. He nodded again and swallowed.

"I sent your momma on her way home. She'll be fine."

He looked back at the hallway. "She'll be on the Night Metro," he said.

"I sent her back in my car. Nothing will happen to her."

Oliver believed her. There was a long, silent moment. He realized he was twisting and wringing his hands before his crotch and he stopped this, embarrassed.

"Your momma's fine. Don't worry about her."

"All right," he said, drawing his shoulders up. "You wanted to talk to me?"

"Yes," she said. "And more."

His nostrils flared and he jerked his eyes hard right, his torso and then his hips and legs twisting that way as he broke into a scrambling rabbit-run for the hallway. The golden eagle claws on each side dropped their candles as he passed and reached out to hook him with their talons. The vast house around him seemed suddenly alert, and he knew even before one claw grabbed his collar that he did not have a chance.

He dangled helpless from the armpits of his jacket at the very end of the hall. In the far door appeared the whore, angry, fingers dripping small beads of fire onto the wooden floor. The floor smoked and sizzled.

"I've let your momma go," Belle Parkhurst said, voice deeper than a grave, face terrible and smoothly beautiful and very old, very experienced. "That was my agreement. You leave, and you break that agreement, and that means I take your sister, or I take back your momma."

She cocked an elegant, painted eyebrow at him and leaned her head to one side in query. He nodded as best he could with his chin jammed against the teeth of his jacket's zipper.

"Good. There's food waiting. I'd enjoy your company."

The dining room was small, no larger than his bedroom at home, occupied by two chairs and an intimate round table covered in white linen and a gold eagle claw candelabrum. Miss Parkhurst preceded Oliver, her long dress rustling softly at her heels. Other things rustled in the room as well; the floor might have been ankle-deep in wind-blown leaves by the sound, but it was spotless, a rich round red and cream Oriental rug centered beneath the table; and beneath that, smooth old oak flooring. Oliver looked up from his sneaker-clad feet. Miss Parkhurst waited expectantly a step back from her chair.

"Your momma teach you no manners?" she asked softly.

He approached the table reluctantly. There were empty gold plates and tableware on the linen now that had not been there before. Napkins seemed to drop from thin fog and folded themselves on the plates. Oliver stopped, his nostrils flaring.

"Don't you mind that," Miss Parkhurst said. "I live alone here. Good help is hard to find."

Oliver stepped behind the chair and lifted it by its maple headpiece, pulling it out for her. She sat and he helped her move closer to the table. Not once did he touch her; his skin crawled at the thought.

"The food here is very good," Miss Parkhurst said as he sat across from her.

"I'm not hungry," Oliver said.

She smiled warmly at him. It was a powerful thing, her smile. "I won't bite," she said. "Except supper. *That* I'll bite."

Oliver smelled wonderful spices and sweet vinegar. A napkin had been draped across his lap, and before him was a salad on a fine china plate. He was very hungry and he enjoyed salads, seeing fresh greens so seldom in Sleepside.

"That's it," Miss Parkhurst said soothingly, smiling as he ate. She lifted her fork in turn and speared a fold of olive-oiled butter lettuce, bringing it to her red lips.

The rest of the dinner proceeded in like fashion, but with no further conversation. She watched him frankly, appraising, and he avoided her eyes.

Down a corridor with tall windows set in an east wall, dawn gray and pink around their faint silhouettes on the west wall, Miss Parkhurst led Oliver to his room. "It's the quietest place in the mansion," she said.

"You're keeping me," he said. "You're never going to let me go?"

"Please allow me to indulge myself. I'm not just alone. I'm lonely. Here, you can have anything you want . . . almost . . ."

A door at the corridor's far end opened by itself. Within, a fire burned brightly within a small fireplace, and a wide bed waited with covers turned down. Exquisitely detailed murals of forests and fields covered the walls; the ceiling was rich deep blue, flecked with gold and silver and jeweled stars. Books filled a case in one corner, and in another corner stood the most beautiful ebony grand piano he had ever seen. Miss Parkhurst did not approach the door too closely. There were no candles; within this room, all lamps were electric.

"This is your room. I won't come in," she said. "And after tonight, you don't ever come out after dark. We'll talk and see each other during the day, but never at night. The door isn't locked. I'll have to trust you."

"I can go any time I want?"

She smiled. Even though she meant her smile to be nothing more than enigmatic, it shook him. She was deadly beautiful, the kind of woman his brothers dreamed about. Her smile said she might eat him alive, all of him that counted. Oliver could imagine his mother's reaction to Miss Belle Parkhurst.

He entered the room and swung the door shut, trembling. There were a dozen things he wanted to say; angry, bitter, frustrated, pleading things. He leaned against the door, swallowing them all back, keeping his hand from going to the gold and crystal knob.

Behind the door, her skirts rustled as she retired along the corridor. After a moment, he pushed off from the door and walked with an exaggerated swagger to the bookcase, mumbling. Miss Parkhurst would never have taken Oliver's sister Yolanda; that wasn't what she wanted. She wanted young boy flesh, he thought. She wanted to burn him down to his sneakers, smiling like that.

The books on the shelves were books he had heard about but had never found in the Sleepside library, books he wanted to read, that the librarians said only people from Sunside and the suburbs cared to read. His fingers lingered on the tops of their spines, tugging gently.

He decided to sleep instead. If she was going to pester him during the day, he didn't have much time. She'd be a late riser, he thought; a night person.

Then he realized: whatever she did at night, she had not done this night. This night had been set aside for him.

He shivered again, thinking of the food and napkins and the eagle claws. Was this room haunted, too? Would things keep watch over him?

Oliver lay back on the bed, still clothed. His mind clouded with thoughts of living sheets feeling up his bare skin. Tired, almost dead out.

The dreams that came were sweet and pleasant and she did not walk in them. This really was his time.

At ten o'clock by the brass and gold and crystal clock on the bookcase, Oliver kicked his legs out, rubbed his face into the pillows and started up, back arched, smelling bacon and eggs and coffee. A covered tray waited on a polished brass cart beside the bed. A vase of roses on one corner of the cart scented the room. A folded piece of fine ivory paper leaned against the vase. Oliver sat on the edge of the bed and read the note, once again written in golden ink in a delicate hand.

I'm waiting for you in the gymnasium. Meet me after you've eaten. Got something to give to you.

He had no idea where the gymnasium was. When he had finished breakfast, he put on a plush robe, opened the heavy door to his room—both relieved and irritated that it did not open by itself—and looked down the corridor. A golden arc clung to the base of each tall window. It was at least noon. Sunside time. She had given him plenty of time to rest.

A pair of new black jeans and a white silk shirt waited for him on the bed, which had been carefully made in the time it had taken him to glance down the hall. Cautiously, but less frightened now, he removed the robe, put on these clothes and the deerskin moccasins by the foot of the bed, and stood in the doorway, leaning as casually as he could manage against the frame.

A silk handkerchief hung in the air several yards away. It fluttered like a pigeon's ghost to attract his attention, then drifted slowly along the hall. He followed.

The house seemed to go on forever, empty and magnificent. Each public room had its own decor, filled with antique furniture, potted palms, plush couches and chairs, and love seats. Several times he thought he saw wisps of dinner jackets, top hats, eager, strained faces, in foyers, corridors, on staircases as he followed the handkerchief. The house smelled of perfume and dust, faint cigars, spilled wine, and old sweat.

He had climbed three flights of stairs before he stood at the tall ivory-white double door of the gymnasium. The handkerchief vanished with a flip. The doors opened.

Miss Parkhurst stood at the opposite end of a wide black-tile dance floor, before a band riser covered with music stands and instruments. Oliver eyed the low half-circle stage with narrowed eyes. Would she demand he dance with her, while all the instruments played by themselves?

"Good morning," she said. She wore a green dress the color of fresh wet grass, high at the neck and down to her calves. Beneath the dress she wore white boots and white gloves, and a white feather curled around her black hair.

"Good morning," he replied softly, politely.

"Did you sleep well? Eat hearty?"

Oliver nodded, fear and shyness returning. What could she possibly want to give him? Herself? His face grew hot.

"It's a shame this house is empty during the day," she said. *And at night?* he thought. "I could fill this room with exercise equipment," she continued. "Weight benches, even a track around the outside." She smiled. The smile seemed less ferocious now, even wistful; younger.

He rubbed a fold of his shirt between two fingers. "I enjoyed the food, and your house is real fine, but I'd like to go home," he said.

She half-turned and walked slowly from the stand. "You could have this house and all my wealth. I'd like you to have it."

"Why? I haven't done anything for you."

"Or to me, either," she said, facing him again. "You know how I've made all this money?"

"Yes, ma'am," he said after a moment's pause. "I'm not a fool."

"You've heard about me. That I'm a whore."

"Yes, ma'am. Mrs. Diamond Freeland says you are."

"And what is a whore?"

"You let men do it to you for money," Oliver said, feeling bolder, but with his face hot all the same.

Miss Parkhurst nodded. "I've got part of them all here with me," she said. "My bookkeeping. I know every name, every face. They all keep me company now that business is slow."

"All of them?" Oliver asked.

Miss Parkhurst's faint smile was part pride, part sadness, her eyes distant and moist. "They gave me all the things I have here."

"I don't think it would be worth it," Oliver said.

"I'd be dead if I wasn't a whore," Miss Parkhurst said, eyes suddenly sharp on him, flashing anger. "I'd have starved to death." She relaxed her clenched hands. "We got plenty of time to talk about my life, so let's hold it here for a while. I got something you need, if you're going to inherit this place."

"I don't want it, ma'am," Oliver said.

"If you don't take it, somebody who doesn't need it and deserves it a lot less will. I want you to have it. Please, be kind to me this once."

"Why me?" Oliver asked. He simply wanted out; this was completely off the planned track of his life. He was less afraid of Miss Parkhurst now, though her anger raised hairs on his neck; he felt he could be bolder and perhaps even demanding. There was a weakness in her: he was her weakness, and he wasn't above taking some advantage of that, considering how desperate his situation might be.

"You're kind," she said. "You care. And you've never had a woman, not all the way."

Oliver's face warmed again. "Please let me go," he said quietly, hoping it didn't sound as if he was pleading.

Miss Parkhurst folded her arms. "I can't," she said.

While Oliver spent his first day in Miss Parkhurst's mansion, across the city, beyond the borders of Sunside, Denver and Reggie Jones had returned home to find the apartment blanketed in gloom. Reggie, tall and gangly, long of neck and short of head, with a prominent nose, stood with back slumped in the front hall, mouth open in surprise. "He just took off and left you all here?" Reggie asked. Denver returned from the kitchen, shorter and stockier than his brother, dressed in black vinyl jacket and pants.

Yolanda's face was puffy from constant crying. She now enjoyed the tears she spilled, and had scheduled them at two hour intervals, to her momma's sorrowful irritation. She herded the two babies into their momma's bedroom and closed a rickety gate behind them, then brushed her hands on the breast of her ragged blouse.

"You don't *get* it," she said, facing them and dropping her arms dramatically. "That whore took Momma, and Oliver traded himself for her."

"That whore," said Reggie, "is a rich old witch."

"Rich old bitch witch," Denver said, pleased with himself.

"That whore is opportunity knocking," Reggie continued, chewing reflectively. "I hear she lives alone."

"That's why she took Oliver," Yolanda said. The babies cooed and chirped behind the gate.

"Why him and not one of us?" Reggie asked.

Momma gently pushed the babies aside, swung open the gate, and marched down the hall, dressed in her best wool skirt and print blouse, wrapped in her overcoat against the gathering dark and cold outside. "Where you going?" Yolanda asked her as she brushed past.

"Time to talk to the police," she said, glowering at Reggie. Denver backed into the bedroom he shared with his brother, out of her way. He shook his head condescendingly, grinning: Momma at it again.

"Them dogheads?" Reggie said. "They got no say in Sunside."

Momma turned at the front door and glared at them. "How are you going to help your brother? He's the best of you all, you know, and you just stand there, flatfooted and jawboning yourselves."

"Momma's upset," Denver informed his brother solemnly.

"She should be," Reggie said sympathetically. "She was held prisoner by that witch bitch whore. We should go get Oliver and bring him home. We could pretend we was customers."

"She don't have customers any more," Denver said. "She's too old. She's worn out." He glanced at his crotch and leaned his head to one side, glaring for emphasis. His glare faded into an amiable grin.

"How do you know?" Reggie asked.

"That's what I hear."

Momma snorted and pulled back the bars and bolts on the front door. Reggie calmly walked up behind her and stopped her. "Police don't do anybody any good, Momma," he said. "We'll go. We'll bring Oliver back."

Denver's face slowly fell at the thought. "We got to plan it out," he said. "We got to be careful."

"We'll be careful," Reggie said. "For Momma's sake."

With his hand blocking her exit, Momma snorted again, then let her shoulders fall and her face sag. She looked more and more like an old woman now, though she was only in her late thirties.

Yolanda stood aside to let her pass into the living room. "Poor Momma," she said, eyes welling up.

"What you going to do for your brother?" Reggie asked his sister pointedly as he in turn walked by her. She craned her neck and stuck out her chin resentfully. "Go trade places with him, work in *her* house?" he taunted.

"She's rich," Denver said to himself, cupping his chin in his hand. "We could make a whole lot of money, saving our brother."

"We start thinking about it now," Reggie mandated, falling into the chair that used to be their father's, leaning his head back against the lace covers Momma had made.

Momma, face ashen, stood by the couch staring at a family portrait hung on the wall in a cheap wooden frame. "He did it for me. I was so stupid, getting off there, letting her help me. Should of known," she murmured, clutching her wrist. Her face ashen, her ankle wobbled under her and she pirouetted, hands spread out like a dancer, and collapsed face down on the couch.

The gift, the thing that Oliver needed to inherit Miss Parkhurst's mansion, was a small gold box with three buttons, like a garage door opener. She finally presented it to him in the dining room as they finished dinner.

Miss Parkhurst was nice to talk to, something Oliver had not expected, but which he should have. Whores did more than lie with a man to keep him coming back and spending his money; that should have been obvious. The day had not been the agony he expected. He had even stopped asking her to let him go. Oliver thought it would be best to bide his time, and when something distracted her, make his escape. Until then, she was not treating him badly or expecting anything he could not freely give.

"It'll be dark soon," she said as the plates cleared themselves away. He was even getting used to the ghostly service. "I have to go soon, and you got to be in your room. Take this with you, and keep it there." She removed a tray cover to reveal a white silk bag. Unstringing the bag, she removed the golden opener and shyly presented it to him. "This was given to me a long time ago. I don't need it now. But if you want to run this place, you got to have it. You can't lose it, or let anyone take it from you."

Oliver's hands went to the opener involuntarily. It seemed very desirable, as if there were something of Miss Parkhurst in it; warm, powerful, a little frightening. It fit his hand perfectly, familiar to his skin; he might have owned it for as long as she had.

He tightened his lips and returned it to her. "I'm sorry," he said. "It's not for me."

"You remember what I told you," she said. "If you don't take it, somebody else will, and it won't do anybody any good then. I want it to do some good now, when I'm done with it."

"Who gave it to you?" Oliver asked.

"A pimp, a long time ago. When I was a girl."

Oliver's eyes betrayed no judgment or disgust. She took a deep breath.

"He made you do it . . . ?" Oliver asked.

"No. I was young, but already a whore. I had an old, kind pimp, at least he seemed old to me, I wasn't much more than a girl. He died, he was killed, so this new pimp came, and he was powerful. He had the magic. But he couldn't tame me. So he says . . ."

Miss Parkhurst raised her hands to her face. "He cut me up. I was almost dead. He says, 'You shame me, whore. You do this to me, make me lose control, you're the only one ever did this to me. So I curse you. You'll be the greatest whore ever was.' He gave me the opener then, and he put my face and body back together so I'd be pretty. Then he left town, and I was in charge. I've been here ever since, but all the girls have gone, it's been so long, died or left or I told them to go. I wanted this place closed, but I couldn't close it all at once."

Oliver nodded slowly, eyes wide.

"He gave me most of his magic, too. I didn't have any choice. One thing he didn't give me was a way out. Except . . ." This time, she was the one with the pleading expression.

Oliver raised an eyebrow.

"What I need has to be freely given. Now take this." She stood and thrust the opener into his hands. "Use it to find your way all around the house. But don't leave your room after dark."

She swept out of the dining room, leaving a scent of musk and flowers and something bittersweet. Oliver put the opener in his pocket and walked back to his room, finding his way without hesitation, without thought. He shut the door and went to the bookcase, sad and troubled and exultant all at once.

She had told him her secret. He could leave now if he wanted. She had given him the power to leave.

Sipping from a glass of sherry on the nightstand beside the bed, reading from a book of composers' lives, he decided to wait until morning.

Yet after a few hours, nothing could keep his mind away from Miss Parkhurst's prohibition—not the piano, the books, or the snacks delivered almost before he thought about them, appearing on the tray when he wasn't watching. Oliver sat with hands folded in the plush chair, blinking at the room's dark corners. He thought he had Miss Parkhurst pegged. She was an old woman tired of her life, a beautifully preserved old woman to be sure, very strong . . . But she was sweet on him, keeping him like some unused gigolo. Still, he couldn't help but admire her, and he couldn't help but want to be home, near Momma and Yolanda and the babies, keeping his brothers out of trouble—not that they appreciated his efforts.

The longer he sat, the angrier and more anxious he became. He felt sure something was wrong at home. Pacing around the room did nothing to calm him. He examined the opener time and again in the firelight, brow wrinkled, wondering what powers it gave him. She had said he could go anywhere in the house and know his way, just as he had found his room without her help.

He moaned, shaking his fists at the air. "She can't keep me here! She just can't!"

At midnight, he couldn't control himself any longer. He stood before the door. "Let me out, dammit!" he cried, and the door opened with a sad whisper. He ran down the corridor, scattering moonlight on the floor like dust, tears shining on his cheeks.

Through the sitting rooms, the long halls of empty bedrooms—now with their doors closed, shades of sound sifting from behind—through the vast deserted kitchen, with its rows of polished copper kettles and huge black coal cookstoves, through a courtyard surrounded by five stories of the mansion on all sides and open to the golden-starred night sky, past a tiled fountain guarded by three huge white porcelain lions, ears and empty eyes following him as he ran by, Oliver searched for Miss Parkhurst, to tell her he must leave.

For a moment, he caught his breath in an upstairs gallery. He saw faint lights under doors, heard more suggestive sounds. No time to pause, even with his heart pounding and his lungs burning. If he waited in one place long enough, he thought the ghosts might become real and make him join their revelry. This was Miss Parkhurst's past, hoary and indecent, more than he could bear contemplating. How could anyone have lived this kind of life, even if they were cursed?

Yet the temptation to stop, to listen, to give in and join in was almost stronger than he could resist. He kept losing track of what he was doing, what his ultimate goal was.

"Where are you?" he shouted, throwing open double doors to a game room, empty but for more startled ghosts, more of Miss Parkhurst's eternity of book-keeping. Pale forms rose from the billiard tables, translucent breasts shining with an inner light, their pale lovers rolling slowly to one side, fat bellies prominent, ghost eyes black and startled. "Miss Parkhurst!"

Oliver brushed through hundreds of girls, no more substantial than curtains of rain drops. His new clothes became wet with their tears. *She* had presided over this eternity of sad lust. *She* had orchestrated the debaucheries, catered to what he felt inside him: the whims and deepest desires unspoken.

Thin antique laughter followed him.

He slid on a splash of sour-smelling champagne and came up abruptly against a heavy wooden door, a room he did not know. The golden opener told him nothing about what waited beyond.

"Open!" he shouted, but he was ignored. The door was not locked, but it resisted his entry as if it weighted tons. He pushed with both hands and then laid his shoulder on the paneling, bracing his sneakers against the thick wool pile of a champagne-soaked runner. The door swung inward with a deep iron and wood grumble, and Oliver stumbled past, saving himself at the last minute from falling on his face. Legs sprawled, down on both hands, he looked up from the wooden floor and saw where he was.

The room was narrow, but stretched on for what might have been miles, lined on one side with an endless row of plain double beds, and on the other with an endless row of free-standing cheval mirrors. An old man, the oldest he had ever seen, naked, white as talcum, rose stiffly from the bed, mumbling. Beneath him, red and warm as a pile of glowing coals, Miss Parkhurst lay with legs spread, incense of musk and sweat thick about her. She raised her head and shoulders, eyes fixed on Oliver's, and pulled a black peignoir over her nakedness. In the gloom of the room's extremities, other men, old and young, stood by their beds, smoking cigarettes or cigars or drinking champagne or whisky, all observing Oliver. Some grinned in speculation.

Miss Parkhurst's face wrinkled in agony like an old apple and she threw back her head to scream. The old man on the bed grabbed clumsily for a robe and his clothes.

Her shriek echoed from the ceiling and the walls, driving Oliver back through the door, down the halls and stairways. The wind of his flight chilled him to the bone in his tear-soaked clothing. Somehow he made his way through the sudden darkness and emptiness, and shut himself in his room, where the fire still burned warm and cheery yellow. Shivering uncontrollably, face slick with his own tears, Oliver removed his wet new clothes and called for his own in a high-pitched, frantic voice. But the invisible servants did not deliver what he requested.

He fell into the bed and pulled the covers tight about him, eyes closed. He prayed that she would not come after him, not come into his room with her peignoir slipping aside, revealing her furnace body; he prayed her smell would not follow him the rest of his life.

The door to his room did not open. Outside, all was quiet. In time, as dawn fired the roofs and then the walls and finally the streets of Sunside, Oliver slept.

"You came out of your room last night," Miss Parkhurst said over the late breakfast. Oliver stopped chewing for a moment, glanced at her through blood-shot eyes, then shrugged.

"Did you see what you expected?"

Oliver didn't answer. Miss Parkhurst sighed like a young girl.

"It's my life. This is the way I've lived for a long time."

"None of my business," Oliver said, breaking a roll in half and buttering it.

"Do I disgust you?"

Again no reply. Miss Parkhurst stood in the middle of his silence and walked to the dining room door. She looked over her shoulder at him, eyes moist. "You're not afraid of me now," she said. "You think you know what I am."

Oliver saw that his silence and uncaring attitude hurt her, and relished for a moment this power. When she remained standing in the doorway, he looked up with a purposefully harsh expression—copied from Reggie, sarcastic and angry at once—and saw tears flowing steadily down her cheeks. She seemed younger than ever now, not dangerous, just very sad. His expression faded. She turned away and closed the door behind her.

Oliver slammed half the roll into his plate of eggs and pushed his chair back from the table. "I'm not even full-grown!" he shouted at the door. "I'm not even a man! What do you want from me?" He stood up and kicked the chair away with his heel, then stuffed his hands in his pockets and paced around the small room. He felt bottled up, and yet she had said he could go any time he wished.

Go *where*? Home?

He stared at the goldenware and the plates heaped with excellent food. Nothing like this at home. Home was a place he sometimes thought he'd have to fight to get away from; he couldn't protect Momma forever from the rest of the family, he couldn't be a breadwinner for five extra mouths for the rest of his life . . .

And if he stayed here, knowing what Miss Parkhurst did each night? Could he eat breakfast each morning, knowing how the food was earned, and all his clothes and books and the piano, too? He really would be a gigolo then.

Sunside. He was here, maybe he could live here, find work, get away from Sleepside for good.

The mere thought gave him a twinge. He sat down and buried his face in his hands, rubbing his eyes with the tips of his fingers, pulling at his lids to make a face, staring at himself reflected in the golden carafe, big-nosed, eyes monstrously bleared. He had to talk to Momma. Even talking to Yolanda might help.

But Miss Parkhurst was nowhere to be found. Oliver searched the mansion until dusk, then ate alone in the small dining room. He retired to his room. as dark closed in, spreading through the halls like ink through water. To banish the night, and all that might be happening in it, Oliver played the piano loudly.

When he finally stumbled to his bed, he saw a single yellow rose on the pillow, delicate and sweet. He placed it by the lamp on the nightstand and pulled the covers over himself, clothes and all.

In the early hours of the morning, he dreamed that Miss Parkhurst had fled the mansion, leaving it for him to tend to. The ghosts and old men crowded around, asking why he was so righteous. "She never had a Momma like you," said one decrepit dude dressed in black velvet nightrobes. "She's lived times you can't imagine. Now you just blew her right out of this house. Where will she go?"

Oliver came awake long enough to remember the dream, and then returned to a light, difficult sleep.

Mrs. Diamond Freeland scowled at Yolanda's hand-wringing and mumbling. "You can't help your momma acting that way," she said.

"I'm no doctor," Yolanda complained.

"No doctor's going to help her," Mrs. Freeland said, eyeing the door to Momma's bedroom.

Denver and Reggie lounged uneasily in the parlor.

"You two louts going to look for your brother?"

"We don't have to look for him," Denver said. "We know where he is. We got a plan to get him back."

"Then why don't you do it?" Mrs. Freeland asked.

"When the time's right," Reggie said decisively.

"Your momma's pining for Oliver," Mrs. Freeland told them, not for the first time. "It's churning her insides thinking he's with that witch and what she might be doing to him."

Reggie tried unsuccessfully to hide a grin.

"What's funny?" Mrs. Freeland asked sternly.

"Nothing. Maybe our little brother needs some of what she's got."

Mrs. Freeland glared at them. "Yolanda," she said, rolling her eyes to the ceiling in disgust. "The babies. They dry?"

"No, ma'am," Yolanda said. She backed away from Mrs. Freeland's severe look. "I'll change them."

"Then you take them into your momma."

"Yes ma'am."

The breakfast went as if nothing had happened. Miss Parkhurst sat across from him, eating and smiling. Oliver tried to be more polite, working his way around to asking a favor. When the breakfast was over, the time seemed right.

"I'd like to see how Momma's doing," he said.

Miss Parkhurst considered for a moment. "There'll be a TV in your room this evening," she said, folding her napkin and placing it beside her plate. "You can use it to see how everybody is."

That seemed fair enough. Until then, however, he'd be spending the entire day with Miss Parkhurst; it was time, he decided, to be civil. Then he might actually test his freedom.

"You say I can go," Oliver said, trying to sound friendly.

Miss Parkhurst nodded. "Any time. I won't keep you."

"If I go, can I come back?"

She smiled ever so slightly. There was the girl in that smile again, and she seemed very vulnerable. "The opener takes you anywhere across town."

"Nobody messes with me?"

"Nobody touches anyone I protect," Miss Parkhurst said.

Oliver absorbed that thoughtfully, steepling his hands below his chin. "You're pretty good to me," he said. "Even when I cross you, you don't hurt me. Why?"

"You're my last chance," Miss Parkhurst said, dark eyes on him. "I've lived a long time, and nobody like you's come along. I don't think there'll be another for even longer. I can't wait that long. I've lived this way so many years, I don't know another, but I don't want any more of it."

Oliver couldn't think of a better way to put his next question. "Do you like being a whore?"

Miss Parkhurst's face hardened. "It has its moments," she said stiffly.

Oliver screwed up his courage enough to say what was on his mind, but not to look at her while doing it. "You enjoy lying down with any man who has the money?"

"It's work. It's something I'm good at."

"Even ugly men?"

"Ugly men need their pleasures, too."

"Bad man? Letting them touch you when they've hurt people, maybe killed people?"

"What kind of work have you done?" she asked.

"Clerked a grocery store. Taught music."

"Did you wait on bad men in the grocery store?"

"If I did," Oliver said swiftly, "I didn't know about it."

"Neither did I," Miss Parkhurst said. Then, more quietly, "Most of the time."

"All those girls you've made whore for you . . ."

"You have some things to learn," she interrupted. "It's not the work that's so awful. It's what you have to be to do it. The way people expect you to be when you do it. Should be, in a good world, a whore's like a doctor or a saint, she doesn't mind getting her hands dirty any more than they do. She gives pleasure and smiles. But in the city, people won't let it happen that way. Here, a whore's always got some empty place inside her, a place you've filled with self-respect, maybe. A whore's got respect, but not for herself. She loses that whenever anybody looks at her. She can be worth a million dollars on the outside, but inside, she knows. That's what makes her a whore. That's the curse. It's beat into you sometimes, everybody taking advantage, like you're dirt. Pretty soon you think you're dirt, too, and who cares what happens to dirt? Pretty soon you're just sliding along, trying to keep from getting hurt or maybe dead, but who cares?"

"You're rich," Oliver said.

"Can't buy everything," Miss Parkhurst commented dryly.

"You've got magic."

"I've got magic because I'm here, and to stay here, I have to be a whore."

"Why can't you leave?"

She sighed, her fingers working nervously along the edge of the tablecloth.

"What stops you from just leaving?"

"If you're going to take this place," she said, and he thought at first she was avoiding his question, "you've got to know all about it. All about me. We're the same, almost, this place and I. A whore's no more than what's in her purse, every pimp knows that. You know how many times I've been married?"

Oliver shook his head.

"Seventeen times. Sometimes they left me, once or twice they stayed. Never any good. But then, maybe I didn't deserve any better. Those who left me, they came back when they were old, asking me to save them from Darkside. I couldn't. But I kept them here anyway. Come on."

She stood and Oliver followed her down the halls, down the stairs, below the garage level, deep beneath the mansion's clutter-filled basement. The air was ageless, deep-earth cool, and smelled of old city rain. A few eternal clear light bulbs cast feeble yellow crescents in the dismal murk. They walked on boards over an old muddy patch, Miss Parkhurst lifting her skirts a few inches to clear the mire. Oliver saw her slim ankles and swallowed back the tightness in his throat.

Ahead, laid out in a row on moss-patched concrete biers, were fifteen black iron cylinders, each seven feet long and slightly flattened on top. They looked like big blockbuster bombs in storage. The first was wedged into a dark corner. Miss Parkhurst stood by its foot, running her hand along its rust-streaked surface.

"Two didn't come back. Maybe they were the best of the lot," she said. "I was no judge. I couldn't know. You judge men by what's inside you, and if you're hollow, they get lost in there, you can't know what you're seeing."

Oliver stepped closer to the last cylinder and saw a clear glass plate mounted at the head. Reluctant but fascinated, he wiped the dusty glass with two fingers and peered past a single cornered bubble. The coffin was filled with clear liquid. Afloat within, a face the color of green olives in a martini looked back at him, blind eyes murky, lips set in a loose line. The liquid and death had smoothed the face's wrinkles, but Oliver could tell nonetheless, this dude had been old, old.

"They all die," she said. "All but me. I keep them all, every John, every husband, no forgetting, no letting them go. We've always got this tie between us. That's the curse."

Oliver pulled back from the coffin, holding his breath, heart thumping with eager horror. Which was worse, this, or old men in the night? Old dead lusts laid to rest or lively ghosts? Wrapped in gloom at the far end of the line of bottle-coffins, Miss Parkhurst seemed for a moment to glow with the same furnace power he had felt when he first saw her.

"I miss some of these guys," she said, her voice so soft the power just vanished, a thing in his mind. "We had some good times together."

Oliver tried to imagine what Miss Parkhurst had lived through, the good times and otherwise. "You have any children?" he asked, his voice as thin as the buzz of a fly in a bottle. He jumped back as one of the coffins resonated with his shaky words.

Miss Parkhurst's shoulders slumped. "Lots," she said. "All dead before they were born."

At first his shock was conventional, orchestrated by his Sundays in church. Then the colossal organic waste of effort came down on him like a pile of stones. All that motion, all that wanting, and nothing good from it, just these iron bottles and vivid lists of ghosts.

"What good is a whore's baby?" Miss Parkhurst asked. "Especially if the mother's going to stay a whore."

"Was your mother . . . ?" It didn't seem right to use the word in connection with anyone's mother.

"She was, and her mother before her. I have no daddies, or lots of daddies."

Oliver remembered the old man chastising him in his dream. Before he could even sort out his words, wishing to give her some solace, some sign he wasn't completely unsympathetic, he said, "It can't be all bad, being a whore."

"Maybe not," she said. Miss Parkhurst hardly made a blot in the larger shadows. She might just fly away to dust if he turned his head.

"You said being a whore is being empty inside. Not everybody who's empty inside is a whore."

"Oh?" she replied, light as a cobweb. He was being pushed into an uncharacteristic posture, but Oliver was damned if he'd give in just yet, however much a fool he made of himself. His mixed feelings were betraying him.

"You've *lived*," he said. "You got memories nobody else has. You could write books. They'd make movies about you."

Her smile was a dull lamp in the shadows. "I've had important people visit me," she said. "Powerful men, even mayors. I had something they needed. Sometimes they opened up and talked about how hard it was not being little boys any more. Sometimes, when we were relaxing, they'd cry on my shoulder, just like I was their momma. But then they'd go away and try to forget about me. If they remembered at all, they were scared of me, because of what I knew about them. Now, they know I'm getting weak," she said. "I don't give a damn about books or movies. I won't tell what I know, and besides, lots of those men are dead. If they aren't, they're waiting for me to die, so they can sleep easy."

"What do you mean, getting weak?"

"I got two days, maybe three, then I die a whore. My time is up. The curse is almost finished."

Oliver gaped. When he had first seen her, she had seemed as powerful as a diesel locomotive, as if she might live forever.

"And if I take over?"

"You get the mansion, the money."

"How much power?"

She didn't answer.

"You can't give me any power, can you?"

"No," faint as the breeze from her eyelashes.

"The opener won't be any good."

"No."

"You lied to me."

"I'll leave you all that's left."

"That's not why you made me come here. You took Momma—"

"She stole from me."

"My momma never stole anything!" Oliver shouted. The iron coffins buzzed.

"She took something after I had given her all my hospitality."

"What could she take from you? She was no thief."

"She took a sheet of music."

Oliver's face screwed up in sudden pain. He looked away, fists clenched. They had almost no money for his music. More often than not since his father died, he made up music, having no new scores to play. "Why'd you bring me here?" he croaked.

"I don't mind dying. But I don't want to die a whore."

Oliver turned back, angry again, this time for his momma as well as himself. He approached the insubstantial shadow. Miss Parkhurst shimmered like a curtain. "What do you want from me?"

"I need someone who loves me. Loves me for no reason."

For an instant, he saw standing before him a scrawny girl in a red shimmy, eyes wide. "How could that help you? Can that make you something else?"

"Just love," she said. "Just letting me forget all these," she pointed to the coffins, "and all those," pointing up.

Oliver's body lost its charge of anger and accusation with an exhaled breath. "I can't love you," he said. "I don't even know what love is." Was this true? Upstairs, she had burned in his mind, and he *had* wanted her, though it upset him to remember how much. What *could* he feel for her? "Let's go back now. I have to look in on Momma."

Miss Parkhurst emerged from the shadows and walked past him silently, not even her skirts rustling. She gestured with a finger for him to follow.

She left him at the door to his room, saying, "I'll wait in the main parlor." Oliver saw a small television set on the nightstand by his bed and rushed to turn it on. The screen filled with static and unresolved images. He saw fragments of faces, patches of color and texture passing so quickly he couldn't make them out. The entire city might be on the screen at once, but he could not see any of it clearly. He twisted the channel knob and got more static. Then he saw the label past channel 13 on the dial: HOME, in small golden letters. He twisted the knob to that position and the screen cleared.

Momma lay in bed, legs drawn tightly up, hair mussed. She didn't look good. Her hand, stretched out across the bed, trembled. Her breathing was hard and rough. In the background, Oliver heard Yolanda fussing with the babies, finally screaming at her older brothers in frustration.

Why don't you help with the babies? his sister demanded in a tinny, distant voice.

Momma told you, Denver replied.

She did not. She told us all. You could help.

Reggie laughed. *We got plans to make.*

Oliver pulled back from the TV. Momma was sick, and for all his brothers and sister and the babies could do, she might die. He could guess why she was sick, too; with worry for him. He had to go to her and tell her he was all right. A phone call wouldn't be enough.

Again, however, he was reluctant to leave the mansion and Miss Parkhurst. Something beyond her waning magic was at work here; he wanted to listen to her and to experience more of that fascinated horror. He wanted to watch her again, absorb her smooth, ancient beauty. In a way, she needed him as much as Momma did. Miss Parkhurst outraged everything in him that was lawful and orderly, but he finally had to admit, as he thought of going back to Momma, that he enjoyed the outrage.

He clutched the gold opener and ran from his room to the parlor. She waited for him there in a red velvet chair, hands gripping two lions at the end of the armrests. The lions' wooden faces grinned beneath her caresses. "I got to go," he said. "Momma's sick for missing me."

She nodded. "I'm not holding you," she said.

He stared at her. "I wish I could help you," he said.

She smiled hopefully, pitifully. "Then promise you'll come back."

Oliver wavered. How long would Momma need him? What if he gave his promise and returned and Miss Parkhurst was already dead?

"I promise."

"Don't be too long," she said.

"Won't," he mumbled.

The limousine waited for him in the garage, white and beautiful, languid and sleek and fast all at once. No chauffeur waited for him this time. The door opened by itself and he climbed in; the door closed behind him, and he leaned back stiffly on the leather seats, gold opener in hand. "Take me home," he said. The glass partition and the windows all around darkened to an opaque smoky gold. He felt a sensation of smooth motion. *What would it be like to have this kind of power all the time?*

But the power wasn't hers to give.

Oliver arrived before the apartment building in a blizzard of swirling snow. Snow packed up over the curbs and coated the sidewalks a foot deep; Sleepside was heavy with winter. Oliver stepped from the limousine and climbed the icy steps, the cold hardly touching him even in his light clothing. He was surrounded by Miss Parkhurst's magic.

Denver was frying a pan of navy beans in the kitchen when Oliver burst through the door, the locks flinging themselves open before him. Oliver paused in the entrance to the kitchen. Denver stared at him, face slack, too surprised to speak.

"Where's Momma?"

Yolanda heard his voice in the living room and screamed.

Reggie met him in the hallway, arms open wide, smiling broadly. "Goddamn, little brother! You got away?"

"Where's Momma?"

"She's in her room. She's feeling low."

"She's sick," Oliver said, pushing past his brother. Yolanda stood before Momma's door as if to keep Oliver out. She sucked her lower lip between her teeth. She looked scared.

"Let me by, Yolanda," Oliver said. He almost pointed the opener at her, and then pulled back, fearful of what might happen.

"You made Momma si-ick," Yolanda squeaked, but she stepped aside. Oliver pushed through the door to Momma's room. She sat up in bed, face drawn and thin, but her eyes danced with joy. "My boy!" she sighed. "My beautiful boy."

Oliver sat beside her and they hugged fiercely. "Please don't leave me again," Momma said, voice muffled by his shoulder. Oliver set the opener on her flimsy nightstand and cried against her neck.

*   *   *

The day after Oliver's return, Denver stood lank-legged by the window, hands in frayed pants pockets, staring at the snow with heavy-lidded eyes. "It's too cold to go anywheres now," he mused.

Reggie sat in their father's chair, face screwed in thought. "I listened to what he told Momma," he said. "That whore sent our little brother back here in a limo. A big white limo. See it out there?"

Denver peered down at the street. A white limousine waited at the curb, not even dusted by snow. A tiny vanishing curl of white rose from its tailpipe. "It's still there," he said.

"Did you see what he had when he came in?" Reggie asked. Denver shook his head. "A gold box. *She* must have given that to him. I bet whoever has that gold box can visit Miss Belle Parkhurst. Want to bet?"

Denver grinned and shook his head again.

"Wouldn't be too cold if we had that limo, would it?" Reggie asked.

Oliver brought his momma chicken soup and a half-rotten, carefully trimmed orange. He plumped her pillow for her, shushing her, telling her not to talk until she had eaten. She smiled weakly, beatific, and let him minister to her. When she had eaten, she lay back and closed her eyes, tears pooling in their hollows before slipping down her cheeks. "I was so afraid for you," she said. "I didn't know what she would do. She seemed so nice at first. I didn't see her. Just her voice, inviting me in over the security buzzer, letting me sit and rest my feet. I knew where I was . . . was it bad of me, to stay there, knowing?"

"You were tired, Momma," Oliver said. "Besides, Miss Parkhurst isn't that bad."

Momma looked at him dubiously. "I saw her piano. There was a shelf next to it with the most beautiful sheet music you ever saw, even big books of it. I looked at some. Oh, Oliver, I've never taken anything in my life . . ." She cried freely now, sapping what little strength the lunch had given her.

"Don't you worry, Momma. She used you. She *wanted* me to come." As an afterthought, she added, not sure why he lied, "Or Yolanda."

Momma absorbed that while her eyes examined his face in tiny, caressing glances. "You won't go back," she said, "will you?"

Oliver looked down at the sheets folded under her arms. "I promised. She'll die if I don't," he said.

"That woman is a liar," Momma stated unequivocally. "If she wants you, she'll do anything to get you."

"I don't think she's lying, Momma."

She looked away from him, a feverish anger flushing her cheeks. "Why did you promise her?"

"She's not that bad, Momma," he said again. He had thought that coming home would clear his mind, but Miss Parkhurst's face, her plea, stayed with him as if she were only a room away. The mansion seemed just a fading dream, unimportant; but Belle Parkhurst stuck. "She needs help. She wants to change."

Momma puffed out her cheeks and blew through her lips like a horse. She had often done that to his father, never before to him. "She'll always be a whore," she said.

Oliver's eyes narrowed. He saw a spitefulness and bitterness in Momma he hadn't noticed before. Not that spite was unwarranted; Miss Parkhurst had treated Momma roughly. Yet . . .

Denver stood in the doorway. "Reggie and I got to talk to Momma," he said. "About you." He jerked his thumb back over his shoulder. "Alone." Reggie stood grinning behind his brother. Oliver took the tray of dishes and sidled past them, going into the kitchen.

In the kitchen, he washed the last few days' plates methodically, letting the lukewarm water slide over his hands, eyes focused on the faucet's dull gleam. He had almost lost track of time when he heard the front door slam. Jerking his head up, he wiped the last plate and put it away, then went to Momma's room. She looked back at him guiltily. Something was wrong. He searched the room with his eyes, but nothing was out of place. Nothing that was normally present . . .

The opener.

His brothers had taken the gold opener.

"Momma!" he said.

"They're going to pay her a visit," she said, the bitterness plain now. "They don't like their momma mistreated."

It was getting dark and the snow was thick. He had hoped to return this evening. If Miss Parkhurst hadn't lied, she would be very weak by now, perhaps dead tomorrow. His lungs seemed to shrink within him, and he had a hard time taking a breath.

"I've got to go," he said. "She might *kill* them, Momma!" But that wasn't what worried him. He put on his heavy coat, then his father's old cracked rubber boots with the snow tread soles. Yolanda came out of the room she shared with the babies. She didn't ask any questions, just watched him dress for the cold, her eyes dull.

"They got that gold box," she said as he flipped the last metal clasp on the boots. "Probably worth a lot."

Oliver hesitated in the hallway, then grabbed Yolanda's shoulders and shook her vigorously. "You take care of Momma, you hear?"

She shut her jaw with a clack and shoved free. Oliver was out the door before she could speak.

Day's last light filled the sky with a deep peachy glow tinged with cold gray. Snow fell golden above the buildings and smudgy brown within their shadow. The wind swirled around him mournfully, sending gust-fingers through his coat for any warmth that might be stolen. For a nauseating moment, all his resolve was sucked away by a vacuous pit of misery. The streets were empty; he briefly wondered what night this was, and then remembered it was the twenty-third of December, but too cold for whatever stray shoppers Sleepside might send out. *Why go? To save two worthless idiots?* Not that so much, although that would have been enough, since their loss would hurt Momma, and they *were* his brothers; not that so much as his promise. And something else.

He was afraid for Belle Parkhurst.

He buttoned his coat collar and leaned into the wind. He hadn't put on a hat. The heat flew from his scalp, and in a few moments he felt drained and exhausted. But he made it to the subway entrance and staggered down the steps, into the warmer heart of the city, where it was always sixty-four degrees.

Locked behind her thick glass and metal booth, wrinkled eyes weary with night's wisdom, the fluorescent-lighted token seller took his money and dropped cat's head tokens into the steel tray with separate, distinct *chinks*. Oliver glanced at her face and saw the whore's printed there instead; this middle-aged woman did not spread her legs for money, but had sold her youth and life away sitting in this cavern. Whose emptiness was more profound?

"Be careful," she warned vacantly through the speaker grill. "Night Metro any minute now."

He dropped a token into the turnstile and pushed through, then stood shivering on the platform, waiting for the Sunside train. It seemed to take forever to arrive, and when it did, he was not particularly relieved. The driver's pit-eyes winked green, bull's head turning as the train slid to a halt beside the platform. The doors opened with an oiled groan, and Oliver stepped aboard, into the hard, cold, and unforgiving glare of the train's interior.

At first, Oliver thought the car was empty. He did not sit down, however. The hair on his neck and arm bristled. Hand gripping a stainless steel handle, he leaned into the train's acceleration and took a deep, half-hiccup breath.

He first consciously noticed the other passengers as their faces gleamed in silhouette against the passing dim lights of ghost stations. They sat almost invisible, crowding the car; they stood beside him, less substantial than a breath of air. They watched him intently, bearing no ill will for the moment, perhaps not yet aware that he was alive and they were not. They carried no overt signs of their wounds, but how they had come to be here was obvious to his animal instincts.

This train carried holiday suicides: men, women, teenagers, even a few children, delicate as expensive crystal in a shop window. Maybe the bull's head driver collected them, culling them out and caging them as they stumbled randomly aboard his train. Maybe he controlled them.

Oliver tried to sink away in his coat. He felt guilty, being alive and healthy, enveloped in strong emotions; they were so flimsy, with so little hold on this reality.

He muttered a prayer, stopping as they all turned toward him, showing glassy disapproval at this reverse blasphemy. Silently, he prayed again, but even that seemed to irritate his fellow passengers, and they squeaked among themselves in voices that only a dog or a bat might hear.

The stations passed one by one, mosaic symbols and names flashing in pools of light. When the Sunside station approached and the train slowed, Oliver moved quickly to the door. It opened with oily grace. He stepped onto the platform, turned, and bumped up against the tall, dark uniform of the bull's head driver. The air around him stank of grease and electricity and something sweeter, perhaps blood. He stood a bad foot and a half taller than Oliver, and in one outstretched, black-nailed, leathery hand he held his long silver shears, points spread wide, briefly suggesting Belle Parkhurst's horizontal position among the old men.

"You're in the wrong place, at the wrong time," the driver warned in a voice deeper than the train motors. "Down here, I can cut your cord." He closed the shears with a slick, singing whisper.

"I'm going to Miss Parkhurst's," Oliver said, voice quavering.

"Who?" the driver asked.

"I'm leaving now," Oliver said, backing away. The driver followed, slowly hunching over him. The shears sang open, angled toward his eyes. The crystal dead within the train passed through the open door and glided around them. Gluey waves of cold shivered the air.

"You're a bold little bastard," the driver said, voice managing to descend off any human scale and still be heard. The white tile walls vibrated. "All I have to do is cut your cord, right in front of your face," he snicked the shears inches from Oliver's nose, "and you'll never find your way home."

The driver backed him up against a cold barrier of suicides. Oliver's fear could not shut out curiosity. Was the bull's head real, or was there a man under the horns and hide and bone? The eyes in their sunken orbits glowed ice-blue. The scissors crossed before Oliver's face again, even closer; mere hairs away from his nose.

"You're mine," the driver whispered, and the scissors closed on something tough and invisible. Oliver's head exploded with pain. He flailed back through the dead, dragging the driver after him by the pinch of the shears on that something unseen and very important. Roaring, the driver applied both hands to the shears' grips. Oliver felt as if his head were being ripped away. Suddenly, he kicked out with all his strength between the driver's black-uniformed legs. His foot hit flesh and bone as unyielding as rock and his agony doubled. But the shears hung for a moment in air before Oliver's face, ungrasped, and the driver slowly curled over.

Oliver grabbed the shears, opened them, released whatever cord he had between himself and his past, his home, and pushed through the dead. The scissors reflected elongated gleams over the astonished, watery faces of the suicides. Suddenly, seeing a chance to escape, they spread out along the platform, some of the station's stairs, some to both sides. Oliver ran through them up the steps and stood on the warm evening sidewalk of Sunside. All he sensed from the station's entrance was a sour breath of oil and blood and a faint chill of fading hands as the dead evaporated in the balmy night air.

A quiet crowd had gathered at the front entrance to Miss Parkhurst's mansion. They stood vigil, waiting for something, their faces shining with a greedy sweat.

He did not see the limousine. His brothers must have arrived by now; they were inside, then.

Catching his breath as he ran, he skirted the old brownstone and looked for the entrance to the underground garage. On the south side, he found the ramp and descended to slam his hands against the corrugated metal door. Echoes replied. "It's me!" he shouted. "Let me in!"

A middle-aged man regarded him dispassionately from the higher ground of the sidewalk. "What do you want in there, young man?" he asked.

Oliver glared back over his shoulder. "None of your business," he said.

"Maybe it is, if you want in," the man said. "There's a way any man can get into that house. It never turns gold away."

Oliver pulled back from the door a moment, stunned. The man shrugged and walked on.

He still grasped the driver's shears. They weren't gold, they were silver, but they had to be worth something. "Let me in!" he said. Then, upping the ante, he dug in his pocket and produced the remaining cat's head token. "I'll pay!"

The door grumbled up. The garage's lights were off, but in the soft yellow glow of the street lights, he saw an eagle's claw thrust out from the brick wall just within the door's frame, supporting a golden cup. Token in one hand, shears in another, Oliver's eyes narrowed. To pay Belle's mansion now was no honorable deed; he dropped the token into the cup, but kept the shears as he ran into the darkness.

A faint crack of light showed beneath the stairwell door. Around the door, the bones of ancient city dwellers glowed in their compacted stone, teeth and knuckles bright as fireflies. Oliver tried the door; it was locked. Inserting the point of the shears between the door and catchplate, he pried until the lock was sprung.

The quiet parlor was illuminated only by a few guttering candles clutched in drooping gold eagle's claws. The air was thick with the blunt smells of long-extinguished cigars and cigarettes. Oliver stopped for a moment, closing his eyes and listening. There was a room he had never seen in the time he had spent in Belle Parkhurst's house. She had never even shown him the door, but he knew it had to exist, and that was where she would be, alive or dead. Where his brothers were, he couldn't tell; for the moment he didn't care. He doubted they were in any mortal danger. Belle's power was as weak as the scattered candles.

Oliver crept along the dark halls, holding the gleaming shears before him as a warning to whatever might try to stop him. He climbed two more flights of stairs, and on the third floor, found an uncarpeted hallway, walls bare, that he had not seen before. The dry floorboards creaked beneath him. The air was cool and still. He could smell a ghost of Belle's rose perfume. At the end of the hall was a plain panel door with a tarnished brass knob.

This door was also unlocked. He sucked in a breath for courage and opened it.

This was Belle's room, and she was indeed in it. She hung suspended above her plain iron-frame bed in a weave of flowing threads. For a moment, he drew back, thinking she was a spider, but it immediately became clear she was more like a spider's prey. The threads reached to all corners of the room, transparent, binding her tightly, but to him as insubstantial as the air.

Belle turned to face him, weak, eyes clouded, skin like paper towels. "Why'd you wait so long?" she asked.

From across the mansion, he heard the echoes of Reggie's delighted laughter.

Oliver stepped forward. Only the blades of the shears plucked at the threads; he passed through unhindered. Arm straining at the silver instrument, he realized what the threads were; they were the cords binding Belle to the mansion, connecting her to all her customers. Belle had not one cord to her past, but thousands. Every place she been had touched, she was held by a strand. Thick twining ropes of the past shot from her lips and breasts and from between her legs; not even the toes of her feet were free.

Without thinking, Oliver lifted the driver's silver shears and began methodically snipping the cords. One by one, or in ropy clusters, he cut them away. With each meeting of the blades, they vanished. He did not ask himself which was her first cord, linking her to her childhood, to the few years she had lived before she became a whore; there was no time to waste worrying about such niceties.

"Your brothers are in my vault," she said. "They found my gold and jewels. I crawled here to get away."

"Don't talk," Oliver said between clenched teeth. The strands became tougher, more like wire the closer he came to her thin gray body. His arm muscles knotted and cold sweat soaked his clothes. She dropped inches closer to the bed.

"I never brought any men here," she said.

"Shh."

"This was my place, the only place I had."

There were hundreds of strands left now, instead of thousands. He worked for long minutes, watching her grow more and more pale, watching her onetime furnace heat dull to less than a single candle, her eyes lose their feverish glitter. For a horrified moment, he thought cutting the cords might actually weaken her; but he hacked and swung at the cords, regardless. They were even tougher now, more resilient.

Far off in the mansion, Denver and Reggie laughed together, and there was a heavy clinking sound. The floor shuddered.

Dozens of cords remained. He had been working at them for an eternity, and now each cord took a concentrated effort, all the strength left in his arms and hands. He thought he might faint or throw up. Belle's eyes had closed. Her breathing was undetectable.

Five strands left. He cut through one, then another. As he applied the shears to the third, a tall man appeared on the opposite side of her bed, dressed in pale gray with a wide-brimmed gray hat. His fingers were covered with gold rings. A gold eagle's claw pinned his white silk tie.

"I was her third," the man said. "She came to me and she cheated me."

Oliver held back his shears, eyes stinging with rage. "Who are you?" he demanded, nearly doubled over by his exertion. He stared up at the gray man through beads of sweat on his eyebrows.

"That other old man, he hardly worked her at all. I put her to work right here, but she cheated me."

"You're her *pimp*," Oliver spat out the word.

The gray man grinned.

"Cut that cord, and she's nothing."

"She's nothing now. Your curse is over and she's dying."

"She shouldn't have messed with me," the pimp said. "I was a strong man, lots of connections. What do you want with an old drained-out whore, boy?"

Oliver didn't answer. He struggled to cut the third cord but it writhed like a snake between the shears.

"She would have been a whore even without me," the pimp said. "She was a whore from the day she was born."

"That's a lie," Oliver said.

"Why do you want to get at her? She give you a pox and you want to finish her off?"

Oliver's lips curled and he flung his head back, not looking as he brought the shears together with all his remaining strength, boosted by a killing anger. The third cord parted and the shears snapped, one blade singing across the room and sticking in the wall with a spray of plaster chips. The gray man vanished like a double-blown puff of cigarette smoke, leaving a scent of onions and stale beer.

Belle hung awkwardly by two cords now. Swinging the single blade like a knife, he parted them swiftly and fell over her, lying across her, feeling her cool body for the first time. She could not arouse lust now. She might be dead.

"Miss Parkhurst," he said. He examined her face, almost as white as the bed sheets, high cheekbones pressing through waxy flesh. "I don't want anything from you," Oliver said. "I just want you to be all right." He lowered his lips to hers, kissed her lightly, dripping sweat on her closed eyes.

Far away, Denver and Reggie cackled with glee.

The house grew quiet. All the ghosts, all accounts received, had fled, had been freed.

The single candle in the room guttered out, and they lay in the dark alone. Oliver fell against his will into an exhausted slumber.

Cool, rose-scented fingers lightly touched his forehead. He opened his eyes and saw a girl in a white nightgown leaning over him, barely his age. Her eyes were very big and her lips bowed into a smile beneath high, full cheekbones. "Where are we?" she asked. "How long we been here?"

Late morning sun filled the small, dusty room with warmth. He glanced around the bed, looking for Belle, and then turned back to the girl. She vaguely resembled the chauffeur who had brought him to the mansion that first night, though younger, her face more bland and simple.

"You don't remember?" he asked.

"Honey," the girl said sweetly, hands on hips, "I don't remember much of anything. Except that you kissed me. You want to kiss me again?"

Momma did not approve of the strange young woman he brought home, and wanted to know where Reggie and Denver were. Oliver did not have the heart to tell her. They lay cold as ice in a room filled with mounds of cat's head subway tokens, bound by the pimp's magic. They had dressed themselves in white, with broad white hats; dressed themselves as pimps. But the mansion was empty, stripped during that night of all its valuables by the greedy crowds.

They were pimps in a whorehouse without whores. As the young girl observed, with a tantalizing touch of wisdom beyond her apparent years, there was nothing much lower than that.

"Where'd you find that girl? She's hiding something, Oliver. You mark my words."

Oliver ignored his mother's misgivings, having enough of his own. The girl agreed she needed a different name now, and chose Lorelei, a name she said "just sings right."

He saved money, lacking brothers to borrow and never repay, and soon rented a cheap studio on the sixth floor of the same building. The girl came to him sweetly in his bed, her mind no more full—for the most part—than that of any young girl. In his way, he loved her—and feared her, though less and less as days passed.

She played the piano almost as well as he, and they planned to give lessons. They had brought a trunk full of old sheet music and books with them from the mansion. The crowds had left them at least that much.

Momma did not visit for two weeks after they moved in. But visit she did, and eventually the girl won her over.

"She's got a good hand in the kitchen," Momma said. "You do right by her, now."

Yolanda made friends with the girl quickly and easily, and Oliver saw more substance in his younger sister than he had before. Lorelei helped Yolanda with the babies. She seemed a natural.

Sometimes, at night, he examined her while she slept, wondering if there still weren't stories, and perhaps skills, hidden behind her sweet, peaceful face. Had she forgotten everything?

In time, they were married.

And they lived—

Well enough.

They lived.

Honorable Mentions: 1989

Aiken, Joan, "Do Not Alight Here," *Give Yourself a Fright.*
Alderman, Gillian, "Country Matters," *Other Edens III.*
Aldiss, Brian W., "North of the Abyss," *F & SF*, October.
——, "Ruins," an Arena Novella (Arrow, U.K.).
Anderson, Kevin, "Family Portrait," *2 A.M. #12*, Summer.
Anthony, Patricia, "The Name of the Demon," *F & SF*, November.
Atoda, Takashi, "Napoleon Crazy," *Ellery Queen's Mystery Magazine*, March.
Ballard, J. G., "The Enormous Space," *Interzone 30.*
Benford, Gregory, "We Could Do Worse," *IASFM*, April.
Bloch, Robert, "Horror Scope," *Fear and Trembling.*
Boston, Bruce, "In the Wake of Sensuous Dreams" (poem), *Grue #10.*
——, "The Eyes of the Crowd," *Nocturne #1.*
Boyett, Steven R., "Like Pavlov's Dog," *Book of the Dead.*
Boyle, T. Coraghessan, "The Devil and Irv Cherniske," *If the River Was Whiskey.*
——, "King Bee," *Playboy*, March.
Brandner, Gary, "Damntown," (novella), *Night Visions VII.*
Braunbeck, Gary A., "Time Heals," *Scare Care.*
Brennan, Joseph Payne, "Vacation Dreams," *Weirdbook #23/24.*
Budrys, Algis, "What Befell Mairiam," *F & SF*, October.
Burleson, Donald R., "Snow Cancellations," *2 A.M. #12*, Fall.
Burns, Christopher, "Embracing the Slaughterer," *About the Body.*
——, "Trying to Get to You," *Ibid.*
Cadigan, Pat, "Addicted to Love," *Wild Cards V: Down and Dirty.*
——, "Dirty Work," (novella), *Blood is Not Enough.*
Campbell, Ramsey, "It Helps If You Sing," *Book of the Dead.*
Cannell, Dorothy, "Lullaby," *Another Dimension (Special report)* August–October.
Card, Orson Scott, "Lost Boys," *F & SF*, October.
Carroll, Jonathan, "Florian," *Weird Tales*, Fall.
——, "Your Tired Angel," *Fear #11.*
Casper, Susan, "A Child of Darkness," *Blood is Not Enough.*
Castle, Mort, "The Running Horse, the High White Sound," *Dark Regions #3.*
Charnas, Suzy McKee, "Boobs," *IASFM*, July.
Cirilo, Randolph, "For Old Time's Sake," *Grue #10.*
Clement, Claude, "The Voice of the Wood," illustrated children's story translated from the French by Lenny Hort.
Craig, Brian, "A Gardener in Parrovon," *Warhammer: Ignorant Armies.*
Craig, Mary Shura, "Caesar and Sleep," *Sisters in Crime.*
Crowley, John, "The Nightingale Sings at Night," *Novelty.*
Cupp, Scott, "Jimmy and Me and the Nigger Man," *The New Frontier.*
Dalkey, Kara, "The Ghosts of Wan Li Road," *Things That Go Bump in the Night.*
Dazai, Osamu, "Crackling Mountain," *Crackling Mountain and Other Stories*, translated from the Japanese by James O'Brien.
Dean, Pamela, "Juniper, Gentian and Rosemary," *Things That Go Bump in the Night.*
de Larrabeiti, Michael, "The Troubadour and the Cage of Gold," *Provençal Tales.*
de Lint, Charles, "The Drowned Man's Reel," *Pulphouse #3.*

——, "Romano Drom," *Pulphouse #5.*
——, "The Sacred Fire," *Stalkers.*
——, "The Stone Drum" (chapbook), Triskell Press.
——, "Westlin Wind" (chapbook), Axolotl Press.
——, "Wooden Bones," *Things That Go Bump in the Night.*
Disch, Thomas M., "The Happy Turnip," *F & SF*, October.
Dowling, Terry, "The Quiet Redemption of Andy the House," *Australian Short Stories.*
Dubois, Brendan, "Fire Burning Bright," *Tales for Long Winter Nights.*
Elgin, Suzette Haden, "Tornado," *F & SF*, March.
Elliott, Tom, "Garden of the Gods," *October Dreams.*
Ericson, J. R., "Vampire" (poem), *Argonaut 14.*
Estleman, Loren R., "Hell on the Draw," *The New Frontier.*
Etchemendy, Nancy, "The Sailor's Bargain," *F & SF*, April.
Evans, Christopher, "Lifelines," *Dark Fantasies.*
Ford, John M., "Troy: The Movie" (poem, chapbook) A Speculative Engineering Production.
Fowler, Christopher, "The Art Nouveau Fireplace," *The Bureau of Lost Souls.*
——, "The Bureau of Lost Souls," *Ibid.*
——, "Cooking the Books," *The Thirtieth Pan Book of Horror.*
Fowler, Karen Joy, "Game Night at the Fox and Goose," *Interzone #29.*
Fraser, Antonia, "The Moon Was to Blame," *EQMM*, December.
Friesner, Esther M., "Poe White Trash," *F & SF*, December.
——, "Do I Dare to Ask Your Name?" *Pulphouse #5.*
Frost, Gregory, "Divertimento," *IASFM*, December.
Fuqua, C. S., "Old Lady Campbell, She is Dead," 2 A.M. *#12.*
Gallagher, Stephen, "The Horn," *Arrows of Eros.*
——, "Life Line," *Dark Fantasies.*
Garcia-Barrio, Constance, "The Monkey Woman," *Talk That Talk: An Anthology of African-American Storytelling.*
Garton, Ray, "Punishments," *Hot Blood.*
Gioia, Dana, "All Souls" (poem), *The New Yorker*, October 9.
Goddin, Jeffrey, "Reflections," *Deathrealm #10.*
Goring, Ann, "Wish Upon a Star," *Weird Tales*, Winter.
Gorman, Ed, "Idol," *The Further Adventures of Batman.*
——, "Stalkers," *Stalkers.*
Gorog, Judith, "The Mall Rat," *Three Dreams & A Nightmare and Other Tales.*
——, "Sad Eyes," *Ibid.*
Grant, Charles L., "The Last Cowboy Song," *Post Mortem.*
Greenland, Colin, "The Traveller," *Zenith.*
Haber, Karen, "The Light of Her Smile," *Phantoms.*
Hall, Melissa Mia, "The Brush of Soft Wings," *Post Mortem.*
——, and Winter, Douglas E., "The Happy Family," *Masques 3.*
Hammell, Dale, "The Affliction," *Argonaut 14.*
Hand, Elizabeth, "The Boy in the Tree" (novella), *Full Spectrum 2.*
——, "On the Town Route," *Pulphouse #5.*
Harris, Geraldine, "Iron Shoes," *Arrows of Eros.*
Harrison, M. John, "The Horse of Iron and How We Can Know It and Be Changed by It Forever," *Tarot Tales.*
Hill, Reginald, "Urban Legend," *EQMM*, March.
Hodge, Brian, "Dead Giveaway, *Book of the Dead.*

——, "Phallusies," *The Horror Show*, Summer,
——, "Skin Deep," *Ibid*.
Hoffman, Nina Kiriki, "Chrysalis," *Pulphouse #3*.
——, "Courting Disasters," *Weird Tales*, Fall.
Hoke, Nancy Simpson, "Habu," *AHMM*, November.
Hopper, Jeannette M., "Sunday Breakfast," *Masques 3*.
Ingalls, Rachel, "Friends in the Country," *The End of Tragedy*.
Ings, Simon D., "Blessed Fields," *Other Edens III*.
——, "Dreyfuss Dogs," *Fear #10*.
Jones, Diana Wynne, "The Master," *Hidden Turnings*.
Jurgens, Kathleen, "Da Goblin Woman" (poem), *Narcopolis and Other Poems*.
Kadrey, Richard, "The Kill Fix," *IASFM*, May.
Kelly, James Patrick, "Dancing with Chairs," *IASFM*, March.
Kilworth, Garry, "Ifurin and the Fat Man," *F & SF*, March.
——, "Island With the Stink of Ghosts," *In the Hollow of the Deep-Sea Wave*.
——, "The Silver Collar," *Blood Is Not Enough*.
King, Stephen, "Dolan's Cadillac" (chapbook).
Kiplinger, Christina, "Dreams Are Born There," *Eldritch Tales #18*.
Kisner, James, "Mother Tucker," *Stalkers*.
Knaff, Jean Christian, "Manhattan," illustrated story.
Koja, Kathe, "Skin Deep," *IASFM*, July.
Kopaska-Merkel, David C., "Wintry Days" (poem), *Narcopolis*.
Kotzwinkle, William, "Django Reinhardt Played the Blues," *The Hot Jazz Trio*.
Kucharski, Lisa, "Meanwhile" (poem), *Dreams and Nightmares #25*.
Lacher, Chris, "The Pet Door," *Scare Care*.
Lafferty, R. A., "Gray Ghost," *Strange Plasma #1*.
Laidlaw, Marc, "His Powder'd Wig, His Crown of Thornes," *Omni*, September.
——, "Uneasy Street," *F & SF*, September.
Lake, Christina, "Wintertime Beauty," *Other Edens III*.
Lamming, R. M., "Candle Lies," *Dark Fantasies*.
Langford, David, "The Motivation," *Arrows of Eros*.
Lansdale, Joe R., "On the Far Side of the Cadillac Desert with Dead Folks," *Book of the Dead*.
——, "Subway Jack," *The Further Adventures of Batman*.
Lawler, Rick, "Solitude Bitch," *Pulphouse #4*.
Laymon, Richard, "Wishbone," *Night Visions VII*.
Lee, Tanith, "The Janfia Tree," *Blood Is Not Enough*.
——, "The Rakshasa," *Forests of the Night*.
——, "Sweet Grapes," *Ibid*.
——, "The Tenebris Malgraph," *Ibid*.
Lehmann, Christian and Kilworth, Garry, "When the Music Stopped," *Other Edens III*.
Ligotti, Thomas, "Conversations in a Dead Language," *Deathrealm #73*.
——, "The Library of Byzantium," *Dagon 22/23*.
——, "Mad Night of Atonement," *Grue #9*.
——, "The Strange Designs of Master Rignolo," *Grue #10*.
Little, Bentley, "And I Am Here, Fighting With Ghosts," *Eldritch Tales #18*.
Llosa, Mario Vargas, "Mouth," *Granta 28*.
Lumley, Brian, "Dagon's Bell," *Weirdbook 23/24*.

——, "The Disapproval of Jeremy Cleave," *Weird Tales*, Winter.
——, "The Pit-Yakker," *Weird Tales*, Fall.
Maclay, John, "Black Stockings," *Pulphouse #5*.
——, "A Childhood Memory," *Deathrealm #9*.
——, "Models," *Scare Care*.
MacLeod, Ian R., "Through," *Interzone* 30.
Manachino, Albert J., "The Green Friends," *Argonaut #14*.
Marten, Eugene, "Allures," *Grue #10*.
Masterton, Graham, "Ever, Ever, After," *Masques 3*.
——, "Hurry, Monster" (chapbook), Footsteps Press.
Matozzo, Francis J., "Why Pop-Pop Died," *Pulphouse #5*.
Mayhar, Ardath, "Trapline," *Razored Saddles*.
McCammon, Robert R., "Black Boots," *Ibid*.
——, "Chico," *Blue World*.
——, "Eat Me," *Book of the Dead*.
——, "Haunted World," *Post Mortem*.
——, "Lizardman," *Stalkers*.
McConnell, Chan, "Blossom," *Book of the Dead*.
Michaels, Barbara, "The Runaway," *Sisters in Crime*.
Misha, "Chippoke Na Gomi," *Witness* magazine.
Morgan, Chris, "Interesting Times," *Dark Fantasies*.
Morlan, A. R., "In the Great Milk White Eye of God," *Eldritch Tales #18*.
——, "This is the Way We Wash Our Clothes, Wash Our Clothes, Wash Our Clothes,"
    The Scream Factory #2.
Morrison, Mark, "In A City of Bells and Towers: A Call of Cthulhu Scenario," *Dagon*
    22/23.
Morrow, James, "The Confessions of Ebenezer Scrooge," *Spirits of Christmas*.
Navarro, Yvonne, "Zachary's Glass Shoppe," *Deathrealm #10*.
Newman, Kim, "Twitch Technicolor," *Interzone* 28.
Nolan, William F., "On 42nd St.," *Masques 3*.
Olsen, Lance, "Family," *The Iowa Review*, Vol. 19, #1.
Osier, Jeffrey, "Catalog," *Deathrealm #8*.
——, "The Face on the Stairs," *2 A.M. #12*.
Page, Gerald W., "Too Much Night," *Weirdbook* 23/24.
Palwick, Susan, "Changeling" (poem), *Ice River*, June.
Picano, Felice, "Spices of the World," *Scare Care*.
Pickering, Paul, "Dream Kitchen," *October Dreams*.
Pierce, Meredith Ann, "Ice Rose," *Jabberwocky #1*.
Pike, Rod, "Twitcher," *Fear #12*.
Pollack, Rachel, "Knower of Birds," *Tarot Tales*.
Ptacek, Kathryn, "Each Night, Each Year," *Post Mortem*.
Rainey, Mark, "La Vita Terra," *Nocturne 2*.
Raisor, Garry L., "Distant Thunder," *The New Frontier*.
——, "The Night Caller," *The Horror Show*, Summer.
Ramsey, Shawn, "The Return" (poem), *Deathrealm #9*.
Ransom, Daniel, "Dark Muse," *Phantoms*.
Reed, Tony, "Beating the Meat," *Fear #8*.
Relling, William, Jr., "Four-in-Hand," *Cemetary Dance #2*, June.
——, "Table for None," *Scare Care*.

Roberts, Giullian, "Hog Heaven," *Sisters in Crime*.
Roberts, Keith, "The Grey Wethers," *Other Edens III*.
Robinson, Gregor, "Metamorphosis," *AHMM*, December.
Robinson, Kim Stanley, "The True Nature of Shangri-La," *IASFM*, December.
Royle, Nicholas, "8," *Fear #4*.
——, "Archway," *Dark Fantasies*.
——, "The Sculptor's Hand," *Interzone 32*.
Rusch, Kristine Kathryn, "Fugue," *Amazing*, November.
Russo, Patricia, "Build It Up with Blood and Bone," *Nocturne #2*.
Ryan, Bill, "The Wulgaru," *Masques 3*.
Ryan, Michael "Milk the Mouse," (poem), *The Nation*, July 13 issue.
Sallee, Wayne Allen, "Corky's Quickies," *Grue #10*.
——, "Third Rail," *Masques 3*.
Sarrantonio, Al, "Children of Cain," *Stalkers*.
——, "The Red Wind," *Weirdbook 23/24*.
Saunders, Charles R., "Drum Magic," *Argonaut #14*.
Sayer, Paul, "Othello's Shadow," *October Dreams*.
Scarborough, Elizabeth Ann, "Bastet's Blessing," *Catfantastic*.
Schacochis, Bob, "Les Femmes Creoles: A Fairy Tale," *The Next New World*.
Schaefer, Amy, "Emeretha" (poem), *Amazing*, May.
Schow, David J., "Sedalia," *Razored Saddles*.
Schweitzer, Darrell, "The Man Who Found the Heart of the Forest," *Pulphouse #5*.
——, "Seeing Them," *The Horror Show*, Spring.
Scoppetone, Sandra, "He Loved Her So Much," *Sisters in Crime*.
Shea, Michael, "I, Said the Fly" (novella), *The Book of Omni Science Fiction #6*.
Sheffield, Charles, "Destroyer of Worlds," *IASFM*, February.
Shepard, Lucius, "Bound for Glory," *F & SF*, October.
——, "The Ends of the Earth" (novella), *F & SF*, March.
——, "Father of Stones," (novella) *IASFM*, September.
——, "Surrender," *IASFM*, August.
Sherman, Delia, "As Blood is it Red," *Weirdbook 23/24*.
Shirley, John, "I Live in Elizabeth," *Heatseeker*.
Silva, David B., "Brothers," *Post Mortem*.
——, "Ice Songs," *Pulphouse #3*.
Silverberg, Robert, "To the Promised Land," *Omni*, May.
Sinclair, P. W., "Getting Back," *Post Mortem*.
Skipp, John and Spector, Craig, "Meat Market," *Dead Lines*.
Sladek, John, "Blood and Gingerbread" (chapbook) Cheap Street.
Sleator, William, "The Elevator," *Things That Go Bump in the Night*.
Smith, E. W., "Under the Dog Star," *Amazing*, November.
Smyth, George W., "Listing," *Grue #10*.
——, "Nothing I Tell You Nothing," *New Pathways*, September.
Sneyd, Steve, "Taken for a Ride," *Back Brain Recluse #12*.
Sonenberg, Maya, "Ariadne in Exile," *Cartographics*.
Soukup, Martha, "Floodlights," *Spirits of Christmas*.
Spector, Craig, "Dead Lines," *Dead Lines*.
Stableford, Brian, "The Will," *Dark Fantasies*.
Strickland, Craig, "In the Trees," *October Dreams*.
Swain, Timothy M., "Lust for Life," *Gorezone*, May.

Swan, Gladys, "Of Memory and Desire," *Of Memory and Desire.*
Tarr, Judith, "Roncevalles," *What Might Have Been* Vol. II.
Taylor, Diane, "The Skull," *Masques 3.*
Taylor, Lucy, "Chains," *Thin Ice #3.*
Tem, Steve Rasnic, "Hooks," *Fear #5.*
——, "Merry-Go-Round," *New Pathways #14.*
——, "Nocturne" (poem), *Blood Is Not Enough.*
——, "The Strangers," *Scare Care.*
——, "The Unmasking," *Phantoms.*
——, and Tem, Melanie, "Resettling," *Post Mortem.*
Tessier, Thomas, "Blanca," *Post Mortem.*
Utley, Steven, "My Wife," *IASFM,* February.
Vachss, Andrew, "Placebo," *EQMM,* March.
Vandermeer, Jeff, "The Color of Chance is Green," *The Book of Frog.*
——, "The Game of Lost and Found," *Ibid.*
Wagner, Karl Edward, "At First Just Ghostly," *Weird Tales,* Fall.
Wainer, Jack, "The Trust Me Game," *The Thirtieth Pan Book of Horror.*
Walker, Larry, "Magic's Price," *Weird Tales,* Winter.
Watkins, Susan M., "The Place Where All Things Go to Die" (novella), *The Horror Show,* Summer.
Watson, Ian, "In Her Shoes," *Fear #13.*
——, "Tales From the Weston Willow," *Dark Fantasies.*
——, "When Jesus Comes Down the Chimney," *Weird Tales,* Winter.
Watson, Sis, "Fatal Condition," *Special Report,* August–October.
Webb, Don, "The Key to the Mysteries," *Eldritch Tales #18.*
Westall, Robert, "The Devil and Clocky Watson," *Antique Dust.*
——, "The Doll," *Ibid.*
——, "The Last Day of Miss Dorinda Molyneaux," *Ibid.*
——, "The Ugly House," *Ibid.*
——, "The Woolworth Spectacles," *Ibid.*
Whetter, Gerry, "Baby's Breath," *Grue #10.*
Whittington, Mary K., "Leaves," *Things That Go Bump in the Night.*
Wilhelm, Kate, "Children of the Wind" (novella), *Children of the Wind.*
Williamson, Chet, "Blue Notes," *Night Visions VII.*
——, "Confessions of St. James" (novella), *Night Visions VI.*
——, "To Feel Another's Woe . . ." *Blood Is Not Enough.*
——, "The House of Fear" (chapbook), Footsteps Press.
Williamson, J. N., "Monstrum," *Scare Care.*
Wilson, F. Paul, "A Day in the Life," *Stalkers.*
——, "The Tenth Toe," *Razored Saddles.*
Wilson, Gahan, "Leavings," *Omni,* April.
Winterson, Jeanette, "The Architect of Unrest," *Granta* 28.
Wisman, Ken, "In the Heart of the Blue Caboose," *Pulphouse #3.*
——, "On the Side of the Road," *Deathrealm #8.*
Wolfe, Gene, "The Friendship Light," *F & SF,* October.
——, "How the Bishop Sailed to Inniskeen," *IASFM,* December.
Won, Park Jim, "The Tiger's Admonition," *Korean Classical Literature,* translated by Chung Kong-Wa.
Wu, William F., "Pagan Midnight," *Pulphouse #3.*

Yano, Tetsu, "The Legend of the Paper Spaceship," *The Best Japanese Science Fiction Stories*.
Yeovil, Jack, "The Ignorant Armies," *Warhammer: Ignorant Armies*.
——, "No Gold in the Grey Mountains," *Wolfriders*.
Yolen, Jane, "The Singer of Seeds," *The Faery Flag*.
Yost, Scott D., "Mr. Sandman," *October Dreams*.

About the Editors

ELLEN DATLOW is the fiction editor of *Omni* magazine, and has edited several anthologies, including *The Books of Omni Science Fiction* (Zebra), *Blood Is Not Enough* (William Morrow/Ace Books), and *Alien Sex* (E. P. Dutton). She has published a number of award-winning stories by outstanding authors during her tenure at *Omni*. She lives in Manhattan.

TERRI WINDLING, a three-time winner of the World Fantasy Award, was for many years the Fantasy Editor for Ace Books. Now she is a Consulting Editor for Tor Books in New York; she also runs the Boston-based Endicott Studio, specializing in book publishing projects and art for exhibition. She created the "Adult Fairy Tales" series of novels (Ace/Tor) and the "Borderland" urban fantasy books for teenagers (NAL/Tor/HBJ), and has edited a number of fiction anthologies. She is currently at work on several fantasy-oriented projects here and in England. She lives in Boston, Massachusetts.

About the Artist

THOMAS CANTY is one of the most distinguished artists working in the fantasy field. He won the World Fantasy Award for his distinctive book jacket and cover illustrations; and he is a noted book designer working in the fantasy, horror, mystery and mainstream fields, as well as with various small presses. He has also created children's picture book series for St. Martin's Press and Ariel Books. He lives in Massachusetts.

About the Packager

JAMES FRENKEL is the publisher of Bluejay Books, which was a major publisher of science fiction and fantasy from 1983 to 1986. Since then he has been a consulting editor for Tor Books and for Macmillan's Collier Nucleus books, and a packager. Editor of Dell's science fiction in the late 1970s, he has published some of the finest new science fiction and fantasy authors, including Greg Bear, Orson Scott Card, Judith Tarr, John Varley, and Joan D. Vinge. He lives with his wife and two children in Chappaqua, New York.